Vampires & Vices

THE COMPLETE SERIES

NINA WALKER

ADDISON & GRAY PRESS

Vampires & Vices: The Complete Series

Paperback ISBN 978-1-950093-43-4

Ebook ISBN 978-1-950093-44-1

Covers by Clarissa at JOY Author Design Studio

Character Illustrations by Kalynne Art

Editing by Ailene Kubricky

"I used to have nightmares, too. There's no shame in it."

"What did you do to make them go away?"

"I became the nightmare."

NINA WALKER

KEEP YOUR CARDS CLOSE &
YOUR ENEMIES CLOSER.

BLOOD CASINO

VAMPIRES & VICES, NO. 1

Praise for Blood Casino

"Deliciously dark, this story is so utterly original and engrossing it's impossible to stop reading. With compelling characters making it a one-sitting read and a mysterious plot, this is my new favorite book about vampires." —**M. Lynn, USA Today Bestselling Author of The Fantasy and Fairytales Series**

"Sinful vampires and a tough-as-nails teen. Walker has woven a tale as addictive as the Blood Casino's vices. Five solid stars for this YA vampire fantasy!" —**Krista Street, USA Today Bestselling Author of the Supernatural Community Series**

"High stakes adventure. Fledgling love triangle. New Orleans casinos. Need I say more to entice you to read Walker's delicious urban fantasy?" —**Olivia Wildenstein, USA Today Bestselling Author of The Boulder Wolves Series and Angels of Elysium Series**

"Blood Casino is a delicious and bold new tale for every vampire fan to savor. Walker shines in this high stakes game of cat and mouse." —**Casey L. Bond, Bestselling author of When Wishes Bleed**

"Blood Casino is nothing like I've read before. Nina Walker takes vampires to a whole new level in this first installment of Vampires and Vices that will have you reading all the way through the book in one sitting! With intrigue, suspense, and sprinkles of romance, you can't go wrong with this series!" —

Heather Renee, USA Today Bestselling Author of The Broken Court Series and the Shadow Veil Academy Series

"Fans of TrueBlood rejoice, your new Eric Northman is here! Walker's intriguing new vampire novel takes a dark spin on the mythical creatures we know and love. In the words of the main character: there are no sparkly vampires here. And I'm all in for it." —**G.K. DeRosa, USA Today Bestselling Author of the Darkblood Academy Series**

This one is for the valiant healthcare workers.
Thank you.

One

Only two types of people frequent the blood casino: gamblers and their children. Standing outside on the steps of The Alabaster Heart, I can safely say that hate isn't a strong enough word to describe how I feel about this place. And okay, maybe there aren't that many of my peers trying to drag their parents out of here, but I've seen plenty over the last few years. Enough to know that once gambling sucks someone in, it's pretty much impossible to get them to stop.

New Orleans Canal Street traffic bustles by in a cacophony of irate drivers. They honk at the slow-moving tourists, who, like slugs on pavement, are too stifled by the humidity to care. The famous street cuts the city in half. On one side is the well-known French Quarter and on the other is the post-colonial builds. I prefer the newer part, even though the older is far more beautiful. Something about the newness feels safer to me, like maybe it's not crawling with centuries-old evil. That's probably wishful thinking.

Guess which side of the street the casino is on?

I clench my hands into fists and sigh. I should be used to going in there by now, but I can't help the nerves from firing in my belly. Out of habit, I check to make sure I'm wearing my crucifix necklace. The dainty thing rests against the hollow in my throat, warm from the sunlight. It's superstitious, I know, but it helps me breathe. In this city, it's better to be superstitious than sorry.

I force myself to ascend the steps. The hotel and casino's late 1800s architecture mirrors many of the buildings down here by the French Quarter with towering white columns, weathered red brick, and ornate metalwork. Since it's the only land casino in the area that has gaming tables, I know my mom will be saddled up to one of them. She's never been keen on the slot machines. "They favor the house," she always says, "doubling down at the tables is the only way to make any real money."

Yeah, like money is the biggest worry in a vampire-run casino.

I wipe my sweaty palms on my jean shorts and open the door. I have to pass through two vestibules to get inside. It's the vamps way of keeping the light out. It could be worse, though. Mom could be on the riverboat casino again. It runs weekend nights and once someone gets on, they can't get off until it docks in the early morning hours. I'm not old enough to step foot on that thing so I hate when she does. I hate feeling helpless. It's something I've experienced a lot lately.

The stale odor of old cigarette smoke hits me like a wall. I blink as my eyes adjust and then I begin weaving through the rows of flashing slot machines. I swear those things are programmed to attract toddlers. *Ding, ding, ding! Winner every hour! Jackpot!*

That's casino speak for, *Give me your money.*

So far I'm under the radar, but my heart rate only skyrockets as I edge closer to the gaming tables. No matter how many times I save her from herself, she always comes back for one more bet . . .

It's not all about money.

It's the game. The addiction.

The thumping roll of the dice, the chance of a win, the dopamine release with each turn of the cards. It's the euphoric feeling of chips being pushed her way. It's taking those chips to the cashier at the end of the night and trading them in for cold hard cash she can slip into her purse, making her feel invincible. Valuable. Loved.

It's too good and it sucks her in every single time.

And I always follow, ready to pull her away when her body can't take another drop. I don't trust *them* to care, even though it's the law. They promise not to bring the gamblers to the brink, but they have ways of covering their tracks. I am not my mother's daughter in that way, I can't handle those odds.

I find her at the Texas Hold'em table, her drug of choice.

It's only four o'clock on a Tuesday and all the seats are filled. Gamblers are cozied up together, talking shop like war heroes. They may look differ-ent--different sizes, ages, ethnicities--but their eyes each have the same glossy sheen, their movements the same practiced calm.

"Mom." I approach her from behind, talking low in her ear. "It's time to go."

She doesn't respond right away, but her bony shoulders still. The middle-aged human dealer shoots me an aloof glance. He deals the hands from the deck, the sound of redemption to these people. I look away. I don't want to be carded. The staff won't get too fussy if I'm in and out fast, but at only eighteen years old, they can boot me in a heartbeat. It happens all the time to those of us under twenty-one who are constantly trying to rescue our parents. Not that the age will stay twenty-one much longer. The vampires are lobbying hard to lower it to eighteen. It's all over the news.

I wait for the hand to finish. Mom drags a pile of winnings toward her and straightens triumphantly, like a fisherman with a tugging line. I cringe. This will only make it harder to get her out of here. She thinks she's the one reeling them in, but really, it's the other way around. "Mom," I try again, "please, let's go. You've played enough."

"Shh–none of that, Evangeline. I'm on a winning streak," she says, brushing me away as she leans over her cards, the IV in her hand tugging at the vein.

My heart drops, but the dealer is quick to push more cards at the players, so I step back again. The cards are thick and gold and shiny, with the swirly heart pattern embossed on the back. The casino's logo. I look away, focusing on the metal drip stand next to us. The plastic bag hangs heavy with blood. I can practically smell the metallic stench of it. She's been playing far too long but the more it fills up, the more chips the house gives her to keep her going. We don't have a lot of money to our name so this is Mom's way of increasing her odds. Another thing she always says, "You have to play big to win big." That and, "The bigger the risk, the bigger the reward." I hate all her little gambling ramblings because the reverse is also true. I study the other five players: two of them have a blood bag slowly filling drip by drip as well, but none are as full as Mom's. Hers is practically bursting at the seams. She needs to stop.

Panic is a beast of claws and teeth, ripping me open and spilling fear out right there on the ugly swirl-patterned carpet. Finally the hand is over, and once again, more chips come clanking toward her. "See, baby," she says, turning to face me, "I'm on a roll." She's as bright as Sunday morning, despite the blood loss. It won't last. Underneath her immaculate makeup, a ghost smiles back at me.

"Nice," I try again, sweet as honey this time. "Let's cash out while you're up, huh? Go shopping or something."

When she turns back to lay yet another bet, I nearly scream. This is ridiculous. I should just leave her and let her deal with her own conse-quences. I twist my foot into the carpet, readying to go. But instead of leav-ing, I remind myself that this isn't entirely her fault. The vampires are to blame, too. They're feeding on her addiction, and I have no doubt, compelling her to come back at the soonest opportunity.

I glare at the dealer. Sure, he's human, but he's still part of the problem. The guy is the definition of forgettable. He has a bulbous red face and beady little eyes. One look and I know he won't help me. They don't call him a "dealer" for nothing. He's a mouse enslaved to the serpent. Speaking of——the pit boss glides toward us. I tell myself it's the casino's air conditioning that causes a chill to run down the back of my neck, not the presence of a vampire.

He comes to stand behind the dealer, observing as gamblers move chips forward like they mean nothing, like they don't amount to mortgages and bills and food in their children's bellies. Everything about this vamp lacks empathy. His humanity is nothing but a relic of an abandoned past. His eyes flash cold when he catches my hard gaze. When he tilts his head, his white-blond hair shines under the neon casino lights.

He whispers something to the dealer and stands back.

"Can I see your ID, please?" the dealer asks, looking up at me grim-faced. The whole table turns to stare now, and anger fills me up.

"I'm not playing."

"There's no loitering allowed around tables if you're under twenty-one."

Right, like we haven't all seen the news talking about how the vampires are lobbying hard to get the gambling age lowered to eighteen. It will be another in a long line of laws changed to get humans addicted young.

"We were just leaving." I tug on mom's shoulder. It really is time to go.

"You go'on out and wait for me, okay, Evangeline?" Mom says, "I'm just going to play a few more hands, then I'll go find the nurse and turn this thing in." She motions to her blood bag.

I don't move. We're both staring at it now. It's *stupid* full. If a fly landed on it, I swear it would pop. My hands are still clenched into fists and begin to sting as my fingernails bite into my palms. Why haven't they cut her off? Of course she thinks she can last a little longer, she always thinks that. I know better. At only five-foot-one and barely a hundred pounds, she can't handle this much blood loss. She's a tiny woman. Simply getting the needle taken out of her hand will exhaust her, and that's if we leave *now*.

I glare at the pit boss, meeting his hollow gaze eye-for-eye. My brain is not fully developed, so we both know I'm too young to be influenced by his vampiric compulsion. He raises an eyebrow as if to warn, *Not much longer, little girl.*

"She's going to pass out," I growl between gritted teeth, leaning over Mom to talk directly to the vampire. Immaculately groomed, he looks to be in his mid-thirties. He's more than likely much older than that. "If you don't cut her off before that happens, you'll break the law." I add, "And I'm here to witness it."

He gives me a sickly smile, fangs extended, and actually sniffs the air. My stomach churns. "She smells fine to me."

"Yeah, well, I know her better than you. She's not fine."

Meanwhile, the dealer has started another hand. The *slap, slap, slap* of cards is followed by Mom pushing out several hundred dollars in chips. In the space of time it takes for me to follow what she's doing, she doubles down.

I swallow a gasp and step back. All in. Fifteen hundred dollars. The exact amount I know we have to turn in to Mrs. Maybee tomorrow for our rent. Whatever she's earned from her blood donation, whatever she's brought along with her, whatever she's won on her streak––she's just bet it all.

"You had enough, already," I hiss. "Why did you do that?"

"I have three aces, Angel." Mom turns to me with a chastized whisper, swiping her auburn curls out of her brown eyes. Her complexion is even worse than it was minutes ago. The longer she plays, the longer she's hooked up to that stupid life-draining thing, the closer she gets to an accident. Drip, by drip, by drip, she plays her game and they collect their blood and the risks grow.

When the dealer flips over his cards, we're as still as the eye of a storm. A straight flush. Everyone around the table deflates, Mom the most.

She lost.

"I can win it back," she mutters as she reaches for the zipper of the purse strung over her bone-thin arm. Enough. I yank her up, and she squeals. Shame prickles through me as I pull her away, the drip stand rolling right along with us. But it's no use, Mom's knees buckle and she collapses in my arms. Not much bigger than she is, I'm only able to hold her weight for a moment. Falling to my knees, I lay her on the floor. The drip stand falls and the blood bag bounces against the carpet. It's a miracle it didn't break. Mom's brown eyes lose focus and flutter closed.

Oh, hell no!

"I told you she would pass out," I yell at the pit boss. "Now what, huh? Should I call the police?"

He seems unaffected, still back behind his table, but I know better. This is a fireable offense. This is the kind of thing that will get him in trouble with the vampires higher up in their royal hierarchy. There are treaties, laws, and rules for a reason.

A team of nurses swoop in moments later. I won't leave Mom. I shift back onto my butt and watch her carefully as they get to work. "She's lost a lot of blood," one of them says. "Virginia's lost a lot before," another adds, "she'll be okay." The fact that the nurses know my mom by name makes me even madder. And they're probably right, she'll probably be okay, but I'm about ready to burn this place to the ground anyway.

The pit boss jumps over the table, the players, and the crowd of gawkers, landing softly to survey the scene. He practically flew, he moved so fast. Maybe he did fly. I've heard some of the suckers can do that. I roll my eyes, unimpressed.

The laws on this kind of thing are clear. Vampires are not allowed to take "donations" to the point that a human passes out and absolutely no bleeding anyone dry. For as much as they need our blood, they need us alive, more.

Vampires use blood bags because feeding directly on human flesh isn't allowed unless there is written consent from the human *and* permission from vamp royalty, which as far as I know, never *ever* happens. The blood-suckers have chosen to keep that kind of feeding to a minimum for their own secretive reasons, thank heavens. And when I say secretive, I mean *secretive*. I've done a ton of research on this subject and haven't found a plausible reason as to why they don't feed directly from us. Sure, there are a zillion theories floating around out there, but the vampires won't confirm anything.

So it's blood bags for feedings, and those nasty creatures like to bite into them when they're as fresh and warm as puppies. Casinos are one of the best places vampires can use human vices against us, and they own them all. So take a seat, but first, you'd better stick out your arm and open a vein. The chance of winning money is too enticing for some people, add that to a nice dose of compulsion layered on each visit to "come again soon," and voila, you have yourself a herd of willing blood donors.

The whole thing makes me sick.

Luckily, I'm not twenty-five, the age that compulsion begins to work. My brain is still developing, which means my prefrontal cortex doesn't rule my decision making, so the vamps can't get inside there quite yet. Note to self, get away from here before the big day. When that happens, I don't want to be anywhere near vampires. Too bad they're in every urban city now and I never pictured myself living in the sticks. I hate bugs and I love fresh sushi. What's a girl to do?

Eyes watering, I lean forward to brush the hair from Mom's forehead. The nurses have been quick to administer their treatment. They must sense the anger still roaring in me because they don't ask me to move.

I can't wait to report this.

"Adrian has requested to speak with you. He wishes to apologize in person," someone is saying. I look up to meet the dealer's beady little eyes. The pit boss is behind him, talking on a cellphone; his voice is muffled and calm, but his expression is mighty strained.

Hello consequences, meet vampire, I hope you two get to know each other very well...

"Who's Adrian?" I ask the dealer, confused why someone would think for a second that I'd be willing to stick around. I'm getting Mom out of here at the first possible second and then we're filing a police report. That alone almost makes the fact that we can't make rent worth what happened. Almost.

At the end of the day, we still can't make rent, and Mrs. Maybee isn't the nicest landlady. We've been late too many times in the past. She'll only give us three days this time. That's it. And then what? Go to a shelter? Those places are cesspools for evil to prey on the weak. The world isn't what it used to be. Ever since the vampires crawled out of the shadows seventeen years ago, nobody is safe anymore. I've never known a world without them. I was a chubby little one year old when it all went down.

"Adrian runs this place," the dealer explains in a rush. "We'll make sure your mom is okay. But trust me, you'd better go, Adrian is not someone you want to say no to."

"And why's that?" I grumble, my mind already out of here and onto the next thing I'm going to have to do to clean up this mess. Maybe I can ask my boss for an advance? *Ugh, that's not going to work.* I just started at Pops and they're a place of *business*, not a charity.

Mom's eyes flutter open. I sink farther into the ground with a sigh. One of the nurses has switched her IV to fluids and she's already starting to look alive again. "You're going to keep a meticulous record of how much she donated, right?" I press the nurse. "So she doesn't donate again before she's safe?"

"Of course," the nurse replies as if that's a given, but I don't know if I believe her. She's human but she still works for *them*.

The dealer waves his hand in my face. "Hey, I'm still talking to you. This is important."

I roll my eyes at him. "What?"

"You really don't know who Adrian is?" The dealer frowns at me like I'm a complete idiot, like I should know everything that goes on in this casino, including who this Adrian guy is.

"Whatever, I'm only eighteen." I shake my head. The fact that I'm even here is total crap, and I blame it on the vamps. They were buying up places like this for decades before they ever went public, all part of their master plan. Places where they could convince humans to trade blood for addiction. And it's as easy as it sounds.

The dealer squats down next to me, getting right up in my face. He stinks of cigarette smoke just as bad as the carpet does. It makes my eyes burn. Another vice, cigarettes. I don't care what it is, if it's an addiction, I don't want any part. "Adrian's one of the North American princes. He doesn't just run The Alabaster Heart, he runs New Orleans and most of the southern United States."

"A prince, you say?" I snort. The idea of this Adrian character is a spark that settles into me, an answer to a problem. I decide to pour gasoline on that idea. Yes, this vampire has the kind of power that could squash me. Yes, he could murder me in a second if he chose. But I'm the one in the power position here. I'm the girl he needs to convince to shut up. My idea started as a spark but it's a full-on inferno now. Will it work?

I only have to strike a deal with the devil to find out.

Two

My sparkly white flip-flops smack on the pearlescent marble tile as I follow the pit boss out of the noxious gaming area and into the attached hotel lobby. Being in The Alabaster Heart is like walking through a time capsule. It's all reflective golden surfaces and polished white accents and deep, dark black everywhere in between. Magnificent crystal chandeliers hang from the ceilings and tufted black and emerald green furniture litter the space. The stunning art deco style is something my interior design-obsessed best friend Ayla would salivate over, but it does nothing but twists me into tight little knots.

"Kelli will help you." The pit boss steps aside, motioning toward a receptionist stand, and strides away. I wish I could follow and go back to mom. I hated leaving her back there, but the nurses insisted she wasn't ready to get up anyway.

A bright-eyed secretary slips me a demure smile. This must be Kelli. She's a California-looking bleached-blonde with big roller-curled hair and high cheekbones. She looks like she would've had glowing tan skin in her previous life but her deadness spoiled that. I catch sight of her gleaming white teeth and try not to stare. At least she has the decency not to extend her fangs. Her beauty is vampiric and unnatural and it sets me on edge. She looks me over and grimaces, as if judging me in two seconds flat and deciding I'm not worth her time or attention.

"Hi," I say, the greeting slipping out of me.

"Adrianos Teresi will see you now," she purrs in response. She nods toward a private elevator and I walk inside, more than happy to put distance between us. I'm surrounded by reflective gold on all sides in the elevator box. Gold ceiling, gold floor, gold walls—super weird. Even weirder is that fact that there are no buttons. I've never been in an elevator without buttons and I can't say I like it. As it rises, inertia settles low in my belly. I suddenly notice the lack of silver in the design. Nowhere in the entire hotel is anything silver. Makes sense, I guess. Vampires hate silver.

When the doors slide open, I'm directly facing a large office.

"First thing you need to know," I announce, stepping inside, "is it's going to take a lot of money to make me go away."

The office itself is a monochromatic cocoon of polished oak. The design is mid-century modern, like that TV show Mom used to watch obsessively, Mad Men. Everything about it screams masculinity and power. A twenty-something man stands before a vast, darkly-tinted window overlooking the Mississippi river. His hands are tucked together behind a crisp gray suit jacket. He's tall, thin, and stoic, with golden-blond wavy hair that's longer on top and cut close to his scalp on the sides. His suit contrasts perfectly against his pale skin like inky night and golden day. When he turns, an undertow of curiosity surfaces within me. It's his eyes. They demand my attention with their glacial blue, biting to my center.

He tilts his head to the side and runs those arrow-eyes down my body. I break out into a sweat. "You want money." His gaze narrows and he sounds almost disappointed. "That's all?"

"Yes, that's right." I steel myself. His people hurt my mother. He owes me. "I want our money back and then some."

"Asking for money is so uninspired, don't you think?"

"That's easy to say coming from someone who has it. Try living without money and you won't be so quick to judge me."

Rubbing his angular chin with his long pale fingers, he slowly walks toward his desk and flicks a hand at the open chair across from it. A businessman in his lair, he smiles wickedly. "Why don't you have a seat?"

"I'd rather stand."

He stops. His jaw clicks, and something that's either lust or thirst crosses his expression. "I'm sure you would."

Something tightens in my stomach. Is he toying with me?

"You're not what I thought you would be," he says. The slightest of Mediterranean accents alerts my basest instincts that he's different. If I had to guess, I'd say the tumbling melody of his tone, his light coloring, and last name Teresi, suggest that he's of Greek descent. He's certainly beautiful enough to have been the muse for those Greek sculptures. How old is he? Any accent he would have had is now watered down, likely through centuries of travel. He must be old if he's in charge of all the vampires in the southern United States.

He catches me staring and chuckles. The laugh rings like sweetgum leaves on a spring breeze, but I know not to trust it. Maybe he's not what I thought either. Maybe he's not the evil bloodthirsty vampire prince who'd suck me dry for dinner if he could, maybe he's something much worse.

Or maybe he's not. Maybe he's more human than I thought. I almost laugh at that stupid thought. It's not possible. I'd be foolish to think it.

"So how much?" I press.

He laughs louder.

"What's so funny?"

"Normally 'how much' is the question I would be asking you."

So he bribes people often. This shouldn't come as a surprise, but my disappointment stings anyway. I don't know why I'd hoped he would be better than my expectations, that he'd somehow care about humans. He doesn't. He can't. They never do.

"Your other guests might like to sit and chat, but I want to get out of here as quickly as possible. So why don't we cut the crap and finalize the money?"

He steps closer. "What makes you think I'm going to give you money?"

I glance down and glare at the lapels of his designer suit, not quite able to hold his gaze. It's probably a vampire thing, that all encompassing "feel it in your bone marrow" type of look meant to ensnare humans, but his eyes are too mesmerizing. "It's clear to me that this casino has more than enough money," I challenge, "and still, your pit boss ignored my mother's obvious distress. Your employee broke the law. If I report it, not only will you have to pay a hefty fine, but I'm guessing that even you, Adrianos Teresi, North American *prince*, will have to answer to an even more powerful vampire than yourself."

He's across the room one second and standing a foot away the next. The scent of warm cedar, bergamot, and honey wash over me. The curls of his golden hair catch the light. Up close, his youthful appearance is more predominant, almost startling. Even though he looks to be in his mid-twenties, there's no possible way that he is. I don't know for sure, but I think someone this powerful had to earn his position through many years of servitude, which is how I know he must answer to someone. Everyone does.

"Are you threatening me?" he snaps, disdain eating his expression. Heat flushes across my cheeks. His pupils dilate and I lose my breath; he can smell my blood. How easy would it be for him to kill me right now? To sink his fangs into my neck and suck the life from my veins?

Don't think about it...

"Maybe I am a threat to you," I challenge back. "And why do you really care for my mother's money? You got her blood. You don't need to take her paycheck, too."

Amusement sparks in his eyes. "And what if your mother faked her incapacitation? What if it was all a stunt to extort *us* for money?"

I gape, wanting to punch the smirk clean off his face.

"That's impossible. My mother loves this place. Besides, there were witnesses."

"Yes." He smiles wide. "There were." His tongue lightly runs across the tip of one fang as they slowly extend. My senses kick into overdrive, my pulse erupting. I need to get out of here.

He's dangerous. Beautiful––they usually are––but deadly as midnight.

"I'm not afraid of you," I lie. "If you kill me, you'll be tried and will face true death."

Okay, I actually doubt that would happen, vampires are good at getting away with things, but still, I have to appear strong in his presence or else I'm going to crumble.

He smiles and retracts the fangs. "How old are you?"

I'm caught off guard by the question. "I'm not even close to twenty-five, if that's what you're thinking."

He studies me as he leans back on his heels, still towering over me by at least a foot. I shrink.

"I'm eighteen," I finally say, irritation spreading through my body like a virus. I have absolutely nothing to hide here. He's the one who hurts people, feeds on human blood. He's the monster. "In case you suck at math," I'm quick to add, "I still have seven more years to make your job difficult if you keep hurting my mom."

Actually, it's closer to six. My birthday is coming up.

"Your mother is a grown woman who is free to come and go as she pleases." He says it like she's to blame here, not like she's a victim to their compulsion and her addiction. It curdles my stomach.

"Don't lie to me. I know your people use compulsion on her. You creeps love to prey on people like my mom."

"Compulsion is illegal." His voice is steel. "I assure you, we abide by the law here at The Alabaster."

Lies.

Sure, it's illegal, but it's also nearly impossible to track. No doubt it happens more often than people would like to believe. No one wants to think they were manipulated, especially not when they refuse to admit to their addictions, and especially not when they're entering into what they believe is a win-win situation.

Blood for gambling.

Blood for drugs.

Blood for sex.

The vampires have no shame.

"Like I said, I'm only eighteen. Let's make a deal, Adrian. Are we going to talk numbers? Maybe I should just go ahead and file that police report now." I raise an eyebrow.

He looks me over for a long second and then steps back, peering down his nose at me like I'm a bug he'd like nothing more than to squash. "I'll play your little game only because I am growing tired of you," he sighs dramatically. "I'll give you five thousand dollars."

I consider the option, ignoring the thrill of it. Be rational. Five grand is enough to get us through August and well into September. Hopefully, even longer. I could ask for more, negotiate, but I don't want to risk more money for what I'm about to do.

I don't want to be greedy like those gamblers down there. Knowing when to walk away is the only way to win.

"Fine by me." I reach out my hand and smile as sweet as my Grammy's pecan pie. Goodness, I miss that woman. She passed away two years ago and ever since it's like Mom's been in the casino nonstop. Grief does horrible things sometimes. We'd like to think so, but not everyone is strong.

Adrian seems pleased with himself, but he doesn't shake my hand.

All the better.

"I'll call down to the cashier," he says coolly. "They already know to look for you."

"Great." I head for the elevator, eager to press the call button. His lingering gaze sticks to me like a tattoo. I stop and turn back while I wait for the doors to open. "If they already knew to look for me, then why play this game?"

His smile is dangerous. "Maybe I like to play games. I do run a casino, after all."

I roll my eyes and turn away.

"You never told me your name," he says just as I step inside.

But I'm already gone.

As soon as I'm downstairs, I swing by the cashier, pick up the cash, and get Mom ready to go all in a matter of five minutes. I wrap her arm through mine, and as we make for the exit, I snatch my cell phone from my pocket. The number is programmed in, and the dispatcher answers on the second ring.

"I'd like to report a crime," I say, as we're about to make our escape.

"Vampires took too much blood from my mom at The Alabaster Heart Casino and she passed out."

As I back up against the first set of doors, I catch ice-blue eyes from across the lobby. *Uh-oh*. Adrian crosses to me instantly, so fast it happens in the space of a single blink, and grips my wrist between his steel-trap hands. They're cold. His touch sends a shockwave through my entire body. Mom shrieks and I shift her behind me.

"What did you just do?" Adrian clips.

"Don't touch me." I shove him away, a feather against a rock. I have zero strength on him, but he lets me go anyway. He shakes his head, angry thunder rolling through him like an incoming storm. I cross the threshold and raise my hand in a wholly inappropriate gesture as my parting goodbye gift.

I can't help it. Like a fool, I look back for one last glimpse. It leaves me with dread in my chest. Adrian is watching me like I'm a whole new kind of game he wants to master, one where I end up dead. The sun is a welcome friend, but it's setting fast. We need to get home. One thing I said I would never do is cross a vampire.

But vampires can be deceived too. They're not the only ones who can play games.

Did we set any terms or conditions? Did we shake on anything? He never once required the money to be an exchange for silence, never once asked for anything from me. All he did was offer five thousand dollars. As far as I'm concerned, this hellish casino has exploited my Mom for years. Maybe now she and I will not only make it through another month, but hopefully Adrian will ban us from the casino altogether.

Wouldn't that be nice?

I made a new enemy today. I know it was reckless, but the money is a thick wad of redemption tucked neatly in my pocket. And the truth is, cheating vampires feels really freaking good.

Three

T he police requested we come into the station right away. I like this place. It's all busy and bustling and no-nonsense. I've been considering looking into law enforcement and being here makes that feel possible, like maybe there's more out there for me. I'm totally excited!

The whole college thing didn't work out. I can't afford it and don't have good enough high school grades or test scores to land scholarships. Plus, growing up with a mom like mine made me scared of debt. It's fine. Right now I'm a server. It's decent money and all, but it's nothing I would want to do for the long haul. Let's be honest here, I'm way too sassy and independent to be in the service industry long term.

As I look around the police station, I imagine myself here instead, dressed in a crisp uniform, packing heat in my holster, and with an important job to protect innocent people. It's a nice thought, offering a chance at meaning in my otherwise murky future.

"This isn't necessary," Mom crows to the officer. "It was an unfortunate accident. My fault, really."

I glower over at Mom. "Stop trying to play this off like it was nothing. The casino took advantage of you."

She waves her wrist around. "Oh, I'd hardly call it that."

"They could've killed you!"

Officer Perez leans closer, tapping his pen against his notebook, worry etched onto his thick brow. "Facts are, Mrs. Blackwood, it's against the human-vampire law to take that much blood. Now, *we* can't go making any arrests in this case because it's outside of our jurisdiction, but what I can do is report the incident to the Vampire Enforcement Coalition. They take these filings very seriously and have their own ways of punishing vampires." His mouth turns down in a grimace. "I'll tell you, I've seen some of it in action and it's pretty nasty. I definitely wouldn't want to be working for the VEC."

Okay, first off, how do I get a job for the VEC? Because I'd love nothing more than to punish the suckers. But second, is this guy for real? Are the police too scared to actually do anything about what happened?

The image of myself working as a police officer slips away in an instant. I don't want to go into law enforcement if this is how it's going to be. I can't imagine how frustrated I would feel knowing someone is guilty of a crime but unable to go after them. I know vampires are scary and all, but humans still need to stand up to them.

"So we're just supposed to believe the Vampire Enforcement Coalition actually cares? Who's running that organization, anyway?" I fold my arms over my chest and glare. I think we all know where this is going...

He shrugs, his face reddening. "A mix of humans and vampires."

I bark out a laugh. "And we're supposed to trust the vampires to punish themselves? Give me a break, man."

"They have a whole watchdog group set up and their own police force for this very reason." He raises his hand in reassurance, but I can tell even he knows it's complete crap. I mean really, the absurdity is like handing a toddler a rainbow lollipop and then telling the child *not* to lick it. Never going to happen.

I shake my head. "But the guy who runs the casino is the vampire prince of North America."

"Adrianos Teresi?" The cop frowns. "Yeah, he's one of the main vamps over there at the VEC and not someone you ever want to piss off. You should stay far away from him."

"Great, so now we know for sure he's not going to get punished. What's he going to do? Slap himself on the wrist?"

"I'm sorry, Ms. Blackwood, but that's all we can do." He straightens in his chair. "And Adrianos isn't the only vampire affiliated with the VEC. They have checks and balances. We have to trust that someone else will punish him."

"If checks and balances actually worked, do you think our country would be in the position it's in?" I scoff. I hate politics because it always fails the exact people it's supposed to help. I think that pretty much goes without saying in a country where vampires are *legally allowed* to take advantage of the people who need protection from them. "You have younger cops, don't you? Officers under twenty-five who don't have to worry about compulsion? Let me talk to one of those guys."

"Yes, well, it doesn't work that way . . ."

"Why not?"

"They have to refer back to the VEC as well. Everyone does."

I blink a few times, absolutely disgusted by this red tape bureaucratic garbage. "This is nuts, you do realize that, right?"

"Think of vampire law like a Native American reservation law. They have their own enforcement, too, and when someone goes onto their land," he gestures to my mother, "or into one of their casinos––they should know the risks."

Mom shrinks in on herself.

"So you're blaming her now?" I point to my mom, even though the man does have a point. A lamb can't expect to walk into the lion's den and come out unscathed. But still, victim shaming is victim shaming, and it doesn't sit right with me.

"No, that's not what I mean," he rushes on. "I'm just saying that there are inherent risks that people take when they go to places like The Alabaster."

"These are vampires we're talking about here," I chastise, "this is not something we should be playing around with, at The Alabaster or anywhere else. If we keep letting them get away with crimes, how much longer until they're the ones in control?"

"I'm sorry that I can't do more for you." He fidgets, and I close my eyes.

I'm so mad I could scream. I don't know if I've ever felt more helpless and disillusioned. Forget about the suckers getting more control of the humans, they already have it. If the laws aren't enforced then what's the point of even having them? To give us the illusion of safety, to make us think we know what we're doing, that everything is going to be okay.

It's not.

"Listen," he whispers under his breath. "We both know compulsion is illegal, but they do it anyway. It allows them to turn the cops crooked if we go near them. Same thing happens with politicians. Even if we could send the under twenty-fives in, we wouldn't want to risk it. We don't know when someone's prefrontal cortex actually forms, the scientists say twenty-five, but there's not an exact date to brain development."

"Fine," I grumble. Maybe he's right. Just because something is illegal doesn't stop the leeches from doing it. The idea that sometime around my twenty-fifth birthday my brain will become permeable to the same tampering makes my stomach slowly harden like drying cement.

I hate them. I hate them all.

"Come on, Mom." I take her hand and we stand. "Let's go home. This was a waste of time."

Mom is all too happy to leave, and despite Perez's assurances that this will be taken seriously by the VEC and that we should stay and answer the rest of his questions, I get us the heck out of there. Deep in my gut I know the VEC won't do anything about this. Everyone is afraid of Adrian, or I guess, technically it's Adrianos. Still, I feel justified in my actions against him. The vamps deserved a taste of their own manipulative medicine, and quite frankly, we deserved to get some of our money back.

Mom doesn't agree.

As soon as we get into the car, she lets me have it. "Evangeline, how could you? We can't make enemies with the vampires!" Her voice shakes. "This is not going to end well."

I laugh bitterly. "Humans and vampires are already enemies, Mom. What are you even saying right now?" I'm driving since she's still weak, and my fingers tighten over the cracked plastic of the steering wheel. My knuckles turn white.

A tear slips down her ashen cheek, and I have to stop myself from lashing out at her even more and remember that she's weak and she's lost a lot of blood today. "I'm so embarrassed. Did you see the way that officer looked at me?"

I hold back a growl. "You don't actually care about that cop. You're embarrassed because you lost face with your casino buddies."

And probably the vamps themselves, but I don't add that part.

We argue the rest of the drive home, and after we pull into the carport, she storms inside, locking herself in her bedroom to pout. I run the rent money over to Mrs. Maybee who lives on the other side of our little duplex, because once again I'm the responsible one in this house. I try to remind myself that it's not all mom's fault, she's an addict and the vampires are feeding off of that, but I'm still mad as hell.

The gambling has always been a little bit of a problem for Mom, but since Grammy died of cancer it's gotten to the point of no return. When Gram was sick I thought maybe Mom would change. She was so busy taking care of her mom, she stopped going to the casino. But then Gram died and Mom went back ten times more often. I honestly don't know how I'm going to fix this, or if I can. I'm terrified she's going to either end up homeless or dead. And where would that leave me? Even though I'm the more mature one in our relationship, I still can't imagine being an orphan.

I stomp into my room, shove the rest of the cash into a sock, and hide it in the air conditioning vent above my bed. Rummaging through my disaster of a closet, I pick out an outfit for tomorrow, pajama shorts and a tank for tonight, find my toothbrush and makeup bag, and toss everything into my raggedy jean backpack. I text Mom on the way out the door. *I'm sleeping at Ayla's house tonight. If someone rings the doorbell, don't answer it.*

Ayla is my best friend. She has been ever since middle school when all the other girls got boobs and boyfriends and we stayed awkward for another few years. Luckily, our boobs and boyfriends came later. Not that I have much of either at the moment compared to Ayla. The girl is voluptuous with a capital V.

I would never answer the door without using the camera. Mom types back. *We'll talk some more tomorrow.* And then a few seconds later. *Why do you always act like you're the parent and I'm the child?*

And then, *I'm tired of your judgement.*

And a quick, *You need to learn to trust me. I'm the grown up here, Evangeline Rose Blackwood.*

I scoff. She could've fooled me! Just because she can yell at me through text by using my full name doesn't make her the mature one here. But that's not what I type. Instead, I type, *I only do what I do because I love you.* And leave it at that.

I'm glad about the doorbell situation though. Vampires can't enter homes without being invited in by someone who actually lives there, but they could easily compel her into letting them in if she answered the door and looked into their eyes. This is common knowledge and the main reason why literally *everyone* has doorbell cameras installed these days. She knows better, but still, I can't shake the rage I saw on Adrian's face when I left the casino earlier. He probably wants me dead for the stunt I pulled, and he seems like the kind of man who is used to getting what he wants.

I shiver and try to erase his image from my mind.

There's a lot of speculation about compulsion in general. Can all vampires do it or only the older ones? Do they really do it often, like I think they do, or not at all like they claim? I wish I knew the answers.

Mom texts back yet again. *Fine, you can go. Have a good time with your friend. Stay inside at her place tonight and don't take off your necklace. I'll see you tomorrow.*

I don't bother with a reply. Protection from a crucifix necklace is only a superstition, everyone knows that. But I feel like it's a declaration to the vampires that I think they're an abomination, so I wear it all the time. Plus, mine's kinda cute and fits in with my whole down-with-the-patriarchy aesthetic, in an ironic kind of way.

The sun is beginning to set, casting everything in a hazy glow of creamsicle orange, so I speed walk down the street and toward my best friend's place. She lives on the other side of our neighborhood, the fancier side, where the houses have their own fenced yards, the garages are all enclosed, and most people don't rent.

Can I sleep over tonight? I text Ayla, already knowing she'll say yes. *Mom and I had a huge fight and I can't be in the same house as her right now.*

Well, shoot! What did you do, Evangeline Rose Blackwood? Ayla immediately texts back, using my full name like she knows my mom does all too often. It drives me crazy, but coming from Ayla it makes me smirk.

Not me. Her gambling again. Is all I say.

It's followed by a quick, *Of course you can stay here. See you soon! Hugs!*

I slide the phone into my back pocket and wipe a bead of sweat from my forehead. You'd think the setting sun would have cooled things off, but it's early August. The humidity is not fun in Louisiana and it's only going to get worse the next few weeks. The heat doesn't let off here until October.

Don't call me by my full name Miss Ayla Elizabeth Moreno, I text again, trying to lighten the conversation before I show up at her door.

Then don't be a menace to society. Her reply is almost instant.

I laugh aloud at the inside joke dating back to a high school assembly in which our crusty old principal lectured us on what was and wasn't appropriate for teen behavior. When I challenged him on the hem length requirement for girls, he called me a menace to society. True story.

My full name is Evangeline Rose Blackwood. Pretentious, right? I hate it. It's way too "Southern Pageant Girl" for my taste, which is exactly why my mother picked it. She's always wanted me to be like her, to pretty myself up for pageants until I was old enough to pretty myself up for a wealthy man. Unfortunately for her active imagination, by age eight I'd rejected her plans, including the name, and have gone by Eva ever since. Mom still calls me Evangeline, or worse, Angel, but she's the only one who's allowed to, on account of the whole "growing me in her uterus, spending twenty hours in labor, and raising me all by herself" thing.

Besides, following in her footsteps was never a guarantee for happiness. Look at how things turned out for her. Mom married into a wealthy family when she was only twenty years old and, from the outside looking in, it seemed like she'd be set for life.

No such luck.

My father was the son of a well-to-do old European family. He was also the black sheep who went off to America for college. They wanted him to return home, but he ended up getting into a medical school in New Orleans and fell in love with the city. It was during med school that he met my mom who was working as a receptionist for the school. He'd fallen even more madly in love with her than he had NOLA and that was all it took for him to commit to staying. After a year of dating, she'd gotten pregnant with me and they'd eloped without the big European wedding or even the blessing of his parents.

Strike one and two, according to his family. They cut him off completely.

When he died in a horrific car accident when I was a baby, his family apparently reached out to Mom and asked her to move overseas so they could help raise me. A Southern girl through and through, Mom had refused, and that was strike three because they put us out of their minds without another word. Just like my father, we were dead to them too.

Nobody from Dad's side of the family has ever contacted me. Not one.

I look like a mixture of my Caucasian mom and the one picture I have of my father. I don't know a lot about him because Mom can't say a word without getting weepy and shutting herself in her bedroom. But their wedding picture still hangs on our living room wall. Judging from his appearance alone, he's got to be Spanish or Italian or something Mediterranean like that. With his creamy olive tone and thick dark hair, it's no wonder she fell head over heels.

I can see myself in him more than I can my mother, and something about that makes me happy and sad all at once.

My inky black hair is stick straight no matter what I do to it, my slightly almond shaped eyes are brown as molasses, and my prominent cheekbones make me stand out among my friends. Sometimes people ask me if I'm Asian or Polynesian. I've even gotten Native American on a couple occasions. I don't mind looking like the personification of the American melting pot, it's not like I've ever been to Europe anyway.

But my complexion is pretty close to Mom's pinky cream, and I have her big pageanty smile too. I've now grown taller and thinner than her because I never inherited her womanly curves, but I'm okay with that. I'm a natural athlete, which is great if you ask me. I was hoping a track scholarship would come my way, but that obviously never happened.

I graduated in May and my plan is to figure out what I want to do with my life, which is kind of laughable at this point. It's been three months since graduation, and my "figure out what I want to do with my life" plan hasn't made an inch of headway. Actually, I'll argue that after that disastrous visit to the police station it's gone backward.

I tuck away the disappointment about that to unpack another day. Right now, the Moreno's cute Spanish style house is a welcome friend, and I bound up the driveway. When I knock on the big blue door and wave to the doorbell camera, I expect Ayla to answer it. But it's Felix who pulls it open. Ayla's older brother by eighteen months, Felix is my longtime crush. One year ahead of us in school, Felix goes to Tulane University in the city. He lived in the dorms his first year and plans to live in off campus housing next year with some of his buddies, but he's been staying at home this summer.

Let's just say, it's been the best thing about this summer. I missed Felix last year.

"Hey, Eva." His smile quirks, and his chocolatey latin eyes sparkle. "You're sleeping over tonight?"

Ugh, why does my brain immediately want to take that question and ask him one of my own? *Like--Yes, Felix, I am. Do you mind if I sleep in your bed?* But I don't have much experience in that department, and I'm pretty sure my best friend would kill me if I started dating her brother. Actually, she has warned me of that many times over the years even though she knows how I feel about him. Doesn't stop a girl from dreaming, though.

"Yes," is all I say about sleeping arrangements as I follow him inside. "How's the internship going?"

He's working at some fancy downtown bank as a paper pusher but doesn't talk about it a whole lot. I mean, what is there to say? It's probably super boring.

"Eh, it's the same old 9 to 5." He winks and immediately changes the subject, "So what's new, Eva? Any guys I need to beat up for you?"

The picture of him beating up some jerk for me is definitely something I can get behind.

"Unfortunately, no." I pretend to think hard. "But I'll let you know when someone crosses me."

"You do that."

My mind flashes to Adrian, and I picture the two battling, Felix coming out victorious for my honor in the end, and then the two of us making out. Definitely an image I want to tattoo into my fantasy memory bank.

"Hey, you." Ayla appears and pulls me into her bedroom, closing the door softly. "Stop drooling over my brother, you hoe."

"Stop having such a hot brother," I retort. And Felix really is a hottie. He's got a bad boy persona with scruffy two-day-old facial hair and dark curly black hair. His eyebrows are stronger than most and his eyes have that deep-set commanding thing going on. He's tall and muscled and he even got a sleeve tattoo this last year. And to top it off, he's an athlete. But not a typical one; he plays lacrosse for the university. Honestly, how can Ayla blame me?

She crosses her eyes and sticks out her tongue. She's basically the girl version of Felix but shorter, with dyed blue hair and lighter eyes and *all the curves.* Ayla's the friend I've always counted on, and now she's leaving me behind to go off to college herself and pursue her dreams. My heart squeezes. "I'm really going to miss you."

"Me too." She frowns and gathers me in a hug, offering the first bit of comfort I've had in ages. Her signature vanilla spice scent wraps around me and I try to commit it to memory. I don't know what I'm going to do when she's gone.

Four

I wake up with a start, my eyes popping wide open. I blink into the shadowy ceiling and freeze. Ayla sleeps next to me, her body curled into a tight ball, her breath soft whisperings in the darkness. Exhaustion grips the back of my eyeballs, but there's no way I could go back to sleep right now. My heart races, the pulse drumming in my neck.

I heard something––a noise that woke me up.

A thump, maybe?

I don't move, don't breathe, listening intently until I hear it again. *Thump, thump, thump.* It's inside the house. Footsteps. Soft, quiet, sneaky, "trying not to wake anyone," kind of footsteps.

I think back to the encounter with Adrian and fear tightens around my neck like gripping murderous fingers. I imagine what it would be like to have fangs sinking into my tender skin, to feel the hot slice of them, to experience my limbs going limp and my body draining of life. Angry tears burn my eyes. Did Adrian come after me? He could have sent his minions to search me out, but that vampire seems like the type who'd want to do the job himself.

I can't believe I played him like that. How stupid can I be? Maybe Mom's right. In the light of day, my actions against Adrian felt empowering, but now in the middle of the night, I feel nothing but vulnerability and fear and the weight of a million what-ifs.

I force myself to sit up and slip from the warm bed, padding softly to the dark hallway. I follow the sound out toward the living room, my eyes slowly adjusting to the darkness. I need to place distance between myself and Ayla just in case the vampires found me here and somehow managed to enter her house uninvited. But also, as foolish and "girl in a horror movie" as it is, I want to locate the source of whatever that thump was that woke me up.

I freeze. A figure is standing near the kitchen counter, tall and unmoving, with the broad shoulders of a man. My throat goes dry.

He moves quickly, taking two steps toward the refrigerator. When he opens it and Felix comes into focus, I let out a breath of relief and sink back into the darkened hallway. I'm an idiot. One encounter with a vampire and I'm already imagining crazy scenarios in my head. I watch Felix for a minute. He puts a lunchbox in his backpack and tosses in a couple bottles of blue Gatorade. He must be getting ready for work. The clock flashes above the stove: 4:10 a.m. I didn't realize his internship started so early. I don't know of any banks that open before 9:00 a.m.

But he's not dressed in professional attire. He's in athletic wear, black basketball shorts and a black hoodie. He's probably hitting the gym before work. Or maybe they have lacrosse practice super early?

Just as I'm thinking that I'm verging on stalkerish behavior over here, he rearranges his bag and lifts something long and wooden from within. The tip glints silver in the refrigerator light and my jaw falls open. It's a silver-tipped wooden stake––the kind used to kill vampires.

Maybe he takes them with him when he goes out at night? A lot of people do these days, it wouldn't be that unusual. Except when he lifts his hoodie and fastens the stake into a holster securely above his waistband, something within me screams that this is more than everyday protection. There's a practiced movement to the way his hands grip the weapon that speaks to experience handling it and handling it well.

I want to ask him about the stake, to emerge from the shadows and confront him, or at least talk about this. What is Felix hiding? And also, how in the heck can I get in on it? Because if he's hunting vamps then I want to do it with him. But just as I'm about to take action and reveal myself, he finishes getting his bag ready and heads out to the garage door, disappearing from sight. Before I can think twice, I race back to Ayla's room, snag her car keys off her desk, and sprint out the back door. Since there isn't room for all the cars in the garage, the Moreno kids park in the driveway. By the time I'm approaching Ayla's prized navy blue Mini Cooper, Felix is already pulling his black SUV around the street corner.

I jump in, start the engine, and follow.

Adrenaline pumps through my veins, enough that every time I start to question my actions, I'm able to push them away and focus on not losing sight of Felix's tail lights. I'm careful to keep my distance, considering nothing about Ayla's ride is inconspicuous. I wish I had my own car at a time like this, but alas, I'm broke. I follow him all the way through the twisting suburban streets, onto the freeway for a few minutes, and then downtown into the banking district. The further we get from home, the more I lose my nerve. Maybe he's not out to hunt down suckers. Maybe there's a gym in this part of town that he belongs to. Executives and business professionals have to workout too.

He pulls the SUV into an underground parking garage. I park at the other end of the garage and watch as he gets out of his car and goes through an unmarked door with a fingerprint keypad to gain access. For five long minutes I stare at the metal door that's now closed behind him, feeling like a stage-five clinger. Why did I think I could follow him and learn anything? The guy is working or exercising or something. So what if he has a stake on him? That's a smart move, doesn't mean he's a hunter. I'm being dumb.

But I still can't forget the expert way in which he handled that stake.

I sigh and lean back into the seat, ready to head back to Ayla's house and squeeze in a few more hours of precious sleep, when the metal door swings open and Felix reappears. He's no longer alone. Two other guys are with him, each carrying a large black duffle bag. The new guys are also dressed in black athletic gear, and they all climb into Felix's black SUV.

It's a lot of black, like a totally suspicious amount. If I didn't know any better, I'd think this was a bank robbery, but I do know better. Felix may look like a bad boy, but he's a good person deep down to the core. He's not robbing anyone. So what's going on here?

They pull out of the garage and I follow him again, this time driving away from the city and back toward the suburbs, then farther to the outskirts of town where the suburbs become the rural areas which then becomes the swamp. As we leave the city behind, I have to drop back even farther so he doesn't recognize Ayla's car. I almost lose them a couple times because of it.

It's after 5 a.m. now. This time of year, the sun will be rising soon. The sky is turning that royal blue color when the sun is making its way out, but it's still pretty dark. I continue to keep back as I follow them––to a cemetery. And let me tell you, there's nothing like a swampy old cemetery at night to give you the heebie-jeebies.

"Okay, guys," I say to myself when I slow the car and park. "What are you up to?"

I'm farther down so I have to jog in. I'm suddenly feeling ridiculous because I'm wearing nothing but the pink lacy pajama shorts and white cotton tank top I brought to Ayla's. I thank the bra god's, or goddesses, that I still have one on, even though I'm so out of my element here. At least the bugs have gone to sleep and aren't having a meal of my legs, which if it was that extra special time around sunset, I'd be a goner. I'm a little cold and I'm *a lot* spooked, but I'm also curious and determined to figure out what's going on.

"We should go back to the car and wait. We weren't supposed to do this until sunrise," an unfamiliar male voice says. He's within the cemetery walls, his gravelly voice catching my attention like a fish on a line. I edge toward it. "We shouldn't break protocol. I don't know if this is a good idea."

"I think it's a great idea," a different voice replies, "maybe we'll get lucky."

"I doubt that. Where did they say it was?" The unfamiliar man speaks again.

"Here," Felix's voice adds. I'd recognize his deep smooth timbre anywhere.

I follow them through the maze of headstones, tombs, and mausoleums. The water levels are too high to bury bodies underground this close to the coast, so our cemeteries are like above-ground mazes. The tombs make it easier for me to follow these three men without being seen, but it's also freaky as hell, and I'm starting to shiver from fear instead of the cold. My sparkly white flippys are going to be ruined from the mud, but that's the least of my worries.

The sunlight will crest the edge of the horizon soon. They're going to catch me and then what?

"Well, if any are in here and wake up," the first unfamiliar voice speaks again, "they'd better hide quickly or the sun will get them soon."

I freeze. They're talking about vampires. They have to be.

"More like I'll get them," the second voice jokes.

I take another step forward and wince when my ankle catches on the edge of a tomb I didn't see in the darkness.

"Shh––" Felix snaps. "Did you hear that?"

They're fast. One second they're several rows of graves over and the next they're coming right for me. Whatever they're hunting, I've now become the target.

I stand there, frozen, really not wanting to be impaled by a silver tipped wooden stake, but also not sure where to even go, when Felix steps between two towering tombs, weapon raised and ready to strike. I scurry backward. "Don't!"

His body goes rigid. "Eva?"

I grimace, caught like a deer in the headlights, but it doesn't matter, because that's when something behind me screeches, something not quite human.

"Get back," Felix growls.

I turn, and standing not three feet away from me, with her fangs gleaming white and eyes bloodshot, is the pale face of a vampire. She lunges for me.

Five

I'm knocked to the ground, the back of my head slamming against a
tomb in the process. Pain rings through my ears, but that's the least of
my problems. I scream as the vampire hurls herself on top of me. Felix
is quick to intervene, wrenching her away before she gets the chance to make
contact. She jumps back just as he swings the stake toward her heart. It's
close, but he misses. She shrieks an animalistic scream, her frizzy blonde hair
a wild mess around her dirt-stained face. She's dressed in a long white gown
and the closer I look at her, the more I realize what she is.

She's not just any vampire. She's new.

The most dangerous kind, because even though it's illegal in the vampire
community to suck blood directly from a human without consent, newly-
sired vampires are too thirsty to care about the laws. Their hunger is even
rumored to be stronger than the blood bonds that forge them to their
masters. The threat of true death is nothing compared to their mind
numbing urgency to feed. This woman is no different. She crouches down
among the grass with flexed fists, ready to pounce.

Male arms grab me from behind and pull me back against a broad chest.
"Stay calm," the young man whispers. He presses something cold and hard
into my palm. A stake. I grip it tight for dear life. It's all I have. It's
everything.

Felix edges closer to the vamp. "You try to hurt us and I will kill you," he
warns. "That's if the sun doesn't get you first."

She hisses, but he's right. The sun will be out soon, and if she's exposed,
the light will burn her alive. But right now, dawn feels a million miles away,

35

each second stretching into eternal darkness. Even though Felix's threats are menacing and we all have stakes at the ready, this woman is probably strong enough to kill the four of us. She'll suck us dry, one by one, until we're nothing but husks.

"You're not my master," she hisses. "Or did my master send you to me as my welcome gift?"

The male arms still wrapped around me shift to push me behind his large frame.

"Oh, yes," she continues. Sick clarity spreads across her moon pale face. "You all smell so good." Her eyes zero in on me. "Oh, and what's this? Virgin blood." She licks her lips.

Hot bile rises to my throat and blood warms my cheeks. New vampires are ruthlessly strong, and this one appears to have barely risen from the dead, literally clawing her way from her grave. The blood of virgins is rumored to have some kind of draw for vamps, but I don't know why.

I'm not going to stick around and find out.

Fight or flight mode kicks in, and I choose flight, taking off at an all-out sprint. I excelled at track while in school, so I'm fast, but even I know I'm no match for a newborn vampire. Even still, I have to try, especially while she's distracted by three aggressive vampire hunters. I don't know exactly where I'm going, just as long as it is in the opposite direction of her and toward the main road. I need to get to the car and get away from this cemetery as fast as possible.

"Wait!" Felix calls after me. He utters a few curse words when I don't respond, but I don't care. I can't be here. I shouldn't have come and I need to go right now.

My eyes have adjusted to the darkness but it's still not light enough to see every obstacle in the pre-dawn misty light. I trip over raised tree roots and graves a few times but scramble back up even faster, adrenaline careening me forward with each hurried step. Behind me, the vampire woman screeches into the night. She's closer—making chase.

Too late, I realize my mistake and the reason for Felix's curses. Earlier, I just so happened to stumble upon her, a lucky break for a new vampire, but now that I'm running, I've started a game of cat and mouse. It's like the advice I heard once about never running away from a mountain lion. You're supposed to make yourself big and scare it away. Running only makes the animal want to eat you even more.

And now this vampire is definitely hunting me down.

I have to choose to fight if I'm going to stand a chance, so I stop and whip around, the stake tight in my hand and poised to strike. I hold my breath in an attempt to hear better, but the graveyard grows eerily quiet, and my blood pumps through my eardrums, reminding me of how vulnerable I am. I ran too fast and too far, and now Felix and his friends are calling out from different directions. They're not close. Not like her scream was.

I look around for Felix anyway. I need him. There's nothing but darkness and shadows and the reality that I'm the idiot who snuck after him in the middle of the night, and because of it, I'm about to become a corpse.

I wait, my breath slowing like silent anguished prayers. I wait for her to come. I wait for the only two options left--to die or to kill.

She appears, jumping from the roof of a tall mausoleum, flying right for me so fast that I almost don't see her coming. She's like a ghostly apparition of death--eyes bloody orbs and fangs long thin daggers. I don't stop to question myself. I just swing the stake and aim for the heart.

It strikes, slicing through the white dress and sinking deep between cracking ribs. She wails, her thin body falling against mine, the tip of a fang nicking my arm. A flash of white-hot pain erupts through me. It feels like the shock of hitting my funny bone, but it's so much worse. The pain subsides as quickly as it came and the woman falls to her knees, reaching up toward the heavens.

"No!" she screams, and then she crumbles into dust.

Gone.

"Holy hell," I mutter. "I can't believe that just happened."

Talk about dumb luck.

Heart thundering, I brush off the dust and study my arm for bite marks where her fang got me. There's nothing but a tiny prick of blood that I rub away with one swipe. Was I bitten? I'm not really sure. I felt her fang pierce my skin, but I wouldn't call that a bite since she didn't get anything out of me. My blood was never taken. But because the vampire royalty has kept their secrets guarded, I have no idea what the consequences of this might be for me. At least I know that I can't be turned into a vampire. Not unless I feed on one who feeds on me, and then I'd have to be buried in a cemetery. Three nights later, I'd either wake up and claw my way out of the grave or the vampire venom would finish me off for good.

That's not going to happen. I'm not rising from the dead any time soon. I'm okay. It was just a scratch. It was nothing.

I let out a shuddering breath as Felix appears. His dark hair is disheveled and horror hangs on his face, followed by anger, and then something else I can't quite read. I prepare to defend myself but I don't have to. The man cuts through the maze of graves and pulls me into a tight hug. He's never hugged me before this moment.

"I thought you were dead," he mutters against my hair.

I release a frightened laugh. "Yeah, so did I."

His heart thuds against his chest, matching the rhythm of my own.

Too soon, he steps back and surveys me up and down, assessing the damage, but there is none. "What were you thinking following me out here?"

I scoff. "Um, excuse me, what were you thinking telling me you're working in banking this summer when you're obviously hunting vampires?"

His two friends trudge from the shadows, chuckling at my antics. "The woman has a point." The attractive African American one nods to me. He's the guy who gave me the stake and essentially saved my life. "But hey, looks like you're a vampire hunter, too."

I shake my head. "No, I'm not."

He points to the bloodied stake in my hand. "Could've fooled me."

I squeeze it tighter. I might never put this stake down.

The third guy frowns, not really watching us anymore but surveying the spooky cemetery. "Let's get out of here." His voice is soft. It's the same voice that didn't want to be in the cemetery at dark.

"The sun is rising soon," Felix says, "we don't need to rush." He points to the black duffle bags I'd forgotten they'd brought with them. "We need to place those stakes before we go."

"Oh . . ." Realization dawns on me. These guys weren't exactly out here to hunt vampires. They were here to place stakes around the graveyard, probably in hidden caches. I've heard this was something vampire hunters do since graveyards are the literal breeding grounds for vamps. It's not a bad idea. I'm pretty sure stakes anywhere and everywhere is an awesome idea, come to think of it.

A chill rolls over my exposed skin as everything comes rushing back to me, my mind unpacking what just happened. I don't want to be here anymore, either.

"Well, the sun's not up yet," the third guy continues in his levelheaded way. "We can place those stakes later because whoever sired that vampire is probably close by."

I thought I was afraid before, but now the consequences of my actions creep over my skin like tiny spiders as I realize what I've done. Killing a vampire isn't just killing a vampire. It's not one and done, and be done with it. Vamps don't work like that. They're connected. They feel each other through their blood bonds and are ruthlessly protective of their creepy little families. The woman I just obliterated hadn't become a vampire all on her own, someone had chosen her, had fed on her, offered their own blood, and then had buried her. This was all planned. Maybe she woke up early, maybe she woke up late, but either way, whoever made her would be coming back.

And that someone might not be pleased to find me standing over her ashes with a bloody stake in my fist.

"We're leaving." I point the silver tip toward Felix. "And you're riding back in my car."

"You mean Ayla's car?" he quips.

"Felix!"

He shrugs. "Fine, but I don't have to answer your questions."

Oh, he knows me so well.

I raise an eyebrow at the boy I grew up with who is apparently someone else entirely. I'd be on the verge of laughing if I wasn't so freaked out. "Umm––you can answer all my questions, and you will answer all my questions."

He smirks. How can he smirk at a time like this? "Yeah, we'll see about that."

Six

╔══════════════════╗

"**G**ive me the keys," Felix says, sliding into the driver's seat. I'm a little too shaken up to drive after having just killed a vampire and all, so I have no problem passing over Ayla's keys. I retrieve a hoodie from her backseat and put it on, slipping the stake into the front pocket, and then get in the front seat.

"What do you want to know?" His voice is strained.

"How about everything?"

He nods once but his mouth turns down. "Well, I'm sworn to secrecy on most of it."

"I'm pretty sure I've already figured out you're a vampire hunter. What group are you with?" There's several that have been talked about over the years, each trying to prove they're better than the last.

His lips twist. "I can't say."

"So that's how it is, huh?"

"We're all under twenty-five if that's what you're wondering."

"Yeah, I sort of guessed that considering your buddies look about your age, but that wasn't what I asked."

"It's not a group you would have heard of."

I lean back against the heated leather seat and sigh. "Now I'm even more curious."

Maybe it's good that I haven't heard of them considering most of the hunter groups I have heard of only came to light after everyone in them had been killed. Vampires live openly in society and have rights now, which means you can't just hunt them down without repercussions, especially when the world leaders and everyday people can be easily compelled. Yeah, we have treaties in place, compulsion was made illegal, and we live our human lives with a semblance of normalcy, but at the end of the day, the vampires have the most power and everyone knows it.

When we turn right and the guys driving Felix's black SUV turn left, I have to ask where we are going.

"I'm taking you home," Felix deadpans. "Obviously."

That doesn't sit well with me. I wanted to know more, not to go home. Even though I was still shaken up, my mind was also whirling with opportunity.

"Take me to your leader," I say.

"E.T. phone home?" Felix rolls his eyes. He's trying to make me laugh and lighten the tension. He can be aloof at times, but he's not a broody person and knows how to crack a good joke; however, right now, I don't want to hear it.

"No, I'm serious, Felix," I continue, passion sparking like a firework. "I want to be a vampire hunter, too." It makes the most sense for me to pursue this. I hate vampires. I want to help humans. Win-win.

The car grows quiet as he flexes white-knuckled fingers over the steering wheel. "That's not a good idea, Eva."

"It's a brilliant idea!"

"Why?"

"*Why?*"

"Yes, why on earth would you want to hunt something so dangerous? Most of us end up dead."

Okay, that was pretty rich coming from him. "Obviously, I'm willing to risk my life if it means getting rid of the vampires. I hate them. I hate them more than you could ever understand."

"Oh, I think I could understand."

I wonder what the vamps ever did to Felix. His family is so perfect and have managed to stay far away from the suckers. Not like me. "So why do you hunt them? You know I have to ask."

He goes still. "Nope. It's personal."

"You're really not going to tell me?"

He sighs, "Maybe someday, I don't know. Please, just drop it. Drop the whole thing. It's a bad idea. You have too much going for you to get caught up in this shit."

"Says the guy going to Tulane. You already know I graduated high school with no prospect of college. I thought maybe I'd go into law enforcement, but one trip to the police station . . . you know those guys are useless when it comes to vampires, right?"

41

He chuckles darkly. "I do know."

"Right. The cop gave our claim over to the Vampire Enforcement Coalition, which is literally run by vampires. What a load of crap."

"What claim?"

I wave him off and continue, "Nonsense to do with my mom, what else?"

His jaw tenses and his face turns into an unreadable mask.

"I need something meaningful to do with my life, Felix. You saw how fast I ran tonight, right? I did track forever, so I'm in shape. And I was good with the stake. I got that one on the first try, didn't I?"

"You did," he grumbles.

"So who do I need to talk to about recruitment?" I don't think I've ever spoken so openly with Felix, but my entire body is thrumming with electric excitement right now and I can't stop myself from going for this new opportunity.

"Eva, listen to me." His voice is tight. "It's too dangerous."

"Well, they'll train me. I'll learn some fighting skills or something."

"It's too dangerous," he repeats, this time emphasizing each word harshly. He turns to glower at me. "Do you have a death wish?"

"Hello pot, meet kettle," I growl. "I'm already in danger. I killed a brand spankin' new vampire sired by someone who's not going to be happy about what I did. What if they can trace it back to me?"

"They can't."

"Don't be so sure. Not to mention, are you ready to hear why I went to the police station to file a claim with the VEC?"

"Okay, why?"

I can tell he's growing annoyed with me, but I can't stop myself from pressing this. Now that I've killed one blood sucker, I need to kill another. They're evil, vile, horrible, and need to go. I don't care if it's illegal and dangerous and maybe even a lot stupid because I could be part of something important. For the first time in ages, I actually feel like I've found some direction in my life. "Yesterday the casino messed with my mom and took way too much blood," I confess.

"I'm sorry to hear that." And he means it. Felix knows all about my mother's vice. It seems like the adults have vices in one way or another, though I still haven't figured out what his wholesome parents are up to in their free time. I'm pretty sure they've eluded the vampires all together. It's not impossible, it's not easy, but if anyone can do it it's the Moreno family. Ayla and Felix's grandparents fled Cuba to immigrate here and have worked dang hard to get to where they are today. They've since retired, and Mr. and Mrs. Moreno now run the furniture and interior design shop. Ayla plans to go to school for design so she can take over for her mom one day. Felix is doing business administration for the same reason. They're good kids, living the American dream.

This guy is the one who has everything going for him, a perfect future all mapped out, and yet he's still a hunter. How can he sit here and tell me I can't do this? I have nothing, literally nothing, to lose.

"And," I press on, going for the kill shot. "I pissed off a vampire prince yesterday."

He whirls on me, slamming too hard on the brakes. The seat belt holds me back from a case of whiplash. "Felix!"

"You did what? Who?"

"Adrian Teresi." I'm being smug about it even though I shouldn't be.

Felix's body freezes. The sun has crested the horizon so I can see his features better, and while he's gone from weary to joking to angry during our conversation, now the man just looks afraid. I don't think it's an emotion I've ever seen him wear. It takes the wind right out of my sails, and my mind flashes back to the terror I felt when the newly sired vampire almost killed me tonight. That was child's play compared to what a vampire prince could do to me.

"Please tell me you don't know Adrianos Teresi." Felix's voice is tight.

"Well, I can explain... " I go into detail about everything that happened at the casino, and by the end of it, Felix is bright red.

"Do you know what you did?" he yells––yes, yells––through the car. "You put a target on your back! Adrian is the most powerful vampire in Louisiana and one of the most powerful in the country, maybe even the world, Eva, what were you thinking?"

"How bad can he really be?" My chest tightens.

"Are you seriously asking me that right now? We've been trying to take Adrian down for years, but the guy is untouchable. He's got his fingers in all the worst vices, Eva. All of them. If you think gambling is bad, you have no idea what he's a part of."

My entire body goes cold and I try not to picture what that means.

"So all the better to recruit me to your hunter group." I lean back in the seat, arms folded and mind made up. "Let me help you kill him." I smirk. "I actually think he might like me."

Felix shakes his head and doesn't speak to me the rest of the drive home. He pulls up to my little duplex and stops the car. "My stuff is with Ayla."

"I don't care. You need to get out."

"Felix––"

"I mean it. You can't do this, Eva. You just can't."

I glare but get out of the car. Who is he to tell me what I can and can't do? I slam the door and storm up my driveway. But soon realize I don't even have my key. Screw this. I whirl around, but he's already driven off, so I head toward Ayla's place on foot. I'm going to get my stuff, at least. He can't stop me from doing that. I need my key and I don't want to wake up Mom to explain why I don't have it.

When I get back to the Moreno's, my bestie is still asleep, none the wiser to what I just went through. I want to shake her awake and tell her every little detail of the horror involved in killing a vampire, but my better judgement stops me. She's leaving for college up north in three weeks. I'm going to miss her like crazy when she's gone, but I also love her enough to want the best for her. Right now, she thinks her world is safe, and it probably is, especially in the small town where she'll be attending college. I'm not going to be the person to take that away.

I quietly gather my things and send her a quick text on my way out the door. *I woke up early and decided to head home. Let's hang out later! Maybe shopping? I want to help you pick out a new bedspread for your dorm.* Her phone is on silent so I know it won't wake her. Offering to go shopping helps ease my guilt a little at keeping secrets. The girl loves shopping; I do not.

When I slip out the front door with my backpack loaded over one shoulder and my house key ring dangling from my index finger, I spot Felix climbing into his black SUV. So his friends came back for him. I run up to the window before I can stop myself.

His friend who had handed me the stake in the graveyard is still in the driver's seat. The quieter one sits in the back so Felix can ride passenger.

Felix motions for them to drive away, but his friend just smirks and rolls down the window. "Good morning, Beautiful," he says, his green eyes sparkling. He's got a southern accent, the kind people don't have when they grew up in the city. This is farmville-speak. I like it. It suits him. And damn, he's gorgeous. Tall, dark, and handsome—has Ayla met him yet? She's going to freak.

"Good morning to you, too." I pop my hip and fold my arms over my chest. I meet his mischievous gaze, then Felix's angry one, then nod to the guy in the back. "Tell your recruiter I want in."

Tall, Dark, and Handsome smiles like the Cheshire Cat. "Excellent. I'll do that."

"No, you won't," Felix spits.

The guy only laughs and rolls up his window, driving off and leaving me alone on the sidewalk. I have a feeling that guy and I are going to become friends. A vampire hunter with a sense of humor seems like the kind of person I'd want to be friends with. I grin to myself. This is going to be fun.

I pull the bloodied stake from the front pocket of Ayla's hoodie and look it over––the silver tip, the finely polished wood, the weight and length of it––all feel right in my hand. Replacing it back in the pocket, I walk home, a mixture of emotions rolling around in my gut. Am I a total idiot? Am I brave? Am I naive to think anything will even come of this? I don't have the answers to those questions, but there is one thing I do know. I killed my first vampire, finally doing something of value with my life, and I'm not going to stop now.

The unsettling feeling of being watched prickles at the back of my neck. I turn but the street is empty. Nobody is there. Of course not, I'm just being paranoid. But as I walk home, that feeling only intensifies. I start to speed walk. The sun is up. This is irrational but I can't shake the feeling...

A car engine revs and a black sedan rolls up next to me. It drives slowly, keeping pace. The windows are so tinted I can't see inside. Can vampires ride in cars if they're not directly exposed to the sun? It seems foolish for them to risk something like that but I don't know the answer. I imagine a human thug jumping from the car and throwing me inside. That's all I need to get thoroughly spooked.

I take off at a run, gripping the stake in my right hand to make sure whoever is in that car can see it. My feet pound against the pavement and my heartbeat thunders against my eardrums like a battle cry. The car speeds away with a screech of tires. When I get home, the scent of burning rubber lingers with me all day.

Seven

The tangy scent of barbecue greets me as I hurry into work that afternoon. And thank goodness it's strong enough to overpower the awful burning rubber smell that's been haunting me. I'm a server at one of the city's oldest and most popular restaurants downtown and I'm beyond grateful for this job. Pops would be a tourist trap if the locals didn't love it so much, but they do and for good reason. We're a greasy spoon kind of place known for authentic Southern food like spicy gumbo, traditional crawfish étouffée, world famous melt-in-your-mouth pecan pie, and so much more.

It's no surprise that the line to get a table is around the block as I weave my way through the crowd to get inside. Serving here comes with excellent tips, I just wish I could get more shifts. I'm one of the newer employees, with only a few months of day shifts under my belt, and tonight is the first time I'll really get to experience the dinner rush. Pops is the kind of restaurant where servers stay on the payroll for years, so I want to impress Eddie, the evening manager in charge of scheduling and my key to making more money.

I'm done counting on Mom to keep a roof over my head. She's in a downward spiral, and even though I'll do anything I can to save her, I refuse to become her collateral damage. New Orleans is probably the least safe place to be homeless in America. Everyone knows it's got the most vampires of any city on the continent, or that's what people say anyway.

I can picture my life the way I want it to be, working the busy evening shifts at Pops, hunting blood suckers through the night with Felix, and sleeping away the day. Who knows? Maybe I'll be able to get my own apartment. Except I have to look after Mom or else she *will* end up homeless or dead, so I should probably keep living in the duplex. Regardless, vampire hunting was a far-off possibility yesterday, but now that it's in my thoughts, now that I've actually done it, I can focus on little else. I have five or six good years left before the vampires will be able to get to my brain, I might as well end as many of them as I can while I still have the chance.

"You've got section four," Marla, the hostess, greets me. "I just sat table twelve."

"Great." I give her a friendly wink and bounce off to take care of my customers.

The shift is so busy that it flies by way faster than my daytime ones. We're a half hour from closing when I'm given what will hopefully be my last table for the night. The men are at least twenty years older than me and definitely intoxicated, if the stench of alcohol and their beady bloodshot eyes are anything to judge them by. I put on an unaffected smile and stroll over to take their orders.

"What can I get for you tonight, gentlemen?"

One of them blatantly checks me out, eyes lingering on my bare legs. Pops' servers wear black shorts and t-shirts, nothing too revealing, but this guy doesn't care and isn't being the least bit discreet. "Any secret menu items you can offer?" His voice is a low jeer and the other three guys chuckle at his sleazy antics. "I've got the money," he continues, "so maybe you can offer a discount?"

What a perv.

I step back and glare. "I can't offer you anything that's not on our menu, but maybe you'd like to speak with my manager?" I motion to Eddie.

Eddie is a massive African American man who looks like a bouncer and is probably packing heat under his oversized clothing. There's a reason he's on the late shift. It's no secret Pops has a lot of money coming in on the daily, and we're right in the middle of the French Quarter, aka New Orleans Party Central. People can get desperate when they're running low on funds.

One look at Eddie shuts these guys up but not without a few grimaces. They leave me alone after that, ordering and eating their meals without any more advances, and leaving without lingering around. As they go, I catch them complaining about a popular vampire-run nightclub nearby called The Crypt that they want to go to. The guy who propositioned me is grumbling about the high cover fee.

Since humans can't give blood every day without wasting away to nothing, the vampires keep meticulous records of how much blood we "donate." Donations equal entrance, so explain to me how it's a donation and not a payment? Anyway, when people aren't eligible for donation they have to pay actual money for their vices, and the prices aren't cheap. The vampires have taken over just about everything seedy––bars, strip clubs, casinos. Rumor has it even illegal drugs and sex work are included on the list.

I've always wondered about blood alcohol levels or drugs tainting the donations, but obviously the vamps don't care because they keep encouraging it. Maybe they even like tainted blood. Could it be more desirable to them? Can they drink alcohol? I have no idea. And I don't really care.

"You did good, kid." Eddie pats me on the back on the way out after I've finished for the night. "I'll make sure you get a couple more evening shifts next week."

I smile brightly and thank him before heading out to the parking lot. Mom's old silver Corolla greets me. I love that car. I'd buy it from her in a heartbeat if she didn't need it for her day job. Scratch getting an apartment, I need to buy my own car so I don't have to keep borrowing hers. At least I didn't have to take the bus today like I do during my daytime shifts when Mom is at her bank teller job at a local credit union. It's a miracle she still has that job, to be honest. If they knew about her gambling addiction, nobody would trust that woman around giant wads of cash.

But Mom has a way about her, a way that can easily fool everyone. Just not me. She's the kind of person who makes you feel at ease while also wanting to impress her. I credit her two-faced nature to all those pageants and to growing up in the South where the phrase "bless your heart" comes second nature. Don't get me wrong, I love my mom deeply and I know so much of what's going on isn't her fault, but I'm also tired. So, so tired.

The back parking lot is usually busy, but by this time of night it's emptied out. The Corolla is one of the only cars left out here. A chill creeps up my spine. It's that paranoid feeling of being watched all over again, only this time it's dark. I ignore it and walk faster to the car, keys ready to go. Something skitters across the pavement behind me. I whip around, but nobody's there. Maybe it was an animal? A racoon or stray cat wouldn't be out of the question.

My mind races a million miles a minute, imagining that table of rough men I had. In my thoughts, they're not at the next bar, but actually spying on me from the shadows, closing in to attack.

Or worse, it could be a vampire...

I do have enemies now and what about that car that followed me? Someone could be out here.

But nothing happens.

I make it to the car, unlock it with the key fob at the last second, and climb inside with a sigh of relief. I'm going to have to ask Eddie to walk me to my car at night next time I snag one of these coveted shifts. That's if I'm not taking the bus home. Or a taxi. All depends on what Mom needs. Considering my pocket is full of tip money, I need to be smarter. That right there puts a target on my back and is definitely worth the nighttime spookiness factor.

I lean back in my seat and slip the seatbelt into position.

The passenger door flies open and a man slides in next to me. Before I can scramble away, he snatches my wrist in his iron tight grip.

"Don't scream," Adrian Teresi speaks low.

His blue eyes and pale skin practically glow in the darkness. My skidding heart turns animalistic, trying to claw its way out of my throat. I can't scream because I can't speak. I can't even move! Everything inside me is urging me to run, to get away, and that this man––*this thing*––is here to deliver my death. Frozen panic doesn't last long as my voice comes rushing back. "Get away from me!"

"Tsk, tsk." Adrian squeezes tighter and glares. "You should have thought of that before you stole from me."

"I didn't steal anything. You gave that money to me."

"I gave it to you under the agreement that you wouldn't call the police, but you did, so the way I see it, you stole five thousand dollars from me." His eyes narrow. "You have caused an issue for me within the VEC and I do not take kindly to it."

I heave my wrist away again, and this time he drops it. Part of me wants to try and make a run for it, but I know I won't be fast enough. The other part of me wants to stay and play Adrian's little game just to see if I can win. Where's that stake when I need it?

My mind fumbles through where I stashed it last, and I remember. It's under the driver's seat, probably inches from my foot. If I can just grab it quick enough, I can kill Adrian and––

"Looking for this?" Adrian holds it up. His blue eyes flash murderous.

Now I've truly run out of things to say.

"I should stake you right here and now," he purrs, "see how you like it." But he doesn't. Instead, he squeezes his hand and splinters the weapon into pieces, hissing when the silver tip of it grazes his skin. It sends a little puff of smoke into the car. He throws the remnants in the backseat.

Geez . . . I'm going to have to talk to Felix about getting me a full-on silver stake because apparently the wood ones are economy class. Then again, I hear genuine silver is hard to come by these days. The suckers saw to that before they revealed themselves. They had ages to plan, after all.

"What do you want from me?" I say at last, staring Adrian back, eye to eye. He's an oxymoron if I've ever seen one. He looks young, mid-twenties at the most, but his eyes and his mannerisms speak of centuries of experience. Not for the first time, I wonder how old he really is. I mean, being a prince must make him ancient, right?

"I already told you what I want, Angel." He nods toward the steering wheel. "Drive. There's somewhere we need to go."

So he found out my mom's nickname for me. I shouldn't be surprised. "Evangeline," I correct.

"Drive!" he roars. "Or do you need me to do it for you?"

"Sorry, buddy, but does this look like a taxi to you?" I glare. "Get out of my car."

Faster than humanly possible, he snatches both my hands and slams them so forcefully against the wheel that pain thunders up my wrists.

Tears spring to my eyes. "What the hell? I'm breakable you know!"

"Drive," he demands again. "Or I will, and you might not survive that. You decide."

I might not survive how he drives? Is he serious with this? Anger burns hot in my chest, but I don't see another way out of this, so I finally do as the man––the creature––says and put the car into drive. I cling to the anger, letting it consume me, because it's better than the alternative: blinding fear!

I go where he directs me and I even think maybe we're going to the casino I hate so much. When we drive right past it, I suddenly don't hate the place as much as I thought I would. At least the casino is known territory, vampiric sure, but known. Whatever this new place is he's taking me to, it can't be good. Vampires own so much property now and if he wants me dead, there's countless places he can take me down without a single consequence.

That sends my heart pounding and my blood pumping. I wonder if he can smell it.

"You know, if I disappear the police will have to look into it," I start to ramble, "I mean, I did just make a report against you."

Compared to mine, his body is still as granite. I'm starting to shake. "And pointing this out will help your case, how?"

"They talk to the VEC and––"

"As I've said, I know all about your little report to the VEC," he cuts me off. "I am the VEC. And now I have shit to clean up in my own house."

My throat goes dry. Of course, he is the VEC. I already knew that. "But if you're the VEC then why are you so upset?"

"It's myself and others." He's not gloating. He's seething mad. And maybe a little annoyed. And possibly nervous. No, I'm totally picking up on my own fears and projecting them. No way is Adrianos-freaking-Teresi nervous. He's just pissed off.

"Turn here." He points to a shipping yard, and my stomach nearly drops to my butt. I stall the car at the stop sign, not wanting to go in there. From the looks of it, it's not good. Places like these are where murder documentaries end, and I really don't want to die tonight.

"I said turn." He grabs the steering wheel and forces it to the left.

In we go.

We drive past huge shipping containers and the occasional ruffian, but otherwise the place is pretty dead. He maneuvers me through the narrow lanes until we reach a tiny parking lot by the black water's edge. The reflection is so dark, all I can picture is spilled blood.

"Get out," Adrian commands. I deflate, because this is it. This is really the end. Some small part of me was hoping I'd have an out by this point, but that's impossible. Where would I go? How would I get away? It's so remote out here, nobody will even hear me scream.

I don't move. I can't.

He throws open his door. "Get out or I will rip your throat out and feast on your corpse right here in this shitty car."

That does the trick. I scurry from the car, and just as quickly, he's at my side. His hand is an iron lock on my arm as he pulls me toward an empty dock.

"What are we doing here?" I croak. "This is it, isn't it? You're going to kill me and throw me in the river." I'll be out to the swamp and eaten by alligators before anyone can find my body. Of course, I'll probably be drained of blood first. My mind races through the scenario, seeing it unravel in horrifying detail. My knees start to buckle and my body goes ice cold. I can practically taste the river water already. Or will his fangs ripping through my throat be the last experience of my life? I try to muster up some courage but it's useless.

"Can you please relax? I'm not going to kill you but if your fear pheromones don't let up soon I might not be able to help myself."

"Oh..." I don't know what to say to that. Neither of us speaks for a long minute. I will my heartbeat to slow and I take long quiet breaths that taste like nightfall.

"I have business to attend to," he says at last. "And you're going to watch."

So I guess I'm not going to die, at least. I blink and look around, finally noticing the rainbow of lights of the classic New Orleans ferry against the surface of the water. I squint to look closer, and recognition hits me like a punch to the stomach. This isn't just any old ferry. It's the floating casino, a giant floating party that takes off after sunset every weekend night and doesn't dock until the early morning hours. I hate it more than The

Alabaster, even though I've never stepped foot on it, because it's where Mom ends up in the most trouble with no one to save her.

Last summer we had a scare where she didn't come home after going on one. She showed up two days later with a black eye and a drained bank account, refusing to tell me what happened. That day was the day I knew that things weren't ever going to get better.

"You want me to go on there?" I frown. "I'm not old enough."

He looks at me like I'm the world's biggest idiot, and maybe I am, but sorry, I have no intention of stepping foot on that boat.

Adrian has other ideas. The casino boat honks its low horn and slows to a creep as it nears the edge of our dock. The noxious sound of music and gamblers in the throws of debauchery drifts over the water. It edges closer and closer, until it's only a few feet from where we're standing.

"After you," Adrian demands.

Realizing I can't fight this, I take a large step and practically jump onto the boat. Adrian is right behind me. We're on––and the dock recedes quickly. The boat never even stopped.

I shouldn't have taken that five thousand dollar bribe. Or maybe I should've taken it but not called the police. But I did both and here we are. I'd really hoped I'd never have to board this boat, but I guess there's a first for everything. I glare at Adrian. "You don't have to do this you know."

"You're right, Angel, I don't." He returns the glare. "But I want to."

Eight

I'm handed off straight away to the woman whom I immediately recognize as Adrian's receptionist, Kelli. She's dressed in a revealing velvety blood-red gown and is downright stunning, but her whole vampire-vibe makes my skin crawl even more than Adrian's does. Nothing about her is warm or kind or welcoming. Nothing. She doesn't speak a word as she directs me into a little dressing room and hands me what can only be described as clubbing attire: a tiny black mini skirt, disco ball sparkly halter top, and towering silver high heels to match.

I don't bother arguing and quickly change out of my Pops uniform and into the ridiculous outfit. I run shaky hands through my long black hair and tell myself not to throw up and to be strong. At least the boat isn't rocking too badly, or I really would lose the little staff dinner I ate earlier tonight.

"Where should I put these?" I lift up my clothes. My phone is tucked inside the bundle. Adrian still has my car keys. Kelli groans like I'm such a bother but hands me a tiny sparkly purse backpack and I shove everything inside.

"Can I pee? I haven't gone in hours."

Her eyebrows draw in on each other. Does she think I'm some kind of animal? Well, vampires probably don't pee, so maybe I'm pathetic in her eyes, but at least I don't drink blood. One of those things is considerably more disgusting as far as I'm concerned, *thank you very much Miss 80's Mean Girl*. I suddenly have the idea to buy her a copy of the children's book *Everybody Poops* and snort to myself.

"Quickly," she snaps and points me to a tiny washroom.

I lock myself inside and consider prying open the window, leaping into the river, swimming to shore, and making a run for it. Total lunacy. Knowing my luck, I'd probably drown. And if I didn't, Adrian would find me and then he really would rip out my throat and feast on my corpse. There's nowhere safe I could go. I'd have to leave New Orleans entirely, but a vampire prince probably has enough power to hunt me down if he really wanted to. There's no place to hide—the sun sets on every last corner of this planet. So instead of jumping, I take care of my business, wash my hands, and return to Kelli.

She looks like a Kelli and like she was turned in the eighties on account of her bad hair dye alone. It's over-the-top brassy bleached blonde but slicked back into a high ponytail so it doesn't look *too* bad. Vamps can't change much about their appearance after they're reborn, so Kelli's bad hair color is stuck with her for eternity and I'm petty enough to care. Her eyes rove over me as if I'm a sad little wannabe and she's the queen bee. Of course, she's no queen, but there you go. *"Hey, sweety, you're a receptionist, so get off your high horse,"* is what I want to say to her, but I would also like to live through the night.

"You don't wear makeup?" She smirks.

"Uh, neither do you."

"I haven't needed it since 1990." She tosses her shiny ponytail to the side. If she's trying to rub her supernatural beauty in my face she doesn't know me very well. "All human women should wear makeup though. Poor pathetic things."

There's that word, pathetic. I totally called it. I shrug. "Like I care?"

"You should."

"I don't."

She raises an eyebrow, moving on from my makeup-free face to assessing my obvious lack of curves, but this time says nothing.

Whatever. I couldn't care less what the leech thinks of me.

"Now what?" I ask, attitude sparking my question. She rolls her eyes as if she'd like nothing more than to crush me under her thin red stiletto. I'm sure she could.

"You got me in trouble with Adrian, you know." Her hazel eyes narrow. "Apparently, I was supposed to watch you or something, like I didn't have other things to do than to babysit a teenager."

Oh, so that explains the animosity. Noted.

"I would say sorry, but I'm not, and I don't like to lie."

Her eyes flash and her pupils dilate. Oh crap, is she going to eat me now?

"Why am I here?" I ask, changing the subject.

I can tell she wants to say more, but she smiles as if she would rather show me. She offers a smirky, "This way," then escorts me to the casino floor.

For one thing, it's smaller than The Alabaster. Much. But that's to be expected considering this is a ferry and not a brick-and-mortar building with an additional hotel highrise attached to the back. It too, reeks of cigarette smoke and booze. And blood. Many of the windows are open to let in the breeze, so at least there's that. It's usually pretty muggy this time of night, and my hair sticks to my neck. The patrons are all dressed up, ignoring the humidity like it's nothing. Fancy dress is part of the requirement for getting on the boat--the regular casino couldn't care less. Either way, the patrons all have that sick sheen to their eyes that speaks of greed, and the pale pallor to their skin that screams of blood loss.

Unlike in The Alabaster, vampires are everywhere. Most have bloody cocktails in their hands, and some of them join in on the gambling. My stomach roils as I look around for Adrian.

I don't see him, but bony shoulders and long auburn hair sure do catch my eye. Sitting at one of the Texas Hold'em tables with her back to me is my mother.

Has to be.

There isn't a blood bag hooked up to her, but there may as well be because we don't have the money to be here and, at this point, I'd almost rather her give blood than money we don't have. Okay, not really, but I can't believe this!

"Ah, there you are." Adrian appears at my side. His familiar scent of warm cedar and bergamot washes over me, but underneath it is the iron of blood, and I want nothing more than to claw his eyes out. "You clean up nicely." His tone is mocking.

"What is she doing here?" I hiss, nodding toward Mom.

He chuckles darkly. "She's the business I was talking about. Your mother is here to teach you a lesson."

"And what lesson is that?" Though I'm afraid I already know.

"You cannot stop her gambling," his tone is no longer amused, "and you cannot stop me from doing anything I wish." He yanks my body around like a rag doll and his stone-like fingertips dig deep into my upper arms. I wince and tears spring to my eyes. I refuse to cry which only makes it harder to push them away.

"You're hurting me," I seethe.

That only makes him squeeze harder. "You are not going to step foot in my casino ever again. Is that clear?"

I should agree to his demands, I know that, but I don't. I hold back a response and meet his steely gaze with one of my own. Just because the pain of his crushing fingers is overpowering and I'm about ready to bawl my eyes out over it, doesn't mean I can't be a defiant brat. He squeezes harder.

"Fine," I say at last.

He releases me and strides purposely toward my mother. His hands are clenched into fists but they might as well be sledge hammers. I know the strength in just those fingers, what could his whole fist do? Is he going to kill her?

"No!" I rush after him.

He doesn't listen.

"Are you Paulo?" He asks the man sitting next to my mother. The man turns and asks, "Yes, why?" Adrian then grabs the sweaty Mediterranean-looking guy, lifts him clear off his seat and snaps his neck.

The body collapses to the floor with a dull thud.

Humans scream and scurry from their seats, but a couple of the vamps are quick to meet them, compelling the humans to sit back down, insisting they didn't see anything. The vamps work quickly; it doesn't matter that there are less of them when they're the wolves and we're the sheep.

It all happens so fast, and my mother doesn't even notice me standing there, gaping like an idiot who should've seen this coming. Within the course of a minute, she's back to playing her game as if there isn't a dead man at her feet.

Something happens to me that rarely happens, if ever; I'm speechless.

Adrian can't do this. He can't kill a man. It's illegal. Vampires are out in society under certain agreements, and they can't just go around killing people. Except, apparently they *can*. Same as vampire hunters can kill and get away with it. Sometimes things that happen at night, stay in the dark.

Adrian motions to Kelli who sashays over seductively. If I didn't know better, I'd think that annoying smirk of hers was permanent.

"Yes, Master?" she asks coyly, batting her lashes.

"Enjoy your treat," he tells her with the flick of his wrist, "but get rid of the body."

"Throw him over the side?" She's giddy now and I'm honestly about to puke.

"As long as he's not going to wash up anywhere, I don't care what you do with him."

She picks up the body as if it weighs nothing, sinking her teeth into the dead man's neck like it's a juicy steak as she walks him out of the casino. His blood drops are the only thing that's left of the guy, but I'm sure those will be gone soon, too.

And none of the humans even give her a second glance. They're entranced by their casino games. It's not their fault, but I still want to scream at them to wake up.

I feel like I'm sinking into the hardwood floor. My entire life is a ticking clock, counting down until my prefrontal cortex is developed and I join the sheep. My legs are weak noodles and I try not to lock my knees. Last thing I need to do is pass out in a place like this. I probably wouldn't wake up.

Adrian steps closer, and I inch back.

"Do you see now, Angel?"

I nod once. "Yes, I've seen all I need." Fear is thick in my tone, but I can't deny it, not for a second. Adrian terrifies me. He is *not* someone I want to cross.

"We have places like this, places where people disappear. Paulo back there chose to make enemies with a friend of mine so I took care of him. Did you notice that you're the youngest one on this boat tonight?"

I nod again. Of course it's for good reason that nobody here is young. The vampires can kill and compel and wash away their sins in the swamp. They can make it seem as if nothing had ever happened. Youth who can not be compelled. We'd be able to expose them.

"Despite our efforts to lower the gambling age, I assure you that this boat will always be reserved exclusively for my older clients. And if I ever have the misfortune to see you in one of my casinos again," his tone slices through me as he delivers the final blow, "I will kill you." And just to twist the knife, he adds, "And I will take my time."

"You won't see me again after tonight." My voice cracks, sounding like it's a million miles away. But I mean it. I am so done.

"Good."

"Who's your friend, Adrianos?" a man questions. He slides up next to us so silently that I nearly jump out of my skin.

I turn to find another vampire, one just as beautiful as Adrian—or maybe I should say Adrianos? *Nah, too fancy for me, I'm sticking with Adrian.* Where Adrian's beauty is light—bright blue eyes and golden hair—this man is dark. His skin is quite olive for a vampire, casting him with an oddly alluring complexion. His jet black hair is slicked back and his eyes are the color of warm brown sugar. He looks older than Adrian, like he was in his mid thirties to early forties when he was changed. The tiny laugh lines around his eyes and mouth are still visible, a tiny snapshot to the human he once was. His stance and smile are welcoming, and he's quite handsome for an older guy, but my senses rise up in warning.

I want to step away. I don't, but only because it would give the wrong impression. He doesn't need to know that everything about him unsettles me to the core.

He can't be trusted--none of them can--but there's something about this one that feels different. I'm not sure how to put words or emotions to it, but it's definitely there, like a painful itch I can't scratch.

"Where's your new child, Hugo?" Adrian asks, changing the subject off of me.

Hugo's body turns rigid. "Dead." His tone turns bitter. "She didn't make it far from her rising. When I went to retrieve her, her grave was empty and I felt no bond."

"Do you think she rose early?" Adrian almost sounds sympathetic. Almost.

"Yes. I'm afraid she rose on the second night instead of the third."

"That's a shame. Maybe the sun got her?"

Hugo raises an eyebrow and slides his gaze over to me. "No, I'm convinced it was hunters."

Nine

My brain catches up to the speed of their conversation. My own prickly fear taints everything they're saying. Hunters killed his new child? Just thinking about a grown adult––someone who had an actual human life––considered a vampire's child makes my skin crawl. There's a good chance that whoever these two are talking about was the baby vampire I staked last night. I was defending myself, but that doesn't mean I have any regrets about my actions. I'd do it all over again if I could.

I have to force myself to keep calm. I don't need my heart rate rising and tipping them off to anything I might be thinking. As far as I know, the old stories about some vampires being able to read minds are just that––stories. I release a slow breath and attempt to clear my mind anyway.

"Hello, dear," Hugo says, his eyes now locked on mine. "Are you Adrian's newest fledgling?"

I nearly choke. "What does that mean?" I ask, trying to keep my voice from shaking, though I have an inkling "fledgling" means next in line for soulless immortality.

He smirks. "Well, if not his, then maybe you can be mine?"

"Brisa will never allow you to choose another child so quickly," Adrian quips, "you know that. Don't push her."

Hugo's face contorts into a grimace, as if he wants to say something but is forcing himself to keep the words locked inside. Finally, he utters a smooth reply. "You're right, Adrian. And it's such a shame, don't you think?"

Adrian doesn't respond, not with words or his face. He's a stone wall.

Hugo's bronze eyes run down the length of me. "We could use more vampires like you. Young. Beautiful." I step back, but he pulls me to him, pressing my body against his in an iron grip. "With a streak of defiance in need of breaking, I see. My favorite."

He wants to turn me? The very idea of it makes me sick, but the revulsion in my stomach is nothing compared to the fear stirring my thoughts. Maybe he assumes I'm one of those pathetic groupie humans hanging around vamps, trying to get turned. Maybe he thinks that I'd readily agree to his offer, that I'd jump at the chance. If he knew who I really was, that I was likely the one who killed his sired vampire, I have no doubt this vile creature would tear me to shreds.

I don't move. I can't. Even if I wanted to, Hugo has caged me in his arms.

"What's your name?" His breath is sweet and metallic. He smiles wide and runs his tongue over the tip of an extended fang, as if to entice me.

Adrian sighs heavily. "We're going now," he sounds extra annoyed, "and Evangeline is my fledgling, so if you wouldn't mind unhanding her, that would be much appreciated."

The two men stare each other down and it's as if I've become the newest toy tossed between schoolyard bullies.

Hearing Adrian call me Evangeline and not Angel doesn't make me feel any better, neither does him calling me the word "fledgling," but him pulling me back from Hugo somehow does. Hugo just laughs and hands me off like it's nothing to him, like I'm one of many possible fledglings and saunters away to go sniff around his other choices.

I'm still stuck on what Adrian just said about me being "his." The term fledgling itself makes me want to punch someone, preferably someone with fangs. But before I can question Adrian on it, he's ushering me from the casino and out onto the river boat deck. The night is quiet and dark, the air has lost some of it's humidity, or maybe the chill is coming from within me. Either way, the boat has docked. It's late. I'm bone-tired, but I'm also more awake than I've ever been in my entire life.

"You'll make sure my mom gets home okay?"

"Your mother is capable of getting herself home. Don't ask me for favors."

I don't speak as he leads me from the boat to a sleek black sports car sitting in the nearby lot. We're no longer near the shipping yard we were at earlier. It's all lit up here, but I don't see Mom's Corolla. Adrian opens the passenger side door to his sports car like a proper gentleman, as if this is a date and he didn't just threaten my mother's life and kill that Paulo guy in front of me.

I hesitate to get in. "Can I please go home then? Or, I mean, can you take me back to my car?" My voice is meek and pathetic, my thoughts are jumbled. He's won, and I want nothing to do with him, at least not until I've trained with the hunters and could possibly take him down like a proper badass.

"I'll drop you off on my way to the office," he says. "You're lucky I'm not angry anymore, Angel. I do tend to take my temper out on the road."

"So I should be thanking you for not having road rage?"

He chuckles. "I have plenty of rage with or without the road."

Sounds promising—not! I slide into the smooth leather seat and force a quick, "Well, thank you, I guess." Thanking him is the last thing I want to do.

He stares at me for a long second, our gazes colliding like fire and water. "You're welcome. But after this, remember, I never want to see you again." He slams the door in my face and all I can think is that I absolutely agree with that sentiment.

Still, I'm met with relief, because whatever that fledgling talk was all about, it must have been a bluff to get Hugo to leave me alone. And thank goodness, because he gave me the absolute creeps.

What else gives me the creeps? The fact that Adrian knows where I live. I don't have to give him directions. He heads the right way as if he's driven these roads a million times before. Maybe he has. Maybe he's lived in this city for ages. Not for the first time, I wonder about his age. Exhaustion weighs heavily, muddling my thoughts, but then it hits me again.

"Wait. Where's my car?" I thought that's where we were going.

"Your mother will be bringing it home later. Kelli will give her the keys."

"I thought you said you weren't going to do me any favors?"

"Don't flatter yourself."

Quite frankly, I find it odd that Adrian wanted to drive me home, odd and worrisome, not flattering. A warning signal tingles down my spine.

When we're pulling up to the driveway, he answers my question as to why he'd want to drive me home with a single, punishing blow. "I can come into your house anytime I like," he says. "And I can kill you." He points to my bedroom window. "I know that's where you sleep. On the other side of that thin pane of glass is your bedroom. And then the bathroom, and then your mother's bedroom is at the back of the hall. I know your little home well."

"You can't--"

"Your mother already invited me in, Angel." He turns on me, baring his fangs. "She gave me an open invitation. And I've been inside every room, I assure you. Don't give me a reason to come back."

I'm frozen. What a total violation of privacy! I want to scream, to run. I want to fight. *Something.*

"Because I will come back if it's warranted." His glacial eyes narrow. "And I'll like it."

I nod once and spring from the car, needing to put as much distance between him and me as possible. He got his point across, threats have been sufficiently made, and I need to protect Mom and myself. So I'll do what he says. I saw what he's capable of. But I also need to find a way to get Mom to stay away from his casinos. She's not going to make it much longer if she keeps living at this pace. Forget about money and being broke, they'll suck her dry.

Adrian drives away, and I groan. I don't even want to go inside. I'm still wearing the clubbing attire Kelli dressed me in and my stuff is shoved into the little bag in my hand. Instead of retrieving my house keys, I dig out my phone.

I leave my house dark and hoof it to Ayla's place, texting her on my way. She texts back immediately, welcoming me with a spattering of excited emojis like she always does. The girl has no idea what's going on in my crappy life, and I want more than anything to tell her, but I can't put this on my best friend like that, especially right before she leaves on her college adventure. I'm seriously going to miss her. How will I get on with my life while she's away? I don't have anyone else like her. I wish she were sticking around town for school like Felix did, but I also can't fault her for following her dreams. If anyone deserves to study at one of the best interior design programs in the country, it's that girl.

The streets are silent and empty. It's almost two in the morning and even though I know I'm an idiot for being out here alone, I kind of don't care. My eyes have adjusted to the darkness and I know the way to Ayla's well enough that I play a game where I decide to keep my phone's flashlight off, walk briskly in these ridiculous high heels, and hope to blend in with the black. At least, I tell myself it's a game and not that I'm freaked out that Adrian will come back for me. Or worse, Hugo.

I don't want to be at home if that happens.

An SUV pulls up behind me and my heart speeds, but then it passes and I let out a shaky breath. I need to chill the heck out. I'm not going to be able to become a vampire hunter if I'm so spooked all the time. The SUV screeches to a stop and flips around, coming right for me. I tense, I don't have a stake on me. The headlights are lighting me up and blinding me. So stupid! I should have gone home. I'm fast, but not fast enough to outrun one of them. What if that's Hugo and he followed Adrian? I'm a sitting duck out here, looking like a glittering disco ball.

The window rolls down and a man speaks low. "Eva, what the heck are you doing out alone at night? Are you trying to get yourself killed?"

Felix.

I kick myself for not realizing it was his SUV sooner. I also praise Jesus!

"I accidentally locked myself out of my house," I totally lie. "I'm heading over to sleep at your place."

The fun African American guy from last night leans over from the passenger seat. "She's going to sleep at your place, Felix." He snickers. "Lucky bastard."

"Shut up, man. She's my kid sister's best friend," Felix quips back. "She's practically a sister to me, too."

Ouch. My heart sinks a little, but I'm not surprised. Alas, once in the friend zone, always in the friend zone.

"Come on," he continues, "get in. I'll drive you the rest of the way."

I'm not about to say no. I jump into the backseat where, again, the quiet guy is sitting. His dusty brown hair and haunted green gaze give him sort of a sexy standoffish vibe. He nods at me once and then stares straight ahead, as if he's deep in thought again and couldn't care less about a girl in a tiny skirt and disco ball top sitting next to him. Heck, a guy like that is probably busy curing cancer in his head––he's that serious.

"So did you talk to whoever you needed to talk to about me joining your little group?" I lean between the two front seats and waggle my eyebrows at Felix.

"No way," Felix replies at the same time that his funny friend says, "I sure did, honey."

"What is wrong with you, Kenton?" Felix glares at his friend. "We talked about this!"

"You talked about it," Kenton replies casually and winks at me "I like this chick. You're one of us now."

"No, she's not."

"I've killed a vampire, haven't I?" I lean back in my seat and cross my arms over my chest. "Pretty sure that should grant me entrance to your little club."

"Our little club?" the quiet guy beside me speaks up. "You've no idea what you're asking to get involved in here, Eva."

"Exactly," Felix interjects.

"I didn't realize you even knew my name," I shoot back at the brooding quiet guy. "And you are? You haven't spoken two words to me and now you have an opinion?"

His face hardens to stone and he doesn't answer.

"That's Seth," Kenton supplies. "He's one of our lacrosse teammates and fellow hunters." He meets Seth's surly gaze through the rearview mirror. "Sorry, but Tate wants to meet her."

Ah, so all three of them play lacrosse. Note to self, lacrosse boys are hot.

"You told Tate?" Seth and Felix say together, both pissed off.

"Hey, he asked me why we left early for our assignment and it came up. You can't get anything past that guy."

"He wasn't mad?"

"At us? Sure. At finding a new hunter? No way. He's excited to meet Eva."

I don't know who this Tate person is, but by the way the other two guys are acting, I can assume it's their boss.

"Hi, Eva here." I raise my hand. "I'm sitting right here, remember?" I lean forward and almost kiss Kenton on the cheek for being awesome but think better of it. "When and where am I meeting this Tate person? Name it and I'll be there."

Ten

A couple days later, I'm dressed in my favorite athletic gear and riding with Felix to meet this Tate character. Felix is pretty pissed that this ball is rolling and there's nothing he can do to stop it. He figures that he might as well be there for the ride so he can make sure I don't get myself killed.

His words, not mine.

He made me lie to Ayla and tell her that I also got an internship at the bank and joined the same gym nearby. She bought it without question. In fact, she was excited for me, which made lying even worse. It's a good thing the woman is going to college soon or else there's no way I would be able to keep that up. I've always told her everything. But Felix is right to not want to get her involved, and if his parents found out about what he's been up to, it would put us all in danger.

"So what can you tell me about Tate?" I ask, fiddling with the air conditioning. I decide I'm really just nervous, so I sit on my hands instead.

"You'll find out for yourself," Felix replies and then goes back to acting like I'm not even in the car. So lame.

I've been wondering about this Tate person for days, but I guess Felix is right.

We wind through the downtown financial district and pull into the same parking garage from before. Felix parks and we head over to the unmarked door. Felix uses both a fingerprint scanner and a keypad code to open it. I'm not really sure what to expect will be on the other side. My brain has conjured up a mix of superhero movies' hidden lairs and squashed them all together. The bat cave would be pretty cool, except for the fact that bats gross me out. So what if they're kind of cute? They eat bugs and their poop is toxic.

We walk through a sterile, blank hallway and then down two flights of stairs. When we open the next set of locked doors, this time using a different keycode from what I can snoop off of Felix's quick fingers, we're greeted by what's essentially an upscale underground bunker/office/gym. It's a huge room--all polished concrete and shining chrome, with sleek gray and white surfaces. There's an open space with workout equipment along the edges and a sparring pad in the middle. Everything is airy and tall, and the second story looks down with glass rooms lining the perimeter. The windows are tinted, so I can't see what's behind them. Offices? Maybe more than that, maybe a kitchen, maybe even bedrooms. There are no windows to the outside. Whatever this place is, it's super nice, super secure, and beyond what I expected. I look around, studying the people here--there aren't many, and most of them are college-aged looking guys. They keep their distance but eye me with blatant curiosity.

I assumed the vampire hunting groups were ill-equipped on account of the fact that adults can't be trusted to get involved. This place--these guys--appear to be anything but.

It's with that thought in mind that an older man descends the metal staircase and my jaw practically drops to the floor.

"Hello, Eva." He sticks out his hand when he reaches our group. "I'm Leslie Tate. It's nice to finally meet you, Eva."

I don't know what to say but I shake his hand. How can he be here? Isn't having anyone older than twenty-five a huge problem for the safety and security of an outfit like this?

"I know what you're thinking." His gray eyes wrinkle around the edges when he smiles. "But I'm immune to vampire compulsion."

"Uh, say what now?" I blurt. "That's not possible."

Tate raises a bushy eyebrow. "I assure you, it is."

Hope loosens my body and I find myself smiling. "Can you show me how?"

"I wish I could," Tate goes on. "But it's an ability I was born with."

"Well that sucks," I grumble, and Felix elbows me in the ribs. "I mean, it's awesome for you, of course, but it sucks for me."

Tate nods and runs his hand through his salt and pepper hair. "Don't worry. I'd feel the same way if I were in your shoes. You're what? Eighteen?"

I can't help but frown. "Yeah, almost nineteen though."

I hate getting older. I should want to grow up, and I do, but every day older is just one day closer to losing my mind to the vamps. What if they turn me into an addict like they did my mom?

"We keep people around until they're twenty-four-and-a-half," he pauses for a second, "that's if they don't die first. I have to be honest about that fact. We lose almost half of our hunters before they age out of the program."

"I know what the vampires are capable of." I swallow hard. "Don't worry about me. I want to be here more than I want to be anywhere else."

Something about that seems to concern Tate. Sadness softens his features. "We will verify your age with your birth records. You can hunt with us until it's time to erase your memory of ever having been a hunter."

Umm . . . My eyes practically bulge out of my head. "Excuse me? Erase my memory?"

This is getting weirder and weirder. How on earth do they have that kind of tech? Did I just walk into the world of Men in Black? I half expect Will Smith to appear with that silver "lose your memory" light pen thingy. I almost want to look around for aliens.

"There's so much more to our world than you know," Felix offers regretfully. Considering he didn't want me to get involved, that sourpuss tone makes sense. Now all I want to do is ask a million and one questions.

"So wait, are you saying other supernaturals exist?"

Tate's sigh is deep. "You'll learn all about that in time."

"Are you a werewolf?" I blurt. I can't help myself. I mean the man has bushy eyebrows and powers and if vampires are real then maybe werewolves are, too.

He chuckles. "No, I assure you I am not a werewolf. It isn't safe for you to know more than that."

"Why?" I look to Felix but he shrugs as if he doesn't know the answer either.

"Well, first of all, we have to see if you're loyal to us and not the vampires," Tate continues.

I scoff. "Loyal to the bloodsuckers? No way. I hate them."

"Unfortunately, it's happened before."

"It won't happen with me." I fold my arms over my chest. "My mom is a gambling addict because of those creeps."

Tate frowns. "I'm sorry to hear that, but we'll still have to confirm that you can be trusted."

"Alright, fine. What do I have to do to prove myself?" Because at this point, I'll do anything.

"A simple lie detector test will suffice."

A trickle of excitement passes through me. I've only ever seen those things in movies and television. I don't mind the thought of it. Not one bit.

An hour later and I end up telling Tate everything he wants to know. He takes a particular interest in my dealings with Adrianos Teresi even though there aren't that many. I never mention that Adrian has threatened my life should I ever step foot in his filthy casino again. I figure if Tate asks me to go to The Alabaster for an assignment, I'll bring up my problem with that then. Sort of an, "asking for forgiveness is better than asking for permission" mentality. I'm careful to be honest while still not saying anything that might jeopardize my ability to get in with this group. If they knew I'd made an enemy of the most powerful vampire around, they might send me packing, and I wouldn't blame them.

"Congratulations, you passed," Tate says as he removes the lie detector wires from where they'd been taped to my skin. We are up in one of the rooms––just us––but I already feel comfortable around Leslie Tate, like he's the father figure I never knew I needed. His energy is warm and magnetic. There's just something about him that's good. I don't know how else to describe it.

"Great." I smile, my mind already three steps ahead. "So what's this group called, anyway?" I've heard names over the years of other groups, like the Midnight Slayers, The Nightwatch Club, The Buffy's, which was a total throwback to the nineties hit television show, and countless others.

"We don't have a name," Tate says. "It's safer this way."

"I guess that makes sense." But honestly, I'll just end up giving it it's own name in my head. The Bank Vault Vampire Hunters has a nice ring to it.

"We're going to start with your training." Tate shoots me back into reality and levels me with a knowing stare. "Are you absolutely sure you want to do this? I can wipe this from your memory now. No hard feelings."

"Yes. I'm sure." Inwardly, I do a little happy dance. I'm excited to get back out there and fight the bad guys, but I understand training will take time and that I need it.

"You have to know what you're getting yourself into," he continues. "You could die. You could be tortured. You will lose the friends you make here because they'll die or they'll age out and forget about your interactions together. And of course, there's always the possibility that a vampire could catch you and turn you into one of them."

I swallow. "Can they turn people against their will?"

"They can and they will. Keep in mind, a situation like that would lead them right to us. This is why it's important you're never caught."

I worry my bottom lip between my teeth and think it over. "If I'm somehow caught and turned, is that it? There's no going back?" These are stupid questions that I already know the answers to but I can't help but ask.

"Well, the bloodthirst will be unlike anything you've experienced as a human. However, I do know of people who were changed against their will and were able to get into the sun before feeding." A haunted expression crosses his face. "But once a new vampire feeds, that's it. They'll never have their humanity back."

It's hard to imagine being burned alive by the sun, but then it's also hard to imagine drinking someone dry and having a vampire master lording over me. If it happens that I get turned one day, I hope I'll be strong enough to seek out the sun too. I think through all these possibilities for a long minute, through everything terrible that could happen to me, then swallow and offer another nod. "I'm in."

"Somehow, I knew you'd say that." He shakes his head. "I've seen your kind before. Let me guess, you feel like you have nothing to lose?"

"I mean, I wouldn't call my *life* nothing, but I don't have a lot of prospects for my future, if that's what you're asking." No college. No boyfriend. Not much of a family unit. Only one close friend in Ayla, but she's going off to live her life. I am probably the perfect candidate for a job like this.

His lips thin and he changes the subject. "Our actual hunters are our best, brightest, and quite honestly, our bravest. Even your friend Felix isn't a hunter, yet," Tate goes on. This revelation is news to me. "He's only been with us for four months. He's still a novice. We recruited him and two of his lacrosse teammates from Tulane. They're on the reconnaissance side of things right now and not considered hunters yet. Once they get more experience under their belts, they'll be able to do the offensive work and start making kills."

Ah, so that's how Felix knows Seth and Kenton. That also explains why those guys were in the graveyard placing stakes in caches a few mornings ago. But that didn't explain why they'd gone out while it was still dark. I suspect they weren't supposed to go in there until the sun came out, so I decide to keep my mouth shut. Something tells me those guys were hoping to find a newly sired vamp that morning. I don't blame them because I want to hunt too.

Tate escorts me back to the gym and introduces me to the hunters and the novice. I count sixteen in all, twelve men and four women. "Everyone, this is Eva. She's new. She's going to be joining the novice crew a few months late, so she'll be working overtime to catch up."

He points to Felix, Kenton, and Seth. "You look out for her like she's your own sister, you got it?" So my guys must be the novice crew, a.k.a., the newest recruits. I can work with that.

I give Felix a sidelong glance. His dark hair is all disheveled from running his hands through it, and his pillowy lips are set in an annoyed pout. I widen my eyes as if to say, "Yay, isn't this fun?"

He glares back.

Oh, yeah, I'm pretty sure treating me like a little sister isn't going to be a problem for him. He's certainly had enough practice.

Eleven

⌘

I'm running through the darkened forest, leaping over fallen logs and ducking under low hanging branches. My boots squash dead leaves like crumpled paper. Between that and my panting breaths, it's hard to hear the vampire chasing me. He could be anywhere by now. My heart thuds against my chest and my mouth goes bone dry. My hands squeeze tight around the wooden stake. The monster is coming for me.

I can't escape it.

I can't outrun it.

So I press my back against a tree, ignoring the rough bark that claws at the exposed skin above my tank top, and try to focus. The metallic scent of blood trickles through my senses and something wet drips down my arm. I've accidentally cut myself.

And now he'll know right where to find me.

I refuse to die today, refuse to let this demon get the better of me. I've been training for this very moment for nearly two weeks, and now that it's here, I'm determined to win. Still, nerves fire warning shots in my belly. What if I fail?

The tree behind me rips away, roots and all. I scream and scramble back as the vampire pounces on me like a sleek cat. His glowing eyes are wide and crazed with bloodlust. His skin is translucent under the moon-drenched night. I swing the stake, same as I've practiced a thousand times, but at the last moment he veers to the left and bears down on me, fangs sinking into my neck. He rips me open, blood arcs and pain erupts. I scream and then drown in my own blood until it's over and I am nothing.

"Damn it!" I growl and rip off the virtual reality headset. I'm covered in little round sensors taped to my skin and I want to rip those off, as well. The dim lights of the small room brighten and Tate slips through the doorway. The treadmill floor below me has stopped. I sit up and shake off the failure. "I really thought I had him that time."

Leslie Tate offers me that same knowing smile he's given me about a million times since I started training in the virtual reality simulations. Okay, not a million, but it sure feels like it. At first I found the smile endearing, but now I imagine it's pitying and all I want is to see it morph into pride. I don't know why, but I suck at this. The others make it look easy. Everyday we get one session with the simulation and everyday I fail to stake the vampire. Tate doesn't want our team to start practicing simulations together until we can all stake the vampire on our own. I'm the last to get there and I worry that the guys are starting to get impatient.

"What is wrong with me?" I ask. "Honestly, what am I doing wrong?"

"It's normal to struggle at first," Tate assures me.

"But from between the simulations, to the sparring down in the gym, and the grueling workouts, I'm still miles behind the rest of my team––way more than a couple months. I'm holding them back."

"Do you know why you're here, Eva? Your friends weren't supposed to go into the cemetery until sunrise. Yes, I know all about how they broke protocol, and they were reprimanded for that, but look what came from it? You."

I guess that's true, but why am I struggling so much? Felix sure hasn't been afraid to let me know I'm behind. On more than one occasion he's encouraged me to quit the program entirely. It's really starting to piss me off. Kenton is all for me being here and is more than willing to help me train, but he doesn't hold back when sparring with me and I've yet to best him. Seth hasn't said anything to me at all. He's the epitome of the silent brooding type, and it's like he doesn't want to acknowledge my existence. Maybe he's sexist? Maybe he just doesn't like me? I can't say I'm his biggest fan either.

"What if I got lucky when I killed that new vampire?" I run my shaky hands through my hair and stand up, peeling the sensors off of me as I go. "Beginners luck and nothing more."

"You're stuck in your head." Tate begins helping me remove the sensors off my back. "Instinct hasn't taken hold yet, but it will. In the meantime, you need to keep practicing and getting stronger. Next week, we'll start training with crossbows, and then we'll move on to silver bullets."

I cheer up. "That sounds fun." A thought occurs to me. "Why don't we start with the silver bullets? Seems easier than having to get close with a stake."

"It's not possible to kill a vampire with a small bullet, unfortunately. It will slow them down and sometimes scare them off, but it's not enough to actually end them."

We walk from the training room and down the metal free-standing staircase. Below me, Felix and Seth are fighting on the sparring mat. They're evenly matched, and from the sweat pouring down each of them, they've probably been at this for a while.

"Silver immobilizes vampires, it weakens them because they're allergic to it, which is why we tip a lot of our stakes with it, but doesn't kill them on its own," Tate continues our conversation. "Always remember, wood through the heart or direct exposure to sunlight are the best ways to kill a vampire."

"Oh yeah, I've seen some videos of them bursting to flame in the sun. Everyone has." A few years ago one went viral online. It was shared millions of times and sparked quite a bit of debate. Facts are, there are people out there who support vampire rights. And then there are even some vampires who are on social media. They're basically celebrities now but I refuse to follow any of them. I chew my lip, wondering how vamps must feel about the sun—the one thing that they'll never ever be able to stop from happening every day. "I'm sure they'd do anything to become immune to the sun, wouldn't they?"

"Oh, they would, and trust me when I say they're researching how to withstand sunlight *and* staking."

Research? I try to picture it and grimace.

The idea of vampires withstanding death would only lead to one thing: human harvesting. There's no other way I can see that going except for us to be treated like cattle while they lord over the world. They may be great at spinning the facade, but they're never going to live peacefully with us since they need our blood to survive. Right now they've got a good thing going with this whole blood bag in exchange for vices thing, but that will be pushed aside if they have nothing to fear. If they can't die, then humans are doomed to a life of servitude.

"Is there another way to kill them?"

Tate looks at me sidelong and I can't help but wonder what he is if he's not a werewolf. He said he wasn't. Whatever he is, I hope he'll tell me soon. "Vampires can rip each other apart. They can also starve to death without blood, which is a slow agonizing death that can take decades."

Huh, well they would deserve it. Same as I've seen videos of them bursting into flames, I've seen videos of them killing innocent humans, not to mention, I'll never forget what Adrian did to that Paulo gambler guy right in front of me as if the man's life meant nothing.

"Do you know why they won't drink from humans directly?" It's the question the world has debated for ages but has never been able to find an answer.

"They do drink directly from humans sometimes. When they do, I can guarantee it ends in a kill or the making of a new vampire. Turning a new vampire is highly regulated by their royals. They're picky about who they allow into their covens."

"Yeah, but what's the big secret with the bites? What does the vampire venom do to humans that would make the royals be so strict about something like that?"

"I have theories, but I don't know for sure." Tate's gray eyes sparkle, like now I've really got him going on a subject he's passionate about. "But we'll save that for when I can confirm one way or another."

I'm beginning to feel like he's dodging my question.

"But--"

He holds up a hand to silence me. "Unfortunately, when it comes to vampires, speculation can mean the difference between life and death. I've learned the hard way to keep my theories to myself until I can prove them."

"Well, that sucks."

"Not as much as vampires do," he cracks a total dad-joke and I roll my eyes.

It also sucks that I still don't know how or why he's immune to vampire compulsion. It also sucks that my team won't talk to me about this either. Anytime I ask about Tate, they tell me I need to take it up with the man himself. For now, I'm being patient, but hopefully I'll have answers soon.

WE START at 6 a.m. and train for six hours every weekday morning, ending right on time for lunch. I've been able to get my schedule moved over to three weekly night shifts at Pops so I'm busier than ever. I make the same amount of money in three night shifts at Pops as I do in five day shifts, so I'm ecstatic about this new development. But since my Pops shifts go from 4:30 p.m. until we close at 10:30 p.m., and half the time I have to take the bus home, it's made for a crappy sleep schedule. Needless to say, by Saturday night of my second week of this, I'm beat and in desperate need of a massage and a good long nap. Neither of which is going to happen.

Luckily, I don't have a Pops shift tonight. It's Ayla's last night at home before she's heading off to college and the two of us are planning to stay in and have a movie marathon of all her favorite romantic comedies. Cheesy unrealistic movies aren't really my thing, but I'll endure them all for her sake, say goodbye, and then crash at home and sleep in until eleven. Sounds like bliss.

I catch a ride home with the guys after training. Tulane started back up a few days ago so Felix moved back into the city but he's still been helping me out with rides when he can since our neighborhood isn't far. All his classes are in the afternoons and evenings to allow for the "internship", plus there are the lacrosse practices. These guys are super busy and I don't take these rides lightly—I know they're sacrificing their time to help me out. Sitting in the backseat next to Seth, my muscles practically melt into the leather and my eyes flutter closed. I don't have an ounce of energy left. Everything is sore. Felix pulls up next to my duplex. "See ya, Eva."

Kenton taps me on the shoulder just as I push open the door. "Hey, we're having our annual kick off party at my fraternity house tonight. Wanna come?"

I turn back to the guys. A slow smile creeps across my face, and what do you know, I'm not so tired anymore.

Felix shifts uncomfortably in the driver's seat and rubs his hand over his face. Seth groans, which I don't even know how to take. Last I heard, Seth is too cool for those parties. It's not his fraternity, anyway. Kenton is the only one who pledged, but when it comes to the big parties, everyone's friends are invited. Kenton waggles his eyebrows and nods encouragingly. "You know you want to."

Actually, I do. I've never been to a college party before, but that doesn't mean I wouldn't be welcome. I mean, this is a fraternity we're talking about here. So what if I'm not enrolled and can't answer when someone inevitably asks what my major is? I'm single, I'm pretty, and I'm not shy. I'll probably fit right in.

"Hmm . . ." I pretend to think about it, like it's a hard decision.

I'll have to clear this new plan with Ayla, but that girl is always down for a good party. I have no doubt she'd ditch the movies and demand we get all dolled up. Felix has never invited us to his parties before. We're only a year younger, but even in high school he managed to keep the line drawn while still being friendly. And I know it's not his party, but I also bet he'll be there. The thought of seeing him outside of the Moreno house and in his friend element makes me giddy. How much longer will he be able to think of me as a friend if I keep showing up around him in places where people can become more than just friends? Time to find out.

I wink at Kenton. "I'm in."

Twelve

The place is packed. Bodies move together to the low bass beat of the music. It thumps through the house so loudly that the walls shake. The people who aren't dancing mingle along the edges of the rooms and in the hallways. They stand around in small groups with red plastic cups in their hands, trying and mostly failing to hear each other over the music. There's so many people here that some have spilled out onto the front and back yards. It's exactly what I'd picture a fraternity house to be with the crimson brick and creeping ivy, columns and balconies along the front, and loads of party boys intermixed throughout the crowd. Honestly, I can't picture Felix or Seth fitting in here, but it's no wonder that a guy as outgoing as Kenton found a place with this fraternity. He's got stereotypical-partier written all over him, but that's not a bad thing, not for him—he's fun!

Ayla and I snake our way inside. She's done her blue hair back in two curly loose braids and sprayed silver sparkles down the part. Her silver crop top, black shorts, and silver gladiator sandals complete the look and accentuate all her natural curves. She can pull off that sexy latin flare like nobody's business.

I'm wearing a little black halter top dress and red Chuck Taylors. Not quite as dressed up by Ayla's standards but definitely by mine. Little does she know, I've got a stake strapped to my upper thigh. A girl's got to be prepared for anything. Since my hair doesn't curl to save my life, I've ironed it extra flat and added my favorite shine spray. Ayla's applied my makeup, complete with winged eyeliner and matte red lipstick, and I have to admit I look as good as I feel--and I feel like a badass.

"Come on." I tug at her, pointing to where Kenton is tearing it up on the dance floor. "That's the guy who invited me."

Kenton spots us right away and waves us over. "You made it!" His short curly hair shines under the dimmed lights and his eyes narrow in on my friend. "Hey Miss Ayla, it's good to see you again."

She grins and then the two start dancing as if they're old friends. They must have met through Felix this summer too. I wonder if Ayla has any idea what Kenton really does in his spare time and what she'd think if she knew he was a vampire hunter. Knowing her, she'd probably find it hot. Ayla isn't a virgin like me. It's not like she's out there hooking up with everyone, but she does like to have her fun as long as she feels respected. She says it's what young people are supposed to do and I need to get with the program, but I can't help that nobody else lives up to Felix's high bar. And I don't know, but the idea of sleeping around has never appealed to me. Maybe it's because I have a hard time trusting people. Maybe it's because I'm protective of my body. But I think it's because I'm holding out for true love. Sappy, I know, but it's important to me.

Large hands clamp down on my eyes from behind and Felix's voice murmurs in my ear, "Guess who?"

I twist around and wrap him in a tight hug. His body is lean and rippled with muscle from all of our gym time. "Hey! It's good to see you outside of work or your house, Felix."

And it is.

He chuckles. "Same."

His energy is looser, but I'm not sure if it's the booze or just catching him in a different environment. Even though the vamps were able to change the legal drinking age to eighteen a few years back, I don't drink because I hate the feeling of losing control. I also didn't miss the lecture from Leslie on the dangers of alcohol while being a vampire hunter. It was one of the first ones I got. The nature of our work puts a target on our backs, and mixing alcohol with that, especially at night, is a lethal combination. It's not that hunters have to swear off drinking, but we know that inebriation could mean the difference between life and death.

I catch the clean mint and rain scent that is Felix's signature smell and notice there's not a hint of alcohol underneath. Smart man. He turns and scans the room full of people, same as I've been doing every few minutes. Felix isn't going to let his guard down. Not really. Neither is Kenton for that matter. He may be dancing with Ayla, but he's not one hundred percent focused on her like he's pretending to be. Not being able to let our guard down is our shared curse it seems. One day, Tate says this will all be washed from my memory, but that's years away, and until then, I can't unknow what I know.

The party gains momentum and an hour later my heart is light with happiness, the muscles in my face have relaxed, and my body is loose and heavy all at the same time. A result from dancing along with my friends song after song after song.

A hot guy moves in on me and we introduce ourselves by yelling over the loud music. Carter has cornflower hair and dimples and good 'ol boy baby blue eyes. We start dancing straight away. Dancing with him sends a little shiver of excitement up my spine when I notice Felix watching us. The music changes, slowing into a low thumping beat. Carter has no problem using it as an opportunity to get closer to me. He smells good, a little heavy on the cologne, but at least it's a yummy one. His hands wrap around my hips and tug me closer.

"Alright, that's enough," Felix butts in.

Carter shoots him an annoyed glare which only grows into a full on grimace when Felix physically inserts himself between us.

"What's the problem, man?" Carter raises his hands, his eyes darting between us.

I pop my hip and smirk up at Felix. "Yeah, what's the problem?"

Over his shoulder I catch Ayla rolling her eyes and mocking throwing up. "Ew, I can't watch you guys flirt-fight. I'm going to pee."

I know she doesn't like that I have a thing for her brother, and it's not like I blame her, *but who can blame me*? Felix is by far the sexiest guy here. Girls have been throwing themselves at him all night. And this whole dominance thing he's doing to me right now just proves my point.

"Do you want Carter's hands all over you?" Felix glowers at me. Okay, so he knows this guy. Maybe they're close, but I like that what I want is Felix's first priority, not what Carter wants. Still, I can't help but like this newfound attention. He's never shown it to me before despite my efforts over the last five years.

I smile ruefully. "Maybe I do."

"See!" Carter moves back in.

"Or maybe I'm just having fun, Felix," I continue, not even bothering to glance sideways at the other guy. Felix is the only one I see. "Haven't you ever heard of a girl wanting to have fun? Or maybe you're too serious all the time to recognize social cues?"

Carter lets out a resigned growl. "Okay, I see what's going on here. Sorry, but not my scene." He turns away, disappearing into the crowd. Gone to find new meat, just like that.

Well shoot, I didn't realize I was being so obvious.

Felix steps back.

"As far as I'm concerned you owe me a dance partner." I raise an eyebrow at him. To my surprise, he slips his arm around my waist and pulls me against his body.

"Don't make me regret this," he says playfully, his earlier tone completely gone. He sounds like the kid I grew up with, but his liquid brown eyes tell a different story. They're older, more experienced, and linger on my lips. It's all I need to know. I've been given the green light--Felix is officially interested. We begin to move together to the beat of the music, our bodies aligned in a way I've only ever dreamed about, and before long it feels like we're the only people in the room.

"Where's Ayla going?" Kenton interrupts.

"Bathroom." My voice is breathy.

"No." Kenton points and we turn to see the back of Ayla's head disappear out the front door. "She's with some guy."

I pause. "That's not like her."

Sure, she likes to party with guys, but she's careful and smart. She wouldn't normally take off with someone random, especially without telling anyone. Felix catches the same train of thought and peels away from me to catch up to his sister.

I'm quick to follow. Kenton, too. Seth isn't here since he's "above" the fraternity parties, but if he were, I'm sure he'd be by our sides. In that moment, it finally feels like we're a team. It's amazing to know someone has my back. Together, we weave in and out of the college students, dodging flinging arms and elbows, many with cups of sloshing drinks in their hands.

When we get out to the front porch, we spot Ayla straight away. Too bad we also spot her with *them*. They're way too beautiful to be human, with skin too pale to be alive.

Vampires.

Thirteen

I reach for the stake strapped high on my thigh, but Felix stops me. "Not yet."

He strolls up to the group as if he either has no idea what these guys are or he doesn't care. "What's up, bloodsuckers?"

Well, that answers that question.

They turn on us with a sneer, and one extends his fangs. Ayla's eyes go wide as saucers and she begins inching toward us. Unfortunately, one of the vamps tugs her back. "Where do you think you're going, Babydoll?" His group snickers. The three of them look like regular college aged guys, except their skin is too oddly pale to be normal, their best features are somehow accentuated to make them more attractive, and their eyes have a slight glow. I want to slap Ayla for not picking up on it straight away, but not everyone does, especially if they're inexperienced with vamps.

Kenton laughs darkly. "You do know you sound like a sexist prick, right? You might be ancient as dirt, but the rest of us are living in the twenty-first century. Go get your breakfast from a willing donor at one of your filthy little blood banks."

"You don't know who you're talking to," the sucker hisses and tightens his hold on Ayla. She squeals and goes white as a sheet.

Kenton lifts his shirt to reveal a stake strapped to his waist. "Right back atcha, buddy."

The vampires' eyes glow brighter at the threat, and all hell breaks loose.

The one who has Ayla arches down to bite her. She screams, and Felix pushes her out of the way. He punches the vamp square in the nose one second and procures his own stake the next. The other vamps have readied their stances, fangs extending. They move unnaturally fast, to the point of almost being blurry. Around us, the front yard partiers scream and scramble away, but I pay them no attention. My mind goes completely focused on the moment which seems to slow everything down as it plays out as if in slow-motion.

We're three on three. The vampires are ten times stronger than we are, but we have weapons and an Ayla-sized load of willpower on our side. No way are we letting our girl get hurt.

"You!" Kenton points to the vampire who tried to bite Ayla. "You asked for this."

He swings his stake with the force of a twenty-year-old who lifts weights on the daily. The vampire deflects his blow, but Kenton was only a distraction. Using the training techniques we've been working on, Felix swings around back to sink his stake into the vampire's heart from behind. The beast screeches and explodes into dust. His two companions hiss and jump at us, as if they didn't just get the memo that attacking us gives us grounds to exterminate them. This is the way the treaties work. We're not supposed to hunt unless we're attacked first, not that we give a crap about the treaties most of the time. If we don't get caught, then we don't get turned into the VEC. Vampires can burn in hell for all we care.

I fight off my attacker and plunge the stake into his heart. I miss. He growls and backs off, his body healing almost instantly. "I'll kill you for that."

"Not if we kill you first." I lunge for him again. By now his remaining companion has also been killed, this time by Kenton. It's three to one, we're hyped up on adrenaline, and this creep doesn't stand a chance.

He must know it because he hisses and bolts.

A saner person would let him go, but I must be a little crazy tonight because I chase after him without a second thought. Something within me can't let him get away. He's a threat to not only my kind as a whole, but also to me directly, and now that he's seen our faces, he won't forget us. Last week Tate taught me that most vampires are excellent trackers. They get a whiff of their prey and they can follow the scent to the ends of the earth. I can't risk this guy having a personal vendetta against me and my friends.

My feet pound the pavement and my hand grips the stake even tighter. All my senses narrow in on the blur of black sinking into the inky darkness of the tree-lined street. He's too fast. I'll never catch up. But that doesn't matter now. I know exactly where he's going; I don't know how that's possible, but I just do.

I continue running, my instincts telling me when to turn left or right. I weave deeper into the neighborhoods surrounding the college, but soon those turn from residential, to businesses that are closed up tight for the night. I run and run and run. I only have one focus now––hunt and kill.

I'm approaching The French Quarter when a black SUV pulls up beside me. "Get in," Felix calls out.

I don't want to. I can feel that my target is closer now. He's slowed down. He's not far. Maybe he doesn't realize I'm on to him, that I'm hunting him. Maybe he thinks he's lost me.

But he doesn't know me.

I ignore Felix and continue to run, going deeper into the The French Quarter until I'm on world-famous Bourbon Street. It's packed and music pulses from speakers. I snake through the raucous crowd until I come out on the other side and it's much quieter and empty again. I keep going, turning down street after street. Many are too small for Felix's SUV and I'm pretty sure I've lost them but I haven't lost the vampire. I can still sense him ahead of me. I end up back on one of the main roads and spot Felix's SUV again. He flashes his lights. I wave but ignore him, darting into another tiny alleyway. I hear my friends getting out of the car in the distance and can't help but feel slightly annoyed that they're making too much noise. I'm going to lose the element of surprise if they don't shut up.

The summertime humidity curls its way up and around my legs under my dress. It's a good thing I wore my Chuck Taylors tonight. I might never wear high heels again, come to think of it. I slow and walk on the balls of my feet, crouching low. I can sense the water in the air, the stillness of the night, the lack of a breeze, the stench of old garbage in the bins, and the acute awareness of everything happening around me.

Voices break the silence up ahead. It sounds like a man is reprimanding another man. "Foolish," he barks.

"But I was ordered to spy on her." The voice is defiant and I recognize it as the one who threatened me. I've found my target.

Maybe there are two vampires now. No biggie, I'll just kill them both. My confidence is growing. I can't help but feel like these kills are a sure thing.

I inch around the corner of the building, listening for the muffled voices. "Did you let her follow you here?"

No more time to think. I jump from my hiding spot and zoom toward my enemy. He doesn't have time to react before I'm sinking the silver tipped wooden stake into his heart. I feel the moment when I hit the intended target this time. The flesh of his heart gives so easily.

He bursts into dust.

Then I swing around, prepared to kill again.

"I thought I told you never to come back here."

I blink up into the face of Adrian Teresi and my blood freezes. It's like all the confidence I just had has rocketed clean out of my body. He narrows his murderous eyes and steps closer. He's going to kill me. It's then that I realize we're in an alleyway behind The Alabaster.

"I didn't realize," I whisper.

Just then, my friends shuffle up behind me, Ayla included.

Adrian peers at them and then back at me, his mouth curling in utter disdain. "What's all this? Did your friends come to kill innocent vampires, too?"

I scramble back. "None of you are innocent."

"And yet you were the one who hunted tonight." He glares at my stake. "And by the looks of it, you've done this before."

I open and close my mouth, unable to find words. I know what Adrian's capable of. How's he going to feel about me being a vampire hunter? And what will it mean for me now that he knows? Will Tate kick us out of the program? Vampires aren't supposed to be able to identify us. I have so many questions, all of which I'm afraid to know the answers to.

"Those vampires showed up at our college party looking for blood. As far as we're concerned," Felix interjects, "they started it."

Kenton nods. "And we ended it." He grips his stake tighter.

What my friends don't know is it sounds like those vamps showed up at the party because they were spying on me. That guy I just staked said someone had ordered him to go. They probably followed me to the party and saw an opportunity to take advantage of partiers, or more likely, lured Ayla away so they could question her about me. Adrian sighs as if dealing with a bunch of young hunters is the last thing on his to-do list for the night. He's not afraid of us. He's inconvenienced.

"I won't kill you," he says at last, like he's doing us a favor. "But only because those idiots weren't my protégés and, quite frankly, had no business in our coven to begin with." He chuckles darkly. "You may have just done me a favor, come to think of it, but that doesn't mean you can show your faces around here again." He flicks a hand toward us. "Now shoo."

And then his body levitates up and up until he vanishes into the darkness.

Ayla yelps. "Did he just?"

"Yes," Felix growls. "I've never seen one of them fly, but I've heard the stories."

"Only the oldest and most powerful, and therefore the creepiest, can do that." Kenton whistles low. "C'mon people, let's get out of here before more fangers show up." He wraps an arm around Ayla's shoulders and tugs her in close. "I think you and I should have a little chat before you head up to college tomorrow about not going off with random strangers."

Ayla doesn't reply as the two shuffle ahead of me and Felix.

"You know what they say, right?" Kenton continues in a lighter tone.

"What?" Ayla's voice cracks.

He winks. "Some guys are only after one thing."

And in the case of vampires, it's nothing good.

Fourteen

⁂

"**H**ow's the new roommate situation going?" I ask Ayla. She's on speaker phone while I sit on my bedroom floor and apply matte overcoat to my freshly black fingernails.

"Getting better. She's cleaning up after herself now that we had that little talk. Hopefully she doesn't hate me, but we're sharing a room, have some decency."

I look around at my cluttered bedroom and snort. Ayla's a clean freak, but her new roommate is the opposite. It's a good learning experience for both of them, if you ask me. Not that anyone has . . .

"How's the training going?" she replies. "Any more run-ins with vampires?"

"Not yet."

It's been a few weeks since my bestie left for school and things have mostly gone back to normal. Well, as normal as they can be with my favorite person gone. Now that the cat's out of the bag, it's been so nice to talk to her about this crazy vampire stuff. Lucky for me, she wasn't mad that I lied about the internship. On the contrary, the woman took it all in stride, saying she'd have done the same thing to protect me and was grateful we were able to save her that night. She'd gone outside to bum a cigarette with that guy, something she does every now and then at parties, but promised she'd never be so careless again.

I believe her. In fact, she's been at school for two weeks and hasn't gone to a single party, let alone left her dorm room after dark. She's going to have to live her life eventually, but right now she's still too traumatized by what happened. I'm glad she's safe, but I also hope that she can learn to trust again. I doubly hope that she can sense vampires better now that she's had direct contact with some. They're not always easy to spot since they look like glorified versions of their human selves.

The phone beeps and an unknown call comes through. I almost send it to voicemail but instinct tells me to answer it. "Hey, I gotta take this call, talk later?"

"Later, babe. Stay safe."

My heart drops a little. The Ayla I know would've ended the call with something akin to "don't do something I wouldn't do" or "make me proud" or even "see ya later, alligator"––not "stay safe." I sigh, switch the call over, and answer with a quick, "Hello."

"Hello, is this Evangeline Blackwood?" The woman's voice is glossy and professional.

"This is she."

"I'm calling about your mother. You're her emergency contact, correct?"

"What's wrong?"

"She's okay, but you need to come pick her up. She refuses to leave and she's already donated well above the allocated amount of blood for her weight."

My body goes cold. "Where are you calling from?"

Not that I have to ask.

"I'm a nurse at The Alabaster Heart Hotel and Casino." Her voice changes from cool professionalism to an urgent whisper. "You need to come quickly. This won't end well for your mom and she's refusing to leave. Vampires aren't great at saying no to blood donations."

Vampires aren't great at saying no to anything they want, who cares who they hurt in the process.

"I'll be right there."

I hang up and jump up with a curse. My nails aren't dry and I don't have the car and I can't even believe this is happening right now. I consider calling Felix to come help, but he's pulled away since the frat party, placing me squarely back in the friend zone, and I don't really want to let him in on my family problems. Mom has the Corolla and taking the bus will take ages at this time of night, so I suck it up and order a taxi. Riding into the city will cost double during prime time, but none of that matters right now. I have to get to Mom.

I blow on my nails and hope for the best, gathering my things and running out the door, making sure to lock it behind me.

. . .

I know what I'm risking by walking in here. The risk was always there before, but this time it's tenfold, and I may as well be signing my own death certificate. I keep my head down, my curtain of black hair covering my face, and power walk toward the nurses station. It's set up right next to the cashier. No surprise there for an establishment that runs on blood and money.

"I'm here to get Virginia Blackwood."

The nurse offers me a grim expression and points. "She refuses to quit. I can't take the bag out without her consent. The vampires have a policy."

Mom is practically slumped over the edge of the Texas Hold'em table and that stupid bag hangs next to her, nearly bursting with her blood. The nearby vampire pit boss eyes her blood bag like it's his dinner. Someone's placed a chocolate chip cookie and a glass of orange juice next to her chips, but the goodies are untouched.

"You're kidding me," I growl at the nurse. "You can't take it out of her? There are laws about this."

"Humans only get to donate every so often, so the vampires don't like us to cut them off once they are hooked up to a bag."

"But the laws––" I press on.

She laughs bitterly and nods toward the pit boss. "He's the law tonight." It's a different guy than the one from last month, but even if it were the same vamp, I don't think it would matter.

Feeling helpless and pissed off, I charge toward my mother. "It's time to go."

She startles and turns on me with a grim expression. "What are you doing here? I'm fine. I know what I'm doing. Did that nosy nurse call you?"

She motions to the pit boss. "You'd better get a handle over your employees. Your nurse called my daughter, who by the way, isn't old enough to be in here."

Mom's never been like this with me. I can't even count on all my fingers and toes the number of times I've come to pick her up here. She always resists, but she's never so volatile.

"Why are you being like this?" I growl at her.

She widens her eyes and motions to her sad stack of chips. "The more blood I donate the more chips the house will give me to play with. Don't worry, I haven't had to touch the ATM yet. It's the weekend," she laughs cruelly, "why aren't you out with your friends? You know, having fun, like I am?" She sighs toward one of the patrons sitting next to her. "You'd think an eighteen-year-old would know how to have a better time than her old mom, wouldn't you?"

The greasy man grins down at her, his eyes traveling to her exposed cleavage and back up to her ruby hair. "Not everyone is as easy going as you are, Virginia." The way he says "easy" makes my stomach twist.

"Gah! Don't be a perv," I hiss at him. He only laughs. "Mom, we need to go. I'm serious. I can't be here and I won't leave you like this."

She turns her back on me and continues playing as if I'm not even there, as if I'm a bother to her and not her own daughter. I can't stick around. Adrian might've been alerted to my presence and on his way to kill me. I also can't make her go, she's a grown woman. "Will you at least let the nurse take that thing out?"

"Fine!" She throws her hands up and the blood bag shakes. "Send that busybody over and then go home, Evangeline."

I turn away with a huff, find the nurse to send her back over to my ridiculous mother, and make for the door. I don't ever want to step foot in here again. Mom is a lost cause because she won't admit the problem, she doesn't want help, and she's going to end up killing herself. Tears well up in my eyes, and my cheeks grow hot. What am I supposed to do? Just let her go? Ditch my own mother? She's the only family I have, but it feels like there's no other choice, and she's never been this mean before.

Arms of steel grab me from behind and lift my feet clear off the floor. I scream just as a black bag is thrust over my head. I claw at my attacker, but something hits me on the back of the head and everything fades to black.

Fifteen

I wake up sputtering to icy water splashing my face. I blink and try to clear my head, but my thoughts are too heavy to catch and my eyes flutter closed again.

"Wake up," the voice is cruel. I know that voice . . .

More water.

I careen back and find my arms and legs tied to a chair. "What the hell?" I force my eyes to stay open this time and take in my surroundings despite the pulsing headache at the back of my skull.

I'm in a small room. I think it's in a basement because it's shadowy and cold and barren. The walls and floor are all concrete. A single light casts most of the small room in shadows. Thick and scratchy ropes bind my wrists. Standing above me is none other than Adrian Teresi. A sour look is plastered to his face as he stares down his nose.

"You kidnapped me?" It's not a question though. It's the cold, hard truth. Is he going to torture me before killing me? I shouldn't have tested my luck by coming to the casino because it's painfully obvious that it's run out, and nobody is coming to save me.

His fangs extend.

They're about half an inch longer than the rest of his teeth. He leans in and breaths in my scent. "Evangeline Blackwood, I can't decide if you're an angel or a devil." His lips brush against the delicate skin of my neck. I lean away, but that only exposes more of me.

"*You're* the devil."

He clicks his tongue. "Careful. Your blood smells hot and fresh. It's practically begging to be mine."

I jerk my head back. "Please . . ." I don't want to beg, but I find myself doing it anyway. "Please let me go or kill me now, but don't play with me."

"Where's the fun in that, huh? You must want to be played with considering you keep coming back to where you don't belong. The Alabaster Heart is a casino, after all. Does the little lamb want to play a game with the lion?"

He twists around until his face is inches from mine. Everything about him is dangerous and beautiful. Gooseflesh prickles all over my body.

"I can hear your heart beating." He possesses my gaze with his. I can't seem to look away. "It's the sound of an invitation. I could rip it from your chest right now."

This time, I don't beg. There's no point. But I won't go down without a fight. I thrust my head forward and crack my forehead into his nose.

He jumps back, growling. "You shouldn't have done that."

Maybe I shouldn't have, and maybe my head hurts even more now, but I'm still glad I did. I smile and glare. I have nothing to say to this sucker.

Procuring a white handkerchief from inside his suit jacket, he mops up his blood. His nose heals right before my eyes. Except for a couple drops on his white shirt, it's as if nothing happened. I heard it crunch, I felt it give, my own forehead hurts.

But he's healed.

"A less controlled vampire would've already killed you for that," he says calmly. "But you're fortunate that I have had centuries to learn patience."

Centuries? Just how old is this freak?

He picks up a stake, the same one I had strapped under my pant leg, and snaps it in half. "Who are you working for?"

"I don't know what you're talking about." It's a lie and we both know it.

"Let's cut right to the chase, shall we? I have your mother. I will kill her if you don't answer my questions, and then I will kill you."

I blink at him, fear cleansing me like boiling water. He's right. He holds all the cards and I've got nothing. What did I expect? This is a casino, he said it, and what do I know about casinos? The house always wins.

"What makes you think I work for someone?" I deflect with a question of my own, even though I know it's useless.

"You tracked that vampire the other night, and you obviously had hunter friends with you. You carry a stake on you at all times. You wear that crucifix everyday, which by the way, is a silly superstition." His jaw tenses and he grabs the necklace, yanking it from my neck and breaking it with an easy flick of his wrist. I yelp as he tosses it to the floor. "You, my angel, are a hunter."

I shrug and try not to hate him for breaking my necklace. Grammy gave it to me before she died but I won't give him the satisfaction of knowing what it means to me. "So? What does it matter now that you've got me. You can't compel me to do anything."

"I could keep you locked down here for years until your prefrontal cortex develops and then compel you. How old are you, again? Eighteen? Oh, but you're almost nineteen. Only two more weeks until your birthday. You humans love to celebrate your countdown towards death."

"What's your point?"

He smiles. "Six years isn't so long a wait for a vampire. It's but a drop in the ocean to me."

My mouth goes dry. He looked up my date of birth and now he's willing to keep me until I'm twenty-five. I imagine myself being a kidnapped girl, living years in this dark, dank room--a vampire as my only link to the outside world.

"But why should I bother with all that when I have your mother?" he continues. "Is her life not compelling enough for you, Angel?"

It is, but he doesn't have to know that. "Stop calling me that."

"Devil, then."

I take a deep breath. "My mother will end up dead either way. I came here to save her, as I've done countless times, but tonight she refused to come home. Did you see how much blood she donated? There's no saving her now, thanks to you."

"*She's* a gambling addict," he scoffs. "How is that my fault?"

"Compulsion!" My outburst echoes through the room.

"We don't need to compel the addicted." His laugh is bitter. "They come to us all on their own. You humans are weak."

"I'm not weak."

His smile quirks. "Trust me, you are. You're mortal. You're breakable. And just like everyone who has come before you, I will get exactly what I want from you when I want it and how I want it. I could even make you beg for it if I desired."

"And what do you want, Adrian?" I twist my neck. "This? You want my blood? Take it then. Get it over with."

"If I wanted your blood you'd already be dead. You already know what I want, hunter. Who do you work for?"

Like I'd tell him. But I need to drag this out while I think of something. "And what's in it for me?" I feign interest.

"Oh, we're back to negotiating, are we?"

"I guess we are."

"Well then, name your price and we'll see what I can do." His liquid ice eyes travel up and down my body, slowly, languidly, and I shiver.

The thought strikes me and I can't stop myself. "Compel my mother never to gamble again."

He pauses. "You're smarter than you look."

"So I don't look smart?"

"You look like a twenty-first century teenager so one can only assume your education and experience are lacking."

"Typical narcissistic male." I roll my eyes.

This time his laugh is genuine and it unsettles me. "If I do this, I'll need more than just to know who you're working for."

I snort. "I'm not going to walk you in there and let you kill my friends if that's what you're after."

"I don't want to kill those hunters," he replies evenly, catching me off guard. "And I already know where you work. Your facility is under the city bank. No, Angel, I have other reasons for wanting to keep my enemies close."

I know I shouldn't believe him even though I want to. But he knows about our location, so maybe he's not lying.

"How can I trust you?"

His eyes flash triumphant. "A blood vow."

"A what now?" I haven't heard of this, but if it has to do with blood and a vampire then it can't be anything good.

"We exchange a small amount of blood and a promise," he says, "if either of us breaks that promise, then we die a very painful death."

"Eww, I don't want your blood! That's so unsanitary." I mean, seriously, that could have terrible complications for me. "Haven't you ever heard of HIV? I don't know where you've been."

"I can assure you my blood is pure, much more than that of a human. The vampiric virus kills off anything that tries to threaten my body."

"Still gross."

"And I can tell your blood is untouched."

If he means that I'm a virgin who's never done a drug in her life, then he has me there. But seriously, that's been *my* hard work and a series of a lot of unpopular choices, and I'm supposed to blow it all now on this guy? *Yeah, right.*

"I won't touch the hunters if you will agree to keep me informed on your handler's goings-on. I want to know when he leaves, where he goes. I want to know what he's teaching. Anything out of the ordinary about him. Anything at all."

"My handler?" My mind flashes to the man who's been nothing but kind to me.

"Yes. Leslie Tate."

I freeze, and he chuckles. "Oh, Angel. Who do you think I am? I run this city. Of course, I already know all about Tate, and if he were brave enough to face me, I wouldn't have to go through you."

I don't know what to say.

"And in return," he continues, "I will agree to save your mother from her addiction."

I think of my mother and the way she treated me tonight. I think of the bag, heavy with blood, of the money, being gambled like it means nothing. I want to save her, I do, but what if I can't? What if Adrian is her only hope? He can fly. He's powerful. He's old and connected and runs the city. If anyone can save her, it would be him. And as much as I don't want to betray Tate or my friends, Adrian is resourceful. He'll find out what he wants about Tate one way or another. At least this way my mom will survive until Christmas. Could anyone really blame me for that? She's the only family I have.

"You can't go after the hunters or Leslie if I do this." The second the words pop out of my mouth, guilt eats at my stomach. I'm not this person. I can't agree to do this. As much as I want to, it's not who I am.

"Fine, I will only fight a hunter if it's to protect myself." I can tell Adrian is getting excited. This isn't going to end well. "How does that sound? It's a good deal that I'm offering. You should take it."

"But––" I can feel the shame pull on my facial features. Adrian freezes. He sees it, too. He knows I'm going to refuse.

"The alternative is I kill you and your mother," he growls, his face going dark. He's not playing games anymore. "You make this vow or you die."

"Those are my only options?"

"Yes. I have no qualms about killing you both. You're lucky I'm even making this deal with you to begin with. Don't think I can't force you to do whatever I want, because I can." He smiles and his eyes shine brighter than ever. "But I'm a gentleman so I'm going to ask you. One. More. Time."

He's not a gentleman. He's a monster.

I release a slow breath, the implications of this conversation pressing down on me with the weight of life or death. He's right. What other choice do I have? Maybe it makes me a horrible person, but I want to live, and I want my mother to have a life free of addiction. I don't see another way out of this one, so I'll just have to hope that I can outsmart Adrian later and help Leslie Tate along the way.

"Fine," I snap. "I'll do it."

Sixteen

ith a flash of movement too fast for my human eyes to follow, the ropes binding me fall to the floor in a stream of ribbons. I jump up and Adrian gives me space to stand and shake out my limbs. I want to run away, to fight, to do *something*, but I can't. So I stand there, frozen to the spot, glaring at the beautiful monster that I'm certain is going to be my ultimate undoing.

"You agree that you'll spy on Leslie Tate for me, and in return I'll relieve your mother of her gambling addiction?"

I nod. I've always been a confident person--I've always loved myself-- but tonight, Adrian has taken some of that away from me, and I'll never forgive him.

His eyes narrow. "And you will speak of this agreement to no one?"

"Fine, but neither will you."

"Agreed." His smile is sinister as he drags one of his fangs across his full bottom lip, splitting it. Blood trickles down his chin.

"What are you doing?"

He answers by stalking in so close that I stumble back. He pushes me up against the hard wall, caging me in with his muscled arms. His spicy cedar smell dances through the air, reminding me of a Christmas tree--if a Christmas tree was sexy and terrifying. The long thin stream of blood continues to trickle down his neck; I grimace. His bottom lip is an entirely different color than his top, red as cherries with the pooling blood. Hunger flashes, lighting up his sky blue eyes like a thunderstorm. Did he change his mind? Is he going to kill me? I should be afraid, but strangely I'm not.

My knees weaken, and I grab hold of his arms to anchor me up. They're like steel beams welded to the wall. His strength is utterly unhuman, reminding me of just how vulnerable I am to be standing here.

"What are you doing?" I ask again, my voice trembling.

"Testing myself." His reply is low and guttural. Is he going to kiss me? *No*, a human man would be testing a kiss, but Adrian is anything but human. The bastard is testing his resolve *not* to drink me dry. I'm a toy to be played with and used, nothing more. He's like a little boy trying to see how long he can hold his breath under water. Eventually, he's going to need air. Eventually, I'm going to get myself killed.

"Test yourself on someone else," I growl. "I thought we were doing the blood vow?"

Something I can't quite describe flashes over his features. It's like annoyance and resolve and laughter all wrapped together. "We are." He snatches his right arm free of my grip and swipes at my face. He's so impossibly fast that his stubby little fingernail slices through my bottom lip, blood spilling to mirror his.

Surprised, I cry out, but he captures the pain with his foul mouth. His lips cover mine, our blood mixing. Metal assaults my taste buds, and I hate him even more than I thought was possible. This feels so wrong, and when he coaxes my mouth open to deepen the kiss, his tongue sliding across mine, it feels downright immoral. What kind of girl kisses a vampire and likes it?

Because I do like it.

My body buzzes and my heart pounds and my fingers crawl their way up and around his cold neck to ruin his perfect Adonis hair. He pushes our bodies against the wall, his hand still above me cracking the plaster. I've never been kissed like this before.

I feel like a wildfire and Adrian is my fuel. I need more.

As if knowing exactly what's going through my mind right now, he chuckles cruelly and peels us apart. He wipes his thumb along his bloodied lip and licks it clean. His has already healed. "Hmm, I thought so."

"You thought what?" I hate that my voice cracks. I hate that I want him to come back and kiss me again and that I'm hoping he'll say something about how good I taste.

"That you'd crumble and I wouldn't." The statement is like a cold shower.

Nevermind, I *don't* want him.

I glare, hating how right he is about me. Here the man stands, completely unaffected by what we just did. He's had lifetimes to engage physically with far more beautiful and experienced women. What am I? I'm nothing but a stupid teenaged girl, a game he played to win. Well, he may be the victor for now, but I'm not giving up. This is far from over.

"And what did you think of our exchange, little angel?"

I shrug. "That I've had better."

He laughs. "So have I." He is so clearly not the liar right now; it would be laughable if it wasn't so embarrassing.

"So that's it? The blood vow is set?" I fold my arms over my chest and tap my foot.

"Yes."

"But I didn't feel anything."

He smirks. "That's obviously not true." His eyes drink me in, and I redden. I also realize just how disciplined and powerful he must be if he could exchange blood with me without actually biting me. I didn't know that kind of restraint was possible for a sucker. Technically what we just did wasn't against vampiric law. There certainly wasn't venom involved.

"How do I know if any of this vow stuff is real?" I challenge. I still can't shake the fact that I didn't feel anything magical happen. Not that it's magic, well, maybe it is, I'm not really sure.

"Well, Angel, it's quite simple. If you don't hold up your end of the bargain, then you'll die. What's so hard about death for your human mind to comprehend? Don't you worry about your mortality on a daily basis?"

I scoff. "Whatever, let's go compel my mother right now and get this show on the road." I raise an eyebrow and try to mask my excitement. I've always wanted this for her––for us––especially since things have taken a turn for the worse, but I never dared to imagine it was possible. Now that it's about to happen, I want it more than ever.

"Patience is a virtue." He strolls away, and I follow, but first I pick up my broken necklace and stuff it into my pocket. "Haven't you ever heard that?"

"Talk of virtues is pretty rich coming from a murderous vampire, don't you think?"

"I can't help what I am, same as you can't help it. It's pointless to fight nature."

"Right. Like vampires are *natural*. I know for a fact you were born human just like the rest of us. You said it yourself. You're a virus."

He says nothing.

"So vampires can't help but kill?" I continue to poke the bear. "Great, maybe we can get that in writing and take it to the idiot humans who signed treaties with you guys in the first place."

He doesn't bother to respond. We continue walking through a labyrinth of hallways until we reach a stairwell. He opens the door. "After you."

He doesn't have to tell me twice. I want to save my mom and get out of here. The thin cut on my lip throbs and I feel completely bruised from his kiss. His mouth is like a brand on me now, one that nobody else will see but that I will never forget. I'm not proud of myself.

As soon as we're back on the casino floor, he points to the nearest bathroom. "Clean yourself up. You're going to attract unwanted attention with all that blood."

I hurry inside and wash my face and neck––even though I refuse to look myself in the eyes––and then scrub everything clean with a paper towel from the dispenser.

Smoothing my hair on the way out, I find Adrian waiting for me. He hasn't bothered to clean our blood off his smirking face. I don't think it's a vampire thing, I think it's a rub-this-in-Eva's-face thing. "You're truly sick, you know that?"

"I do know that." His eyes are sinister but playful, a terrible combination.

I have to look away. I gaze out at the casino floor with it's golden art deco style, totally bugged that it's more crowded than I've ever seen it before. These people are idiots for being here and I want to shake them all and scream in their faces, not that it would matter one iota. "Okay, let's go find my mother. Knowing her, I'm sure she's still here somewhere."

"You mistake me, little angel. I'm not going to do anything for your mother tonight."

I stop short and gape at him. "But you have to."

"No, the vow we agreed on is that you'll spy for me and then I'll relieve your mother of her addiction." He clicks his tongue, smiling ruefully. "We never set a time limit on when that relief would come, but we did set an order."

Realization burns bright as the midday sun. "That's not fair!"

He backs away. "Neither is taking my money and still reporting me to the Vampire Enforcement Coalition, but you did that, and now I'm doing this. Two can play the game of twisting words, Angel. Now get out of my casino and don't return until you have valuable information to report."

He disappears into the raucous crowd, leaving me to wonder why on earth I ever thought I could trust a vampire.

Seventeen

I regret everything. What was I doing? Why did I give into him like that? I'm a terrible person. A better hunter—a stronger hunter—wouldn't have agreed. They'd have died before engaging in a blood vow with a sucker, especially Adrian-freaking-Teresi. I may not know Tate well, but I do know that he's been nothing but gracious to me, and here I am betraying his trust. And what if it ultimately comes down on my friends, too? What if I'm the weak link that causes the downfall of the whole organization?

I can't follow through with this. I just can't.

My mind whirls with regretful thoughts as I fail to find Mom in the busy casino. I look everywhere before finding the nurse who tells me she already left. I hope she's safe and okay. She probably ran out of money and went home. At least she's not in a hospital or dead somewhere. Defeated, I wait on the front steps of the casino for a cab to arrive. I know it's counterproductive, but I really hope Mom won some money tonight so she can pay me back for all this cab fare. September's rent is paid and I'm saving the last of the hidden sock money toward our next payment and my own money for a car.

I stare at my phone for too long and then sit on the steps. Exhaustion is heavy, and all I want is to be in my bed and for this night to undo itself.

But what if...

What if I do it, though? What if I find something valuable to tell Adrian about Tate and he saves my mother from addiction? I'd never have to come back to this casino again.

But I can't.

I won't.

So then, what? I'm going to die? I don't want to die.

Adrian is the one who said there wasn't a time limit on our blood vow, so maybe I can hide from him, and hold off telling him anything valuable. I mean, eventually I'll be old enough that Leslie will do whatever he does to erase my memory and that will be the end of it. The blood vow can't possibly work if I don't remember it, right?

Ugh, I don't know.

And now that I'm really thinking about it, something isn't adding up. How, exactly, is Tate going to magically erase my memory? And why is it that he's the only adult I've ever met who's immune to vampire compulsion? Felix said there was more to the supernatural community the first day I met Tate. Tate said I'd learn more soon. But he hasn't mentioned it again in the last month of training. There's got to be something else going on with that man. He claims his immunity isn't something he can share, but maybe he's lying, or maybe he just hasn't tested it enough.

I can't help but wonder if he's some kind of warlock. Are those a thing? There's enough voodoo witch-doctors in New Orleans for me to believe it's possible. But I don't know, Tate seems too level-headed for that. Or maybe he really is a werewolf, but with powers? Maybe he's something else. Elf? Are elves a thing? I know enough bookworm girls out there who would hope so, who'd give up their firstborn for a chance to be kidnapped by a High Fae and taken to some magical realm.

I snort and the sound rings out into the darkness. I'm starting to get away with my imagination, here. None of that is real. In my experience, the sparkly stuff doesn't exist. It's the things that go bump in the night that you have to worry about.

Well, when I get home––another fifty bucks poorer thanks to Mom––I don't want my mind to be a complete mess about this. I may not know the right thing to do, or if I even have a choice in the matter, but I'm going to climb into my warm bed with the decision that I'll deal with this problem when it comes back to bite me in the butt. Until then, I'm going to pretend this night never even happened.

Fat chance.

I tap my shoe against the concrete step and double check my phone that the car I ordered will be here soon, when a smooth voice behind me says a low, "Hello."

I jump up and turn to the man descending the casino's steps toward me. My hand presses against my chest. "You scared me."

"I have that effect on people."

My throat tightens when he approaches close enough for me to recognize him. "Hugo."

"Hello, Evangeline. I'd hoped I'd run into you again."

He sniffs the air and grins. "Are you hurt?"

Without thinking, I raise my hand to my injured lip. That only causes him to chuckle again. Everything within me is telling me to get far away from this one. He's not here to be my friend.

"There's something very familiar about you," he goes on. "Do you feel it, too?"

"We've met before," I try to keep my voice from shaking, but it's useless. "On the ferry, remember?"

"Oh, I remember." His eyes narrow into little slits. "But there's something more to this . . . connection."

"If this is some kind of pickup line, sorry but I don't date vampires." My tone is dry. This is my attempt to change the subject. Sarcasm usually is. The last thing I need is for this guy to realize the reason we might have a connection is because I killed his baby vampire lady a few weeks back. I'm sure now that it was her. Tate had said that vamps rarely make kin, so it stands to reason that the one I staked was Hugo's.

He doesn't take the bait. "This isn't about romance and you know it."

I swallow hard just as my phone dings and a car pulls up. "That's my ride. Gotta run!"

I dash down the remaining steps and into the car. Hugo doesn't follow me, though I can't let go of the horrible suspicion that I haven't seen the last of him.

When I get home, Mom isn't in bed. I check the garage and the car isn't in the bay. It's well past 2 a.m. which means she's either still at the casino and the nurse lied, or she went home with somebody else. I don't want to think about that one because she's never left me alone at night before. But there's a lot that's changed with the woman. Maybe I shouldn't be surprised.

I send her a quick check-in text and fall asleep waiting for her to reply. She never does.

I SLEEP through my alarm the next morning and not by a little, by a lot. When I eventually peel myself out of the bed and realize I'd turned it off this morning in my sleepy stupor, the time on the screen catches me by surprise. I'm three hours late for training. I've never been late before. I'm also used to catching rides with Felix, but he never bothered this morning, it seems. There's no missed call or anything.

Cursing my mom and Adrian, and Felix for that matter, I speed through the quickest shower of my life. I need to get the cigarette smell from the casino out of my hair. I don't want anyone guessing where I was last night. I finish up and hastily french braid my long wet hair back, slide into workout clothes, and run to the kitchen to grab a banana and fill up my water bottle.

Mom's car keys sit on the counter. I guess she made it home after all. She should be at work by now.

"Mom." I pop my head in her darkened room. "Are you okay?"

She mumbles something about calling in sick to work and rolls over, her little red head burrowing under a mountain of pillows. I don't have time to lecture her about the stunt she pulled last night, and it wouldn't matter anyway. Taking her car, I zip downtown to training and hope that I don't get into too much trouble for showing up late.

Well, I try to zip over, but I get caught in terrible slow-moving traffic and by the time I'm actually pulling into the underground parking garage, I'm four hours late. Half the day is gone. I wish I'd applied some makeup because I can already tell I'm blushing from embarrassment and probably look like I lost as much sleep as I did. They're going to think I'm hungover, and with my lip still healing, they may even think I ended up in a bar fight or something.

I do the fingerprint scan first and then number code my way into the facility, racing over to the gym area where I expect to find my teammates sparring. But it's empty. Taking the stairs up to the classroom areas, I find a group of hunters gathered outside of Leslie's office.

"What's going on?" I ask.

One of the girls turns on me with a frown. "He's gone."

"What do you mean, gone?"

She shrugs. "He wasn't here this morning so we started working out on our own. Finally someone got worried enough to break into his office. He wasn't there. He's not anywhere in the building. This has never happened before. Did you know he lives here? He has an apartment and everything. He's very careful about when he leaves and where he goes.."

I did not know that. "Thanks," I mutter to the girl and push my way through the crowd until I find Felix, Seth, and Kenton whispering in the corner.

"What's going on? Tate's missing?"

They go quiet and turn to me. "There she is," Seth says. "Hello, Eva. Nice of you to join us." He peers down at his watch. "A little late, don't you think?"

I wave in his face. "Uh, yeah, hi! I'm your teammate, remember? You're supposed to be on my side, not giving me crap for being late."

He rolls his eyes. "Giving you crap for being late proves I'm on your side. You can do better. Who else is going to tell it to you like it is?"

Fair point.

I turn to Felix, punching him in the arm. "Why didn't you wake me up this morning? You were my ride."

"I rang the doorbell twice."

Well, shoot. "You could've called."

"I'm not your personal alarm clock," he bites out. "And I drove across town for you not to answer your door."

Fair point.

I ball my hands into fists. "Why are you acting so rude to me? It's been this way for two freaking weeks."

"Really, Eva?" Felix shakes his head. "Think about it. What happened two weeks ago?"

"I don't know." That's a lie. Two weeks ago we danced and got close and I thought for sure we'd end up a thing, but then he backed off. It still stings to think about it. Rejection sucks.

He laughs bitterly. "Come on, Eva. Say it."

I'm not going to say it. What? That he rejected me? That's cruel. I've never known Felix to be cruel but maybe he is.

"Break it up, Mom and Dad." Kenton steps between us. "We have bigger fish to fry than your stupid argument."

I fold my arms and turn on Kenton. "So then what's the problem with Tate?"

"The guy wasn't here when we arrived this morning." He points to the desk. "And look at what he left."

Centered on Tate's desk is a single piece of paper. Instead of a neat scrawl, the black words inked against the white appear to be written with a hurried hand.

I'm safe. I don't know when I'll return. Be careful. Stick together but trust no one. Things aren't as they seem.

My face goes white hot. Surely this doesn't have something to do with me, does it? He can't know about my deal with Adrian. That would be impossible. But what if he did? It makes sense, actually. He somehow knows about the blood vow and took off. A shard of guilt cuts through my gut like broken glass. Maybe I caused this. Maybe it's my fault. And what happens when the others figure out I'm the one to blame?

Eighteen

❦

I study the other hunters, measuring their faces for any possible suspicion that could be pointed in my direction. So far, there's nothing beyond what I'm also feeling––they are freaking the freak out. Because, seriously, what are we supposed to do now? Tate runs this operation. He's our leader. He tells us where to go, what to do, and teaches us how to do it. He's like the captain and the life-jacket *and the boat* and suddenly we're floating in the ocean on a flimsy raft.

"Listen up, everybody." One of the older hunters jumps up onto the desk where everyone can see him, or at least hear him considering it's crowded in here and there are still several people in the hallway. "I'm Cameron Scout, and I'm pretty sure I'm the oldest one here. I'm supposed to age out of the program in a few months."

Cameron is a muscled and stocky guy with spray-tanned freckled skin and flaming red hair. He reminds me of a grown up Chucky doll who went to hang out on the Jersey Shore for the summer. He's a little scary, a little hot, and a *lot* creepy, and I wouldn't want to be on his bad side. Or his good side. Or any side, actually.

"Being the oldest here has to count for something, right? But hey, I'm not saying my seniority puts me in charge." He smiles, and my hackles rise.

"That's exactly what it sounds like," Felix mutters.

"But I'm a team leader and I've been around the longest, so I know how things are supposed to work around here," he continues. "So let's just keep things going business as usual until our fearless leader returns, okay?"

A bunch of the hunters nod, and considering my team and I are newbies, it's not like we have a dog in this fight. We'd be looked at like little yappy chihuahuas who think they're ten times bigger than they really are. My guys and I end up nodding along with the others even though this Cameron person is a tool.

"Team leaders, raise your hands, please," Cameron commands.

Next to me, Seth raises his hand. I'm surprised. I assumed our leader was Felix. I never thought to ask, and nobody said anything, but Felix is usually the one to drive us around and make demands and all that jazz. Felix doesn't bat an eye at Seth's raised hand. Once again, I'm reminded that I was late to this party and missed a few important things.

Also, if Seth is my leader, I might be in trouble. Seth doesn't like me. He's not a jerk, he doesn't say anything bad about me, but that's the point, *he doesn't say anything*. He doesn't even act like I'm here most of the time. Today was one of the only times he's even acknowledged my existence and it was to tell me how late I was.

"Okay guys," Cameron motions to the leaders, "hold back so we can have a conversation. The rest of you can go workout until we figure out our next step."

We shuffle out the door and Kenton curses. "We're so screwed. You guys know that, right? Does anyone even know how to work the simulations that's not Tate?"

"And don't forget we were supposed to be learning crossbows this week," I add and the guys groan in unison. Looks like I wasn't the only one looking forward to crossbows.

"Hopefully Tate will be back soon," Felix grumbles.

"But if he's not, we're going to turn into all those other hunting organizations that end up going south and everyone gets killed," Kenton goes on. I've never heard him be so negative and something about that makes this feel even worse. "Tate is what made us different and kept us safe. He's the only damn reason I agreed to do this job in the first place." He motions to the large state-of-the-art gym as we amble inside with the rest of the group. "I mean, the man single-handedly secured all of this without the vampires knowing. With him gone, it's only a matter of time before it falls apart."

There's at least one vampire who knows about our facility.

"Well, then we're just going to have to train harder than ever to make sure we don't get killed, now won't we?" I raise my eyebrows at Kenton. I hate seeing him like this but I don't blame him. We're all here for a cause, not a death wish.

"The woman has a point." Felix sighs, raking a hand through his curly dark hair. His bicep flexes and I have to look away. I'm mad at him. No more drooling.

"Fine, you two go first." Kenton points to the mat. "I haven't seen you spar yet."

"That's because we haven't sparred." Felix's tone is warning.

"Yeah," I add. "Felix is too holier-than-thou to spar with me."

"It's not like that." He glares down at me, but behind that glare I catch hurt. I have to stop myself from rolling my eyes, because if anyone should be hurt about the iciness that's been going on between us, it should be me.

"Then what's it like?" I fold my arms and pop my hip.

"I don't want to hurt you." He says it like it's obvious.

"Maybe you avoiding me is what's actually hurting me. Did you ever stop to think about that?"

Felix just stares at me. He knows I'm right. Did he really not catch on before?

Kenton chuckles and intervenes. "You know that if she doesn't get good sparring partners then you're only weakening her for the suckers, right?"

"Yeah. What he said! Or maybe you're scared I'm going to kick your ass?"

Felix shifts his glare to Kenton. "Fine." He picks up two of the rubber stakes we use to practice with and tosses one to me before stepping back onto the black mat. "But I'm not going to go easy on you."

"You wouldn't dare," I tease.

And then he lunges for me.

I'm quick to dodge him, jumping out of the way and landing in a fighter's stance. As we circle around each other, I'm reminded of two wolves challenging each other for the spot of alpha. Adrenaline spikes my blood. Everything around us blurs as I become hyper-focused on Felix. I'm quick, quicker than I've ever been before, dodging his moves milliseconds before they should strike. Deciding that I don't just want to be on the defensive here, I make my own move, dropping low and kicking out my foot, hooking it around the back of his ankle and pulling. It catches him, and he falls. I pounce forward, stake prepared to strike, but he blocks me with his forearm and flips me onto my back. Before I can react, the tip of his rubber stake presses to my ribcage, just over my heart.

I lost.

His body is weighing mine down and every inch feels like an answer to all my teenaged birthday candle wishes. This is what I've been waiting for. I blink up into his chocolatey eyes, daring him to take this further. He shouldn't kiss me here, not where everyone can see, but I want him to want to kiss me anyway. I want him to think about my lips and nothing else. My hope leaps when his gaze flicks to my mouth and then holds.

He feels it, too.

"What happened to your lip?" He sits back up, rolling off me.

Oh, that . . .

"Why were you looking at my lip so closely?" I deflect, and he glares. It's not like I can tell him the truth of my healing lip, but I don't want to lie to him either.

"Eva," he challenges.

Well, maybe I can tell him part of the truth. "Someone got a little excited when he kissed me last night." I wink. "Don't worry, I liked it."

Also, not exactly lying because I did like that part.

My words cause the reaction I was hoping for. Pure unfiltered jealousy creases his brow and fires up his eyes. It ignites something primal in me. Before I can react, he jumps to his feet and stalks away. I guess this is his way of not wanting to show me his true feelings, but it's too late, I already know what I saw. Meanwhile, Kenton is busy laughing his head off from the sidelines.

I get up and brush myself off, ready to go another round, when Seth shows up.

"Evangeline, can I speak to you about something?"

His request catches me by surprise, but I decide to give the guy the benefit of the doubt. Also, I don't want to look as guilty as I feel today.

"Sure. Here?" I nod toward the mat. "Wanna talk while we spar?"

"No, let's go somewhere more private."

I follow him back up the stairs and into one of the smaller classrooms. We turn to face each other. I almost expect him to tell me to back off Felix, and I'm prepared to lay out all the reasons why it's none of his business who I date. Of course, I know that's a load of crap considering he's the leader of our little novice team.

"There's something I've been meaning to ask you." He levels me with that all-seeing gaze of his, and I try to appear causal.

"What's up?"

He studies me and it feels like he's looking into my soul or something. Geez, this guy is so freaking intense for only being twenty years old. "That night at the party when you tracked that vampire from Kenton's fraternity house all the way into the city . . ."

"Yes?" I let out a little breath.

"How did you do that?"

This isn't what I expected. In fact, I hadn't given much thought to that night since it happened. I've been so busy. "I don't know," I shrug, "I just did it."

"You have no idea how you were able to do that?" He's skeptical. "I wish

I was there to see it for myself. Kenton and Felix told me about what happened. Felix has been going on and on about it. "

I shrug again and realize that's what Felix was talking about earlier. He's been upset because I ditched him to track that vamp. "I don't really know how I did it. The sucker pissed me off, I knew he was a threat, and when he ran, I followed him. It was like I just sensed where he was. Hunter's instinct, I guess."

He frowns. "Instinct?"

"Well, I don't know what else to call it." But now that he brings it up, it is kind of odd. I thought it was normal but now I realize it's anything but normal. People can't just track vampires like that. So, why me?

"Do you have any idea where Tate could be? Do you think you could track him, too?"

I try to keep my face clear of any guilt I feel when I think about Tate and shake my head. "I don't know if it was a one time thing with that particular vampire, but I don't have any idea where Tate is or any kind of instinct as to where to look. I'm just as worried about his disappearance as you are."

And for more reasons than I'll admit.

"Okay." He nods once. "Well, if you think of anything, or if anything else comes up, will you let me know?"

"Sure thing, boss." I don't say it sarcastically, but maybe he takes it that way because he frowns.

"I didn't choose to be the group leader, you know. Tate assigned me."

"Tate's a smart man." I pat him on the shoulder. "I'm sure you're a great leader."

He hums to himself and frowns. "Actually, I don't think I have been the best leader. I'm sorry I haven't been more welcoming to you. I'll do better."

"I definitely wasn't expecting you to say that, but I'll take it." I try to hug him but he escapes me by ducking under my arms and makes a break for the door.

"Baby steps, Eva," he deadpans, and I snort.

We go back downstairs with the others and train like we normally do, all the while wondering about Leslie Tate's disappearance and what that might mean for our futures.

A COUPLE DAYS later and things have almost returned to normal, except for the fact that Tate's still MIA. I'm back to getting rides to and from hunter practice with Felix and the guys whenever Felix has availability. Sometimes they have lacrosse practice that intervenes with our gym time, and I hate those days, because I hate to train by myself. I'm so used to doing things independently, that this feels different and special. I like that I'm not all alone in this thing. Being on a team has become a lifeline.

Felix has dropped his attitude and I suspect Seth has something to do with that. Today I'm sitting in the front and sneaking glances at the boy whom I've had a not-so-secret crush on for ages. He's still as gorgeous as ever. He's still this mysterious code I'm dying to crack. He's still fun and alluring. But... but I'm starting to get tired of waiting for him to make a move. I deserve someone who wants me as much I want them.

I know, shocker, right? This is what Ayla's been preaching to me forever, and it's what I've believed too, but I still couldn't shut my feelings off. Maybe it's time I find the switch and stop worrying about him like that. I have enough going on without having to add a complicated romantic relationship to the mix.

The thought makes me a little sad, but a little relieved at the same time. Mostly sad.

When we pull up to the duplex, my entire body goes cold.

"The door is open," I croak.

Felix and the guys are out of the car in all of two seconds flat. I follow behind as we quietly creep up to the duplex. Sure enough, our front door has been kicked clear off the hinges. It lays in our tiny living room, parts of the painted red wood splintered across the beige carpet.

Nineteen

S eth points to Kenton and he takes off to run the perimeter of the
house. Then he and Felix escort me inside.

Our stuff is everywhere--literally everywhere--and tossed
about like trash. A couple of our kitchen cabinets have been kicked in. Our
round hallway mirror is smashed in the middle, splintering out like spiderwebs. I catch my stunned face in the reflection, a fractured image of a girl I
can hardly recognize.

Something's happened to Mom. I'm sure of it.

We edge along the hallway into her room, but she isn't there. It only
takes a few more minutes to case the rest of the tiny two bedroom duplex
and realize she's not here at all. Am I too late? Is she dead somewhere?

"Mom?" I call out, helpless.

Silence.

At least there doesn't seem to be anyone else here, namely whoever
destroyed my house.

"I'm going to call her," I croak and then dial her number. To my
surprise, she answers right away.

"Evangeline, baby," her voice is breathy, like she's been running. "I was
just about to call you."

"Mom, what happened? Have you been home? The house is a disaster.
Were we robbed?" My mind starts racing, imagining her hurt. "Do we need
to call the police?"

"No!" she barks out. "Do not call the police."

"Mom, what's going on?"

"Listen, baby, I did something stupid." She goes silent. "I'm okay though. I wasn't there when they came to the house, but--"

"Mom! What did you do?"

"I borrowed some money from the wrong people, that's all. I'll pay them back. I'm working on it, but in the meantime I'm hiding out with a buddy, and you should hide out, too, okay? Go stay with Ayla."

I'm shaking. Shaking with fear. Shaking with rage. I want to yell at her that Ayla isn't even in the state anymore, but then I have to remember that this addiction isn't all entirely Mom's fault, even though it certainly feels like it right now. I still don't believe Adrian when he said they don't compel people because they don't need to. Maybe I'm looking for the best in people instead of looking for the truth.

"Are you okay?" Felix places a gentle hand on my shoulder.

I don't know what to say. He carefully removes the phone from my hand and finishes up the conversation with my mom before hanging up.

"You're coming to stay at my parent's house," he says, "you can take Ayla's room. It's fine. My parents will be happy to have you. They've been super weird about being empty nesters anyway."

My face has got to be candy apple red by now. I don't know if I've ever been more embarrassed, which certainly doesn't make the anger or fear feel any better. While Felix tells Kenton and Seth what's going on, I go to my room to pack up what I can from the mess of my things. I don't have much to begin with, but a lot of my stuff has been destroyed by whoever is after my mom. Tears burn my eyes and stream down my face but I force myself to work through them anyway.

Once I'm all done, I go to the air conditioner vent where I've got my sock of money hidden away, but when I reach inside, there's nothing there.

Of course, it's gone. What did I expect? The whole house is a mess, they probably took anything of value and whatever money they could find. It's not like a vent is the most original hiding spot. I want to scream, to riot, to find whoever stole that money and demand it back. But I know it's hopeless. There was only a grand left in the sock but I was counting on that money. I should've put it in the bank. I should've been smarter.

"What happened here?" I recognize Mrs. Maybee's shrill voice and cane thumping against the floor from the duplex entrance. My heart sinks. And as usual, I'm the one who has to fix this with the landlady. Just great.

I wipe away my tears and go out to the living room. "I'm so sorry, Mrs. Maybee," I say. "I'll clean this up."

"Where's your mom?" Her face is scrunched up like a prune.

"Umm--I don't exactly know but she's safe."

"Were you robbed?" She thumps her cane against the floor to emphasize each word. Her face is no longer a prune and has turned ghost white.

I should lie, I know I should, but I freeze up and don't say anything.

"Get out," she finally snaps. "Just get your things and get out. Consider this your eviction notice!"

I don't know if she can legally do that because it's not like we're late on rent anymore and we still have plenty of time left on our lease, but I'm not going to stick around for her to call the cops and try to deal with this legally. If Mom is worried about the police then there must be a reason. Whoever she owes can't be happy with her. This isn't my mess, it's hers, but once again, here I am trying to clean it up.

"Now!" Mrs. Maybee growls.

Mortified, I glare at the woman but pick up my duffle bag and scurry from my house, the guys at my side.

"And don't bother coming back," she yells after me. "I'm fixing the door, changing the lock, and using your security deposit to repair these damages."

"You could fight her on it," Seth says, "there are laws to protect you in these situations."

"I'm sure there are laws to protect her, too," I reply, dejected, thinking about all the damages. "But it's a moot point considering my mom has taken off and my name isn't on the lease."

"It's going to be fine." Felix wraps an arm around my shoulder and leads me back to his SUV. He's trying to be nice, but even he can't make everything better. I've lived in that duplex for four years, and before that, in an apartment building a few streets over. This neighborhood is my home, my stomping grounds, and now what? Now I crash at Ayla's? Felix isn't even living there anymore now that school's started. And last I'd heard from Ayla, her parents are trying to make sense of their new life as empty nesters by remodeling a bunch of stuff. They're talking about turning her room into the guest room and have started transforming Felix's into a home gym. Ayla's been sending her mom mock-ups and helping them design everything. Who am I to come in and ruin their grand plans? I'm going to have to figure something else out. And in the meantime, Mom is heaven knows where, with heaven knows who, and loan sharks are after her.

My life is a mess, but I'm not going to cry about it anymore. I hate crying. I'm going to fix it. It was the last of Adrian's money that I had stashed in that vent, over a thousand dollars now gone. Luckily everything I've been saving for a car is still in my bank account. I'll just have to use that money to find an apartment rental instead and keep taking the bus and bumming for rides.

When we get to the Moreno house, Felix runs inside to discuss the situation with his parents. Not surprisingly, his mom Yanet comes out to usher me into their home like I'm their long lost child and there's nothing they'd rather do than take care of me.

"Eva, honey," she says, pulling me into a warm squishy mom-hug. "I've always thought of you as a second daughter anyway. Don't even worry for one second." She's the middle-aged version of her kids. The whole family looks like gorgeous Cuban cookie cutters of each other. I sink into her for a second and then we're walking into the house.

"You don't know where your mom is?" She glances around, as if looking for something or someone. Who am I kidding? Of course, she's worried. My mom is an idiot and people are after her. They could be watching us right now. Yanet has to be wondering if her house is a new target.

"I'm sorry," my voice cracks, "she won't tell me where she is but she sounds okay."

"Well, that's a good sign." I can tell she doesn't believe her own words. "Come inside."

Yanet begins cooking dinner for our crew, and while they all hunker down on the couch to watch football, I go lay on Ayla's bed and begin searching online for rooms to rent but don't find anything. I was hoping maybe someone would need a roommate near the college, but it's looking like it's too late and everything is filled.

I could stay here. I could use the Moreno's generosity until my mom shows up with a solution. But what if we bring trouble to their doorstep? Whoever is after my mom could decide to use me as collateral to get her out of hiding. I can't risk their safety. I would never forgive myself if something happened to anyone in this household. I shouldn't even be here at all.

My bag is still packed.

I open the window, toss the bag with everything I own onto the lawn, and crawl out, leaving the comforting smell of Yanet's signature arroz con pollo dinner and the cozy feeling of family behind.

Twenty

❧

"**B**ack so soon?" Kelli raises a perfectly groomed eyebrow from where she sits at her receptionist desk. She sniffs the air and cringes. "Humans really should shower everyday, you know."

"Is your boss in?" I drop the duffle bag at my feet and rub my aching shoulder. "I need to talk to him. It's important." And yeah, I wanted to shower after practice, but things took an unfortunate turn, none of which is Kelli's business. I totally want to punch the nasty smirk off her perfect face but I'm not going to fall for the bait.

She rolls her eyes and sighs dramatically, like it's such an imposition to do her job. "Is he expecting you?"

"I know you don't like me, Kelli," I snap. "But I've had a hell of a day and I'm not going to put up with your attitude. Just get me Adrian."

She stands and her fangs extend. "Do you know who you're talking to, little girl?"

Maybe I should feel fear, but I don't. I have a stake strapped to my stomach under my baggy t-shirt and I could end her if I wanted. Of course, that would be the end of me too considering where I am right now. And anyway, I'm tired, I don't want to fight her. I just want to get Adrian's help. That's it.

But dang, I'm in a pissy mood. I can't help myself.

"I said please. Are you his receptionist or not?"

"Executive assistant," she growls. "There's a difference."

"Oh, so you pick up his dry cleaning *as well* as answer his phone? My bad."

A dark voice chuckles.

"Two things," Adrian's voice cuts through the tension and I turn to see him standing not a foot behind me. I didn't even sense his approach. He holds up a finger and whispers low in my ear. "First, you're foolish to bring a stake in here. If a vampire catches you with one of those, you're dead." He leans back.

Note to self: the vamps must not have the amazing hearing I assumed they did. Or maybe that's only for when they're hunting? Or maybe he wanted to whisper in my ear for dramatic effect and Kelli heard every word. Whatever it is, I don't ask.

"And second," he says aloud, "you two need to get along."

Kelli scoffs.

"Because you both work for me now."

I elbow him in the stomach and then immediately regret it because I hit my funny bone and it burns like a mother. "Ouch!" Kelli laughs as I lean over and try not to cry. His chest is hard as rock, no exaggeration. Vampires are too strong for their own good. Also, how does he always know when I have a stake? The man is too good at spotting them. Maybe that's why he's managed to stay alive for so long.

"That's between us." I glare up at him.

"Kelli can be trusted." Adrian shrugs. "She's my protégé. She is bound to me."

Again, creepy.

"So you're saying I can trust you, then?" I roll my eyes. "Yeah, I'm not dumb."

"Do you have information for me already? Because if you don't, then I'd beg to differ." He stares down at me, his blue eyes swirling with excitement.

"Unfortunately, I do." I pick up my bag. "But we need to chat in private."

He eyes my duffle bag, curls his lip, and nods to the elevator bay that leads to his office.

"Let me guess," he says once we step inside. "You need a place to stay."

I pat my trusty old blue duffel bag with it's frayed edges. It's seen better days, but I still love it because I associate it to years of fun track tournaments. "Unfortunately, I'm currently homeless. It seems my mom borrowed some money from gangsters and now I have to hide out."

He glowers at me. "Angel, did someone drop you on your head as a child?"

"Excuse me?"

"You really think hiding out among vampires is a good idea?"

"I don't." I swallow hard. "I know I could get a cheap hotel room in a seedy part of town and probably be safer there than in a vampire casino. And sure, maybe I should do that, but I needed to talk to you anyway and I figured you could help me for a night or two until I find a place to rent. You've got to have empty rooms available. This place is huge."

The elevator stops and the doors open to his gorgeous office. The last time I was here, I was terrified and angry, and now I'm just . . . tired. Adrian ushers me into a plush leather chair. Outside the river sparkles under the blue sky. He leans against his desk, studying me like he thinks I'm either courageous or stupid or both.

"So do you have information on Leslie Tate?"

I grimace. "I do."

"And?"

"Mr. Tate has left the building."

"I assume he does that from time to time. During the daylight hours to avoid people like me, of course." He glances out at the highly tinted windows and frowns. "Did you follow him somewhere, perhaps? Maybe somewhere interesting . . ."

I follow his line of sight outside. It's the afternoon, so it's the time of day when he's stuck indoors. When was the last time that this man was able to feel the sun on his face? No, I can't think about those things. He's not a man. He's a monster.

"Leslie Tate is gone," I continue and Adrian's eyes narrow into slits. "He left a hurried note on his desk saying that he had to leave us, and that he's safe, but he doesn't know when he'll return. Oh, and he also told us to trust no one and that nothing is as it appears." I release a slow breath. "So that was fun."

He growls, slamming his fist into his desk with a bang. I flinch and gape at the cracked oak finish.

"And you're probably wondering what this means for our blood oath?" He rakes a hand through his Greek god-like hair and levels his gaze on mine. There's something so otherworldly about the fluidity of his movements; it reminds me who I'm dealing with, reminds me to be careful. He's not human. And I'm nothing more than food.

"There is that." I sit up straighter.

"The vow hasn't changed. You will keep digging up what you can, and when I get what I need, I'll release your mother from her addiction."

I'll admit, I do like this situation better now that Tate is MIA, and I want to help my mother, but right now I have to think about getting a roof over my head and food into my belly. I hate Adrian, but the guy has more resources than anyone I know. When the time comes for him to compel

Mom, maybe I can get him to get rid of her gangsters, too. In order to do that, I need to get on his good side.

I need him to like me. Vampires can like humans, can't they? I mean, some must like them enough to turn them. That's not going to happen to me but maybe I can get him to think of me with something other than utter contempt.

"Come." He strides back to the elevator and we return to the lobby. He tries to hand off my raggedy bag to a bellman, but I refuse.

"If you must carry that thing then fine, but let's go, I have a meeting in an hour."

I smile, channeling all that pageantry in my blood. "So you're going to help me?" I bat my eyelashes, feeling like a complete idiot. But hey, men like to save women and feel like we can't survive without them. This is a universal and timeless fact about the opposite sex.

He glances sidelong at me. "If your hunter friends know you're staying here, they're going to be mighty suspicious."

I frown. "Crap, you have a point."

"You can hide out here for a few nights until you find a place, but do not go out onto the casino floor, do not talk to any vampires––especially not my brother––and don't let your people know about this arrangement."

Considering I snuck out of the Moreno's house to come here, this secret is going to be difficult to keep from Felix, but I bite my tongue. Adrian doesn't need to know about Felix. Something he said hits me as we stride toward another bank of elevators.

"Your brother?" I try to imagine another man who looks like Adrian and my insides almost spontaneously combust. Is Adrian awful? Yes. Is he also the most attractive creature I've seen in real life? Also, yes. Take Greek-god features and add vampiric beauty and make him look mid-twenties forever? Genetic lottery.

"You've met Hugo."

Eww, Hugo . . .

"Hugo and I are sired by the same master which makes him my brother."

"Trust me." I shiver. "Hugo is creepy on a cracker. I'll stay as far away from him as possible."

"Creepy on a cracker? Can't say I've heard that one before, Angel." His eyes travel up and down my body. "But it's not really him I'm worried about."

"What's that supposed to mean?"

"It means if he knows I'm interested in you, it's only going to make him more interested in you as well. You might try to stay away from him, but if he wants to find you, he will. His tracking skills are the best I've ever seen."

He's expecting the reaction that I'm feeling, which is fear of Hugo, but what I give him instead surprises him. I waggle my eyebrows. "You're interested in me, eh?"

He laughs. The sound makes me smile. It's stupid.

We climb into the hotel elevator and zoom to the top floor. There is a small hallway and two hotel doors opposite each other.

"This way." Adrian uses a real key instead of a hotel card to open the door on the left. He stares at me for a long minute. "Can I trust you with a key?"

I don't know what to say so I nod. He shakes his head and mutters something about being foolish.

My jaw actually drops open when we enter into what has to be the presidential penthouse suite. The room seems to take up an entire floor, similar to his massive office. But it doesn't have the same businessman feel of the office. It's not intimidating or mid-century or sharp angles. This place is warm. The floors are dark hardwoods with turkish rugs. The couches are plush and welcoming. The cream colored walls have beautiful paintings hung on them, many of which have to be famous. I don't know much about art, but even I can recognize a Van Gogh when I see one. There's a small kitchenette that looks untouched, a couple of closed doors, a mammoth-sized flatscreen television, a fireplace, and of course, a view of the city behind thick bulletproof darkly tinted glass.

"If you're staying in my hotel then you'll need to stay close to me." He saunters to the kitchenette, removes a blood bag from the refrigerator, and plops it into the microwave as if it's the most normal thing in the world, as if he's making a freaking Hot Pocket. I can only stare as I watch him prepare his meal. The microwave dings and I imagine him biting into the bag like I've seen Felix drink directly from the milk jug. I can picture the rivulets of crimson that might stream down his face and neck. Instead, he slices the top corner of the plastic and pours the blood into a black water bottle, sealing the lid. It appears so natural. He walks back toward the door to leave.

"You can take whichever bedroom you prefer. Vampires don't use them for sleep, anyway. But you should stay in here when you're at The Alabaster if you're not with me. Don't go anywhere else. And let me or Kelli escort you to and from the hotel. You can call her using the phones in the bedrooms." He retrieves a key and hands it to me. "You can have this, just in case you need to get in and Kelli or I aren't available. Don't try to make a copy. I plan to replace the locks once you leave anyway."

The weight of the gold key feels heavier than it should, like it's attached to a million expectations. I shove it into my pocket. "Is it really so dangerous for me to be here? I've come to this casino many times to get my mom."

"It's always been dangerous, Angel. Your virgin blood makes you more desirable to my kind and they will seek you out. I may run a casino, but I'm not always a betting man. I need you alive to get use out of you."

He pushes open the door and steps into the hallway.

Realization dawns on me. "Wait, is this *your* penthouse?"

"Welcome home." He chuckles.

The door slams.

Twenty-One

⌒⌒⌒

My phone buzzes in my back pocket but I ignore it. Again. It's probably Felix. He's been texting me nonstop for the last twenty-four hours, trying to figure out where I'm staying so he can check on me. He's all worried, but I can't exactly tell him the whole truth. I texted back last night that I was safe at a hotel and that I'd see him on Monday at our "internship." Apparently, that's not a good enough explanation for sneaking out of Ayla's bedroom window because he keeps sending follow ups that I don't know how to answer. Meanwhile, the person I want to hear from––my mother––is totally MIA.

I wipe a bead of sweat from my forehead and refocus on what I'm here at work to do: work! I load table fourteen's order onto my arms and stroll out to deliver the food. I head over to my next table that was just sat by the hostess only to find Felix, Seth, and Kenton there waiting for me. Felix stares at me hard, his eyes roving over me like he's looking for flesh wounds. Seth is unreadable. And Kenton already has his face stuck in the menu.

"Hey . . . guys. I didn't expect to see you here tonight. Can I start you off with some drinks?"

"We're here because you apparently forgot how to answer your phone." Felix's eyes narrow. "What's going on with you, Eva?"

"Would you recommend the ribs or the brisket?" Kenton interrupts.

"Shut up, Kenton," Felix growls.

Kenton looks up with wide eyes. "What's your problem, man? I'm hungry." He flexes his right arm and kisses his bicep. "It takes a lot of food to fuel this body."

I laugh, Felix and Seth roll their eyes, and the tension dissipates. "Definitely the brisket. Ours is amazing. But save room for the pecan pie because it's the best thing on our entire menu."

"That good, huh?" He waggles his eyebrows. "I'm not normally into sweets. You know I like it savory."

"Dude, don't be gross." Seth punches him in the arm but they laugh.

"Trust me, Kenton. You want this pie."

"Hello?" Felix waves his hand in my face. "Can you please tell us what's up with you? Why'd you ditch us yesterday?"

"I'm at work, Felix." I motion to the busy restaurant. "Can't this wait?"

Suspicion flashes behind his chocolate eyes, and I sigh. "Okay, fine. If you must know, I didn't want to stay at your parent's place because what if the people after my mom show up there looking for me? You saw what they did to my house. I love your mom and dad and can't risk anything happening to them."

He folds his tan arms and I have to keep myself from staring. What is it about his manly arms that has me so attracted? He's looking good today, but I've sworn myself off of the Felix-train. "Fair enough, but you could have told me that. We'd have helped you."

"Hotels are fine until I find a place," I rush, catching the eye of my manager Eddie heading our way. "What was I supposed to do, crash at your party house?"

I haven't been inside his house but I have been with them when he dropped Seth off once since they're roommates. The place looks like a typical off-campus party-house man-cave dump. I'd rather take my chances staying with Adrian, scary as it is.

"You could've stayed in my room at the frat house," Kenton says, his tone completely serious. "Plenty of girls do." He waggles his eyebrows to break character.

Seth gives him a sidelong glance and Felix looks about ready to rip his head off.

"Hello, gentlemen." Eddie approaches the table with that happy-go-lucky smile on his face, but I know this is his way of checking up on me. "Is everything okay over here?"

"Yeah, we're just having a debate about the menu." Kenton grins ruefully. "Ribs or brisket? What say you?"

"I'm normally a ribs man myself, but nobody makes brisket like Pops." I smile at Eddie, mentally thanking him for saving me from this conversation.

Kenton hands me the menu. "Great. I'll take the brisket with a side of coleslaw and hush puppies. Oh, and a sweet tea and let's finish it off with that pie." He winks.

The other guys order and I get back to work while Eddie hangs around for a few minutes to chat. Eddie sometimes has to do this for the servers. It's his way of keeping us on task while also keeping the customers happy with his lively conversation and saving us from flirty or just overly chatty customers.

Later, when the guys pay their check, they give me a big tip and ask if I'll be needing a ride on Monday. I insist that I'm fine. I tell them not to worry, that I got it handled, and I'll let them know when I need something. I'm an adult. I can take care of myself. But it's not until they leave that I finally relax and get focused on my job. Being faced with that suspicion in Felix's gaze, not to mention Seth's unreadable intelligence, I know I need this money now more than ever. Adrian was right last night, I can't stay at The Alabaster for long, and I can't let the hunters figure out I'm there.

I TAKE the bus back to the casino even though I hate the bus. I get a little carsick each time because it's way too hot and smelly and bouncy, but taking a taxi to and from work isn't going to do me any favors when it comes to saving money and I'm not walking alone through these neighborhoods at night. At least there's a reliable bus system. I have to be grateful for that. When I finally get off and walk into the lobby of the hotel, I veer away from the elevator bay and toward the casino floor. Adrian doesn't want me out here, but I'm just going to take a quick peek to see if Mom's gambling. She's hiding out, so I'm guessing that includes staying away from The Alabaster Heart, but I also know my mother. She won't be able to stay away for long, and I want to talk to her, to find out the full situation she's gotten herself into. Maybe it's not as bad as she says. Maybe I can help.

I've still got on my little black shorts and t-shirt from work, and the AC bites at the exposed skin. I keep my head down, the curtain of black hair a pathetic disguise, and fold my arms in on myself. I do a quick once around the area where the tables are set up but don't see her here. On one hand, I'm relieved she's not here. On the other, I hope that doesn't mean she's on the riverboat. It is Saturday night, after all. And on the other, other hand, I'm just hoping she's staying away from casinos and staying safe in general.

But I really wish she'd return my calls. I'm on the verge of giving up.

I also don't see Adrian down here and the only vampire is the pit boss, who's busy working. It's fine. It's not like someone is going to jump over the tables and bite me just because I'm a virgin which somehow makes my blood yummier. I recognize one of the regulars at the Texas Hold'em table and saunter over to his side, positioning my back to the dealer and keeping my head down. It's a full table, a full casino really, and the music is annoyingly loud. Hopefully, I won't get carded and sent away.

"Hey," I say casually to the guy, "you know my mother, right? Virginia Blackwood? She's the petite redhead who's at this table a lot."

He peers over at me from under bushy black and silver eyebrows. His eyes are red rimmed and his breath reeks of alcohol, which tells me he has more than one vice. The guy doesn't stand a chance. He'll probably be dead before the year's end. "Sure, I know her."

"Have you seen her recently?"

He ignores me for a minute to place a bet. I put a friendly smile on my face, waiting patiently, even though I'm far from patient right now.

"Saw her a few days ago. What was it?" He thinks back. "That was Wednesday."

"Yeah." I nod. "Me too. But I can't find her and haven't seen her since then. She said she's staying with one of her casino buddies. Do you know who that might be?"

He doubles down on his bet and stares at the cards as the dealer finishes the hand. "Yes!" He pumps his fist and pulls his winnings toward his stack of chips.

"Good job. You're really good at this." I'm trying to stroke his ego here, even though I know that he's probably going to blow through those winnings before the night is out.

He smiles for the first time and really looks at me, some of that alcoholic haze melting away. "Virgina has a lot of friends around here, not just me. I don't know what to tell ya, kid."

"Thing is, I'm worried she might be in trouble and I really want to find her."

He stiffens. "In trouble? If she's in trouble then keep me out of it."

Some friend.

"Let's say you needed to borrow money from someone around here. Who would that be?"

Please don't say vampires. Please don't say vampires. Please don't say vampires.

He laughs. "Vampires."

I frown. "That's what I was afraid of. I didn't realize casinos were keen to give out loans."

"Not the casino." he whispers and looks around, making sure nobody is listening in on us. "But there are others who have their little fangs mixed up with the mob, if you know what I mean."

I feel like sinking into the floor and disappearing. How am I supposed to handle vampires *and* the mob, especially if they're working together? I don't even know anything about mobsters beyond what they show in movies and television, but I do know that they are a law unto themselves and they're not the kind of people my mom should've borrowed money from.

"If you're smart, kid," he goes on, placing his next bet. "You'll stay far away from your mom and her troubles. Let her deal with them. You don't want to end up as collateral damage."

"Thanks." I grimace and walk away, my heart strumming against my ribcage because I know he's right. For as many times as I tell myself I'm going to give up on her, that I try to convince myself to do it, I also know it'll never happen. I can't. She's the only family I have left, she's my *mom*. Besides, I'm already in too deep to turn my back on her now.

I make a beeline for the elevator and sigh with relief when it arrives and nobody is inside. I hit the button for the top floor and close my eyes all the way up. When I get back to the room, I'm going to take a hot bubble bath and then go right to bed. Sounds heavenly. The elevator dings and I step off into the hallway.

I stop short and freeze. I'm not alone.

Twenty-Two

There are two penthouse suites up here. They take up the entire top floor, swanky enough for a prince. I already know the one on the left belongs to Adrian.

And the other...

A man in a black tuxedo has a woman in a silky ballgown pressed up against the door on the right. He's kissing her hungrily, she's groaning, and they definitely need to get a room. I try to sneak past, but my footsteps snap them out of their bubble.

"Ah, if it isn't Adrianos's little pet." Hugo turns to me and smirks, wiping a smear of lipstick from his mouth. He leans down to whisper something to the human woman. She murmurs a response and opens the door behind her to disappear into the dark suite. "I heard you were staying with my brother but I'll admit, I found it hard to believe."

"And why's that?"

He chuckles but doesn't reply.

"So I guess I don't have to wonder who has the other penthouse suite in this place, huh?" I shrug and point after his woman. "I think you'd better get in there and take care of her." My smile is fake as I pull out my key to unlock the door on the left.

"Before I do," Hugo appears in front of me, blocking my way and nearly making me jump, "I have something I wanted to talk to you about."

"Geez, do you have to do that vampire Speedy Gonzales shit?"

His black eyes narrow. "You haven't seen anything yet, my dear."

I don't know what to say to that, so I just raise an unimpressed eyebrow and try to appear aloof. Inside, my heart is pounding wildly and I'm certain he can hear it.

"You're staying with Adrian," he continues. "Nobody stays with him."

"So? It's not like the guy is here all that often, and you people don't sleep anyway. He's doing me a favor, that's all."

"You two are not involved?" He says "involved" like it's a filthy word.

"We're . . ." Oh, crap. What do I respond with here? That I'm working for the sucker? Do I lie and act like I'm in love with Adrian? Do I pretend to be his fledgling wannabe vampire groupie? I'm at a loss. "I don't know what we are."

He clicks his tongue. "Romance isn't my brother's thing. Sex? Often. Business? Always. So what is it?"

"Business." One word. One simple word. Business. And yet it has so many implications when it comes to what I've wrapped myself up in these last few days.

"I appreciate you telling me the truth." He smiles and steps impossibly close. "I can still smell your virgin blood. Had you lied to me, I would have punished you."

"I work for Adrian. Not you." I wrinkle my nose. His eyes flash with anger one second and then with amusement the next. "And how can you people smell virgins? That's so weird, do you know that?"

"It dates back to when priests used to send virgins into graveyards to find vampires to stake. Virgins are attracted to us and we to you. Think of it like the biblical Adam and Eve story, only we're the serpent. We can't help but want to tempt you, young Eve. You can't help but want to be tempted. I can't explain it beyond that."

But maybe that explains why I was able to track that vamp from the frat party.

Yuck.

"I find you quite intriguing." He runs a piece of my hair between his long fingers. I don't move. I'm suddenly very aware of how vulnerable I am in this moment. With Adrian, I'm the angel making deals with the devil. With Hugo, I'm not Eve, I'm the simple field mouse standing at the mouth of the serpent. "Now tell me, Evangeline, what would you do to have your own car? To have your own home? What would you do to be able to pay off the Italian mobsters who are after your mother?"

My body goes cold. "You know about that?"

"You made me curious, so I had you followed." My eyes bug, but he shrugs like the disgusting invasion of privacy means absolutely nothing to him. "I know why you're in that little uniform. I know you work for a bank during the day and at a restaurant at night. I know your mother is a colossal disappointment, failing you time and again. And I know your best friend in the whole wide world is away at college." He tilts his head in sympathy. "You're lonely."

"I'm not lonely," I whisper. Even as I say it, a pang stabs in my chest. He doesn't know me and yet he's somehow managed to uncover my deepest wound—the fear I'm not enough for people to love me.

"What did I say about lying, hmm?" He drops the piece of hair. "Evangeline Rose Blackwood, my my my, what a name. I do like it. It would be a great vampire name."

"I go by Eva." I glare.

"Well, Eva, I probably know more about you than Adrian does. What makes you think he's going to protect you, to help you? Leave him. Come be mine, and I'll give you anything you desire. I will *never* leave you."

His eyes shine with passion. His body radiates power. He plays a convincing character but I can't trust him. Deep in my gut, I know it. This has nothing to do with me. I don't *really* interest him. This is a pissing contest with Adrian and nothing more.

"You obviously don't know everything about me."

"Oh, what did I miss?"

"I'm loyal." I push past him and slip the key into the lock, letting myself inside. He doesn't follow.

"Think about it." He walks away as I close the door.

My knees go weak and I crumple to the floor, every inch of me shaking. Who am I kidding? I'm not loyal. If I was loyal, I wouldn't even be here. I wouldn't have ever agreed to the blood vow, no matter how precarious my situation was at the time. I'd have died before agreeing to be Adrian's spy. But then my mind flits back to what Hugo said about Mom owing money to the Italian mafia, and just the thought of her reminds me that when it comes to my family, I am loyal to a fault. How many times have I dragged her out of this place? How many times have I helped her? Defended her? Tried to save her? And I never seem to learn that she doesn't want to be fixed.

And where is she now, huh? Where is she while her daughter is hanging out around deadly vampires and making deals with them on her behalf? I retrieve my phone, knowing I'll find nothing from her, but hoping there will be something. Anything. A lifeline for me to hold onto for dear life and believe that she still loves me and that I matter to her more than the addiction.

There's nothing.

She hasn't called. She hasn't texted. I drop my phone into my lap, my face into my palms, and burst into tears. I don't know how much time passes. Minutes? Hours? Eventually, I lay on the floor. All the emotions I've knotted up inside of me are unraveling one by one. Anger. Sadness. Fear. Guilt. Frustration. Betrayal.

And yes, loneliness. Deep, deep loneliness. Hugo was right about that one.

I gladly fall asleep in it, letting unconsciousness replace the pain.

Sometime later, cold hands wake me up, lift me into cold arms, and carry me to a cold bed.

WHEN MY EYES flutter open the next morning, I long to feel the sunlight on my face. I peel myself from the bed and pad over to the window to throw open the curtains. It hardly makes a difference. These bulletproof tinted windows are too dark and only remind me of exactly where I am. I don't have anything going on today, but I don't want to stick around the casino either. The vampires roam around the city at night and are often gone, but since they have to stay out of the sunlight during the day and they never sleep, that means this hotel is probably full of them. Hugo included. I don't want to run into him again.

I shower and get dressed, trying not to think about last night, my conversation with Hugo, and especially not about my breakdown and Adrian finding me in a ball of sleepy tears on the floor. He'd carried me to my bedroom and tucked me under the covers. Why on earth would he do something like that? It's mortifying and confusing and not something I want to ever think about again.

I need to get out of this place. If I could go anywhere, I'd go to the beach. I'd swim in the surf and lay out on the sand and let the sun warm every inch of my body. But New Orleans isn't very close to good beaches for someone without a car. So instead, I brush my hair up into a wet ponytail and dress in a simple t-shirt, shorts, and sandals. I'm going to walk along the touristy boardwalk today. It's only a street away. It will be fun. This whole area of New Orleans is historic and draws in tourists from all over the world. There are so many fun places where I can window shop and people watch. It sure beats the alternative.

When I walk out into the family room, Adrian is sitting on the sofa with a newspaper in his hand and what would be a cup of coffee if he were human. I'm sure it's blood. If it weren't for his impossible Adonis Grecian beauty, his too-perfect movements, and the aura of danger that oozes off of him, he could pass for a normal man. I suddenly wonder what he looked like before he turned. I want to know his story but I don't ask.

"Good morning," I chirp.

He peers up from his paper. "Is it?"

My memory flashes to how he found me last night. "Look, I'm fine, okay? I've never been better."

He returns to his paper. "You're a liar, but fortunately for you, I don't care." As I go toward the door, he clears his throat. "I had some human food stocked in the kitchen for you."

Hmm, you don't care, huh?

As if on queue, my stomach growls. "Well, I'm not too proud to turn down a meal. And oh, look at you, you even got a toaster." It's sitting on the counter. I go to the cupboard to see what he got. I peel apart a bagel and plop it in the toaster. "I don't know, Adrian, some might say you're warming up to me."

He rolls his eyes. "I can't get warm, remember?"

"No need to remind me."

He saunters over and opens the fridge, retrieving a tub of cream cheese from between the stacked blood bags. I turn away and try to scrub the image from my mind. "We only have one coven in New Orleans. Most of the vampires live here in the casino. People are talking."

"And?" I plop the hot bagel sides onto a plate as he hands me a butter knife.

"And I don't like anyone knowing my business but me. How much longer are you going to be staying here?"

My heart sinks. "I don't know. I haven't made a plan yet."

"Do you need Kelli to help you find a place? She's rather good at her job."

"No offense, but I don't want Kelli or any vampires knowing where I live."

He levels me with a heavy gaze. "And yet here you are."

"Give me a couple days. I want to find a room to lease with one of the off campus college kids. I figure that'll be cheaper than getting my own place, and I should be around people my own age." I take a bite of the bagel. "No offense."

He laughs. It's real, not bitter or dark, but golden around the edges. It loosens something in my chest. I don't like it. "Fair enough. I'm the oldest vampire in all of North America after all." I choke, and he whacks me on the back. "Try not to look so surprised."

"I'm not. You've definitely got old man vibes about you." I look him up and down. "Total dinosaur." That's the complete opposite of the truth. He doesn't look a day over twenty-five and he's got sex appeal for days.

His eyes do the same—rove up and down my body. They linger on my legs. "Where are you going today?"

I shrug. "Walking the boardwalk. Taking some me-time. You know, self-care is self-love and all that? It's my day off."

"Good. Finish up and get changed. There's a dress in your wardrobe. You're coming with me."

"Uhh––what? Why? Where?"

"Downstairs to meet the rest of the coven. It's time we put the rumors about us to bed don't you think?" He walks toward the other bedroom, the one that I didn't claim. "Unless you'd like to put me to bed?" He says it like it's a dare. Is he flirting?

I glare. "Virgin blood, remember? I'm not losing it with a sucker. I'm already at rock bottom, no need to dig a hole."

He chuckles again. "Well, you might want to think about losing it soon, Angel. You're too attractive to us for your own good." He winks. "I'll even provide the shovel."

"Eww! In your dreams." He's totally flirting and I don't know what to do with that. I've never seen this side of him and I want to kick myself for enjoying it.

"One cannot dream if one cannot sleep. Never forget what I really am."

"You mean you're what nightmares are made of?" I bat my eyelashes.

"Exactly."

Twenty-Three

An hour later, I've curled my hair and brushed it into long Hollywood-style waves. It probably won't stay this way for more than two seconds, but it looks amazing, if I do say so myself. My face is made up with perfectly dark smoky eyes and bright red lipstick. I try not to think about the color too much or the last time my lips were this red. I slip into the little black dress hanging in the closet with the matching strappy high heels. The designer labels make me want to scream. Here I am, homeless, barely scraping by, and Adrian dresses me up in an outfit that probably costs more than a month's worth of tips.

"You can't bring that." He says the second I step into the family room.

"Bring what?"

"Don't play dumb." He flashes forward in that speedy vampire way, reaches under the hem of my dress, and rips the stake and holster clean off my thigh, throwing it to the hardwood. "I've told you. If one of my kind finds you with that, you're dead."

"So I'm supposed to walk into your creepy little coven lair with nothing to protect myself?"

"Not nothing. You have me."

He shoves a necklace into my hand. "Put this on. But you're not keeping it."

It's certainly not the dainty little crucifix I normally wear, which I'd decided to forgo today. Plus, I already had to buy a new chain thanks to this guy. Adrian's necklace is heavy and dripping with huge sparkly white diamonds. It can't be real. Can it? I snort. Who am I kidding? Of course, it's real. The vampires have billions of dollars because they've been around forever, and Adrian is their little North American fanger prince, after all.

I stop short. "If you're a prince, does that make Hugo a prince, too?"

Adrian offers a clipped, "yes" and goes stone-faced. He clearly doesn't want to talk about this more, so I clasp the necklace around my neck and follow him out the door. We ride the elevator down to the level below the casino floor. I don't want to think about the fact that we're now underground. This is a restricted area and Adrian uses his fingerprint to get the elevator to open. We're greeted with dark lighting, a spicy incense scent mixed with the undercurrent of copper, dramatic classical music drifting from a live orchestra, and beautiful people dressed up in suits and gowns. Some are humans, but most are vampires. There's probably two hundred vampires in this ballroom alone. I didn't know so many lived in New Orleans and a cool shiver rolls up my spine.

"Stay close to me," Adrian says, tucking me against him like we're on a date. Maybe we are? I don't like it, but I'll pretend I do for both our sakes.

We circle the room as he introduces me as his fledgling. It's not true––it will never be true. Fledgling is the term they use for humans who are trying to get turned, and it makes me want to scream to be called something so degrading. I try to hide my frustration and go along with it because it's not like I want these vamps to know I'm actually an aspiring vampire hunter and Adrian's little spy, but it's hard.

"Ah, there she is." Hugo appears next to us. A wine glass filled with inky blood rests in his hand and I have to look away. "Came for the fledgling announcement, I see? My my, you two are closer than I thought. Remind me, how did you meet?" Adrian glares and Hugo laughs. "That's right, how could I forget? She turned you into the police and you formed some kind of enemies-to-lovers bond over it." He pats me on the back. "You sure know the way to a vamp's heart."

"Careful," Adrian warns.

"Oh, come now, brother. I find it quite amusing! All that VEC nonsense is water under the bridge now that you've got your girl, isn't it?"

Adrian relaxes and cracks a smile. "What can I say? Eva's beautiful and smart. A winning combination for my next child."

I had no idea that Hugo had figured out that particular piece of our history. He knows all about the complaint I filed. At least Adrian is trying to play it off like it's all part of my charm. He smiles down at me like he finds me adorable. "Anyone who would dare to challenge me like that is someone who gets my attention."

"And she's just your type." Kelli approaches with her hand on her hip.

"That's why you turned me, isn't that right, Master? Because I'm beautiful and smart."

He smiles at her adoringly. "That's right, daughter. I don't like to be encumbered with protégés, so I'm incredibly choosy." Kelli smirks and kisses him full on the mouth like a lover would, like they've kissed a million times, before sashaying away in her tight silver dress. I definitely catch a hateful scathing look from her on her way out. She's playing me up to please Adrian, but underneath the smiles is a savage beauty who wants me dead. *I didn't ask for this!* This whole family coven stuff they've got going on here is beyond weird. He calls her daughter but they kiss open-mouthed, and I don't even want to think of what else they do together.

"Come," he says, "you're sitting with me and Kelli up front."

Hugo stops us. "I find it so strange that you don't grow your family as large as the queen allows. Here I am petitioning for more children, and you only have one protégé left, and a young one at that."

"Differences of opinion." Adrian shrugs.

"Perhaps I can use a new angle to convince Brisa to reconsider my proposition. If you don't want to multiply your family, let me pick up your slack." His eyes bore into mine.

Adrian stiffens. "Did you not hear me? I'm announcing Eva this very day."

"But think of all the years you choose not to take a child," Hugo argues.

"Don't be a fool. You've asked Brisa many times, and her answer is always no. Perhaps, brother, you are overlooking one important factor."

"And what's that?" His tone turns sour and he finally tears his gaze from me.

"Our mother loves me more than you." Adrian doesn't say it playfully. He means it, and then he pats Hugo on the back to rub it in. My mouth drops open in shock. These two aren't engaging in sibling rivalry like I'd thought. They're straight up enemies.

They hate each other.

"Oh don't look so offended. I'm only kidding," Adrian laments, his tone, however, says otherwise.

Hugo looks about ready to rip Adrian's head off. "Are you doing this because of what happened at that damned VEC meeting last month? It's not my fault you can't control what goes on in your own casino."

"Enough," Adrian stops him. "I don't have time to bicker with you yet again. Eva and I are expected somewhere else." When Adrian turns away to take us to our seats, Hugo directs that seething look my way. If he can't have me, maybe he won't want Adrian to have me either. Maybe he'd rather I be dead. This is not good.

"How often does your coven meet like this?" I whisper to Adrian, desperate to change the subject. We walk between aisles of chairs, his arm still around me.

Adrian doesn't take the bait. "Like I would tell you that. Now come on. I'm going to announce you as my fledgling to the queen."

"What?" My eyes bug out and I nearly stumble on my heels. "To your *queen*? I didn't agree to this," I hiss. And I didn't know the Queen was even here. I thought she lived in Europe somewhere!

"Quiet," he snaps back. "Do you want to survive this casino or not?"

"I was only supposed to stay for a few nights."

"And you will be leaving soon, but in the meantime, I need you to do this for me." He whispers against my ear, his soft lips featherlight, making my body tense, "Please."

"Geez, Adrian, you make me so uncomfortable."

And in so many ways I don't want to admit.

"Feeling's mutual."

We sit down at the front of the room, facing all the other chairs with the vampires and humans who are beginning to occupy them. He needs me here? Why? The prince brought me, someone he knows is a hunter, into his coven's sanctum. There's something more happening today than he's letting on, and he's definitely using me for some political game with Hugo and now his queen.

He stands and strolls over to a podium with a microphone. A camera is set up on a tripod to face it and another is set up to face the crowd. I feel like I'm at a conference or a school assembly. Dread settles low in my stomach. He begins to speak and the room falls silent. "Welcome to our family meeting. Tonight we announce our newest fledglings. Over time, as they prove themselves to us, and to Queen Brisa De La Cour, of course, they will have the honor of joining our ranks."

The crowd claps and my heart skitters. It feels like hands are gripping my throat. I shouldn't be here. *Squeeze.* This isn't right. *Tighter squeeze.*

The room darkens and a projector lights up a huge screen on the wall behind us. A young woman flickers to life, transforming the white backdrop to something else entirely. She's got a worldly European look to her, complete with a narrow face, pale smooth skin, long caramel hair, and large amber eyes. She looks cool––she also looks like a mean girl. While it's day here, she sits outside where she is in the darkness. An ancient looking city is lit up in the distance. I wonder where she is. I don't recognize it immediately but I feel like I should know, like I've seen pictures before. Going by her last name, I'd guess somewhere in France. Even though I'm still freaked out, I let out a breath of relief that the woman isn't actually in the building.

"Hello, my posterity. I miss you!" Her voice is wind chime sweet with a slight French accent. It sounds to have been watered down over her many years as a vampire. She's probably traveled the whole world many times by now.

"Your Majesty," Adrian purrs. "It's so wonderful to see your face again."

"Adrianos, my son, you are looking quite handsome tonight. It's good to see you in such a cheerful mood." She thinks this version of Adrian is cheerful? I try not to roll my eyes. He seems pretty sour to me. "Do you have the fledglings ready to announce? I've got another call with Saint Petersburg in an hour. You know how those Russians can get, not an ounce of patience in the lot of them."

"They are ready." He sweeps his hand toward the crowd. "Fledglings and their sponsors, please line up and introduce yourselves to Queen Brisa."

I sit frozen, watching as one by one the humans approach the camera at the podium and introduce themselves. At least we have to introduce ourselves to her via televideo. I don't know how I'd react to meeting a vampire queen in person. I wonder if she's the only queen. I assume so but I don't know much about their royalty since they keep as much as they can to themselves.

"What's this Hugo? Another one?" Brisa hisses when Hugo approaches with the woman I saw him kissing last night. "But you just turned that other girl, what happened to her?"

Hugo's face goes stony cold. "She woke early and hunters killed her."

My face warms. I want to sink into the floor and disappear.

"And so that makes you above the rules? No, no, this simply will not do. You know better than this, my son." Her voice turns razor sharp. "We do not allow too many fledglings. You are aware of the reasons."

"But we should want to grow our numbers."

"Hugo––"

"We should take over and harvest the humans in farms."

"That is not necessary or smart." Her eyes are daggers. "They will rise up against us."

"I'm not the only one who feels this way," Hugo bites back. The crowd gasps. Brisa goes silent and her cheeks flare red.

Adrian flies forward in a flash of movement, picking Hugo up by the neck and lifting him off the floor. "You forget your place, brother."

"I'm sorry," Hugo sputters, showing weakness for the first time since I've met him.

"If you are sorry," Brisa says bitterly, "you will kill your proposed fledging and offer her blood as an apology to me. As I am not here, I'm sure Adrianos will stand in as my proxy."

Adrian shoots the camera a dark look and drops his brother. Gone is the flirty man—he's all thirsty vampire now. Hugo's woman, dressed to the nines and staring with horror at the scene, holds up her hands and backs away. "Hold on, this isn't what you said would--" Hugo cuts her off, jumping on her and ripping her throat from her body in a matter of seconds. Blood sprays in a sickly arc. He throws the body at Adrian.

I hold back a scream, biting my fist as I whimper. I reach for the stake strapped at my thigh only to remember it's not there.

Nobody else screams. Not one.

Maybe that's the sickest part of it all. Not even the humans seem fazed by this horrific murder. It's as if they expected it to happen. Adrian scoops up the body and sinks his fangs into what's left of the woman's neck. Nobody reacts to that, either.

"You may go now, Hugo. Who's next?" Brisa calls out through the screen. "Hurry, please. I don't have all night."

Hugo storms from the room as twelve more vampires approach with one fledgling each and Brisa approves them all. When the last of them steps forward, my stomach flips.

Standing with Kelli is none other than Cameron Scout. I wouldn't be able to miss that flaming red hair anywhere. He holds himself tall and proud, and when he catches my eye, he winks.

"What's your name, dear?" Brisa coos.

"Kelli. I'm Adrian's only living protégé."

Brisa laughs. "I know that, darling. I was talking to your beefy arm candy."

"I'm Cameron Scout, Your Highness."

"You're a perfectly built specimen." Brisa grins. "Well done, Kelli. This is a good choice for your first child. You've waited the required thirty years for this, I know."

"Thank you." Kelli beams. "He's very eager to be here and actually, there's something special you need to know about Cameron." I freeze.

No. No, don't do it.

"He's a hunter."

The room goes eerily still seconds before the other vampires start hissing. Kelli speaks above it all, unfazed. "I wanted to bring you someone extra useful to prove my devotion to our family, Your Majesty. Cameron is willing to turn over his team of hunters when we make him one of us."

The lying, disgusting, little Chucky doll twerp! I want to go over there and rip off his head myself!

Brisa's cool demeanor breaks into a wicked smile. "Well aren't you resourceful. But he better not be trying to deceive us, Kelli, or it's true death for you."

"He's the real deal," she assures Brisa. "We will prove it to you when he delivers his comrades to us."

"We'll see." She's skeptical, but she's pleased. I stare at the people standing before me and wonder—did Adrian tell Kelli to find Cameron? Did she do it herself? Or maybe Cameron came to her? I need to know what's going on. I just hope that my being here didn't somehow create this. First the blood vow and spying on Tate, and now this? As her maker, Adrian is bound to want to help Kelli now that she's got the threat of true death looming over her.

We're all screwed.

My hands are shaking and I have to hold them together against my stomach in a tight ball.

"And what about you, Adrianos? Did you take my advice?" Brisa asks, turning back to Adrian.

He's been watching everything unfold with his fangs still in Hugo's woman, drinking from her like he can't stop. Her skin is unnaturally snowy white and my stomach lurches to see it. At his master's question, Adrian drops the body into the pool of her own blood and wipes his face, turning back to the camera. His blond curls hang low over his hooded eyes. He looks like the devil.

"Of course, Mother," he says. "How could I not?" There's an edge to his voice and I'm reminded that vampires are bound to their makers. Adrian has to do whatever she asks. And so does Hugo for that matter. That's why Hugo was so quick to kill his lover, and Adrian was quick to make a meal of her body.

Well, that and they're vampires. They deal in death. Adrian had to have liked drinking from that body. It's his nature.

It now makes sense why Hugo can't just do as he wishes and make as many vampire babies as his evil heart desires. Someone else is pulling the strings. Queen Brisa. Thank goodness she's in charge and not Hugo or I'd be living in some dystopian blood harvesting farm right now.

"Evangeline." Adrian motions to me. I stand even though my entire body is suddenly made of sand. "Come forward, fledgling; come and say hello to your new queen."

Twenty-Four

❧

I feel as if I'm on a rowboat in the middle of a hurricane. I can barely keep my balance as I go to stand in front of the camera. Like dangerous waves, my heart slams against my chest. Like pouring rain, fear pelts my nervous system. My every thought is met with the horrible feeling of drowning, because if Brisa doesn't approve of me, she'll order me dead and that will be the end of it. I remind myself to kill Adrian if I make it out of here and force a pageant-girl smile to my lips.

I stare directly into the lens, knowing that on the other side, the queen of all the vampires is staring back and deciding my fate. After what feels like an eternity, her voice rings through the speakers. I never take my eyes off the lens. I can't bear to see her expression.

"You've outdone yourself, my son. She's unusually beautiful."

"Yes, she is."

My stomach goes hard. I don't like them talking about me like I'm some kind of prized race horse. Unusually beautiful? What, because my ethnicity is hard to pinpoint? I hate these people.

"Well, good, I'm glad you've finally decided to bring another child to our family." Brisa levels me with a daring expression. "I hope she proves herself worthy."

"She will."

"And what do you think of all this, dear? Is this what you want?"

It's a trick question. Of course I can't tell her the truth. "I'm honored to be here," I say, my voice silky with the lies. "I won't let you down."

"Good girl." The queen sighs and my eyes hold the screen. She looks

137

truly pleased. "Evangeline. Pretty name. I'll be sure to check back on your progress. It's not often that Adrianos takes on a fledgling. Do as he says and you'll be his protégé. Don't, and well," she chuckles, "you saw."

I smile and nod, all the while wanting to strangle Adrian for bringing me here. That's after I kill Cameron Scout first.

And here I thought the bagels were him being nice. Vampires don't *do* nice.

The queen signs off and the room buzzes with conversation, everyone eager to discuss all that just happened. Nobody seems to care about the body on the floor. They're desensitized from death. Humans are food and nothing more, and even the humans here act like they're thinking that way. But what did I expect?

I stroll right up to Cameron. "Hey, buddy, you and I need to talk."

"That we do." He grins happily. "I was surprised to see you here, but now I'm glad to have someone else I can trust during this process. I'll be at the Neon House tonight at nine. Come, and we can make plans on how to help each other."

He winks again and then he slips into the crowd with Kelli on his arm. Bile turns my stomach. I'm going to be sick.

"Let's go," Adrian demands. He takes hold of me and steers me toward the elevator. It's the private one that goes to the penthouses, so we don't have to worry about a line. Once we're inside and the doors close, I vomit into the corner. I can't keep it in for another second.

"I'll get someone to clean that up."

I wipe my mouth, then turn and glare.

"I'm sorry I blindsided you, but I knew you'd never come otherwise," Adrian says. "I needed to take a fledgling, my Queen asked and I can't deny her. It's impossible. Don't worry, I won't turn you. This was all for show. Brisa will forget all about it. She's extremely busy and doesn't care if we choose to turn our fledglings as long as we keep the number of vampires where she wants them."

This is all a bunch of political crap that means nothing to me. "I hate you."

"Good," he purrs. "You should hold onto that hate. It might keep you alive. No matter what happens, don't stop hating me, and remember this, Angel: I will always put my needs before yours."

THE NEON HOUSE is a popular eighteen and older nightclub smack dab between The French Quarter and Tulane University. The music is too loud, the neon lights too bright, and the foggy smoke cough-worthy thick. I weave my way through throngs of dancers and search for Cameron. Sure enough, I find him near the bar with a group of douchebag-looking friends. I don't recognize any of them from the hunters' gym. They probably have no idea who the real Cameron Scout is. For all they know, he's going to be the one to kill them one day when he's a vampire. He well and truly is a snake.

"Hey," I say, sliding up next to him and smiling as brightly as I can manage to fake. "What's up?"

"You came!" His voice is too loud and a little slurred. He's been drinking. For a vampire hunter, he's sure not doing his job. And to think he took control of our teams when Tate left as if he were the best man for the job. Anger burns me up and I hate that I have to pretend that it doesn't. He hugs me like we're old friends. "Let's dance."

"I came to talk." I fold my arms over my chest and resist the urge to tug at the short hem of my white minidress. I fit right in with this scene, but I don't love the outfit. I can't help but wonder how different my life would be if I'd gotten that track scholarship. I'd have gone away to school and none of this would've happened. I'd be a normal girl, like Ayla, like everyone else here.

"We can dance and talk at the same time. It's called multitasking." Cameron grins like he's just realized he's a rocket scientist. I roll my eyes but follow him out to the floor.

"Mutual assured destruction," he says, putting his hands on my hips and tugging me against him to dance.

"What?" I yell over the pounding music and back up a bit. I have no intentions of making this "a thing" with him.

"That's what this is, you and I. You can't turn me in and I can't turn you in. We're in this together. If you go down, I go down, and vice versa. Might as well form an alliance."

I grimace. This Chucky doll is the last person I'd want to form an alliance with, and that's saying a lot considering my many recent lapses in judgement. "So why'd you do it, Cameron?" I pretend to be genuinely interested and not wildly pissed off.

"I could ask you the same question."

I can't show all my cards here. I don't know what to do, so I go with a semblance of the truth. Easier to keep my story straight that way. "I need to help my mom. She's in trouble with the Italian mob. Adrian can save her for me. The hunters can't."

"Woah, that's intense."

"Yes," I level, "it is. And what about you? What's your excuse for turning on the hunters?" It comes off a little too jaded but Cameron is far too pleased with himself to notice.

"I realized that the vampires are the winning team." The green glow of the neon lights gives his red hair a sickly filter as he stares down at me. "I'm a realist and I want to win. It's simple."

It's evil is what it is, but I can't let him know what I really think, so I nod. "I get that but how can you be certain?"

"There's more to this war than you realize. It's not just vampires and humans, you know. Leslie Tate is using us."

I stop short. "What do you mean?"

"Do you trust me?"

I snort. "Not as far as I can throw you."

"That's fair." He smiles. "But I like you. And I think we should talk about what happened to me so you understand me enough to maybe start trusting me."

"Okay, what happened to you?"

"I joined the hunters because I thought vampires were the evil I needed to fight but I was wrong. Something else is a lot worse than the vamps."

"Something else?" I sound skeptical even though deep down, I believe him. There aren't other supernaturals that we know of, just vampires, but wouldn't it stand to reason that if vampires are real, then other things are real, too? I've always thought so.

"Just hear me out, okay? Let's go over there." I nod and we move to a quieter corner of the room and stand side by side, looking out at the club. We're up on a platform so we can see everything going on down below. These people are having the time of their lives and here I am with creepy Cameron. My life sucks.

"My kid brother got sick with cancer," he says, and suddenly I feel like a brat for coining his new nickname. "Tyler was fourteen and I was seventeen at the time. It was terrible. The doctors did everything they could but Tyler was terminal." His voice cracks and he stares at his shoes for a minute. Part of me feels bad for the guy but the bigger part is still angry about what he did today. "So anyway, my father got desperate so he found a vampire and made a deal. The vampire would turn my brother immortal and in exchange my parents would be willing blood donors."

I grimace. "That sounds pretty brutal." It also sounds like something the vampire royalty wouldn't condone. Brisa doesn't seem like the charitable type.

"I didn't know anything about it until after Tyler's funeral when my father broke down and admitted to me what happened. He said that the vampire came to see Tyler on his deathbed. He watched him cry out and die, but refused to help. He just stood there watching it all unfold like he enjoyed it or something. And then when it was over, he left."

My heart hurts for the family. Nobody should have to experience something that horrific. "I'm sorry. That's terrible."

"Yeah, it was messed up. So you can imagine that when I went to college and got the opportunity to hunt vampires, I jumped at it. It was my way to heal through the pain of losing Tyler. But my parents? They never got over Tyler's death. They ended up getting divorced a couple years ago."

Okay, I still hate Cameron, but he's doing a good job of making me feel bad about that. This story just keeps getting worse.

"Here's the thing," he continues. "My mom never knew about the vampire. So she starts dating this guy, right? Something was off about him but I couldn't figure out what it was. Well, one day my dad comes around and starts freaking out, accusing the guy of being a vampire, saying this is the same guy that was supposed to help Tyler."

"Was it?"

His face hardens. "Same guy? Yes. Vampire? No. Remember, I'm a hunter by this point so I know how to spot a vampire a mile away and this thing definitely wasn't a vampire."

"So what was he then?"

"I still don't know for sure, maybe a demon, a fae, some kind of warlock, I don't know. But I do know this; that guy was truly sick. He fed off Tyler's illness and then my parent's grief to sustain him."

I scowl. "That doesn't make sense. What do you mean by fed?"

"It's hard to explain and that's why I wanted to show you." The song changes and techno music blares through the room. The neon lights shift to blacklight and Cameron points. "The blacklight allows you to see what they're doing."

I gaze out into the crowd, unsure what I'm supposed to be looking for.

"Whatever they are, they're real and they're even more dangerous than vampires. They hide their true selves easily, blending right in with humans, but they feed on us, too. The day I decided to turn on our group of hunters was the day I found out Leslie Tate is one of them."

Twenty-Five

I blink rapidly, realizing the implications of this information. Tate is immune to vampire compulsion. Tate can erase memories. All this time I've been obsessing over the vampire threat when maybe I should have been questioning my leader. "Leslie Tate is one of... *what now*?" I ask for clarity. I still have no idea what Cameron is on about and he's starting to sound a wee bit delusional.

"He's one of the vampire's mortal enemies, the demons, or whatever they are. I'm still not sure. In my mind, I call them demons."

"I always thought werewolves were the vampire's enemies." I lean back against the wall and keep staring out into the crowd of dancers. Sure, they're lit up with the blacklight, a sea of blue and white, but there's nothing strange going on that I can see. Certainly no *demons*.

"The werewolves were enemies with vampires but they were hunted to extinction hundreds of years ago. It's whatever *these things* are that are the bigger problem." He points again.

"Cameron, I'm so confused. I don't see anything."

"Look harder," he growls. "Look! Don't you see? They feed off of us. There are some doing it right now. Use your eyes, Eva, and you'll understand why I'm done being a weak and pathetic human."

I'm starting to think this guy is on drugs and never listened to his DARE officer.

"Kelli knows what I'm talking about. It's how she got me to be her fledgling. And once I'm turned and she can trust me, she's going to tell me everything."

"Talking about Kelli isn't going to help your case," I say. "She hates me."

"Adrian then. Ask Adrian."

I close my eyes and gather a breath deep into my lungs, trying to focus. I push away the fear bubbling just under the surface--Cam is really starting to scare me--and open my eyes again. I blink out into the room of dancers, looking for a change, anything at all.

And that's when I see it.

Most of the people here are the same.

But some are not.

Their features are the same as ours. They laugh and dance and kiss and are clearly here to have fun--just like us. But there's something different about them. There's something lacking. I don't even know what it is exactly.

"Okay, I think I see them."

He laughs with relief.

"But how are they sinister?"

"Look closer," he whispers against my ear. "See the energy?"

I squint and catch on to what he's talking about. It's so subtle I didn't notice it at first. The humans have light glowing around them. The others-- whatever they are--do not. "Are you talking about the glow around the humans?"

"Those are auras," Cam says. "All humans have them. They're supposed to be all different colors but we can't see all that. We *can* see the outline of the aura in the blacklight. And we can see the ones who are being fed on."

I rub my eyes and look again. Still there. "This is so weird."

He leans back against the wall and for the first time tonight, his vibe isn't so frantic. "Tell me about it. I never thought that woo-woo shit was real. Kelli says it's the human's soul energy. Suckers don't have auras, which makes sense considering they already died. And whatever the demon things are, they don't have them either. And do you see what they're doing to the humans?"

He nods toward a tall man who is dancing close to a human girl. He smiles down on her like she's the only person in the room. She's beaming, and her energy is clinging to him like a magnet. Not just that, but some of it flows from her and into him. "You're right. He's feeding off of her energy."

"Yes. Exactly that. He is sucking away her life force. I believe this is what makes humans weak. This is why we get sick and why we're frail. These things are everywhere and they feed on us all the time. I wish I could carry a blacklight everywhere I go so I can spot them. One of these things came to feed off of my brother while he was on his deathbed, and then came back to feed off of my parents in their grief."

"What happened to him, this demon thing?"

He releases a long sigh. "My dad killed it and then he went to prison."

My mouth falls open. I have no idea what to say.

"And this, Eva, is exactly why humans are going to lose in the end. We don't stand a chance."

"Are there a lot of them?" In this room of hundreds, I can spot six, but it's hard to tell because they don't look much different than humans except for the no aura thing. The music changes and the blacklight switches back to the neon. Everything appears as it was before.

"Yeah, I come here every weekend and count. There's always at least ten by the end of the night and it's usually different ones, too. That tells me there are a lot. The vampires and these demons are fighting a war over their food source and guess what, babe? That's us. One feeds on our blood, the other on our energy. Since it's impossible for me to become whatever this is," he motions toward the dancers, "I'm going to become a vampire. I'm done being at the mercy of more powerful creatures. If you can't beat them, join them, right?"

"Right," I mumble once and then say again louder.

What Cameron is saying makes sense, and I need him to think that I agree. But to betray his team––his friends––in order to become part of the evil he claims to hate? That's dead wrong.

THE NEXT NIGHT as I'm riding home on the bus, I try to stay awake despite feeling as if I've been run over by a herd of elephants. This morning I had to drag my butt into training super early and then had a long dinner shift at Pops. Exhaustion paws at me like a demanding toddler. I haven't slept well at all during the three nights I've been staying at the casino, and I have *at least* one more to go. I'm stressed out about Mom who still hasn't answered my calls even though she has the freaking mafia after her. And the cherry––or rather cherries––on top is all this fledgling crap, the blood vow, and now everything going on with Cameron Scout. I know what I saw, but I still have a hard time believing him. I need concrete proof of what he's claiming and that there's actually a war going on. I mean, sure, he calls them demons, but he doesn't know what they are.

I scroll through the rental ads on my phone, but there's just nothing in my price range. Putting on my big girl pants, I send a group text to Seth, Kenton, and Felix.

Hey guys. This hotel situation sucks. Can you ask around to see if anyone you know has a room for rent?

Kenton replies immediately, **You got it. I know people.**

Seth pops in with the all annoying, **K**

And Felix adds an, **We will find you something by tomorrow. Hang tight.**

I smile. It feels good to let someone else help me for a change. I'm so used to doing things myself and being Miss Independent that I sometimes forget that there are people out there who care about me. I slip my phone into my pocket and get off at my stop. If the guys come through, and knowing them they will, then this really will be my last night at The Alabaster. I just hope that Adrian is right and Brisa forgets all about me. I don't want to get my hopes up, but I can't help it. That place is toxic. Those people are toxic. All the things I regret lately are things I've done there, things that have involved them.

I have to walk a block to get to the hotel, which isn't normally a big deal, but it's later than usual and much, much quieter. This area is tourist central, but right now there isn't a soul in sight. Vampires are probably nearby. I won't be able to hear them coming––they're too silent––and I don't have a stake on me. It's colder than normal for September, so maybe that's why I feel weird. Maybe I'm just imagining things and freaking myself out for no reason. Goosebumps crawl across my skin. The streetlight above me flickers and goes dark. I walk faster.

Arms grab me from behind, one around my waist and one over my mouth. My scream is muffled. A man drags me into an alleyway and shoves me up against the wall. The back of my head cracks against the bricks. Tears fill my eyes as I fight, clawing and kicking, but he's twice my size and my efforts are worthless. He keeps his hand pressed against my mouth.

I don't know him, but he looks like a mafia thug. He's human. Middle-aged and balding, the man is dressed in all black except for the gold chain around his beefy neck. It's like he's trying to live up to a henchman stereotype. "Listen closely, Princess." His voice is that deep thunder that comes before a storm and I'm suddenly very, very afraid. "You tell your mother that if she doesn't give Armondo his money, then not only will we find her and kill her, but we'll kill you right in front of her first."

Tears blur my vision.

He slams me against the wall again. "You got that?"

I nod against his hand and he smiles like this is any other business trans-action. "That's great, Princess. Get it done."

My knees give out when he releases me, and I drop to the filthy concrete as he disappears into the night.

My head throbs. I reach around and gently press my fingertips to the back of my scalp. I wince at the pain, fingers coming away wet. My mind swims through mud as I try to process what just happened. The guys after my mother know where I am. I was just assaulted by one of them. I'm wounded. Bloody. And I'm sitting outside of the building where over a hundred thirsty vampires live.

Twenty-Six

‿‿‿

Why am I always the poster child for what not to do around the vamps? I need to make some better life choices. I hiss as I try to hold back the tears. And now I have to get inside and upstairs to the room so I can take care of this. That's if I don't get eaten first.

I stumble out of the alleyway and around the corner, up the long set of stairs, and through the double vestibules. I keep my hand pressed to the back of my head the entire time even though I can feel the blood dripping. I'll be fine once I'm alone. Head wounds are bloody. Everybody knows that. I just have to keep going and get to safety. One foot in front of the other. Head down. Move quickly. Adrian's private elevator to the penthouse floor will help as long as I don't run into Hugo.

Blood splashes onto the marble floor.

Well, it's a blood casino, right? It's not like people don't bleed in here all the time. *It's fine. I'll be fine,* I tell myself, simply because thinking of the alternative is terrifying.

Across the lobby, Kelli sits behind her receptionist desk. She watches me carefully, her nostrils flared, but doesn't say anything. She tilts her head, inhales deeply, and then picks up her phone. I make it to the elevator bank and press the button for the one I need. There are four more elevators here that go to the other hotel floors. The one next to mine dings and opens; a young man steps out. He's pale, vampire-beautiful, and looking right at me with unimaginable hunger.

"You're bleeding," he speaks each word slowly, like they're the punchline to a joke.

"Yeah, I'll be fine. No big deal." My voice is shaking. He wouldn't attack me, would he? It's not allowed. We're in public. I know that the vampire hierarchy is a definite thing after yesterday, and, for whatever reason, the higher ups don't want humans to have their venom in us under any circumstances unless we're going to be turned or going to die. That's why the whole blood bag thing even exists in the first place. Sure, they'll kill us when they can get away with it, but otherwise they need us alive. We're no good to them dead.

Where is my elevator? I uselessly press the button again and blood smears against that, too.

"You smell good." The young man circles me like a shark.

"Uh--thanks." I press my hand harder against my skull, but that just makes it worse. "The blood bank is back that way if you need a meal." I nod toward the casino.

Footsteps echo through the lobby. "Tray, what's going on here?" Hugo approaches, and for once I'm actually happy to see the guy.

"She's bleeding. Doesn't she smell amazing?" Tray's voice sounds far away. "I've never had the pleasure of virgin blood before."

Hugo stares at me. He steps forward, runs a finger along my cheek, and then licks the blood clean. His eyes go dark. "You," is all he says. One word--it obliterates my confidence.

Tray pounces.

He's so fast I don't even register what is happening until I'm on the floor and the guy is on top of me. He holds my arms down as his fangs extend. Hugo rips him off and throws him clear across the room. He crashes into a couch, breaking it in half, but rebounds lightning fast. He comes running back at top speed, diving for me with outstretched arms. His fangs glint under the golden lights.

I'm dead.

But I'm not going down without a fight. I ready my stance, prepared to defend myself to the bitter end, when the elevator dings. A flash of white and black flies out. Adrian Teresi is on Tray, ripping his head from his body, the blood splattering across Adrian's crisp white shirt. Tray disintegrates into a cloud of dust.

"I had it under control," Hugo screams at his brother.

"Clearly you didn't," Adrian roars back.

"He was my child, I would have been able to get him to stop. You can't kill what belongs to me. Brisa will--"

"You won't speak of this to Brisa! You have no case with her considering your protégé tried to sink his fangs into my fledgling."

Hugo growls, "I could have stopped him. I could have saved them both."

"Not since his bloodlust was so strong." Adrians voice lowers. "This is exactly why you can't take on too many protégés. They're weak and they make you weak."

Hugo points at me. "It's her fault. She's bleeding. And she's--"

"Enough!" Adrian sneers. He grabs me and flies us into the elevator. My vision blurs again. As the elevator is closing, I catch the bitter end of Hugo's glare.

As we rise, I finally find my breath as I sink into Adrian.

"Are you okay, Angel?" He turns me around and hisses at the mess of my bloody hair. "You shouldn't have come here like this. What happened?"

"I was jumped outside of the casino. I didn't have anywhere else to go."

"Who did this to you?"

"Whoever works for Armondo." I grimace as I turn back around, catching Adrian's confused look. "Remember? The whole reason I'm staying here is because my gambling addicted mother got herself mixed up with the mafia."

He sighs and runs a hand through his hair. A little bit of my blood sticks to the curls, turning them pink. "I shouldn't have let you stay here. It's too dangerous."

I laugh bitterly. "You think!" I press myself to the far side of the elevator; we are in a small space, I am covered in blood and need distance between us.

"You asked to come here. I did you a favor."

"And what did I get for it? You're no better than the rest of them. You used me to gain favor with your queen, just like all vampires use all humans. I'm leaving tomorrow. My friends are finding me a safer place to stay."

And at this point, I can't be around here anyway. Mafia. Vampires. It's all too much.

His face is a mask. "Good."

When the elevator doors open, I walk ahead of him to the penthouse and head straight into the bathroom. The blood is starting to clot now, but it's worse than I thought. I'm practically covered. I'll need to shower, but first I've got to get this wound sealed. Where's duct tape when you need it, huh? Adrian knocks on the door.

"Kelli is sending up one of the nurses. You need stitches."

I don't have it in me to say thank you to him, so instead, I sit down on the cold floor and wait. The nurse arrives quickly and stitches me right up as if she's done this a million times before. Adrian watches her like a hawk, asking question after question. If my blood is bothering him, he doesn't show it. He almost seems normal, and for a minute, I forget what he is, then immediately chastise myself for the slip up.

After the nurse finishes, I send them out so I can take a warm shower. I finish off with a tall glass of water and an extra strength Tylenol. I go right for the bed, too tired to care about pajamas. When I slip into the sheets sans clothing, the cool fabric feels like heaven against my aching body. To be all clean and unencumbered like this is a treat.

A light knock on the door is quickly followed by Adrian letting himself into the room. He has changed into a clean shirt and looks like he's ready to get back to business as usual. Good thing I'm neatly tucked in already––a minute earlier and he'd have walked in on me naked. Nothing he hasn't seen, I'm certain, but my heart races anyway. He needs to get out of here and let me have my privacy.

"Do you need anything else before I head out?" he asks curtly.

"Sleep." I reach toward the lamp, knowing I'm exposing my bare shoulder enough for him to realize I'm naked, but I don't care anymore. I turn it off the light. My eyes flutter shut and I bury myself into the blankets. My racing heart begins to slow and I release a long, slow breath. I'm so drained, I can hardly think straight. What must it be like to be Adrian and never sleep? It's all I want in this moment and I can't imagine an eternity without the peace it offers. "Goodbye, Adrian," I mumble. I don't say good-night. I say goodbye, and I mean it.

He doesn't reply, but he does leave, closing the door behind him with a soft thud.

The next morning, I pack my things and move out.

IF A GIRL LEAVING a college party house early on a weekday morning is considered the "walk of shame" then is me showing up here the reverse of that? 'Cause I feel like a total loser, but I'm fresh out of options. I even checked my bank account balance this morning just to be sure I couldn't swing my own place, and yup, I'm still broke as a joke. It's barely sunrise and Felix and the guys should be out any minute to head to the gym. I sit down on the lawn next to my duffle bag and shoot them a group text.

Look who's outside. . .

A minute later, Felix comes through the front door. His expression blossoms into pleasure when he spots me. "Eva, is that you?"

I wave. "Hey, good morning."

"What are you doing here?" Concern etches his tone and I hate that I put that there. I hate being vulnerable or seen as needy. I want to be strong, maybe even admired, but maybe that's not practical. Life is messy.

I sigh. "Let's just say I had a bad night at the hotel. I needed to get out of that place. Can I get a ride to the bank vault?"

His lip quirks. "The bank vault?"

"Yeah, sorry, I know Tate doesn't want it to have a name but that's what I call it in my head. We're the Bank Vault Vampire Hunters." I wink and he chuckles.

"Sure. You didn't want to meet us there?"

I pat the duffle bag. "Too proud to let everyone at the gym know I'm officially homeless." That and I have Cameron Scout to consider. He doesn't need to know any more of my business. "Can I keep my stuff in your car while we're there?"

"You're not homeless. I found a room for you with some girls who live off campus."

"Oh, thank you!" I pump my fist and we both laugh.

Felix lifts the bag over his shoulder and helps me up. When our hands touch, warmth spreads through my entire body. I inhale his minty rain scent and long to get lost in it, despite my goal to quit wanting him. He doesn't let me go but actually tugs me closer. Hope swells in my chest.

"I've been really worried, Eva. And I've been thinking about you a lot." His voice is gravelly, his eyes liquid.

I inch closer until there's no space left between us, *screw my goal.* "Have you?"

He nods once, running his warm palms up my arms, over my shoulders, and finally cupping my face and tilting it upward. He doesn't know about the stitches, and I have to force myself not to wince. Luckily, he must not notice them. They are pretty small. He towers over me and I lift onto my toes while he leans down. *Finally.*

Twenty-Seven

"**E**va!" Kenton appears, bounding up the front steps. "How's my girl?"

Felix and I both shoot him a scathing look. He holds up his hands. "What?" His fraternity house is only a few blocks from here so I guess it makes sense that he'd walk over to catch a ride, but his timing sure sucks.

The house door bangs open and Seth comes out with a sour expression on his face. He points at me and Felix. "Don't even think about it. We're a team, remember? There's no room for error, which means there's no place for romance or friends with benefits or whatever you two are doing."

Kenton's eyes go round. "Oh snap! Did I just cockblock you guys? My bad."

I want to sink into the lawn and die, but then I wouldn't be able to kiss Felix, which I am going to do at the next possible opportunity.

"Let's get coffee on the way in," Seth adds, strolling past us. "My treat."

Felix snorts. "Doesn't make up for the interruption." He gives me a wink and a bright smile; I relax instantly. Okay fine, we can't hook up right now, but if Felix wants me after all, then I'm in. This is what I've been waiting for, and no way is Seth going to get in the way of that. I don't care if he's our team leader. He's not the relationship police. I've always known I was meant to be with Felix––he's been my crush for years. I've pushed every other possible love interest away in favor of this man. It's finally time to make Felix + Eva a reality.

. . .

"Luckily there's no lacrosse practice so I'm skipping class today to help you," Felix announces after dropping the others off at campus after training. "Jasmine and Olive have furniture already, but you need to bring your own bedding and towels and that kind of stuff. So let's go pick something out, and then I'll help you get settled."

I feign shock and fan my face. "A man going shopping? You're my hero, Felix Moreno."

"Hey, not all straight men hate shopping." He laughs. He's so macho and broody most of the time that it's fun to see this side of him.

"So. . .Jasmine and Olive, huh? Are they nice?"

"They're great. They're good friends of mine. Don't worry, you'll like them."

I hope he's right, but at least these girls are human. If only I could room with Ayla, then my life would be made, but that's impossible. I'm happy for her and hope she's having fun. Last I checked, she's still hiding out in her dorm room between classes, but I think she's starting to chill out again. Thanksgiving break can't come fast enough. I need my Ayla-time. Hopefully she doesn't murder me for what's about to happen between me and her brother.

During the next hour of shopping, I can't keep the grin off my face. With Felix, my troubles fade into the background, and even the stinging reminder on the back of my head doesn't bother me too much. I worked out this morning but didn't spar, and my high ponytail has kept everything safely hidden under a mound of messy black hair. The nurse had to put seven little stitches in and said they can come out next week.

Lucky number seven, yeah right.

But considering I had no signs of a concussion, maybe I am lucky. I could have died last night. Being alive and with Felix only solidifies what's most important to me. I'm not going to let this chance pass me by.

It takes a while to find parking close to the apartment, but since I don't have a car that's not a deal breaker. Felix and I carry everything a few blocks over to the building. It's not super close to the college campus but that's no problem for me. As we walk up to the historic row house central to almost everything in downtown New Orleans, a smile stretches across my cheeks. This building has been engineered from old gray stone blocks with black metal ironwork along the windows and an iron staircase leading to the front door. Ivy climbs up one side of the entire building, giving the place a total gothic vibe.

It's love at first sight.

"Pretty cool, huh?"

"This is what I love about this city," I sigh. "This building is amazing. How did your friends land an apartment here?"

"The building is actually super old and needs some work, plus they're on the ground level so when hurricanes come they always have to evacuate. A lot of renters don't like ground levels."

"Hey, I'm no stranger to hurricane season." In fact, we're in it now, but luckily we haven't had any come our way this year. "Whatever this place lacks in renovation, it makes up for in charm. I'm already obsessed."

We go inside to find a little mailroom, laundry room, and a staircase that leads to the other three floors of apartments. Under the staircase is a shiny black door and a welcome mat. Felix knocks.

The tiny girl who opens it has candy apple red hair and the palest skin I've seen on a human. At least she's human. If I never see another vampire again I will die a happy woman. Not likely.

"You must be Eva. I'm Olive." She hugs me right away, bouncing up and down on the balls of her feet. I can already tell this girl is the definition of extrovert. She instantly reminds me of Ayla.

"Hi, Olive." I beam. "Thanks so much for taking me on short notice."

"No prob, you're doing us a favor too. Our third roommate ditched us after only a month for a spot in some stupid sorority house. Ew, sororities, am I right? I wouldn't be caught dead in one." I chuckle because I'm not sure how else to respond. I don't care either way. I'm not the type to go for something like that but I don't begrudge those who are, though ditching your roommates with a lease hanging over their heads is pretty messed up. "She didn't even give notice. Anyway, let me show you to your room."

We follow her into the apartment. The kitchen, living, and dining spaces are all squished in together and about the size of my old bedroom. The walls are painted deep purple, and the furniture is a hodgepodge of styles that somehow works to create an eclectic design.

"What you see is what you get," she says, "we're pretty busy, so we're not here as much as we'd like, but we're proud of our little home."

"It looks great. Very thrift store chic. I love how all of these pieces don't match but still somehow look perfect together." And it's true. I'm going to have to send some pictures to Ayla.

Olive smiles knowingly at Felix. "Okay, you're right, I like her."

"I told you." When he smiles, my day gets even better.

"The bathroom's back here and so are the bedrooms. Rent is six hundred dollars a month and includes utilities and wifi. You'll pay me by the end of the month so I can pay the landlord on the first. Does that work?"

It's a tad more expensive than I was hoping, but definitely less than anything I could swing on my own, so I say yes. I haven't even seen my new bedroom, but I already know I'm going to love it because at least it's my own. Finally, I feel like I haven't been left behind by all my peers anymore. I'm a grown-ass woman who can take care of herself.

"Jasmine's a pre-med student and studies at the library all the time so you'll probably barely see her. I'm an art major so I come and go depending on what's going on at the studio. You work nights, right?"

She leads me into one of the bedrooms. I take it all in with a smile. It's got a four-poster queen-sized bed tucked into the corner with a matching black dresser. The walls are painted the same deep purple as the rest of the apartment, which I can definitely work with. Sure it's tiny, and the window is barred and faces a brick wall, but it's got a great energy about it. It feels safe. Welcoming. *Mine.*

"Yeah, I'm a server at Pops at night and am in an internship with Felix in the mornings, so I'm pretty busy too. But I'm not a student. You Tulane kids are way too smart for me. I hope that's okay with you guys."

"We don't care," she hands me a key, "so long as you're reliable and supply us with free Pops sometimes." She winks her huge fake eyelashes playfully, and I can't help but admire her makeup skills. Maybe she'll teach me her ways. "That place is the best. But Jasmine's a vegetarian so maybe bring her pie or something."

"That I can do."

"See, I like her." She raises her eyebrows at Felix and leaves us to it.

We make up the bed with my new white coverlet and hang the matching curtains. Tomorrow I'm going to find some cute throw pillows and a tie dye linen wall hanging to bring it all together. Ayla can give me advice on where to find the perfect things. I probably shouldn't spend any more money, but I want to, I need to. It's helping me take my mind off of everything, especially Mom. I've been trying to get ahold of her all day, but she's still missing. I'm starting to wonder if I should file a missing persons report, not that it would do me any good. And at the back of my mind is that mafia man's face from last night. I never want to see him again.

I unpack my clothes into the pocket closet while Felix sits on the bed, watching me lazily. Electricity fills the little room with him in it, and all I can think about is our almost-kiss this morning. I finish up and turn to look at him, instantly knowing he's thinking about the same thing.

"Hi."

"Hi." He grins.

This is the part where I hope he stands up and pulls me to him and kisses me, but he doesn't. He continues to sit there as the tension grows thicker. He knows what to do, I know he's capable of making a move. He's always had girls orbiting him and never shied away from them as far as I could tell. If we stay in the friend zone, before long it's going to get too awkward, and I can't let that happen.

"You know what, Felix?" It only takes three steps to go from standing by the closet to standing between his legs. He's so tall that I'm only a head taller even though he's sitting down on the edge of the bed.

"What?" He peers up at me. The dark lashes frame his yummy brown eyes, and from this close I can see the gold specks around his pupil. I get the answer I need in those eyes. He wants this too.

"I'm just gonna go for it." And I do––I lean down and press my lips to his. His response is instant, opening his mouth to mine. I can't help but moan. He wraps his hands around my waist and tugs me closer. It's not close enough for me, so I end up sitting in his lap. Much better.

I'm careful to keep his hands away from my scalp, not that he minds. They tend to travel lower anyway. Our kiss becomes an epic makeout session that lasts at least twenty minutes before my phone buzzes and ruins the fun. I groan and peel myself off him. "Ugh, no. . ."

"What's wrong?"

"I have to get ready for work."

"It's fine. I've got to go study anyway." He presses one final kiss to my lips and I walk him to the door.

I don't know what any of this means, but I'm not going to ruin it with questions or labels. I finally know what it feels like to have butterflies in my chest. It's as cliché as anything, but it's the perfect descriptor for how he makes me feel. For the first time in ages, I'm happy. I can't stop smiling.

He leaves, and not even a minute later someone knocks on the door. Assuming Felix forgot something, I open it. I want another kiss, too!

But there's nobody there.

At my feet rests a black box tied with a velvet red ribbon. Only thirty seconds ago this hallway was completely empty and now this? An inner warning bell wipes the smile off my face. I pick up the box to find a little white envelope tucked under the ribbon *Evangeline* scrawled in elegant handwriting across the front.

Twenty-Eight

E verything about this box screams vampire. Who else would be dropping off presents in black boxes all tied up with red ribbon? It might be daytime, but they have plenty of humans to do their bidding, like delivering mysterious packages to unsuspecting women. I haven't even lived here for a day and they already know where I landed. I groan and bring the box inside. I don't have time to deal with this. I need to get ready for my shift, but I know myself—if I don't open it now, I'll go crazy thinking about it.

I take the box into my room and open the card first. The handwriting is unfamiliar and perfect, but it's the words that make me sick.

I have your mother. If you ever want to see her again, wear this dress to the riverboat casino tonight. Be there by eight.

There's no signature.

I scream in frustration and tear open the box. Inside is a black and gold flapper-style beaded party dress and shoes in my size. There's even jewelry to match. The only person who's ever done anything like this is Adrian-freaking-Teresi! I don't want to believe he'd take my mom but that makes me a fool. Of course he would. I'm still not sure why but there's got to be a reason. He told me he'll always do what's best for him and not for me. He warned me. I should have listened the first time. There's no time to debate this though. I'm going to have to save my mom—story of my life—so I pick up the phone and call Pops.

"This is Eddie."

I take a deep breath and try to steady my voice so it's not as frantic as I feel. "Hi, Eddie. It's Eva. I'm so sorry, but I can't come to work tonight. I'm having a family emergency."

He takes a long pause and suddenly I'm all too aware that even though he likes me, and even though he's had my back at work, he's my boss and he has a job to do here. "Are you sure you can't come?"

"I promise to make it up to you. I have no choice."

"You're putting me in a bad position here, Eva. Cami is out on maternity leave and Tennison is on vacation. If you don't show up I'll be understaffed."

"I'm so sorry." My voice cracks and tears burst from my eyes. Pops is always busy––being understaffed is a nightmare. I hate to disappoint anyone.

"Alright," his tone is unreadable. "Come in early for your next shift so we can talk about this face to face."

He hangs up, and as much as I'm worried about my only source of income and that I might have just lost my job, that is not my biggest problem. With shaky hands, I wipe away the tears and change into the dress.

THE PIER IS CROWDED TONIGHT. A sleek banner hangs across the ferry indicating it's been specially booked for a Roaring Twenties themed fundraising event. Who books a vampire casino boat for an event? Our city's mayor, Robyn Cox, that's who. All of the government is in bed with the vampires, they can't even help it, and the whole thing makes me want to scream. But I don't. I smile like a good little girl and give the person checking names at the door mine. She lets me right in without asking about my age. The laws are a joke anyway. The vamps already had the drinking age dropped. It's only a matter of time until the gambling age is lowered, too. It's been the big push during the last election cycle and nobody will be surprised when it happens.

The Roaring Twenties theme is carried throughout the boat to the max. All the decor is in metallic gold and inky black, reminding me of The Alabaster Heart's design. People are dressed up in gorgeous vintage frocks and suits and it's as if we've been transported back in time. My own dress hangs loosely just below my knees, the gold and black beads sparkling under the lights. I hate that I fit right in with the decor, like a prop. A full band plays lively big-band music and part of the casino floor has been cleared out for dancing. Waitstaff amble through the crowds with trays of hors d'oeuvres and glasses of bubbly champagne.

It's still a little light out so the vampires haven't arrived yet, but the pier isn't far from The Alabaster Heart and I know they'll be here soon. I want to find my mom and get us out of here, but I don't have much time to do that since the boat will be disembarking soon. And anyway, she's probably going to show up with Adrian.

I circle the room, avoiding making eye contact with anyone because I'm not in the mood for conversation and I shouldn't even be here. It's not like the mayor invited me. I'm not the least bit tempted by alcohol or gambling, unlike all of the adults. Quite a few of the young women hang off of older men, and I wonder if they're paid call girls. I wouldn't be surprised. Vampires have their fingers in everything seedy along with constantly meddling with the law, politics, and real estate to gain more control.

I spot the mayor standing at one of the craps tables. Wearing a sophisticated black dress, she blows on dice, throwing them to the table. She's not even playing, she's the "good luck" girl. Everyone screams and raises their hands––of course she just secured a win. I've never seen her in person before, only in political campaigns that I've barely paid attention to. I think I had better start paying attention. These people are going to ruin New Orleans even more than they already have.

The sunset finally gives way to darkness and we're joined by a procession of vampires. They're welcomed with open arms. Most people swarm them. I know that many want to be close to their enigmatic force, it's a pull the vampires have to their prey. They may look like us, but they aren't us, and to lose sight of that is deadly. To see vampires and humans mixing so easily makes my toes curl.

I stay far back and watch for my mother.

Adrian Teresi descends on the boat like some kind of God and I want to go slap him. It's impossible to leave a red mark on a vamp but I'm mad enough that I think I may be able to be the first. Kelli trails close behind her boss, and the mayor rushes over to them like they're all old friends. He smiles in his wicked way that is unique to him, and the two chat it up. Should I go over there and confront him? I'm not sure that's a good idea, and I don't see my mother anyway. So where is she? Is he hiding her somewhere? Kelli must feel my eyes boring into them because she spots me and her face goes slack. She whispers something in Adrian's ear. He looks up, and when he catches my gaze, I can feel him like an electrical energy pulse. A flash of confusion crosses his features. He seems upset that I'm here, which is odd considering he sent the note.

Didn't he?

My body goes cold as I realize Adrian isn't behind Mom's kidnapping. As if on cue, Hugo glides into the room with an older red-headed woman perched on his arm. She's classically beautiful and completely enamoured by the man. She's also human. And my mother.

The world tilts off its axis. What is he doing with her? How does he even know who she is? He leans down and kisses her gently on the mouth. My mother, kissing a vampire. I never thought I'd see the day. But then, I don't really know her like I thought I did. And that's a dull knife right into my heart.

I can't move. I can't breathe. All I can do is watch in horror.

The crowd thickens and I lose sight of them. The engines rumble to life. The boat starts to move away from the dock. Someone walks onto the little stage with the band and speaks into the microphone to introduce the mayor. Like a true politician, Robyn Cox glides up onto the stage as if it's the most comfortable place on earth for her to be. She smiles down at us, her perfectly styled short black hair and brown eyes shining under the lights.

"Thank you all for coming!" Everyone cheers, and she jumps into an impassioned speech about improving the city and the importance of vampire-human relations. This is a fundraiser event for her own campaign, so of course everyone here already supports her and is eating it up like a kid with a bucket full of Halloween candy. "And I'm excited to announce that the bill to lower the gambling age will be taken to Capitol Hill during the next session and all our projections indicate it will pass." More cheers. My cheeks burn at that. She's supposed to be helping her constituents, not feeding them to the vampires! When she points to the police commissioner and he cheerily holds up a glass of champagne to acknowledge her, I've had enough.

I edge my way along the crowd, trying to get closer to Hugo and my mom. The mayor says something about him and he leaves my mother standing by the side of the stage to go speak into the microphone. I still don't understand why Hugo would want me here. What's he going to do to Mom? My mind flashes to the quick and ruthless way he murdered that woman the other night and how Adrian sucked up the mess. Bile burns my throat with the hateful words I'm dying to scream.

"Thank you, Robyn." His cruel energy blankets the room. Or maybe I'm the only one who thinks he's cruel? Others look up at Hugo like he's some kind of savior. "As the co-chair of the VEC and the head of the government relationships board on behalf of the North American vampires, I've had a lot of experience on these matters. Now, more than ever, it is critical that we keep our lines of communication open. The last thing anyone wants is a war." He winks and the crowd quiets. His tone is all business, but his words are a threat. Do they see it now? Do they sense his cruelty like I do? "We need each other. This is a two-way relationship," he continues his speech. "And my brother and I will stop at nothing to ensure the best quality of life for vampires *and* humans."

I'm only a few paces from Mom. She's gazing adoringly up at Hugo like he's the sun in winter. Shouldn't she be hiding from the mafia right now? I clasp her hand in mine and whisper in her ear. "Hey, Mom, can you come with me?"

She turns and blinks at me, her eyes confused. "Evangeline, what are you doing here?"

I shake my head and tug her backward. Luckily, for once in her stubborn life, she follows. We move to the farthest edge of the room so that we can whisper without drawing attention from Hugo's speech. Every once in a while his eyes flick over to us. He's not mad that I've found her. Triumph sparkles in his eyes. This is all a game to him––one I don't know the rules to.

"What are you doing here with Hugo? He's a vampire."

She blinks at me, confused. "Umm––no, he's not. Hugo's my date."

"How do you know him?"

"Umm––" More confusion. "We met at––umm––I know him from––" Her voice trails off. She doesn't know because she's clearly been compelled to believe something that doesn't exist. She's not afraid, she's still sending adoring looks in Hugo's direction, but it's obvious he's brought her here as bait for me. She's a pawn and she doesn't even know it.

"Aren't you supposed to be hiding from the mafia?" I whisper-hiss. "I've been trying to get ahold of you for days. They're going to hurt me if you don't pay Armondo."

She blinks rapidly and a knot seems to untangle in her mind. "Oh, I'd forgotten." Fear mars her features and her hand presses against her chest. "I can't believe I forgot. I don't know how I could have. I'm so sorry, Evangeline. I'm working on it. I almost got the money, I swear." She opens the little purse on her shoulder. There's a wad of cash shoved inside. "See, I used what was left of the sock-money and got someone else to lend me some more and I just need to take some of this and win a few hands and we'll be free and clear."

I blink at her. "*You* took that money from my room? And now you think gambling it away is a good idea right now?"

"You don't understand. I'm out of time. I'm desperate."

Oh, I think I understand desperation.

Hugo finishes his speech, the crowd cheers, and then everyone disperses to chat or play or dance or whatever people do at these things. Meanwhile, Adrian stays centered in the room, connecting with acquaintances, but his bright blue eyes never stray from me for long. The last time I was on this boat with him, he also used my mother as a pawn. And then he killed a man. I can't forget it. I've been too lax around him since the blood vow, but I need to remember who he really is. What he really is.

Hugo appears. I can smell the blood on him from here. My stomach knots. I hope he hasn't been feeding on my mother. She doesn't have any bite marks and that would be illegal. "I see you got my invitation."

"Unfortunately. What are you doing with my mother? Do you even know her?"

He runs a finger across her cheek. "She was easy to find. I have contacts everywhere."

She peers up at him adoringly, but with a question in her eyes. "You found me?"

He chuckles low. "Sorry, doll, I don't actually know you. We're not together. A little compulsion to get you here was all I needed." She goes rigid, and he stares at her with a little smile on his lips. "Don't be afraid." His voice sounds different. Deeper. Certain.

Wrong.

She instantly relaxes, the fear melting like butter. To see how quickly and powerfully his compulsion works is unlike anything I've witnessed before. I step back, terrified for my mother, for every human on this boat.

"So what's really going on here, Hugo?"

"I'll explain it all in time, don't worry." He ushers my mom toward the gaming tables, and I follow. "First, there's someone else here that I think we need to have a little talk with."

We approach the roulette table. The wheel spins, the little white ball dancing across the numbers. Around the table, gamblers are busy placing their bets. The ones who want to take the biggest risk but possibly gain the biggest reward bet on the numbers. The ones who want to play it safe bet on the outside edges, on the even and odds, and mainly black or red.

A middle aged gentleman in a pinstripe suit and bowler hat turns to us and addresses Hugo. "You delivered the goods."

"I always do. I hope we can call this even for what my brother did to your man, Paulo."

That name rings in my ear. Paulo. Who's Paulo? Then I remember he's the gambler Adrian killed right in front of me. Apparently, he was also a mobster.

Mom stumbles back.

"Uh oh," Hugo chuckles, "care to introduce our mutual friend to your daughter?"

Mom shakes her head, and her eyes go round as marbles.

"I can introduce myself," the man says. When he smiles, an old scar on his left eyebrow cuts deep into his face. He's a large guy with a sinister energy and a depth to his eyes made by years of corruption. He sticks out a thick hand with a big gold ring on one of the fingers. "I'm pleased to finally meet you, Eva. I'm Armondo."

Twenty-Nine

～∾✦∾～

"**Y**our mother loves to gamble, doesn't she Eva?" Armondo continues. "So why don't we play a little game?"

"What do you want?" I rush. "She's got the money on her. She can pay you back right now."

Armando laughs bitterly but offers his hand. Mom shoves the purse at him and he peers inside, greedy eyes assessing. "This might be half of what you owe me, Virginia."

"I can get more."

"Time's up."

I always thought it would be the blood loss that would be my mom's ruin, but it's not, it's the gambling. It's what that *need* to play––the addiction––has led her to do. It's this man who has no qualms about hurting her, maybe killing her, maybe killing me too. Hugo grips Mom's upper arm and she winces.

Armondo goes on, "How about your daughter makes a bet for you. Beginner's luck, right?" He chuckles. "If she wins, I'll take the money and we'll call it even. If she loses. . ."

"What?" Mom's voice is barely a whisper.

"Then you both die."

Hugo shakes his head adamantly. "You can't touch the girl. She belongs to the vampires now. She's ours."

Panicked, Mom shoots me a questioning look that I can't answer.

Armondo leans back and curls his lip before taking a long drink of his liquor. He sets the drink back down and assesses the three of us. "Fine. Virginia's life then."

"I won't do it." I shake my head and plead. "Please, I can't do this. Don't make me do this." I'm not a gambler, I hate it, and to have to gamble my mother's life is out of the question. It's so loud in here, so busy and lively, that nobody seems to notice our little group conversation. If they did, would they care?

"If you don't place a bet, then I'll kill her. This is her only chance." He means it. I have the wound on the back of my head as proof. His henchman was just a taste of what he's capable of and to think that he'll hurt my mom sends me over the edge. I lock my knees so I don't weaken and glare daggers at the man.

Hugo raises an eyebrow at me. "Sweetheart, you better do what the man says."

The next bet has come and gone and the little white ball is spinning around the wheel again. I watch it, my stomach going hollow. It slows and lands on the green double zero. Everyone around the table groans as the winnings are swooped up by the dealer. This is the fail-safe for the casino, the assurance that more often than not, the house wins.

"It's a simple game of odds," Mom whispers to me, her eyes pleading with me to give her this chance. "Make the safest bet."

Hugo shoves her against the table and she cries out. "No more talking."

Is there such a thing as a "safe bet"? I don't think so. The whole point is the risk. But I take the rolled wad of money and set it on the table. The dealer calls something out and the pit boss zips over. It's the same vampire from my first run-in weeks ago. His eyes light with recognition, but this time he doesn't tell me to leave. He nods to the dealer who counts out the cash and replaces it with a stack of pink chips.

"Double the money," Armondo says. "You have options. You can put it on a number and if you win, the payout is thirty-five to one. I'll let you keep the extra. Doesn't that sound nice? You'd be a wealthy woman. Or you could play the outside thirds, giving yourself a third share of the spoils if you win there. That's a lot of money too."

"Or I can play it safe and take the two to one odds." I move the pile onto the red rectangle. It reminds me of blood and vampires and all the reasons why we're here tonight. At the last second, I switch it to black.

"Black it is," Armondo says.

Hugo smirks. "Not much for gambling?"

"No." I fold my arms and glare.

By now we've attracted a crowd of onlookers. There's got to be at least ten thousand dollars on that single bet, and people are excited to see the result. I spot Adrian and Kelli standing not too far off. Adrians face is an unreadable mask. I can't tell if he's happy to see me or wishes I were dead. It could go either way, and I wouldn't want to bet on that, either.

Mom levels me with a hard look. "Eva, whatever happens, I want you to know this isn't your fault." But it feels like it. If I win, I double the money and get Armondo off our backs. I don't even want to think about what will happen if I lose.

The dealer spins the wheel and the little ball goes *plop, plop, plop* with no concern for what its movements mean for the future. It slows and slows, until finally lands on thirty-six, red. My heart plummets. At the last second, it bounces once more, and lands solidly in number eleven.

Black.

I crumple to my knees as the crowd explodes in cheers. I've never been so relieved in my life, every ounce of anxiety leaving my body in that moment. Mom crouches and wraps her arms around me. "I'm so sorry, baby. . .so sorry," she whispers over and over. She promises to get better, promises things will be different. But I know nothing will change unless Adrian comes through with the compulsion and gets her to stop.

We stand, and I wipe away tears.

"It's your lucky day." Armondo sounds disappointed, but he's a man of his word, collecting his winnings and moving on to another table.

"That money isn't much to him," Hugo says, pulling me up to standing. "He'll blow it by the end of the night. If only you'd made a better bet you could have pocketed some of that for yourself."

Like I care about that right now.

"Then why did he do it? Just to punish my mom?"

"In part, but mostly to prove a point to me. The vampires and the mob have been at odds in this city for years. This wasn't about the money so much as it was about honor and asserting dominance in front of vampires. He knows he'll never have what we have." His fang extends and he sips from a glass of blood. My stomach churns. "Immortality."

"When does this thing dock? I'm ready to go home."

"The party is just getting started." He retrieves his wallet and hands my mother five crisp one hundred dollar bills. "Go have fun, Virginia. I have business to attend to with your daughter."

I expect her to tell him off, to insist that she's had enough excitement for tonight. Once again, my expectations break my own heart. Mom takes the money. Avoiding eye contact with me, she heads in the direction of the Texas Hold'em table. I see her sit down and place her first bet, then rub her hands together as if she's preparing for a fun night ahead. If my heart was broken before, now it's in absolute shatters. I can't believe it. And yet, I can. And lying to myself is the worst part. *She took the money from my room.* My eyes burn with tears––I force them back.

"Come. . ." Hugo places a hand on my lower back and leads me toward the dance floor. "Let me cheer you up. Aren't you happy to have that mafia trouble behind you?"

I can't answer that.

My body follows even though my mind is back with Mom, begging her to reconsider. It doesn't matter that she is now gambling with Hugo's money. Soon it will be hers again. She's been in hiding for days, and now she's back to doing the thing that landed her there in the first place.

We end up on the dance floor where the music is a loud noxious riot of instruments. I can't keep up as he swings me to and fro like a paper doll. I have no idea what I'm doing and I don't want to be here. "Can I go home now? I don't want to dance."

"This isn't about what you want, Eva, it's about what I know." He laughs. "Don't you realize that by now?" I try to leave but his hands hold me back, fingers biting into my flesh. He's too strong. I'm confused by his statement, what he knows. It doesn't make sense.

The music slows, and a silky voice brushes across the back of my exposed neck. "May I cut in?"

"You're so predictable, Adrianos." But Hugo hands me over to Adrian and takes Kelli in his arms. "Let me guess, you were responsible for what happened back there at the roulette table?"

Adrian doesn't say anything. The music is a slow sultry tune and he pulls me against him, the steps taking us farther and farther away from Hugo and Kelli.

"I didn't expect to see you here," he says at last.

"I didn't expect to be here. Hugo threatened my mother, so I came." I look up into his blue eyes. They're so reflective in the golden light that I can see myself staring back. "What did he mean about the roulette table?"

"It was nothing."

"Please just tell me," I sigh. "I don't think I can handle any more deception in one night."

"Then you've come to the wrong place." Emotion shifts through his irises and they're no longer blocked. Suddenly, I can see into the oceanic depths of them. I could get lost there if I'm not careful. I would drown and it would not be pleasant. At least, I don't think it would be. I wouldn't want it to be. What if it was?

"I'm the only vampire in North America who can fly," Adrian relents. "I'm also the only vampire in North America with telekinesis."

The reality of what happened sinks in and my mouth pops open in awe.

"You saved her. You moved the ball at the last second to black. Thank you." I can't help it. I hug him. I never thought I would be grateful to a vampire but I am. I misjudged him.

Adrian freezes and doesn't hug me back.

"That's enough." He dislodges himself. "Let's go find out why Hugo really brought you here. I'm growing tired of his little game."

"What do you mean? It was all to appease the mafia guy."

"Trust me. I know my brother; we've been at odds for centuries. The only person Hugo cares to appease is himself." He slips his hand into mine and tugs. "Now come on."

"Centuries. . ." I swallow, once again questioning his age.

Adrian catches the question in my expression and tilts his head at me, his eyes narrowing. "As far as I know, Brisa is the oldest vampire alive and I'm her oldest son, Angel. I'll let you guess what that means for my age." But I can't even wrap my mind around that kind of eternity. How many wars, how much pain and suffering, and how much technological advancement has this man experienced?

When we make it back through the dancers to Kelli and Hugo, Hugo looks at our clasped hands and smiles with glee. "This is going to be fun."

Thirty

❦

"L et's go down to the VIP room and discuss a few things, shall we?" Hugo leads us through the maze of people and to the back of the boat. Along the way, we're stopped several times by eager humans. Adrian and Hugo shmooze them over like it's nothing, like we're not on some important walk to discuss *whatever*. These guys really know how to turn on the charm, and it seems to take forever to shake off all the humans. All the while my mind is buzzing with thoughts of what could be coming next. Truth is, I haven't a clue. I feel like all my cards are showing and none of them are aces.

We finally make it to a tiny stairwell that descends into the bowels of the ship. Kelli isn't anywhere to be found. It's just me, Adrian, and Hugo. I follow them down the stairs because there's no other choice. What am I going to do, run away? Jump into the river? I can't tell these creatures no. Their power is on another level.

We walk down a long thin hallway with little metal doors on either side. Some have words inscribed on them with "restricted" or "crew only." One says VIP in gold lettering. That's our target. The room is small, the lights are low, and we're not the only ones in here.

A woman with shiny black hair is pressed up against a man in a police uniform. Her dress is hiked up around her waist and his hands roam her backside. She groans and shifts closer just as I realize who they are. Mayor Cox and the police commissioner! To walk in on them engaging in an affair is so stereotypical that I almost laugh. Both have wedding rings on their fingers. Both have spouses upstairs.

"Get out," Adrian deadpans like he doesn't have the time for this.

The two jump apart and offer their apologies. Hugo smiles with even more glee than before, and all I can think is that this juicy piece of information is going to help him in his quest to control the city.

They scamper out of the room.

"And then there were three," Hugo says.

I take in the small polished space and try to relax. The windows are the waterproof bolted-in kind, typical on boats. Outside, the top of the water laps against the bottom rims. The river is black and sparkling under the moon. On the near distant shore, the city lights crawl past. The room itself is wallpapered in deep maroon with black foil accents. There's a minibar in one corner, a flat screen television on the wall, with two black leather chairs and a couch evenly spaced out.

Hugo closes the door and motions for us to take a seat. I sit next to Adrian on the couch and Hugo sits across from us in a chair. He lounges back and smiles. "I don't think I've had this much fun at a party in a hundred years. You remember that time when we--"

"Why are we here, brother?" Adrian cuts in. "Get to the point."

"You know, Ardrianos, for someone who's lived as long as you have, you'd think you would have learned patience by now."

Adrian's eyes narrow. There's hatred for his brother in those eyes. It's clear as day. "Believe me. I'm patient," he says, "I'm more patient than I ever planned on."

Hugo snickers and slaps the arm of his chair, then stands and crosses to the minibar. He pours two bourbons. "Would you like something, child?" he asks me. "What's your drink?"

I'm parched, I could use water, but I don't want to take a thing from Hugo. After the way he toyed with my mother, he's my new favorite fanger to hate. "No." My voice is clipped.

He smirks and hands the glass to Adrian, sits back down, and the two drink. I knew vampires could drink but it seems pointless. "It's one human thing that we can still have," Hugo says when he catches me looking. "Not that the alcohol affects us. It doesn't do anything to our blood but it's a different taste and it doesn't make us ill. I'll admit, I prefer my alcohol mixed with blood but sometimes it's fun to switch things up every now and then." Hugo smirks at me, lazily swirling the amber liquor in his right hand before taking another sip.

"Vampires don't eat food or drink water. Alcohol is a luxury, and blood is a necessity," Adrian adds. "What's your point, brother?"

Hugo raises an eyebrow in my direction. "Are you prepared for that, Eva? Are you truly willing to give up your humanity?"

My body goes hard. He's calling my bluff.

I'm not going to become a vampire. I never had any intention of doing so, and it's the last thing I want. I'd rather die than feed off of other's blood and abuse their addictions so that I can survive. But this is a floating casino and I came prepared to lie and cheat and game my way out of here. "Of course." I smile happily at Adrian and take his hand in mine. He flinches. "I trust you. From what I understand, I'll be bound to you and unable to defy you." I bat my eyelashes. "But I know you'll take good care of me."

"Lucky me." He frowns, peels his hand away, and takes a sip from his drink.

Hugo laughs. "It will be a lucky man who has the opportunity to break a strong-willed woman such as yourself, Evangeline. It's unfortunate for my brother, but that man won't be him."

I shake my head, confused. Adrian freezes.

"Do I have your attention now?" Hugo's face turns stony. "Good. Listen closely. I take a new protégé every year as my queen allows. There's a reason I've lost five of my protégés in a single month and that my queen won't grant me more children, and that reason is you, Eva."

A weight crushes down on me and I try not to sink under the pressure. How much does he know?

"What are you talking about?" Adrian asks sharply. "Do not waste any more of our time. Explain yourself."

"First was my newest child, Roxy. She didn't even make it past the grave-yard. Hunters got her. Or the sun. Then I lost three more a few weeks later; those men definitely weren't killed by the sun. And of course we know about what happened in the lobby with my bloodthirsty child whom you killed without consulting me." He counts them off his fingers. "All deaths that were caused by Eva, here."

The two exchange heated glares before turning them both on me. The pressure is too much. My hands are shaking. My heart is racing. I don't know what to do.

"The lobby wasn't my fledgling's fault," Adrian spits. "And the others have nothing to do with her. Do not make false accusations or I will see that you are punished. You have no proof."

Hugo laughs gleefully. "Ah, but you're wrong. I figured it out in the lobby when her blood was spilled. She's connected to my line, but yet she's human. So how can that be?" He leans closer to me and his voice goes low. "There is only one way a human can connect into a vampiric line and that is through venom. If our venom enters your human bloodstream it makes you able to feel, sense, and track the vampires within the family of the vampire who bit you. It also makes us far more attracted to you and your blood more desirable."

"This is forbidden information!" Adrian growls. "Brisa has only allowed you to speak of this to Eva because you've made up lies. My fledgling is no hunter."

"This is why you don't drink directly from human flesh unless you intend to kill or turn," I whisper breathily.

"Indeed it is one of the reasons," Hugo confirms. "I knew it the second I smelled your fresh blood in the lobby, and I confirmed it when I tasted it for myself. So tell us, Evangeline, how long have you been a vampire hunter, and which one of my children bit you before you killed them?"

Time stills. Everything slows. I don't know how to lie my way out of this.

Adrian watches me closely. I expect him to defend me or keep denying this, but he does neither. Hurt crosses his features, then anger. He turns on me with a sneer, "Answer him!"

"I--I was defending myself." Fear prickles over every inch of my body. "I followed a friend to the cemetery because I suspected he was a hunter, and then this new vampire attacked me and I staked her with one of his stakes. Her fang barely grazed my arm. I thought it was nothing. I didn't know." My voice comes out shaky. I hope they don't think it's because I'm lying. Surely, they hear the adrenaline racing through my veins and the pounding of my heart.

"And what of my other children?" Hugo snarls. "You were connected to them. You must have killed them."

"That wasn't my fault! We were at a party. Vampires came. I think they were following me. They had no place showing up at a human college party, but they were there and they attacked my friend. We were defending ourselves and--"

"It is not easy to kill vampires!" Hugo stands and flies at me. Adrian lets him. In two seconds I'm slammed up against the wall and choking under his stony hands. They grip my throat and squeeze. "They were following you because I ordered them to, I had suspicions about you from the beginning. You are a hunter! Admit it!"

Tears stream down my face. My vision blacks at the edges. There's no choice. Either way I'm going to die.

"Tell the truth or I'll kill your mother and then I'll kill you!"

"Yes," I mouth.

"Do you confess it?"

I try to nod but it's hard. "Yes," my voice is strained under his death-grip.

He drops me to the floor and my lungs burn as I gasp for breath. Adrian stands rock still and peers down at me like I'm a bug in need of squashing.

"So here's what we're going to do," Hugo continues. "You've already been approved by the queen to be a fledgling." I look over his shoulder at Adrian. "She knows of my suspicions and said that if I can get a confession, then I can have Eva for myself."

"And what do you intend to do with her?" Adrian raises an eyebrow. He stands back with his arms over his chest. Anger rolls off him in waves, filling every crevice of the small room. "Because I don't care anymore, brother. I am tired of family drama. This is why I never want to take any children. They are a liability, not an asset, and I am done."

He's done. The words feel like a battle axe to my chest.

But wait... why is Adrian pretending not to know who I really am? He already knew I was a hunter. And why is he so quick to hand me over to the brother he so obviously hates? There's something more going on here. With my eyes alone, I will him to save me, to intervene, to do something, because he's my only hope. But he does nothing. He turns away, appearing well and truly done with me. Maybe this is it. Maybe he'd rather turn me over to his brother than deal with me any longer.

Hugo peers down his nose and his fangs extend. They're like two little daggers--two little promises of pain to come. "I intend to turn her. Tonight."

Thirty-One

E verything happens in a blur of blind panic. Hugo binds my hands and feet and mouth with thick black fabric and Adrian carries me off the floating casino and onto a speed boat that has been tied to the side of the ferry. My oversized flapper-style dress hangs around my knees and I pray that it stays that way. My life depends on it.

Adrian drops me on the floor and I lay there curled up in the fetal position as the boat flies down the river. I try to maneuver through the bindings at my wrists and ankles but it's useless. I start to cry. My tears blur the stars, the moon, and the rare glimpses of city and freedom. Even though it should barely register on my list of worries, I'm cold and starting to shiver. Before long it consumes my thoughts. I let it, at least it's something to focus on that doesn't terrify me. My dress is loose enough and long enough that I can tuck my legs up into it. I make sure to stay on my left side even though it's extra painful to lie this way. The beads of the dress bite into my flesh, many of them probably cracking where I lie on them. I can't believe this stupid gown is what I'm going to be wearing to my death. That's if I don't find a way to get out of becoming a vampire. I'm going to fight to the death. But if they win, if I rise up as Hugo's new child, I will join the sunrise. I don't know if that's possible, if the thirst will overpower me, but I vow to try to die before I hurt someone.

Vow––the word shocks me back to the present. I look at Adrian. He's driving the boat. The wind blows his dark blond hair behind him and his biceps flex when he makes a turn. I have vowed to help him, haven't I? Not Hugo. Maybe that's why Adrian is going along with this. Maybe the blood

173

we already exchanged will somehow bind me to him instead of his brother. He might be playing the both of us. What if I wake up as Adrian's child, after all?

My stomach hardens. If I had food in my belly, I'd throw up. These brothers are truly evil. I'm nothing but a toy for them to fight over.

After a while, the boat slows, and Adrian drives it to the shore. Hugo picks me up like I weigh nothing and I grit my teeth when his arm gets too close to my upper thigh. He smells of expensive cologne and alcohol and blood. I don't want to smell him, I'd rather smell the water and the dirt and the cold air. He carries me off the boat and into a wooded graveyard. There are no underground graves here this close to the water. The tombs are above ground, ranging from dark gray stone to cream limestone, with inscriptions too old and weathered to read. Moss covers many of them. The moon is bright enough to see by, but the vampires have no issues either way. They can see in the dark. Soon I will too. The thought makes me whimper.

"Have you already prepared the grave?" Adrian asks. It's the first I've heard from him even though he trails behind us like a dark shadow. I meet his eyes. They glow like two little blue orbs in the darkness. I murmur pleas for help against the fabric gagging my mouth, but he only watches.

"I have," Hugo replies. "Why are you not fighting this? It wasn't long ago that you were defending your little Angel." He snickers. "Yes, I've heard your pet name for the girl. Maybe I'll call her the same."

Adrian rolls his eyes. "You know I don't like to take children. I thought I wanted Eva but she betrayed us. There's no way I would turn a hunter into my child. I'm surprised you're willing to after she killed some of your family. If I were in your shoes, she'd be dead already."

Hugo tightens his arms around me. "Then I guess that's where you and I differ. I will always take a new child. My family bond is stronger than most. She will be loyal after the change."

"Because she'll have to be," Adrian challenges. "But won't you always wonder if she'll hate you?"

"She'll love me," Hugo snaps. "Children always love their fathers, even when they hate them. Now come on, it's this way. I had to get farther from the river to find a place I could dig."

Hugo moves like liquid smoke through the crowded graveyard and I'm carried along with him. Adrian levitates and flies above. I wonder if it's a talent that makes Hugo jealous. I would be. We arrive at a spot with a pile of disturbed dirt. Hugo walks me right up to the hole and tilts me so I can look inside. There's a coffin at the bottom. The lid is already open and a white silk lining glistens up at me.

I shake my head and try to yell through the fabric but it's useless.

He sets me down on the cool grass and unbinds my limbs. "You need to be able to claw yourself out of the coffin or it won't work."

He stares into my eyes and says, "If I remove this and you scream, I'll be forced to put it back on." He unties the gag from my mouth and I cough, sucking in the foggy air. I don't scream. Nobody would hear me anyway. "After I bite you, you will have my venom in your bloodstream. It might hurt at first but it will feel good soon after, so don't be afraid. After that we will exchange blood, and then I will bury you. In three nights you will rise as my child and I will be here to greet you."

I shake my head. *No. Please, no.*

"Shh—don't worry, child. Once it's all done, you will be thanking me." He runs a calloused finger down my face and wipes away a tear. I bristle under his touch. "And you will love me."

What does that mean? Love? Does it mean I will want to be around him like a daughter and father, or that I will want to be with him like a lover? He's older and scary and awful, and this can't be happening. It can't.

Adrian hovers above us, viewing the dreadful scene like a voyeur, like it's nothing he hasn't seen a million times before. He almost looks bored. I hate him for that look, maybe even more than Hugo.

"Let's begin." Hugo's fangs extend once again, but this time he lunges for me and they sink into my neck. I do scream, I can't help it. The pain is blinding and white hot, but my eyes flutter closed and it soon transforms into utter and complete ecstasy. The warmth of it washes through me like a salve to a wound. I've never done drugs, but perhaps this is why people get addicted. I could get lost in this. Forever. It's a cruel kind of beauty and I want more, more, more...

Hugo releases me and sucks in a greedy breath. Vamps don't even need to breathe but he does it for show. "Virgin blood. Mmm, it's been a while since I've had some as sweet as yours." He licks his lips. "I must be careful or I'll kill you." He wipes the red from his face and turns to Adrian. "I would offer you a taste but we can't have her blood bond confused with the wrong master. Sorry."

He's not sorry. It's a taunt. Adrian may have exchanged blood with me, but he never bit me, so my earlier theory is out. This really is happening with Hugo.

"I would never give my venom to a traitor," Adrian says nonchalantly, but I can see the crazed look in his glowing eyes and wonder if it's from a thirst to taste my blood or something else.

I start to cry again. "Shh––Eva. It will be okay." Adrian's voice is smooth and easy. "Sometimes you lose when you play a game of high stakes."

There it is. That word. Stakes. *He knows.*

Adrian lands on the grass a few feet from us and sits back on his heels. "Are you going to get this show on the road or are we going to be here all night?"

Using his fangs, Hugo rips into the pale flesh of his wrist. Crimson liquid gushes down his arm. "I have to admit, it may make me a sick bastard, but this is my favorite part of the process. I love knowing part of me will always be with you."

He extends his wrist toward my mouth and his eyes move heavenward. This is my chance, what I've been waiting for, and what Adrian alluded to with his comment.

Adrian's bluff.

My ace.

I gather my courage, tap into weeks of training, and slip my hand under the fold of my dress. The long thin wooden stake I've had strapped to my upper thigh has been waiting for me this whole time. Adrian always warned me not to bring this around the vampires, always said they'd kill me if they found it. He demanded I stop. Good thing I didn't listen.

The stake is cool salvation in my palm and I grip it with all my might. I spring forward and sink it directly into Hugo's chest. It slices through the ribcage and into his spongy heart. He gasps and looks down at me, shock seizing his body. He never expected to be bested, not by me. But it's not just me, it's Adrian. He knew the stake was there the whole time, his satisfied smile says it all.

"No. . ." Blood seeps from Hugo's mouth.

"You should have known this could happen, *Father*. I am a hunter after all." I'm a sarcastic bitch. Adrian laughs. I push Hugo off of me, and he crumbles into ash.

It's over.

I stand and brush myself off. The pile of Hugo-dust blows away with a gust of wind and I watch it go with relief. My legs are shaking. His venom is still racing through my body. It makes me feel stronger, more powerful, *better*, but I want it gone. I imagine it racing through my veins like a dirty virus and hope my body can fight it off soon. I press my fingers to the bite on my neck. There's blood but the wound has already healed over thanks to the venom, sealing away that last shred of Hugo into my body.

Adrian hovers above me and that damned satisfied smile plays on his face. "See, my brother was wrong. I am rather patient."

"You're sick, too."

He doesn't care. He's barely even listening. "I've wanted to do that for ages, but I couldn't. My maker forbids us from killing our siblings or ordering our progeny to do it." He laughs. "It does make me sick, I know, but I thank God you walked into my casino. You *are* my Angel."

I glare. "How dare you speak of God. You're vile."

He stills and his eyes narrow. "You have no idea."

"You wanted him dead and risked my life in the process. You allowed him to bring me here and get this far so that I could kill him for you." I'm boiling over with anger and have nowhere to direct it but at Adrian. "You played me. I almost died!"

"You're alive. Don't be so dramatic." He nods toward the stake, his demeanor returning to business-as-usual. "Please, let's dispose of that. It's evidence and I'd rather not have it around, though I admit I would love to keep it as a souvenir of Hugo's demise. It would be my most-prized possession."

I scoff. I don't want to get rid of the only weapon on me, but if Adrian was going to kill me, he would have done so already, not to mention, what if one of the vamps was able to smell Hugo's blood on it? I shouldn't have the murder weapon on me, that's like Crime 101. So I do as Adrian wishes and walk back to the river and toss the stake in. "Can we go home now? I'm so done with vampires."

"Hmm, does that mean you're going to give up hunting?"

"Yes," I bark out. I would be happy to never see another bloodsucker in my life. But even as I say it, I don't know if I can give up hunting or abandon my friends.

"You're such a liar."

"Takes one to know one."

He laughs and lands gracefully in the boat as I climb inside. I sit in the chair across from the driver's seat, the same one Hugo just occupied. It's cold and I'm still shaking. I tuck my legs up into my dress again and try to banish Hugo from my memory.

Adrian drives us back to the city slow enough that we can hear each other over the engine. The story he plans to tell the queen and the others is that when we arrived at the graveyard, hunters showed up and killed Hugo while we escaped. He will insist that I am not a hunter myself, that Hugo wasn't able to prove anything or get me to admit to anything. He'll say that he was going to gift me to Hugo out of pity for all his recent losses and because he'd decided he didn't want to take a child after all. But since Hugo died, Adrian invited me to continue on as his fledgling.

"As if I would agree," I snap.

"Well, wait," he continues. "I haven't gotten to the best part. You see, after such a terrible ordeal, you were spooked by the hunters, and decided to go on living your life as a human. And I, in all my infinite mercy, decided to grant your wish."

I scoff. "Good. Consider this the end of our relationship."

It's a great story, but this is the oldest vampire on earth we're talking about, and I'm a little skeptical our story is going to land. "And you think Queen Brisa is going to buy that? What if she orders you not to lie?"

"You let me worry about Brisa." He sighs happily and rakes his hand through his hair. "She's busy with other matters and Hugo has been out of her favor for quite some time. The vampire court is full of problems, and this will mean little to any of them. She'll be upset about Hugo's death because it's one less child for her, but that anger will be directed toward the hunters and not us."

"Oh great," I scoff, "so just send her after my friends. Wonderful."

"She doesn't know about your little gym under the bank. I'm the only one who does and I won't be telling her."

"I hope you're right. I still think she'll just order you not to lie to her. If I were her, I'd do that all the time."

His fingers dance over the steering wheel as he looks at me for a long moment. "Oh, and do you want to be the vampire queen, now, Angel?"

"Ew. Never."

He nods. "You're right, she can order us about, and she does it quite often, but I've built a tolerance to her over the years. My words are very easy for me to control. It's actions against her will that are hard to take, especially something as final as killing one of her other children when she's told me I couldn't."

I fold my arms and sit back. "Interesting."

"What's interesting?" His pale face glows under the moonlight. "You'll forgive me, but I've been around too long to find much interesting anymore."

"Your worldview is truly sad." I deflect the question. "It's a wonderful world if you know where to look. It would be even better without vampires, no offense."

"I've lived long enough to know with certainty that this world is rather bleak." He narrows his eyes. "Now tell me, what's interesting?"

"Just that you hate your maker even more than you hated Hugo."

He leans back. "Ah––that. Yes. I love her and I hate her. It's a rather complicated relationship that mostly errs on the side of loathing."

"For her or yourself?"

He stills in that vampiric way of his and doesn't answer. I change tactics. "You called me on my bluff back there. You knew that even though I said I'd stop bringing stakes around vampires that I would still do it. I think it's time I call you on a bluff, Adrian."

"Oh? And what's that?"

"We don't actually have a blood vow."

"Hmm. . . what makes you think so?"

"You wanted me to believe it was real so I would spy for you, but I haven't done a thing we agreed upon and nothing has happened to me. I'm supposed to take your word for the blood vow, that it will somehow kill me if I don't comply." I sit up straighter. "But I believe it was all a fabrication."

"Hmm. . ."

"What are you thinking? Am I correct?"

"I'm thinking that Hugo was right, you would make an excellent vampire. It's too bad you hate us so much, not that I blame you." He sighs and shakes his head. "I'm also thinking that you are smarter than most humans I've met because you're right. There never was a blood vow. Bonds forged in blood only exist between vampires themselves."

"I knew it." I pump my fist. "I can't believe you played me like that. Wait, scratch that, I totally can."

"The deal still stands if you want it. You give me information about Leslie Tate and what's going on in his organization, and I'll break your mother free of her gambling addiction."

I go quiet and think about the offer the rest of the boat ride home. I consider it from all angles. "What is Leslie Tate?" I finally ask. "Cameron is convinced he's some kind of demon."

"Hmm, if we work together, maybe I'll tell you."

Should I work with him? There's reasons to do it, plenty of reasons. But when we get to the dock and see the ferry with all the people still on there, still partying and reluctant to leave, I know my answer. I never want to be in bed with vampires, literally or figuratively.

"I'm out," I say at last. "I can't betray my friends for my mother, as much as I want to. I just can't be that person."

"And why not?"

He ties the boat to a post and we climb onto the dock. I'm a bloody mess, but it's dark and there's nobody else out here. They're all still on the boat, gambling their souls away. I stop and turn, taking in his beautiful face and hoping it's the last time I see it. "Because I want to be better than vampires. Not physically, not mentally, I'm talking about morally, Adrian. I want to be a good person."

"And vampires can't be good?"

"You know they can't." Even the times he's tried to help me, the times he's brought feelings out in me, or been on my side, he's still used me in his games.

Hurt cracks through his hard exterior. It's nothing I've seen on his face before. "You're right. I'm a lost cause. Best to stay away from me." And then he levitates into the moonlit sky and flies away.

Thirty-Two

I n the days since Hugo bit me, I've become a different woman. All of my senses are heightened in the best possible way. I feel invincible and so, so alive. If this is what vampire venom can do for a human then I'm certain people would do just about anything to get their hands on it. It's no wonder the vamps are so adamant to keep this a secret. Every day this week I've woken up thinking the venom will have dispersed but every day I feel as invincible as the day before.

I stroll through City Park, marveling at the enhanced colors, the cleaner scents, and the brighter and warmer sun. It's as if I was wearing a filter over my senses all these years and now that it's been taken off, I don't ever want to go back.

This is my favorite park in New Orleans. It's filled with tree-lined paths, grassy knolls, ponds, bridges, and artistic statues. The place attracts tourists, families, photographers, sunbathers, and just about anyone looking for some peace and calm in an otherwise lively city. The Spanish moss trees here are my favorite, and it's one of those that I'm heading over to now. I chose this sundrenched area in a public spot and picked a time in broad daylight to have this meeting with my friends. I can't risk any vampires or their human minions overhearing. There's no way a vamp could be out here and a human wouldn't be able to get close without notice.

All week at our practices I've been avoiding talking to them and it's eating me up inside. I can't do it anymore. I have to be honest and explain everything from start to finish if I'm going to lose some of this guilt and hopefully get the guys' help. They might hate me after what I'm about to confess. Part of me fully expects that they'll never speak with me again and the idea of losing Felix is killing me the very most.

I spread out the pale blue picnic blanket that I borrowed from Olive and set down the sack of food in the center. Maybe another girl would have brought along a basket of bite-sized cucumber sandwiches, pita bread and hummus, fancy olives, crackers, cured meats, and expensive cheeses. But not me. I picked up cheeseburgers and fries on the way over. I have no place spending my money on other people's meals, especially considering Eddie's still mad at me, but I need a win with my team. I'm hoping greasy food will do that for me.

"Well well well, what have we here?" Kenton is the first to arrive. He runs over and plops down on the blanket, quick to dig into his burger. From afar, I spot Seth and Felix strolling across the field, chatting like old friends. Felix's eyes dance with flirtation when they lock with mine. We share a delicious secret, definitely yummier than anything I could have brought to the picnic. My thoughts fill with memories of our time kissing earlier this week. I want to do it again. I'm certain he does, too, because we have plans to meet up tomorrow—just us.

What will it feel like to kiss him now that I've got vampire venom in my veins? The thought excites me way more than it should considering the guy might never talk to me again. Another kiss isn't guaranteed.

Felix purposely doesn't sit close to me, but his lingering gaze says it all. He wants to keep our relationship private between us until we can work out how to explain it to the others, especially Seth who thinks he's got some kind of say in it as our team leader. Keeping quiet is probably a good idea, what with the bomb I'm about to drop.

"Is this a bribe?" Seth questions, ever the observant one. He's the last to sit down. He skips the burger, going right for the fries instead. My smile falters into a slight grimace and that's all it takes. He knows. "What is it, Eva? Spit it out."

"You're good at reading people, you know that? You should play poker," I say. He bites into a long fry and raises his dark eyebrows. "Except don't because you'd be corrupted by the vampires."

"And how much do you know about that?" he questions, pointing the fry in my direction. The little dab of ketchup on the end reminds me of blood.

I lean back on my hands and summon my courage. My heart is racing and I'm certain my face is betraying my every thought. I've never been good at disappointing people. "I have to tell you guys a story, but I need you to let me tell it from beginning to end before you interrupt me."

I've got their full attention now. Everyone but Kenton puts down their food.

"Agreed?"

They exchanged worried glances but they each nod.

"Alright, so you know Adrian Teresi?"

"Everyone knows *of* Adrian," Seth says slowly, his hackles obviously rising. Kenton blinks at me and Felix stiffens.

"Well, I *know him* know him." Here goes nothing. "I was working for him."

"You were what?" Kenton sputters, nearly choking on his food. He coughs and I hand him a water bottle. The color has drained from Felix's face, and mistrust ignites in Seth's eyes. I get it. I'd feel the same way.

I hold up my hands in surrender. "You agreed to let me tell the story from beginning to end, so please let me."

They don't say yes, they don't say no, they don't say anything. I start from the beginning and don't hold a word of it back. I explain it all. The problems with my mom, getting nicked by that fang that night I followed them, and how the tiniest bit of venom connected me into Hugo's bloodline without my knowing. The worst of it is the blood vow with Adrian. As I tell them how it all unfolded, shame slices me up into a million guilty pieces. I'm not proud of what I did, but I am proud that I didn't follow through for Adrian in the end. I'm super lucky it wasn't a real vow and that I was able to call Adrian on his bluff. When I tell them about Hugo's toying with me and the eventual staking in the graveyard, I can tell they're impressed but don't want to show it cause they're also pissed. And I finish it all off with why Leslie Tate is so interesting to the vampires, because whatever he is, he's something that feeds on humans too, and how Cameron Scout is a two-faced twerp gunning for eternal death.

"Okay." I pick a piece of tiny lint from my shorts and stare at my knees. "I know there's a lot to unpack there. So, do you have any questions?"

I'm met with a wall of guarded expressions. Nobody utters a word.

"Umm--okay. Well, I think I need your help," I say at last. "Cameron is going to screw us over and there's still the issue of Tate being MIA and--"

"Eva," Felix stops me. "Why didn't you come to us before? I'm not happy about any of this, but mostly I'm hurt that you didn't think you could trust me."

"Yeah," Kenton adds, "we would've helped you."

"Really?" I never thought they'd understand, let alone want to help me.

"Yes," the two say in unison.

"I guess I was worried you wouldn't believe me or if you did you would hate me." I peer over at Seth who's being awfully quiet. "And what about you?"

He considers me for a long moment. "I am partially responsible here. Had I welcomed you into our team like I should have from the start, you might have felt more comfortable telling us the truth in the beginning."

I want to ask him why he didn't welcome me, but I decide to leave that conversation for later. I have a feeling it has something to do with my crush on Felix, like maybe I'm not the only one who has feelings for our mutual friend. I don't know if it's true, but if it is, it's not my place to bring it up now.

A gust of wind rustles past us and takes the weight of my secrets away with it. I smile. The back of my eyes burn with tears and I want to kick myself for that--I am not a crier--but it feels good to have people who care about me. I've been so alone. Hugo was right all those nights ago when he called me out as being lonely, but my isolation was only because I was the one not letting others in, not the other way around.

"So will you guys help me?"

"Of course we'll help you," Seth says, "we're a team. But this isn't just about Cameron and Tate. Don't you see the opportunity you have here?"

I blink at him. I'm not sure where he's going with this.

"You need to go back to Adrian and take him up on his offer. We'll figure out how to stall on the Tate stuff, but this is your opportunity to learn secrets about the vampires"--his eyes gleam ruthlessly--"and take that bastard down."

"You can't ask her to do that," Felix hisses. "It's too dangerous."

Kenton stays quiet. He's become far more pensive than usual. "It's up to you, Eva," he says finally. "I'll support either decision."

"Are you nuts?" Felix isn't thinking clearly. He's thinking about me romantically, not about me as a vampire hunter, a member of this team, and someone who does have an edge that no other hunters have.

Seth is right.

I never wanted to go back to the casino or see Adrianos Teresi again. As much as I want to hate Adrian, as much as I try to convince myself that I do, I don't. He's helped me and I've developed a bit of a soft spot for the man. It makes me weak and part of why I've wanted this whole thing to be over. But I also want to save the humans from the vampires, even if that means besting Adrian. It's not everyday I'll get a chance like this. This idea is a crazy gamble, one that might cost my life, but the payout could change everything.

My heart picks up speed and against my better judgement, I decide to take the chance. "I'm in."

. . .

I HAVEN'T SEEN my mom since she chose Hugo's money over me. My heart is broken over what's happened to her, but she's not the person she once was, and I don't think there's anything I can do to save her. Of course, there's always a chance now that I'm going back to tell Adrian we've got a deal, but I'm not going to get my hopes up again when it comes to Virginia Blackwood. The let down is too painful. Too much damage has been done. I need to move on and let it go.

My job is still on shaky ground, but luckily Eddie is a total sweetheart and is letting me keep it as long as I promise not to leave him in a lurch again. I'm thinking about my lunchtime picnic and walking to work for my next shift. It's a nice evening, the sunset is casting everything in a golden light, and it's not too far to walk from my new apartment so I choose to forgo the bus.

"It's now or never, Eva. Just do it," I mutter to myself. I slip my phone from my pocket, call the casino, and ask the customer service rep to direct me to Kelli.

"How may I assist you?" Her voice is polished indifference.

"Hey, Kelli, it's Eva Blackwood, I'm wondering if I can have a meeting with Adrian sometime tomorrow or Monday. Is he available?"

She sighs heavily. "Haven't you had enough?"

"Apparently not."

She smacks her lips. "Can't say I blame you. The man is a force of nature." I can hear her fingernails clicking against her keyboard. "I'm only giving you a meeting because he's told me I have to look out for you, and I can't disobey my master. But just so we're clear," she adds in a sing-song tone, "I still hate you."

I can't help but laugh. I don't love Kelli either, but I'm starting to warm up to her, which says a lot. "I wouldn't have it any other way, Kelli."

"Tomorrow at noon. Don't be late. There's something Adrian would like to discuss with you, too."

I wasn't expecting that, and part of me wants to take it all back and cancel. Who knows what's going to happen when I step foot in The Alabaster if Adrian wants to "discuss something" with me. I've never had a positive outcome in the past, that's for sure. But I take the appointment and end the call. I have to get my stitches out anyway, so I'll kill two birds with one stone when I go to the casino tomorrow.

I round the corner and stop short when I see who's leaning against the wall of Pops. I don't know where she's been staying or what she's been up to, and seeing her here catches me off guard. I nearly trip over my own feet.

"Evangeline." My mother rushes forward and wraps me in a tight hug. Her familiar rose scent hits me like a slap to the face. It's usually mixed with a tinge of cigarette smoke and booze from being in the casino, but today she smells fresh from a shower. I want to hug her back, want to instantly forgive and forget the events of the past month, but I can't. "I'm so sorry, Angel," she whispers against my cheek. "But I'm all better now."

I sigh and remove her arms, stepping back. "No, Mom, it's okay. You're an addict and the vampires only make it worse. That's what they do. To everyone. But you are who you are too, and I need to accept that and love you and stop holding it against you." Now for the hard part. My voice shakes. "But I'm also done trying to save you. And I can't be a big part of your life when you're like this. Sorry, Mom, but I have to save myself."

"You're right." Her eyes shine. "You're absolutely right. And I'm proud of you for saying that, I know it was hard, and I am ashamed for what I've done. But, honey, I mean it, I'm better now. I'm clean."

My heart clenches and I sidestep her. "I have to get to work."

She grabs my hand. "Please hear me out." Her voice goes low and she whispers excitedly. "Last night I was at The Alabaster and something incredible happened."

"Let me guess, you won big."

"No, that vampire guy, Adrian something, he took me up to his office and compelled me to give up gambling."

"What?" I gasp. I blink at her in confusion. Why would he help her? I backed out of the deal.

"I know! I couldn't believe it either! I have no idea why he would bother. I asked, but he wouldn't say." She smiles brightly, looking a good ten years younger. "It's not just gambling either. I'm free of any unhealthy addiction for the rest of my life. And it worked. I have absolutely no desire to do anything like that again. Just the thought of that awful casino makes me upset."

"I'm really happy for you, Mom. I don't even know what to say."

She whispers. "And what's more, he said I couldn't tell anyone this but you, but he also compelled me to be free of other vampire's compulsion. Nobody will ever be able to get in here ever again." She taps her forehead.

I'm floored. It's as if everything I thought I knew about the world was a lie—it all tilts to reveal something brand new. "He can do that?" And also, how can I get in on it? I've never heard of such a thing. The very idea of it offers the freedom I've been searching for. This is *everything*.

"I mean, I don't know, but I guess so?" She laughs and her Southern accent grows thick. "It's not like I'm dumb enough to go test it, but he was pretty confident about what he was doing."

She hugs me again and I can't help it, a million emotions overwhelm me and for the first time in ages, I let myself cry over my mother. She shushes me and pats my back, and I let her do that, too. I bury my face into her shoulder and let it all out, years of frustration and sadness, and that newfound bright spark that Adrian has given me. He gave me my mom back. Why would he do this?

I don't know what's going to happen with him tomorrow. I no longer have a deal to strike since he's already given me what I wanted. I will need to think of something else he'll believe, some other reason why I would agree to be his little spy. But I also want to thank him, and maybe that's the craziest part of this whole messed up situation. Never in my life did I think I would be thanking a vampire, but Mom always said never say never, and it turns out she was right.

He *saved* her.

He didn't have to do that, and yet he did. For me.

There's got to be a reason besides the kindness of his heart. Adrian's heart doesn't even beat. He kills. He lives his eternal life––or death––from drinking our blood. He runs the city and deals in addiction and plays dangerous games with his ruthless queen. No, this move with my mother is a play for something bigger, and I intend to find out his endgame before it's too late.

The next day, I march into The Alabaster Heart at exactly twelve-noon, with my head held high, and what I hope is a brilliant plan up my sleeve–– one that had better work or we're all dead.

A Letter From The Author

Dear Reader,

Would you like to read the blood vow kissing scene from Adrian's point of view? You can get that bonus chapter and other fun goodies by joining my Facebook reader group called "Nina's Reading Party". Thank you for taking a chance on *Blood Casino*. I've been dreaming of this world for over three years, so to finally have it in your hands feels a bit surreal. If you liked it, please leave a quick written review on Amazon and Goodreads, and please tell your friends. Word of mouth is to an indie author, what blood is to a vampire—seriously, I can't do this without you.

Much Love,
Nina Walker

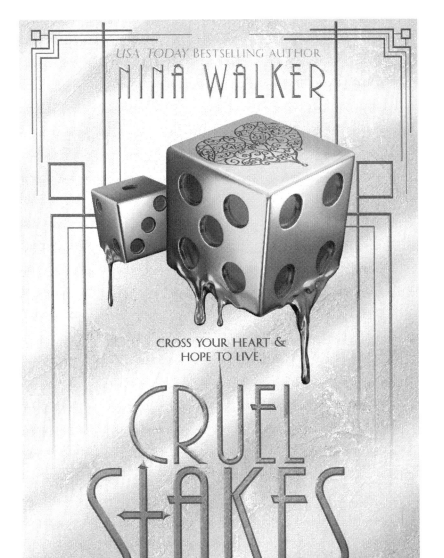

USA TODAY BESTSELLING AUTHOR

NINA WALKER

CROSS YOUR HEART &
HOPE TO LIVE.

CRUEL
STAKES

VAMPIRES & VICES, NO. 2

To the ones who saved me.

One

ADRIAN

I swirl the wine glass until the blood licks the edges. Then I drink, trying to ignore the taste and force my mind somewhere else. As always, it's impossible. The blood fills my mouth with delicious sensations, and I automatically savor every drop. My fangs burst forward as I swallow, aching for more. My mind goes blissfully numb.

My thoughts travel back to my childhood until I lock on a safe memory--one of the many times I devoured a pomegranate. Every autumn they would come back in season, and I would break them open to gorge on the seeds like they were candy. I cling to that thought as I drink from the wine glass, eyes closed, imagining the blood is the same as that tangy-sweet fruit I once loved so much. The plump crimson seeds would burst, and the juice would run down my cheeks and neck, often staining my tunic or my chest.

In most of my early childhood memories us boys only wore clothing when it was cold. Nakedness was normal for the Hellenes--the Greeks. Another reminder that so much has changed since those far off days of youth. Nakedness has come and gone out of style over the centuries, same as nearly everything else. With every resurgence fads will slightly change, molded to fit the current generations' tastes, until they eventually no longer resemble the original.

But the pomegranates still grow in Greece.

The buildings corroded, the treasures were stolen by new empires, the culture changed, the language evolved, and even my devout mother's religion became nothing but myths for twisting into cautionary tales--but the pomegranates stayed.

I finish off the glass and set it down, watching the last beads of blood slide into a little pool at the bottom. I eye it, reminded of a time when I'd have licked the glass clean. There was also a time when I'd have thrown the full glass and shattered it in a fit of rage, going hungry as the blood grew cold. That is, when I drank from a glass at all. Things also used to be entirely different between the vampires and humans. We used to take their lives freely, killing with almost every meal. We're much more civilized these days . . . well, mostly more civilized.

For now, I find myself settled somewhere between self-loathing of who I've become and bitter acceptance of everything I've lost.

Blood will always be my tormentor as it is my liberator.

I will always crave it and need it, like an addict bargaining for his next fix. It will always bind me to an afterlife I did not choose and to a woman I hate. Most vampires love their makers, but how could I love Brisa when she took away my agency and made me immortally thirsty against my will? She may claim to love me, I may be one of her eldest sons, but I'm still a single root in her tree, a lone bee in her nest, and a thin thread in her rope.

I close my eyes for another moment, gathering my thoughts as the fog clears, then open my computer and pull up the video conferencing software. It's a good thing Brisa's paranoid and refuses to leave France, because if she were here to question me about Hugo's death, she'd probably sense the truth.

And the last thing the vampire queen needs to know is the truth.

The screen brightens and there she is, the creature who followed me home from The Lyceum after another day of studying at the feet of master philosophers all those lifetimes ago. She'd sunk her teeth into me and stolen my mortality as well as a bright future among my peers. I'd been in agony, begging for my life, when she'd buried me and left me to my own devices three nights later. I crawled from the grave in a wave of bloodthirst and made my way back home. I was lucky the sunrise didn't get me. Or maybe not, because the deaths that followed have haunted me for centuries.

I had killed my own family––ripping the lives from my wife and our unborn child. And I've never forgiven myself or Brisa since.

Pushing those thoughts aside, I smile warmly at her now. "Hello, Mother. You look stunning."

And she does, she always does. So that's not a lie. But I will lie to her today, as I learned how to do quickly under her tutelage. I'm still not able to refuse her commands outright. However, lying is a skill I've developed as one would slowly introduce poison to their bloodstream in order to become immune. It was painful, slow and terrible, but it was well worth it. Now there's little she can do to control me unless it's an outright command.

"Do you find it strange that you call me mother considering we've been lovers?" she asks, batting her eyelashes.

My stomach hardens. I was her lover, at first, because I was lost to the bloodlust as many new vampires are. She came to me in my weakest moment and offered me answers and a warm bed. When the years passed and I was able to rise above the bloody haze of youth, my hatred for her grew like an infection, and then I was only her lover because I didn't want her to question my loyalty. She would've killed me if she thought I was a threat. I've seen her do it countless times. And I didn't want to die until I could enact my revenge for what she did to me.

Even to this day, if she calls me to her bed, I will go. And I will hate her even more.

"I will stop calling you mother if you wish." I laugh, playing her game, and actually I would like nothing better. She commanded me to call her mother when she first found me, and I've had no choice but to comply ever since. My real mother was nothing like Brisa. She was kind and warm and spirited. And even though her bones are dust, I often think of her and what could have been.

And then I think of all those I killed, and force my mind blank.

"Hmm," Brisa muses, "let's keep "mother" for now. And speaking of, when are you going to visit me?" She smirks at the screen and raises an eyebrow. "I do miss you, darling."

I've been in New Orleans for a handful of decades, and while part of me misses traveling, I've already seen all there is to see on this earth while being limited to darkness. As for now, I rather enjoy running the businesses. It gives me something purposeful to do. And as much as some humans hate it––Evangeline comes to mind––our setup protects the humans. If we didn't have willing donors, we would be forced to go back to murdering for our food. We'd be relegated back to the shadows, hiding among the fringes of society, and most vampires would never stand for that. We've gotten a taste of this new way of living and we like the control. Take it away and there would be war, chaos, and endless bloodshed.

And we absolutely can't bite a human and leave them alive with our venom running through their veins. It makes them far too dangerous to our kind, ruthless hunters who can track our movements and fight us with nearly equal strength. Again, Eva comes to mind.

"Adrian!" Brisa cuts off my thoughts. She turns to face the camera head-on and glares. "Are you paying attention, or are you wasting my time?"

"My apologies." I'm quick to recover. "As soon as you order me back to France, of course I will come, but for now I am rather busy here. I think you'd like modern day New Orleans. Are you sure you can't come visit me instead?"

I know she'll refuse, but I'd love to get her into a position of vulnerability. She is the queen because she is the head of the remaining vampiric bloodlines. She's worked hard to ensure there are no vampires left to challenge her, and her own maker is long dead. She's placed strong and loyal princes around her--always sons--but none of us would be able to assume the position of king unless the entire family was gone, save for one.

That will never happen.

And there are no princesses to angle for queen. Brisa has never confessed why she doesn't turn women, but I know it's because she doesn't want anyone to rival her beauty and power. That, and she doesn't sleep with women, so she can't use them up the way she does her princes.

"You know I can't travel anymore," she sighs dramatically. "I did this to myself."

And that's true.

"But at least my new home is beautiful." She shifts the camera to reveal a room gilded in gold, and my mouth falls open--something that hasn't happened in ages. I've been around so long that I can't remember the last time I was surprised, but this is truly unexpected. "Isn't it amazing?" she coos. "The French people were finally generous enough to hand over my favorite city." Her eyes gleam, and she leans forward, her voice lowering. "It belongs to us now."

City.

I recognize exactly where she is--the famous city of Versailles. The very same one that King Louis XIV built and was named the capital of the country for years. I always believed in my maker's ability to get her way but even I'll admit I didn't think she'd manage this one.

But she did.

She's set up in the palace and, if she's taken over the city, then that means she has achieved a lifelong goal of hers: to compel enough of the governmental officials in France, forcing them to turn over France's prized jewel. This is something she's been trying to accomplish since well before we first came out of hiding, but the French people have been better at eluding us compared to many of the others.

"*You* are amazing," I respond coolly. "Honestly, Mother, I am in awe of you."

Her weakness is her own vanity.

"Yes, yes." Her face relaxes. "Now, what was it you wished to speak to me about?"

This is it. Although she may already know. Makers can sense these things through the blood bonds, but with an ocean between them, it's a bit diluted.

"Hugo is dead."

Her face stills, turning to stone. "How did it happen?" she finally asks. Her voice is eerily quiet, a sign of the rage behind her calm exterior.

So she didn't know. That's interesting—and promising. Now it's time to tell her the story I've created to protect Eva. The human girl killed Hugo exactly as I had orchestrated, and I'd feel bad about how I manipulated her if she hadn't come asking for trouble.

"You told him that if he caught my fledgling in a lie, then he could have her for himself," I say, narrowing my eyes.

She laughs. "That's right. I almost forgot about that." I dig my fingers into my chair to keep from outright glaring because I highly doubt that's true. The woman never forgets anything. "And he succeeded?" Her eyes thin into knowing slits. "Did you bring a hunter into your own home?"

"The girl was foolish and was trying to get in with both groups. The hunters ambushed us in the cemetery and killed Hugo. They almost got me too." My voice grows angry, "I will avenge my brother, of this I swear."

She doesn't say anything for a moment, and the tiny flame of worry ignites in my chest. If she can sense the inferno, then I'm already dead. "And what of the girl? Please tell me she's dead too."

"She's not." I shrug as if I couldn't care less about Eva either way. "She wishes to be freed and to live out her life as a human." I smirk. "I think we scared her away, Mother." I don't say anything more. Sometimes it's imperative to know when to stop and this is one of those moments.

Brisa considers this, and for a moment I'm certain she's going to order me to kill Eva. I'd have no choice. "Keep her as your prodigy," she says at last. "We need to watch her closely, but I have a feeling she may be of more use to us. Anyone who has the guts to play both sides is someone I want to entertain."

"You do enjoy playing games with human lives."

"Always." She winks.

Keeping Eva close is the opposite of what I had planned, but at least I don't have to kill her yet. I nod readily, my anxiety uncoiling like a spring.

"Are you absolutely sure those were hunters who killed Hugo?" she questions.

"Of course." The lie sounds a little shaky, and I grind my foot into the floor. I'm losing my touch, I can't let that happen, especially not over a ridiculous human. "Could they have been something else?"

We both know what that something else is I'm referring to. Brisa never likes to talk about them, she says it gives them power. I find that a foolish approach.

"I don't know." Her lips thin. "But Hugo isn't the only prince to have been murdered in the last few weeks."

This is news.

This is news that could change *everything*.

Brisa knows it. I know it. And we don't have to say anything more about it. If I were to question her further, she might suspect me. There are normally seven princes––one for each continent––but Brisa had eight when she sent Hugo and I to North America. He should've stayed in Mexico City as we planned, but a few years ago he decided he wanted to be in New Orleans just to spite me. So if he's gone, and at least one other too, then there can't be more than six of us left. I'd kill to know who else is gone, but I want to live so I don't ask.

"Watch your back, Adrianos," she offers before ending the call abruptly.

I close the computer, my mind whirling with possibility. "You'd better watch your back as well, *Mother*," I whisper to the dark. Then I pick up the phone and instruct Kelli to set up a meeting with Evangeline.

Two

One thing I've learned in my nineteen years--vampires are excellent lie detectors. Their heightened senses allow them to smell when adrenaline enters the bloodstream. They can hear when a heart beats faster, and even detect the slightest change in a human's voice or mannerisms. Lying to one is about the most ridiculous thing a human can do, which is all I can think about as I ride the elevator up to Adrian's office prepared to lie my butt off. I've got to be either the bravest or the dumbest person I know. And I'm leaning toward the latter, but hey, nobody's perfect.

I was done with him--I never had to come back here ever again.

And that's the truth. Adrian and I had parted ways. I'd gotten what I wanted, my mother was free of her addictions, and Adrian had no hold over me anymore. I'd figured out that the blood vow was a complete lie, so there was no obligation for me to hold up my end of the deal, and Adrian wasn't going to make me. Hugo was dead, which was enough to make him happy and forget all about me. Plus, he was going to cover for me with Queen Brisa. It was all tidied away, and that was supposed to be the end of it.

So then why am I surrounded by the familiar reflective gold mirrors of his elevator, heading up to meet with him again? Because like I said, I'm an idiot. A brave idiot, but still an idiot. I never should've let Seth convince me to do this, but he knows as well as I that I want to help the hunters--even to my own detriment. I'm pretty sure I am about to regret that entire ideology pretty soon.

I gaze up at the ceiling, and a slightly distorted version of my face reflects back at me. I'm wearing a simple, red tank top and black pants with a wooden stake strapped under my pant leg just above the ankle. Adrian is probably going to freak if he notices it, and he will notice. He always does. Or maybe he doesn't actually sense the stakes I wear, maybe the man can read me like a book and knows I'm unlikely to go anywhere without one.

I groan and lean back into the corner, biting my bottom lip. I really shouldn't keep taking these chances. Adrian is a ruthless killer, a vampire prince with centuries of experience in staying alive and killing others to do it. No way am I going to keep getting away with lying to someone like that. He'll know better. He'll figure out that I am here as a double agent and he'll kill me without hesitation. Sure, I can fight--I've been working hard in training and this venom from Hugo has enhanced my senses--but I'm still outmatched by Mr. Adrianos "Runs the City" Teresi, aka Adrian.

I reach out toward the red button, ready to turn this elevator around and never look back.

Too late--the elevator dings, and the doors slide open as if to mock me.

I slow my breathing, square my shoulders, and step into Adrian's office.

Nothing has changed. It's still polished oak and professional and not welcoming for someone like me. I shouldn't have come the first time, and I shouldn't be here now. This is a lion's den. Actually, Adrian is less of a lion and more of a snake considering what he does with his mouth. *Don't think about what he does with his mouth.*

I inhale--nice and slow--willing my heart to slow the heck down. He can't know I'm here to lie. *He can't know, he can't know, he can't know--* unless he already does.

"It's my birthday today," I say, making sure my voice has the snarky quality I reserve specially for him. "Last night I went to bed as a salty eighteen-year-old, and today I woke up a salty nineteen."

And that's true. Maybe if I sprinkle in truth with the lies he'll believe every word.

But probably not.

The man is sitting at his desk, his face unreadable and his eyes glued to his computer. He doesn't acknowledge me. The elevator doors close. I stand there, afraid to move.

Finally, he looks up, those glacial eyes locking with mine, and does the last thing I expect. He smiles. It's such a rarity, I'm momentarily stunned. He's already beautiful considering the vampire DNA enhanced those attractive Greek features, so it's not my fault that I'm staring because humans are hardwired to be attracted to vampires. Not. My. Fault. He's still a sucker and a murderer, and I'll continue to hate him . . . even if he did save my mother.

"Well, you never claimed to be sweet," he says at last.

For a moment I forget what I said about being salty, but it comes back to me, and my cheeks warm. "True." I shake myself from whatever trance I'm under and sit down in the chair across from him. "You know, it amazes me that in this messed up vampire world there are still people who celebrate their birth. Do you know some humans celebrate their entire birthday month like it's some kind of holiday? I can't even stomach thinking about growing older for a single day, let alone for all of September."

He leans back and steeples his fingers together. "This world has been messy long before vampires came out to play. Are you sure this"––he pauses for a moment, considering–– "tantrum isn't because of your personality?"

I'm not sure if he's joking using that word "tantrum" but maybe I am being childish. Is he joking? I'm not even angry about it, though, and against my better judgement, I laugh. "True that. Those astrology-obsessed people out there would say my saltiness is typical for a virgo."

"Do you know how much astrology has changed over the years, Angel? You shouldn't put too much stock into something as pliable as astrology."

Don't let Ayla hear you say that. My bestie loves that stuff. To her, the stars are forever and they make the rules.

"Trust me, I'm not. I already know I'm feeling extra salty today because I'm one year closer to my prefrontal cortex developing and my brain becoming vampire playdough."

He laughs, and something loosens in my chest. This is weird. This banter feels like normal interaction between friends, or maybe even flirting. Part of me wants to soften into it, but the smarter part of me listens to the inner-alarm bells: danger, danger, danger.

Adrian is not *Adrian*.

Adrian is *Adrianos Teresi*––vampire prince and ruthless killer. End of story.

"Do you know what amazes me? That you're still coming into my casino with stakes strapped to your ankle." He stands in one fluid movement.

"Are you going to take it from me?" I don't move. Besides, I expected this.

He circles, coming up behind me, and whispers low in my ear. "No, you keep it." And then he straightens and is back into his chair before I can blink. I'm not sure what to do with this information, but him letting me keep it is unsettling. He's never done that before.

Actually, that's not true. He was happy to let me keep it when he wanted me to kill Hugo for him. I'm still mad about being used like that, but I guess we're even considering what he did for my mother.

"So what did you want to talk to me about?" I ask. When I called yesterday to set up this meeting, Kelli had said Adrian wanted to speak with me as well. I'd be lying if I said that hadn't piqued my interest.

"Better question is what did you want to talk to me about?" He's staring. I don't know what to do with a staring Adrian. I wasn't planning on this kind of attention from a man who's always been so aloof with me.

But I know what I have to do, even if I'm terrified to do it. "Nope, I asked you first."

He opens his drawer and pulls out a black box. "I got you a birthday present."

Of all things he could've done right now, this one surprises me the most. My mouth pops open. What the heck? He knew it was my birthday? He's giving me a present? What alternate timeline did I step into, because I'm pretty sure this can't be my life?

"I don't know what to say except what have you done with the real Adrianos Teresi? Are you his long lost twin or something?"

He tosses the box at me with an annoyed sigh. "Just open it."

"Well, there's the vampire I know and hate."

"At your service." He chuckles under his breath and my stomach tightens.

The gift is in what looks like a jewelry box, so that's what I'm expecting when I open it. Nope. Not jewelry. "Are you kidding me right now?" I pull out a set of car keys and turn them over in my hands. They're heavy, and when I read the Porsche label, I drop them on the desk with a metallic clatter. "No, no freaking way. I can't accept this."

He has the audacity to look offended. "You can and you will. It's waiting for you in the garage. You need a car, don't you? I figured this would be a suitable gift."

"Okay, first of all, you getting me a gift at all is beyond weird, but second of all, this is way too extravagant. People are going to ask where I got it."

Not to mention, a gift from a vampire has to be a trick, especially one this nice.

"Are you worried about your hunters? Tell them you won it." His eyes are unreadable. "That's not so unbelievable."

"Uh, yes it is. People don't really win cars, Adrian. They give away their email addresses hoping to win cars and then spend an eternity unsubscribing from the same scammy dealerships." I can't believe I'm doing this, but I plop the keys back in the box and slide them across the desk. "I'm serious. Forget the fact that a Porsche is way too nice for a girl like me; I'd never be able to make up a story that people would believe."

His eyes darken. "It is *not* too nice for you, so I don't ever want to hear you say that again."

I snort. I don't know how to take that.

Adrian eyes the box for a moment. "Fine. How about I play you for it? We are in a casino after all." He opens his desk drawer again and produces a set of shiny dice. They look like silver, but they can't be since vampires are allergic to it. The metal doesn't kill them, but it weakens them. There's no silver in this entire place, save for the little crucifix under my shirt. The dice must be made from a different kind of metal since he's handling them easily. They shine under the warm lights with undertones of gold.

"We'll play it craps style. You roll the dice," he says, "if it's a seven or eleven, you win, if it's a two, three, or twelve, then I win. And if it's something else, you keep rolling."

"I already know you have telekinesis, so nice try, but no."

He reaches out and cups my hand in his cold ones. A pulse of electricity shoots up my spine, and my senses grow to double. For a moment, my mind goes so sharp it almost hurts, but Adrian doesn't seem to notice a thing. "I promise I won't cheat," he whispers. When he releases my hand, the dice are resting in my palm.

"But you have the advantage," I protest, already finding myself giving in to him. "You have three numbers to win on, and I only have two."

"Ah, but statistically, seven is the most common number rolled between two dice." He winks. "And besides, you know the house has to keep some advantage. That's the way gambling works, but it doesn't mean you can't win."

Well, the fact that vampires are running this place is already advantageous enough, but I don't say that. He's not going to let this go, and as much as I hate to admit this, I'm intrigued. And part of me, surely the foolish part, the part that grew up poor, the part that never had anything nice for herself, the part that desperately wants to feel loved and worthy and maybe even wealthy--really wants that car.

"Okay," I whisper, and then I roll the dice.

Three

⟅⟆

A three and a five. Nobody wins.

"Again," he says.

I repeat the process and we get another roll where nobody wins, but this time it's a six. I've been dancing around a winning roll, and despite my better judgement, I'm ready to beat him. *No.* No, I'm not. I'm not ready to beat him. I know what I want but I also know what I should want, and they're two very different things. I close my eyes for a second, unable to untangle my thoughts, then shake them away and blow on the dice for good luck.

I roll.

They clink across the desk, landing on two ones--snake eyes. Adrian wins.

Or maybe we both do . . .

He hands me the black box and says, "I don't want to hear another word about it."

I want the car--I don't want the car--I'm mixed up and wouldn't even know what to say about it. Everything is brighter, somehow. Impossibly bright, like the sun is blasting through those tinted windows. I blink rapidly. Maybe I should leave.

"Now, what was it that you wanted to talk to me about?" he questions.

This is the fun part. Not.

"I want to be your fledgling." I swallow hard. "For real this time."

He freezes, a bewildered expression crossing his face, and I think maybe I'm the one to surprise him this time. His eyes narrow into two blue orbs--

again, snake eyes. "You're a vampire hunter. Don't forget that I know what you are. Why would I trust you with this request?"

I sit up taller. "Because Cameron was right."

"Cameron?" He says it like the name means little to him.

"Yes, Cameron. You know, Kelli's prodigy, the one who is also a hunter?"

"Of course I know who he is, but what does he have to do with you?" His tone goes sour.

Maybe he doesn't like Cameron, which is interesting considering he's in line to join the family tree. I tuck that information away for later. "He showed me something that changed everything." I boldly recite the words I'd rehearsed at home about fifty times this morning. "I know there are some kind of energy demons out there who are your enemies, and that's why you wanted me to get information about Leslie Tate. He's one of them. I thought I was working for the good guys when I joined the hunters, but I realize now that's not true. Cameron was right. If I don't join you, then eventually I'll end up dead. I'd rather have immortality than become some demon's meal."

Lies. Lies. Lies.

And in all honesty, learning about these demonish energy stealers only made me want to protect humans even more, but Adrian doesn't have to know that. He stands again and saunters over to peer out his window. Since windows at the Alabaster Heart are heavily tinted and bulletproof, he can see the sun without being burned by it. I wonder how many years he lived in the dark and what that must have been like for him. I couldn't do it, myself. The sun means too much to me. I watch him as he looks down on the Mississippi river and let myself drink him in. He's tall and handsome and tortured. And in his suit, he almost looks human.

Not for the first time, I wish he was.

"Come here, please," he says softly.

I don't know if I've ever heard that word from his mouth, but if he's going to believe that I want him to one day become my maker, then I'd better lose the attitude and start doing what he asks. Damn, I should've thought this one through more. Attitude is sort of my calling card. And now I have to suck up to a blood sucker? I can't think of anything worse.

But I go stand at his side.

Between the blinking of my eyes, he's beside me one second and in front of me the next. My back presses to the warm window as his cold hand grips my throat. It's not so tight that he's strangling me, but it's a promise of what's to come if I don't get the next few moments right.

"You're a terrible liar," he says, his voice low and dangerous. "The last thing you want to become is like me." He's so close now, glaring down at me, his fangs extending.

"That's not true," I hiss. But I know he's already won.

"Really?" He nods toward my leg. "Then why are you still carrying a stake with you?"

My mind races for an answer. "Because this building houses a vampire coven, and I'm not a complete idiot."

"That's debatable." He shakes his head. "You're here to double cross me."

I don't know what to do. He's figured me out in about point-two seconds flat, and now he's going to kill me. My heart pounds, and my hands clench and unclench. I want to run, but there's nowhere to go. His hand tightens, and my breath goes shallow. I automatically reach up and grab onto his wrists, trying to get free. It does nothing.

"You saved my mother," I whisper-hiss. "You were the only one who would've done that for me. And after everything, I think maybe vampires aren't so bad after all."

"Vampires aren't bad after all?" He laughs but doesn't release me. My air supply is dwindling fast. "Like I said, you're a terrible liar."

"Why don't we roll the dice? If I win, you let me stay as your prodigy, and if you win, I'll leave you alone," I squeak out in little bursts.

He frees me, and my knees weaken. I lean back against the window for support and gulp in big breaths of the overly conditioned air. He's lightning fast, returning for the dice and dropping them at my feet. "You keep those. Take them with your car."

"You don't want to roll dice?"

"I am tired of games," he snaps. "You need to leave now."

I jut my hip and raise an eyebrow. "What about being your prodigy?"

He slinks into his desk chair. "Fine, Angel. I'll take you up on whatever this foolish venture of yours is, but don't think I believe this will end well for you."

"So--"

"You can be my fledgling."

"Thank you." I shoot him a winning smile, but it doesn't faze him one bit.

"Don't thank me, yet. I haven't turned you into my prodigy, and I doubt I ever will." His fangs have receded into his gums when he smiles grimly back at me. I have no idea what he's thinking, and I'd give my right leg to be able to crawl into that brain of his and know every last thought. "But we will continue this charade and see where it leads us."

"I won't let you down," I say cheerily, like a girl scout who made her biggest sale. Quite frankly, it's no wonder he's already called me out. We both know this is a farce, right? And if that's the case, his agreement should scare the snot out of me. "So, you'll let me know what I'm supposed to do next, right? Like, is there some kind of initiation or a test or something?" This right here is information I'm dying to take back to my hunter team. He probably knows that.

"Kelli will get in touch soon. And, Angel, this means you're still spying on Tate for me."

"When he gets back." I nod, because what else can I say at this point?

"Yes. And he will be back, I'm sure of it. The man wants to see me dead and he can't very well do that without his hunters, now can he? In the meantime, I need you to do something else for me as well."

My heartbeat speeds up, which I'm certain he can hear. "Anything," I say brightly. Okay, I'm totally a *lying* girl scout because I'm not willing to do anything. In fact, I'm willing to do very little for vampires, even sexy ones with arctic eyes and golden wavy hair. Even ones who saved my own mother.

"Lose your virginity."

He speaks of my virginity like it's an item on a checklist.

"Excuse me?" My cheeks prickle, and my senses jump up again. I'm keenly aware of everything in this room, my own embarrassment most of all.

He holds my gaze and tilts his head slightly. "You heard me, Angel. I can't have you around my coven with your blood smelling like that, it's too . . . distracting."

"Uhhh--" My face reddens. "Sorry, but I'm not going to lose my virginity until I'm ready."

He tries to look surprised, but mostly he just looks smug. "Oh, but you said you'd do anything."

"Yeah, but--"

"Then make yourself ready and take care of it." He sweeps his hand toward me in a leave-me-alone-you-peon motion. I glare at him, but I do what he says and get into the elevator. What else can I do? The doors close, and I find myself looking up again at my reflection.

Absolutely nothing about this meeting went as planned, but at least I made it out alive.

Four

Kelli meets me in the hotel lobby, and considering her puckered lips and sour gaze, I realize I'm not out of the woods quite yet.

"You know, you'd be gorgeous if you didn't glare all the time," I say, half-snarky and half-honest. She's absolutely stunning, smiling or not, but everytime I'm around her she's as angry as a cat in water––and that anger is usually directed toward me.

"Who says I care about being pretty?" she barks at me. Okay, maybe she's an angry dog––a possessive one, pissed that her master has allowed me to infiltrate her territory. "Or that a smile is a prerequisite."

"Sorry, that was rude of me to say." I give her an apologetic smile. "And actually, I like where you're going with that. Makes sense to me. Honestly, Kelli, I think you're a woman after my own heart. We could be friends."

"Ew." She rolls her eyes. "Come on then, let's go get your birthday present."

I follow her through the casino to the parking garage, my mind whirling with everything I've gotten myself into. Is the dice game simply that—a game? Did Adrian call Kelli while I was taking the elevator down from his office? Part of me is disappointed that Adrian isn't showing me the car himself, but that's a ridiculous thing to be disappointed about.

The vampire's parking garage isn't the same one that's open to the public for the hotel and casino guests. First of all, it's the nicest parking garage I've ever seen. The walls are painted a gleaming white and the ceilings and floor are matte black tile. There's gray carpet along the edges, and it even smells clean and welcoming. The lighting is terribly dim, but my eyes adjust far quicker than they used to—a side effect of Hugo's venom. As I take in the rows and rows and *rows* of collectable cars, I try not to salivate. They're in all colors and sizes, from SUVs to race cars to muscle cars and everything in between. Even a whole bunch of pretty motorcycles are mixed in and I wonder what it would be like to drive one. I've never even ridden on one before, but I'd love the chance.

"This way," Kelli nods toward the back of the garage, "and stay close to me. We don't need a repeat of what happened in the lobby."

She's referring to one of Hugo's baby prodigies smelling the wound inflicted on me by the mob. The vamp had tried to eat me.

"I don't plan on ever coming here with an open wound again," I say.

And it's not like people don't bleed in the casino all the time. They do. But apparently my virgin blood mixed with the tiniest amount of that vampire venom from my first kill had made me irresistible to Hugo's bloodline. Now that he's dead, they're beholden to Brisa, and I wonder what she'd do if she found out about me.

I can only imagine that bloodlust has grown considering how long Hugo had his fangs in me that night he tried to turn me. The memory slices like a knife and I shiver. I hate to think of how close I came to becoming one of these monsters. And now, here I am, signing up to be Adrian's fledgling. What was I thinking? I'm still not sure how I'm going to get out of it in the end, but I have to lock that thought away or else I'm going to lose my nerve.

Kelli looks at me sidelong. "Honey, if I were a bee, then you would be the sweetest flower in the middle of spring." She says it like it's the most annoying thing on earth.

"Ah, thank you," I bat my eyelashes, "nobody's ever called me a flower before."

"Don't flatter yourself," she grumbles, "let me think of a better analogy."

"Don't worry." I touch her arm. "I liked that one."

Her skin is ice cold, reminding me of when Adrian took my hand, and also reminding me that I could be exactly like them soon if I'm not careful. She brushes me off, ending the conversation. Maybe she can't think of a better analogy, or maybe she's warming up to me.

I laugh to myself because the thought of a sucker getting warm is ludicrous.

"What's so funny?"

"Nothing."

"I swear, I'm going to kill Adrian," she grumbles, but I know she doesn't mean it. Her love of her master is evident. I don't detect jealousy from her, only annoyance that she has to keep dealing with me. Hey, maybe even for an eternity.

We approach a line of cars at the back of the garage, and I can't help but gawk. They're definitely the nicest ones down here. I can't say for sure how I know that they're the best of the lot, but I can just tell by looking at them—they scream money.

Old money.

Big money.

Blood money.

"I guess congratulations are in order," she sighs. "Honestly, I don't know how you pulled this off, but I have to hand it to you. You've got Adrian wrapped around your finger."

"Uhhh, what?" I frown at her. "I didn't do anything, and I certainly never asked for a car. I refused it, if you must know, but he——"

"That's for you," she cuts me off and points to a gorgeous black sports car. I blink in surprise. I don't know what I was expecting, especially considering everything else down here, but it certainly wasn't this. The car is beyond beautiful and has to be wildly expensive. It's little and curvy and sexy as hell. I've never thought of cars as sexy before but I've been corrected in my ways. I stare at it, suddenly caring very much about this piece of machinery. "You did something. Let's see . . . Hugo's dead, and the story is that hunters killed him." Kelli looks at me sidelong. "Which is quite interesting considering your background."

"I can't——"

She holds up her hand. "Don't say anything. It's better that I don't know the details." She runs the tips of her fingers across the shiny finish of the car. "This is a brand new Porsche 911 Carrera 4." She may as well be speaking Russian. "Which is completely lost on you, isn't it?"

I nod, but this time I grin. "I know less about cars than I know about astrophysics."

"What do you know about astrophysics?"

"Absolutely nothing."

Her lips quirk. I don't know why, but I want her to like me, and I'd love to make her laugh. It doesn't really make sense since she's the enemy, but I can't help but tease her. "Well, don't get too excited. This is not even close to being the nicest car Adrian owns," she continues, nodding toward the other cars in the row, "but it's still way too nice for someone who doesn't appreciate cars."

I'm starting to enjoy our banter far too much. "Oh, honey, I can appreciate this one." I wink. I click the unlock button on the key fob, open the driver's door, and climb inside. The maroon interior leather smells new and expensive. It kind of reminds me of the inside of a wallet.

"He didn't really give this to you." Kelli leans in through the open door, her ghostly face inches from mine. Her movements are fast and fluid and vampiric in a way I'll never get used to. "Adrian's name is on the title, and it's insured under his policy, so don't think you can go sell it." As if I would! Okay, maybe I would if I really needed to because this is way too expensive and completely unnecessary. Before I can utter a response, she slams the door in my face and dashes off.

"Well, that went well," I mutter to the steering wheel.

I wait there for a while, trying to figure out my next step. Should I go back upstairs and refuse to take something so fancy and ask for something more normal? Should I demand Adrian put the car in my name since it's a gift and I don't want him to lord it over me later? But no, I can't bring myself to do either, because every second I sit down here alone is another second a vampire could sniff me out and decide I'd make a great lunch.

I'll have to deal with whatever strings come attached to this beauty later.

I turn it on, and the engine is so quiet and smooth that I almost don't believe I'm doing this right. I carefully drive from the dark underground parking garage and out into bright sunlight. The second that warmth brushes my face I roll the windows down and breathe in deeply. The sun feels better than it ever has, and the idea that I could lose it leaves me cold. I can't let them turn me. I shouldn't have made another deal with Adrian. The guys will kill me if they find out what I'm doing. I know Seth is my leader and he wants me to work with Adrian, but we never talked about it going this far. He doesn't know what I've asked.

And if Felix finds out––I don't want to know what he'd do.

The day is getting away from me, but I think back to everything so far. I feel old, but I know I'm not. Nineteen is nothing, but it's also everything. I started the day with a lovely breakfast with my mom at our favorite diner, and it was amazing. I have her back, and I still haven't processed it. Everytime I think of her actually being *her*, tears burn my vision.

Even now.

I wipe them away. I have to drive over to Felix and Seth's house. It's near the Tulane campus which is only a few miles up from the casino. Unfortunately, the drive through New Orleans is lovely but doesn't provide enough time to think of a plausible explanation for why I'm driving a Porsche. I've already forgotten what model Kelli said it is, so I'll just have to call it The Porsche.

I end up parking it down the road a little so I can walk over to Felix's place and allow the guys to assume I took the city bus here. I'm still not sure what Felix has in mind for my birthday date, but I'm super excited. We haven't had one-on-one time all week, and I need this. I'm still unsure if we're a real couple, though, considering we're hiding our relationship from

Seth. That bothers me, but I agree with Felix. It's a necessity. Seth is our team leader and insists that dating between teammates should be off limits. And normally I'd agree with him, but Seth doesn't understand my heart or my history with Felix. I've been wanting this forever, and now that Felix finally wants it too, nothing is going to stop us.

I smile to myself. This secret can be sexy and fun if we let it. We'll tell everyone eventually, but for now, it's safer to keep it between the two of us. I knock on the door, and Felix opens it, takes my hand, and pulls me inside with a conspiratorial smile.

Five

"Surprise!" A chorus of voices crash over me, and I step back, momentarily stunned. Streamers in various shades of blue are ribboned across the tiny living room and helium balloons float in bunches.

I take it all in with a laugh. "Are you kidding me? You planned a surprise party?" I've never had one before.

Felix wraps me in a hug and whispers, "Happy birthday. There's someone here to see you." Then he turns me around and standing there in a blue party dress that matches her vibrant curly hair is none other than my best friend in the whole wide world.

"Ayla!" I scream, launching myself at her. I practically tackle her with my hug, and she hugs me back just as tight. "Oh my gosh, I've missed you so much," I gush. The last month has been the longest we've ever been apart since she up and moved on me to become a college girl.

"You have no idea," she replies in a tone that says *we need to talk*.

There are other people at this surprise party, like Seth and Kenton, my two new roommates, and a handful of people I have yet to meet who I'm guessing often come over to this house to hang out with their college friends. Some of these guys are built like they're definitely on the lacrosse team, too. But none of them really matter to me right now, not even Felix. All I want to do is talk with Ayla. Something is going on with my girl, and I have to know what it is.

"Later," she whispers, sensing exactly what I'm thinking. "Please, let's try to have fun."

And with that request, I do as she asks over the next couple of hours. Felix has set up a couple of drinking games, karaoke, and even got one of those massive sheet cakes from Costco. I don't drink and neither does my team, but I play along with everything else and end up having a great time. When they sing to me, I want to simultaneously crawl into a hole and hug everyone. After things settle down and I've met all the new people, Ayla and I finally get a chance to talk. I'm worried she's going to call me out on the sexual tension between me and her brother, and I feel bad keeping a secret from her. But maybe she hasn't sensed anything? Felix and I stayed apart most of the evening and Ayla took credit for the party. And maybe it really was all her idea, but I have a feeling that's not entirely true.

Arm in arm, we go up to Felix's room. It feels a little weird because I didn't think the first time I'd be up here would be with her, but I don't say that. The fact that she still doesn't know we've kissed is killing me. She's my person. But I'm not even sure what I am to Felix, so I pretend not to be extra interested in the posters on the wall or all the study materials on the desk as I sit down on the bed with her. What will she do when I tell her I've started something with her brother? I send a little prayer up that she'll support us, and I'm not even the praying type. Mom always said church wasn't her thing, though my grandma sometimes took me when I was a kid on the major holidays. Beyond that, I don't have much belief in a higher power. Especially one that would let vampires roam the earth.

I turn on my friend with a huge conspiratorial grin. "What are you doing here? And don't tell me you only came for the day because we both know a Sunday afternoon in September isn't really feasible for you to leave college. You're supposed to be long gone and having the best time of your life."

"Am I?" she teases, but she won't meet my eyes. I can sense the emotional wall she's built around herself, something that I've never experienced with my best friend before. She's always let me in. But then again, it's not like I'm one to talk ...

"So, are you going to skip class for a few days or something?" I venture.

She sighs and tugs her hair behind her ear. It's greasy, which isn't like her either. Neither are the dark circles under her eyes.

"Listen, don't judge me okay?" Her eyes go round, and I grab her hands and squeeze. She returns the gesture but her grip is weak.

"I would never," I whisper.

"I know, but I also know how excited you were for me and everything, and I don't really know how to say this, so I'm just going to say it," she rushes. "I decided to drop out of school."

I squeeze her hands again, but she lets go. "Are you serious?" I wish I could do something to help her. This is the last thing I was expecting her to say--she was so excited to go.

"Yeah, I really hated it. I've never been so depressed in my entire life."

"I'm so sorry." I don't know what else to say. It's barely been a month.

"It's okay. Mom and dad support me coming home, at least for now. I went to a therapist and she said that a lot of kids get depression their first year of college and it can be really unhealthy for them." Her mouth wobbles and those round eyes fill with tears. "I guess I'm not as strong as I thought I was, huh?"

"Are you kidding me?" I want to shake her. "You're so strong. Admitting something was wrong and taking action on that was super brave."

"Thanks." She shrugs. "Anyway, I'm going to stay home until I figure out what I want to do next. It's not like I need a college degree to do interior design at my own family's business, you know? But I'm not even sure I want to do interior design anymore. I'm not really sure about anything."

When I say my friend has been obsessed with home design since she was in preschool, I am not exaggerating. Her Sims houses are unbelievable, and her bedroom has changed about ten times over the years, each time better than the last. She was the kind of kid who asked for new bedding for her birthday instead of toys and rearranged furniture for fun. To this day she loves nothing more than to walk around IKEA and critique the displays. She's a total natural at this stuff, and to think that she'd give it up so quickly breaks my heart.

I wrap her in the tightest hug, wishing she would've confided in me about this sooner, but I am not about to make this about me. And it's not like I've been the world's greatest friend lately. So much has changed in my life, too. "I'm really sorry, Ayla. I know how much you were looking forward to your college experience. Are you sure this is the right decision?"

She pulls away and shoots me an annoyed glare. "You sound like Felix. He doesn't get it either. But honestly, I hated college. I never even wanted to leave my dorm room."

I nod, but I don't think she didn't want to leave her room because of being away from home or being shy or life changes or anything like that. I think the reason she wanted to stay locked up in her room was because she felt safe there and nowhere else. But I don't say that. Could my friend be going through post traumatic stress disorder after the vampire attack? Those guys had almost murdered her, and then we killed three of them right in front of her while she was still processing almost being vampire food. Not everyone is cut out to be a hunter, and my sensitive bestie might be hiding her true fears.

She stands. "I'm gonna head home before it gets dark. Happy birthday."

And sure enough, the sky outside has turned to bright creamsicle orange. She doesn't give me a present or a card, she simply leaves. It's not like I'm expecting a gift or that I'm mad that she didn't have something. It's that I'm even more concerned because this is not like her at all. My friend has always known I don't have much, so she goes all-out with her gifts. One time she even redid my wardrobe, saving up money meant for herself to use on new school clothes for me. And when I hadn't wanted to accept such a big gift, she'd already removed all the tags.

That's my Ayla. But I guess so is this girl. And I have no idea what to do.

Felix taps on the door and peeks inside. "Are you doing okay?"

I fake a happy smile. "Of course, thank you for this party. I know Ayla helped but you were the mastermind, weren't you?"

"I'll never tell." He winks and sits down next to me. "I have something for you."

He pulls a little box from the drawer of his nightstand. It's wrapped in blue paper to match the decorations downstairs. If I had to guess, Alya set him up with all of the party decor, which gives me some hope for my friend. But then again, maybe not. Maybe it was all him.

"Open it," he says, handing it over. I do and find a solid silver chain tucked neatly on top of a black velvet pillow inside.

"I saw that you broke the chain of your favorite necklace and had to replace it with something cheap," he says, his gaze dropping to my neck, "you know, the one that you wear all the time with the cross your grand-mother gave you? Well anyway, I hope you like this replacement."

"It's one of the most thoughtful gifts anyone has ever given me," I breathe. Sure, driving a Porsche over here was one of the most surreal moments of my life. It's beautiful and brand new, and I'm still not sure why Adrian gave it to me . . . and I can't trust it. "Thank you so much, Felix. This is perfect." I've been wearing my cross on a crappy chain since Hugo broke it. It rests below my collarbone in its usual spot, half the time under my clothes. I pull it off to switch it out with the nice silver chain, and Felix clasps it to my neck for me. As he does, my thumb glides along the stamped insignia of two tiny feathers crossing over each other on the back of the cross. The stamp belongs to the artisan who made it, a signature of sorts.

I turn back to him, and the energy between us completely shifts. His eyes flick to my lips, and before I can think about the consequences, I'm pressing my mouth to his. My senses have grown so much since having vampire venom in my blood, and even more since seeing Adrian, and it immediately kicks in with the kiss. I feel and hear and sense everything deeper than I ever have before––the hum of the ceiling fan, the warmth of Felix's soft mouth, the smell of his heady aftershave, the whoosh of my blood, and the swell in my breathing.

Maybe I'm not so mad about Adrian's orders to lose my virginity. My hands find a courage of their own, sneaking up under Felix's t-shirt to spread across his hard chest. He groans into my mouth. He tugs his shirt off, and then his hands are asking a question of their own. "This okay?" he whispers, tugging at my shirt as well. I nod against his kiss.

"Are you kidding me?" Ayla's voice breaks us apart like a bucket of ice water. She's standing in the doorway, her blue silhouette lit by the bright hallway behind her. And the look on her face is one of utter betrayal.

My heart drops.

"I can explain," I say at the same time Felix declares, "We were going to tell you."

"Don't bother," she snaps, and then she's gone before we can see her cry.

Six

"That went well," Felix grumbles as he slips his shirt back on. "I'd better go after her."

"I'll come with you."

But by the time we make it out to the front lawn, Ayla's nowhere to be seen. Felix runs to the sidewalk, peering up and down the street, his shoulders going limp. She probably parked around the corner because of the surprise party––I'd recognize her prized Mini Cooper anywhere––but there's no telling where that could be.

He stops abruptly. "Kenton, what are you doing?"

"Imagining myself in this sweet ride."

Kenton's voice sends a little nervous thrill through me. I rush over and, sure enough, my friend is standing next to my new car, staring at it like it's the most beautiful thing he's ever seen. Seth's got Kenton's phone out and is taking pictures of Kenton with the Porsche like it's a display at an amusement park. From Seth's bored expression, this photoshoot was not his idea.

"Well, I guess now is as good a time as ever," I mutter. I tug the keys free from my pocket, dangling them for the guys to see. "Anyone want to take a ride?"

They gape at me.

"You told me you were taking the city bus here," Felix laments.

I look around to make sure it's only the four of us on the little tree-lined street. "And that was the plan, but you know how you want me to get in with the vampires?" At once, all of their expressions change. Seth looks concerned, Kenton impressed, and Felix downright pissed off. "Well, Adrian agreed to keep working together and loaned me this car."

I leave out the fact that by "working together" I meant becoming his next *prodigy*, and that by "loan" I meant *give*, but hey, I'm working in baby steps here.

"Is it safe?" Felix asks as I unlock it. He's upon that car in all of two seconds flat, looking under the seats and in every nook and cranny like there's got to be a hidden camera or a bomb or something. "Can you pop the trunk? The hood too while you're at it."

Kenton and Seth are right there with him.

"Don't you think you're overreacting a bit?" I fold my arms over my chest and tap my foot on the pavement.

"No," Felix barks. His dark eyes land on mine from across the car. I'm not sure if he's mad that I took the gift or that Adrian gave the gift or what's going on exactly. Could it be jealousy?

"What if there's a tracking device on this thing?" Seth breaks my train of thought. "Or a camera or something worse?"

"What could be worse?"

"I don't know, a bomb?"

I laugh. "If Adrian wanted me dead, I'd be dead. Trust me."

"So what? You shouldn't have brought this here where your teammates live. You should've called me first and made a plan."

My cheeks warm. "Okay, you have a point," I relent, "I'm sorry." But what they don't realize is that if Adrian wanted to know who they were, then he wouldn't need to go to these lengths. He saw their faces that night behind the casino. He does his due diligence. It's very likely he already knows all about them. He could probably tell me their favorite breakfast cereal if I asked!

"Promise me one thing," Kenton says with a cheeky smile that breaks the tension. "Once we know it's safe, please let me be the first to drive her."

As it turns out, Kenton gets his wish. After about twenty minutes of investigating, they can't find a single thing wrong with the Porsche. Kenton and I climb in together for a joyride.

"But first, we need to set the tone," he says, connecting his phone to Bluetooth. He turns on one of my favorite hip hop albums and we take off. He goes right to the freeway. "We gotta see how fast this girl can go."

"Oh gosh, don't get us pulled over."

"I won't." He leans back in the driver's seat and tightens his grip on the wheel.

There's not a lot of traffic tonight, so he hits the gas and takes us up to the speed limit in seconds. I'm laughing the entire time.

Twenty minutes later we're back and Seth is next.

"Mind if I go alone?" he asks.

I shrug. "Go for it."

The request is a little weird but not unlike Seth, so whatever. Kenton gives me a hug and goes back to the party. I stay on the sidewalk with Felix. I'm not sure what to do. Hold his hand? Kiss him? Stay away because Ayla's obviously unhappy about us being together?

He calms my worries by wrapping me into a tight hug and kissing the top of my head. "It'll be alright," he says.

We stay like that until Seth returns a couple minutes later. As soon as we hear the car coming, we break apart. Seth doesn't need to know about us just yet. He parks and hands me the keys. I smile at Felix, dangling them in front of him.

"You ready?" I'm interested to know what he thinks about the car and to have another moment alone with him. "We can go together." And maybe we can go somewhere pretty even though the sun has already set. It's flat in New Orleans but there's got to be somewhere we can see the lights of the city. Or even just drive around for a while and talk. That would be nice. Ayla and I did that all the time when she first got her license.

"Sorry, I've got to get some homework done and we have training tomorrow, so I'd better not. Go enjoy your party though. It's all for you." He leaves me standing on the street, wondering what happened as he goes back inside with Seth. I want to go after him and demand . . . something.

But what?

It's only ten o'clock on my birthday, and I'm not ready for this day to be over. Everything has become so intense lately that getting this car and having some fun have felt like a dream. At least Kenton and I had a good time, but I wanted to experience it with Felix, and my feelings are a little hurt. I decide not to stick around the house any longer even though the party seems to be taking off again. I feel weird hanging out with a bunch of college kids when Felix is done for the night, so I say goodbye to everyone and check to see if my roommates want a ride home, but they don't. They're fun girls, and nice to me, but they're older and focused on school. I get the feeling that I'll never really get in with them, not the way real friends can. Not like with Ayla.

I slide into the driver's seat and retrieve my phone, wanting to call her. I call my mom instead. She picks up after the first ring. "Hi, Evangeline. How's my birthday girl doing?"

Mom's been staying with a work friend on the outside of town since we got evicted, so getting to see her this morning was really nice. Ending the day in my own apartment instead of somewhere we live together? It's . . . weird. Not bad. Not good. Just--weird.

"I'm doing good, Mom." She still doesn't know much about my involvement with Adrian, and she definitely doesn't need to know about the Porsche, so I decide to leave that out.

She pauses for a second. "There's something I've been wanting to tell you."

I don't know if I've ever heard those words come out of her mouth. I sit up straight as my heart speeds up. "Why didn't you tell me at breakfast?"

"I didn't want to worry you on your birthday."

"Worry . . . are you kidding me? It's still my birthday, Mom." I roll my eyes. This is typical Virginia Blackwood, so I guess I shouldn't be surprised. At least she's not arguing with me about her gambling anymore. I hope we never have to talk about that again.

"Can I come by before your shift at Pops tomorrow? What time are you working?" Her voice is relaxed, which is not like her either. But maybe I haven't known the real her in a long time. She's probably going to be a lot different now that she's been compelled never to become addicted again, and I can't wait to get to know the person she is without all that, but I have to remind myself she's still Virginia. And she's never going to be perfect. Nobody is. And I'm okay with that.

I tell her when to meet me and we finish up talking as I drive over to Ayla's house. If my best friend isn't ready to talk, I'll go home, but I can't end this day knowing I've hurt her. I need to make this right, so I park out front and knock on the same front door that I've knocked on a million times before.

Mrs. Moreno lets me in. "Honey, it's so good to see you." She hugs me right away.

"Can I see Ayla?"

She steps back with a little frown and whispers, "I hope you can get through to her. She's in her room."

Which is actually a guest room now. Ayla already helped her mom convert it to something new when she took most of her stuff to school. My heart does a little pang. Nothing went as planned. I wonder how she feels about everything. But maybe she's right, maybe she doesn't need a degree. Maybe college isn't for her. Maybe I'm completely off base about why she left.

I find her laying in bed with all the lights on and her laptop opened beside her. She's streaming an old sitcom with a terrible laugh track and doesn't acknowledge me when I come in and say hello. I sit on the edge of the bed for about five minutes and she doesn't move a muscle or look up once. When the audience members on the show laugh, she doesn't join them. "Are you really going to pretend like I'm not even here?" I finally ask.

"Sure am. Same as you pretended like I wasn't there anymore."

Yeah, we fight every now and then, but this seems pretty childish. And Ayla knows I've always had a thing for Felix. She didn't like it, didn't think anything would ever come of it, but she still knew and it's not like she ever seriously told me to stop. "I've called or texted you almost every day since you've been gone," I say.

"Yeah, and during all that you never once mentioned that you've been hooking up with my brother." She glares up from her computer. "How long has that been going on? Were you waiting for me to leave so you could shoot your shot?"

I hold up my hands. "First of all, I'm not hooking up with him. We've only kissed a few times. And second of all, you know I've always had a thing for your brother."

"Yeah, and I was cool with it because I thought you'd never act on it and that you'd always put our friendship first. You're *my* best friend, not *his* girlfriend."

"Why can't I be both?" I'm trying to hold my anger down, but she's not making it easy.

"Are you really asking me that?"

"Why wouldn't I be? You're being unfair."

"Because, Eva, if you date him, what happens when you break up? It'll force me to pick a side, and as much as I love you, he's *Felix*. I can't not pick my only sibling."

That hurts. She's already assuming Felix won't want me and is planning for a dramatic breakup. "You don't think I haven't thought about that?" I whisper. "I know you'd pick him, and do you realize how much that sucks for me? Because I *don't* have a sibling or another best friend. I have you. That's it."

"Apparently you have Felix."

I clench and unclench my fists, growing more and more frustrated. "Don't twist my words." We go quiet for so long that I'm forced to fill it. "I'm sorry, okay? I didn't mean for you to find out like that. This thing with Felix is brand-new."

"He had his shirt off. I'm not stupid, okay? So, did you finally lose your virginity then?"

I stand up, growing exhausted by this argument. "No, and even if I did, it shouldn't be such a big deal. A girl shouldn't be defined by her decisions about her body."

"Are you kidding? It's a big deal because you've always made it a big deal. I know what it means to you."

"Okay but--"

"And it's a big deal when it's your best friend who's keeping secrets from you."

Silence stretches between us, pulling us further and further apart. "You don't understand," I grumble.

"You're right, I don't."

"Ayla--"

"I think you should leave."

And I think maybe she's right. I go to stand in the doorway. I'm burning mad, but I also understand where she's coming from because I know her better than anyone, and I know she was already hurting when she came home and now I've added to that pain with my secrets. I wonder if this is less about Felix and more about me keeping something from her. "Please, get help, okay? You need someone to talk to about everything. Are you going to be seeing that therapist regularly now?"

"So you think that because I dropped out of school that I'm somehow defective? Well, at least I tried, Eva. I don't see you trying."

"That stings." My voice goes low. She knows how I was brought up, and she certainly knows I'm doing my best. I wasn't raised like her with two parents, a steady income household, a beautiful house to grow up in, a legacy and cultural traditions and, and, and . . . I take a deep breath. "I'm actually talking about the vampire attack last month. You haven't been the same since that awful party. You're attributing your unhappiness with going away to college, but I just want you to talk to someone who can help you separate the two because maybe it's the vampire thing that's got you feeling this way. A professional is trained to help you get closure on things like that."

"Closure?" She rolls her eyes. "How am I supposed to get closure when suckers are still out there? And now I have to think about you and Felix going out and hunting them every night when you're not doing God knows what else."

"Not every night." In fact, we haven't even gone out on a first official mission. Tate still isn't back. Cameron is running the show like the little twerp he is, and he hasn't authorized our team to actually do anything but train. We can't even drop stakes in graveyards right now because the last time the guys did that, they went at night when they weren't supposed to. It was the night I followed them and got attacked by a newly turned vampire, but I don't think Cameron knows anything about that.

"Hunting is our way of coping with this messed up world," I say at last, "you need to find your way of coping too."

"Can you go now?" She's being mean, and I could serve it right back, but I'm tired and I don't want to fight. Hopefully she'll soften over time and forgive me. But I'm not going to stop seeing Felix now that I've started. And

I'm not going to give up the hunters. And I'm certainly not going to give up on Ayla's mental health or our friendship.

"You know," she says right before I close the door. "It's best if you don't come around here anymore. It's safer for me considering your questionable life decisions."

Tears prickle in my eyes, and I don't know what to do or say because she's right. She might not be safe around me. It's the reason I didn't stay here when the Morenos' offered after Mom and I got evicted. And that was a good decision considering Hugo had me followed, and that Adrian knew the details of my home's layout and where I slept. Who's to say other vamps aren't after me? And now that I'm actually Adrian's fledgling, I'm going to have even more eyes on me.

I close the door and refuse to cry.

On the way out of the house, I give her parents a hug. "Contact me if you ever need anything or if Ayla needs me."

Their eyes widen in surprise but they nod their agreement. I leave before they can start asking questions. I really hope Ayla will come around to my way of thinking or at least forgive me soon. But I'm not so sure she will. I know my friend--she's as stubborn as I am.

Seven

"**G**uess who's back?" Kenton greets me as I amble into the gym the next morning after a terrible night's sleep. At first, I'm confused by the statement, but then I see *him*––Leslie Tate. He's standing on the stairs chatting with a few of the other hunters. The older man looks the same as he always did with his gray, inquisitive eyes hooded by bushy eyebrows. He was only gone for a few weeks, but to me it feels like an eternity. It also feels like something is wrong.

"Well, what did he say?" I remove my hoodie and toss it into one of the cubbies, heading over to the weights area with Kenton at my side. We've fallen into a routine where we workout together in the mornings. First we spot each other, then we spar. Felix and Seth are already out on the mat, paired up for the same thing. Once we're all done, we have to do some of the simulations upstairs, maybe a lecture or two, and then we're out before lunch. I know the guys are chomping at the bit to get real assignments, but I'm starting to get a little nervous about the prospect of actually hunting.

"What do you mean what did he say?" Kenton asks, genuinely confused by my question.

I widen my eyes. "Oh, I don't know, maybe about the fact that he ditched us, only leaving behind a cryptic note like we're all in some kind of murder mystery novel?"

Kenton shrugs. "Didn't think to ask."

"Right . . ."

He changes the subject, and we go about our training. The craziest part is that everyone I talk to about Tate throughout the morning gives me a similar answer. They don't seem to care where their leader has been or why he left, only that he's back. Surely Tate isn't infallible to scrutiny. Do they follow this man blindly no matter what?

I corner Cameron by the drinking fountain. We're alone so I need to be quick. "Hey, do you know what's going on? Everyone's acting like it's no big deal that Tate is back."

"Why don't you talk to Tate yourself?" Cameron says, shooting me an odd look. "That's what I did."

"Uhh--what about the whole energy demon thing?"

"The what?" Cameron raises his eyebrows. They're bushy today, reminding me of orange caterpillars.

"You know." I make sure nobody is around us and then whisper low. "The whole reason why you're a prodigy for Kelli."

Cameron steps back, his face going slack. "I don't know what the hell you're talking about. What's your name again? Aren't you a novice?"

Huh? "Eva, and yes, but that's not the point. I'm talking about the night-club and Kelli. Remember when we were at the casino and--"

He shakes his head, holding up his hands. "Alright, Ava. I don't know what you're trying to do here, but whatever it is, you need to stop."

"It's Eva."

"Whatever. Don't make up lies like that."

I open and close my mouth a few times. "But what about your little brother? Avenging his death and all that *if you can't beat them, join them* stuff?"

Cameron's face pales. "My brother died of childhood cancer." His voice is dangerously low, like he's close to erupting. I catch sight of his clenched hands and step back. "And what are you doing looking into me like that? I don't even know you. Are you doing this to everyone?"

I stare at him, completely flabbergasted. Did he really forget everything? It's hard to believe, but then I know what Tate can do. He told me from day one that he can make people forget things. Has he done that to me? My mind whirls with the possibilities, and suddenly I want to run far, far away from this secret training facility and never look back.

But my friends are here and I can't leave them vulnerable.

"Everything okay here?" Seth slides in next to me. He assesses Cameron with a hard stare.

"Is this girl on your team?" Cameron asks. He's short and stocky, but his bulk is considerable and his hands are fisted.

"Yes." Seth's tone darkens to match Cameron's, and I'm grateful that Seth decided to get over his annoyance and welcome me to his team. It feels good to be wanted. It's not a feeling I've had too many times before.

"Your little girl here is digging into people's backgrounds, and you need to get her to stop."

Seth turns to me. "Is this true?"

I don't know what to say to get this to make sense, but my team knows about Cameron, who he really is and what his plans are. At least, what they were before his mind was washed clean like a window. In the end, I decide to go with Cameron's side of things just to get him to leave us alone. "Yeah, I guess so. Sorry about that, Cameron. It won't happen again."

Cameron huffs and stalks off, his eyes still on me as he crosses the gym to join his teammates.

"Okay, so what was that really all about?" Seth is never that interested in me, but right now he's looking at me with scrutinizing eyes. There is also sympathy in them. And trust. And I love that he trusts me. I didn't realize how much I needed it.

"You still remember the stuff I told you about Cameron before, right?" I whisper.

"Yes."

Relief floods through me. "Good, because the guy was just acting like he had no recollection of any of it."

"Nothing? Do you think he was bullshitting you?"

"Could be, but I really don't think so. His memory was wiped."

"Hmm . . ." Seth turns, and we both watch Cameron as he starts to spar with one of his teammates. They're not in the gym a lot because they're usually out hunting, but today it's like everyone's here. Maybe Tate told the leaders to call all their teammates in.

"I asked him about Leslie Tate, and he acted like it's no big deal that Tate is back. Same with Kenton. Do you think something's going on?"

Seth's eyes go from hard to soft. "Nothing's wrong. You can trust Tate. Go talk to him yourself and see."

"Well, Tate obviously wiped Cameron's mind, so you'll excuse me if I don't want to talk to the guy."

"Nah, trust me, Tate is a good guy. If he did anything weird, he did it to protect us."

Okay, so now Seth is acting the same way as everyone else, and I am certain something is definitely up with Tate. Maybe I should stay away, but it feels inevitable. Against my better judgement, I take to the stairs, determined to get answers.

I find Tate in his office, sitting at his desk, business as usual.

"Hi, Eva," he greets me with a smile. "How are you doing?"

I sit down in the chair across from him and glower. "I'm fine. More interesting question——how are *you* doing? And while you're at it, where have you been? And why did you ditch us like that?"

Tate nods once, understanding framing his eyes.

"And for that matter, what happened to Cameron? He's wiped. You took his memories away, I know you did."

"I helped Cameron." He leans forward. "Do I need to help you?"

Does he know about Adrian? I blink and my heart speeds up.

"All your questions are valid." He smiles. "But they're questions you don't need to ask or think about anymore."

There's something about his words that sink into me like an anchor. He's telling the truth. Even if there's something about that truth that's not entirely ringing true, it's still trustworthy. I try to grasp on to what could be off about this moment, but my mind goes a little fuzzy. I need to remember that he's doing something to me, that he's using his powers somehow. I need to cling to the fact that he himself admitted to being something other than human the first time we met. I need to hold on to Cameron's words at the nightclub, that Tate is some kind of energy demon, and I need, I need . . .

The fuzziness takes over my thoughts and then clears, leaving nothing behind.

"Okay," I say simply. My mind is at ease, so I get up to leave. "When will we be resuming training together?" He takes new recruits under his wing, and I've really missed having that one on one time with him. He's a great guy, like the father I never had.

"How about tomorrow?"

A little burst of happiness releases in my chest. "I'll be here."

FELIX WRAPS me in his arms and kisses me one last time. "It's been fun having you around today."

I smile and nod. We're standing on his front porch after having spent most of our Monday together. After practice this morning, he apologized for turning in early last night, and asked me to hang out at his house in between his classes so he could hop over and spend time with me. Since I wasn't working until later, I figured it was a good idea. And I'd been right. The whole day was amazing, so much so that I think I'm almost ready to take Adrian up on his request and finally cash in my v-card with Felix. Not today because I've got to get to work, but soon.

We hug and then I reluctantly walk down to my car. Whatever jealousy Felix had about the Porsche, he hasn't said another word about it. Maybe he realized he was being a jerk.

I wave goodbye and slide in, then pull out on the road and turn toward downtown. I have to go home and change into my work uniform, and I'm keenly aware that my mom wanted to swing by first to talk to me about something. I'm super curious about whatever it is she wants to tell me--and nervous. I didn't like the tone of her voice, it reminded me too much of the days before Adrian compelled her.

As I turn the corner, I catch sight of Tate walking through a parking lot. Seeing him out in the wild like this makes me pause at the stop sign and watch him. I shouldn't worry about what he's doing, but something deep within warns that's a false thought. I'm filled with mixed emotions, but I follow that little warning bell, pulling into the same parking lot. I jog over to the sidewalk to catch up with him, but he doesn't see me in time and walks into a revolving door before I get a chance to call out his name.

I want to say hi and to thank him for coming back after he had left and ask . . .

There's something else, something important, but my mind has gone fuzzy again. I don't know if it's out of curiosity or a suspicion I can't quite name, but I find myself following Tate inside the building.

I look up at the sign above the glass door and frown a little: Tulane Medical Center. What could he be doing at a hospital? I hope he's okay. My first thought is he's probably visiting someone and would appreciate his privacy. But my feet keep moving forward, and I walk right past reception, following him to an unmarked door. I find myself in a plain hallway, Tate's footsteps echoing ahead. Again, I want to call out to him, but a deep sense of knowing crawls up my throat. It seals my mouth shut, and all I can do is follow him.

Eight

O nce again, my senses grow, everything prickling to keen awareness. The scent of antiseptic, the clacking of shoes on polished tiles, and the air conditioning running through the vents all seem to surround me at once. I'm not sure why it's so strong right now because Tate isn't a vampire or connected into Hugo's bloodline. Maybe it's because I'm sensing something is off or because I'm hyper-focused. I'm still not sure how this venom works yet, but I'm certain that I have to keep it a secret. The vampires will kill me if they find out I have it. Adrian still might. And I don't want Tate to know.

Pieces of my mind still want to relax and let Tate go, but clarity has peeked through like sunbeams in thick clouds. Clarity that says, *it's time to learn the truth about Tate*. I grit my teeth, realizing the only reason why I want to trust Tate is because he *told* me to, and that has more to do with his secret abilities than it does with how I actually feel deep down. I've been manipulated, plain and simple.

Growing angry, I push through double doors and end up inside a bustling emergency room floor. I wouldn't have known how to get back here without asking at reception, and I find it odd that Tate did. What's a guy like him doing sneaking around a hospital? If he were visiting someone, there wouldn't be a need for secrecy.

A middle-aged woman with blurry red eyes rushes past, and I catch sight of the bright blue visitor sticker on her shirt. I fold in on myself, hoping nobody will notice that I don't have one of my own. What I'm doing might be illegal, but luckily the place is busy, and it seems the doctors and nurses aren't concerned with me, not when they have ten places to be at once. A sign at the far end of the hall reads *Blood Donation Center*, and I recoil. I shouldn't, it probably has nothing to do with feeding vampires and everything to do with saving humans, but I'm turned off by any kind of blood donation at this point. There's a reason the top ailments in our society have become anemia, restless leg syndrome, fatigue, brain fog, and more—all symptoms of donating too much blood.

I've lost sight of Tate and can't very well start opening doors to look for him, so instead I casually stroll down the hall, keeping my eyes open. I've never had to be admitted into an ER before, but I did bring Mom into one once when she donated too much blood, and I know hospitals well enough from when my gran died. I've avoided those memories, but being here now makes me think that maybe it wouldn't be such a bad idea to go into medicine. I've always wanted to help people, and since being a police officer turned out to be a bust, maybe I could go to nursing school or do something in the medical field. I like the buzz of this ER and the thought of responding to people in immediate need. Maybe I could find my way into working here and keep hunting vampires on the side, at least until my brain fully develops and it's no longer safe to be near vampires.

The idea seems . . . impossible.

But maybe it's not.

There's a huge glass door marked ICU for Intensive Care Unit in bright red lettering. The unit inside is surrounded in glass and lit with sunshine, as if all that light helps the people in there heal. I peek through the glass, my breath catching when I spot Tate. He's standing with his back to me next to someone in a hospital bed. The patient has so many tubes and wires taped to him that I can barely make out his face. Whatever is going on with this guy, it looks like it's pretty bad.

Something catches the light, and I blink rapidly and then squint. Just like that night at the Neon House, the humans have auras again. This time I don't need neon to see the energy––I can see it in broad daylight––another sense heightened. They're all sorts of colors, but the person lying on the bed has a very weak yellow glow around them, and exactly like Cameron claimed, Leslie Tate is syphoning the energy away from the human. It flows from the person in the bed directly into Tate's body.

I have to run in there, to rip him away from that innocent person, but when I yank on the glass door, it doesn't budge. I curse, realizing it's because I don't have access. I really don't understand how Tate got inside because surely he doesn't have access either. It's like the man went to a hospital looking for the person in the weakest state and zeroed in on them. It's horrific. Cameron was right. If I don't stop him, Tate's going to kill that guy.

I bang on the glass door, but nobody inside hears me, and Tate doesn't stop or even flinch in my direction. Is that why they come here--these energy vampires/demons--to prey on humans at their very weakest? Do they get some kind of extra boost when they take a life? Is that why Cameron's brother was targeted?

"Stop!" I yell.

"Excuse me, you can't go back there," a nurse cuts me off sharply.

I turn to her, panic growing. "See that man?" I point to Tate. "He's hurting your patient."

Her eyebrows furrow and then she's through the door, closing it in my face before I can follow after her. I expect her to stop him, but as she approaches Tate, her body language softens, all urgency evaporating into thin air. She doesn't even bother to speak to him. In fact, she moves past the patient and Tate as if he's not even there, as if the patient is completely fine and peacefully dreaming about sugar plum fairies.

"Are you kidding me?" I hiss, looking around the hallway for someone else who could get me access into the ICU.

This must be part of why his kind--whatever they are--have gone undetected for so long. Nobody can stop them because the second a human questions them, they're able to turn our minds to peach fuzz.

I can fight it, but that must be because of the venom.

I still don't agree with Cameron's whole "if you can't beat them, join them" attitude, but I can understand why he's so concerned about these things, why he made it his life's mission to stop them after the things he witnessed. I make a mental note to grill Adrian about these *things* next time I see him because surely he knows. This must be why he wants me to spy on Tate for him, so I can give him more information on his enemy. This is far beyond humans hunting down vampires. Maybe the vampires don't fear human hunters at all, maybe it's these *other things* that are the true targets.

My mind whirls with the implications, and questions sprout in my mind. What if it's not only humans in that gym every morning? What if there are others like Tate working with us? How many are out there like him? Could Seth or Kenton be one of them?

I used to think I knew everything. I've since realized I know nothing.

I turn around and spot a grumpy looking security officer charging right toward me. Maybe banging on an ICU door wasn't the best way to keep myself inconspicuous. Not my smartest idea, I'll admit. I take on a relaxed posture and walk briskly in the opposite direction. He follows, but before he can get to me, I'm strolling through the waiting room, and then I'm on the front sidewalk, and then I'm sprinting back to the Porsche.

I jump in and peel out of the parking lot, my heart rioting in my chest.

Maybe there was nothing I could do to help that one person in the ICU, and it kills me to even think about leaving them vulnerable like that, but now I know that Cameron was right about one thing: there's definitely more out there than vampires. And maybe he's right that vampires aren't the worst of them. That's hard to believe with what I know of the suckers, but at least they're out in public and open about their vileness. At least they have weaknesses, like the sun and silver and wood through the heart. And at least they don't lie about who they are.

Because Tate is a liar. And now I really want to know where he disappeared to and why. I drive home with my knuckles white on the steering wheel and more questions than ever racing through my head.

Nine

I lean against the side of the brick wall, aimlessly watching the cars in the street and the people on the sidewalk. I have to go into work but I've been standing out here in the evening sun waiting for someone who will never come.

My mom stood me up.

And even though she's done it a million different times before, this one stings the most. It's my own fault for caring so much. I'd dropped my guard and allowed myself to hope. I shouldn't have done that. I know better, have *learned* better. Experience is the best teacher, as they say. I hate that I was foolish enough to let this happen.

Because hope is cruel. It rips your heart out. It breaks promises and doesn't return phone calls and treats you like an afterthought and makes you late for work.

I was stupid to trust her again. All it took was one conversation with her, one happy birthday breakfast, one promise that things were going to be different this time, that she was better, that it was impossible for her to be sick again.

Adrian obviously didn't compel her to be a better mom, and it's sad that I wish he had.

And as I march into Pops, pissed off and ten minutes late for my shift, all I can think is that I should've refused to celebrate my birthday altogether. That would've been my preference! That's what I had wanted. I'd been content with not celebrating in any way, shape, or form. As the day had approached, I had not allowed myself to think of it. Why should I? I didn't

238

want to grow older, and I certainly didn't want to be disappointed. It was always better to set expectations low because that way nobody could hurt me.

"You okay?" Eddie frowns when he sees me. I assumed he would give me a stern talking to about being late, but maybe he caught the expression on my face because he only seems concerned. I don't really get it. I'm here to do a job. This is the second time I've messed up. First, I had called in with an emergency and had no coverage, and now, I was late and in a piss-poor mood.

"Yeah, I'm fine," I say. "Sorry I'm late."

He nods. "You're okay. Go clock in."

And that's it. He doesn't question me, which is exactly the slack I need right now in my tug-of-war life. Maybe it's another strike against professionalism, but I give him a big bear hug. I can hardly get my arms around him, but the man pats me on the back and tells me to take better care of myself. Maybe he can see the bags forming under my eyes from all the late nights and early mornings. Or maybe he can sense the stress I'm under, especially when it comes to worrying about my mom. Or the sadness from losing my best friend.

I go about my shift, and Eddie walks me to my car afterward. He raises an eyebrow when he sees the Porsche. I can't claim it as my own, I just can't. Maybe because of who really owns it, or maybe because I don't think I actually deserve it. I don't know. "It's a friend's car, not mine," I explain sheepishly, "he's letting me drive it for a while until I can get my own."

Eddie whistles low. "Some friend, huh?" I climb in, and he pats the roof. "Be careful, okay? Sometimes a gift isn't really for the giftee as much as the gifter, know what I'm saying?"

I nod, knowing exactly what he's saying and wishing I didn't.

"So then you have to ask yourself, is it really a gift?"

His words follow me the entire drive home, and when Mom texts apologizing and wanting to reschedule for a lunch date instead, I don't respond.

A WEEK PASSES BY, and I don't hear from her again. I don't hear from Adrian either. Or Ayla. I find myself hanging out at the guys' house more and more, which has become a little tricky for me and Felix. A few nights ago we agreed to be official, but we're still pretending to be just friends whenever Seth is around. And considering Seth is his roommate, that happens to be a lot.

"Alright, level with me," I say the next chance we have to be alone. We're sitting on the living room couch watching SportsCenter. I couldn't care less about sports, but I don't mind it since Felix enjoys it so much. But there's something I've been meaning to talk to him about. "Why have you been avoiding coming over to my apartment?"

Because that's the thing. We could be alone there any chance we wanted. But Felix keeps wanting to hang at his house, and I don't get it. I've thought about this a lot and I want to take things to the next step with him, but it's like he's pushing it off.

Felix tugs at the tips of his curly hair nervously and his cheeks go red. "Well, I guess it's because I used to hook up with Jasmine."

One sentence from those pretty lips of his and my world tilts off its axis.

He's referring to my roommate who I almost never see, the pretty Latina girl who's always at the library studying for her pre-med degree. I like her from the few interactions I've had with her, and she came to my birthday party, but I never expected to get this news. I sink into the couch and take it in. I guess I shouldn't be too surprised since Felix is a twenty-year-old college student. He's sexy as hell with his sleeve tattoo and that Cuban ethnicity girls love around here. He's a star player on the lacrosse team so he's built like a model. And don't forget he's super smart and going into business, where he'll surely become the CEO of some Fortune 500 company one day. Sometimes I can't believe he wants me. He's got his life together. I don't.

"Well, I could see how that could be a problem." My throat goes dry.

"Her and I are just friends, I promise." He leans over to wrap me in a hug. "And I'm exclusive with you now."

Right. I want to believe him . . . I do believe him. The simple fact that he was the one who found me a room in her apartment is confirmation enough that he's not into her anymore. He wouldn't have done that if he had something to hide. He's helped me, been kind, looked out for me, and finally seen me as something other than a kid sister. This is everything I've been wanting for years. I can't screw this up.

"Well, we're alone now, aren't we?" I scoot in closer and run the tips of my fingers along the little curls at the back of his neck. "Why don't we go up to your room?"

There's no denying my meaning.

It takes more courage than I care to admit. Maybe it's because I've been holding onto my virginity for so long, or maybe it's because for so many years I fantasized it happening with Felix and nobody else, but I've been thinking about this a lot, and I think Adrian is right. At first I was angry at him for acting like he should get a say in what I do with my body, but I realize now that he's a logical creature and logic says I need to take care of this to be safer among the vampires. I don't know what my blood smells like to them. Even Kelli, who hates me, said I smell like the sweetest flower.

For some gross unexplainable reason, virgin blood smells better to vampires than nonvirgin blood. And now that I'm planning to be around vampires a lot more--who better to lose it with than the one guy I've pined over for ages?

Felix leans over and kisses me, long and slow and deep. Butterflies tickle through my stomach and my heart speeds up. I imagine that at any second he's going to scoop me into his arms and follow through with my request.

He doesn't.

He pulls back and stands. "I actually need to get to class."

My heart drops. I didn't know he had a class coming up. He never said so, and a little voice in my head says he's making up an excuse to get rid of me. I stand up, annoyed, and an angry fire rushes in to snuff out the insecurities.

"What's a girl got to do around here to lose her virginity, huh?" I throw my arms up.

Felix doubles over in laughter. I don't know what I expected Felix to do, but laughing? It makes me even angrier.

"Sorry." He tries to pull me into a hug, but I dodge him. "I don't mean to laugh at you."

"Sure," I deadpan.

He calms down. "You just reminded me of why I like you so much."

"Oh, you need reminding?" I put my hands on my hips and shoot him a glare.

"No, I don't." He turns serious. "But this isn't easy for me."

"And why is that?" Now I'm even more offended. I don't want to be some chore to him. "You've slept with loads of girls before. Do I repulse you or something?"

"No, Eva. You're the most tempting thing I've ever laid eyes on and I've thought so for a long time. But you're my sister's best friend, and she's mad as hell at me right now."

"She'll come around."

"Will she? I'm not so sure. Not to mention, you're on my hunter team, and my best friends are telling me to back off."

"I thought they didn't know about us."

"They're not stupid." He grins sheepishly. "They see the way we are together. And you have been hanging out here every day lately."

He makes good points, but I still don't care. This is about us, not everyone else. "Why are you letting other people dictate *your* life?"

The front door swings open, and, as if to mock me, Kenton and Seth bulldoze inside. "Who's hungry?" Kenton asks. "I'm ordering pizza."

"Actually, we were leaving," I reply.

"Together?" Seth questions, his tone accusatory.

"If you must know, your boy here claims to have a class coming up. And I have . . . things to do." I don't have things to do.

"I thought it was your night off?"

"Fine. If you must know, my thing to do was supposed to be Felix." I go to the door and turn back, giving all the guys my dirtiest glare. "And by the way, my dating life is my business. I'm a grown ass woman who can make her own choices."

Kenton yells at Felix, "Damn, son! What did you do?"

I leave, the door banging behind me. Seth follows me. Which, I gotta admit, only adds fuel to the fire. Felix should be out here, begging for my forgiveness, not Seth to rub it all in.

"Hold up, Eva," he calls after me, "I think we need to talk about this."

I spin on my heels. "Oh, you mean about how you've decided that you get a say in what goes on in *my* relationship?"

His face hardens. "This is to protect all of us." But there's something else in his meaning, and I can't quite put my finger on it.

"What aren't you telling me?"

Then Seth does something I've never seen him do--he blushes.

And I know.

He looks away, and I drop it, because I'm not going to make him say it. *But I know.* All the signs are there. The way he treats his friends, the way he acts around Felix, the attitude he gives me and how he's tried to push me away . . .

Seth is in love with Felix.

How did I not see it before? Does Felix know?

"Don't say anything." Seth's voice is raw with emotion. "Please."

I nod once. I would never out someone. I don't know Seth's reasons for staying closeted.

He runs his hand through his hair and shakes his head. "Look, I know I can't have him. I'm not stupid enough to think he's going to switch teams for me or anything like that. Guys like me? We've been in this situation before."

"Seth, I don't know what to say."

"It's fine. Whatever. But that doesn't mean I magically approve of your relationship because I don't."

"But Felix means as much to me as he does to you."

He holds my gaze. "I know, okay? I'm a hypocrite. And I'm sorry I haven't been the kindest to you. Now you know why. But that aside, the two of you dating is a horrible idea."

I shake my head. "Felix and I have known each other for years. We

242

wouldn't get involved if we didn't really care about this working out. Don't you want him to be happy?"

"You really don't get it, do you?"

Pretty sure I do get it. He's jealous—to the point of ruining our happiness.

"I don't care about Felix's happiness," he says, practically reading my mind. "I care about his *life*. I want to keep him alive. And you. And all of us. Hunters aren't supposed to date each other, and there's good reasons for that. The vampires could use Felix against you. And don't think for one second that your buddy Adrian wouldn't do that, because he would."

He wouldn't.

Maybe he would.

"Go home," Seth continues, "think about it. Take your emotions out of the equation and really think this through using your brain and nothing else."

"I have."

"No, you haven't, because if you had you'd already be at the same conclusion." He sighs heavily and steps back. "I already know Felix is willing to risk everything on you, so he hasn't thought this through enough either." My heart does a little happy dance at his confession, despite what he's trying to say. All I want to do is go back in there, work things out with Felix, and then drag him up to his room and tell everyone else to stay out of our business.

Seth must see my thoughts written all over my face because his voice turns angry. "Are you honestly that selfish that you're willing to risk Felix's life? You think you know Adrian better than the rest of us, but don't forget what he is, and don't forget that you *don't* really know him. You can't."

"He's encouraged me to be with Felix, actually," I jut in. "He wants me to lose my virginity."

"So lose it with someone else!"

"Are you kidding me?"

"You just proved my point that your vampire already knows about Felix." His voice goes dark. "If it were between Adrian's life and yours, Adrian would choose his own, and he'd drink you dry to do it. Now imagine Felix mixed up in that. Imagine what it would feel like to have your boyfriend and your best friend's brother killed because of your choices. Choices that could be avoidable if you treated Felix like a teammate and kept things professional."

A tear burns down my cheek—one that I didn't even know was there until it brands me with the truth.

Because Seth is right.

My heart breaks, but I walk away without another word. I don't go back in there to work things out with Felix. I get into my car and go home to my apartment alone. After a few hours of thinking it all through, I send Felix a text asking for us to stick to being friends. When he calls me back immediately, I don't answer. And when he blows up my phone with texts, I don't respond to any of them. And even when he shows up at my doorstep later that night, begging to talk to me, I have my roommate Olive send him away.

Ten

By the next morning, Felix gives up, and that hurts the most. I cry into my pillow and then I scream into it. Once that's done, I wipe the tears and sit up, phone in hand.

I need some time off, I text Seth. *I'll see you guys when I'm ready.*

So you're quitting?

Of course not, but I'm taking a short break.

Fine, but we need you by next Monday. We can't miss more than a week. I think we'll be getting assignments soon.

"Yeah, I'll believe it when I see it," I grumble out loud.

Going back to the gym at all seems like a huge chore, and honestly, I'm angry about everything. I'm angry about the guys, about Tate, and about being a hunter in general. Becoming one of them was supposed to be rewarding, and so far we haven't even been on a single mission. Seth may think we'll be sent out soon but I'm skeptical. We're training and learning, and we need time to get prepared so we don't end up dead. I have to keep reminding myself that it's only been a little over a month, and I'm not being very patient.

But I'm ready.

Hugo's venom has enhanced my senses, gaining strength each day and adding to my confidence that I could hunt down vampires with ease. This has nothing to do with simulations. This has to do with blood. I'm linked into their bloodline, which means that I can sense them better than anyone. And maybe if I accomplish what I set out to do, I won't feel so guilty about everything else.

It's too bad Tate can't be trusted. I've avoided him ever since seeing him in the ICU. If I could trust him then I'd tell him about the venom in my blood so he could send me out. I'd be able to help the mission. But then, who's mission? The humans or the energy demons? I'm confused and indecisive, which isn't like me. I'm not sure I like the person in the mirror these days.

Going to Adrian for help late Friday night is the last thing I ever thought I'd do, but the phrase "never say never" hits me right across the face as I walk into the Alabaster Heart Hotel and Casino uninvited.

Kelli sits at her office reception desk and doesn't seem surprised as I approach. She looks me up and down and smiles devilishly. "You didn't dress up."

"Hello to you, too." I look down at my high-waisted cut-off jeans and forest green baggy t-shirt, wondering what the big deal is. My little silver cross necklace is tucked under my shirt, and I've got my wooden stake strapped to my ribcage. I'm sure Adrian will notice, but at this point he'd probably find it more out of character if I didn't have one.

"I need to talk to Adrian."

Kelli stands on five inch heels and motions for me to follow. I expect her to lead me to the elevator, but she doesn't. We must be going to Adrian's suite, or maybe out on the casino floor, or even downstairs to the ballroom the coven uses for meetings.

I'm wrong on all counts because we cross the opulent lobby and go outside.

The sunset has given way to an inky black sky, the city lights blotting out the stars. The energy bustles around us with evening partiers, many of which are probably tourists. Even though it's known for having more vampires than a lot of cities, people still flock here. A group of intoxicated girls wobble past us on high heels, heading toward the nightclub across the street. I catch a whiff of booze mixed with a cloud of perfume and I grimace.

I wonder how many of the people in there have donated blood instead of paying a cover fee. They can't possibly feel safe. Why do people keep doing it, keep exchanging their safety for a night of fun? We follow them to the club. They go to the back of the line that wraps around the block, but Kelli and I head right past the massive vampire bouncer.

The moment we step inside, I want to turn back around. Suckers are everywhere––behind the bar, in the seats, dancing on the floor. There are far more vamps in here than there are humans, but several of the humans have a nurse with them drawing blood. Opening a vein to gain free drinks for the night must be too good to pass up for many. Before I was around vampires, it wasn't always obvious what they were, but now that I know what to look for, it's impossible not to see them. It's a knowledge I wish I didn't have.

Canal Street separates the city, the old from the new, and we're on the newer side of town. It's all shiny black surfaces and purplish-red lights here, unlike the casino which has obviously been renovated but still clings to the old charm. Kelli leads me to the back of the club where a spiral metal staircase twists up to the top floor. Another bouncer lets us through to what must be the VIP area. We climb, and I become acutely aware of how underdressed I am.

"I need to talk to Adrian about something," I say, uneasy. "And then I can leave."

"Oh, did I forget to tell you?" She laughs. "You've been invited to a special coven meeting."

My face burns. "This is the first I'm hearing of it, and you know it."

"Too bad Adrian didn't give me a deadline to inform you about it," she muses, "but I'm telling you now."

She has to do as her master says, but she found a way to make it harder for me. I wonder how Adrian will respond when he finds out what she's done. "And what were you going to do if I didn't happen to walk into the casino tonight?"

She lifts a shoulder. "I know where you live."

"I moved."

She only laughs at that. Of course these suckers are going to keep tabs on me wherever I go. I'm not surprised that she knows about the new address, but my stomach hardens anyway.

"By the way," she goes on, "what's the deal with my fledgling? I went to pay him a visit last night and he practically tried to kill me."

"There's a reason for that and it's exactly why I want to talk to Adrian."

"I guess it's your lucky night." But her tone has darkened, and I wonder how important it is that she gets Cameron to follow through with his promises. Brisa loved the idea of having a hunter working on their side. If Kelli's lost that, Brisa won't be happy. Does Kelli know Cameron's already long gone?

"I don't think it's anyones lucky night," I mutter.

The top floor is two stories above the rest with a balcony looking over the dance floor. It's a little bit quieter up here, and less packed, with black velvet couches placed around the edges of the room. In the middle are three long metal poles. Dancers swing around them, their toned bodies moving to the music. They aren't nude, they're in tiny bras and underwear, but once my eyes catch on Adrian, I can't look at anybody else.

And he's staring right back.

"Remember, Eva," Kelli whispers, "you're his now. This is what you wanted."

I brush past her and go to Adrian, sitting next to him on the couch. I can feel the sets of at least fifty pairs of eyes on us. All the vampires who took fledglings this year are here, as are their humans. Kelli sits on his other side and leans back, appearing disinterested.

"Where's Cameron?" he asks her.

"He's out." Two words and his entire demeanor goes frigid.

"And this is the first I'm hearing of it?"

"Sorry," she mumbles. "I don't know what happened."

"I can tell you what happened," I speak up, "and it's not Kelli's fault." I don't know why I'm helping her when she continues to treat me like trash, but maybe I feel bad for her.

"Is that so?" Adrian turns back to me. "I see you didn't bother to dress for the occasion, nor have you taken care of your little problem, like I asked."

I narrow my eyes. "It's my choice, asshole. It's my body and I decide what goes on it and who touches it."

"Come." He stands, hauling me up. "We need to discuss this in private."

When Kelli stands, he points to her. "You stay here. Keep an eye on things."

There's a little hallway at the back of the room and he leads me into one of the unmarked doors. It's some kind of VIP suite for privacy. I can only imagine what it's usually used for, and my cheeks flame. I don't want to be alone with this guy anymore. I shouldn't even be here.

I turn on him. "You need to be nicer to Kelli." Here I go defending her again when she screwed me over.

"Oh, you mean the woman responsible for your poor choice in outfit tonight?" He motions to me. "Because I can assure you I'm no fool. I know she didn't tell you to dress up."

I shrug. "I like how I look."

"Is that so?"

I square my shoulders. "Yes."

"Very well, though I find it strange you're defending Kelli. Do you realize she's mad that you're my fledgling?"

I narrow my eyes. "Well, tell her it's not really going to happen. That's what you said, right? You'd entertain this game but didn't actually plan to turn me."

He slaps his hand over my mouth and pushes me against the wall, glaring. "Keep your voice down. Do you know how many listening ears are around anytime I'm in public? If that got back to Brisa, you'd be dead."

I push him off. "Fine, but don't touch me."

"What is this about Kelli's fledgling? What do you know?"

"Tell me what you know about Tate," I return. "Why is he messing with people's memories?"

"I suspected this but you just confirmed it for me." He begins to pace the little room. "I knew they could sometimes wipe minds like that, but I didn't think anyone had developed the ability in over a century."

"What are you talking about?"

His eyes land on me. "It's better that you don't know."

"Says you, maybe." I frown. "But am I safe going there? Are my friends safe training underneath Tate?"

"Probably not," he supplies, "but they're humans, so they're not safe anywhere." He comes closer. "And neither are you."

Closer. Closer. Closer. I'm back up against the wall, and he's leaning into me. I think maybe he's going to bite me. My heart rate speeds up, and my mouth waters. I kinda, sorta, maybe ... want him to bite me. It must be the venom. It's reaching out, clearing my mind of any objections.

He runs the cool tip of his nose along my neck and then up to whisper in my ear. "What have you seen him do?"

"Huh?"

He chuckles and pulls back. "What have you seen Tate do? What else do you know of him?"

"He returned last week. Everyone's acting like he never left. Nobody questions him. He brought me into his office and told me to trust him. I did, but part of me fought back, I think because of Hugo's venom." I whisper that last part. "So I followed him to a hospital ICU. He did some kind of energy exchange thing there. Do you know what I'm talking about? Where they steal energy from humans?"

He nods once.

"So, what are they?"

"Like I said, it's better if you don't know."

"You're really annoying."

Someone knocks on the door.

"Come in," Adrian says, albeit a little reluctantly.

I'm expecting it to be Kelli.

It's not.

Eleven

"**I**'ve been looking for you," the man says.

Hugo.

Not Hugo. Hugo is dead.

Hugo is dead.

But this man looks eerily like Hugo. I want to run, to scream, to fight—anything. But I'm frozen to the spot. My senses grow the most they have since I was bit, almost drowning me with smell and sight and ... I can't think. I need to go.

"Sebastian, I didn't expect to see you here," Adrian says. His voice comes at me loud and fast, but also like he's speaking through a wall of glass.

"Brisa is allowing me to investigate my twin's death." The man saunters into the room, his lip curled up like he just smelled something rotten. So that's why I thought it was Hugo. Sebastian looks exactly like the dead vampire—Italian, broad-shouldered, handsome, middle-aged, and creepy. And now he's here to *investigate*?

"That's good," Adrian says smoothly, "I hope you can catch the hunters who did this. I've been looking for them myself but so far have no leads."

Sebastian's eyes flick to mine. "Why do you smell so good?" His fangs begin to extend. Oh, so maybe not rotten.

"Virgin blood." Adrian positions himself in front of me. "She's mine."

I'm his—it's the same thing Kelli said. What have I gotten myself into?

I flash back to how Hugo figured out I was connected into his line. My blood had spilled, and that's all it took. That could happen again. One wrong move and it'll all be over. Being here is more dangerous than ever. I

250

never should've pushed for this. What do I really think I'll learn that can help the hunters? So far all I've done is put myself in danger.

Sebastian's fangs retract, but his pupils stay dilated and his eyes remain on me. "You know, I've always found it frustrating that so much of the archaic vampire lore happens to be true. We can't go in the sun. We're allergic to silver. We're killed with a stake to the heart. We're even adverse to garlic––it smells horrible and I'm Italian. Such a pity."

"And you're born in cemeteries," I add, trying to make my voice sound light.

"We are." His head tilts. "But being attracted to the blood of virgins? That's one I've never minded."

"What's so special about it?" Adrian stiffens when I ask the question.

"Nobody knows," the man smiles, "but it works both ways. Did you know that? We're more attracted to you," he steps forward, "and you're more attracted to us. Back in the day, priests used to have virgins walk through graveyards at night looking for vampire graves. The girls could sometimes spot our newly buried prodigy's graves, and the priests would dig them up and stake them before they had a chance to fully change." His smile turns mocking. "Now, tell me, who's more barbaric?"

I've always hated vampires, but maybe this explains part of why it was easier for me to track that one. I had venom from the same line and virgin blood. Maybe I really am special. I shoot a charged look at Adrian––no wonder he wanted me to "take care of it."

"So what would happen if a fledgling was turned into a prodigy while still a virgin?"

"That's––"

"Let's go," Adrian cuts him off, "we have business to attend to."

I want to object and ask Sebastian to finish but the two are looking at each other now like they hate each other, like their history is even worse than Hugo's, and it's as if I'm no longer in the room.

"Ah, that's right."Sebastian wiggles his fingers. "Pretend I'm a fly on the wall."

As if that were possible.

Adrian takes my hand and squeezes, his way of telling me to stick close. I wonder what the implications of Sebastian being here means for me. Is he going to figure out what happened that night? Will they turn me? Kill me? What will happen to Adrian? If Hugo was a prince, then surely Sebastian is one as well.

When we get back to the main room, it's filled up with more vampires and their fledglings. Standing room only. Adrian sits me next to Kelli, who's now got Cameron at her side. I gape at him. He forgot everything so why is he here? Kelli nods toward him. "He showed up here a couple minutes ago. Apparently it all came back to him and he's on our side."

But how? Is Tate's ability not as strong as I thought?

"Hey," Cameron whispers when he sees me.

"You remembered?"

He nods curtly. "Yup."

I don't have a good feeling about this. Something isn't adding up.

"Get all the humans who aren't prodigies out of this building," Adrian instructs one of his minions who takes off in a flash––literally. These creatures can move so fast that sometimes they look like a flash.

We mingle for a few minutes, but I don't offer much to the conversations. I'm listening intently though, hoping for something I can bring back to Seth. My eyes keep going from Adrian to Sebastian and back again. Sebastian is even more charismatic than his brother was, the creepiness factor not quite there. That's got to make him more dangerous. People flock to him, and he engages a crowd with practiced ease, moving through them like I imagine a prince should. He's a true diplomat.

Adrian seems annoyed. This is his territory, after all. And his coven. But he hides it well, or maybe we're all used to Adrian being annoyed. The dancers have long been sent away by the time Adrian strides to the center of the room and then levitates, hovering above the busy crowd. Everyone falls silent, their leader commanding attention without having to say a word. Several of the humans gaze up at him like he's a god or something. It's hard not to glower at them.

"Thank you for coming," Adrian says. "Many of you already know how this is going to work, but some of you have waited for me to explain it to your humans." His blue gaze seems to glow as he surveys the room, making a point to look at us fledglings. Right now we're nothing, but soon we'll be their prodigies. Maybe. "You are not guaranteed a spot in our coven even though you've been selected to be the next prodigy to your masters. You must prove your loyalty and utility. When your master feels you are ready, he or she will petition the queen. Only Brisa can decide who joins our fold and when."

Damn. I knew Brisa was controlling, but this is next level.

"There is no set rule in our coven about how, when, or where to test you. We do things a little differently each year so that the playing field stays level. Once you are ready, you will be turned. If you are deemed unworthy, however," his voice drops an octave, "well, let's just say you don't want to find out what happens to you then."

They kill us.

He doesn't have to say more, it's apparent. Maybe because we know too much. Probably because they can get away with it. Either way, my mouth grows dry. Nervous whispers ignite throughout the room, spreading to every corner. The fledglings are all young, athletic-looking, beautiful people. Everyone has a chance. And I hate them all. They're here because they want immortality, even at the cost of human lives. If I look hard enough, I can see their auras. The colors are dingy, dark, and not bright and happy like so many other humans I've been able to see. I wish I could see my own aura, but I can't. Would mine be pretty or would mine be dirty? At least I'm only here because I'm a double agent, sent to help the humans.

"Your first test starts now. You will go out into the city and bring back a human to do a willing blood donation within the hour. What we do with that donor is up to us." The vampires laugh as we sit here, letting this challenge sink in. Shouldn't be too hard, right? Except what do I have to offer someone to get them to come back here? It almost sounds like we're supposed to go find someone to sacrifice. "Well, go on." Adrian flicks his wrist. "The clock is ticking."

"Come on," I get up, nodding to Cameron, "are we going to do this or what?"

We go outside, and Cameron veers off without me. I shake my head and shoot a middle finger to his back. "Jerk," I mumble.

I don't want to do this.

I'm not really going to be a prodigy, I hate the fledglings, and I take zero delight in finding someone to become a vampire's snack. What will happen if I go back there empty handed?

I don't know what to do. If it were only Adrian here, I'd refuse this request. But it's not only Adrian here, and there are eyes on him now, eyes reporting back to the queen, eyes looking to avenge their dead twin brother.

And I'm all alone. I'm keenly aware that I'm a young woman alone at night in a very dangerous city. This is not a place I want to be.

I can't do this.

I can't bring someone up there. What if they kill them? Sure, they may only get willing donations, but I've seen vampires kill before. I saw Adrian do it. I later figured out that it was a mobster he'd killed, and maybe someone who deserved it, but Adrian hadn't wanted me to know that. He'd wanted me to believe that it was someone who didn't deserve it. That he was a ruthless killer. He wanted me to see who he really was so that I wouldn't be stupid enough to keep coming around. I should've listened.

That's when the idea strikes me.

Twelve

❧

I walk across the street to the casino, heading past the tables and right for the nurses' office. "Hey, do you guys know who I am?"

The woman at reception stares at me blankly and shakes her head. I sigh and head for the tables, looking for one of the pit bosses. Sure enough, I find the very same guy who pissed me off the first day I met Adrian. *Well, this is going to be fun.* I motion to him with my finger and to my delight, he comes right away.

"You know who I am, right? You can vouch for me?" I ask.

He groans under his breath but nods.

"Great. Follow me. We have to do something for Adrian."

I turn and stride back to the nurses' station. I don't bother to see if he followed because I can sense him at my back.

"Me again," I say to the same lady from before. "He can vouch for me. I work for Adrian."

She raises an eyebrow and the vampire answers. "Adrian instructed us to keep her safe and do whatever she needs." With that, he shoots me a glare and then turns and walks away.

I don't care. I've perked up at his confession, warmth spreading through me. More news and this time it's actually good news.

"Right." I smile back at the woman. "Adrian says I'm supposed to bring one of you across the street to do blood donations over there at the club."

The lady frowns. "Are they short-staffed again?"

Okay, I can work with this. "Oh, you know how it is. There's always another human in line. Can I walk someone over?"

"Hold on," she says, "I'll grab a nurse for you."

Five minutes later, I'm walking back across the street with Nurse Giggi at my side, hoping this isn't a huge mistake. My nerves are like a coil of angry snakes raging in my belly, but I can't think about that right now. Technically, this is what Adrian asked for, and he should know I have a way with twisting his words.

When we get back to the nightclub VIP area, we're one of the first to arrive. Adrian is sitting with Sebastian, their heads bent together in deep conversation. Nothing about Adrian's demeanor exposes his guilt. He's had how many years now to perfect his lying capabilities? I need to remember that next time I want to believe him about something.

"Here you go," I say, interrupting them. "The human you asked for."

They stop and stare up at me. Adrian's mouth thins. "Who's this?"

"You told us to bring you a human for blood donations." Poor Nurse Giggi stiffens at my side as I continue. "Well, that's what she is, right? She's trained in taking donations."

The room is quiet, the waiting vampires watching our exchange, when Sebastian bursts into laughter. His energy is so different than Hugo's had been, so open and charismatic. I can't imagine Hugo ever had a sense of humor. Adrian doesn't have much of one either, because his mouth is still thinned and his eyes are glued to me.

"Do you not need my services?" Giggi balks and steps back.

Adrian holds up a hand to stop her. "Actually, I think you should stay. We can always use more help." He nods over to the corner of the room and tells her to wait over there.

"Your lady is something else." Sebastian gives me a wink. "You sure you want to be with this guy? I could get you into my bloodline during my next prodigy cycle."

Hmm, I've heard that one before.

"Very funny." Adrian grabs me, pulling me down to sit in his lap. My heart rate speeds up, and he leans down to whisper against my cheek. "You like to push my buttons, don't you?"

I elbow him in the chest, which does nothing but hurt my funny bone. I try not to wince but I do and he chuckles darkly. "You make it so easy. How is that my fault?"

He tightens his grip around my stomach but doesn't say anything more. I could move. I could slide to his side or get up--anything--and I'm certain he'd let me. But I don't. We have to appear like we want this to work. I'm more than a little grateful he didn't kill me for skirting around his dumb assignment. I'm not sure I'll be able to keep doing that.

"You're quite clever," Sebastian says, turning on me with his dark gaze. "Tell me, did you have the opportunity to meet my brother?"

I nod.

"Right answer," he says. He must already know. Adrian said he was going to tell Brisa that I was there that night. I try to get the story straight in my mind, but it goes annoyingly blank. "Lying to a vampire is a terrible idea."

I'm not going to let this guy get the best of me.

"I don't have a death wish. Well, that's unless it comes with a three night stay in a graveyard." I wink playfully. "So ask me anything. I was there that night Hugo was killed by those hunters. I have nothing to hide."

"So forthright," Sebastian says. "Okay, how did it happen? I want every detail."

"Now is not really the time," Adrian says, "we can schedule an appointment for this if you'd like."

"Now is the perfect time." I elbow Adrian again. "Like I said, there's nothing to hide. I was supposed to be Adrian's fledgling, but Hugo took over and was going to be my master instead. They took me to the graveyard together, but hunters showed up, killing your brother before we could do anything. Adrian saved me and then stepped in to be my master once again. And that's about it, Sebastian. I'm sorry about your twin. We tried to help, but we were ambushed."

"Hmm," Sebastian says, "I can see why you picked her, Adrian."

"I didn't pick her," Adrian replies, "she picked me."

"Well isn't that adorable."

"You know what I mean. I don't believe in building our family lines. We're more vulnerable when there's too many of us. We're too open to mistakes, especially our younger spawn. But it was time to add another to my line and this one asked for the role."

The two men stare off like they're either about to debate with words or with fists.

"Whatever." I slip off Adrian's lap and sit at the end of the couch. I'm not getting between those two. "I'm a woman who makes her own choices, and I wanted to become a vampire. What's so wrong with that?"

"And as a woman who makes her own choices," Sebastian's tone shifts, turning slightly accusatory as he glares at me, "why would you choose to become a vampire? You'll be beholden to Adrian, and through Adrian to Brisa, for the rest of your existence."

That's if they don't die first. But I don't add that thought. "Because I'd rather be immortal. I want to be able to feel and experience the world to its fullest, like you can."

"That's a clichéanswer." He gets up and comes to stand above me, leaning in close. His pupils dilate, and his fangs peek through his lips. "What's the truth?"

I dig deep, searching for a better answer. The truth? I hate vampires. I want them eradicated from the planet. But why? So I can feel safe. So I can live without looking over my shoulder. So I can have all the things I deserved to have that were stolen from me when my mother became an addict.

"Tell me," he demands, inching closer.

Adrian holds him back. "Leave her."

"Because I want to feel safe," I grind out. "Because I want to be taken care of. Because I want a real family."

Both men relax. Pity creeps into Adrian's eyes, and I have to look away.

Sebastian points at me as he steps away. "The truth will set you free."

Okay, lame. Who does this guy think he is? Jerry Maguire?

"That's enough," Adrian says. "We need to move this along." He motions to the room, which has filled up with people. They're mingling among each other, the humans easy to pick out in the crowd. Some seem nervous, their eyes darting from sucker to sucker, and some seem excited. Cameron is there, a young woman in club attire at his side. They chat casually, but his body language is stiff and uncertain.

The vampires stand and circle the humans, their eyes growing hungry. This might not be what I thought it was. What if this is a bloodbath? What if they kill all these humans and dispose of the bodies discreetly? There's got to be at least twenty humans who aren't fledglings. Surely they can't cover up twenty deaths. The Vampire Enforcement Coalition wouldn't allow it.

Or would they?

I'm starting to suspect the VEC is nothing but a farce and a way for them to pretend like they're behaving, and another way to assert power over each other––big egos versus even bigger egos. Because if a human gets bit, they're as good as dead. Vampires don't want humans to have the senses that I have and I can see why, now that it's burning through me. It would make us all excellent fighters, able to track them, able to kill them easier. What if every human in the world was able to get the venom injected into them, kind of like a vaccine? We'd become strong enough to fight them, maybe even end them all.

If I could somehow get the word out, somehow find a way . . .

"Well done," Adrian says, "now let's eat."

I expect the vampires to pounce, for blood to fly and bodies to hit the floor.

Nurses appear with all the necessary supplies and begin taking blood. They even have little handheld devices to see who's eligible to give and how much. The entire thing is completely legal and anticlimactic. Nurse Giggi is among them and she gives me a little wave when we make eye contact.

I don't think I've ever been more grateful for an anticlimactic moment.

This was a test. Would we risk another's life for the vampires? We passed, but I don't feel any better than I did before.

Just as I start to relax, start to think that everyone is going to get out of here alive, everything changes. Cameron dives on Kelli with a guttural scream, a silver stake firm in his hand. It sinks right through her center. She screams.

Thirteen

K elli evaporates into dust.

I scream.

It's not like those other times I saw vampires die. There's no joy in this. I feel her loss immediately, like the stake went through my own heart. Kelli wasn't a friend, per se, but I liked her and thought maybe . . .

I don't know what I thought.

But she's gone, and my senses burst to life once again. Cameron stands against the railing, stakes in both hands, ready to fight. He sneers, looking right at me. "That vile sucker showed up last night and insisted that I was hers and told me to come here. And so I do and here you are––"

He never finishes his sentence. Adrian flies at him, ripping the stakes from his hands as if they're children's toys. He tosses them to the ground with a clatter.

Cameron opens his arms wide, accepting his fate. But his eyes are frantic––death isn't what he wants. It's too late. Adrian pushes Cameron over the railing. Cameron doesn't even scream on his way down. He disappears from view, followed by a quick dull thump. Adrian growls savagely and jumps down after him.

Sebastian follows.

As do several others.

I stand frozen, unwilling to look over the railing and see for myself. A few of the humans run over to watch, while most of us crowd to the back of the room. We can all hear what's happening. Personally, I don't need to see it, too.

A couple minutes later, Adrian flies up, hovering midair. His appearance causes a ripple of gasps from almost everyone in the room. Not me. His eyes are bloodshot. I didn't know that happened to vampires. Does it have something to do with anger rather than bloodlust? Or maybe it's because he just fed from human flesh, not a blood bag. Whatever it is, the sight sends a chill right through me. Blood drips from his mouth and stains the top of his crisp white shirt.

"Go home." His voice is eerily calm, but I can trace the grief there. Kelli was his only prodigy, and now she's nothing but dust. "Go home and tell everyone what you saw here. Tell them how a hunter tried to take us out when we were obeying the law. We did nothing wrong. He murdered one of our own in cold blood and would've killed more if he had the chance. Tell them exactly what happened." His eyes land on me. "And let them know we will root out anyone who hurts us. And when we do, we will kill them. No hunter in this city is safe."

He zooms away, practically disappearing into thin air.

I leave with everyone else, guilt wracking me as I do. I want to go to Adrian and explain what I think happened here, to make sure he doesn't blame me. But maybe he should blame me. I failed to protect Kelli, didn't I? I should've known this could happen. The moment I saw Cameron in here, I should've stopped him. In his mind, all he knew was that vampires were bad and he should kill them. Tate made him forget the rest. So Kelli showing up and telling him he's her fledgling last night must have freaked him out. But he did come, and then he acted on his training. And now they're both dead.

And here you are . . .

What was he going to say? Was he going to reveal who I am to everyone? Was he expecting me to help him? I'll never know. Maybe it's better that I don't.

I go to the casino. I want to head up to Adrian's office so we can talk about this but the elevator won't open. I try the penthouse elevator, which does work, and I head up to his room instead. I knock on the door, but he doesn't answer. I'm sure he's probably in there, but he won't come to the door. I don't have his number either. My only contact is calling The Alabaster when I need to relay a message through Kelli. I'm not sure what to do now.

"Listen," I call through the door, "I'm sorry about what happened. Do you have my number?" He doesn't reply and maybe I'm talking to thin air. I tell him the number anyway, assuming he can memorize it. And then I leave.

When I locate my Porsche in the parking garage, Sebastian appears next to me; I nearly jump out of my skin.

"Geez! Do you have manners? You shouldn't sneak up on someone like that." My heart beats wildly and my senses grow.

"It comes with the territory." That's true. I don't think vampires know how to be loud.

I fold my arms over my chest. "How can I help you, Sebastian?"

"You can explain what happened back there."

None of your business.

We stop and stare off. This is the part where I lie and tell him I have no idea. But I don't. I know I can't be compelled, and I know I can't trust this guy, but something inside of me spills the truth.

"I'm a hunter, too. Adrian knows." I hold up my hands before he rips my head off. "I'm working for Adrian. How do you think I got the guy who insists he doesn't want a family line to agree to take me on as his fledgling?"

Sebastian looks me up and down. "If you're lying, I will find out, and I will kill you."

I laugh. "Believe me, I know."

"So is this how my brother died?"

"No, he died as we said he did. Hunters ambushed us and killed him."

He studies me for a long while. "You know, someone is going around and killing off the princes. Brisa has lost almost all her direct prodigies, Hugo included. It's my job to find out who's doing it and deliver them to her."

My mouth falls open a little. "I've not heard anything about this."

"There will be dire consequences for the humans if the bloodlines are severed," he goes on. "Brisa is the best thing that's ever happened to humankind."

It takes everything in me not to snort because this guy has got to be delusional. She's the reason vampires are out in public, the mastermind behind this system of trading blood for addictions. I hate her with everything in me. Killing her would be my dream come true. "And how do you figure that?"

"Because without her, our one strong vampire bloodline would splinter off into several independent lines. Do you know how many vampires would love nothing more than to feed and kill whoever they wanted? And they would be free to do that because nobody would be able to tell them not to."

I have no response to that and feel stupid that I'd never thought of it. But it makes sense, and it flips my entire world upside down. I should get out of this. Return the fancy car, refuse to be a fledgling anymore, drop the hunters, everything. Just be done.

I should, but I won't. I'm not sure I even can at this point.

"Adrian is going to be grieving his child," Sebastian continues, his voice growing cold. "So it's a good thing he has you to tend to his broken heart. Can you imagine how he'd feel if you had died tonight as well? If someone wanted to get back at him, say someone who lost his twin recently for no good reason, well, I think your death would be the perfect move."

I widen my stance, my mind racing to the thin stake under my shirt. Could I get to it in time?

"But don't worry," Sebastian continues, "I'd never do such a thing to my own brother." He strolls off, whistling as he does, as if he didn't just threaten my life to get back at Adrian. He rounds the corner, disappearing, but his nasally tune echoes through the parking garage for another full minute.

I DON'T HEAR from Adrian. September crawls into October, and life continues as if I weren't a vampire's fledgling at all. Felix and I go back to being friends with*out* benefits, even though it's hard. So many times I catch him staring at me in a way that sends my heart fluttering. I want to kiss him––to do more than kiss him––but I don't. Things have gotten too complicated. Between his past with my roommate, Ayla refusing to talk to me, Seth telling me to back off, and mostly because I'm not a very safe person to date right now, it's better that I go back to waiting.

Waiting for Felix is something I'm used to, even though it's killing me.

I keep expecting the venom to wear off, but it doesn't. I've quickly become the top member on my team, able to fight faster than anyone else. Even the simulations are easy for me now. And the more I grow in my abilities, the more I can sense things I never could before. And the more I can see things. But I know the simulations aren't the real thing, and I'm eager to hunt.

Too bad I'm in an impossible situation. Being a double agent sucks.

One day, I'm driving back from a dayshift at Pops, marveling at the swirls of colors surrounding all the people as they walk down the sidewalks. It's crowded today, and the auras remind me of misty clouds bouncing into each other. There's roadwork on my usual route, so I follow the GPS down a curvy side street. It's narrow with tall buildings that cast cool shadows down below. There are shops here I haven't seen before, so I drive a little slow and look at the pretty storefronts. There's an eclectic gift shop, a clothing boutique, an independent bookstore, a little bakery, and a voodoo shop.

A lot of the businesses down in this part of town say they deal in voodoo as a way to bring tourists in. I don't know how much of it is authentic, but either way, it's something I've chosen to stay away from. Growing up in New Orleans, a lot of the parents and grandparents teach their kids that voodoo is dangerous. I'm not sure what parts of voodoo are considered a closed-practice and what aren't, what's safe or even real. I'm not going to judge anyone who practices religion, but it's not my thing. Never has been. Never will be.

Never say never, right?

Because something catches my eye, a bright flash of golden reflective light in my peripheral vision. The window display of the voodoo shop is filled to the brim with little dolls and trinkets, nothing unusual. Except there's also a golden metal decoration. It's two crossing feathers in the same shape as the little stamp on the back of the silver cross I wear around my neck. It seems far-fetched, especially since a cross is typically a Christian symbol, but maybe my grandmother bought the necklace there.

The same grandmother who made me promise to stay away from voodoo. So why do I have the feeling she was hiding something?

I parallel park like a pro. It was the one thing I spent hours practicing for the driver's exam and aced with flying colors, which is important living in a busy city. I climb out of the car and head into the shop before my sweet gran's voice in my head can stop me. The bell chimes as I enter, but nobody comes to check on me. It doesn't seem like anyone's even in here. The shop is tiny and packed. Skull candles, jewelry, herbs, crystals, loads more of the dolls, and a bunch of other things that I'm not sure how to identify. I go to the window display and crane my neck to try to get a better look at the golden feathers.

Just as I thought, it's an exact match for the one stamped on the back of my cross. Upon first inspection, it looks like any other simple design of feathers and nothing too special, but there's a little hook at the bottom of the left feather that makes it distinctive.

Mine has the same one. I pinch it between my fingers and an eerie sense of foreboding prickles down my body.

"Can I help you?" a scratchy voice croons.

I turn to find a tiny middle-aged woman with creamy tanned skin and long braided hair staring at me. She's beautiful but immediately I can sense her anger. It reminds me of Kelli and my heart drops.

"I was wondering if you could tell me about these feathers?" I ask politely.

She glares at me, which is certainly an odd way to treat a customer. "What do you want with that talisman, girl?"

My mouth pops open, but I recover quickly, folding my arms over my chest. My politeness was short-lived. "Listen, I don't know what your problem is with me, but I'm a potential customer and––"

"No, you're not." She shoos me to the door. "Get out of here."

I gape at her. I've never had such a strange interaction with a salesperson, and it's obvious the woman is trying to get me out of here before I can learn what that talisman is for. I've watched enough CW shows to know a talisman is an object that holds a spell.

I pull the cross out from under the neckline of my shirt and flip it over, showing her the little stamp. "My grandmother gave this to me. She wore it her whole life as far as I know. Her and my mom have insisted I wear it now, too."

"A lot of people wear crucifixes to ward off vampires, which is silly because it doesn't work."

"I want to know about the feathers. My gran is dead or I'd ask her myself."

"What does this have to do with me?" The woman stomps past me and opens the door. "You need to leave or I'll call the police."

"No, look," I press, "on the back of it, see? There's a little feather. It's the same one."

The woman stares at me for a long moment, her eyes going from my face to the necklace and back again. Her demeanor stays hard. "It's for protection," she barks out.

"The feather or the cross?"

I already know the cross is supposed to be protection, but Adrian had no issue ripping it from my throat. It didn't do anything to hurt him, but maybe that's because the chain wasn't real silver. Maybe it was, I'm not sure, but it easily could've been something else. I definitely think the new chain is silver though, Felix wouldn't mess around or lie to me about that.

"Superstitions run deep around here," she says. "Both."

My eyes start to water. "My grandmother was my favorite person in the whole wide world." Losing her nearly killed me and Mom.

"I'm sorry for your loss," she grinds out. "Keep wearing the feathers."

So really, it's the feathers that mattered to gran, not the cross like she led me to believe.

"Protection from what?"

She swallows and then whispers. "Listen, I don't want anything to do with this. You shouldn't have come here."

"Are you talking about vampires?" I whisper. "Or something else?"

She stills. That's it then. Does this symbol have something to do with the energy demon things? Is this protection from them? I always thought it was for the vampires, but maybe I was wrong. I wonder how much my gran knew. I wonder what would happen if I showed it to Tate. Would he freak out? Would he be fine?

"Please . . ." My voice cracks. "I have nowhere else to go."

"You don't have a place here either, and trust me, you do not want to get on my bad side," she hisses. She points to one of the dolls, which I know are used for hexes, and that's when I decide maybe I'd better listen. I can't even leave a bad review online for fear of retribution. I never thought I believed in any of this stuff, but turns out I sorta do.

I go back to my car and stare at the window display for a few minutes. How could a question about a feather symbol cause such an upset? The answer is because they mean something important, something to do with protection that she doesn't want to discuss with me. I wince, realizing that the more I look for answers, the more questions I end up with. Hours roll by and I'm still thinking about the necklace.

Fourteen

$\mathcal{G}\!\!\!\!\sim\!\!\!\!\mathcal{D}$

I knock on the Morenos' door, and a few minutes later Mrs. Moreno opens it. "Eva, it's so good to see you honey." She hugs me, but she comes out onto the doorstep to do it. It's the first time she doesn't immediately invite me inside.

"Is Ayla here?" I ask tentatively.

The woman steps back and frowns. "I'm sorry, she's not seeing guests right now."

I blink at her, unsure how to respond. Ayla has been my bestie for ages and I still can't believe this is happening. "Nobody?"

Mrs. Moreno shakes her head with a little frown. "We're trying to respect her wishes," her voice cracks and she whispers. "We don't know what to do. She's refusing to leave the house. The therapist says it's an anxiety disorder called agoraphobia."

"But she won't let anyone visit her either?"

Her eyes water. "Not even Felix. She won't talk to anyone. We don't know what to do. At this point, our main concern is keeping her alive." She wipes a tear. "I never thought this would happen to one of our kids."

I wring my hands behind my back, my emotions torn to shreds. I should probably tell her about the vampire attack, but that would involve revealing Felix's secrets. And I'm pretty sure Ayla would be upset if I did, but my friend's safety and happiness is important. I want her to heal. Ayla's made of tough stuff, always has been, so to see her like this is terrible.

In the end, I decide to go half way. "Is the therapist doing house calls?"

"They're doing video conferencing. Ayla gets upset at the thought of anyone coming into the house."

Yeah, because she's afraid of vampires, and vampires have to be invited into a private residence. It makes sense. It doesn't make sense that she's turning humans away, but her mind is probably having a hard time separating it all.

"You should tell the therapist to talk to Ayla about a possible fear of vampires."

Mrs. Moreno's face goes pale and she does the sign of the cross, muttering to herself in Spanish. "Has Ayla seen a vampire?"

"I have to go," I say, backing away. "But trust me, there's something there."

I go back and sit in the car for a while. Then I get out and go to the side of the house where I can knock on Ayla's window. The curtains are drawn, so I can't see in, but I know she's got to be in there. I pull out my phone and text her.

Are you okay? We should talk.

I told you not to come back here, is her immediate reply. She knows I'm out here which is probably why she replied to me at all.

I have something to tell you. Please, at least come to the window.

A minute later the curtain moves and Ayla cracks the window. Not enough for me to go in or anything, but enough so we can talk. I jog over and study her through the reflective glass. Her hair is in a messy bun on the top of her head, her eyes are sunken, and she's wearing oversized pajamas.

"Hey," I keep my voice low and smooth. "Are you okay?"

"What did you want to tell me?" She folds her arms over her chest and lifts a messy eyebrow. It's another reminder of how much my friend has changed. She's hurting, sick, and I want to help her. I wish I knew how to rewind everything.

"I broke it off with Felix, but that's not all I wanted to say."

"Trouble in paradise? I could've told you he's a player." Her voice is annoyed.

"I broke it off because I don't think it's the best idea right now."

"Oh, right now, huh? So you're still going to hook up with my brother later on?"

I sigh heavily and grind my sandal into the grass. "Ugh, I don't know, Ayla, that's not what this is about."

"Okay, fine, what else is so important that you had to disrespect my wishes by coming and knocking on my window? You already know how I feel. I don't want you hunting, and you're hunting. I don't want you dating my brother, and you did it behind my back. What else is there to talk about?"

My eyes water. "You're my best friend."

"Not anymore."

"What?" My voice cracks.

"Because I've changed." Her eyes narrow. "People change and grow up and move on. You need to get over it."

Despite everything I've gone through with my mom, this is the worst betrayal I've ever experienced. My heart squeezes, and the hot tears finally release, running down my cheeks. "I was going to say sorry and that I am here for you. I wanted to show you my apartment. I wanted––"

"Just go home." Her voice is regretful. "I wish things were different, okay? But as long as you're involved with hunting vampires, I can't be your friend."

"So you're asking me to choose?"

"You already did." And then she slams the window shut, the curtains sliding back into place. My heart shuts down equally hard.

I never thought this would happen. I completely took our friendship for granted. But I'm angry, too. Because this is Ayla's choice, and she's not even going to try. One scary experience with vampires and that's it, she's shut out anyone and anything she can that could possibly put her in danger again. I don't blame her, but this extreme isn't healthy. She's locked herself in her room during the days now too. Vampires can't go out in sunlight, so what does she think is going to happen?

And yet . . . my gut says something is off––that there's more to the story. I want to help her fix the ending, but she won't let me.

"Nobody knows what happened to Cameron?" Tate asks. We look around at each other, but nobody speaks up.

He's called us in for an emergency meeting because it's been so long since Cameron has disappeared. There isn't room for everyone in his office, so we're sitting on the gym mats in our teams. Each team consists of three to five people who were recruited together. We're all young enough that our prefrontal cortexes haven't fully developed, ranging in age from eighteen to twenty-four, and Cameron was getting near that cut off. Soon Tate would've been wiping his mind clear of any memories of his time with the hunters, except that's impossible now that he's dead.

I look around, really hoping that we're all humans here. I blink a few times, concentrating, and the auras start to materialize. As far as I can tell, everyone has one. Everyone except for Leslie Tate, that is.

Someone in the back raises his hand. "I think I might know something," he says with a regretful tone.

My heart riots against my ribcage, adrenaline racing through my limbs. I'm frozen, my breath trapped in my lungs. I feel as if everyone is staring at me, but I know they're not. I wish I could debrief my team on everything that's happened, but I don't trust Tate anymore and they're too close to him. What if he was able to get information out of them that I didn't want him to know? I hate that Cameron's death is something I've had to keep to myself.

"What do you know, Kevin?" Tate walks toward the guy, and once he passes us, I relax a little. I exchange worried glances with my team. Kenton reaches over to squeeze my hand. It's completely platonic, we've become great friends, and I'm struck by how grateful I am for him. Nobody will ever replace Ayla, but it's nice to know I have a friend like Kenton in my corner.

"I've only heard rumors." Kevin stands up and addresses the room. "But apparently a hunter tried to attack vampires during one of their meetups. He killed one of them." He swallows hard. "That's the good news."

"And the bad news?"

He doesn't have to say it--everybody knows--but he does anyway. "They ripped him to pieces. By the time they were done with him, there wasn't anything left."

We're all quiet. Nobody's surprised. It's part of the risks in doing what we're doing, and nobody is stupid enough to come here thinking they'll be the exception. We hope we'll survive and assume we won't. It's the life of a vampire hunter.

"Thank you," Tate says. He turns back to all of us. "This is why we do what we do. We have to defeat these monsters."

But how? Honestly, how are we going to end them? They're all over the planet. They're everywhere. And they can turn more of us into them anytime they want. Sometimes this mission seems helpless.

"We're going to take back our city," Tate says, "we've been too soft, too slow, and too careful."

Careful? Cameron is dead, and Tate's telling us we're being too careful.

"It's time we get them in one swoop," Tate continues. "There's a meetup tomorrow at the Alabaster Heart with the entire coven. Every vampire in New Orleans will be there."

His gaze locks us in. "And we're going to pay them a visit. It's time to end this coven and take back our city. Are you in?"

It's a death wish. We can't do this. We may be able to get some of them, but there's no way we could get them all. And even if we did, the vampires from other cities would retaliate.

There's no way to win.

"Our target is Adrianos Teresi. I'll be emailing you all a breakdown on him. He's the heart of the operation. We take him out first."

Everyone stands up, and I follow. What else can I do? But my legs are shaking and Adrian's face fills my mind.

"Who's in?"

We cheer our agreement, but I know how foolish this is. We're going to end up like Cameron, every last one of us.

Fifteen

"We can't go through with this," I announce the second we're back to Seth and Felix's place. "It's going to be a bloodbath."

"It'd better be!" Kenton laughs. "This is what we've been waiting for. This is our chance."

"I hardly think a few months of training is enough," I scoff. I plop down on the couch and press my palms into my eyes, trying to think. "What benefit would Tate have to take Adrian out?"

"This isn't just about your little vampire prince," Felix interjects. It's the first time he's spoken to me directly since we broke up, not that we were really together for long. But he's avoided me and it's been awful. "Tate wants to clean up New Orleans."

I shake my head. "This has more to do with the vampire royalty than it does our city." I stand and begin to pace the little room. "Vampire princes have been turning up dead all over the world the last few weeks."

"Good," Felix mutters.

Are they even listening to me? "No, not good," I retort. "It's not what you think. If the royals fall, the vamp hierarchy collapses. And that means anarchy."

"What are you saying?" Seth speaks up.

"I am saying that vampires will go back to killing humans for meals. They only follow all these rules about biting and feeding and making their children because the bloodlines are so strong and the queen makes the rules. If the princes die off and the queen is killed, everything they've created will fall apart and not in a good way."

Everyone goes quiet for a while. "And why would Tate want anarchy?" Felix asks.

"I don't know yet." I swallow hard. I don't want to say too much but I have to say enough to get them to understand. "And I know you guys trust him, but I promise you, that feeling is part of his abilities. We all know he's not human, but has he ever told any of you what he is? Have you even asked?"

They stare at me blankly, their faces too relaxed. This is exactly the problem. Tate is powerful enough to get people to believe whatever he says. They know he's different, but they don't question him because he tells them not to. It's only because of Hugo's venom that I'm lucky enough to see through the lies. I never thought I would be grateful for that creepy vampire trying to turn me, but here we are.

"This is getting dangerous," Felix says at last. "Maybe you should stay away."

"Me? How about all of us?"

"No, you."

"Oh, not this again. We already established that I'm part of this team."

"Last I checked you're probably invited to that coven meeting?"

I bite my lip and try not to scream. He's missing the point, trying to make this about something that it's not. "I honestly don't know yet."

"I think Felix has a point," Kenton interjects. "I'm sorry, Eva, but think about it. What if the vampires catch you with us or vice versa? You could end up killed."

I lean forward. "So what do you want me to do? Should I tell Adrian I'm out?"

"No," Seth's voice of reason cuts in, "I think you should be careful about being seen with hunters in public and skip the raid tomorrow. There's got to be something you can learn from that sucker—something that can help us."

I throw my hands up in the air. There shouldn't be a raid tomorrow, but I'm talking in circles with these guys. It's not their fault they're so influenced by Tate, but I'm not about to let my closest friends, the only friends I have left, walk into that casino tomorrow to be slaughtered. So I get up to leave.

"Please, don't go tomorrow. I promise, you won't win. You will die and I can't lose you."

Nobody moves. I leave before they can see me cry. I hate crying. I'm not a crier, damn it.

Felix catches me by my car. He gives the car a frown but I get a sweet smile. "Why are you running off so fast?"

I don't want to explain this to him, there's no point. And the last thing I need is for any of this to get back to Tate. "I've got stuff to do," is all I say.

He steps closer, his warm scent surrounding me. "Are you sure you have to leave?"

"Don't you have to get to class?"

"Not for another hour," he says. "Maybe we could hang out? Talk about things?"

He hasn't brought up the breakup since that first day, but it all comes flooding back now. Most of all, I'm overcome by the feelings I've had for him for so many years. They're so layered that I have a hard time sorting through them. Which ones are old? Which ones are new? Which ones are real?

"I don't want to hurt Ayla," I blurt out.

"Ayla is going through some tough stuff," he says, "and you and I both know it doesn't really have anything to do with us."

I don't know if that's true, but I desperately want to believe it. He leans in closer, trapping me against the car. I like it. A thrill of electricity races up my spine. "And what about the danger? What about the risks?" I whisper.

"We're already putting our lives on the line," he leans in, whispering against my ear, "shouldn't we be allowed to have some fun?"

I don't know if I've ever prioritized fun in my entire life. But I do deserve to have fun. I also need to get rid of my virginity so the vampires stop pestering me about it. Kelli's words float through my head again, and then I remember she's dead, that Cameron's dead, that any of us could go at any time.

Life is short--kiss the boy.

And so I do.

His body presses against mine, his arms wrapping around me, his mouth warm and soft. We kiss for a while, the tension between us growing. For once, I let myself have exactly what I want. I hope Ayla will forgive me and that this choice won't put anyone in danger, but it feels right, and I haven't felt right about anything in so, so long.

This is it.

When we break for a second, I whisper against his soft lips. "Take me upstairs." There's a huskiness to my voice and no doubts about my intentions.

"Are you sure?" he asks.

"Yes."

He peels us apart. "I may sound like I'm an asshole, but I'm trying not to be one for once," he says sheepishly, and I think he's rejecting me. "But I think we should take a little bit of time. I want you to be sure."

Oh.

My cheeks burn. "I said I was sure. I know how I feel."

"But you've had weeks of indecision about us." He wraps me back into a hug and kisses me on the top of the head. "Trust me, this is what I want too. Why don't we meet later tonight after you've had a little more time to think about it? Are you working?"

I shake my head. I guess a few hours isn't the worst thing. "It's my night off."

"Great, tomorrow night we will take down a coven. And tonight, that's for you and me. I promise, okay?"

I'm equal parts annoyed and excited––but I am sure about him, I really am. A couple hours, a couple days, months, or even years won't change my mind about this man. Even if Felix and I don't work out in the end, he's the guy I've been waiting for and the one I want to be my first. I'm not going to let this go. "I'll be back tonight then."

Famous last words . . .

Sixteen

⌥

The best way to save my friends is to stop this coven meeting from happening. If they show up to ambush the vampires and there's nobody there to fight with, then hopefully they can walk out of there alive. I may be making a horrible mistake, but once again, I find myself going to Adrian's casino uninvited. When I walk from the sunny outside world and through the double vestibules, the energy shifts. It's opulent inside the casino lobby and I'm used to that. But I'm not used to seeing someone else behind Kelli's desk.

I walk up to the young man and offer a winning smile. "I'm here to meet with Adrian. I'm Evangeline Blackwood." The young man stares at me with a blank expression. He's a vampire alright, and thoroughly creepy. His blond hair is slicked back, and his eyes assess me with dark intentions.

"You don't have an appointment," he says coolly.

"I don't need one," I respond, "I'm his fledgling."

He scoffs. "Honey, all of us were fledglings once upon a time. You think that makes you special? I have news, it doesn't."

I fold my arms over my chest and glare. "Maybe that was your experience, but Adrian treats his fledglings much differently. Do I need to show you my brand new Porsche?"

That was probably the wrong choice of words because the guy's face turns sour. "If you don't have an appointment, then you don't get to demand one without notice. I can fit you in next week, assuming Adrian agrees to take it."

I tap my foot on the tile, growing impatient. "I can't wait until next week."

"That's not my problem."

I grumble and sit down on one of the couches, my eyes trained on the elevator bay. He has to come down eventually, right? Well, that's assuming he's even up there. Hanging out in a vampire's den is not the best idea I've had in a while, but I'm not sure what else to do. So I wait and wait and wait, and the afternoon fades into evening. I'm supposed to go to Felix's place soon, and I need to go home and shower first. But that date seems so unimportant compared to this. I've got to get the vampires to call off their coven meeting tomorrow.

What if I'm making a mistake? What if Adrian uses this information against the hunters? Would he do that? Asked this question a month ago and I would've said yes without a moment's hesitation. But the same question now, and I don't think so. He's not interested in killing the hunters if he can't get to Tate.

And Tate's little plan?

He wants us to kill Adrian without his help. As per the little email that went out, Tate's not even planning to come tomorrow night. So essentially, he's sending the hunters in as sacrificial lambs. I don't know if he cares about our lives, but I kind of doubt it.

Screw this.

I rummage through my wallet, finding the metal key, and smirk. I shoot the executive assistant a dirty glare as I head for the elevators. Assuming he hasn't changed the locks, I still have what I need to get myself into Adrian's penthouse. The ride isn't solo. A human woman gets in with me. She's wearing the tiniest dress I've ever seen. The fabric is a little sheer and I can see her black undergarments.

"Oh, hey," her eyes narrow on me, "aren't you Adrian's fledgling?"

"Yup. I'm Eva."

She extends her hand firmly, and I shake it. "I'm Fiona. I'm Sebastian's fledgling this year. I travel with him wherever he goes."

"Very cool."

Though I don't think it's cool, and the more time I spend around these types of humans, the less I like or understand them. They're not doing this because they think it's right or because they want to help anyone. They're doing it because they have a sick fascination with vampires and want power. Maybe they want to feel safe, too, but even that is no excuse for signing up and jumping through hoops to impress these suckers.

We make it to the top floor. She goes to the door on the right, and I go left; Sebastian must have taken over Hugo's penthouse. He's a prince, it makes sense. I don't know what to think of Sebastian. Hugo was obviously creepy. Sebastian has charisma for days, but he's kind of like a slimy politician. She knocks softly, and I find it interesting that she doesn't have a key.

When I slide my key into Adrian's lock and turn it easily, I give her a parting goodbye. She doesn't say anything at first, but she does give me a curious look. "You know," she adds, her voice low. "It's weird that Adrian doesn't have a prodigy anymore. Kelli was his only one for years. It's good he has you. People talk."

I scrunch my face up at her, as if anything about that is okay. Like Adrian is so bad because he doesn't turn a human into a monster every chance he can get.

"Let them talk," Adrian's voice cuts sharply from the crack in the door.

The woman freezes.

Adrian snatches me from the hallway, tugging me into the penthouse so fast that my head spins. He slams the door and presses me back against it. "You shouldn't have come here," he hisses.

It's dark inside the room. The shades are drawn over the thick UV-proof windows, and the lights are all off. I can barely see the whites of his eyes, but his presence surrounds me––commanding me to take notice.

"And why's that?"

"Because I'm hungry," he growls under his breath.

"Then eat something." I know he keeps blood stocked in his fridge, and he lives above a blood bank. It's not like he's without food.

He disappears.

Okay, not really, but he flies away so fast that I can't see him do it at all. Then he's in his room, shutting the door and shutting me out. So is this how grief looks in vampires? Shouldn't they be used to death by now? But Kelli was his only "child," and now she's dead. I can't judge him for locking himself in his penthouse, assuming that's what he's doing here.

"That new guy you have sitting in Kelli's desk down there is a real prick," I call out.

"Good," his voice is muffled through the door, "I told him to field all my calls for a few weeks while I grieve."

I don't know why I'm surprised, but I am. I guess I expected Adrian to carry on like business as usual. He's always so in control, so dark and stoic and impenetrable. I never expected him to grieve as humans do, or to call it that. He seems so cold, like nothing could hurt him. Do vampires have therapists?

I flip on the lights.

The place is clean, but it's stuffy as hell. So I turn up the air conditioner since I can't crack a window. Then I rummage through the kitchen drawers until I find some air freshener and spray it around. I go to the fridge where rows of blood bags are stacked inside and plop one in the microwave. Vampires can drink it cold, but I know from observing Adrian that he prefers his warm or room temperature.

Super gross, but here we are.

I try not to think about it when it's done heating, and I pour it into a large glass. I pretend that the coppery scent is actually sea salt and that the red is tomato juice. It does *not* work. I hold my breath and go knock on Adrian's door. He doesn't answer, but he left it unlocked, so I push it open and tiptoe inside. The lamp is on and he's laying on the bed, his eyes trained on the ceiling. He's wearing nothing but basketball shorts. I've only ever seen him in dress clothes, and it's hard not to stare at his body. His muscles are lean and strong, his shoulders are broad, and his skin is perfect without a single blemish. His golden locks are curlier than normal, like he's run his hands through them a million times. Those bright blue eyes track me as I walk in and set the glass on the nightstand.

He doesn't look at it, he looks at me.

"I'm sorry about Kelli," I say at last.

He sighs. "Do you know why I chose her?"

I shake my head.

"I rarely turn anyone into a vampire." His voice is faraway. "It's not a life I would condemn to anyone, despite what you might think."

"I don't know what I think anymore."

He's quiet for a while and then picks the conversation back up. "I met Kelli after she'd been attacked by one of my brothers. He left her for dead. I was going to end it for her, put her out of her misery. She begged me not to."

"So you turned her?"

"Not right away. Plenty of people beg for death, for life, or to make it stop. I was used to that."

"So what was different about her?"

"I knew her," he says simply, "she'd been someone else's fledgling for years, trying to get turned. I despised her for it, as I do all of them. I only take a child when my queen demands it."

"So Brisa demanded you take her?"

"Not that time. I did it to spite the brother who'd promised to turn her only to leave her for dead." He laughs bitterly. "Don't pretend to be surprised. You know how much I hated Hugo. I've had several enemies over the years, but he was perhaps my least favorite."

I don't expect this. I assumed he picked her because he liked her, not because he wanted to spite the brother who meant to kill her, to spite Hugo. "So I bit her, making sure my venom was strongest, and then I buried her and made her mine. The next time I saw him and she was on my arm, the look on his face was worth the effort."

My stomach sours, and I sit down on the edge of the bed. "You like to play games with people, don't you?"

He shrugs. "Sometimes. But I'm glad I turned Kelli. She proved her loyalty and became my closest friend over the years. I could trust her with anything. And when we were assigned to New Orleans, she offered to be my assistant. She didn't have to. I could've gotten almost anyone for that job, but I trusted her the most with the inner-workings of my day, so I was grateful she offered." His voice goes ragged. "She deserved better."

"I'm sorry."

He sits up and takes the glass of blood in his hands, scowling down at it. "Sometimes, when I'm angry with myself, I don't eat."

Well, damn. There's some serious self-loathing going on here. I never expected it from Adrian of all people. And I never expected to feel bad for a vampire, but I do. I reach over and place my hand on his back. It's cold, but I don't flinch. "It doesn't do you any good to starve yourself. If anything, it makes you more dangerous to innocent people."

He doesn't respond, but he drinks, downing the glass in one go.

His lips are stained red when he turns to me. I drop my hand and take a deep breath. "There's something I need to talk to you about . . . Is there a coven meeting tomorrow?"

His eyes narrow, and he nods. "How did you know that? It's not for fledglings."

"You must have a spy somewhere in your organization because I didn't know that, Tate knew it."

His mouth curls and his eyes brighten, as if lights are being turned on in his head.

"What *is* Tate?" I ask, growing desperate.

He doesn't answer. He sets the glass down and goes to his bathroom. He keeps the door open and turns on the shower.

"Come talk to me while I get ready," he says, "it sounds like we have a lot to discuss."

Okay, I've never seen a man shower before, and he probably knows that. But he's acting like he's back to business as usual.

"Don't get any ideas." I fold my arms over my chest.

"Oh please, Angel. I can get willing partners anytime I want and I've never been a prude about nudity. I am Greek, remember? But if you're uncomfortable, we can discuss this later. It's no problem."

I don't have time for later. I want to do this now. "Fine." I go sit on the bathroom counter and close my eyes. "But I'm not peeking."

He chuckles, and a few seconds later I can hear the shower door open and shut.

"So, tell me what Tate is?" I say, "And why are you enemies with him?"

"I cannot speak about what he is as my master has expressly forbidden it." His silky voice mixes with the steam. "But I will say that he and his kind are my enemy."

"They take energy from humans. That I do know." He doesn't reply. Maybe he can't. "Okay, so he's got this plan to send the hunters to ambush you at your coven meeting. His number one goal is to have you killed. I don't think he really cares all that much about what happens to the hunters."

"He's been after me for years," Adrian says. "He can't compel people, but if he could, I'd be fighting off humans every day."

I'd wondered about that with Cameron. I guess I know my answer.

"Don't worry, Angel. He won't succeed. If he wants me dead, he'll have to face me himself."

"So why doesn't he?"

"Because he knows he can't defeat a vampire with skills such as mine."

Adrian can levitate, aka fly, and has telekinesis, plus he's able to compel humans. He may have other abilities, too.

"So call off the coven meeting," I say. The room is thick with steam now; it coats me like a second skin. I carefully open my eyes, looking at my feet. My curious eyes want to travel to the glass shower, but I don't let them. Why does Adrian have to be so distracting? This would be easier if he were hideous.

"Why would I call off the meeting?" His voice grows angry. "Thanks to this insider information, I can kill the hunters. This is a good thing for my coven, not a bad one."

I stand, my hands fisting. "That's not why I told you this and you know it."

"So?" He steps from the shower, completely naked and dripping wet. I don't look down nor do I blush. I glare at him, keeping my eyes on his, and he glares right back. "Your hunter killed Kelli."

"Cameron killed Kelli because he was confused."

"How was he confused?" Adrian seethes. "He used her to get closer to me. He failed to kill me, but managed to kill her. That's what happened."

"Cameron hated Tate," I shoot back, "but Tate messed with his mind and made him forget all about that."

"More reason to kill Tate's little hunters."

"So he can just make more of them? Because he will. You're not mad at the hunters. They're humans trying to protect their families. You're mad at Tate. Go after Tate."

"Maybe I'll use one of the hunters to get to Tate."

"How? They're all too young to be compelled."

He growls a little and grabs a towel, storming from the bathroom. I'm assuming he's going to his closet to get changed. I stay behind to cool off, even though the bathroom is sticky hot with condensation. I lean over the bathroom sink and wipe away at the mirror, staring at myself. I look tired. I look angry. Defeated.

No.

I won't let this defeat me. I can't give up. If this is how it's going to be, if he's going to turn into the monster he is, then I have to warn my friends.

I make for the exit, power walking through the suite. But when I pull open the door, Adrian's hand slams it closed. "You're not going anywhere, Angel," he growls against my ear. "You're mine."

Seventeen

6∽9

If there's an award for the world's most gullible idiot, engrave my name on it because I've officially proven myself worthy. I shouldn't have trusted Adrian with this kind of information. My stupid plan to get deeper into the vampire organization and somehow save the world has completely backfired and soon my friends will be dead.

Not to mention, Adrian's grieving Kelli's death, so of course he's not going to call off the coven meeting because I asked him to, not when this is the perfect opportunity for him to get revenge. He's going to come out ahead on the war between hunters and vampires, and it's very likely that my friends will get killed. And if not, well, they'll for sure be turned into the VEC who will imprison them since hunting vampires is illegal. No matter what happens, it's going to change everything. And it's all my fault.

Adrian picks me up and takes me to his spare bedroom, tossing me onto the bed like a sack of potatoes. "Hand it over," he demands.

I glare and jump up before sprinting to the door. He blocks me. "Give me your phone," he seethes, "and your stake while you're at it."

I know better than to argue about having a stake, he knows I always carry one. I'm wearing long linen pants today that hang wide around my legs. The stake is strapped to my calf underneath. My phone is in my handbag, which happens to be in his kitchen. I'd forgotten all about it when I ran for the door. I know that seems improbable for someone of my generation since our phones are like a fifth limb, but try running from a vampire and then come talk to me.

"Fine, I'll do it myself," he growls.

I scream in frustration as he grabs onto my pants and rips them clean off my body, the seams splitting apart with ease. So now I'm standing here in my underwear and t-shirt.

Just great.

I'm fast, my own senses speeding up to try and match his. When he reaches for the stake, I block him. It's like blocking a stone wall, and my forearm aches, but I hold strong.

"Do. Not. Touch. Me."

He laughs bitterly. "I told you exactly what I was and warned you never to forget."

And I didn't. Or maybe I did a little because I trusted him. My mind fills with guilt, and he uses that moment to grab the stake. It's wooden and it's tipped in silver, but he's careful to avoid the silver. "I'll be disposing of this," he says. "Now, where is your phone?"

"In the kitchen. It's obviously not on me. What, do you want me to strip naked so you can make sure?"

He smirks. "Oh, Angel, don't be surprised if you strip naked for me all on your own one day."

"You're vile," I seethe between gritted teeth. "I would never."

"And you're staying here until I decide what to do with you." He steps through the doorway and slams the door shut, the lock clicking into place.

Panic hits me. I don't remember the lock being on the outside, but sure enough, when I pull on the handle it doesn't budge. Could he have added it? This man is truly sick.

"How could you?" I pound on the door. "I came to warn you, to help you, not to let you kill my friends."

But he doesn't reply, and a few seconds later, I hear the door to the outside hallway close.

So that's it?

No, that can't be it.

I close my eyes, willing all of Hugo's venom to surface, channeling it into me stronger than ever. I slam against the door, expecting it to break. It doesn't. I do it again. And again. Each time hurting myself more. I'm going to have bruises. I may even fracture something. But I don't care. I have to get out of here. I have to warn the hunters.

I do it again. This time I lose my balance and my head accidentally gets most of the impact. My vision narrows and then fades to black.

I don't know how much time passes before I wake in a bundle of cold limbs on the floor. I pick myself up and wait and wait and wait. The only way to pass the time is to watch the world go by outside the tinted glass. At least there's water in the bathroom but I have a pounding headache and my stomach starts to growl for dinner. I desperately want out of here, but that's not going to happen, so instead, I stare at the city below. All those people out there, what would they do if they were me? Would they be able to think of a viable plan? I wish someone could see me, but I'm too high up, and the windows are too dark to see through, anyway. I'm stuck.

A prisoner.

And I'm at the mercy of the man I foolishly trusted. I have nobody to blame but myself. I knew what vampires were capable of, knew humans didn't really matter to them beyond a source of food. And still, look at what I did.

As it always does, the world keeps turning, and time keeps marching on. The evening fades to night, and then the blackness takes over––an endless night. I lay on the bed and stare at the ceiling until I eventually fall asleep.

Morning comes and I expect Adrian will stop by with food and I'll have an opportunity to beg him again or maybe a chance to escape.

But none of that happens.

The day stretches and my stomach turns hollow. At least I can drink from the sink so it's not like I'm going to die up here like my friends will tonight.

For most of the day I think of their faces, imagining what they're doing right now to prepare for the attack. I wonder what Felix thinks of me standing him up last night. Does he assume I didn't show up because I got cold feet about sleeping with him? Or does he suspect something is wrong? Maybe he and Kenton and Seth are looking for me right now. Maybe they've already figured it out and are confessing to Tate.

There's no way to know, and being helpless is destroying me.

Eventually, night descends, and I know this is it. Somewhere below me in the hotel, the coven is meeting. And somewhere outside, the hunters are gathering. Their directive is to storm the ballroom. They'll work in teams, killing as many vampires as they can, with Adrian as their number one target.

It will never work.

I pace the room with a racing heart for what feels like hours. The night grows darker and darker. At one point I hear movement in the suite. I jump up and go to the door. "Adrian? Is that you?"

The movement stops and then starts again.

"Please," I beg, banging on the door, "please don't do this."

"Eva?" The voice doesn't belong to Adrian. No, it belongs to the man I hate almost as much as Adrian: Tate.

"Yes!" I scream, hopefully he's here to save me. "Let me out!"

"I'm afraid I can't do that yet." A door slams and then there's nothing but silence. He left me here.

I lay on the bed and cry. What was he doing in here if not to help me? But he's gone and I'm alone. When there are no tears left and the salt warms my mouth and my cheeks are streaked raw with the aftermath, my eyes finally begin to close on their own. I don't like that. I refuse to go to sleep. How can I?

And yet . . . I do.

My dreams torment me. Nightmares that tumble, one into another, over and over. I see my friends dying. I see some of them being turned. I see blood. Anger. Fear. I hear it, smell it, feel it. It's like I'm there, but I'm not there.

I'm not there.

Felix appears before me. His eyes are lovely brown, and then they're murderous red. And then he's kissing me. Fangs cut at my lips. I pull back and scream.

"Eva," he says, his hands cupping my face, "I'm still me."

"No," I reply, but the word gets trapped in my throat.

"Wake up," he snaps. No, not him. Someone else . . .

The hand is still on my face––a cold hand.

My eyes flutter open, and I'm looking up into Adrian's glacial eyes. He's so close. Too close.

"Get off!" I scream, pushing him away. My strength has gathered while I slept, the senses coming back all at once. He flies back against the wall and falls.

He's quick to recover and brushes himself off, smiling. "It looks like you're starting to get used to that venom," he teases. "But you should be careful with that. If the wrong person finds out about it, you'll either be turned or you'll be dead."

I can still be turned? Of course, I can still be turned. "I'd rather die." I glare.

"Hmm, I thought you'd say that. Your little request to become my prodigy was a lie from the beginning." He sighs. "Well, do you want to know about your friends or not?"

I jump out of the blankets, not caring that I'm hardly dressed. "What happened?" My voice comes out like sandpaper. "Are they dead? What did you do to them?"

"Nobody is dead," he says, and I nearly burst into tears.

"Arrested?"

"Not that either."

"So, what happened?"

He pauses for a second, considering. "They showed up, and we detained them. They're being held downstairs." He runs his thumb along his bottom lip for a moment. "Eva, I need you to do something for me, something important. And if you do, I'll let them all go. It will be as if nothing ever happened."

I don't want to hear what this request is because I'm afraid I may already know, but I have to face it. "What do you want?"

"I want you to come to France with me."

I blink at him; this was the last thing I expected him to say. "What's in France?"

"Who's in France," he corrects. "Brisa. She wants to meet you. I need you to be on your best behavior."

"That's all?" My eyes narrow. I don't believe him. I never will.

"You're still my fledgling, in case you've forgotten. We're being called to go to France where . . ." He stares at me, eyes softening, "where I'm going to turn you."

I feel as if I'm sinking into the ground, as if I'm already being buried alive, as if I'm already dead. No. I can't agree. I can't go to France. I can't meet the vampire queen. And I can't become one of them.

But what other choice do I have? It's me or it's all of them.

"Do I have your word?" My voice is so much stronger than I feel, and I can't imagine how I'm managing it when I feel like I've been shattered into a million razor-edged pieces. "You will do no harm to any of the hunters? You will set them all free?"

"Yes."

"I'll agree only if you promise to do that right now."

"But––"

"No, Adrian. I mean it." I fold my arms over my chest and give him a hard stare.

"Take the deal or leave it," he replies stonily.

Anger seeps into my tone. "You'll give me nothing?"

"I need leverage to make sure you behave in France." He's such a logical creature and I hate him for it.

"We have to come to a compromise."

"Do we? Because I'm the one holding the aces."

I throw my hands up. "I'm so tired of all your stupid gambling sayings." We're at an impasse and I don't know what to do. I can't trust him, he's already proved that. There's no telling that he won't take me to France and turn me into his prodigy no matter what I agree to. He's used to getting whatever he wants. "Please," I whisper. I'm truly defeated this time. He's won.

"Fine," he spits out. "I'll release them when we get on the jet, but I need you to go along with this in France. There's so much more on the line than you realize and I can't have your bad attitude getting in the way."

I scoff. "I think giving you my life should be good enough."

"This isn't about your life," he says, "it's about so many others."

"What does that have to do with me?"

"I need to go where I've been called and I need to take you with me before someone kills me here."

I raise a brow. "But you've got the hunters detained."

"The princes are being killed across the continents. There are only three of us left."

"I didn't know..."

"Don't you think your little friend Leslie Tate has something to do with that? He didn't show up to the casino, by the way. He sent in all the humans, exactly as you said he would."

I swallow. Should I tell him that Tate was in his suite? But I don't want to give him a single thing extra, so I keep my secret and reach out my hand. "Give me your word, and I'll give you mine. That's going to have to be enough for you."

"I rather preferred the blood vow." He chuckles, but I don't find it amusing. There's no way I'm ever kissing this man again, especially not for a fake vow which he would've let me keep on believing was real if I hadn't figured it out.

"Really? Because I'd rather prefer honesty."

He shakes my hand.

Eighteen

⤜⧼∽

A couple hours later and it's time to leave. "I don't have a suitcase or my phone back or anything." I give him a pointed look. "And what about my job? I have shifts, you know. I can't leave them in a lurch and disappear. And my apartment? I have to pay rent soon."

He responds by holding out his hand. "You need to leave your necklace here and forget about everything else. It doesn't matter. You have a new life now."

"Maybe it doesn't matter to you but it does to me." My voice wobbles. "Can I at least call my Mom?"

He winces but shakes his head. "The necklace, Eva."

He didn't use my pet name. Somehow it makes this all the more real. And maybe it's stupid, but this little necklace is the only thing I have left.

"I'll put it in my safe," he offers. "It'll be fine, but you can't take a silver cross to meet Brisa. It's offensive to vampires. You already know that."

I unlatch it with a grumble of reluctance. He produces a glove from his back pocket so he can handle the silver. He takes it in his hands and studies it for a minute, his face unreadable. What does he think of the feathers on the back? I want to ask him what he knows of it, but keep my thoughts to myself.

He leaves and returns with a pile of clothes. "Those are some of my sweatpants and a t-shirt to keep you comfortable for the plane ride. You'll have everything provided for you once we arrive at the palace."

The palace.

I didn't know the royal vampires lived in a palace, though I guess it makes sense. They're pretty private about things when it comes to that—one big mystery that the world is equally fascinated with and horrified by.

I'm tired and broken, so I don't ask any more questions.

We take a private jet with UV-proof windows. It looks like the ones in the movies with plush seating and decadent catered food. The pilots are humans, and when we climb aboard, Adrian compels them to keep us as safe as possible. Vampires have enemies the world over, what better way to take a prince down than by plane crash?

"Prove it," I say when he comes back into the cabin. He doesn't have to ask what I mean. He retrieves his phone and fiddles with it before handing it over. The screen shows what the cameras all over the casino are seeing right now. The hunters are walking out the front door, free and clear. Felix turns to look up at the camera almost like he knows I'm watching him.

And then he's gone.

I hand the phone back to Adrian and buckle myself into my seat. I have nothing to say and I'm only half relieved. It's not like I wanted to sacrifice myself.

The flight is boring and quiet. I devour the pre-catered food even though my stomach is in knots. When Adrian apologizes for forgetting to feed me, I throw a baguette at his head and tell him not to speak unless spoken to. He rolls his eyes but proceeds to work on his computer without acknowledging me again. I don't even have a phone to play games or read an ebook or even a television to keep me company. I'm stuck staring out the tinted window at the expanse of white and blue sky between restless naps and finishing off the food.

When we finally fly over Paris, I'm practically glued to the window. It's daytime—been light out for hours now, part of the wonders of transatlantic airline travel. I catch sight of the Eiffel Tower standing vigil over the winding river and smile to myself. The city is gorgeous, and I'd love to explore it one day. I have a feeling this won't be the trip. But if the vampires succeed in turning me, I guess I'll have an eternity to explore.

My smile falters as a tear slips down my cheek. I don't want to explore the world in darkness. I've always loved the sun—the light, the warmth, the energy. My freedom means more to me than just about anything else and now it's gone. I hope wherever my friends are, they're safe and not trying to come after me. As much as I'd love to be rescued, I can't have them in danger because of me and I don't want all this to be for nothing.

We're on the outskirts somewhere, and I'm not sure how we're going to get from here to wherever we're going in broad daylight. But the plane drives slowly along the tarmac and pulls into a massive building—a huge garage door closing behind us. We climb out and immediately get into a waiting car. It's sleek and black, with no windows in the back.

"No windows?" I turn on Adrian.

"It's bulletproof but there's always a higher risk with windows," Adrian says. "We'll also be surrounded by a detail of human armed forces. Nothing will happen to us. We'll be fine."

"I hope you're sure about that because this thing is obvious. Anyone wanting to hurt vampires will know one of you is in here. What cars don't have windows?"

He doesn't respond, probably because he knows I'm right. Expose a vamp to sunlight and that's it. What a perfect way to do it. I try to imagine it happening to Adrian, but my mind won't let me go there. He's a pawn in all this too, isn't he? A pawn I'll never forgive, but a pawn no less. I've only seen Brisa once through a video call, but I'll never forget her face. I wish I could kill her and have it all be over, but Sebastian made a lot of sense. If she dies the vampires will have too much freedom.

I climb inside and it's like a coffin in here.

"It's a good thing I'm not very claustrophobic," I complain. When Adrian locks us in from the inside and a strip of red LED lights along the ceiling immediately brightens the enclosed cab, I relax a little. There are two rows of leather seats facing each other. He takes one and I take the other and the car begins to drive.

I've avoided eye contact since leaving New Orleans. This time I let my gaze linger over him and don't hold anything back about how I'm feeling. I'm angry. I'm frustrated. I'm scared. And I'm also attracted to him, which I hate, but there it is.

He stares right back. Something grows between us, thick and confusing.

"I'm sorry," he whispers, breaking the silence.

I have nothing to say to that. I don't know if I even believe him. Maybe it doesn't matter anymore.

He leans forward and then something slams into the car, metal hitting the metal like a bomb, and we're flying. I'm simultaneously kicking myself for not putting on my seatbelt and trying to grab onto Adrian. He can't get hit by sunlight. We're suspended in air as the vehicle flips over and then rights itself again.

Everything stops and the red lights flicker and then turn off.

"Are you okay?" I ask.

He hisses but his hands are on me, running up and down my body.

"What are you doing?"

"Checking for injuries. Hold still."

"Dude, I'm fine," I say and he stops.

"But I can smell blood." His voice whispers through the dark, taking on a sinister quality.

"It's my head." I can feel something wet dripping down my forehead and wince when I try to touch it. "I really should've worn that seatbelt."

"The venom will heal it fast."

"Oh, nice perk. Now tell me, do you have any guns stashed in here? I'd like to be able to defend myself." I never thought I'd hunt the vampire hunters but I don't want to die today.

He growls low. "Why do you have to smell so good?"

"Are you serious right now? We're under attack, someone is obviously trying to kill you, and all you can think about is my blood?" I keep feeling around the seats but there's nothing of use. I hate that I can't see in here!

He groans in frustration and when my hand accidentally brushes his, he catches it and tugs me into his lap. He wraps his arms around me in a cage and I freeze. "One taste," he whispers in my ear, "I promise not to bite."

I elbow him in the chest. "Don't be a creep." But he doesn't laugh and he doesn't let me go. He's breathing hard, fighting the instinct to feed on my wound. He resisted before but this time we're in close proximity and he may be minutes away from dying. What's stopping him?

I should, but I don't fight back. I lean into him and can't reason away why part of me is completely okay with this, maybe even wants to see how he reacts. "Fine, but I swear if you bite me, I'm going to rip your head off."

He chuckles and then his mouth is pressing against my cheek and moving upwards. He stops when he reaches the blood, tongue trailing along a line, cold and hot intermixing. He groans with satisfaction.

Gunfire sounds outside and it seems to shake him from his task because he stops. I use that as my cue to peel away from him and find the other bench. Little pops blast into the side of the car but nothing has a chance of getting through so far.

Someone knocks on the side of the car. I want to unlock it and go out there, but I know I can't expose Adrian like that. A French voice says something I can't understand and Adrian replies.

"What happened?" I ask.

"Hunters," he offers with a little growl. "They're gone now and we're continuing on."

The engine starts and the lights brighten. "What did I say about this car again?" he asks. Under the lights I see my blood on his lips. He smiles, licks them clean, and teases me with a wink. "What did I say?" he presses.

"That nothing would happen to us when clearly it just did."

"I said we'd be fine and we're fine."

I hold my hand to my head wound and glare. "Speak for yourself."

Nineteen

"We're going to the palace of Versailles," he tells me. "Act impressed. Queen Brisa will love that. But don't be needy, she hates needy."

"You're kidding," I whisper. "Versailles?"

Adrian looks at me sidelong. "Brisa's been wanting to take up residence there since Louis XIV built it. She even infiltrated his court for a few years and nearly succeeded in her efforts."

"She really doesn't know how to let things go, does she?" I lean back and close my eyes, trying to sort through my thoughts.

"No." The single word speaks volumes. I need to be careful from this moment on, more so than I've been in the past. If I'm going to get out of here alive, I must pretend that I'm here because I want to be here. The last thing I need is to get locked up, or worse, murdered because Brisa figures out I'm full of shit and want nothing to do with her creepy little vampire family.

The car stops again. Adrian pulls out his phone and looks at something. "There's cameras on the car," he says. "We're in a garage. It's safe to get out."

I scoff. "Why didn't you use that before?"

His eyes flick to my forehead. "I was distracted."

Right ...

My fingers play at the wound. It's mostly healed right now, but I'm a mess. "I can't walk in there like this."

"You're with me," he says, "you'll be fine." He wrenches open the door and steps out.

We're met by household staff, a mix of humans and vampires. A vampire greets us, bowing to Adrian. I've never seen anyone bow to him, not even at his own coven meeting. Things must be pretty formal here. The vampire eyes the mess of blood but doesn't say anything. Then he's back to Adrian again. "Your highness."

Adrian clears his throat. "Casper, you don't need to call me that. How many times have we been through this?"

The older looking vampire doesn't even bother to respond to that. He stays professional as ever. "I must apologize. As Brisa recently acquired our new palace, it's not fully renovated yet. There's not a lot of space for everyone during the daylight hours."

"I'm sure it's fine," Adrian mumbles. "Can you direct me to a shower, please? I'd like to freshen up before meeting with Brisa. I think Evangeline would like to as well, given her current state."

I shoot him a little glare but nod my agreement because I probably smell like garbage and I'd like nothing more than to scrub off the dried blood.

"Of course." Casper turns and leads us through an unmarked door, then down a wide hallway and a sweeping staircase. "Most of the windows are boarded over as a temporary measure until we can get them all turned into bulletproof UV-proof glass." I bite my tongue from saying what a shame that will be. The building is stunning, even from the tiny slice we've seen so far. I'd love to explore it in all its grandeur sans tinted glass, and now I never will, not really, not now that the vampires have already started modifying it.

"Here you are." Casper's voice is apologetic. "Again, I'm truly sorry for the lack of space, but we did outfit the closets for you."

A human woman opens two large wardrobes which are bursting with clothes––but not modern day clothes. This is the stuff of fairy tales. "I'll be your personal maidservant." She smiles at me. "I'm Remi."

The vampire shoots her a pointed look and she rushes from the room. I think I like her—I don't like him.

"As I was saying, Her Majesty doesn't want any of the princes staying in the rooms with the boarded up windows. You are to be in the rooms with the new ones already installed. Oh, and don't be alarmed by the increase in guards when you roam about the palace. They're there for your protection."

"Thank you," Adrian cuts him off. "Don't worry. We'll be fine"

Casper leaves us to it, and we take in the room. It must've been a guest room from long ago, much of the decor has been meticulously cared for over the centuries. Either that or restored, because it looks like we could've time traveled right into France during the seventeenth century. I seriously hope the bathroom has running water. It must, because Casper probably would've said otherwise about the showers.

There's a grand four-poster bed in the center of the room with a loveseat and dressing table by the tinted window. Wallpaper lines the walls in textured blue and gold fleur-de-lis designs, and the crown molding is at least six inches thick.

Adrian strides over to the armoires and grumbles at the contents inside the one clearly meant for a man. "So she wants to play dress-up, does she?"

"What do you mean?" I join him, my heart squeezing when I get a better look at what's inside. The gowns are from what I think is the Renaissance age, or whatever age it was that this palace was built. I should've paid more attention in history class, not that we went into European history all that much in school. His clothing is in a similar fashion. I spend a good five minutes looking through all mine and then move to his. It reminds me of the princes from movies and television shows. "Wait a second," I let out a little snort, "do you have to wear tights?"

"They're called hose," he grumbles and I laugh again.

"Excellent."

But really, I'm only teasing because the outfits are pretty cool.

"Admittedly, this wasn't my favorite era for fashion," he says.

"And what is?"

"Nice form fitted suits from a tailor as you often see me in or as close as I can get to nudity, take your pick."

I punch him in the arm. "Ew, did you really have to go there?"

"It's the truth. I don't like to feel constricted."

And wearing a suit isn't constricting? I roll my eyes. And then my mouth pops open when I finally put the pieces together that Adrian and I are sharing this little room. It's not that big of a deal, it's not like vampires sleep, but it still feels way too intimate. I'm only here because he blackmailed me into coming. My hatred for it all is no surprise, and I hate him too for manipulating me. And now I'll have to be turned into one of them while wearing a massive ball gown.

I carefully close the armoires and spin around to plead with Adrian. "You can't turn me." My voice wobbles. "Please."

"We have a deal."

"One I was manipulated into making."

"I don't want to turn you, Angel, but I have to follow her orders." He looks away.

"Please. Promise me you'll at least try to save me from it."

"Vampires can't promise anything, least of all me." He walks to the bathroom. "Don't try to run away. You'll be killed if you do."

He closes the door, and I fall back onto the bed, staring up at the canopy over the bed. There's no way this is happening. There's no way. It can't be.

But it is.

. . .

AFTER ADRIAN FINISHES in the bathroom, I go inside. Turns out there's no shower in this room, but there is a beautiful clawfoot bathtub. I soak in it until my fingers turn to prunes, and the blood on my scalp is gone, then I slip into silk pajamas––the only thing that's not a dress––while I'm still in the bathroom because I desperately want to get out of Adrian's sweatpants and do so in privacy. I come back out into the bedroom to find Adrian lying on the bed with his hands behind his head and his eyes closed. I know he's not sleeping but perhaps he's resting his mind. All the more reason to disturb him.

I stomp through the room, throwing the old clothes down next to the armoire because I have no idea where else to put them, and settle into the couch. This isn't an enemies-to-lovers, only one bed, will-they won't-they situation. This is an enemies-to-allies-to-enemies, and I refuse to go near that bed when he's on it.

"You know," I say loudly, hoping to disturb him, "the least you could do is let me enjoy one last hurrah in the daylight." It's late afternoon, and there may only be a few hours left for me. Adrian doesn't move. "What would you give to have one more hour in the sun?"

His eyes open, and he peers over at me.

"Well?" I fold my arms over my chest and raise my eyebrows.

"I'd do anything."

"Exactly." I nod toward the door. "Do you think I care about those guards out there? Give them an excuse and help me get outside."

"You're not leaving this palace during the sunlight and it's not your last night as a human."

"You don't know that," I say sharply, "and I don't appreciate being lied to anymore."

He sits up and runs his hands over his face. "You're right. I don't know that. But I do know that Brisa will want to test you for a while first. I also know that if she thinks for even one minute that you're not loyal to me, and thus to her, then you won't be turned. You'll be dead."

"And what does sunlight have to do with that?"

He flashes through the room so quickly I nearly fall off the loveseat. He's on his knees, leaning over me. I'm average height, but he's tall, and he dwarfs me in both his size and his presence. His fangs extend, and fear seizes me. I have no way to protect myself. "The sun has everything to do with that. You should want this so bad that you'd be eager to throw away the sun. You should worship the darkness. And if Brisa suspects how you really feel, I can promise you'll be wishing you were dead."

"But you said she'd kill me." Okay, now I'm just being a smart ass.

"She will, but she won't hurry to do it. She'll take her time. And then she'll go after your family and anyone you've loved." His eyes flash silver. "The last person you want to cross is a vampire, and Brisa is the worst of them all."

"Sebestian said there were worse ones than her." There I go again.

He stills. And then he stands. "There may be." He starts to pace the room. "Someone has been killing off princes, and when they can take over those bloodlines, they will target Brisa next. I know vampires that would like nothing more than to enslave the human race. Hugo was one of those. I suspect Sebastian is as well, though I don't know for sure; he's always been disgustingly loyal to Brisa."

"And so have you."

He nods, but he knows what I mean. He's loyal to her as a defense mechanism. There's a knock on the door, and Adrian opens it. "Sorry to interrupt," a woman says, "but we're to get her ready for the ball."

"Is that you Remi?" I ask, strolling to the door, grateful to find a human and not another vamp.

"Yes, Miss."

"The ball?" Adrian frowns. "Are we seriously doing one of those again?" He sounds as if he's a duke and a million mamas are after his hand for their eligible daughters. I fail to bite back a laugh.

"Oh yes. Queen Brisa insisted we have one every night the first year she's here." First year? Remi looks pointedly at me. "Come along now, there's much to do."

Twenty

❧

I stop laughing abruptly. This is so not my scene. But I have to play the part, that much Adrian has made clear. I really hope that I can trust him this time. I snort again and he shakes his head.

"Lord help us all," he moans.

The young woman looks to be in her twenties—probably old enough to be compelled so she can work here. She takes me to a dressing room, and I'm descended upon by five other human women of varying ages. I seriously wonder if they work here because they want to or if they're here because they've been compelled. I wouldn't be surprised by either. Too many humans have accepted vampires as part of everyday life. We've become complacent and desensitized, treating vampires like part of society instead of a stain on it. Maybe the vamps pay well? They certainly have the money.

The maidservants don't make me bathe again, but they do my nails, style my hair onto the top of my head, apply way too much makeup, and then fit me into a corset that makes my waist tiny and my boobs big. Then comes the heaviest gown I've ever worn, times a million. "What is this thing?" I complain, already getting hot. It's itchy and huge. It's also a striking sapphire blue that compliments my tanned skin tone. The bodice is cut in a low sweetheart shape, and the twins are on full display, having been pushed up by the ridiculous corset underneath. I think of Ayla, and my heart hurts. I'd love to share this with her, sans vampires of course. She would absolutely love it.

At least, the old her would have.

She still hates me. She knows I've dumped her brother but still doesn't want to talk to me. She hates that I joined the hunters but she doesn't seem to get that I'm doing it because I love her and want her to live in a safer world. If only I could text her.

"Do any of you have a phone?" I ask the ladies. They frown. "I want to take a picture of myself like this." I hold the universal symbol of phone to my ear by extending my thumb and pinky.

"*Non, Non,*" one of them says. "*C'est interdit!*"

"I'm sorry, I don't speak French."

"She said it is forbidden. Privacy is of the utmost importance here," another replies, speaking English with a thick French accent, "there are no phones allowed in the city for us humans."

"So what do you tell your families when you get home? Do they know you work here?"

"We live here," another supplies. She barely has an accent at all. "This is our home. We are each other's family now."

She sounds a little robotic, and I know the answer to my earlier question. These humans have been compelled, probably multiple times. The only one that seems to have any spirit left in her is Remi, but she keeps quiet about the phone thing, shooting me an apologetic look.

"Sorry," I mumble.

They finish off the job with white gold jewelry adorned with diamonds and sapphires. The sparkling jewels settle around my neck and hang off my ears like prison chains. And when it's time to go, I don't want to move.

Adrian meets me at the door. When he sees me all dolled up, his face darkens. "Get out," he commands the women. They scurry away, and then we're alone in the little windowless dressing room.

"Please," I ask one last time, "please don't make me do this."

When he doesn't respond, my breathing starts to speed up and my vision blurs. My hands begin shaking and waves of anxiety crash over my body, drowning me alive. "I can't . . . I can't breathe." My knees buckle, and Adrian catches me before I'm on the floor. He sits down and holds me in his lap, trying to shush me. I can barely even tell he's there. In a corner of my mind, I'm aware that I'm having a panic attack. I've never had one before, and they're as terrifying as people say. But even though I'm partially aware of what's going on, I can't seem to stop it, nor can I distance myself from it.

No, I'm stuck right here in the middle of it, forced to feel every bit. The more I think I can't breathe, the more it comes true. I claw at the back of my dress. I have to get out of the corset. I can't have something choking my lungs like this. My fingers fumble with the laces, but I'm completely stuck. "Get it off me," I beg, tears streaming down my face.

In one quick move, Adrian rips the back of the dress completely in two and then the corset underneath. The sound of fabric tearing is right here but it's also like it's a million miles away. Everything slows and then speeds up as I'm freed from the gown. I scramble out of it, wearing only the cream slip the ladies use for underwear here. I gasp for breath and let it filter through me.

I lie back on the floor.

"Here," he says, lifting my knees up, "try to talk to me. What's your favorite color?"

The question is so out of left field it catches me off guard a little. "Umm." I swallow hard, trying to clear the panicked haze from my mind. "Green."

"Any particular shade?"

"Nature. Any green that comes from nature."

"Good choice," he replies, "I feel that way about all colors."

Except he can't see nature anymore, unless it's in the dark. And who would want to go enjoy everything our beautiful planet has to offer in the middle of the night? Something nags at me, a memory from his penthouse suite. "Is that why you always have a bouquet of fresh flowers in your living room?"

"I enjoy it how I can, even if it means killing it first."

I sit up, my breathing finally stabilized. "Spoken like a true vampire."

"I have a plan, you know," he says, "I don't want to turn you, either."

"So don't."

"I won't if I can help it. Like I said, I have a plan."

"So tell me about it." My voice cracks.

"I can't tell you everything," he says, "it's not safe for you to know. But I'll tell you that Brisa likes us to use the catacombs for the business of making our prodigy. When we take you there, you have to stay for three days and nights."

I shiver, thinking of The Cask of Amontillado. We had to read the ominous short story by Edgar Allan Poe in high school about a man who buries someone alive in a catacomb. The final line was "in pace requiescat," which our teacher said meant "may he Rest In Peace." Yeah, guy was still alive in there!

No, thank you.

"But what about Hugo's venom?" My heart squeezes. "Will I be yours?"

He shakes his head. "This isn't easy for me to explain." He grimaces in pain. He's fighting whatever it is that keeps him from going against his maker's wishes, and when he speaks again, it's through gritted teeth. "You'd have to be down there for three days and nights before you'd rise as one of us. Sometimes vampires can rise a little early or a little late, and they're still one of us, but they may be a little weaker or even stronger. Three days, though. Remember that number."

He won't say more but I can tell he wants to.

"What if someone were to be able to leave before their time was up?"

He opens and closes his mouth, then groans in frustration. He can't speak it. So I'll say it for him.

"Would they stay human?" I study his face as memories flood him.

He nods and then shakes his head. "They'd be human, but they'd have . . ."

"Heightened senses," I whisper.

He just looks at me, but I know what he's trying to say and something loosens in my chest. I take a deep breath and think back to my own experience. "Heightened senses and an ability to be able to hunt down the vampires in that bloodline."

Because I'd done it before. That's how I was able to kill Hugo's children so easily.

And then Hugo himself.

Sure it had been a fight, but if I hadn't had that venom, I would've been far more disadvantaged.

"I can see why this information is a guarded secret among your kind."

He gives me a hard look. "And if it were to get out and be traced back to me, I'd face the true death. Brisa wouldn't stake me either. That's too clean. She'd most likely put me out in the sun to burn alive."

He's trusting me with something that he shouldn't. I mop up my tears and straighten my shoulders as I speak. "I don't understand why you're telling me all this. You used my friends against me to blackmail me into coming here and get me to agree to be turned, and now you're telling me how to get out."

"Things aren't always what they seem," he says.

I roll my eyes. "Seriously? That's your answer?"

"It's time to go." He stands and helps me up, looking me square in the eyes. "Please go along with whatever Brisa says. You must. If you don't, we'll both die."

"What did she do to you?" The question I've been dying to ask for weeks finally bursts out. I know the bloodlines make it so he has to obey her commands, but there's more to the story. I see it in his eyes every time he speaks of her.

Adrian *hates* Brisa. It's a loathing that I've never seen before.

His shoulders go rigid, and he glares at me as he speaks. "Brisa is charming and beautiful, but never forget that she's cunning and cruel."

"You can tell me," I say softly. I take his hand in mine and squeeze. I don't know what's come over me, maybe it's the lack of oxygen to my brain or something, but I want to comfort him.

"She never gave me the choice to be her prodigy," he bites out, "and I will do everything in my power to make sure I never do the same to another human." But there's got to be more. I drop his hand, willing to let the conversation go, but he keeps talking. This time he doesn't look at me. "I woke up in darkness. I didn't know what had happened to me. I was so thirsty and confused. I dug my way out from my grave and stumbled home. When I got there, my wife was asleep in our bed and I––" His voice cracks, and he doesn't say anything more. He doesn't have to. I already know.

Adrian killed her.

But it wasn't his fault, not really. He'd been turned without even knowing what a vampire was and had no direction or help from his master when he awoke.

"She was pregnant," he continues, and my heart drops. "Brisa found me later that night and made me think she was helping me. For years, I didn't understand what had really happened. But when I eventually lifted out of the bloodlust, I knew what a monster I was. And I knew it was because of her."

I would hate her too. "You're not a monster," I lie. And maybe it's not totally a lie. Like he said, things aren't always as they seem.

He finally looks back up at me. "Don't worry, Angel. I don't need you to make me feel better, but I do need you to do this for me. We're going to this ball tonight, and tomorrow, and every night we have to, and when Brisa decides it's time, I turn you. You will lay in your grave, and you will act happy about it. And if you do those things, I'll do everything in my power to make sure you don't stay down there for three nights."

"I thought you said vampires can't make promises."

"We can't."

Twenty-One

~⁓~

Th e servants have to get me dressed again. I expect them to be upset, but they're not. They don't really seem to have many emotions at all. I wish I could free them from this place, and maybe someday I will.

I want to kill Brisa.

So badly.

I know that it's not a smart idea, that cutting the head off the snake will breed many more with even worse venom, but I hate that I can't just drive a stake through her heart and end her tyranny over her "children" and so many others.

I force all of that to the back of my mind as I prepare for what comes next. The servants keep the jewels on me, but choose a silver gown instead. At first, I think it's not as pretty as the blue one, but once it's on and I look in a gilded mirror, I change my mind. I'm dressed like a winter princess. It's not my style in the slightest, but considering how drafty and cold the palace is, I decide to count it as a blessing.

"I got this for you," Remi says, handing me a notebook and pencil. "It's not much but it's a drawing pad. You can use it to sketch or journal. Whatever you want during the times you're not otherwise occupied."

It's a small gesture but it means everything. "Thank you," I say, wrapping her into a hug with the book between us. "Will you put it in my room for me?"

"It's locked," she says sheepishly, stepping away. We're probably not supposed to hug given the way Casper glared at her for speaking out of turn.

"Adrianos has made it very clear that nobody else is allowed in there. I'm not even sure he'll give you a key."

"Oh, he will," I supply, "I'll make him."

Her smile quirks and she takes the notebook and pencil back. "Either way, I'll leave these here and you can come back tomorrow to find them. Right now it's time to go meet the queen."

I swallow hard and nod. Remi offers a smile of assurance but I catch the sheen of worry in her hazel eyes. Her hair is tucked up into a bonnet, her would-be curly blonde locks hidden away. I need a friend here--I feel so alone--but I'm not sure it's safe for anyone to be my friend at this point. All I do is bring friends down and put them into danger.

Adrian is back to his stoic self when I'm ushered into the hallway. He doesn't say a word about my appearance, and I don't about his either. He's heartbreakingly, earthshatteringly beautiful. And I'm aware "earthshatteringly" isn't even a word. But it is one in my book now, and right next to it is a picture of Adrianos Freaking Teresi.

It's not fair that he makes it so easy to hate him while simultaneously making it hard.

The orchestra music, melodic and sweet, leads us to the ballroom, and we enter with our heads held high.

My hackles rise instantly. Vampires of all ages, shapes, and ethnicities are scattered throughout. More than I've ever seen in one place! They watch me with hungry eyes, and, for the gazillionth time, I'm reminded of my virginity. It's not like it's hard to go find some willing guy to lose it with, but I'd been holding out for someone I love. I thought I loved Felix. Maybe I still do love Felix. But I'm not sure we'll ever find the right timing.

The crowd splits like Moses parting the Red Sea as we head toward Brisa. The queen is like a beacon unto herself--everything about her glows. From her warm-honey colored hair, to her sparkling eyes, soft skin, hourglass figure, and the natural way she carries herself--commanding the room with both power and grace, Queen Brisa is everything I'd imagine a vampire queen to be.

She's surrounded by what I can only assume are guards. They are vampires dressed in all black garb, and their eyes constantly scan the room. They have huge guns. I've never seen vampires with guns before but it makes sense. Vampires can't be killed with bullets, but humans certainly can. And who are their enemies if not humans?

And whatever the energy demons are--maybe guns can kill them too. One day, I will find out what Tate is, and I will find out how to protect my friends from whatever his kind is. Tate won't get away with continuing to put innocent young human lives at risk for his own goals. But right now, I have to focus on Brisa. As we approach, I dress myself in my most winning smile and cling tighter to Adrian's arm. I want her to think I'm enamoured with him, with this life––the true mark of a fledgling.

Brisa turns, as if sensing I'm there, and looks right into my eyes. Her gaze is mesmerizing, locking me in like a hypnotist. Her posture hardens, and her mouth frowns for a second. Is she jealous? Territorial? Hard to please? Maybe I shouldn't hang off of Adrian. I relax my arm and slip away from his hold. Brisa notes the move and tilts her head at me, as if studying that too.

I wonder what kind of abilities she has, what her strengths and weaknesses are. If Adrian can levitate, can move objects with his mind, and can compel humans better than most other vampires, then what does the queen have in her arsenal besides her obvious power over the bloodlines?

"There she is." Her voice is smooth like butter, with a silky hint of a French accent. "I've been looking forward to meeting the girl who's convinced my Adrian to add to our family again."

"Hello." My voice comes out too nasally. I offer a curtsy. "Your Highness."

"Hello to you too, Mother," Adrian's voice is light and playful. It's nothing I've heard from him, it has to be fake, and I almost lose my nerve right then and there. "Please, don't forget about my Kelli so soon."

She hugs him, her arms slipping around his neck. "How could I? She was a lovely woman who will be missed." She steps back, her voice growing icy. "It's a real shame those hunters in New Orleans have grown so strong lately, Adrian. How many deaths are there now? By my count, you've lost six vampires from your coven in less than two months."

He frowns at that and she turns to me. "You wouldn't happen to know anything about that, would you, Evangeline?"

Can she tell if I lie? Will my heart speed? I don't know what to do because I don't know how much Adrian has told her, but Sabastain came on her errand. So she must know enough by now. I can't lie to her.

But before I can speak, Adrian cuts her off. "Mother, you know Evangeline has infiltrated the hunters for us. She happens to be an old friend of one of them and convinced him to bring her into their organization. She's spying on that vile Leslie Tate for me."

Well, that answers that. I nod in agreement, hating that my cheeks are burning the entire time. I always thought I could play it cool, and then I met vampires.

"And what have you learned of Leslie Tate?" she asks me.

"I know that he wants Adrian dead," I say, gaining courage, "and I know that you've lost some of your princes recently, haven't you? I'd wager that Tate and his organization have played a large part in that. In fact, Tate left for a little while last month and didn't tell anyone where he went. When did you say your sons died?"

The question hangs between us for far longer than I'd like. "Very astute observation," she says at last, and then she waves us away. "But this is supposed to be a party. Please, go enjoy yourselves."

We're dismissed for now.

So we end up dancing and trying to enjoy the party, as per Brisa's wishes. It's not easy for me, but Adrian lets himself relax in a way I haven't seen before. I think back to Brisa's instructions and wonder how far her commands reach into these people. If she told them all to go jump off a bridge or to walk out into sunlight, would they?

Adrian introduces me to the vampires who inquire after us––a sea of beautiful new faces––but otherwise it's just the two of us. He's probably used to coming to these things with Kelli, and I wonder what he thinks about being here with me.

"What's that look on your face for?" he asks, pulling me against him for a slow dance. We sway to the music, and I'm surrounded by him to the point that I can hardly think. "This is supposed to be fun."

I sigh. "You know this isn't easy for me."

He nods once. "But you're doing a good job."

"When do you think it's going to happen?" He doesn't have to ask what I mean. All I can think about is the turning ceremony and being taken underground in those catacombs, laying among a bunch of old bones. I want to scream just thinking about it.

"I don't know. Could be tonight, could be tomorrow, could be in a month from now."

A month! "How long are we going to be here?" I swallow hard.

"As long as she wishes. Time is different to vampires, especially one as old as our queen."

I sneak glances at the others as we dance. Everyone is dressed in the same fashion, like we've traveled back in time. The other guests occasionally look our way, but mostly keep their distance and mingle amongst themselves. I wonder what kind of reputation Adrian has. He's a prince, so he's important, but that's all I know.

"I haven't even gotten to say goodbye to my mom," I whisper. "I want my phone back."

"Your phone is in New Orleans." He pulls me even closer until our bodies are flush against each other. "You already know Brisa doesn't like technology."

"That's pretty hypocritical––"

He cuts me off, literally putting a hand to my mouth. My eyes go wide at the fury in his expression. "Come." He leads me from the ballroom and out into the midnight courtyard. Even in the darkness, it's stunning and smells like fresh spring flowers despite it being early October. There are lawns that seem to go on forever, and more gardens than I could possibly count. Off in the distance, a shoulder-height hedge maze weaves endlessly. Party guests roam about out here, some couples finding the darkest corners, but most have stayed inside where the action is.

He keeps walking me out until we're well away from the glitter of lights. "There are listening ears everywhere," he says, voice dark and low, "so I will only say this once."

Twenty-Two

"**Y**our mother is safe," he continues, "and your friends are fine. If you wish to have a life as a human, you'd better listen closely. It's not going to be easy and I can't promise you anything. But I will try my best. If I'm to succeed, you must go along with everything I ask of you." He squeezes my hands. "One misstep and you're dead."

I let out a frustrated breath. "Fine."

"Brisa is living out a fantasy right now. She's been trying to gain control of this palace for ages, and now that she has, she wants to pretend she's Marie Antoinette for a little while."

"Didn't Marie's own people assassinate her?"

His eyes flash. "You know the story then."

Is he trying to tell me something? I step back and he drops my hands. "Yeah, let them eat cake and all that."

"Brisa won't even let *me* have a phone here. She's decided that she's the only one who can have access to the outside world, at least for now. She's paranoid about someone trying to usurp her. This is as much a test of me as it is for you."

"But don't you have business to run in New Orleans? You can't hang around here."

"I do," he grits out, "so let's get through this as quickly as possible so we can get back to our lives."

His life. Not mine.

He drags me back to the party and I put on my best show. I smile happily and chat with everyone, though never leaving Adrian's side. We act as if we're more than friends, as if we're in the process of falling madly in love, holding hands constantly, dancing too close, his arm or hand never straying from my body for even a second, his lips grazing my cheek or nuzzling into my neck. Everyone seems to buy it, and for a few moments throughout the night, I buy it too.

And that scares me, because I don't always know what's real and what's fake with Adrian. I know what my head wants--to get out of here. But my body betrays me, enjoying every touch. And my heart? I don't even let myself go there.

We're in the middle of chatting with a group of vampires who are sucking up to Adrian--vampires sure are good at that--when a couple strolls into the ballroom and everyone quiets down. We're all watching them with rapt attention, and I can't blame anyone, can't even blame myself.

They are hands down the most beautiful couple I've ever laid eyes on-- and also the most in love. I can tell by the way they look at each other, the way they hold each other's hand, and the glow in their eyes. They're abso-lutely mad for one another. I didn't know vampires could feel that way and the realization makes me feel a little conflicted.

"Who's that?" I find myself asking. The woman looks Japanese with glossy long black hair that curls and shears off at her waist. Her beauty could rival Brisa's on a bad day. The man is her equal, with coppery-blond hair that spans to his chin, broad shoulders, and a uniquely masculine face--he could be a model for a cologne commercial. "He kind of looks like a Viking," I add.

"That's because Magnus was a Viking," Adrian replies. "And Katerina is his wife."

There's a subtle shift in the air when the couple greets the queen. I wish I could listen in on their conversation, because from here it looks like Brisa doesn't like Katerina one bit.

Adrian takes my hand and leads me through the crowd toward the couple, whispering in my ear as we move. "Magnus is another of Brisa's princes. We aren't allowed to marry, but he met Kat during the Second World War and brought her back to our mother, and insisted they make it official. It was a scandal, but Brisa eventually agreed to let them wed."

"That's romantic," I hear myself saying. No, it's not! Kat's a vampire now.

"Make no mistake, they have fallen out of favor with the queen and have spent the years since trying to prove themselves. Let's just say they still have a long way to go."

I wonder how they're even alive. Adrian makes it sound like Brisa gets her way no matter what. The exception she made for Magnus must have caused a huge upset in her court.

"My brother!" Adrian turns on the charm as we approach, slapping the Viking on the back. I wonder how much of this is real, but Adrian does seem happier around Magnus than he ever did with Sebestian or Hugo. "It's been too long. What have you been up to?"

"They've been helping me," Brisa interrupts and everyone gives her their complete attention. "Traveling, and such." She waves her hand around vaguely. I thought all the princes ran different areas of the world and find this interesting––likely another blow to the couple.

Magnus is one of the last princes left right now and I wonder what that will mean for him and Katerina. Maybe they'll be brought back into favor simply because they're the only ones still standing. Or maybe Brisa will make more children, giving them better roles to spite Magnus. But I don't see any fledglings around Brisa and I haven't all night.

"It's good to see you happy, Adrianos." Brisa's rich voice turns on the two of us.

"Thank you, Mother."

She smiles and my hackles rise. There's something amiss in her expression. Her gaze turns to Adrian. "Come to my chambers with me, please. We have some catching up to do."

"Always," he says, his tone going hollow.

I can't be certain of her meaning, but I think she is letting me know that even if Adrian and I were to be in a relationship, she still has the power. She can call him to her "chambers" at any time, and he will go. She's the one in control, and there's nothing I can do to stop her. Even killing her is off the table now that I know what the outcome would be.

She kisses my cheeks goodbye, reeking of fresh blood and roses. She doesn't pull away. Her fangs extend, and I freeze. She could bite me, and then what would happen? Would she know I already have vampire venom in my veins?

But she pulls away, taking Adrian's hand and wrapping it around her waist, sashaying from the room. He never looks back.

I'm a human girl alone in a room full of vampires. Most of them have taken lives like mine without a glimmer of remorse. Maybe all of them have. Brisa changed things in order to allow them to come out in public, but their base nature has stayed the same. If anything, my association with Adrian has proved that I can't forget what they are and I shouldn't trust them. I swallow hard, wanting to get away.

"She did the same to us before we were married," Katerina says, jarring me from my thoughts. I shake my head and she tilts hers. "Oh, are you and Adrian not together?"

"We're not like that. I'm his fledgling only."

"Hmm..." She raises a thin brow at her husband. "What do you think of this one, Magnus?"

He peers down his nose at me and I feel about two inches tall. The loving gaze he had for his wife has turned to one of cool indifference as he looks at me. "I liked Kelli better."

Shock prickles at my cheeks.

"Kelli was lovely. Such a shame." They turn and walk away, leaving me gaping.

What on Earth?

I don't know if I've ever been so openly insulted like that. And to think I instantly liked them at first! It goes to show that vampires may be attractive to us humans, but that doesn't mean they're something we should seek after. At the end of the day, we're food, sometimes potential servants or lovers or maybe even prodigies, but we're not on their level. And in their minds, we never will be.

I need to get out of here. The exit is on the other side of the vast ballroom and I start that way, but somehow end up being tugged into the dance floor. I'm nearly knocked to the marble floor and a group of vampires laugh as they trample over the hem of my gown.

Fakers! They acted as if they liked me when Adrian was around and now I'm nothing but a useless human for their cruel amusement. The stakes are higher than ever for me. One false move and I may end up dead. I guess that makes me a faker too.

"It's good to see you again." A voice purrs into my ear, and I spin around into Sebastian's arms. This is the first I've seen of him since the day we met. I step back involuntarily. "May I have this dance?" His lips quirk at the corner and he tugs me back in. "Don't worry, Adrian won't mind. He's not even here."

"What about Fiona?"

"Ah, that's right. I forgot you met her." He nods to another dancing couple and I catch sight of Fiona in a man's arms. "She's busy. Now let's dance."

Realizing people are watching us, I settle into his arms, and we begin to circle around the room in a waltz. I don't know what I'm doing, but he's an expert lead, his eyes never straying from my face. I don't say anything, I'm not sure what to say to this creature. The sight of him makes my skin crawl--he's too much like Hugo.

"Aren't you curious?" He tilts his head.

"About what?"

"About my findings," he continues. "You know I came to New Orleans to investigate the death of my brother––a death you witnessed."

I hold my chin high. "And what did you find?"

But really, I want to know how long he stayed in town and what else he did there. Was he part of the raid when the hunters tried to take down the coven a few nights ago? Because if so, he's bound to know too much about me. Or maybe not. I wasn't there and my story might still stand.

Maybe that's why Adrian locked me in his suite.

"You know, it's funny," he continues, his grip suddenly tight, "everyone I spoke with all denied having anything to do with my brother's death. But they certainly knew who you were."

His fangs extend, and his eyes flash murderous.

"It was hunters," I hurry to supply, "but none that I recognized." I mix lies with truth, hoping it all comes out sounding real. "Brisa and Adrian already know about me. I'm a spy for them. But you do realize there are other hunter groups in Louisiana, right?"

"I know you are lying," he hisses, "and the only thing keeping me from tearing your head off is an order from my queen to keep Adrian's pretty little new pet safe. You'd better be grateful to Brisa. She's the reason you're still breathing."

I try to pull away, but he keeps us spinning round and round the dance floor like a puppet master. And I'm nothing but a helpless doll. The crowd seems to have thickened, and the party has grown obnoxious since Brisa left. I need to get out of here. Faster and faster we go, my feet start to drag on the marble floors, the heels at an odd angle. My ankles scream in protest.

"You're hurting me," I squeal.

He stops abruptly and releases me. "I apologize. Sometimes I forget how weak you humans are." But I read between the lines. This is a threat, the equivalent of telling me to watch my back because he'll kill me if he gets the chance.

Twenty-Three

∽∽∽

I hurry back to the room and pray I don't meet any more vampires along the way. Even in low candlelight, the palace is stunning with tall ceilings painted with Renaissance scenes, intricate tapestries on the walls, and plush rugs underfoot. There is lovely furniture and every shade of gold, blue, and white imaginable decorating the open spaces. And pastels as far as the eye can see.

My outfit blends right in, even down to the slippers on my feet. They have tiny heels at the bottoms and clack softly as I walk. I wish I could enjoy this palace more, but it's impossible. I want to find a way out of here, but Adrian's right. There are too many guards and it's too risky. His plan is the only way, but it doesn't feel like much of a plan to me. More like a hope and a way to keep my mouth shut so Brisa stays happy.

Flickers of light lead the way since the place is lit up solely with candles. Save for a few exceptions like running water, the guards with walkie-talkies, and I'm sure the Wi-Fi that Brisa uses, this place is authentic to the old French courts. Adrian said that Brisa infiltrated it for a while so she must know how things were done. She has one foot firmly planted in the past and one in the present day, allowing her to control her bloodlines while still living her life in the luxury she prefers. But at what cost? Someone has to pay for all this, and I'm not talking about the literal money the vampires have acquired over the years like mythical dragons hoarding piles of gold, I mean the countless lives that have been lost to Brisa's ambitions.

Outside, the black sky is giving way to the starless navy that comes minutes before sunrise. The vampires will be leaving the party now and retreating to safer places in the palace. They don't sleep, so I'm sure their celebrations will continue, but I'm ready for bed. I quicken my step, rounding the corner toward the room Adrian and I share.

But it's not the corner I thought it was.

And I don't know where my room is.

A wave of panic crashes over me the moment I realize I'm lost. I look around, desperate for a servant to help me. Surely they'll know every nook and cranny and can lead me to safety. But they're nowhere to be seen. Maybe they're smarter than I am. The vampires are retreating into the shadows, drunk on blood and rowdy. I can hear several yelling at each other through the halls. I step into a darkened alcove and wait for them to pass, but they never do.

Nobody comes in this wing. Why is that?

In a book, this is where I'd stumble upon a secret passageway. It would lead me to uncovering a mystery, or even better, a way out of this palace.

Of course, that doesn't happen. I'm no heroine in some nicely laid out story. I'm nothing but a weak and foolish girl who keeps making mistakes. I never should've agreed to come here. A smarter person would've figured out how to save her friends and get away from the vampires. Better yet, a smarter person would have avoided the vampires from the very beginning. But I'm not that person. I'm the girl whose dad died when she was a kid, the girl who had trouble making friends until she found the one true friend that mattered. And then I lost her, too. I'm the girl who got herself bit by vampires and ended up here because of it.

But maybe I need to stop blaming myself. Maybe I was taken advantage of by others and was only trying to do the right thing. Maybe I need to give myself more credit.

A fluttering sound pulls me from my thoughts. It's followed by a bird's sweet chirp. The melody echoes through the grand hallway, suggesting that the bird is stuck in here and not outside. I decide to find it, following the sounds. I'm still lost, but maybe I can at least save this bird. Even better, maybe this bird will show me a way out of here that's not guarded.

It sings, welcoming the morning, and I follow until I catch sight of the tiny thing and smile. It's barely larger than my thumb, with blue and green feathers. It sits perched on the arm of a chair, shiny black eyes blinking as I approach. But I get too close and it flies away, further down the hall. I continue to follow it until I hear a little thump and find it sitting on a windowsill.

It hops on one leg, feathers spread around it in a little arc. It's injured, must have tried to fly through the window even though it's tinted.

"Oh no," I whisper to the bird, "don't be scared. I'm going to help you get out of here."

This time it has no choice but to let me approach, and I push on the window. It doesn't give. It's bolted to the frame. I look down at my dress, trying to figure out how to use the material to safely pick up a bird. I don't want to touch it with my bare hands in case it's diseased.

A hand appears, snatching the bird so fast that I jump.

Brisa's hand.

"You snuck up on me," I gasp. I hurry to curtsy, hoping I'm doing this right.

"I have a tendency to do that." She holds the bird in her palm and pets its tiny head with her dainty finger. "They get in here sometimes when we leave the doors open at night," she says, smiling at the bird. "Tell me, Evangeline. Should I let it go free?"

This feels like a trick question. I swallow hard. "It's a bird. It's not meant to live indoors."

"Oh no? What about in a beautiful bird cage? We have several throughout the palace. I could keep it as a pet."

"Maybe if it was raised in captivity, but it would be cruel to put a wild animal in a cage."

"Hmm." She nods. "But it's injured. Wouldn't it be cruel to let it go back out there where it will surely die?"

Would she rather I agree with her or speak my truth. I straighten, standing tall. "You don't know that for sure."

"I've been around long enough to know it's very likely." She raises an exposed shoulder. She's not dressed in the gown from the party anymore. She wears a silky cream nightgown, and I have to force myself to not think of Adrian in her bed. She commanded he go to her chambers, so it stands to reason sex had something to do with it.

"It's your choice," I say finally. "I trust you to know what's best."

Her smile quirks. "I wish I believed you." And then she squeezes the bird. It cries out with a mangled squawk and goes silent in her stone-like hand. I stare, horrified. She drops it to the ground like garbage, feathers bent and broken. "Sometimes," she says, "it's better to end a life than to allow it to suffer." She steps closer and runs fingers along my cheek; my stomach twists, revolted by the feathers stuck to them. "If you continue to live as a human, that's what your life will be. Pain and suffering. What we're offering you is a second life, a better life. Very few people get that offer."

"And I'm grateful," I whisper.

"We'll see," she replies, and then she floats away like a ghost in the night. She's levitating a few inches off the ground and I wonder if she was the one who taught Adrian how. Or maybe it's because she's his master? No wonder she was able to sneak up on me! I swallow hard and stare down at the dead bird. If it weren't for me, it might still be alive because I'm certain her actions weren't to put the bird out of its misery, it was to let me know how much power she has over me.

I hope she believes me––that she thinks I want this and she wants this, too.

But I don't and I never will.

I don't care if her offer of a second life is filled with all the riches in the world. And like that bird, she wants to put me in a pretty cage. I can't let it happen.

"There you are," Adrian calls to me as he strides down the hall. "You're not supposed to be in this wing of the palace. This is Brisa's wing."

I nod. "Yeah, I just found that out."

He frowns and stops when he notices the dead bird. He doesn't say anything, and neither do I. He takes my hand and leads me away.

"Sorry, I got lost after the party," I whisper. "Do you know Sebastian's here? He thinks I killed his brother."

Adrian gives me a look that says, *"Well, you did kill his brother,"* so I return with one that says, *"Yeah, but only because you forced me into the situation."* He rolls his eyes as if to say, *"My, you're so ungrateful."*

Or something like that.

It's not as if I can read his mind with only a look.

"Come on," he says suddenly, "we need to move." He picks me up, dress and all, and we're flying through the halls. It's only when I catch a glimpse of the sunrise outside a window that I realize why. He doesn't want to get stuck anywhere else in this building for the day. He wants to be stuck with me.

When we make it back to the room, he sets me down simply as if the levitating trick is a normal occurrence for him. I'm still a little stunned but I'm also really tired. I strip out of my dress, not even caring that Adrian has a full view of my undergarments. My mind is thick with oncoming sleep. Between the flight and the time change and staying up all night to party with scary vampires, I'm done. I keep my slip on because it's easier than finding pajamas, and crawl into the blankets, pulling pins from my hair and tossing them to the floor. I burrow down into the fluffy pillow and close my eyes. Adrian lays down beside me. I don't know what I was expecting him to do, but it wasn't that. Before I can read anything into it, sleep takes me away.

I dream of birds.

Beautiful little green and blue birds. They descend on me like a cloud of locusts, clawing at my face, drawing blood. Wings flutter all around me, a tornado of feathers and claws and beaks. I scream and swat them away, but they keep coming. More and more. I fall to my knees, and they start to peck––little knives stabbing me. Over and over. I continue to scream and fight, but it's no use. There are too many of them. Beautiful little monsters.

Something cold shakes me. "Angel," a voice says. "Wake up."

My eyes pop open, and I bolt upright. I'm covered in sweat, and my heart pounds. My eyes try to adjust in the darkness, searching for the birds.

"You're okay. It was a nightmare." Adrian's voice reaches through the panic like water to a flame. He pulls me into his lap and rubs my back, shushing me. As sleep lifts, I find myself leaning into him.

This is not good.

This is so good. This is––

I scurry away and jump off the bed. "I'm okay now. Sorry." I run my hands through my hair. They're still shaking.

"You don't have to apologize to me." His voice drifts through the darkness. I can barely etch out his figure, but he's still sitting on the bed. "I used to have nightmares, too. There's no shame in it."

"What did you do to make them go away?"

"I became the nightmare."

Twenty-Four

S ometime later I fall back asleep, and then the day repeats itself. And it happens again, and again, and again. I spend daylight hours sleeping off the nightly parties that Brisa requires us all to attend. Each seems to grow more wild than the next. We dress in the attire of courtesans to dance and mingle. It's mostly vampires, but there are a few humans as well. There's always food and drinks for us and endless blood for them. They mix it with all types of alcohol, creating their own versions of champagne and wine and more options than I can count. The vampires don't seem to be affected by the alcohol all that much, but it creates different tastes and ways for them to enjoy the blood.

And still, I can't help but notice the way they look at me and the other humans. No amount of blood bags will compare to drinking straight from our veins. They want us. We're the temptation they're not allowed to have. Not only are they forbidden from feeding on humans, but the bloodline from Brisa makes it harder for them to break her commands. However, I know from experience that there are ways around it. Vampires can drink when they intend to turn us, they can drink if they're instructed to kill us, and they can push past Brisa's commands when they're so young that the bloodlust takes over.

I don't let myself forget that, given the chance, every last one of them would eat me alive. Adrian doesn't either. He stays close to my side at all times unless Brisa orders him away. When she does, I force myself not to think of what they might be doing. I don't walk back to my room alone again and Adrian never gives me a key. Night after night I wait for him to come for me and he always turns up right before dawn. Even though I hate it, I learned the first time that it's better to stay where the crowds are, especially since Sebastian always seems to be around. He doesn't talk to me anymore, but he watches, and he listens. He's building his case against me, I'm sure of it. He wants me to pay for Hugo's death with my life.

Adrian and I are still staying in the same room, but he doesn't show affection for me in private like he does for the court. I prefer it that way. When I sleep, he usually works from a laptop. After a week here he convinced Brisa to allow him a computer with internet connection so that he can continue to do business with his coven back home, but he keeps the laptop locked up in a safe whenever he's not using it. She's expressly forbidden me from touching it, but I still keep waiting for the opportunity to get my hands on it, hoping I can get a message to my friends and family back home. It never happens. And so the cycle continues––parties and sleep.

"What are you always writing in there?" Adrian asks me one evening. I'm sitting on the bed with a tray of fruit for breakfast at my side and the notebook Remi gave me open in my lap.

"Not always writing," I say, "mostly I'm doodling. And I'm surprised you haven't spied on it."

"I have no interest in invading your privacy."

I snort. "Sure, keep telling yourself that."

I've been writing out some of my feelings but I'd never show anyone those. I'm mostly drawing pictures from home, which aren't quite as embarrassing. They're the things I want to commit to memory in case I never see them again. I tried to sketch Felix and Ayla and my mom, but they all turned out terrible. Eventually, I'll get my hands on some electronics and can cyber stalk their lives from afar.

I moved on to objects, and lately I've been trying to get the feather talisman right. I know it's only a symbol of feathers crossing with the little hook on the bottom of one, but I can't seem to get it exactly right. I like what that woman said it represents: protection. I could use some of that right about now.

I decide to go out on a limb and flip the notebook around so Adrian can get a look at it. He's sitting on the loveseat with his laptop in his lap, typing away. Apparently he already forgot that he cared about what I was doing with this notebook because he doesn't even look up.

"Whatever," I say, and flip it back around.

"You should be careful who sees that," he speaks up. So he did see it. "Why?"

He lifts a shoulder. "Because it's not what you think it is."

"So what is it?"

"You ask too many questions."

"You started it."

He closes his laptop and sighs. "It's to do with those energy demons as you like to call them. That's all I can say but it should be enough."

As I suspected.

I close the book and take it with me to get ready that night. Remi is my only friend here and I don't get a lot of time with her. I want to ask her about the symbol, see if she knows anything more about it. When it's time to go to the dressing room, I do just that.

"I see you brought your notebook." She beams. "I'm so happy you're using it."

"Every day. This is saving my sanity. I can't thank you enough for giving it to me."

"It's my pleasure."

I hand it over to her. Despite it containing my deepest thoughts and loads of bad sketches, I hope this step will help me in some small way. "Take a look."

She's been busy pinning my hair up, but she stops to take it. Half my hair hangs around my face and the other half is artfully swirled on top of my head.

She flips through it, stopping at a few of the journal entries, eyes roaming the words.

"They're really bad. So are the drawings," I interject. "But that's okay, I like it anyway. Keeps my mind busy and helps me process everything I'm going through."

She makes it to the pages I've been waiting for—the talisman images—and immediately hands the sketchbook back to me. "Turn to the right for me, please."

"Wait." I flash the pages at her. "Do you know anything about this symbol? Have you seen it before?"

Her face is impossibly blank as she studies it for a minute. "I don't. Sorry, Eva."

There's something different about her tone, something fearful, and I know she's lying. I want to question her more, but she insists she doesn't have any answers for me, so I eventually put the notebook away. When it's time to move onto my makeup and wardrobe, she says she has a headache and leaves me with the other servants. What is Remi hiding?

She doesn't show up to dress me the next night.

. . .

IT'S ALMOST a month into my stay here that I wake up in the middle of the day, sitting upright with all sleepiness gone. My internal time clock has completely flipped from day to night. Since Brisa keeps me busy with her parties, I always end up sleeping the day away.

Not this time.

I blink the haze away and look for Adrian. He's not here. I've been waiting for this to happen. The idea came to me after that night I accidentally stumbled into Brisa's wing of the palace and Adrian swooped me up and flew us back to our room before I could blink twice. Fact is, this palace isn't completely ready for vamps, and that means there are places I can go to during the day that they cannot.

Still in my pajamas, I go to the door and peer out into the hallway. It's empty. This part of the palace is safe for vampires and I know they get up to stuff during the daylight hours, but I stay far away from whatever it is they're doing. I'm almost afraid to find out.

But someone is responsible for the deaths of all those princes. My first thought is Tate, but now that I've met Brisa, I can understand why she'd have many more enemies and some in her own court. I don't know what I'm looking for exactly, but I brave the hallway and hurry in the direction I committed to memory. I hope Brisa hasn't outfitted her entire wing with UV resistant windows yet, or I'm screwed.

"Fiona, are you hungry, my love? What are you doing awake?" I jump into an alcove when I hear Sebastian's voice up ahead.

"Bad dream. I wanted to find you." Her voice is sultry and welcoming, but he doesn't take the bait.

"You know the rules. Go back to the room. You can't be out during daylight hours."

So it's not just me. Maybe all the humans are relegated to our rooms during the day. There was a night during one of the parties that I tried to "wander" off and guards stopped me from getting very far. They seemed pretty angry with me then. I don't think I could get away with it twice.

I hold my breath when Sebastian and Fiona walk past. He's got his hand wrapped tight around her wrist and whispers harshly in her ear. I don't know what he's saying, but she's in trouble.

Maybe she's like me. Maybe she's here because she has to be, not because she wants to be. I never thought about that, I always assumed the other humans were traitors to their own kind. Could it be possible that I'm not the only one here pretending?

When they're gone, I'm faced with two choices. Keep exploring and risk discovery, or go back to safety. Me being me, I keep going.

A couple minutes later and I'm in Brisa's wing. It's quiet and sunlight streams through the windows, golden light that brings tears to my eyes. I didn't realize how much I missed it. I want to go to it, to soak in it and close my eyes, but I know I can't.

What am I even looking for? I don't know. Something. There's got to be something, some kind of clue. That's when I see two human maidservants walking by. If anyone knows about the secrets of this place, it would be them, right?

"Excuse me?" I wave them down. "I'm wondering if you could help me with something?"

They look at me like deers in headlights. One points and starts yelling, "Guards!"

I guess that's my cue to leave.

Vampire guards aren't like regular guards. They're so much faster. A human wouldn't have a chance against them, so it's a dang good thing I'm not like other humans around here. I channel the venom and take off at incredible speed, rounding the hallway corners and diving back into the room before they can catch me.

I'm gasping for breath when I look up to see Adrian. He stands towering above me, his hands in fists at his sides.

"I know," I gasp out. "You don't have to lecture me."

"If you break Brisa's rules and they find you out there, they will kill you."

"How unfair is it that I'm here of all places and I can't even explore?"

"Is that what you were doing? Don't lie to me."

I shrug. "I was hoping to figure out whoever's been killing the princes. In case you forgot, that includes you." I point. "Someone wants you dead."

"A lot of people want me dead," he replies. "I'm used to it. Now get back to bed."

I roll my eyes but do as he says, adrenaline making it impossible to fall asleep. I wish I did, because it's that very night, at one of Brisa's monotonous parties, that everything changes.

The French people don't typically celebrate Halloween, but Brisa announces that we're going to anyway--with a masked ball. I can't believe it's still October and that we're not well into November by now. Time has started to draw in on itself and I don't like that--I feel disoriented and want to demand to look at a calendar. But I don't demand anything. I can't. Not here.

True to Brisa's tastes, we're required to wear historical outfits. I don't get to choose what I wear. Ever. The servants always take care of that, and I never complain to them since none of this is their fault. I'm assuming Brisa is choosing my outfits, like a little girl playing with her dollies. Of course, I'm not the only doll, I'm one of at least a hundred. And all of us have painted smiles on our faces because we know the alternative could mean death.

Tonight, they dress me in a bright white gown. It's looser than the others and doesn't require a corset underneath––finally! I smile as the fabric sparkles under the candlelight.

"Wow," I whisper, appraising myself in the mirror. "This is my favorite one yet."

"Just wait," Remi says conspiratorially. "We're not done."

I hate that she's the only human servant here who I suspect isn't under a compulsion. The woman simply has too much fiery life left inside her. I hope she leaves this place one day and never returns. I can see her hatred of Brisa in her hazel eyes and hear it in her careful voice when we talk about the queen, even if she does her best to keep it hidden. She produces a set of sheer angelic wings and fastens them to the back of the gown. Then she paints gold shimmery dust all over my neck and on the bridges of my cheekbones. My hair is braided intricately down my back with little gold gems twisted throughout. Lastly, she ties a gold Venetian mask over my smoky eyes. I stare at myself in the mirror because I don't think I've ever looked more beautiful.

"Good luck tonight." She hugs me, whispering in my ear. "Keep your eyes open."

She leaves me in the dressing room before I can question her, the others scurrying after her. I watch closely as they go, looking for the auras as I often do. They're dim, but they're always there when I make an effort to see them. I hope that means one day they can be saved from the compulsions. I squint to get a better look. Does Remi have one? For a moment, I think maybe she doesn't. She turns back and winks at me, and then closes the door.

I gape after her, wide awake despite my lack of sleep. Is Remi one of the energy demons? But she's so kind, so helpful. How did she get in here? Is she planning to help me? Hurt me?

I start toward the door to follow after her, but it opens into me, nearly knocking me over. I stumble back and then Adrian is there, catching me. He steadies my body, and I gaze up at him, momentarily mesmerized. He's dressed completely in black, from the doublet vest and fine tunic, down to the breeches, tights, and boots. He's grumbled over the clothing here enough times that I know he hates everything about them, but I've grown to like him this way––my dark prince. His mask matches mine, elegant shape, but is matte black. And at the top of his head, resting in his curls, are two crimson horns.

"So, your true self is revealed," I tease.

He smirks and sets me upright. My body burns in each place he touches.

"I thought it would only be fitting if we went as a matching set."

So he picked this dress for me. My cheeks warm at the realization. "The devil and an angel?" I raise an eyebrow. "Aren't they supposed to be enemies?"

"That's what makes it interesting." He takes my hand and leads me to the ballroom as he's done so many times before. But there's something about tonight that feels different. I'm unsettled, trying to figure it out. Is this the night the vampires turn me? Is it when hunters come to save me? Or are the demon-things here on some sort of mission?

I can't figure it out, but I'm certain there's something going on. Like a change in the weather, it can be subtle at first and then one day a new season blankets the world. It's happening.

I squeeze his hand. "You promise you'd help me, remember?" I whisper. We haven't spoken of it again since arriving, not since he took me out into the garden and demanded I keep my mouth shut. When he takes me to the catacombs to turn me, I will be saved the next day, pulled from the grave before I can turn. I'll be free to run away. It's not the life I would choose but it's better than becoming a permanent fixture in this court. I'm still not sure what will happen after that, but with Adrian's venom also in my human veins, I'm hoping it will be enough to keep me one step ahead of Brisa.

He squeezes my hand back and nods once.

I know I shouldn't, I know it's completely foolish, that he's tricked me time and again, but I think this time he's being honest.

"I trust you," I say. "Please don't hurt me again."

He stops abruptly, turns, and stares into my eyes. There is nobody else in the hall save for a few guards down at the far end. He doesn't speak or frown or smile. Nothing. His expression is unreadable, eyes hooded in shadows behind his Venetian mask as he takes me in. I'm certain he wants to say something, but the moment passes without a word. My heart skitters for reasons I can't name.

Twenty-Five

⤛⤜

The ballroom is decorated in a gothic style with dark red roses and black candles dripping long rivers of wax. Gauzy black fabric has been draped across the ceiling so that only the center crystal chandelier hangs down. The candles burn softly, the shrouded light creating an air of mystery to the event. It's perfect for Halloween, but I'm not sure I'll be able to enjoy myself tonight. I'm way too nervous. Adrian runs a thumb along the edge of my wrists, as if he can sense my emotions and wants me to relax. Trepidation is probably written all over my face despite the mask.

We mingle with the other guests for a few minutes, and I turn on my charm as best I can despite the nerves.

"You look lovely tonight, Evangeline," Katerina says. She's on Magnus's arm and they're also a matching set––dressed in peacock colors with feathered masks. They've warmed up to me a little in my time here, but I still think they'd rather it be Kelli on Adrian's arm tonight. They begin to talk with Adrian and my mind wanders.

"Did you hear? There are only three princes left," someone whispers behind me. I make a point to listen.

"I heard that it was a rumor. Are you sure?"

"I'm sure. Someone's been killing them off. That's why Brisa brought all her courtesans here. The princes, too, of course."

"To protect us or investigate us?"

"Both."

I never turn around to see who's talking. I don't need to. If it's gossip among the courtesans then everyone will know. I'd foolishly assumed they already did--Adrian did. I wonder if this will change things. I imagined myself to be a bit of a detective when I arrived here, thinking I'd uncover things of my own, but that proved impossible. Is Sebastian creepy as heck and possibly the killer? Sure. But it could be Tate and whatever organization he's with, or it could be Magnus and Katerina. Or anyone else for that matter. What worries me the most is eventually he or she or they will get to Adrian. I won't survive without him.

Eventually, the crowd separates and quiets as Brisa sweeps into the room. She's ruthlessly beautiful in an emerald colored gown that's cut low to show off her supple curves, but that's not what's so eye-catching about her costume. A long green snake is wrapped over her shoulders and around her arms. It curls into its master, body slithering as it inspects us with beady eyes. My stomach clenches when she walks toward us, and I instinctively step back. Snakes are so not my thing.

"A devil and an angel," Brisa greets us with a coy smile. "How fitting."

"And let me guess, Medusa?" Adrian bows.

"Well, I couldn't fasten snakes to my hair, so I decided this would have to do." She winks playfully. "But you'd better stay back, Evangeline. The snake is venomous and deadly to humans."

My stomach coils. Her pet eyes me like I'm either a threat or a treat, and I take another step back. "At least your eyes can't turn me to stone," I joke shakily.

She grins. "Don't be so certain that I'm not a gorgon and a vampire."

It's a good thing gorgons are a myth because if she were both, she'd be unstoppable. She's already unstoppable. She ends the conversation by walking away, going to the front of the room, and clears her throat to speak. The chatter dies off as the guests take notice. Everyone turns to their queen.

"Welcome, my lovelies. I'd like to make a toast," she purrs and opens her arms wide.

The human servants enter at once, streaming through us in a line with trays of champagne flutes and hors d'oeuvres for the humans. Aside from a few regular glasses for the fledglings, the drinks are dark red from the blood mixed in. We take the drinks, and I grimace at the outfits the waitstaff are wearing. They're dressed in black overcoats with plague doctor masks, the creepy bird beaks strapped over their mouths and noses. Their wide brimmed hats cast shadows over their eyes, making it hard to distinguish any identifying features. I thank the man who serves me a drink, but he doesn't respond. I sigh and take a tentative sip. The carbonation burns my throat as it goes down.

"As many of you know by now, someone is after me." Brisa's voice sharpens. "So let's toast to the demise of my enemies, especially the pretenders of my own court."

She raises her glass, and we do the same, some with more enthusiasm than others. She's just watered the distrust among us. The seeds were planted long ago, but tonight, things have shifted in a matter of a few words. There are only three princes left and by now everyone must know. The rest of the vampires here have other titles modeled after the French courts of old, but they're not tied so closely to Brisa as Adrian, Sebastian, and Magnus. As a human, I'm nothing, and I'm okay with that. Except for Sebastian's, not a lot of eyes have been on me during my time here. They see me as Adrian's newest accessory and nothing more.

"Now, have fun," she coos, "or I'll think you don't like me."

The orchestra strikes up, and people move into formation, some on the dance floor, others to the edges of the room to mingle. It may be dressed differently, but it's like every other night, and I'm weary. I don't want to party. I don't want to gossip. I don't want to pretend that I'm happy here for another moment. It's been weeks, and nothing has happened. We're all stuck here in an endless loop, like snowflakes being tossed about in a snowglobe.

"Come on," Adrian whispers, taking my hand. "You know what to do."

And it's true. I've learned the dances by now. We begin the group waltz, and the champagne settles in my blood, making me feel lighter. I'm passed from Adrian, to other vampires, and even another human fledgling. It's a little more fun than some of the other dances, and I try to enjoy myself. But the music gathers speed. This hasn't happened before. Faster and faster, until I'm being tossed about like a ragdoll. Someone brushes up against my wings and they tug on my shoulder blade.

I cry out as Sebastian pulls me into his steel-like arms. He's dressed in gray and wearing a wolf mask that covers the left side of his handsome face. "Let me help you," he says roughly, then he dances with me so fast that my feet catch and I trip over the hem of my dress. He picks me up *after* I hit the marble floor. "Sometimes I forget how klutzy humans can be." He laughs as if this is all a game.

"Your costume is perfect, by the way," I bite back. My knees ache, and I long to sit down. I look around for Adrian, but his back is to me as he dances with another woman. "Adr––"

Sebastian's hand clasps over my mouth as he continues to dance with me. Round and round we go. My hands itch for a stake so I can end him, but I haven't touched a stake since I left New Orleans. "Don't think such awful things." He laughs in my face. "You claim to want to be a part of this court, don't you? Adrian's little angel."

My eyes go wide. Does he know what I'm thinking? Since he's a prince, he's got to be old. Adrian told me Brisa made all her princes centuries ago and hasn't turned anyone else since. She surrounded herself with men she could trust. It was a strategic move on her part not to make any vampire princesses. She didn't want anyone who could compete with her beauty. What does she think of the female vampires in her bloodlines? What does she think of me?

"That's enough." Adrian appears beside us, and we blessedly stop dancing. The other dancers have no trouble continuing around us. Adrian's mouth is drawn into a thin line as he glares at Sebastian, anger radiating from him. "I'll take my date back now."

Sebastian releases me easily, as if this were all a fun joke. "You really are a bore sometimes, Adrianos. All that Greek study did you no good if you ask me."

"Nobody asked you," Adrian bites back.

Greek study? I'm keenly interested in Adrian's past but after his confessions of killing his wife and unborn child, I haven't asked him anything. From what I learned in school, the ancient Greek people were really into philosophy and arts, so it must have something to do with that. Maybe one day he'll tell me all about his life before immortality.

"If you care about her so much, why aren't you more affectionate with her?" Sebastian questions. "Maybe Evangeline wants to dance with other men."

"I don't," I'm quick to say.

Adrian continues to glare. "I have nothing to prove to you."

"Don't you?" Sebastian's mocking tone dissolves into one of accusation. "Because everyone is wondering what's going on with you, Adrian. You rarely take on any prodigies and you recently lost your only child."

"Don't talk about Kelli!" Adrian roars.

"And now, you're here with this new girl, and you're dragging your feet. Turn her already. You can turn her at any moment. Brisa told me she gave you permission the first night you arrived. So what are you waiting for?"

I blink at them, my chest tightening. Adrian's been protecting me, but in doing so he's also keeping me here in an endless loop. If he'd go through with our plan, I could be free by now.

"Oh, she doesn't know . . ." Sebastian laughs. "Well, it sounds like you have some explaining to do, brother." He pats Adrian on the shoulder and then strides away, taking another human dance partner. He whispers into her ear, and she laughs, her cheeks becoming pink. I turn back to Adrian and blink up at him.

"Is this true?"

He doesn't say anything, which says everything I need to know. I turn and stride away.

Twenty-Six

~❦~

I'm done with this party. I wish I could be done with him and this palace and the stupid little room we share. I wish I'd never walked into that casino. I wish I'd never met Adrian. I wish none of this had ever happened.

I run back to the room, attempting to slam the door behind me, but Adrain catches it. "You have to go back to the party," he hisses to my back. "Brisa wants us all to be there."

His voice aches like it's painful for him to disobey her. I know it is. And yet, he's here. I wonder what kind of order she gave. Was it a command or a request?

"I'm risking everything to follow you here," he goes on, "don't you see that I care for you?"

I turn to face him. "All I see is a liar in a mask."

He rips his mask off and tosses it to the floor. "I shouldn't be in here, but I am, with *you*."

"Tell me why."

He grabs my hand and tugs, shaking his head. "It doesn't matter right now. We have to go back."

"Leave me alone! I'm not under Brisa's or your command," I growl. "You can't make me do a damn thing."

"Why do you have to be such a pain in the ass?" He changes direction, stalking toward me.

"It takes one to know one."

He pushes me up against the edge of the four-poster bed. My back presses into the pillar of wood, but I hardly notice it because every part of me lights up. The venom in my blood sparks to life, and I can feel, see, and sense everything. And it's all directed toward Adrian like he's the storm on the horizon. The electricity between us is unmistakable. It draws my breath from my body, and I try to look away.

"Look at me," he whispers. He takes my face into his cold hand and turns me to face him. His fingers wrap around my jaw, featherlight. His thumb tilts my head upward to look at him. "What is it about you that draws me to you?"

My lips part, but I don't know what to say. It's the same for me, and I hate and love it equally. It's an enjoyable pain, and I'm sick for liking it.

"My winning personality and kickass combat skills?" I respond. "Or maybe it's my wit. Or maybe it's because I'm an innocent little virginal angel. I know how you like my blood."

"You're insufferable." His blue eyes wrinkle at the sides, anger dissipating.

"Don't do that." I press my hands to his chest and try to push him back. He doesn't move. It's like pushing into a stone statue.

"Don't do what?"

"Flirt with me," I growl. "Play with my heart. Lead me on. Lie to me. Hurt me."

I don't know what I expect him to do. Apologize? Pout? Weave more lies? He does none of those things.

"I don't take orders from you," he says, eyes darkening.

"So what will you do, huh?" My hands press into his chest again. "Go back to your little party?"

"Brisa can wait." His voice is clipped.

"Like how you waited to let me go free?"

He grabs my wrists, wrenching my hands away and pushing me back against the post even harder. He holds my arms above my head and inches close, like a predator about to pounce on his prey. His body comes closer still, until it's flush against mine, until I can feel every muscle. I can sense something in him fighting off Brisa's instructions to enjoy the party. He should be there, but he wants to be here, and that changes things.

My body betrays me, longing pooling low in my stomach. Everything buzzes—my skin is alive with his presence. His cedar and bergamot scent wraps around me, and I breathe him in. He shifts his hands so that he's only got one holding my arms above my head. This time, I don't fight him. His other hand trails down my arm, fingertips feathering around my shoulder, up my neck, and around the back of my head. I shiver as he unties my mask.

The second it falls to the floor and his fingers claw into my hair, I forget everything.

I know what's happening. None of this takes me by surprise, not as it should. Not even for a second. The moment his lips claim mine, I finally admit that I've been waiting for this moment for months.

It's inevitable.

And wrong.

And so, so right.

The kiss is not tender. It's demanding and claiming and exploring.

We move right for the bed, and things progress quickly. I let it. I want it. We continue on a brazen path until it's time to lose my virginity. Not only will it keep me safer around the other vampires, but I'm tired of waiting for this to happen. *I need it.* My mind is ready. My body is pleading. And my heart is wanting--wanting this to work, wanting it to be real, for him to feel everything I'm feeling right now.

And I'm scared as hell.

But not for the reasons I thought I would be. The physical act itself is inevitable. I'm a grown woman, and this is a natural part of growing up. No, that's not what scares me. It's everything else, it's what will change between us, it's my own emotions, and especially his. I'm foolishly opening myself to be vulnerable with someone who could ruin me with his coldness. He can have me and just as easily destroy me. But despite all that, I still want this with him.

My hands tug at his layers of clothing, eager to get the last of them off. When there's nothing between his body and mine, he stops for a moment, staring down at me. He's frozen, and I don't know how he does it because I'm burning up. Something unreadable flashes in his eyes, and then it's gone as quick as a falling star. "Are you sure?" he asks, searching my face.

I laugh. "You're the one who said I needed to take care of it."

He growls a little. "I'm sorry for that. I was thinking of your safety among my coven and not your feelings as a human woman."

I nuzzle into him, kissing along his collarbone. I speak between kisses. "Wow, I never thought I'd see the day that Adrianos Teresi would apologize."

"Don't get used to it." He laughs back and then descends on me, kissing down my collarbone this time.

It sends another bolt of electricity down my spine, and I arch into him, ready for more. "Yes, this is what I want."

His kisses continue for long agonizing minutes, some gentle and others not. Emotions flood my body, and I don't know if my heart can take another second. I try to cloud them over, to focus on the physical motions only, but my feelings for Adrian shine through with the force of the sun. There's nothing I can do to stop my falling for him, not falling––*jumping*. I'm doing this to myself. He may have gotten me here, but this moment is my choice and one I'd choose a thousand times over. When I told him I wanted this, I meant it. To not have this moment would hurt too much, would rip me open and leave me for dead.

Adrian takes his time, and it's evident he's done this countless times before. Maybe I'm like every other woman who's been in his bed, but I tell myself that can't be true. I break away for a moment to gaze at him. I want to see into his eyes, hoping I'll find something real there. An answer to a question I've been asking my whole life. Why does he have to be the most beautiful man I've ever seen? As evil as she is, I can't blame Brisa for picking him because anyone would want him. His blue eyes are hooded with desire, as if it's killing him to hold back, as if this is tormenting him as much as it is me.

"The power you hold over me," he whispers low, "it's . . . " His voice trails off. He doesn't have a word for it. It's perhaps the most relatable thing he's ever said, and he didn't actually say anything.

"I know." I smile and laugh, that power filling me up like a woman possessed. "You don't have to explain it to me. I know."

Because I feel the exact same way.

We kiss again, and then we're doing more than kissing.

It's surreal, but it's also the realest moment of my life. As he takes me, I simultaneously want it to end and to last forever. It would be easier if he treated this like a transaction, like another one of his deals. But he worships my body, bringing it to life in a way I never knew was possible. No other man could make me feel this good. Nobody. My emotions build at the same time my thoughts melt away, until everything is taken over by pure sensation, like ocean waves crashing into the shore.

He holds me as those sensations begin to ebb away, whispering into my ear in a language I don't know. He runs his nose down my jaw and to my neck, kissing there as he speaks. His breath tickles, and goosebumps dance over my skin. His cool hands freely roam over me until I can't take it. I turn so our legs are entwined and press into him.

"Are you okay?" he asks. I gaze up, noticing his fangs have appeared. I'm not afraid. In fact, I'm overcome with something I never expected––a need for my lover to bite me.

"Yes," I whisper, followed by a whispered, "please."

He whips away with a groan.

He can't. I know that. It might even be impossible without Brisa's permission, might be too much for him to fight this time. And it's stupid to want it. Dangerous. Foolish. But I remember that euphoric feeling when Hugo bit me, and I can only imagine what it will be like with Adrian, especially with my senses so alive as they are. Allowing him to feed on me may even trump what we just did, as impossible as that seems.

He manages to get his fangs to retract, and then he's kissing me again. It's as tender as a lover's confession, and I'm paralyzed by it. Am I already in love? Has it already happened? Is he in love?

No he's not, and I'm not, but . . .

Someone pounds on the door.

Adrian pauses only long enough to yell, "Go away." It doesn't work. Whoever's at the door keeps knocking. With a frustrated sigh, he peels himself away and slides into his leggings. He pads over to open the door, peeking his head through.

"This had better be important," he hisses at whatever unfortunate soul has interrupted us.

"Brisa has commanded everyone to join her outside for a special surprise," someone says apologetically. He sounds like one of the male servants.

"We'll pass," Adrian growls.

"You can't," the voice continues, "she specifically asked to make sure you and Eva are there. She's agitated that you left her party."

There's a long pause, but I already know this moment is over. "We'll be there." Adrian closes the door and turns on me with a regretful expression. "Get dressed, my angel. We have to go."

Twenty-Seven

 ⟨✦⟩

One thing the palace of Versailles isn't lacking is gardens. They're the kind of impressive that's hard to comprehend in real life. I haven't been allowed out to explore them during the day, but at night Adrian and I have ventured into their sweeping grandeur during a few of the parties. I'm sure it's not the same experience without the sun, but I've let Adrian become my sun without realizing it. Maybe that was stupid, maybe it was a mistake, but it was also inevitable.

The gardens stretch around the palace for two thousand acres. Adrian says they're twice the size of Central Park. I've never been to Central Park, nor do I want to. Rumor has it New York City is rampant with vampires, far more so than New Orleans. All the best cities have a vampire infestation at this point. Any travel bug I would've had has been ruined by them. Truthfully, I'd love to see the world, and being in Paris without really being in Paris hurts my soul. But after this experience, the only places I'd feel comfortable traveling to are tiny boring towns without enough humans to keep vampires satisfied. But the suckers have even popped up in Hawaii and on most of the Caribbean islands, which aren't even all that populated. I don't know how the people stayed; I wouldn't want to be stuck with vampires on a little plot of land surrounded by a vast ocean.

This palace sort of feels like an island most days—these gardens are my ocean. And instead of sharks to watch out for, I've got vampire guards with big guns and a queen I still can't figure out. Some days I think she hates me, others I think she likes me, and most days I don't think she cares one way or the other.

Adrian and I walk down the hallway hand in hand and my romantic heart leaps. I'm still so mixed up. I know how I feel about him, know that I want him, but I'm still aware of how messed up that is. He's the enemy, they all are, and I'm toeing a very dangerous line.

When we stride outside, the guests are gathered around the ballroom terrace. The thin crescent moon hangs high, and darkness covers the landscape. Brisa stands on a little podium, a grassy lawn stretching behind her. She's already started a speech, and Adrian and I sneak into the back of the onlookers. He squeezes my hand tighter. "Come on," he whispers, "let's go up front."

I'd rather not be here at all, let alone to go up front, but Adrian's already weaving through the crowd and tugging me along after him. Maybe he wants to make sure Brisa sees us so she isn't angry that we ditched her party. Awareness needles my cheeks as I realize these vampires can probably tell what Adrian and I did. They wouldn't know except that the scent of my blood would have changed with the loss of my virginity. But it's not like these vamps aren't enjoying themselves whenever and wherever they wish. Why should I care? I hold my head up high and smirk at anyone who gives me a knowing glance or a sly smile. There's no reason to be ashamed. Besides, the whole vampires loving virgin blood thing is creepy and their problem, not mine.

Brisa falters when she sees us, her voice slipping for the slightest moment. She blinks it away and returns to her speech. "There's a reason I called you all here," she says. "You're my closest friends and family, and I wanted you in my presence again. You've all been living at my new court for at least a month now. Have you enjoyed yourselves?"

People cheer and nod along, but the enthusiasm is a bit mixed. Like Adrian, so many of these vampires are eager to get back to their covens and manage their work. Time may be arbitrary to Brisa, but it's not to the many businesses and humans outside of the palace. Brisa's gaze surveys the crowd, appraising us like jewels in her collection, some of us more shiny and valuable than others.

"I have news." She motions for someone in the crowd to join her. When Sebastian climbs onto the podium next to her, my stomach hardens. "Go ahead, tell them what you know," her voice goes sharp, "tell no lies."

It's a command.

If he tells no lies, will he have to out himself as being the killer? I've wondered if he's the one who's been responsible, acting like he was on Brisa's errand when really he was working against her. I have no real proof, just a thought that led to another and another until I started to become convinced. When Kelli died, Cameron had targeted Adrian, and I've wondered if he was in part compelled, because any hunter in their right mind wouldn't have tried that alone.

I've kept this to myself, but now I suddenly wish I'd told Adrian my suspicions.

Sebastian speaks as if he knows everything. "I've rooted out the person responsible for going after the princes. The traitor has been successful in killing all but two of us." Two? What about Magnus? "That's right, unfortunately earlier tonight during the party Magnus faced true death."

"I felt his loss the moment he was taken from me," Brisa says angrily, her eyes watering. "And Sebastian witnessed it."

I squeeze Adrian's hand at the news. This can't be good. What if they're going to blame me for it? Adrian and I left the party early, something everyone who cares to know will know by now. And I can't forget Sebastian's many threats toward me. When his eyes land on me and he points right in my direction, I refuse to believe it. He's not really accusing me, is he? It's true about Hugo, but he doesn't know that for sure. And how could I possibly have killed princes who weren't even on the same continent as me?

"Katerina!" he calls out, voice cracking like a whip, and all hell breaks out.

I'm pushed to the ground, my knees hitting the stones first. Then Adrian is on top of me, protecting me with his body. The woman is directly behind us and screaming out obscenities between sobs. "You're a liar, Sebastian! I *loved* him."

But it's no use.

Guards detain her and nobody defends her. Adrian helps me up, and I rub my palms on my dress while trying to locate the woman. Her cries were anguished and I believed she loved her maker and partner even more than the rest of us are supposed to. What if she is innocent? I don't think it would matter. Brisa has already made up her mind.

Katerina is a beautiful woman, and possibly became a threat to Magnus's loyalty. If he had to choose between his lover and his maker, I genuinely believe he'd have chosen Katerina. And Brisa knew it too. At this point it doesn't matter, Brisa seems happy to be rid of the couple.

"Katerina wants to take out our monarchy, and I have proof," Sebastian continues, "She recently traveled to every location where the princes were murdered. When I went to confront them, I caught her with the stake."

Katerina gapes at him. "I didn't see who killed him and neither did you. I only picked up the stake after he was gone. And I was doing my job when I traveled." Tears run down her cheeks, makeup smearing. "We both were."

"That's enough." Brisa flicks her wrist toward Katerina and the guards. "You know what to do."

So that's it? She's going to believe Sebastian just like that? He was commanded not to lie but Brisa never questioned his story. It's perfect--if he's the real killer, he now has a scapegoat and only one more person standing between him and Brisa. And that person is Adrian.

The guards drag Katerina out toward the gardens, which makes no sense to me. Wouldn't they put her in a dungeon? Kill her on the spot? What's out in the gardens? We stay in place, everyone silent on the terrace.

"Well, don't be so glum, this is a party!" Brisa opens her arms wide. "And I have another surprise for you in a few minutes, so don't go anywhere."

She turns away, eager to watch the gardens and see if she can spot what's happening to Kat. To please Brisa, we talk amongst ourselves. Some people here seem glad that Katerina is gone. Others . . . not so much. Their mouths are set and eyes are glum. Katerina was a favorite at court. Is this what happens to the female favorites around here?

I stick close to Adrian's side as we mingle through the crowd. I'm never letting him go again. Well, that's if Brisa doesn't command him to leave me. Since that first party, she's called him to her chambers on multiple occasions. We never talk about it. Now I suddenly want to talk about it and to demand he never entertain her again, but I don't.

"Come up front. Both of you," Brisa says, appearing at our sides. She slips a slim arm around my waist as well as Adrian's and directs us to the balcony at the head of the large terrace. I'm aware of the snake resting around her shoulders. It lays its little head on Adrian's arm and he pets it gently. I shiver, wishing that thing was long gone.

Brisa stands between us, a tiny woman with the power to ruin everything. I breathe slowly, filling my lungs with cool air, hoping to slow my heart. She needs to like me, to want me here, or I'm dead.

We lean on the railing and she whispers to the snake, "Go home now, Precious. You did good." It slithers down the steps.

"You can compel animals?"

"One of my many talents," she replies.

"She's the only vampire who can do it," Adrian adds. "The rest of us can compel adult humans and that's only if we're strong enough. Brisa is an incredible queen."

She waves the compliment off but I can tell she's pleased. It's dark, but my eyes adjust thanks to Hugo's venom. I squint anyway, to be safe. She knows I was involved with hunters but she doesn't know about Hugo's venom. Standing this close to her kind of makes me want to throw up--I'm so nervous.

"What are we looking at?" I ask.

Brisa laughs and turns to Adrian. "Is she always this impatient?"

"Always."

"All humans are." Brisa smirks and pats me on the back. "It's okay. I was the same when I knew my time on this earth was so limited. You remind me a lot of myself, actually. Now tell me, are you glad you switched sides?"

I smile, putting on my best mask. I wish I still had the Venetian one covering my eyes but it's still back on the bedroom floor. I hope she can't see the worry on my face. "The hunters can't give me all this. Nobody can but you and Adrian can."

She nods. "He's been taking his time, hasn't he?"

It all comes back to me in a rush, the entire reason I was angry at Adrian in the first place. He could've put me in the catacombs weeks ago. My spine straightens and I'm not sure what to say. I don't want to make it sound like I don't want this. I do, but only so I can escape before the venom takes hold forever.

A woman's frantic screams roll across the gardens.

"Ah, that would be Katerina facing her mortality." And then the screams are swapped for thunderous booms. Fireworks light up the sky, glorious and sweeping through the darkness. The next ten minutes are filled with one of the most impressive shows I've ever seen, but I can't find it in myself to enjoy it. Not when I realize the truth--Katerina is dead, and those fireworks are what ended her. I'm not exactly sure how, but if I had to guess, I'd assume she was tied down to them. I always thought vampires had to be killed with a stake or the sun, but I guess there are more creative options. Blowing someone to pieces seems to do the trick. Or maybe my imagination is getting away with me and the guards simply used the noise of the show to muffle her death. Somehow, I doubt it.

The show ends, and I'm antsy to get back to the room and forget about this ever happening. Brisa smiles brightly and squeezes my shoulders. "Welcome to the family, Evangeline. It looks like our Adrian finally made you his tonight." She winks playfully, but there's an undercurrent of venom in her tone. "It's okay, I don't expect him to be celibate. Besides, you'll be one of us in three days anyway." I blink at her and then at Adrian. He smiles grimly and looks away. The corner of Brisa's mouth lifts. "Oh, didn't he tell you? Today was your last day as a human."

Twenty-Eight

I can't move. I'm numb. I glance at Adrian, pleading with my eyes for answers, but his are downcast, and his face is unreadable. Brisa grabs my hand and tugs me after her. Her grip is vise-like and far too strong, crushing my fingers without care. "We'd better get going before we run out of time," she says. Adrian follows behind us, and all I can hope is that his plan is still in motion. Did he ever find someone to get me out of there? Is he going to come back himself?

I knew this was coming, watched it coming, even. But no amount of knowing and waiting and watching could've prepared me for this moment. My heart slams against my chest like a drum, and I'm sure the vampires can hear it. Maybe that makes them more excited, maybe it's that beat that makes them the most hungry. And maybe I'm lucky that they're taking me to the catacombs and not feeding on me right here.

"And between you and me," she whispers, "I will let you feed directly on humans, and I'll even let you end some of their lives. It's cruel to keep new vampires from their base instincts but it's done for the betterment of our kind. You will get special privileges since you'll be a royal, but they have to stay a secret or the other vampires will get angry with me."

"What?" I balk at her. I wonder where they keep these humans. The palace is so big, they could be hidden anywhere. No wonder why I was forbidden from exploring! Plus, the vampires own property all over the world. It's almost comical that I thought she wasn't allowing this for her favorites, and surely for herself. I should've caught on before.

"I know, I'm nothing if not generous. We go for criminals and people who deserve to die. I have cultivated special relationships with prison wardens across the globe. They give me the ones who have no friends or family to ask after them." Brisa chuckles. "We're not complete savages. It's not like we're killing innocents anymore. We've learned, and we do better now."

Wait . . . my thoughts roll back to something she said before. "Royal?" I ask. That doesn't make sense. I'm going to be Adrian's prodigy, which would make me . . . what? What is the daughter of a prince? I don't know enough about this stuff to have the title off the top of my head, but I know it puts me far enough away from the crown that I'm not considered royal anymore. Or maybe it still does? I guess the royal family in England, the ones who are always all over the tabloids, call their grandchildren princes and princesses.

So maybe that's what she means. *Please let that be what she means . . .*

"What's Adrian's is mine," she answers.

This whole vampire family dynamic is twisted.

"Come, this way." The group moves around the edge of the palace toward the same area where Adrian and I were brought into a garage weeks ago. Everyone is laughing and cheerful, acting as if they didn't just witness one of their very own being brutally murdered. I'm having a hard time thinking or breathing, knowing that my life is about to end as well. I keep clenching and unclenching my fists, not sure what to do. How can I go along with this? I feel like I'm a kid marching up to the diving board for the first time, only this is one of the tall ones reserved for professionals. I don't know how I'm going to make it out alive!

I'm seriously praying that Adrian was honest when he said he was working on a way to get me out of those catacombs before my third day. Luckily, being down there should be better than trying to dig myself out of an actual grave. As we come around the corner of the palace, several of the human servants in the plague doctor costumes appear with more drinks to greet us on the driveway. The area is surrounded on three sides by the palace and one by a large golden fence. The stars twinkle above.

We raise our glasses. "A parting goodbye," Brisa says right before someone screams.

The plague doctor humans throw their trays at the vampires. They rip off their masks and drop their long coats, and time seems to stop. I recognize several of them; they are the hunters from New Orleans. My hunters––and my friends. But I don't have time to process much, because time speeds up again and the fight breaks out.

These hunters are prepared, with loads of stakes strapped on their bodies and crossbows in several of their hands. Adrian grabs me and pushes me back. "Stay here," he yells, and then he's flying out to meet the hunters. Stakes slice through the air, going right for him, but he dodges them all with practiced ease. He's so much faster than the rest of them.

There are far more humans than I've ever seen before. Somehow they have infiltrated the palace. Are they here because of me? I'm not sure how they figured out how to find me, but they must have. Part of me wants to go to them, and to be saved and rescued and to get far away from Brisa and Adrian and the rest of them. And another part of me wants to scream that they're here at all, because they're not going to survive this. I have seen for myself how cruel this court is––there will be no prisoners. It's dead or alive and that's it.

But they are here now, and if I can get away from Versailles, I would be stupid not to take my chance. I run toward them, hoping someone will give me a stake so I can fight at their sides. I catch sight of Seth and hurry to him. "Hey, what are you doing here?"

He gives me a hard look. "Get out of the way, you're not our target."

And then he's gone.

Okay, so maybe this isn't a rescue mission. But what the heck? Why did he talk to me like that? Am I just meant to stand back and watch?

And that's when I realize how much they are going after Adrian over anyone else. I would think they'd be going after the queen herself, but nope, everyone seems to have Adrian as their target. As the fight explodes into blood and chaos, vampires go down and so do humans. It's hard to watch, and I would give anything to join in.

Felix's face appears as the crowd surrounds me. He picks me up around the torso, dragging me to the edge of the fray. "We have to get you to safety," he mutters. "You should get out of here."

Once we're out of the craziness, I have to ask, "What are you guys doing here? Are you trying to kill Adrian?"

He sets me down abruptly and steps back. His eyes narrow into little slits and he stares at me as if he's seeing me for the first time. "Are you sleeping with him?"

I don't know how to answer that. My cheeks warm and I look away. It's all he needs to know. He takes another step back and lets out a small breath.

"We're here for Tate. Our target is your boyfriend. Funny, I thought I would save you in the process and we could go back to the way things were before you disappeared."

"I'm sorry," I whisper.

"Did you come here willingly? Just answer me that."

"Of course not."

His lips thin and he looks away, hands back on his stakes.

"Why do you want to kill Adrian? There are worse vampires here."

Those words turn his attention back to me and he glares. "You know what, Eva? Why don't you save yourself."

Twenty-Nine

A nd then as if I'm nothing to him, he's running back into the fight and my heart is breaking and it's all my own fault. He's right and he should hate me. I've become too soft, too trusting, when my heart should've stayed guarded. I dig my foot into the grass, because you know what? I thought Felix was my friend.

Another hunter comes barreling toward me, his eyes wide and his teeth bared. "You! This is all your fault!" He actually has the stake pointed at me, death in his eyes.

I ready my stance and channel my training. I'll fight him off if I need to. But I don't have to, because Adrian gets to him first, knocking him unconscious. He lands a foot away.

"Why does Tate hate you so much?" I demand.

"It's a long story."

"Where's Brisa?"

"Her guards already got her out of here. We need to get you to safety too."

"I don't think so," I say, my heart dropping as I point back to the drive. The tide has shifted and it has become painfully clear that the vampires are the stronger of the two groups here.

"Move out!" Felix calls, and the hunters take off, sprinting into the darkness.

But the remaining vampires are angry, and hungry, and they'll kill anyone they can. I can't let them kill my friends! I turn on Adrian. "Please don't let them kill them," I cry, "please, they don't know what they're doing. Tate set them up to this. They're not bad people."

Adrian shakes his head––and it sets me free. I'm done with him, with the lies, the manipulations, and the disappointments. I have to take matters into my own hands. I run toward the hunters, hoping to save whoever I can. Something metallic rattles through the air––a machine gun. Everyone drops to the ground, myself included, and my heart beats in my ears. Is that coming from the guards? Or from the hunters? Either way, this is it. We're all going to die right here at the foot of the palace.

The gunfire stops and I uncover my head to find a silver bullet embedded into the earth a mere two inches from my face. I remember what Tate said about silver bullets being used to slow the vampires down. My hope rises–– does that mean my friends got away? It's hard to hope these things, when hope has been taken away from me so many times before. But when I look up, I find that most of the hunters are gone.

I don't see Seth or Felix.

I stand and wander through the bodies of what hunters didn't make it. When I see Kenton laying among the dead, my heart stops. His leg is twisted back behind him at an awkward angle and his eyes are wide open and staring into nothing.

No. No no no no no. This can't be happening.

I want to fall to my knees and sob, but Remi is at my side and pulling me away. "Don't feel sad," she says, "don't let anyone see you sad."

"What are you doing here?" I turn on her.

But she doesn't have an answer and I can't help but wonder if she had something to do with this attack. "What are you? Are you a human or not?" I ask her point-blank.

Her face shuts down and then she turns and runs away. I want to chase her down and demand answers but I can't seem to move with Kenton lying at my feet. The vampires will stred him to pieces before he even gets a chance to grow cold.

"Death is part of being a vampire." Brisa appears at my side. "You will get used to it. Come, I'm not going to let this deter us from our intentions for the night."

I blink at her as she leads me to a car, the first I've seen in a month, and we climb into the plush leather backseat. At least it's not one of the ones without windows. That other one felt like an early grave, but I guess that's fitting considering where I'm about to go. There are other cars waiting on the wide driveway as well, and other vampires that are left climb into those. I notice some of the other fledglings are along for the ride. Did everyone know about this night? Did they know this was their last day as a human, and Adrian decided not to let me in the loop?

I've always hated surprises . . .

Adrian climbs in, too, and I'm sandwiched between them in the back of the vehicle as we head toward Paris. Maybe I'm in shock, but I can't believe any of this is happening, or that the hunters just attacked and now we're back to business as usual minutes later.

Versailles is on the outskirts of the city, and I've been longing to go into the city itself since the moment the jet hit the runway. Maybe some of the people of the court have been allowed into Paris, I'm not sure, but Adrian and I have been ordered to stay put. It's one more thing I can add to my long list of resentments against Brisa.

As we drive through the beautiful historic city, it reminds me of New Orleans at night, and that reminds me of my friends. It's hard not to cry, but I don't let myself. Instead I focus on the view and keep pointing out the similarities of the cities to myself. It's not just in the architecture of some of the buildings, but in the small groups of people tittering down the sidewalks on their way home from the clubs and bars. Who cares if vampires are involved when the vices are served? It's a horribly brilliant exchange, and I'm sitting next to the mastermind.

Guilt wracks through me, because I put myself in this situation, because I was a fool. And now people are dead, my amazing, vibrant, funny, cute, awesome friend Kenton among them.

For a moment, I pretend that it's daylight, that we're on our way to enjoy the city like any other tourists. I try to imagine the last couple of hours as if nothing notable had ever happened. If I had my choice, we'd be going to the museums, to the top of the Eiffel Tower, to wander the treasure of the Louvre, and stop off at a bakery or a café to enjoy wonderful food and people-watch. If I could only be gifted a semblance of a normal life before . . . before . . . before . . .

We pull up to a church that I instantly recognize but whose name eludes me right now. My brain has gone fuzzy as the nerves have taken over. "If the humans would've allowed us to take over their landmarks sooner," Brisa says, "we would've never allowed a *fire* to destroy such a historic building." She says fire as if it's an avoidable nuisance and not a sad accident. "I've always loved Notre Dame, same is true of all the gothic architecture that is mostly gone now. France is my home. I've traveled the world, of course, but I always come back here. There's simply nowhere like France."

Notre Dame, that's right. Looking at it now is like coming to a church with a confession and being told I'm not forgiven. My eyes water again. I can't cry in front of her, and that makes it even harder.

The lights of the city twinkle on the inky black river. What's left of Notre Dame looms over us like a dark gothic mountain, gargoyles perched on its ledges. Through the haze of sadness, I recall what she's talking about, how years ago huge parts of this historic church caught on fire and burned to the ground. Investigators later said it was the fault of bad electrical wiring or maybe even a stray cigarette butt. Either way, it had been a tragedy that the whole world had watched from their television screens.

But do vampires really think that they could prevent something such as a fire? And what about an act of God? Could they stop a natural disaster like lightning from striking or a storm from raging? "You've seen it all, haven't you?" I ask numbly. "And you prefer the old ways to the new?"

"In some ways, yes." She smiles demurely. She's acting as if the hunter attack did nothing to ruin her good mood. What is wrong with this lady? "Do you know I've never made my own princess? I've only made sons and raised them to be powerful princes." I did know, but I don't say anything. She muses to herself as she continues. "Some say it's because I get jealous of women, but that's not really why, I just find that men are better company." I swallow, not sure what she means by that. Is she talking about sex? Should I take offense? Should I be grateful that I'm even in her presence right now? In the end, I decide it's best to keep quiet and let her continue. "Adrianos knows all about that. Don't you, Adrian?"

She's obviously talking about sex and it makes my stomach roll. For the first time since we climbed into this car, he makes eye contact with me. The pained look in his eyes does not bode well for me. "I do." Two words. That's all he says.

I look away.

We walk into the church with about thirty others following us. A lot of it is still roped off, but it doesn't matter. Brisa leads us to a staircase, and we immediately descend. "There are all sorts of entrances to the catacombs in Paris," she explains, "but I prefer this one. I like to keep things dramatic." She laughs at herself and most of the minions laugh along. She certainly does know how to put on a show.

It's too dark for humans to see, but I can. I don't say anything. I hold onto Adrian's rigid arm and act like I'm as blind as the rest of the humans. Someone lights a few torches and the catacombs light up in an eerie warm flickering glow. And same as we learned in school, the long hallways are lined with human bones, centuries of skeletons stacked upon each other in intricate patterns. I've never been one to spook easily, but this place gives me the absolute creeps.

Brisa and the other vamps know exactly where they're going, as if they've done this countless times. They probably have. "We have a safe place that the hunters don't know about," I hear one of the other vampires say to his fledgling. I swallow hard, for the first time praying that hunters don't show up. They wouldn't want to save me, not the way I am now. They'd count me as one of the vampires, a traitor to human kind. And I wouldn't blame them.

But they won't come, at least not mine. I already know they're weaker than ever.

There are eight fledglings by my count. Seven other humans who are choosing this life . . . or rather, this afterlife. One that will stretch on and on and on if they're lucky, filled with adventure and travel and darkness and blood and death and answering to somebody who has more control over their free will than maybe even they do. I don't understand how anyone could willingly sign up for this. It doesn't matter what I feel for Adrian, I still wouldn't want this. When I was younger, I read that book where the girl begs her vampire boyfriend to turn her, where turning eighteen felt like a horrible old age. I didn't understand it then, and I still don't now.

Why are people so afraid of death?

It's not like I have a death wish. I don't. But I want to live––*really* live.

I want to live a full life. That means having the sun. It means enjoying real food and drinks and going on vacations to discover places with blue skies overhead. I want to feel love and heartbreak and family––my own children––and time passing by as I grow old.

I never thought I wanted children, not in this horrible world, but maybe I would someday.

Not a family that is made from adults turning into immortal blood suckers, but real families with human problems and joys. The way that vampires create their families can't replace the real thing. I want to be a parent, I want my kids to have siblings and hopefully cousins and aunts and uncles and everything that goes with it. All the things I never got to have, those are the things I want my kids to have one day.

I've never really thought too much about a full human life, or maybe I've spent countless hours thinking about it.

But now it's all about to be taken away, and I can only desperately pray that Adrian's plan will work, that he was being honest, and that I can trust him. I can trust him, right? But then, why didn't he tell me that today would've been my last day? Why keep that a secret? He knew I had been waiting for this to happen and was growing impatient, so what isn't he telling me?

Maybe he just wanted to be with me. He could've waited until I gave into my attraction for him, but I don't think he'd be that selfish.

We reach an area with several small openings in the walls and stop. These are obviously the crypts we're to be placed in. They'll take our blood and give us theirs. They'll put us in that wall and allow the vampire venom to do its job, and in three days when they come back for us, we'll rise as one of them.

"This is where the transformation will happen." Brisa sounds like a proud parent. "We are taking care to separate you all because we can't have one vampire waking before the others. Let's just say you'll be very thirsty." The vampires chuckle at that, and my mouth goes sour.

Brisa turns to me. "And you, my darling, are the very first. Are you ready?"

No, of course I'm not ready, but I don't have a choice.

I smile down at her, she's so petite and beautiful, but worldly and power-ful. I wish I could stake her and hate that I can't. She smiles back. "Please, my darling, keep your angel wings. I rather like them. I find it kind of ironic, don't you think? I mean, what better outfit than that of an angel for my very first princess."

I blink at her, reality snapping into place. "Your princess?"

"Oh, didn't Adrian tell you that? This agreement was made ages ago. Before you even came here, actually. The whole reason I wanted you to come was so I could vet you and see if you would be worthy of the title. So sorry we lied to you and said it would be him to do it. I wanted to make sure I liked you. Plus, I was waiting for him to take your virginity." She scrunches her nose. "I rather dislike the idea of a virginal vampire as my daughter, no offense."

My heart shatters and disbelief overtakes me. I stare between the two of them, and Adrian offers me nothing. Not an apology, not anger, not regret. *Nothing.* And suddenly, in the worst way, I know the answer to my recurrent question.

I cannot trust Adrian.

I never could.

And I am a fool to have believed him for even a second. I had weeks of chances to try to get out of this place and I didn't because he fed me some ridiculous plan about having someone get me out of here before the third day. What a load of crap that was. And I wanted to believe him, I chose to ignore the stupidity of his plan because the truth was that I wanted to be with him. I was falling in love with him, and he played that to his advantage. I'm nothing but a stupid little girl to him, someone to be used in whatever way he saw fit to please his queen and meet his own agendas. Maybe he never turned on me. Maybe he was never on my side to begin with.

And my virginity. Maybe that part hurts the most, because I gave him something Brisa wanted him to take. He never cared for me. It was all a lie. All of it.

"You've handed me over to your queen like a prize?" I ask him, a wobble in my voice betraying my attempt at stoicism.

"Brisa needs to build her line back up. You should be grateful she chose you," he responds, and then he melts into the crowd of vampires surrounding us. It doesn't make sense. I thought he hated her. Maybe he does, but he still did what was best for her over what was best for me––what he promised me.

"So, you'll be my master?" I ask Brisa, even though I already know the answer. I'm stalling. I'm in disbelief. I'm––

She answers by extending her fangs, grabbing hold of me, and sinking her teeth deep into my neck.

Thirty

~❦~

My limbs go numb and then limp. Excruciating pain shoots through me, followed by exquisite euphoria. The bliss seemingly heals me, sending me away. One second I am standing, and the next I am on the ground, Brisa leaning over me, feeding on me like she's probably done to countless others before, but to me, it's like falling in love for the first time. I smile at her, enjoying every incredible second. I don't care that her venom stings because it's so wonderful, and much stronger than Hugo's was. Perhaps that's because she's the queen, and the oldest vampire alive.

The last of my thoughts run as dry as my veins.

She is lost to me, everything's in a fog, but my body is still incredibly alive. It's as if every cell is being rattled, shaken, burned, and transformed by her venom. Brisa sucks and sucks, drinking my blood until my vision blurs, the edges going black, and everything tunnels. I don't like that, so I close my eyes. I don't scream because I don't want her to stop. So I sigh, letting it happen, willing it to happen, whatever *it* is.

But somewhere, somehow, there is still a part of me that is fighting this, a part of me that's the little girl, that's the teenager, that's the grown woman. All of them are Eva, and she is lashing out. She wants her life back. And she wants Brisa dead.

I am that girl.

She is me.

But I am also this new thing, this soon-to-be vampire. Brisa finally pulls away but stays leaning over me, her amber eyes ablaze like hot coals. "I can taste Hugo's venom in you," she whispers low, eyes growing angrier by the second. She knew that he was going to take me as his own that night, but she didn't know that he had already fed. At least I don't think so, because with her, it's so hard to know what she's thinking. "I have half a mind to kill you right now," she sneers as her lips softly caress my cheek. "But once you are mine, Evangeline, you will be unable to resist anything I ask of you. You will be loyal to me through our bond. And perhaps that will be your punishment. Because if you hate me, this transformation will force you to love me instead." She inches back and smiles wickedly.

My mind slowly rolls back to me, and I search for Adrian, but he's not here. Where could he have possibly gone at a time like this? Does he really feel so little for me that he'd leave me here in my most vulnerable moment? But no, my most vulnerable moment already happened, and he was very much there for that. My heart crumbles all over again. Tears burn in my eyes as I search the faces of the people watching me. It's a sea of faces with predatory claims in their hungry eyes, as if they can smell the last of the human blood still left in my body. I look away and try to sit up, but it's useless. I've lost too much blood. I was strong once, and now I can hardly remember what that felt like.

Brisa holds her slim arm to my lips and blood fills my mouth. I start to choke on it and try to turn away but she's too strong and holds me in place. It flows down my throat and I gag on it for what feels like ages. When it's over, she lifts me easily into her cold arms as if I were nothing but a small child. Even though I've got at least twenty pounds on her, her vampire strength is unmatched. She walks me into the little crypt and lays me down on a flat slab bed.

"Sleep now, my little one," she coos like a madwoman, "for when you wake, your past will be nothing but a burdensome dream, and your true life will start." She steps away, watching me for a long moment with a satisfied smile. It's like she's tucking her child into bed, not killing a human. This is sadistic. This isn't what I want. The tears release from my eyes and stream down my cheeks, mixing with the wetness of my bloodied neck.

No. This can't happen.

She can't leave me here. Where's Adrian? Why can't I speak?

Will I be able to fight this on my own? Somehow, I know I won't.

A sob racks through me right as something burns, prickling at my hands. Is it the venom working its way through me? The fiery pain gets hotter and hotter, crawling its way up my arms.

Brisa steps back.

I finally find my voice. "What's happening to me?"

"I knew from the first moment that I saw you in person and had a chance to smell your blood that you were different," she says, "and I was thrilled. You had to be mine. Adrian agreed."

"Why?" My voice scratches at my throat. The burning continues.

She leans in and whispers against my ear. "Just between you and me, it's time for a new generation of royal children. Soon they'll all be replaced by worthier sons and daughters, even my precious Adrian must be culled. You think you hate me but, darling, that will change. Don't you see? You're exactly what I've been searching for."

Realization is like a sharp arrow to the chest. Brisa's the one who's been killing the princes––and pinning it on everyone else.

"But why me?" The question still remains.

"Because you're special. You're part of them, but now you'll also be part of us. You're both––exactly what I need."

"I don't know what you're talking about." The pain intensifies, and I scream out, "Please stop this!"

A light flashes so bright that my eyes cannot handle it and I squeeze them shut. There's a scream––Brisa's scream––and then more screams that aren't hers. All the vampires, the fledglings, everyone . . .

And then there's nothing.

And I'm nothing.

Thirty-One

![ornament]

I don't know how long I'm lost to the heat. Hours? Days? Or maybe it's merely minutes. But I'm there for all of it, and I don't know what it means. Fear wracks me for the eternity that I lay waiting, terrified that I'm transforming into one of them. If I could crawl out of here I would, but I can't move. Finally, the burn dissipates enough for me to open my eyes and not be blinded by the light. I peer at my hands, but there's no sign of scorching. They're not even red.

I look around, expecting to be walled in here since that was the plan. Brick by horrid brick, we were to be locked into our crypts like a child in a mother's womb until it was time to be born again. But there's no wall keeping me in, and I stand, heading toward the entrance. When I peer out, I don't know what I'm expecting, but not this. Because it's nothing––nobody is here, no vampires to watch over us, no lights, no torches.

Just emptiness.

But I can see everything, every crack in the cobbled walls, every old bone stacked up, every booted footprint in the dirt, all of it. It's as if I've walked outside in the middle of the day rather than far under the city of love. Doesn't matter––I'm out of here.

I sprint my way down the stooped hallway of musty old bones and back up into the church and then outside, moving faster than I ever have before. The sun has already crested over the horizon and I immediately jump back into Notre Dame's shadows. Could this be it? Could this be my opportunity to end my life now instead of starting a new one as a monster? I always thought I would be able to offer myself to the sun if this happened, but now that I'm faced with the reality of my situation, I'm not so sure I'm strong enough.

I reach out a tentative hand, one finger pointed, prepared for it to burn into dust. I imagine the pain to be similar to what it was in the crypt, or maybe even worse, but when it slides into the sunlight, nothing happens. The light wraps around my fingertips, same as it always has. I slowly step the rest of the way out, and still nothing happens. I sigh in relief, sobs once again wracking my body. I fall to my knees and tuck my head against my chest, crying. I've never been much of a crier, but this moment is perhaps the one I'm most grateful for in my entire life. Because I'm alive. I'm here. I'm safe. And I'm still me.

And at this point, all I can do is cling to the hope that Adrian didn't lie to me about this one important thing. He claimed that if I didn't stay for the three nights that I could avoid this transformation. I growl to myself because how can I trust anything he's ever said? And how could I have been so stupid as to let him manipulate me like he did? I walked into his trap willingly! He's proved who his loyalty is to, and it isn't to me.

I sigh and stand back up, walking out to the sidewalk. My transformation hasn't happened, and I'm worried that maybe I have too much venom, maybe it will kill me, but maybe it's exactly what I need to set me free. My senses are full-on. With Hugo, they'd come and go, but now that I have Brisa's venom in my veins, I am ablaze with power.

And it's time to run.

There isn't a snowball's chance in hell that I'm going back into that crypt or anywhere near a graveyard ever again, nor am I going around vampires anytime soon. I'm about to become a hunted woman, is my guess. Thank goodness it's daylight because I have to get out of here. I need to find a way to escape Paris and never return. Where should I go? Where can I be safe from them? They can smell me, that I already know, but will they be able to smell me enough that I can't take on another identity? Because if they find me, I'm as good as dead. I can fight and I'll take down as many as I can, but I know what Brisa is capable of, and I know her numbers.

My mind whirls with possibilities and then it hits me; I can't go back to New Orleans. Ever.

The realization hurts perhaps more than anything else. Maybe even more than realizing Adrian betrayed me, had kept important secrets from me. He knew I would resist the moment when his queen took me, and so he never said a word. He knew, and there's nothing he could ever do or say to make me forgive him. I'm done trusting vampires, and I'm done with him.

My hands continue to burn, but no light escapes from them. I think back to what I saw with that blinding light, not wanting to admit it, but forcing myself to anyway. My palms had light exploding from them, the brightest light I've ever seen. I fist my hands at the thought, wishing they were cool. Maybe I'll find a place where I can dip them in the river. The sidewalk I'm on is wide and stretches for miles. The river is below, but unreachable from here. I keep walking. Take this one step at a time. First, wet my hands and cool the burn. Second, get out of here and find somewhere safe to hide. And finally, figure out what is happening to me.

A little red convertible sports car with the hood back pulls up next to me, screeching to a halt. The face that peers up at me from the driver's seat makes me stop in surprise. I don't know who I expected to find me. Felix, maybe? But I saw the look on his face, he'll never forgive me for what I did with Adrian. In my weeks at Versailles, I kept imagining my friends busting me out of the palace. What an idiot I was to give up on them. When they needed me most, I was useless. And Kenton paid the ultimate price.

No, it's not them smiling at me, and it never will be again.

It's Leslie Tate. "Climb inside, Eva," he says wearily, "we have so much to discuss."

I step back, about ready to jump into that river to get away from him. The last thing I need is another man intent on using me for his own agenda. "Did you send them in there? Was that your doing?"

"They would've with or without my help," he insists.

"How would they even know where to look? You came into Adrian's suite that night of the attack. What did you take?"

"Join me and I'll tell you."

I glare.

He puffs out his breath. "Listen, Brisa's takeover of Versailles is international news. Once your friends figured out that's where you'd most likely be, they came to me. Not the other way around."

"I'm done with you," I growl out, and then I start walking again. He drives beside me and I keep talking. "Look, I know you're something different, okay? I know you were willing to slaughter my friends to get at Adrian. And that tells me all I need to know about someone like you."

"Get in the car, or I will make you get in the car," he calls back, "this isn't a negotiation."

"I can't trust you." I laugh maniacally. "You can go now."

"Believe me, Eva, you can't trust anyone. But that's not what's important right now. Right now, we have to get you to safety, and I know how to do that."

"I can take care of myself." Other vehicles go around him and some of them honk. It's early enough that he doesn't slow traffic down too much, but try telling that to the taxi cabs. Not that he's the type to care.

"Don't you wanna know what you are?" he calls out. "Do you want to know what's happening to you?"

I don't look at him even though my interest piques. I open and close my hands, but I already know the light has vanished. My hands are normal, and maybe it's a good thing that he didn't see what I saw in that crypt.

Or maybe it's all in my head. Maybe it was some kind of hallucination from Brisa's strong venom. But no . . . that couldn't be. Because I wasn't sealed into that crypt. Because Brisa responded with words about who I was. Because when that prickling happened in my hands, the flash of light followed. And then the screams. And then nothing.

I stop short with a gasp.

Is it possible? Did I kill the vampires? What kind of light did I emit down there?

And if she's dead, then the vampires of the world are now subject to whoever their highest masters are in the bloodlines, masters who might want to hurt the humans far more than she ever did. And if word gets out about what I did, then I'll become the most wanted person on planet Earth.

For once, I hope a vampire is alive and well . . .

I stop and walk over to Tate, leaning over the edge of the car. "Can you really help me?"

"I can really help you." He nods. "Now please, Eva, get inside because we don't have much time."

I have nowhere else to go.

No one else is willing to help me but him.

And most of all, I need answers.

So against my better judgement, I do what he says, opening the car door and sliding into the passenger's seat. He speeds away before I even have a chance to buckle myself in. The air whips through my hair; it's mostly down by now. And my makeup must be a mess. And my dress is torn and bloody. I'm still wearing the sheer angel wings. I reach back and untangle them from my dress, then toss them out. Let someone else have them or let them be garbage, but I don't *ever* want to see them again.

As we drive out of the city, we sit in silence, nothing but the wind to listen to. We drive and drive and drive, a race against the sun. And somehow, deep down, I know that he's taking me somewhere I've been waiting to go my whole life—because whatever Tate is must be whatever I am, too. I didn't want to face it, but it explains why I was never able to see my own aura, why the vampires took such an interest in me, why Remi gave me that wink, why Brisa said what she said before the light took over.

Her last words echo in my mind: *Because you're special. Because you're both.*

Adrian

NINA WALKER

SOMETIMES YOU WIN,
SOMETIMES YOU BURN.

WICKED SUN

VAMPIRES & VICES, NO. 3

This one is for all those brave souls battling chronic illness, seen and unseen.
You are not alone.

One

ADRIAN

I'm halfway back to Versailles when the royal blood bond breaks. It stops me in my tracks, a chasing wave of unbridled relief and incredible loss. I don't have to see it to know that it's happened--my maker is dead. I press against the nearest building and breathe in deep. It's a learned behavior from a mortality long since abandoned, but right now, *I need to breathe.*

I drop my head low between my knees and try to rid myself of unwelcome emotions. The stone at my back is winter-cold, the night smells of ice and dirt and city. It's everything I can do to keep upright when a bulbous Frenchman appears next to me, inquiring as to why I'm here. A demanding finger taps me on the shoulder. He smells of flour and booze. He's either a concerned citizen or an angry bakery owner or both, but he's most assuredly a fool. Does he not see who I am--what I am?

I can't deal with humans right now. I can't. *"Laisse-moi tranquille,"* I snap, growling at him as my fangs spring from my gums.

The man freezes, eyes going wide and glossy. So glossy I see the monster reflecting back. I'm primed to kill. And I could.

I could--what a revelation.

Brisa is really gone. I have no master, nobody to tell me no, and it's enough to ruin me. His blood smells delicious, but not as good as his fear-- that scent is intoxicating. It's the middle of the night in a back alley in Paris. Nobody would see. Nobody would know it was me. What consequences would I have? None.

I want to lunge for him, but I hesitate, and it's enough of a break for him to run. Bad idea. The predatory urge to chase prey rears its ugly head, and I almost do. "No," I demand of myself aloud. "You're stronger than this."

He runs, and I don't follow because that's not who I am anymore. Or maybe it is, maybe it always will be, but it's not who I *want* to be, who I *can* be. There was a time when killing an innocent for sport was natural, but it's been ages since that game, and I've grown to pride myself on my restraint. I don't have a choice in what I am, but I can choose who I am, and I'm not a murderer anymore.

Just because I'm a predator let free from my cage doesn't mean I'm going back to that. I can't say the same for my kind. Whoever that Frenchman is, I hope he sounds the alarm. Humans need to be on high alert.

Gathering myself together, I continue on foot back to Versailles. I'm a blur of motion that the human eye can't catch. Speed allows me to think while running from undesirable emotions. I've always been good at multi-tasking like that. But I'm angry––that hasn't left me yet, and I'm not sure if I even want it to. "I warned you!" I yell out to a Brisa who no longer exists. "I warned you this would happen, and now you're not here to clean up the mess you've made!"

For as much as I hated Brisa, I hadn't wanted her dead. Not yet, anyway. Not when it would unleash so many of her children to feed as they please and undo decades of hard work. No amount of immortality will make up for the dark shadows we must hide in during the daylight, but having the freedom to live among society and build a life for ourselves has been more than I ever thought possible. In the years since we came out of hiding, I've been happier than I've ever been since becoming a vampire. And for what? For it all to be undone because Brisa wanted a hybrid child? Something she herself had expressly forbidden others from doing?

She of all people should've avoided the risk. Avoiding risk is what allowed her to keep her crown as long as she did. When I'd left for France, I'd expected Evangeline to be my prodigy. I should've seen this coming––Brisa never was good at sharing.

Then again, neither am I.

I scale the palace wall and levitate across the gardens. Not many vampires can fly, so most won't think to look up. I need to get a feel for what I'm dealing with here, a plan before I reveal myself. I don't have children now that Kelli is gone, so there's nobody to sense if I'm still alive or not. I could use this opportunity to slip away, but that's the last thing I want. Even though the New Orleans coven I lead isn't mine through a blood bond, they're still my family, and I will protect them with my life. I hate that I'm not there right now. They need me. Many will be wayward and will get themselves killed.

I expect chaos at the palace. What I don't expect? Stillness. Quiet. Utter Silence.

Where is everyone? Most of the court hadn't been invited to the ritual tonight, only the most select were ushered along to spectate. And of those, surely they didn't all die. They should've scattered when Brisa died but, like me, they would've come back here to see their children and send word to their covens back home. And maybe even to fight for Brisa's place, though it will never be what it was.

Nobody could ever truly replace Brisa, and that had been her true power, and why I'd never found a way to kill her. Oh, I had wanted to try, had dreamed about finding a work around for the blood bond, had fantasized watching her burn . . . but I'm logical. Her death means disaster for my kind.

I enter through an open window on the third floor to a sparse empty bedroom that must belong to one of the human servants. I find her immediately, hearing her thudding heartbeat before I see her. A middle-aged stick of a woman is squashed into the corner, her eyes hollow and her mouth pinched.

"Are you okay?" I ask, first in French and then in English.

She blinks up at me through round fearful eyes. She's lost whatever compulsion Brisa had put over her. I'm surprised she's still here and hasn't run off by now. She starts begging for her life in gasping French––she's still here because she's hiding from the vampires in the palace.

"I'm not going to hurt you," I say in her native French. "You're safe with me."

She nods, but I can sense she doesn't believe me because her heart rate speeds. Tears break from her eyes to stream down her cheeks. "The others . . ." Horror corrupts her tone, and I don't need to ask for clarification.

I already know.

When the royal blood bond broke, any humans in close proximity to the vampires here were likely sucked dry. I don't have time to deal with this, but I'm not going to leave her to be slaughtered either. I gather the tiny woman into my arms and fly her back out to the street. If I can do one good thing tonight, then let this be it. Why should she have to die? I don't compel humans to be my servants like Brisa did. I pay them well. I've built a business I can be proud of, lead a coven I love, have a home I want to keep.

Merde . . . I like my life, enough to compel this human to slow the news of what happened tonight from spreading. But what difference will it make? Brisa's bond lorded over all of us, and now that's gone. Many coven leaders will continue to enforce our customs, but not all. Some will use this opportunity for blood, and if it gets out of hand, vampires will be forced back into our holes.

Like where Eva is right now.

Thinking of her sends a frenzy of worry through me coupled with an aching need and a hollow fear that I can't will away. I had this stupid idea that she and I could make it work somehow, that I could be with her, really be with her. But that was foolish. She'll never forgive me. Why would she? I wouldn't forgive me.

It was self-preservation, a skill I picked up long ago. When I learned to conceal my emotions, tucking them away to gather dust. When I made Brisa love me. And when I left Eva in the catacombs to face our common oppressor without me.

Damned self-preservation.

No vampire lives as long as I have without being a selfish prick. I had to leave her, I couldn't risk staying. But there's just one problem--what starts as self-preservation can quickly become self-sabotage, and that shit gets old. And lonely. There, I said it. *Lonely. Lonely. Lonely.* I didn't realize how bad it had gotten until I met her.

Eva is my own personal sun. I've found her warmth, and I love it.

And I hate it.

But what if she refuses me? What if I have to feel this aliveness all on my own? Every pain, every hope, every emotion that I've locked away for centuries is now staring me in the face without a way out. She's the only way out. She's it.

The sun.

I have half a mind to forget Versailles and get her out of the catacombs this very second. And I will, as soon as I know what I'm dealing with, what *we're* dealing with. She has three days before she'll turn, but I'll intercept her before that happens. I'll keep her safe. And then I'll kiss her and hold her, and she won't turn into a monster like I am. She'll be wholly herself, and she'll forgive me, and maybe she'll love me, but even if she doesn't love me I'll be content just to have her.

I drop the trembling woman off with instructions to hide and then rush back to the palace. This time, though, it's not quiet. Not even close.

Two

The wind twists my hair back as the car zips down the two-lane highway. My fingers dance on the torrents of air--up down, up down--until the rattling fear in my chest loosens. Even though I'm one step closer to freedom, I'm beginning to question if freedom really exists. It's a strange resignation that my life isn't what I thought it was. It's not like I have lived wearing rose-colored glasses, but things have turned out to be crueler than I imagined.

"You're not planning something stupid are you?" Tate asks, his weathered eyes twinkling with observation. Sometimes it feels like he sees far more than he lets on. It's unsettling in the best of times and terrifying in the others.

When I left Paris this morning, part of me imagined I'd be free, but I know deep down that was wishful thinking. I've traded one prison for another, but escaping an eternity as a vampire is worth whatever Tate has in store for me. It has to be. I'm at his mercy--a man who has manipulated me and lied to my friends, who hid his true identity for his own gains.

I could make him squirm a little with my answer, but I decide to go with the truth because lies feel like quicksand right now. "Nope, even though I want to run away, I won't. I have literally no plans, nowhere to go, and am counting on you not to screw me over."

"You don't like losing control," he prods. "Can't say I blame you. I don't like it either."

My mind flits to Ayla and how she'd say wanting to keep control was a trait of being born in September. I miss her weird zodiac ramblings so much and don't know if I'll ever get to make things right between us. "Yeah, that control freak thing is a problem. That, and I can't stop thinking about the freedom I'll never get to have."

"Ah, freedom." He nods as if he understands how I feel, but I'm the one being held hostage in this situation, not him. "It's such an American concept, you know. In other countries, people care more for unity and the collective good than for individual freedom."

"Well, you have an American accent, so are you saying you're not the same way?" I fight to roll my eyes.

"I was born in Spain, spent many years in Italy, but I've lived all over since I was a small boy." He smiles ruefully. "I guess that makes me a citizen of the world." Sounds pretentious. "I spent most of my formative years in New York City, but I do think I've held onto my sense of community over individual expression."

"So you're a rule follower?" I raise an eyebrow.

He doesn't answer that, and I let it go, trying to relax into the leather seat. It's cool enough that my skin doesn't stick to the upholstery and late enough in the day that I'm starting to grow chilly with the convertible top down. I don't ask him to put it up, though, because I don't mind the cold. It's actually quite refreshing. I breathe it in as if this is the natural state my body prefers. I don't let myself think about it for too long because enjoying the cold isn't my norm. It's actually another thing to add to my freak-out list. Vampires love the cold because they *are* cold, but I'm not going to turn. I refuse.

"Well, I used to think that freedom existed in my own mind," I explain, deciding this conversation with Tate is the best way I'm going to process my emotions. "That no matter what happens to me, I'd be able to control my thoughts and feelings, and that nobody can take that away from me."

"And do you still believe that?" A ray of sunlight glints off his sunglasses as he turns to study me.

A knot forms in my throat, and I shake my head. "I wish I did, but I've come to realize that our thoughts are biased. We see what we want to see, believe what we want to believe, and feel what we want to feel. Sometimes those things keep us more trapped than anything else ever could."

Because even when all the evidence pointed to the contrary, I still allowed myself to fall for Adrian. Not even fall, *I jumped*. And I wanted to believe I was making the right choices with him, that he'd protect me, that he was falling too . . .

I was wrong.

"Ah, now you're catching on," Tate replies.

There's a smugness to his tone that makes me want to punch the smirk off his face. Normally I'd say something snarky. I could point out that he uses young and impressionable human hunters for his dirty work, but I don't. It's not a good idea to poke the bear, and it's not really what's bothering me right now anyway . . .

The truth is, I fell in love with a cold-blooded vampire. I trusted Adrian. I gave myself over to him, offered my heart and my body. And where did it get me? Betrayed. Heartbroken. And worst of all––infected.

Gah! Why can't I get him out of my mind?

Tate has the forethought not to comment further, and we continue on in silence for the next hour. He's been driving all day, and we've only stopped once to go to the bathroom and pick up snacks. We're in a hurry to get to our destination, and as the sun sinks into the horizon, my heart rate accelerates. It would be so easy for me to give in, to go underground and let the venom take control, snuffing out my mortality like a flame starved of oxygen.

I can picture the venom spreading through my body––my olive skin going waxy, my warm muscles hardening like concrete, my limbs growing cold, and fangs bursting through pliable gums. Presumably, I'd become far more beautiful than I am right now, every imperfection smoothed over like a glossy varnish, but I have a hard time imagining that part to be worth it. Human mortality is something so many vamp wannabes would give up at the chance to be powerful and gorgeous. Not me. I can only focus on the bloodthirsty monster that would lurk underneath the false exterior, and it makes me want to scream and cry and hurl myself from Tate's speeding car.

I shake my horrible thoughts away and turn on him. "Where are we going?" I ask for what is probably the hundredth time. The man hasn't given me a straight answer.

"I told you, it's safest for everyone if you trust me to handle this."

Here we go, another man asking me to trust him. "Trusting you got me into this car, didn't it?"

"No, necessity did."

Okay, he has a point. "But why can't I know where we're going? Unless it's somewhere you know I won't agree with, and that's the true reason you won't tell me."

He sighs heavily, as if I'm such a burden when he was the one who sought me out. "You're going to have vampires on your tail for a while. I'm taking you to safety, and I'd rather not disclose the location until we get there."

"Why, though?"

"Because I have more than just you to protect."

"Pardon me if I have a hard time believing you. You haven't been totally honest."

He doesn't respond, and neither do I because I don't have a lot of options––and we both know that.

The man got me out of Paris, and I'm not sure I would've been able to do that on my own. I do know that we're somewhere in the Italian countryside because we had to go through customs between the neighboring countries. I don't have a passport, but the Italian border control officers waved us through without stopping us. My heart had been a riot in my chest, visions of getting stuck in France dancing through my mind, but they must have recognized Tate's vehicle. The vampires are powerful, but whatever Tate is? He's powerful too.

Rolling hills and sweeping vineyards pass by us in a stunning blur of greens, oranges, and every color of beige that Ayla could have easily named. Autumn has come to Italy, and it suits the country well, casting the landscape in a dusty gold and adding texture. The countryside is dotted with little old farmhouses and small towns. I can easily imagine what it must have been like to live in a place like this a few hundred years ago.

We stick to the back roads, never getting near any big cities, which takes us longer to get to wherever we're going. I would normally love this road trip––it's the kind of thing I used to dream about––but it's hard to enjoy with all the questions floating around in my brain and Brisa's venom heating my veins. I'm anxious, and I don't know what's going to happen to me. Is Brisa dead? Did I kill her? Where's Adrian? What about the other vampires, did I kill some of them too?

What if . . . what if . . . what if . . .

I don't have to wonder about our destination for too much longer because an hour later, just as the sun begins its descent and lights up the sky like a fireball behind the mountains, we turn off the two-lane highway and roll into a quaint village. Tate navigates the cobbled streets with familiarity, approaching the edge of town where a gorgeous limestone castle rests on a cliff's edge. Yellowing ivy crawls up one side, and a vast lake twinkles gold and blue at the base of the cliff. The tallest mountains I've ever seen in person tower like ancient giants beyond the lake. These are the kind of mountains that have seen civilizations rise and fall.

"Waiting wasn't so bad, was it?" Tate asks, pulling me from my thoughts.

"Feels like a power play if you ask me," I reply honestly.

He frowns at that. "I'm sorry you feel that way, Eva, but again, I had to be certain we'd make it here in one piece. What if someone intercepted you? God forbid you'd tell them where I was heading."

I fold my arms in on myself, hating that he's right.

"Switzerland is on the other side of these mountains," he points out.

"Well, I'll be honest, I don't know much about northern Italy, though, it is beautiful. Whenever I think of Italy, I think of Rome and Venice and places I've seen touristy photos of." There's a whole wide world out there that I haven't gotten to explore, and I'm suddenly filled with the desire to see it all.

"We own this castle. It's a historical landmark," Tate continues, voice dripping with pride. "My family has more real estate in Italy than any other country in the world, though we do have holdings all over the globe. Rest assured, Evangeline, you're safe with us."

Safe with you as long as I do what you want . . .

"And who is this 'us' that you're referring to?" When he doesn't answer right away I add, "You know I have to ask. You'd be asking the same things if you were in my shoes."

His fingers tighten on the steering wheel for a second and then relax. "All of your questions will be answered when you are ready for the answers."

That's his response? Is he serious right now? But he smiles at me like he's the most trustworthy dude on the planet, and my spidey senses kick in. "You're trying to do your voice manipulation trick," I scoff. "It won't work on me anymore."

Even without my feather talisman, I have no trouble blocking the manipulation. Must be the venom. His jaw tightens. Maybe I shouldn't have said anything. "I figured as much."

"Listen, I'm not sure how much time we have together for you to answer these questions," I point out. "What if the vamps get to me before you can tell me the things I need to know? You were the one who warned me that I'll have vampires after me for the rest of my life."

"Hmm . . . I did say that, didn't I?"

Not only do I want to know what Tate is, but I wanna know what I am as well because I'm starting to suspect that we might have a few things in common. It's scary to even consider it, and I can't know for sure, but Brisa's words keep ringing in my head about how I'm "both." She acted as if I would've been a valuable piece on her chessboard, knocking courtesans and even princes out of my way.

Looking at my hands, I remember how they'd glowed. Why had they done that? What did it mean? They're completely fine now, just small hands with long fingers and shiny black nail polish. From the outside, I look like a typical nineteen-year-old girl, but I know that can't be true. I gaze up at the approaching castle and sigh. The fortress is intimidating, and Tate's people can't be trustworthy, but hopefully, I'll find answers here.

Three

⚬～⚬

The castle has a tall outer wall with only one arched opening visible. We pass through it, and I note the guards with semi-automatic weapons who wave us on by. These types of weapons used to be illegal in most of the world, but ever since the vampires came out of hiding, gun laws stopped being enforced. I can't say I blame people for wanting to pack heat, but the sight of guns makes me nervous. Hopefully, they're here to keep me safe, but I kind of doubt they can stop a determined vampire. Fangers are much stronger than bullets, and even the silver ones only slow them down.

We wind up a thin cobblestone drive lined with olive trees that have lost most of their leaves this late in the season. The fallen leaves crunch under our tires like scraps of paper bags. We approach the castle, and I frown at a large gravel parking lot off to one side. Tourists climb onto buses and several of them stop to gawk at us as we round the corner. I end up gawking right back. This is so weird.

"So do I get an official tour?" I ask, only halfway sarcastically because, even though I'm surprised to see tourists, I actually am curious to explore the castle. I never got to explore Versailles, which is a shame.

"Tomorrow," he replies, bullish, and a little smile greets my lips.

We continue to the backside of the castle and pull into an automatic garage. It's a surreal reminder of my arrival to Versailles. A chill zips through my body––I'd rather forget that place ever happened, impossible as that is. Every time I close my eyes, I see the gilded palace and the garish parties and Queen Brisa and her raucous court of nightmares. And then it's Adrian's face that's behind my eyelids, and it's his calloused hands on my body, and those possessive kisses staining my lips . . . and then I *remember*.

"Are you locking me up in here like some kind of princess?" I think of those huge guns and wonder if they're not to keep people out but to keep people in.

Tate doesn't answer as the garage door closes behind us, which sets me on edge. We climb out of the car, and I shake out my sore limbs, then follow Tate to a thick metal door similar to the one back in the hunter's gym. The vampires were all about security too, which I've learned to appreciate only when I'm on the receiving side of security.

"If vampires can't enter a building without being invited in," I question. "Why so much security?"

Tate looks at me sidelong. "Did you learn nothing under my tutelage?"

He's right. It's a silly question. Vampires always find ways to get what they want.

"This is private property, but it's not a proper home. It hasn't been for so many generations that even if we tried to make it one now, it wouldn't stop the vampires." He gives me a level-headed look. "You learned this during your studies. I distinctly remember the lesson. Besides that, vampires get into the homes they really want to get into. There's always someone they can compel."

I hold up my hands in surrender, and my mind floods with the faces of the friends I made while training to become a hunter. They must hate me by now. They came all the way to France to save my ass only to find me playing house with the enemy. They wanted me to go with them, they came to save me, and I'd refused to leave Versailles. If they find me now, no doubt they'll kill me. Would I even blame them? It's what I would've done once upon a time. I never thought I would have allowed Adrian to get to me as he did. I just hope my friends are okay––that Felix and Ayla are doing well and that Seth has found a better team member to boss around. I was never any good at being a team player.

My thoughts move to Kenton, and my heart breaks all over again. Why do the brightest souls have to be the ones here for the shortest time? It's not fair. He deserved so much better. He had his whole life ahead of him––a family who loved him, a promising talent for lacrosse, and a few years away from finishing an engineering degree at a prestigious university. His laugh was infectious, he was so kind, wicked smart, and made everyone happier. My eyes fill with held-back tears. I'll mourn him when I have a moment alone, but right now I don't want to cry in front of anyone.

And I hate that I can't be vulnerable, that I can't cry, that I can't be myself. Then again, I don't even know who I am anymore.

"We like to keep things authentic for the tourists. It's all part of our cover. Hiding in plain sight, you see? But rest assured, there are many parts of this castle that are renovated with modern conveniences and stay off-limits to the outside world," Tate says as we approach a set of stairs. I wonder what he thinks of losing Kenton and if he even cares. He's lost hunters before and will lose them again. The man purposely puts them in harm's way. "You'll be safe here, and that's what matters."

His words directly oppose my thoughts, and I snort. "Safe somewhere that is open to tourists? Because I've seen enough movies to know that people have ways around guards and locks, and here you are letting them get in the building."

"Don't believe everything you see in films." He chuckles condescendingly, and I fight off the urge to slap him. "Only part of the castle is for tourists and only during the daylight hours."

"Vampires have loyal humans working for them, humans who could have come here today. You know that."

"Yes, but I also know how the vampires think. They'll be looking for you somewhere much more remote. They won't think to track you to a public landmark. And if they do, we have plenty of guards, security cameras, silver bars on all the windows, weapons . . ." His voice trails off when he sees the worried look on my face. "Come along, we need to keep moving."

We climb stairs with no railings, and I pray I don't fall. They're incredibly narrow, and twist up steeply like the turret staircases in medieval films. I can almost see myself carrying an oil lamp while dressed in a sweeping gown, rushing off to solve a mystery or meet a lover. My sorry calves burn with the effort, but I don't complain because the higher we climb, the less anxious I feel. It's like being lifted from a trance or waking up from a too-long nap. My thoughts become clearer, and I feel more like myself. But part of me––a tiny part that surely belongs to Brisa's venom––wants to go back and dig myself a grave in the nearest graveyard, to make the earth my bed and the soil my blanket. I'm ridiculously tired, and I could sleep one last time and wake up with a new life, one without human restraints.

"Right this way," Tate cuts into my thoughts, and I snap out of it. He directs me to a tiny room, but I can hardly pay attention, I'm so bothered by the daydream. No, not just a daydream, it was a fantasy of being a vampire. Why would I think that? I hate vampires. I can't let myself go there ever again, and yet it's something that's been happening in the back of my mind on and off all day.

"Everything you need is already here."

I step inside and blink, trying to take it in and clear my mind. The room is sparse. There's a fluffy full-sized bed with a white duvet blanket on the far wall with a stack of pillows, a square window opposite with a view of the lake and the alps beyond, and . . . that's it.

"I don't need much, but a toilet would be nice," I say dryly.

He points to the corner where a wooden bucket sits next to a roll of toilet paper. I blink, confused and then horrified. "Sure, I can picture myself in another century here, but I wouldn't go so far as this."

"Forgive me, Eva. But this room is the safest we could outfit for you on such short notice. We need to make sure you're locked up tight and above ground tonight."

I turn on him and glare. "Excuse me?"

"It's for your own good," he says, and then he's backing through the doorway, the lock clicking into place.

Four

My first instinct is to panic, but I force myself to stay calm. Terror grips my mind. How far am I willing to go to do the right thing?

Maybe Tate has it right––minutes ago I was fantasizing about finding a graveyard and finishing where Brisa left off. If locking me up in here means that I don't do something crazy, then so be it. But couldn't they have at least given me a television or a book?

I wander over to the window and brace myself against the glass, watching the last of the sunset fade away. As Tate said, there are thick silver bars crossing over the glass, but I try not to think too much about those––I'm not allergic to them, but they remind me of what I've come so close to becoming.

The sunset reflects off the water in a sea of melted honey. I've never met a sunset I didn't like, but this one is proving otherwise because as the sun slides behind the horizon, my body starts to buzz again. I groan and clutch my arms to my chest, trying not to scratch what feels like angry ants burrowing into my skin.

A familiar pain shoots through my head––the beginning of a migraine.

I squint and hurry to the bed to sprawl out on top of the duvet. I don't want to climb inside the fluff because it's way too hot up here. It wasn't so hot when I arrived a few minutes ago, but now it's like I've been trapped in a sauna. Could Tate have turned on a heater? Sweat begins to bead along my forehead.

"This is just the venom," I whisper, trying to reason this out, to talk myself down from letting the ball of panic in my chest explode and send shrapnel through my body. "Brisa's venom is trying to get you to do what it wants, which is *not* what you want."

Because it's not what I want . . . right?

The reasonable part of me knows that these horrible pains won't last forever, but that part seems to be growing smaller by the second. I open my eyes to blinding light. Since the sun has officially set behind the mountains, the light should be dimming, not brightening. It must be another ridiculous side effect of the venom and only strengthens my pounding headache. The agony grows until I throw my head into the closest pillow and scream. I scream for everything I've been through, for the lies I've believed, the people I've lost, and the many mistakes I've made.

And then I scream because I don't want to be here.

This is *not* where I'm supposed to be. This isn't right. Every bit of me can't take being locked away in this tower for another second. I jump off the bed and hurl the pillow against the stone wall. It erupts in a plume of white feathers.

I have to get out of here.

My headache is only getting worse, and if I stay up here, it's going to cook my brain. This isn't a migraine. I was wrong. This is much worse. This is death. I force my eyes to stay open in the blinding light as I gaze around the room again, frantically searching for something I could use, but it's too sparse. I kneel at the bed and lift at the frame, my muscles pumping with adrenaline and something else—something not human. I'll throw the furniture through the door if I have to. Whatever it takes to break free of this misery, I'm game. I don't care who I hurt or what I break as long as I can get out of here.

I can picture it now. I'm breaking down the door and careening down the spiral staircase until I can find a way out. Or I'm smashing through the window and diving into the lake below. It would take a long jump to reach it, and there could be rocks down there that would kill me on impact, but I'm willing to take that risk. Death would be better than this torture, and if I don't die, then I'll be free and can find a graveyard. This is an old village surrounded by similar ancient cities, so there's got to be loads of graveyards nearby. As soon as I step foot in one, I'll dig if I have to, or I'll find a crypt. Are there crypts that go underground or catacombs in Italy like there are in France? I hope so, that would make it so much easier, but either way, I'm not staying here.

My hands shake, and sweat beads on every inch of my skin. "How is it getting hotter?" I scream as I heave at the heavy bed.

It won't move. I kneel down to inspect it closer and growl. The frame is bolted to the floor and, even with my superhuman strength, it's not going anywhere. I dive for the bucket instead and throw it at the glass, but it bounces off with a thud. The glass doesn't even crack, but the bucket sure does. I jump up and storm toward the windows, grabbing hold of one of the bars and wincing. They're made from silver, but they hadn't hurt me earlier. I'm not a vampire yet, so why are they hurting me now? I shouldn't be allergic. I try again, but it's the same outcome. The metal is way too hot. It's like trying to hold onto the edge of a sizzling frying pan. I can't do it for more than a second or two.

It must mean the transition has begun.

I don't know what to do or how to get out. My panic builds, but there's nowhere for it to go, so I scream, and then I cry. And then I get back up and bang on the door.

"Hello?" I yell. "Is there someone out there?"

It's thick wood--way too thick for me to break through even with my added strength. I stop and listen intently, my hearing kicking up a notch. Someone shifts their weight on the other side.

I calm my voice to a more reasonable tone. "I really need to get out of here."

Whoever is over there clears their throat. "Sorry, but the boss says you can't come out until morning."

I grit my teeth together. According to Adrian, I need to be underground for three nights after being bit to become a vampire. Does that mean I have to be underground all three nights in a row? Last night I was passed out in a French catacomb, which was a step in the right direction. This? This is not going to help me! I only have two more nights to get this done, and the idea of morning feels a million years away. I need to take care of this now. What if I'm not underground long enough? What if I can't find a cemetery in time? What if Tate hunts me down again? No, I can't take any chances because I'm absolutely certain that this venom is either going to transform me or it's going to kill me.

And I don't care about the naive do-gooder girl I used to be--she seems like a shadow of a person, a girl who didn't know anything about the world. Who I am now would rather give in to my fate than try to fight it a moment longer. But I have to be smart because the people holding me captive will never see things my way.

"That's not what Tate told me," I lie, keeping my voice steadier this time. "He told me that we'd be going to dinner and to get changed." I force a smile and hope the man on the other side of the door can hear it in my voice. "Well, I'm all ready now and getting hungry."

"Don't listen to her," another voice says——a voice I know like the back of my hand. "She's a liar."

"Felix," I cry with relief, "you're here. I'm so glad you're here. You've got to help me." He doesn't respond, and I continue, hoping he can recognize the desperation in my voice and will want to free me from it. "There's been a big mistake. It's not what you think."

He scoffs bitterly, and I can picture his face full of shame and anger. "Am I going to have to listen to you all night? Because guess what, babe, there are five of us out here and more throughout the castle and outside. Everyone is on duty tonight. You're not getting out of that room."

I deflate, and then rage takes over. Did he just call me babe like it's an insult? "You have no right to lock me up! If you ever cared about me, you wouldn't allow this bullshit to carry on."

"I *cared* for you. Past-tense." My heart twists at his cruel words. "But it turns out, I didn't actually know the girl I cared for, so shut up because you'll get no more sympathy from me."

I growl and bang on the door again, but it's useless. I can't get out. I'm locked away like Rapunzel in her tower. But Rapunzel was a princess who needed a prince to save her. Not me. I'm a powerful woman destined to become an even more powerful vampire, and no man is going to stop me from my destiny. My headache starts to ease, and it gives me a chance to think this through. I sit down on the bed and close my eyes, my mind whirling with everything that's happened and everything that needs to happen. I've got to come up with a plan. There's got to be something I can do.

And then it hits me. I haven't been patient enough. Tonight's a lost cause, but I'll get another chance tomorrow. In the meantime, I think I'll punish Felix.

Five

I spent all day in the catacombs searching for Eva, but she's gone. So I return to Versailles again, hell-bent on finding Brisa's blasted laptop. When I couldn't find it last night, I'd left in frustration, but now I can't figure out my next steps without it. My plan had been to find Eva and get back to New Orleans. Things were going to be a mess for a while, and getting control over my city was my priority.

But now that I can't find Eva, I need the information from Brisa's servers. She's the only one who had the kind of access I need to figure out where Eva could've gone. I know for a fact she'd tapped into the CCTV cameras all over the world, Paris included.

I storm into the palace, no longer caring what I may face, stopping by the throne room first because that's where things really got out of hand yesterday. I wonder if any of them are still in there, still fighting for something that means little without a royal blood bond. The one person I don't expect to find?

Mangus.

I stop in my tracks, staring at the very brother who was announced dead by my queen only two nights earlier. He's lounging on Brisa's old throne, long coppery hair a mess, his Victorian clothing wrinkled, and blood glistening on his lips. He blinks up at me through hazy red-rimmed eyes.

"I know," he says, raising his glass of blood-wine. "Don't tell me. You thought I was dead."

If I didn't know better, I'd think he was half drunk, but alcohol doesn't do much to our systems, not unless consumed profusely. It could be that my brother has been on a binge since his wife was murdered.

"So Brisa lied?" It doesn't make sense. Why would she lie about him dying? Did she want to punish him somehow? Sebastian was ordered not to lie, so he must've truly believed Katerina killed her husband. It's a puzzle with pieces that don't fit.

He nods, long and slow and tortured. "In a way, she lied. Truth is, brother, she really thought I was dead."

"How?"

He cuts me off. "And then she killed Katerina." His voice is hoarse. Murderous. "I'm glad the queen bitch is dead. Good riddance."

He spits and then sinks further into the throne. I eye it warily, a pit forming in my stomach. He must see my trepidation because what he says next surprises me. "Come to take it?" His tone is lazy. He stands and sways to one side. "It's yours."

"I don't want it. I know better than to put that target on my back. You should too."

"What's the point?" He scoffs. "Let them kill me."

"You don't mean that."

He shrugs. "Maybe I do."

He's really broken up about his mate, but I understand and I can't say I blame him. So many times I have wanted to end this endless existence, but I was forbidden from ever doing so. Now that my maker is gone, I could. I won't, there's too much to do, but Mangus can, and he very well might.

"Nobody has been crowned," he goes on, "and from the ashy scene I stumbled into yesterday, nobody will be."

He's right, of course. Even if someone were to try and make a go of ruling our court, they'd be doing it through force and not a royal blood bond. Everything has been splintered, and taking that role would be like signing up for an early death. Even for a prince such as myself. *Especially for a prince.*

"Four of the lower vampires went at it right after she died and ended up killing each other." I'd stayed back, letting them pick one another off while I looked for information. Mangus hadn't even been there. But he's here now, and it's a marvel he's still alive in his state. Anyone with a grudge against him could easily take him out. The man is barely standing.

"Where's Sebastian?" I ask. "Did he die too? Do you know?"

"No clue. Maybe. Who cares? Technically you and I are the highest-ranked left," he says. "I half expect you to kill me." He raises his hands wide and smiles. "So please, do me the honor."

"I won't be killing you, Mangus," I say. "And if Seb is alive, then he's ranked just as high as we are."

Mangus frowns. "True. Ugh, our other siblings were always so awful, weren't they? I truly hope Seb is gone too. He was no better than Hugo, and Hugo was the worst." He cackles, and then his energy shifts from drunk and disorderly, to full of rage. He's not as affected by the alcohol as he wants me to believe. "But I didn't kill our brothers, and neither did my wife. We were framed. You know that, right? It was a setup. Had to be."

"I believe you." Against the odds.

I've never seen him so upset, never seen him cry. Until now. "Who would do that to us?" Tears cut down his cheeks, mixing with his stringy unwashed hair.

I'm momentarily stunned, and then I speak. "Someone interested in toppling the vampire court. Look at us now, brother. We're prime for a take-down. But that's not why I'm here." Mangus and I aren't close, but we haven't had any quarrels either. He worked with Brisa in a traveling capacity and may be just the person to ask for help. I hate asking for help, but I'll do it for Eva. Anything for Eva. Underneath his grief, there's a powerful and vengeful creature––one I can use to my advantage. "Come," I nod toward the exit. "Let's discuss our next move in private."

Most of the court has fled, but a few wayward vamps still stick around, waiting for someone to tell them what to do. Many have lost their masters, and therefore their way. But that will change once they get a taste of freedom.

Mangus leads me from the throne room to his private quarters, throwing open the door and plopping down on the rumpled bed. The man is normally so well put together, so stoic, so hard. This is not the Mangus I know. But I understand––when Kelli was murdered, I had been lost for a few weeks. I'd lose my mind if something happened to Eva. And my dead wife has haunted me for centuries. But we also don't have time for him to unravel completely, not if we're going to secure a future for our cause.

I close the door behind me. "We need to control this." I don't lead with my goal of finding Eva. There's another angle I go for instead.

He stares at me with unblinking eyes. "I thought you said you didn't want the throne."

"I don't. It won't work anyway. Anyone who dares to take it will end up staked."

"Exactly why I was sitting on it." He says it like it's a joke, but there's truth in his words.

"You really want to die?" I point outside. "Then step into the sun."

"Maybe I will, brother."

It's a common command from masters to their prodigies to forbid them from attempting anything suicidal, and the depression of immortality fades after enough time. I didn't think it would, thought that the adage "time heals all wounds" was bullshit, but I had been wrong. Still, I don't know what to say to Mangus right now, so I say nothing. We stay in silence for a good five minutes before he speaks.

"Okay, I'll help you," he relents. "But I can't make any promises."

"That's fair."

"So what's your big idea, Adrianos?" Only those who've known me the longest call me by my full name. It reminds me of when I first met him in the 10th century. He'd been so different back then. So *angry*––Katerina had softened him.

"We need to establish a council of coven leaders."

He sits up with a rueful smile. "Brisa forbade us to even speak of this."

"So you're glad she's gone, too?" It's a gamble to talk about her this way to another one of her children, a gamble that pays off.

He jumps up from the bed. "Of course I hated her, but didn't know you did as well, you were always such a kiss-ass."

"We all were, Mangus. But yes, I hated Brisa for centuries." I level him with a stare. "What she did to your vampire wife? She did the same to my human one." This is hard to talk about, but I press on. "And orchestrated it to be by my own hands."

I'm grateful he doesn't ask for clarification, but his face falls, and rage flashes through his eyes. If anyone gets it, he does––I hate that he does, but I can't do this alone. "Okay, I will help you so I can have a measure of revenge on Brisa's legacy before I join Katerina in death."

My spirits fall. I don't want this for him, and Katerina wouldn't either, but I know better than to argue with Mangus. He's even more stubborn than I am.

"We need to break into Brisa's files." I give him a knowing look because while it's a secret the man has made a point to adapt with technology, it's not a secret he's been able to keep from me. If we can't find her computer, then surely she has a cloud of information somewhere. And if anyone can hack into that, it would be the man who's taken it upon himself to learn every-thing possible about technology. "We won't be able to form a council if we don't have the names of every coven leader."

Part of his job was to travel around and enforce Brisa's laws, so he's got more connections than I do, but even he doesn't know everybody.

He strolls to the armoire, throwing it open and retrieving a black laptop. "How could this have gotten here?" he teases.

I laugh. It's like every holiday has been wrapped into one. "You're the one who stole the laptop?" I rush toward him with an outstretched hand, but he holds it away from my grasp.

"First thing I did when I felt her die." His eyes glitter with rage and despair and the littlest bit of triumph. "I busted into her office and snatched it. Had to kill a few of her guards to do it. You're not the only one who knows that what Brisa has access to will be useful."

I step back, leveling him with a hard gaze. "We need to call a gathering of the coven leaders. Virtual or in person, I don't care, but it must be done."

His eyes narrow. "What's all this about, really?"

"The safety of our covens and preservation of everything we've worked for," I'm quick to respond.

That's only part of my reasoning. Finding Eva is dependent on getting Brisa's CCTV access. I'd tried to find her scent but couldn't, so it's this or let her go, *and I can't let her go.*

But besides that, I really do want to establish a council rather than grapple for a hollow throne. Vampires need to hold onto our prosperity in order to keep our people well-fed without the unnecessary bloodshed of humans. That's the only way we're going to stay alive——because if we start a war with them, they'll rise up against us. So many of my kind have forgotten just how many humans there are.

But as much as I should be worrying about that right now, I can't keep my thoughts away from Eva's well-being. She's out there somewhere, scared and full of Brisa's venom. If I don't get to her, something terrible could happen. God willing, I'll be able to track her down and get her to safety. She has no idea what she's dealing with, and if I don't find her soon, then I've already lost.

Six

"How's our girl doing?" Tate's voice wakes me from a fitful slumber, and I sit up in a sweaty pile of torn blankets and white feathers. The morning sun filters through the windows in streams of golden light, and I have to blink a few times for my eyes to adjust.

"Last night was horrible." My voice cracks. Tate nods in understanding and hands me a tall glass of ice water. The condensation alone makes me want to weep.

"Drink this. It'll help." He sits down on the edge of the bed, and I gulp the water down like I've been days without a drop. "What happened last night? Is there anything you need to tell me?"

"You already know . . ." my voice trails off as I catch sight of Felix in the doorway.

He won't meet my eyes, and I can't say I blame him. Bits and pieces of last night rush back to me, and I grimace. I said so many things to him that I wish I could take back. I told him about Adrian, about the things we had done together and how it felt to be with him, and I spoke as if becoming a vampire was so much better than any human life I could have. I stand to shake out my limbs, but I don't go to him because I know I don't deserve his forgiveness or sympathy right now.

"I'm so sorry, Felix." That's all I can say, but it won't be enough. It wouldn't be if I were in his shoes.

He doesn't reply, and his gaze still doesn't reach my eyes. A hollow sadness seeps through me because I know this is the biggest turning point in our relationship so far. We'll never be lovers, and we'll likely never be friends again either.

"The venom will do horrible things to people," Tate cuts in. "It'll make you say and do things that you wouldn't otherwise."

I nod. "It was like being burned alive. I would've done anything to make it stop, but that's no excuse for the things I said."

"The desire to turn is not going to go away until you make it past night three. But the good news is, you only have to get through one more night of this."

"And then what? I really won't turn into one of them?" Because what if on night four it starts all over again? I don't think I can take a lifetime of trying to fight this off. I'm one person during the day and someone else entirely at night--and that nighttime Eva will eventually succeed in her efforts.

"No, you really won't turn into one of them unless one were to get its hands on you and start the process all over again."

A huge weight lifts from my shoulders. "I'll do everything in my power to stop this from happening again, but you have to understand that I never wanted Brisa to try and turn me in the first place." My voice catches. "They lied to me. I should've known they were going to lie to me." The room goes quiet for a minute, and I remember what he had originally asked. He wanted to know if there was anything I needed to tell him, and there is. I hate that there is--I want to scrub everything about last night from my mind, but I have to face this. "The thing is, Tate, last night I made a plan to run away today, but now that the sun is back up, running away is the last thing I want to do. In fact, I'd rather you keep me locked up until we're sure this is behind us."

Felix's brows furrow, and a flash of annoyance mars his face. He thinks I'm lying, or that I'm sucking up to Tate, but I'm not doing either. This is the real me, not that monster from last night who said horrible things to him. I'm not that girl who planned it all out, imagined every scenario of getting out of here. Those scenarios frighten me now because I'd been one hundred percent serious about getting to a cemetery and killing anyone who got in my way. I would've killed Felix, no questions asked, and he knows it.

"Can I go to the bathroom?" I nod toward the broken bucket on the floor. "And maybe I can get a few things to eat?"

"Of course," Tate says, "we'll make sure you get three square meals while you're with us." He points to my tattered dress. It's been through so much over the last two days. "And I'll get you some clean clothing. I'm sorry that we didn't have time to take care of that yesterday. I should've had them leave you pajamas in here for when we arrived, but it slipped my mind."

That doesn't matter to me so much as food does. My stomach rumbles, and I sigh because I know what I have to say next. "But besides those few things, I think it's going to be better if I stay locked in here most of the day, just in case."

Tate nods approvingly. "I'd hoped you would say so. We don't have a lot of experience with this kind of thing. Believe it or not, most people who get turned don't leave their graves unless it's because we find and stake them."

A shiver runs through me as I imagine what a stake through my heart would feel like. I sigh, grateful to be alive. "Well, I'm glad I made the cut." And I can't help but wonder why . . .

"It was like I turned into a different person." I shiver inwardly, remembering how quickly my personality had changed. "Last night was . . ." I trail off because I don't have words for my behavior and I'm ashamed of how it all went down, even though I know it wasn't entirely my fault. The venom was stronger than I ever could have anticipated. No wonder new vampires are bloodthirsty little demons. If that's what it feels like to be turning into one, then actually being one would be ten times worse.

"Where's your thanks, huh? If you were anyone else, we would have killed you by now," Felix chimes in, his eyes finally meeting mine, and I shrink back.

"I hate vampires, and I always have. You know that about me, Felix," I challenge him with a hard stare.

"Do I?" His glare is pure fire as memories flash between us.

"Nothing I've been through has changed that," I say. "In fact, it's made me hate them even more."

"Keep telling yourself that," he replies bitterly before storming away.

My mouth pops open as I watch him walk away from me, and Tate squeezes my hand. "Give him some time. He'll forgive you."

I snatch my hand away and shake my head because I know that's never going to happen. Felix hates me now. In trying to save him and my other friends, I ended up betraying his trust. Worst of all? I betrayed myself as well. I may have learned my lesson the hard way, but at least I learned it. I'll never trust a bloodsucker again, especially not one with golden blond curls and bottomless blue eyes.

THE DAY GOES by excruciatingly slow, anxiety gaining traction with every passing hour. Last night was the most painful night of my life, and my gut tells me tonight's going to be worse. The phrase "it gets worse before it gets better" is the one thing I'm clinging to because once I'm through with all this I'll be a more powerful vampire hunter. I'll be able to better defend myself, and hopefully nothing like this will ever happen again.

I can feel it's true--my vision is crystal clear, my senses are unimaginably heightened, my muscles are relaxed but strong, and my mind is razor-sharp. Maybe this is why Tate is taking such great lengths to keep me human. If he succeeds, I'll be a powerful weapon against the vampires. I hate the idea that he's using me, but right now, he's the only protection I've got. If I run away from here now, I'll be a vampire by morning. There's zero doubt about that.

By early afternoon, the lack of quality sleep catches up with me. I ease into a long nap, but it's ruined by the venom because when I dream, it's of Brisa. In the dream, she's a mother figure to me and I love her deeply, and when I wake up, I hate her even more. Even if she's dead, her venom lives in me, and I'll never be free of her.

Hugo's bite had made me stronger, but Brisa's venom is on another level. She not only bit me, but she exchanged our blood as well. As the queen, Brisa was the most powerful vampire in the world, surely staying human with her venom in my blood will have unintended consequences. I just wish I knew for certain if she is dead or alive. I think I burned her up when my hands glowed, and if I didn't, she's going to hunt me down and kill me.

A hulking guard opens the door and offers me a steaming bowl of pasta with tomato sauce. "Are you hungry for dinner?" he asks in a thick Italian accent.

My stomach growls in response, and he hands me the warm bowl.

"The chef is a local woman who uses a family recipe, so you know everything is fresh and authentic." He smiles, and I almost can't believe it. Shouldn't he hate me too?

"Thank you." I return his smile and twist the fork into the noodles, lifting a bite to my mouth. The rich flavors caress my tongue, and I devour the food. "Please give her my compliments."

The guard beams and waits by the door for me to finish up, then takes the bowl and leaves me locked up again. Despite the panic building, my stomach is finally relaxed. A few minutes later, the guard returns to offer me some water and to escort me to the bathroom one last time. I take it all in stride, returning to my Rapunzel tower for my final night.

Tate greets me at the door. "We're going to have more guards here tonight. We've had time to bring in as many reinforcements as we could spare. You have nothing to worry about. We've got your back."

"And who is 'we'?"

"We are a family that is highly invested in you, and that's all I can tell you for now."

I roll my eyes but don't try to fight him because I need the investment.

Who else is going to lock me up in a castle so I don't end up killing myself? But I'm no fool, I know there's going to be a price to pay later. He's going to want something from me when this is over. But right now, it's one step at a time: focus and survive the night.

I thank him and head into the room. "You can lock me away now."

"Is there anything else we should do to protect you?" His bushy eyebrows rise considerably. "Anything else you can think of that we may have missed?"

I gaze around the room. Everything is sparse and neatly in order, but that only reminds me of the mess I made last night. Someone came in and cleaned it up while I was eating breakfast this morning, but I don't want them to have to do that again. "Actually, I think you should leave me the mattress with the top sheet and that's all."

He chuckles like I just made a joke, but I don't find anything about this even remotely funny. I bite my tongue from lashing out while I pull up the blankets and begin throwing them into the hallway. Felix is standing there when I do, the pile of fluff landing at his feet. I haven't seen him since this morning, and my heart lurches. He's so handsome, so familiar, and so very hurt by me.

"You're back," I say tentatively.

"Not for your sake," his response is cold. "It's my job."

"Really? Because I think you should be in New Orleans attending university."

"I don't expect you to understand loyalty to a cause," he quips. "My education can wait, this cannot."

Sure, school can wait, but that doesn't mean it should. Felix deserves better than to be standing guard over me. "Shouldn't you be loyal to your lacrosse teammates? To your studies? And your future?"

"Everything I'm doing is for my future." He turns away and folds his arms over his broad chest, effectively ending the conversation. There's nothing I can say to get through to him, and my skin is starting to buzz like it did yesterday on the drive into this place, so I leave him to pout and go back into the tower room.

"Good luck," Tate says, locking me in once again. A sense of foreboding crawls up my spine and sinks into my chest, pounding on my heart. This night is not going to be easy, and there's nothing I can do about it. I just have to force myself through it, because the alternative is out of the question.

Seven

⁋

The sunset feels like a doomsday countdown, and I wonder if I'm about to say goodbye to the sun forever. Could this be my last sunset? Am I really going to make it to the other side of this night with my humanity intact?

I know what's about to happen, but that doesn't make it easier when it hits me. A headache slams into me like a freight train, quickly transforming into a migraine and then into something much worse. It's so excruciating that I have no words to describe it. Maybe I should've kept the blankets because the room is brightening, and even though I'm squeezing my eyes shut, light is still assaulting me. Tears spill from my eyes, and I pray for numbness to take me.

That doesn't happen.

It's as if my soul is clinging to me for dear life and I don't know how to save it. Either I die a human or I lose my soul because this pain can't be tolerable. It just can't be. My body is impossibly hot, and I scream out in frustration. I'm frantic, and that feeling just keeps getting worse with each quick breath of my lungs. I can't handle this. I can't, I can't, I can't. I thought I could be strong enough to do it again, but I'm not. And it's not what I want.

I want to be a vampire.

The thought hits me with stark clarity, easing the pain enough for me to focus on it. I want immortality. I want power. I want what they have, whatever is on the other side of being a human who can hurt and feel too much. It's going to be so much better than *this*––I'll do anything to get it. Whatever I'd said to Tate was foolish and naive. I was a stupid girl who feared the very best thing that had ever happened to her. Queen Brisa gave me a gift. A queen wanted me as an heir, and who am I to squander the chance?

I sprint to the door and begin begging for someone to let me go. "Please," I gasp, "I've changed my mind. I promise I won't hurt anyone, but I need to get out of here. I'm going to die if I stay up here." My voice rises. "I'll die. Do you want me to die? Are you murderers now? You can't just keep me against my will!"

Nothing.

I don't expect Felix to understand, but whoever else is on the other side of this door doesn't say anything either. I should've asked the guard who brought me food to give me his name. He seemed kind, like maybe he would help someone in need. And he's huge, probably big enough to take on the other men if needed. "Please," I go on, "I swear, I need to go to the hospital. I'm not going to make it." I know they're there. They have to be. But they ignore me, and I hate them for it. Maybe I will kill them when I get out of here. I'm going to make them regret leaving me in this kind of pain. Anyone who can sit there and keep me trapped in hell doesn't deserve to live.

I scream in agony and then go quiet, scurrying to sit next to the door and wait for an opportunity. If I don't make a sound, they might check on me. I need to be in a prime position in case that happens. But waiting is excruciating. My blood burns through my veins, quickening with each breath. My gums hurt so bad that I can picture two little fangs trying to break through them, and I wish they would already.

If I could rip off the door right now, I'd set them on Felix for locking me in here. He should know better than anyone else. He's supposed to be my friend, and here he is, putting me through something as terrible as this. I picture myself ripping into his lovely flesh and striking a thick pulsing vein. His blood would pour into my mouth like liquid salvation, offering me a new life. It would taste divine, and I wouldn't stop until I'd sucked up every last drop. He'd have to die, of course, but that's all part of the life cycle. Everyone dies. It's sad but inevitable, and what are humans for if not meant to feed vampires? And Felix smells so, so good.

I'm lucky to have been bitten by Brisa. I'm going to get out of here and become a vampire without anyone to tell me what to do. Brisa will be my master, but she's not here, and she might be dead. And if that's the case, then I'll be free to feed as I please and do whatever I want. I don't have any blood bonds to anyone else who could tell me what to do or force their ridiculous vampire rules on me. Felix will be my first kill, but he won't be my last.

There's a commotion outside the door, and my hackles rise. Someone yells, footsteps pound, and shots are fired. I jump to my feet and ready myself.

"They went that way." I hear Felix say as his voice fades beneath the sound of his retreating footsteps.

I stay impossibly still as the blood rushes through my veins. A long minute later, the handle wiggles, and then the door creaks open. I blink in surprise at the vampire standing in the doorway. I immediately recognize her as one of Brisa's many minions, but I don't know her name. She's tall and slender, with warm brown skin and thick ebony braids. She's dressed in all black and sporting a wicked grin. Whoever she is, I instantly love her.

"There you are," she says coolly. "You need to come with me."

I'm quick to follow her out. "Does this mean Brisa's alive?" I ask with trepidation as we hurry down the stairs. The woman doesn't answer me as she practically floats down them, but I don't have that ability yet, and my humanness makes me slower than she is. I can't wait for that to be gone. Part of me is hopeful my maker will be able to greet me upon my transformation, but the other part wants to live my vampire life as I wish, including feasting on as many humans as I can. I know Brisa's way of things, and I don't like the thought of them.

When we make it to the basement garage, the vault door is wide open, and a cool breeze greets us. I sigh in relief. We step through the door, and I grow giddy with excitement. The garage door has been blown clear off its frame, and the promise of night and graveyards and warm sweet blood calls me forward.

The woman points. "East of the city is a graveyard, but they'll find you there come morning."

"Won't I already be a vampire by then?"

She shakes her head. "You might, but we can't risk it. We need to go further in case you need more time underground to make up for what you've lost." She lifts me easily into her arms even though we're probably the same weight. Of course, that means nothing to a vampire, I'm light as a feather to her. "There are several places I can take you."

"Does this mean Brisa is alive?" I repeat my question as she takes off. To human ears, my voice would be lost on the wind, but with her excellent hearing, that doesn't matter.

"No," the woman replies sharply, and my mouth falls open. I knew it was a possibility that I had accidentally killed her, but to have it confirmed leaves me feeling mixed up. It's like I'm waiting for a favorite meal and watching it cook behind glass oven doors. I can smell it, imagine it, wait for it––but I won't be satisfied until I get to taste it on my tongue.

The woman continues to run with me in her arms. She's impossibly fast, and the landscape blurs around us. With a jump, we're over the castle wall like it's nothing. And then we're running along a path on the cliff's edge.

The lights of the village twinkle, and a soft smile plays at my lips as I watch them fly past. Soon this will all be a memory.

Something as dark as the sky appears in our path and knocks us to the ground. I cry out in surprise as pain shoots up my arm when I land on it. On one side of us is a farm field, on the other is the cliff with the lake below, and standing over us is a man. I adjust to his presence and growl under my breath.

"You!" the woman screeches. "Where have you been? Sebastian's been looking for you."

"I don't answer to Sebastian," he replies in a gruff tone. "But I can see he sent you to do his dirty work. Where is my brother? I thought he might have died with the others."

My heart tugs at the sound of that all-too familiar voice, and I scramble to my feet. Anger is quick to grab hold. "Adrian," I sneer, "what are you doing here?"

Because it's him––and I am so damn angry at him. Despite wanting to be a vampire now, I'll never forget what he did. Maybe I should be thanking him for giving me over to Brisa like a piece of meat, but thanking Adrian has never been my forte.

He turns to me and smiles softly, his light eyes practically glowing. "Nice to see you too, Angel," he says, "but unfortunately, not under these circumstances." He's so fast that his movements blur. He knocks the woman out with a single blow to the side of the head, her body crumpling to the ground, and then he pushes her over the cliff. Her body hits the lake with a splash. I jump up just as he turns on me with a fierceness I've come to recognize.

"What are you doing?" I growl.

"She was going to make sure you turned," he snaps. "Or she would've killed you. One or the other."

"Did you just kill her? You can't kill her. She's helping me."

"She'll be fine. Now tell me, how exactly was she helping you?"

I hold up my hands. "You wouldn't understand." All he knows is the girl who hated vampirism, he doesn't know the real me.

"I think I understand perfectly," he frowns, a look of regret passing over his sharp features. "I feared this would happen."

"I want to be a vampire," I challenge, "I know better now."

He shakes his head once and pins me with a cold glare. "That's not happening."

I have two choices. I can stay and fight him, or I can run. I choose the latter, taking off in the opposite direction.

Eight

The cold soil and pointy sticks of the empty farm field fly out around my bare feet. I'm in nothing but thin cotton pajamas, but that doesn't matter. I am free, *finally free*, and Adrian is threatening to take that away. I'm fast--the speed at which my muscles are pumping me forward is far beyond anything I've experienced before. I was a track star in high school, but this is a zillion times better. It's a taste of what my life will be like soon, and I'm reveling in it. The world around me fades to the background as I run at such a high speed that it's almost as if I've already made the transformation.

This is it. I'm going to outrun my captors, outrun the man who betrayed me, and find a graveyard all on my own. I have the whole night to do it. Since it's November, the sunset was early, and there are hours of night left. I smirk and urge my body to move even faster, Brisa's venom fueling me. It doesn't matter that I've hated vampires all my life, that everything about me will change, and that I will lose the friends and family I have left. This is right where I'm supposed to be--and I get to spend an eternity with total control.

Too bad Adrian is faster.

He jumps on my back and we tumble to the ground. "You need to stop this nonsense, Angel. This isn't what you want," he commands as he lands on top of me. His flesh is a welcomed cold, but only because I can't wait to join him in immortal life--not that I will have anything to do with him in my next life. I want nothing to do with Adrian now, and I'll want nothing to do with him later.

"You have no more say over anything I do ever again," I snap, shoving him off me. I jump up to run again, but he isn't having it. He growls like a damn wolf and pulls me into the cage of his arms. His body is solid steel–– despite my own amazing strength, it's not enough to match his. He holds me tightly against him and levitates us into the air.

"No," I scream, kicking out and trying to wiggle free. "Unless you're taking me to a graveyard, you need to let me go."

"No can do."

My mouth goes dry. "What are you doing?"

"I've never seen anyone take to the venom quite like you have," he grumbles, almost talking to himself. "If I'd known you were going to be so adamant about turning, I would've . . ." He doesn't finish his thought.

"You would've what?" I snap, angry at his antics. He's acting as if he isn't the reason I'm here in the first place. "Nothing. You wouldn't have changed a thing."

"That's not true."

I don't believe him, but I don't say anything more, and neither does he as he flies us back toward Tate's castle. As we get closer, though, I give into my fear and start to beg. "Please, Adrian. Please, if you ever cared for me, even a little, please don't take me back there."

"This isn't you talking."

"It is," I squirm. "It's me. You know those people can't be trusted."

For a moment, his arms loosen and I think he's going to let me go, but instead, he leans in close and whispers hotly against my ear. "As much as I hate Leslie Tate, that man has the safest place for you to make it through tonight."

"You can't be serious." My heart thuds wildly in my chest at the mere thought of being locked up in that Rapunzel tower. It will ruin everything.

"Do you think I want this?" His voice sounds pained, but I don't feel sorry for him. He's the one taking my choices away, not the other way around.

"I don't know what you want," I seethe, my hatred of him growing tenfold. "And that's all that should matter. What I'm telling you right now should matter."

My mind races back through my time with Adrian. I'm disgusted by the vulnerability I showed him. He didn't feed on my blood, but he fed on my emotions, and it was only a couple of nights ago that he happily took my virginity, all while spinning lies to deliver me to his queen. Brisa didn't want her newest vampire princess to be a virgin, and Adrian had seen to it that she'd gotten exactly as she'd asked for. I know now that she'd planned to kill her princes off––and had already gotten started––but Adrian didn't know that when he'd taken her orders. He probably still doesn't know seeing as she had whispered that confession to me.

"I hate you!" I scream. "You've done awful things to me just because you wanted to do them. You're vile!"

"I'm saving you now, aren't I?"

"You should listen to what I want. This isn't saving me. This is ruining me."

He tightens his grip, not responding to that. But it's true, it's all true. He's done what *he* wanted all along. Sure, the royal blood bond made it so he had to do what Brisa asked, but he's worked out ways to lie to her before, and he certainly seemed willing to take me to bed. The very least he could've done was find some way to warn me about what was going to happen, or at least act upset when she revealed her plans. The man didn't even apologize. "The truth is, you don't love me and you don't even care for me. You made me into a fool!"

A fool who fancied herself in love.

A fool who gave her body and heart over to her enemy. A fool who cherished that night as if it had actually meant something real. Turns out I was wrong, but I will never make that mistake again.

Anger rolls through me like a tidal wave. He doesn't get to win again. As we near the castle, I thrash out, trying to gain purchase––one last ditch effort to get away. But it doesn't work because he's simply too strong. Adrian has already broken my heart once, and now he's doing it again. It never seems to matter what I want, everything he has done in our relationship has always led to him getting what he wants and me getting screwed over.

"If you're smart, you won't let Tate know that I'm alive," he whispers against my ear. "They still don't know what vampires survived your attack, and it's better that it stays that way."

My attack? I was laying there on my deathbed with light blasting from my hands, and he's calling it an attack. "You've got to be kidding. I'm definitely going to tell him you were here," I reply, sounding childish but far past the point of caring.

"Do that, and you'll be facing the consequences more than I will." He doesn't even have the decency to sound bothered.

I'm not sure what he means, but the truth is, I probably won't be telling Tate squat about anything. I don't trust him either. He's only helping me because he wants something from me. Fact is, nobody has my back in this world. Nobody. Not even Ayla, because she broke off our friendship. And not even that vampire woman who's currently passed out in the lake, because no doubt she only helped me to suit her own plans.

I hope she comes back for me.

Adrian clamps his hand over my mouth as we slow to a stop. We're still flying––at least fifteen feet up. His scent normally makes me want him, but right now it makes me hate him. I look down to find we're hovering over a group of Tate's guards. They are standing just outside the castle, talking about where I could've gone. If only they'd look up, they wouldn't sound so worried by my disappearance.

Why do they care if I become a vampire, anyway? I'm not going to bother them. Sure, I have no plans to be chummy with vampire hunters, but I plan to keep to myself. Maybe I can get enough control over my thirst that I'll eventually only feed on the bad humans. I can hunt them down and make them pay for the awful things they do. But I won't be feeding on blood bags. The idea of it seems so lackluster, like having a rubbery fast-food hamburger instead of a prime filet mignon.

A thought strikes me––if Brisa is really dead, does that mean vampires are free to feed as they want? The bloodlines won't be erased entirely because they'll fall to whoever is highest in the pecking order. Adrian doesn't have any vampires below him because he hates taking on prodigies, but other vamps have suckers under their control. Will they enforce blood bags and stick to Brisa's laws? Or will they give in to their base instincts? The human part of me fears what this could mean, but that's nothing compared to the thirsty part of me, and that part agrees with the old way of doing things.

"Don't say I never did you any favors, Angel," Adrian whispers, his lips soft against my cheek, and then the bastard drops me.

The inertia of falling shoots a tremor of fear through me. I cry out before I can tap into my common sense and keep my mouth shut. I hit the earth hard, landing on my butt and getting the wind knocked clear out of my lungs. It isn't more than two seconds before Tate's guards are on me. There are at least ten of them, and they surround me on all sides, pinning me to the ground like I'm a common criminal.

"Where the hell did she come from?" someone asks. I recognize Seth's voice straight away. He sounds like his usual angry self. I'm surprised he's here, but I guess I shouldn't be.

"She fell out of the sky," another adds with a laugh. "Lucky us."

"Doesn't matter, she's here, isn't she? Carry her back upstairs and lock her up again," Felix's voice rings out, and my stomach turns to rocks. There isn't an ounce of sympathy in his tone.

"No!" I scream, "You can't––"

Seth clamps a large hand over my mouth and glares down at me. I glare right back, thinking that he never did like me. He's probably loving this. I thrash my limbs about, trying to get away, but I can't fight these men off. It's no use. There are too many of them and only one of me. My only hope is that another vampire will break me out before sunrise, but with Adrian hanging around to see to it that I stay put, my chances are eroding to dust.

They carry me upstairs and throw me back into my tower. As Felix slams the door in my face, terror rips through my body. I run to the window and scream obscenities into the darkness.

Nine

ADRIAN

I hover outside of her room, my black cloak camouflaging me into the blustery night. Her light is off, but that doesn't matter, I can see everything as if it were the middle of the day. To say she isn't doing well is an understatement. She's livid and attempting to break free, but it's not going to work. I'm keeping watch over her and won't let her transition to my kind even if she hates me for it. And maybe she will hate me, maybe she already does, maybe she always will, but I can't go back on my promise.

And yet . . .

The second I wrapped Eva in my arms tonight, I knew my suspicions were correct––saying no to this woman is next to impossible. It's never been easy, but something about tonight felt vastly different. It felt like she had finally taken control of our relationship, and in a way that left me defenseless.

Could it be because we've slept together? Reminders of what it feels like to have her, even though I don't deserve her, keep returning to my mind and warming my body. Or maybe it's because she's becoming more powerful than me. I can't stop thinking about that either. Either way, this woman has a way of getting me to do what she wants. And this need to go to her and free her from that tower? It's killing me, but I refuse to give in. I live on my own terms and always find a way to make my life what I want of it, and that includes keeping my promise to the bad-mouthed woman who stomped into my office months ago, hating vampires more than anyone.

No, I'm sticking to what I know is best, so I won't go to her. My hands ball into fists and my chest aches with frustration, but I stay where I am, determined to see this through. I will not allow her to sway me in this. I will not let her change my mind. Nobody will have control over me ever again. Not even Eva.

I spent centuries building up a tolerance to Brisa's bond and now that she's dead, my problems are even bigger, and Eva is the center of them all. Asserting my free will is more than important to me––it's everything. Losing that was what I'd hated most about having to answer to a master, and yet here I am completely undone by a nineteen-year-old *human*. Alright, turns out she's not entirely human. Her blood is mixed, but it's still close enough.

And nineteen? *Nineteen!* What is wrong with me? I can't have someone my own age because nobody my age exists, but I make a habit of dating women older than nineteen. Doesn't matter that my body is permanently frozen at twenty-four, everything else about me has grown the kind of bitterness that can only come with age. Eva isn't a child, but she's vulnerable and soft under that hard exterior. She deserves better than me.

But damn it if she doesn't bring something to life that I've not felt since I was a mortal man. I don't often think about my human life. The memories are tainted, and it's so far in the past that sometimes I forget what it had even been like to have those mortal needs. But when I do remember, I'm reminded of everything I've lost. Some in my coven like to call me a sadist, but even I can't wallow in that kind of misery for long. Those horrors aren't something I seek out because when I think of my lovely wife Eleni and our unborn child in her womb, the images of their bloody deaths claw at me, taking me to my darkest places.

They'd died at *my* hands.

I'd murdered them. My bloodlust had been too much. Brisa had turned me and set me loose on them without me having any clue what was happening, and then she tricked me into believing she could help me feel better. I've lost so much because of that monster, but she's gone, and I am still reveling in her death. I wish I could have seen the moment it happened. Her loss is both devastating and exhilarating. My vampire nature makes it impossible not to grieve, but I'm free of her too, and she'll get no tears from me.

Nor from the sick bastards out there who will use the opportunity to undo everything Brisa has built––that I helped her build. We've only been public for eighteen years, but preparing took decades longer. And now what? How many vampires feast on human flesh? Will they kill their donors or let them live? Will they turn whoever they please, sending us back to the Stone Age? Mangus was able to get his hands on the genealogy, and a meeting has been called for one week from today. I'm worried things won't go the way I need them to, but I have to try.

Mangus was also able to get me access to the CCTV, but I'd had to tell him who I was looking for. He didn't bat an eyelash. I was surprised––I'd had the impression that he didn't care for Eva. But he said he understood and left it at that, and then I'd come here on my own. I'm not even sure where Mangus is now. The man doesn't have his own coven to keep his death wish at bay.

I shake my head, once again angry at Brisa for all she's done to those I care about. It's the emotion I can't seem to be rid of. Here I'd spent the weeks in her palace trying to convince her to hold off on making Eva one of us, and she did it anyway. Clearly, Brisa hadn't worried about the risks enough to see reason. I'd suspected what Eva was, and Brisa had confirmed it the moment they met. So why didn't she leave well enough alone? Eva isn't meant to be one of us, and in trying to turn her, she could become our biggest threat.

I watch her now, pacing in her little tower like a mouse in a cage, and plan ways to kill her or turn her. I won't, but I should, and so I plan. Does she realize how much trouble she's in? And how much trouble she could cause? My vampiric nature urges me forward, and I move closer to her window. I'm strong enough to get in there. I could do it before talking myself out of it. It would simplify everything. With her gone, I could return to New Orleans and take control of the city. Who knows what will happen with the rest of the world, but my coven is my coven, and they'd stand with me. As the most powerful vampire in New Orleans, the other vampires will be given a choice: swear their allegiance to me or get out.

Some will leave. Most will stay.

Eva stands at the window, eyes searching the darkness. When they land on me, she stops and sneers. "Let me out of here!"

She can see me. The guards will assume she's talking to them, but I know it's me she hates right now. And she shouldn't be able to see me in the dark like that until she's turned, but then again she has a lot of venom in her system. The desire to kill her morphs into the urgency to turn her––make her one of us, so I can have her forever. She could come work by my side, making her hometown into whatever we desired. We'd have so much control, nobody would dare cross us. Time is so fleeting, moves so quickly, and I could––

"––Please," her voice softens, a whisper meant for my vampiric ears only. We stare at each other across the space, and I want to go to her, the need is so heady, my fingers itch.

"No," I whisper back, and then I levitate up above her tower, looking down so that I can see and hear everything below but she can't see me.

She spews obscenities that sound nothing like her, and I force myself to calm down. I need to be stronger. Better. I'd almost gone through with turning her twice tonight. The second I'd picked her up and flown away with her, those thoughts had raced through my mind. I'd fantasized about burying her in a cemetery and being there when she rose as one of us, welcoming her into my arms. Right after I'd pictured giving in to my basest desires to sink my teeth into her soft flesh. Now that Brisa's commands are null and void, it's something I could do, something maybe I should do . . .

Stop it. I shake my head, trembling with my lack of self-control.

I will do none of those things because Eva has gotten under my skin and into my cold dead heart, and it's become my job to keep her safe. It no longer matters if she hates me, that's unavoidable, and I'm used to being hated anyway. I am a man of my word if nothing else, and I'd promised her she won't be turned. I intend to keep that promise.

She continues to yell, but I close my eyes, drowning her out. I can't listen to this, it's too tempting. Too heartbreaking.

My thoughts return to two nights ago. It had nearly killed me to leave Eva there with Brisa and the others, but I couldn't watch my failure happen either. Brisa hadn't commanded me to stay, so I'd slipped out like a coward. Since that moment, it's been days of self-loathing. Days of plotting.

"So help me, Adrian!" Eva's voice startles me. "I need you."

I don't respond. She has no idea who's after her or of the trouble she's caused, because if Sebastian is after Eva, that means the others haven't forgotten about her either. They'll be wanting revenge on the beautiful creature who murdered their queen. Or they'll be wanting to use her for themselves.

"This isn't my fault. Why should I have to suffer?"

She's right, it isn't her fault, but by tomorrow night she'll be in the clear. I'm going to get her out of here and away from Tate. This little tourist trap certainly isn't the fortress I expected of his kind. It'll be simple. But for now, Tate has the best place to keep her under lock and key while this third night passes and her humanity is preserved. She needs to be locked above ground, and as much as I hate to admit it, I can't get close to her right now. My urges are too strong. To feed. To kill. To turn. To do anything but let her become my greatest enemy.

It's better than being one of us. This fate is evil, and I've hated giving it to others. Kelli was the last. And now that Brisa can't control me, I'll never turn another human again. Certainly not Eva. Never.

I observe Tate's guards assembling below the castle. The man himself must be close by, maybe even under this roof, though I can't be sure. This could be my chance to kill him once and for all, but that would require I leave my watch over Eva. I can't do that. Nobody else can keep her as safe as I can. Nobody else can see as much as I see, or hear, or smell, or sense . . .

At least I know what Tate's people are up to. I know his family and what they're capable of. No doubt they will use Eva against the vampires––and so many others. I can't have that. My coven needs me, and I need her, alive and mortal and by my side. Tomorrow night. One more day. I can be patient. I'll kidnap her if I have to, take her kicking and screaming, but she's leaving Italy.

Evangeline Blackwood is mine.

Ten

I stay awake until dawn, as salty beads of sweat drip down my face. I feel as if I'm trapped in the Sahara instead of sitting in Northern Italy on a blustery November evening. My body is stiff with panic and slumped with exhaustion. Bloodthirsty thoughts swirl in my mind, and it isn't until the night disappears that I relax.

The sky fades from black, to navy, and then lights up with hues of pinks and golds like a promise at a new life. One thing is for sure––I'll never ever let something like this happen to me again. I don't care what it takes. I go to the window, testing the silver bars against my fingertips. They don't burn. I lean against them with a long sigh. I can't see the sun from my tower, but I can feel it wash through my body like a healing balm. Tears blur my vision.

I survived. I can't believe I survived.

Relieved, I stumble back to the bare bed and drift away into sleep. I'm too tired to think about everything that happened last night for another second. I know Felix and Seth will never forgive me, Adrian saved me from myself, and Tate is only helping me for some long term gain––but none of them matter more than my desperation for sleep right now.

When it greets me, I don't dream of Brisa. Instead, I dream of Adrian, of his hands on my skin, his lips on my mouth, and the heated way his gaze lingers on me. I've never seen him look at anyone else the way he looks at me. It's like I'm a puzzle he can't quite figure out, but he wants to. He's not bored or annoyed. He's intrigued. He's amused. Does he love me too? My heart believes I'm in love, but that emotion quickly shifts to anger when I wake up. Our relationship was built on lies, and seeing him last night brought that to the surface. The truth still remains––Adrianos Teresi is no good for me.

"Knock, knock." Tate pokes his head in the door. He's all fresh in business casual clothing, and his pepper hair is slicked back. He looks like he had a much better night than I did. "Are you okay?"

I groan and sit up, rubbing the remaining sleep from my eyes. "Nope, but I'm still human, so at least there's that."

He enters the room, followed by more guards than he had yesterday. They crowd in around me, eight in all. The fit men and women are dressed in black with guns and stakes strapped to their bodies. I guess Tate was serious when he said he was calling in reinforcements.

"You did it." He smiles broadly. "Congratulations."

I nod once, but at my primal center, I know that I'm not meant to be locked away. It's not who I am. But I also know I'm not meant to be some disgusting bloodsucker. "Thank you for helping me survive the venom."

"It's my pleasure, Eva. And now that I know you're safe to be around, we're leaving here. This location has obviously been compromised." He pauses. "Do you know what happened to you? Who helped you and why did you fall out of the sky like that?"

"Vampires." I shrug. "One helped me leave and one intercepted me and brought me back."

His eyes flash with surprise and he rubs his chin. "Do you know who they were?"

"No. I didn't get a good look and they didn't speak." My cheeks heat with the lie.

He considers this for a long moment and I'm not even sure why I'm keeping Adrian's name out of my mouth, except that I don't trust Tate.

"Very well," he says at last.

"So where are we going next?" I don't expect him to be forthcoming, but I can't help but ask the question. The guards back up to give me space, and my cheeks warm when I realize they're all staring at me like I'm a ticking time bomb. Felix and Seth are among them, and they're the only ones who aren't staring at me like they're afraid of what I'll do next. In fact, they don't look at me at all.

"We could keep moving you every day or two and try to stay ahead of the vampires," he says, "we have enough real estate."

"That sounds kind of fun, assuming I could see Italy along the way." I smile ruefully. I already know it's wishful thinking, but I'm trying to be positive here. And I really am grateful I'm still me. I wouldn't have made it through this without Tate. Whatever he is, at least he's good enough to have helped me survive.

"But . . . I think it's best if we take you to one safe stronghold and hide you there."

"I had a feeling you were going to say something like that."

"Yes, well, it's for the best. The family helicopter has been made available and will be here within the hour. We'll be at our new location within three."

Family helicopter? I swallow hard, trying to imagine what kind of family has a helicopter. But then again, Tate had enough funds to set up an elaborate hunting organization in New Orleans, so he must have deep pockets.

"Okay," I agree to the plan, the idea of playing tourist deflating like a birthday balloon.

Tate must see it on my face. "The vampires will still want you. They could try to turn you again, though, I don't expect it to work." He frowns at the thought. "You may not know this, but there's only so much your body can take, and you've already lost a lot of blood. If they tried again anytime soon, you could end up dead."

My stomach hardens.

"But my guess is they won't attempt to make you a vampire again."

I know exactly what he's getting at. "If they can't have me, then they'll want me dead?"

He nods, and we don't say another word about it.

According to the vampires, I'm too powerful to be anything but one of them––well, except for Adrian. He obviously doesn't want me to become like him. And maybe I should tell Tate about Adrian showing up last night, but I decide to keep my mouth shut. I still don't know Tate's angle.

"Let's get moving," Tate announces, heading for the door in two purposeful strides. I follow him out and spend the next hour showering, changing into comfortable clothing, and eating breakfast. When we head out to greet the shiny black helicopter, I think what a shame it is that I never got to tour the castle, swim in the lovely lake, or explore the quaint village. I hope that's not foreshadowing what the rest of my life will be like–– watching the world from behind the safety of Tate's protection.

The chopper lands in an open field, and four of us climb inside. My heart lodges in my throat as we rise quickly into the cloudy sky. We zoom over the rocky countryside, and I hang on tight to my seatbelt, simultaneously uneasy and exhilarated. I've never had an experience like this, and it's too bad it's under such crappy circumstances.

A few hours later, we descend toward our destination. I didn't recognize much of northern Italy––it was stunning, and I'd love to return someday–– but this landscape? This, I *do* recognize. For some reason, I'd expected to go to Rome, visions of the Colosseum dancing through my head, but we're quickly approaching the colorful Amalfi Coast. Even in the off-season, this view is right out of a storybook. A smile bubbles up as I take it all in. I've seen the famous coastline from viewing travelers' viral posts on social media, but to witness it in person is an entirely different experience. It steals the breath from my lungs.

The imposing mountains are dotted with granite rock faces, with white and tan buildings nestled between. Some of the rooftops are yellow, orange, and blue, but most are muted natural colors that blend into the rocky cliffs. The Tyrrhenian Sea sweeps over the horizon like a blue blanket, even more pristine than the lakes up north. The air is slightly warmer here too. Italy must be wonderful during the summer months, and I envision the beaches full of happy tanned people who get to lay out under the sun before venturing into the historic city to enjoy the rice Italian culture.

Too bad I need to stay hidden from the vampires. As much as I'd love to explore this coastline, I'm sure Tate won't allow it. And anyway, I can't stay for long. I need to find a way back home. I need to call my mom and make sure she's okay. I need to check in on Ayla because even if our friendship is on the fritz, I still care for her and want to repair things between us. I have a life to get back to, no matter all the crazy things that have happened to me.

We've got headphones on to protect our hearing, but they're not offering much support, and I foresee a headache on my horizon. I look to Tate where he's lazily reading an Italian newspaper. Pressing a button on the side of the headphones, I'm able to speak to him. "I need a phone," I say, "I need to call my mom. She's got to be sick with worry."

He drops the paper and gives me a nod. "One step at a time."

"You can't keep me from my friends and family."

"And I won't." Then he's back to ignoring me, this time reading something on his cell phone, seemingly unaffected by the picturesque landscape zipping past us and by my demands. Except for the pilot, there are only two hulking guards sitting with us. I know they're here to keep us safe, but they still make me a little uncomfortable.

Tate said the other guards will be driving over to our new location, which means Felix and Seth will be showing up again soon. I appreciate that they came to save me from Versailles, but I don't want them here on my account. I don't want to mess up their lives anymore.

Tate gazes up from his phone and nods to a building that stands apart from the rest. My jaw drops. "Is that where we're staying?"

"Now that we're sure you're not a vampire, you can join us in our family home," he responds. "This place is special."

"I'll say." It's not a quaint castle with a tower up top that could double for a princess's hideout, and it certainly doesn't look like a home either. It's a fortress––big enough to be a grand hotel and surrounded on all sides by a massive stone fence with silver pickets all across the top. There are guard towers at each corner of the fence, and when I squint I can make out the people there standing watch. The footprint of the structure itself takes up most of the space, but I catch sight of a few courtyards and a green lawn off the back. The building's walls are a sleek whitewashed limestone with rows of silver-barred arched windows. This place screams "old money" and "no vampires allowed" at the same time.

I turn on Tate. "You aren't mafia, are you?" I immediately regret asking so openly. People who value their lives don't just go around asking their captors if they're in the mafia. Even though Tate's helping me, he's still my captor. I couldn't get away if I tried. Unease gnaws at my chest. This isn't good.

He raises his bushy eyebrow and smirks. "We don't need to resort to criminal enterprises to keep our lights on."

I swallow hard, remembering how my mother got involved with the mob back in New Orleans. The memory of getting my head slammed into a wall echoes at the back of my skull, a reminder of what it felt like to lose control over my life. I'm lucky to be alive after everything I've been through. More than lucky.

"I know you're wondering who 'we' are," he says ruefully, "and I've said that we couldn't tell you until it was safe." I sit up straighter, ready to hear more. "Answers will only have to wait a little longer." He holds up his hand to stop me from interrupting. "Be patient, Eva. I promise it's all going to come together soon."

Eleven

"**E**va, welcome to Casa Del Sole!" A young woman with a slight French accent bounds from the house, and I immediately recognize Remi, one of my servants from back at Versailles. I blink at Remi in surprise, stopping in my tracks. She laughs and tugs me in for a quick hug. "In case you hadn't figured it out, I was a spy," she stands back and winks at me. "And I'm so glad you got out of there. I was getting worried about you."

Her curly blonde locks gleam in the sunlight, and behind her is the endless blue sky. Like Tate, she doesn't have an aura. I already knew that about her, but the confirmation that she isn't human puts me on edge. I inch back, unsure if I can trust her. Being a spy just means she's good at lying. And she's Tate's spy, not mine.

Tate was willing to sacrifice my friends. He'd sent all of those hunters into the casino for a chance to get at Adrian knowing full well people were going to get killed. It's only because of my deal with Adrian that they weren't slaughtered. Whatever he and Remi are, they're not human. They risk lives, they haven't been honest with me . . . and I'm probably one of them.

Whatever that means, I still don't know. If I ever want to find out, I need to play their game, so I plaster on a fake smile. "Oh, right, Remi, it's good to see a familiar face." My voice comes out weirdly chipper, and I have to stop myself from cringing.

"Come on," she says, "I'll show you to your room."

She takes my hand and tugs me after her, guards following at our heels. Tate's phone rings, and he stays back, nodding at me to go with Remi.

"You're here early enough in the day that I can show you around first," she says.

"Sounds good."

Casa Del Sole is even larger than it appeared from above. It really could be a hotel, except I'm sure it's not. Tate called it the family home, and with the guard towers and loads of silver accents, I'll bet whoever lives here is mortal enemies with the vamps. Silver is hard to come by, it's expensive, and the suckers have a vested interest in getting rid of it, but these people have an abundance. We walk into a grand entrance through silver doors twice as tall as I am. I don't know what I expect, but it's not what I find . . .

People.

There are people walking through the corridors––at least twenty. They look at me and smile, and some even wave hello.

"Is this place open to the public, too?" I ask, confused that Tate thinks this is their most secure location. The touristy castle ruse obviously didn't work, so to try another tourist destination seems like a bad idea.

She shakes her head, her hazel eyes widening. "Not a chance. Tate really didn't tell you anything, did he? Casa Del Sole is . . ." She ponders on her words for a second. "Well, think of it like someone's home where they've also set up an exclusive boarding school."

Okay, what? "This day is full of surprises."

She laughs. "Come on, let me show you around."

"How old are you?" I ask as she leads me into a library with golden light streaming through the windows. "You look too old to be in boarding school."

"I'm twenty-two. I finished my time here already and stayed on to work for the family."

"Oh yeah, tell me about this family."

Her smile beams. "You'll meet them soon, I'm sure. Don't worry, you're going to love them. They're an old Italian family, and they find people like us and help us."

"People like us?" My fingers itch, so I ball them into tight fists.

She winks but doesn't say more on the matter. I drop the subject for now and let Remi show me from room to room. There are two classrooms, a grand dining room with a long table that seats at least fifty people, a state of the art gym, a light-filled center courtyard that doubles as a greenhouse and is brimming with exotic plants, and even an elegant indoor pool.

"There's an outdoor pool too," Remi says dreamily as we stand at the edge of the chlorine-blue water. "We spend loads of time there in the summer, but it's already closed for the season."

"Just my luck." Summers in Italy would be my fantasy. It's hard to believe people live it in real, everyday life. "How many people live here?"

"Well, the family comes and goes, but this is their main residence. There are eleven of them in total, including the matriarch who is the actual owner of Casa Del Sole. Her husband passed away, but she has three grown children, two of which are married, and five grandchildren."

"Tate's one of these people?"

"He's the son-in-law. His wife has a couple of brothers."

"And then they invite people like us to stay here and study with them?"

"Yup. Right now, there are seven students under their tutelage. And then there are tons of security guards who live here full time, plus the household staff, two teachers, some admin people for the school like myself . . ."

"So you're an admin who moonlights as a spy?" I raise an eyebrow, and she goes pink.

"Come on. I'll take you to your room." Her abrupt change in subject is so jarring that I don't say anything more as she grabs my hand, but I quickly shake her off. I'm sure my hands are sweating.

"Are you okay?" she questions. She stares at me, and I realize my mind has softened against my will with that one touch of her hand. I so want to tell her I'm not okay, to unload all my worries on her, but I don't let myself give in. If she's trying to do something similar to what Tate can do, I don't want any part. But I also don't want her to be suspicious that I know what she's up to, so I nod and lie through my teeth.

"Yeah, this pool just looks amazing. I was thinking of how nice it would be to jump in right now. I don't normally like swimming, but this summer was so busy that I missed out on the fun." I'm totally rambling.

"There will be plenty of time for swimming," she laughs. "Come on now, let's go to your room."

I stare longingly at the cobalt blue pool as she drags me away. A strange feeling comes rushing right back with her touch, but I don't shake her off again. I'm still not sure how I feel about her or this place. On one hand, Casa Del Sole is beautiful and welcoming, the kind of home that existed only in my dreams. But on the other hand, I'm not sure how safe I am here. And I want to go home. I miss my mom, and I really miss Ayla.

A thought strikes me as we pass by a pair of what I think are students. They're close in age to me and say hello as we pass, then scurry off around one of the many corners. "You know I'm not enrolling here, right? I'm only staying for a little bit to get away from the vampires until things die down. I'm going home soon."

Remi gives me a pitying look. I know what she's thinking, that I don't have a home to go back to anymore, that nowhere is safe for me now that vampires are after me. But she doesn't understand how badly I want to return to normal. Why should I be punished for something Brisa did? I was forced to leave New Orleans––but what about my new apartment? What about my mom? My life? I've got to find a way to get it back.

"Think of this place as a vocational training program instead of a school. People come here at all sorts of ages, but most are college-aged young adults like us, which makes it more fun. You might actually be interested in what we do here after you learn more about it." Her voice drops. "And about yourself." Her eyes are practically bugging out of her head, and I know she wants to tell me more.

My mouth turns to sawdust as I consider her words. If I'm like them, that means this is a place for energy demons like Tate. Are they here to learn how to drain humans? I'm not about to trade becoming a bloodsucking vampire for an energy one. So far, I haven't seen a single aura, so I can safely assume these people aren't regular humans, not even the guards or the staff. And just because I may fit in here, doesn't mean I want to.

"Does this have something to do with the fact that none of y'all have auras?" I blurt out, then my mouth pops open, and I drop her hand. "Maybe I shouldn't have asked that. I'm not good at knowing when to shut my mouth."

She grabs my hand *again* and tugs me into my room, closing the door. The room is on the top floor and bigger than any bedroom I've had before, with pretty wood furniture and white linens. A large window overlooks the coastline, and same as at the castle, there are silver bars fastened across it. But I barely have time to take any of that in, I'm more concerned with whatever Remi's doing to me. Her touch makes me want to talk, to trust her with all the fears I normally keep to myself.

"How much do you know?" she demands in a whisper. "Tate said you don't know anything, but you obviously do."

My hackles rise, but I can't help from spilling my guts, hoping this burden won't be mine to carry alone anymore. "I know that Tate sucks energy from humans and that he's not the only one. I've seen people like you without auras doing it before." My voice goes impossibly low, and my heart pounds. "I also know he can make people do things or forget things. It's a lot like vampire compulsion."

Her lips thin, and guilt shadows her pretty face. "Okay, so you know a lot. Full disclosure, I'm supposed to report anything you say back to him," she says, holding up her hands and finally dropping mine.

"So don't," I reply. This time, I fold my arms and tuck my hands against my sides.

"I have to do my job," she says sheepishly.

"So can Tate do that manipulation thing on you too?" I tilt my head at her. "Is that why you have to do your job? Or is it that you want to do your job?"

"Both," she shrugs, and that's all I need to know.

No more telling my feelings to someone who's going to go blabber them all to Tate. At least now I know not to trust her with any secrets. "Fine, but at least tell me what he is, and what I'm guessing you are too? Because in my head, I've been calling you people energy demons."

She gasps and murmurs to herself in French. "We are not demons!"

I shrug. "Then what are you?"

A knock sounds on the door, and we both jump. Leslie Tate strides into the room. "How are you settling in, Eva? Feeling okay?"

"I'll leave you two alone to talk," Remi squeaks out, and then scurries out the door. I can't come to grips between the woman who was my maidservant back in Versailles and this jumpy girl. How could she have been so brave in the face of vampires but acts so skittish around Tate? Is she afraid of him? Intimidated? He must have more power over her than he does over me, which I'm pretty sure has something to do with the venom.

I turn on Tate and rest my hands on my hips. "To answer your question, I'm fine, but I'm ready for you to tell me what's really going on."

"Remi explained what we do here?" he asks, circling the room. Is he going to ignore the fact that Remi practically ran out of here?

"In a way." I raise a brow. "She showed me around and said it's like a vocational training program." I level him with a hard stare. "But she wouldn't say what for."

He stares right back, as if weighing all possibilities in his mind. I'm waiting for him to do his manipulation trick on me to test if it will work again. I don't think it will work as well as he would want it to.

"You're to stay away from the students and out of the classrooms for the time being," he says abruptly. "You're here because we need to keep you out of the vampire's hands, and that's all for now."

I scoff. "Why can't you just tell me? I already told Remi that I know about you sucking energy from humans, I've seen it. And I know that you can compel people similar to the way vampires do."

"That's a special talent of mine personally," he answers. There's frustration lacing his tone. This man isn't used to being talked back to. "So you can see why the family has decided to make sure you can be trusted before letting you in on the secrets."

I balk at him. "See! This is what I mean. Do you know what I am? Am I different from other humans?"

He heaves a heavy sigh. "It's not all up to me to give you these answers. But again, once we're sure you can be trusted, you'll be the first to know. In the meantime, you'll be safe here."

"Really? Because it feels like I'm here to be your prisoner. The same thing happened with the vampires."

His eyes flash. "And does any part of you miss the vampires? Do you feel yourself being drawn to them in any way?"

Memories of Adrian come to mind, and I squash them.

"No, of course not, but I feel like we're in a game of chicken right now. I can't trust you until you tell me the truth––so how am I supposed to act like I can be trusted? You already know I hate the vampires, but you act like I don't."

He laughs at that.

"What's so funny?"

"You left New Orleans with a vampire prince! And then you played dress-up with the queen and her court. And now you have the oldest and most powerful vampire venom in your veins. So forgive me for being skeptical."

"You picked me up, not the other way around." I glare, a fury building inside me, but I have to admit his reasoning makes sense. That still doesn't make up for the fact that I did those things because I was forced to. "None of that was my choice."

My face heats remembering my time in bed with Adrian, something that was most definitely my choice. A bad one, but still mine. Everything else, though? Not my doing! A little voice in the back of my head is yelling at me to cut the shit and take accountability for my part, but I silence her.

"Be that as it may, my family has an obligation to protect our interests."

Here he goes again with the "family" talk. I step back and release the wind from my sails. This conversation is going in circles. If I act appreciative, then maybe Tate will loosen the reins a bit and I can figure out what an energy demon actually is. Remi acted like calling her a demon was a slap in the face, so they must be something else.

"You win," I say, defeated, "tell me what to do, and I'll do it."

Words I never thought would come out of my mouth. But the more I'm around him, the more I'm reminded that he's in the power position. He brought me to this fortress, and I'm not sure if the monsters outside of its walls are any worse than the monsters inside them. I have to play nice and get his family to trust me, which means I'll have to hang on to his every word and act as if he walks on water. The man has an ego the size of Texas, and I should've realized this about him the day we met.

He smiles like he's just won our little game, but I'm not done playing. "Today, you will lay low and keep to your room." He heads for the door.

"And tomorrow?" I ask, hopeful.

He stops and turns back to me. "Tomorrow, you will meet the family."

Twelve

After a long nap, I wake up renewed and ready to take fate into my own hands. There's a walk-in closet and a chest of drawers filled with clothes in my size and, figuring they must be for me, I rummage around until I find a black one-piece bathing suit and matching cover-up. I change and set out for the indoor pool. I'm not really interested in swimming as much as I am looking for a good excuse to explore this place on my own.

When I leave my room, however, I'm met with the same two guards who accompanied Tate and me in the helicopter this morning. Neither of them have auras, both are middle-aged and rippled with muscles, and they've practically got "no-nonsense" written on their foreheads.

"Where are you going?" the first guy asks in a thick Russian accent. The second one just grunts and looks me up and down like I'm a security threat.

I motion to my outfit. "Swimming."

"Did Tate approve this?"

I roll my eyes and play it cool. "I need some exercise, and Tate only said the classrooms and other students were off-limits, so the swimming pool should be fair game." I turn on my heels and head in that direction, half expecting them to drag me back into my new room, but they follow behind and don't say another word.

So much for exploring, they're not going to let me out of their sight. I guess I shouldn't have expected anything different, but I'm still disappointed. I remember where the pool is, but I take a wrong turn on purpose to see what the guards will say. They're quick to correct my error.

"I thought you said you wanted to go swimming?" the Russian asks gruffly.

My cheeks redden as I turn around. "I do."

"This way then." He nods toward the opposite corridor, and I follow after him. I've got myself sandwiched between these guards, and I'm itching to get away from them. They're here to watch me more than to protect me, and I'm not used to being around anyone this much. I've been a lone wolf type of girl for years. I was good with Ayla when I needed a friend, but enjoyed being by myself a lot. Being followed like this isn't something I'm too keen on.

When we get to the pool room, it's blissfully empty. I release a sigh, thankful that I don't have to deal with even more people. The large room is lined with gleaming white tiles and the pool is long, thin, and bright turquoise. It's only a lap pool, but that's fine by me. It's also deep, and the reflection of the water bounces off the low ceiling. If I watch it for too long I'll get dizzy.

I remove my cover-up and dive in. The cold water washes over me, and I'm instantly able to let my worries go. I'm not big on the cold, so normally I would screech like a drowned rat in this temperature, but something about today feels infinitely different. Maybe it's the venom or the change in scenery, or simply doing something as normal as swimming, but I love this cold pool.

I swim laps for a while, getting lost in my thoughts before allowing them to wash away with the water. My body is fluid as I pump from side to side of the pool, and my muscles warm up. I've never gone this fast. I feel like an Olympic swimmer and imagine myself in a race. Maybe I should've joined the swim team in high school instead of running track because this is amazing. I could be off winning championships with some university scholarship right now.

I know it's the venom, but it's still fun to imagine.

"Hey, watch out!" A voice breaks me from my daydream, and I stop, my head bobbing on the surface.

"Do you mind?" another voice adds. Staring down from the side of the pool is a group of two guys and two girls about my age. One of the girls points to the pool water. It's swishing so hard that big waves have lapped up onto the pool deck. "You're going to get the towels wet."

I blink in surprise. I hadn't realized I'd been swimming so fast and had displaced so much water. It must be the venom that's made me stronger than I'm used to. "Oh, sorry." I sink back down into the water. I don't know why I'm embarrassed––I usually don't care what people think––but I am, and it's annoying. They strip down to their swimsuits and jump in, and I wade to the ladder to climb out.

"You're the new girl, right? Evangeline? We've heard about you." One of the guys catches me before I go. "I'm Gentry." He has an American accent, and something about that makes me feel like I'm not so out of my element here.

"Gentry, don't talk to her," the girl from before chastises him. "My family hasn't approved of her yet. You know the rules."

So she's one of them . . .

I'm not surprised that they've been instructed not to talk to me, and it's not like I need to talk to them either. They may look like normal humans, but I know better. None of them have auras! I can't let myself get manipulated again, and who knows what kind of powers they have. Tate can manipulate minds, and Remi was trying to do something to my emotions. The girl got me to admit my energy demon theory. My hackles rise as I realize I'm not safe around these people.

Gentry shrugs and grins at me, dimples popping in both of his cheeks. He's a home-grown American boy type, and nothing I can't deal with if we're just talking about appearances. But who knows what kind of powers he could have. I suck it up and return his smile, shaking his hand and testing to see what happens when I touch him.

Nothing. *Thank goodness.*

"Hi, Gentry. Yep that's me, but call me Eva. Only my mother calls me Evangeline."

"It's nice to meet you."

"That's enough," one of my guards cuts him off and points to me. "Time to go."

"That's what I was doing." I roll my eyes and climb from the pool, shooting Gentry a genuine smile. "It's nice to meet you too."

Is it nice to meet him, though? I don't think anyone here can be trusted. It's not lost on me that seeing human auras was an ability that came with venom, but I'm glad I have the ability now. It's one of the vampire defenses to be able to tell humans apart from whatever these enemies of theirs are, and now I can tell the difference too. But if these people are the suckers' enemies, does that make them my allies?

Ugh . . . I don't even know anymore, and I certainly don't want to face the reality that I could be one of them, even though it's time I face it. It's not as if I want to sign up for this school, but it would be nice to have some answers for once.

I dry myself off with one of the fluffy white towels and leave these kids to it. I hurry back to my bedroom and shower just in time for a late lunch to be delivered to my door. Four mini triangle sandwiches are piled next to a handful of berries and grapes, and my stomach grumbles just looking at it.

The guard hands me a couple of water bottles. "Do you need anything else for the night?"

"Oh, so I guess this is dinner too." I sigh and set the food and water down on my bedside table. I know Tate wanted me to lay low, but I didn't expect to be so shut off from everyone. "How about a phone?"

"No can do." He shakes his head. "Anything else?"

"You people are really starting to piss me off." I widen my eyes. "I need to call my mother, and nobody has a right to keep her from me, not even Tate."

"Sorry, kid. This place is a sanctuary for a reason. None of the students have phones."

"I'm not a student."

"Nope."

I throw my hands up. "Alright, what about television? Or books? Something to keep me from dying of boredom?"

He strides past me and opens the nightstand drawer, retrieving a thin remote. With the push of a button, a gold-framed print of the Italian countryside flickers on. I had no idea it was a television; who has a television that looks like artwork? This place is next level.

He hands the remote over. "We're not trying to make your life harder," he says, "in fact, we're doing the opposite. Think of how hard your life would be if you weren't somewhere safe the next time you want to complain." With that, he leaves, locking the door behind him.

I roll my eyes, hating that he's right, and get to eating while flipping through the channels. Most of them are in Italian, so they're no use. Why is it that most Americans only know English, myself included? Other countries teach people multiple languages in school, but ours doesn't. I find that quite annoying at the moment. Sure, I picked up on a little Spanish from the Moreno family, which sounds similar to Italian, but I still have no idea what the people on the TV are talking about. I study the remote harder and locate a button for a streaming service.

Thank heavens it works. I settle into a new series, hoping it's binge-worthy enough to get my mind off everything. Luckily the show is funny, and the best part? It has absolutely nothing to do with supernaturals. I think I've had enough of them for today.

Thirteen

~~~

Darkness comes, and I go to bed relieved that I'm not trying to make myself into a vampire tonight. I sleep better than I have in weeks, but I wake up the next morning feeling like a different girl—one who is angry at herself for being so selfish.

Here I've been, worried about the venom in my veins, when innocent people are in trouble. It's time to stop resenting the venom and see it as the asset it is. Humans are my priority, and that isn't going to change. In fact, I'm more determined to end the vampires now that I know how cruel they can be. And heartless. They'll always see humans as food to be played with and then consumed. It's not going to change, and neither will I.

I can run and hide, spend the rest of my days trying to keep away from them now that I'm a weapon against them, or I can turn that weapon on them just as they fear. I'll do more than just defend myself. I'll become the best vampire hunter the world has ever seen. I'll hunt them down, one by one if I have to, until they're wiped from the earth. And what's more?

I'll get the word out about the venom. There have got to be more people like me out there that would do anything to transform into badass vampire hunters. Why not let everyone know the big secret? It may get me killed, but it would be worth the risk. We could end vampirism once and for all. That impossible goal suddenly seems less impossible, and I grin wickedly to myself.

This is it. I can feel it.

But first, I need to know exactly what I am.

I haven't wanted to face the facts, but Tate brought me here to stay among his people because I must be one of them. And if I am some kind of energy demon soul-sucker, I need to know so I can get back to what I'm meant to be doing: hunting vampires.

I sit up in bed and eye the television. Brisa is dead, so the world must be dissolving into chaos. I turn it on and scroll until I find the BBC. I turn up the volume, listening intently to the anchors' reports on elections, natural disasters, high-profile criminals, and what seems like a typical news day. I watch for a few minutes, searching for news of Brisa's death, but there's nothing. The story must not have broken yet, but it's only a matter of time. When it does, it's going to be huge.

I watch for a few more minutes, searching for clues until a headline catches my eye. On the bottom of the screen where the smaller stories scroll by in text is one that sends my nervous system into a panic.

Breaking: 12 dead in an apparent killing spree in Zurich, Switzerland.

That's all? There's got to be a report on this. A killing spree is a big deal, but the story slides by with little fanfare. I twist my lips and sit back on the bed. I need to look into this further because my gut says it could have something to do with vampires.

And it doesn't help that the suckers have their fingers in everything, especially the news. Could someone be holding off news of Queen Brisa's death? Then again, most people don't understand how blood bonds work, let alone the royal one.

But I know the truth.

The vampire alliances would've splintered with Brisa's death. Whole covens of vampires are probably reverting back to their old ways, and it's only a matter of time until the news of everything breaks. Maybe it will turn out to be a good thing and cause a much-needed war between humans and vampires? But with compulsion working on anyone over twenty-five, humans might not come out as the victors. In the meantime, vampires can't keep this news hidden forever. Somebody needs to warn the world. I wish that someone could be me, but I don't know how I can sound the alarm when I'm locked up here. Besides, I do need to stay away from the vampires until I'm ready to fight them.

I spend most of the day in isolation. The guards take me to the dining hall to eat meals, but only after everyone else has finished up. I don't see Remi again, and when I ask to go swimming, I'm told the pool is already in use. By the time the stylist comes to my room that afternoon and introduces herself, I'm eager for something to do. I find it strange having a stylist considering I'm perfectly capable of doing my own hair and makeup, but she insists this is the way things are done for special gatherings.

"The family has no shortage of funds and likes to enjoy the finer things in life," Kaylee says with a grin as she brushes out my hair. "Might as well enjoy it."

"The family, huh?" I look up at her from the vanity chair in my massive bathroom. "What can you tell me about this family?"

Her cheeks pale and she shakes her head. "I can't say anything, but you're lucky they're showing such an interest in you. Don't worry, you'll do great."

"You're making me nervous."

She doesn't say another word about it as she curls my hair and applies my makeup. She uses way too much bronzer for my liking, but I have to admit the woman knows what she's doing. When she's finished, I've been transformed from a nineteen-year-old who uses dry shampoo more often than she should to a sophisticated socialite. I change into an emerald green evening gown with matching strappy heels. Kaylee finishes the look off with a string of pearls.

This is so not me. And even though it's a gorgeous look, I've had enough of playing dress-up. I only want to be myself. No more pretending. Just as the sunset is painting the sky a cotton candy pink, the guards enter my room and tell me it's time to go.

"Good luck," Kaylee beams, but I can't return more than a polite thank you. My stomach tightens and my hands shake as the guards lead me downstairs and through the hallways into a much more intimate dining room than the one I've used. Unfortunately, I'm the last guest to arrive.

Fourteen

⟨⟩

Tate's the only one I recognize, but the entire family must be in attendance because I quickly count eleven people. The matriarch herself sits at the head of the table, an imposing woman with thick white hair swept on top of her head and knowing black eyes that send a shiver through me.

The grandchildren aren't young. All are probably older than I am, or close to it. I don't know why that catches me off guard, but it does. I'd assumed when Remi had said "children," that she actually meant children.

Tate stands to greet me as all eleven pairs of eyes assess me from head to toe. Some are welcoming, but most are not. They're all dressed as well as I am, and all look as if they're used to these types of gatherings. "Ah, Evangeline, please come in," Tate says, "let me introduce you to the De Luca family."

I frown at the surname before remembering that Leslie Tate is the son-in-law. I stride forward to the intimidating woman at the head of the table and extend my hand. She takes it, shaking it with a firm hold while gazing up with a sharpness in her eyes that is either judging or protective or both. It's immediately apparent that this woman is not one of those who loses her touch with age. She's quite the opposite, and can't be fooled by the trappings of youth.

"Hello, child," she says in a syrupy Italian accent. "I'm Camilla De Luca. Lovely to finally meet you."

"It's nice to meet you too," I return, and she drops my hand.

"Everyone, I'd like you to meet Evangeline Blackwood." Tate points to the people seated around the table and begins introductions. "This is my wife, Bianca, and her older brothers Fredrico and Dario."

Bianca is much younger than her husband, with a sultry untouchable energy about her. She probably married Leslie when she was fresh out of high school and had her children shortly after. Either that, or she's had a lot of plastic surgery. She gives me a tight smile––they all do. It's pretty clear that they don't trust me, but she seems particularly bothered by my presence here.

"And these are my kids, Bella and Greyson." It's strange that Tate has been living at the hunter gym without his family, but I don't comment on it.

I recognize Bella as the standoffish blonde girl from the pool who told me not to get the towels wet. Her hair is obviously dyed because her complexion is as dark as her family's. The contrasting colors suit her well. She turns up her nose and shifts away. Greyson is a bit older with long dark curls and pouty lips that turn into a full-on scowl.

"Fredrico is the oldest De Luca son, and his wife is Lainey." Tate points to the couple. Fredrico reminds me of the male version of Camilla, and Lainey is a soft plump woman who gives me a sweet hello in an American accent. She's not nearly as intimidating as the rest of them and appears the same age as her husband.

"Enzo and Nicco are their twins." Identical men in their late twenties nod to me. They're built of so much hulking muscle that they barely fit into their chairs.

"And Chloe is the baby of the family."

Chloe is the only one who offers me a genuine smile and also the only one who looks to be my age or younger. She matches her family, Italian and beautiful, with the sweet roundness of her mother. I can immediately tell she's the kind of girl who fits right in wherever she goes. When she says hello, her accent is more American than Italian, like her mother's and her uncle's.

"Thank you all for having me," I say. My voice comes out a bit shaky, and I want to pinch myself.

"Are you sure about this, mother?" Fredrico says darkly, bypassing me altogether. "She's an outsider. We can hardly trust her to join us for our family dinner."

I want to roll my eyes at that. What's so special about a family dinner that an outsider can't be invited in for a meal?

"I trust Leslie," Camilla croons back. Fredrico's sitting right next to her, and she motions for him to move. "Go further down the table. I'd like Evangeline to sit by me tonight."

The tension in the room grows thicker, and I feel awkward as hell. This family is nothing like what I grew up with. They're the complete antithesis of my childhood. Sure, my mom and I have had a strained relationship, but we don't play games. I'm keenly aware that these people are incredibly competitive while still being close-knit.

Trying not to let my face reveal just how uncomfortable I am, I sit down in his still-warm chair. A staff member is quick to change the drinks around, pouring me a glass of wine in the process. I'm parched, but I don't touch it. If there's one useful thing I've learned from Tate, it's that alcohol is never a good idea for a vampire hunter. I go for the glass of water resting next to the wine instead. The condensation wets my hand––a wake-up call of sorts for me to not forget who I'm with. *These people could be worse than the vampires.*

"How are you enjoying your time here so far?" Camilla asks.

"I'm safe, and it's a beautiful place to hide out," I reply with the truth. "But I'd appreciate some answers to my questions. Your son hasn't exactly been forthcoming."

"Son-in-law," Camilla corrects, and Tate shifts uncomfortably.

Further down the table, someone scoffs, but otherwise it's quiet as midnight in this room. Nobody says a word for a long minute, and then the silence is interrupted by staff with trays of food. They get everyone situated with heaps of roasted lamb and vegetables.

"Leslie, will you offer the prayer?"

Everyone bows their heads, and I do the same, but I'm so startled by the fact that these people are praying that I can hardly hear a word of it. Does praying make them good people? Not necessarily. Plenty of people pray one minute and then go off to do horrible things the next.

"Please enjoy," Camilla says when the prayer is over, and everyone digs in. I do as well, but I find myself picking at the food despite my gnawing hunger. Something about this dinner feels like a test somehow. They're all watching me intently, as if I'm eating the wrong way. I frown at the silver forks, wondering if I should've picked up the small one instead of the big one.

"So, do you go by Evangeline or Eva?" Bella asks coyly, a gleam of mischief in her big brown eyes. "Or perhaps it's Angel?"

Hearing Andrian's nickname for me on her lips makes me pause. "Eva, thanks."

"Tell us about yourself," Enzo asks. He and his brother have piercing blue eyes that turn on me at once, and I nearly fall out of my chair, I'm so uncomfortable. It's like they can see into my head.

I clear my throat, half expecting someone to save me from talking about myself, but of course, nobody does. Talking about myself is my least favorite thing to do. I've always found people who talk about themselves instead of asking questions of others to be dull. The most interesting people are usually the quietest ones.

"There's not much to say." I shrug.

"Oh, I doubt that," Lainey replies. She's nice, but I can't help but keep my guard up. Her apparent niceness could be an act.

"Well, I was born and raised in New Orleans, Louisiana. I'm nineteen. I'm not in college right now, but I'd like to go eventually. I'm considering nursing or something that will allow me to help people. I work as a server at a popular restaurant, and I've been training with Tate to be a hunter."

None of these things are actually true anymore considering it's been over a month since I left home without a trace.

"Do you have any family?" Bianca asks innocently, and a few of the others look away.

"I'm the only child to a single mother," I say it like it's no big deal because to me it's not. "It's just the two of us."

"I can't imagine what that would be like," Chloe pipes up, her fork midair as she addresses me. "It must be so quiet."

"You're lucky to have so many family members," I say, "but then again, I'm lucky too."

"And why is that?" Dario asks. It's the first time he speaks directly to me, and there's something about the man that gives me the creeps. Maybe it's because he's a single man looking at me like I'm fresh meat, but I don't think so--it's more than that. Something I can't quite put my finger on.

"There are pros and cons to everything," I supply but don't elaborate because I don't have to defend myself.

He raises a dark eyebrow. "And what are the pros to being in such a small family?"

I level him with a stare, anger burning deep. I can't believe he has the audacity to ask me such a rude question. "When it comes to my mom, I get all the attention, all the money, and all the time. There's no one for me to compete with, now is there?"

The room goes silent, and I know I've gone too far. If they didn't already hate me, they're going to now. They have to compete for Camilla's love--of that I'm certain.

Dario glares, but Fredrico smiles, raising his glass. "Fair point."

"You're not getting attention if you're sharing it with her gambling problem," Greyson juts in, and the guy may as well have punched me in the gut. I go ghost-still, blood pooling in my cheeks. How do they know about that? I shoot Leslie Tate a scathing glare, and he frowns apologetically.

"We've done our research on you," Camilla cuts in as if her son and grandson aren't complete asses. "Don't be surprised that we had you vetted before inviting you to our table. Why do you think you weren't brought here straight away?" Her eyes narrow. "My family is under my protection, and one can never be too careful these days."

There's an undercurrent to her words I don't quite understand, a double meaning that I'm meant to uncover. All at once, she grabs my hand and squeezes. I yelp as pain shoots through me––white-hot unexpected agony that drops me to my knees beside her, my chair long forgotten. The sounds of the room fade to white noise as my head buzzes.

My life flashes before my eyes. Memories of my mother, of Gram, of Ayla and Felix, and everyone else that mattered. Early childhood and holidays and memories of school come barreling to the surface, and then I'm reliving the last three months of my life. The hell. The excitement. The mistakes. The whirlwind of falling for Adrian's tricks. The foolish agreements I made with him. The incredible joy I felt when Mom beat her addiction, thanks to him. The unruliness of Versailles. The ecstasy of sleeping with Adrian after weeks of yearning for him. The terror of being bit by Brisa. The darkness of the catacombs, and then the light bursting from my hands.

And Brisa.

Again, I see Brisa––this time, she's consumed by the light.

Camilla releases me, and I scramble back, falling to my butt. "What did you just do to me?"

Fifteen

"I read your memories," she answers, her gaze digging into my very soul. My dinner threatens to come up as those four words sink in. I didn't know that ability was possible, but it's a violation I'll never be able to get past. I glare at the woman, wanting to spit in her face and run far away from this place.

Lies. It's all lies. They promise safety and then do *this*.

"I didn't give you permission," I growl.

"I don't need permission. This is my house you're in, and my protection you're under."

"But I'm your guest."

"You're here for a specific reason, Eva. Do you want safety from the vampires? Fine. I believe you. I can see how you were fooled by them. Adrianos broke your little heart."

Someone laughs, and I'm so angry, I could cry.

"You need me, and I need you." She leans down to get a better look at me. "I'll give you the safety you're craving, and the answers, the training . . . I'll give you everything you need if you choose to stay here with us."

I blink up at her in surprise. If I'm being honest, I'd never thought they'd let me walk out of here. I'd assumed that, once again, I'd been imprisoned by those in the power position. The fact that she's offering me a choice doesn't fit with her character, but it gives me an opportunity to test the waters.

"So I can leave?" I stand up, heading for the door.

"You can leave," she calls after me, "but if you do, you'll be dead by sunrise."

I stop and glare at her. "I'm stronger than you give me credit for."

"Oh, darling, I know all about your strength. Do you not think we have also taken the venom? We have. All of us."

Again—another revelation. Tonight is proving to be full of them.

"Our family has been draining fangers for generations," Dario adds with a satisfied smirk.

I throw up my hands. "Fine! If you're so great, then why don't you fight the vampires? Why train innocent humans to do your dirty work?"

"Because there are so few of us left, and we can't make more of us as quickly as they can. And, if you can't tell, I rather like my family, and I'd like to see them alive."

"So what do you want with me, then?"

"Stay here. Work for us."

I want to call her bluff, so I push my way out the door, stomping toward the exit. I need to see if she's being honest with me or if she's going to swoop in at the last moment and drop me in some prison cell somewhere. It's easy to get outside of the mansion, but not so easy to get past the wall. I ask that Russian guard who's always following me around, and he leads me right to a gate.

"Are you sure about this?" He scratches the back of his neck.

I turn on him. "If I go, are you instructed to chase me?"

He shakes his head. "You can go, but you shouldn't. Camilla will help you. She's helped all of us."

I stand there, staring out into the street beyond. Who knows what I'll find. Whatever it is, I might not survive it. I might not survive this place either.

With a groan, I march back into the dining room. I was never going to leave because I don't have a death wish, but I wanted to make sure I could. When I return to the dining room, the family is all still sitting in their chairs, enjoying their dinners as if I hadn't just left and then returned in the span of five minutes.

I point at them. "Okay, I'll stay if you answer my questions."

Camilla pats the place where I had been seated. "Come, sit back down. Have dessert with us, and we can discuss anything you like."

I return to my chair, but I'm on high alert now. Not even the decadent cheesecake the staff brings out can distract me.

After a few bites, I set down my fork. "What are you?"

"We," she raises her eyebrows and points at me, "are not the monsters that you think we are. And you are one of us, in case you haven't figured that out, but I think by now you have."

"You steal the humans' energy and suck their lives away. I've seen it."

Her lips thin. "Then you saw wrong."

"I don't think so." I point at Tate. "I saw him in the hospital ICU. He was taking someone out with the energy-sucking thing."

"I was helping them," he counters, his voice booming across the table. He turns to his mother-in-law. "This is exactly why I wanted to tell her earlier. She's been confused. No wonder the vampires got to her."

"I had to check her memories first," Camilla challenges. "And do you know that she was spying on you for that vile Adrianos?"

His cheeks pinken, but that's the only indication that he's angry or embarrassed because his words are as smooth as satin. "I'd figured as much, but I wasn't worried about it. She didn't see anything."

"She saw you in the hospital ICU," Greyson is quick to point out, much to his father's annoyance.

Camilla releases a slow breath. "Regardless, I need a full picture before ever welcoming someone into my home. You all know that."

Tate nods once and looks away. I can tell he wants to say more. Greyson's smirk is triumphant, and it's obvious the kid resents his father. What a great family this is turning out to be . . .

Camilla levels me with soft eyes. "Eva, what you saw in the hospital was Tate helping a human. It's what we're here to do."

"I don't understand. I know what I saw."

"You saw wrong," she snaps. "Tate goes to the hospital because when someone is close to death, we can help them transition back to spirit with less pain and suffering."

"Come again?"

"We transmute painful energy, feelings of fear, grief, anger, and so on," she says. "That's what Tate was doing. He wasn't hurting that patient, he was helping them. We can't save someone from death, but we can make it easier for them to cross over."

"And that does what for you?"

"You're right that it feeds us in a way. It makes our abilities stronger."

I have to fight to roll my eyes because I also know what I saw in the nightclub and I'm sorry, but none of those humans were on death's door. They want me to believe it's all sunshine and rainbows when I know that's not true.

"Okay, so that takes me right back to my question." I raise an eyebrow. "What are you? Don't make me keep asking." And really, I'm asking what I am too. My heart beats faster, and I'm equally terrified and eager to know the answer. I really hope she doesn't say werewolf because they're supposed to have been hunted to extinction and I really don't want to be howling at the moon anytime soon.

They exchange nervous looks, and then Camilla nods.

"We are the descendants of angels," she says. "We're nephilim."

I'm waiting for someone to laugh, for a punchline to be dropped, but that doesn't happen. Looking around the room, it's clear everyone here is absolutely serious.

"Is that hard for you to believe?" Tate questions. "Many humans didn't believe in vampires when they first came out eighteen years ago, and now the whole world has accepted their existence."

"I mean--I guess--yeah, makes sense, I guess." I stumble awkwardly through my response. How the heck do I respond to something like this? And what does it mean for me?

"She's not human," Fredrico says. "She shouldn't be so surprised."

"But she was raised as one." Camilla takes my hand, and I wince, expecting to be violated again. But nothing happens. This is just one person taking the hand of another and nothing more. "You are special. Didn't you always feel that deep down you were special?"

I shake my head. The truth? I felt ordinary. Actually, I felt less than ordinary. I was nothing but a normal girl living a normal existence in a messed up world. And now I'm supposed to be some kind of angelic descendant?

It's all too much.

"Okay, so not special," Bianca says. Her eyes are cruel, and Tate gives his wife a deep frown. There's something amiss between him and his family. "But maybe you felt like you didn't belong? Like nobody ever truly understood you?"

Damn it. She's right.

Her smile lifts and she nods. "That's because you didn't belong."

Camilla tugs on my arm, and I'm forced to turn back to her. Her eyes are softer now, compassion filling them. "But we understand you, darling. We know how it feels to be different, to be underappreciated, and to have your light dimmed by the world. But you don't have to worry about that anymore because you're one of us now. Welcome to the family."

Sixteen

ⱺ

Angels? It's not lost on me that my nickname is Angel, and now I'm supposed to believe I'm descended from one. I don't know much about angels except that they're talked about in the Bible and they work for God. That's about it. And I still don't know if I even believe in God, but I guess He or She must exist if angels do. This is all so weird . . .

Despite everything, I'm still waiting for them to all start laughing, to tell me that they're pulling my chain and that I'm actually something else, but they never do. They just stare at me with equal parts expectation and the kind of seriousness that means they believe they're exactly what they say they are. They want me to believe it too. And part of me does—the part that's lived among vampires and has seen things she can't explain. But the other part of me—the normal girl who didn't grow up with this stuff, she doesn't know what to think.

"Come," Camilla motions to Chloe, "show her."

Chloe stands and approaches me with glittering hopeful eyes.

"What is she going to do?" I ask.

"I'm the record keeper," is all Chloe says. She grabs hold of me and everything goes white.

Blinding white.

Then I'm thrust backward, my entire body prickling with the inertia of falling impossibly fast. All at once, it stops, and I blink as the scene around me begins to form into a desert and stone buildings and people dressed in strange clothes. Chloe is standing with me, still holding onto my arm. Her hand slides down into mine and she squeezes. "They can't see us," she says, "this is only a look into the past. None of this is here anymore. It's all dust."

"I have questions," I mutter. "So many questions."

She grins. "I know, but watch. You'll see."

A scene materializes before us. There's a man standing over a group of people. He doesn't see us because we're not really there, or this is all some crazy hallucination. The man doesn't look like he belongs in our time or in their time. He doesn't even look like he belongs on Earth. He looms at least ten feet tall with massive fiery angelic wings and a long silver sword swathed at his side. He's dressed in a white tunic and is barefoot. His skin seems to glow, and his golden curls brush his shoulders.

Someone asks him something in a language I don't understand. The people here are so ordinary compared to the angel, but he doesn't seem to mind. In fact, he looks down at them with nothing but unbridled love and compassion in his deep blue eyes.

"I'm a messenger of God," he says in a rich voice. There's something about his tone that is unearthly and I'm not even sure he's speaking English, but I somehow know what he's saying.

"He can be understood in all languages," Chloe whispers, sensing my confusion.

The people fall to their knees as if to worship the angel, and he commands them to stand. "My siblings and I have been directed by the Father to spread our seed over the earth. Those seeds will grow into an army meant to guide and protect the human race from the evils of the serpent."

The people erupt in prayers, questions, tears, and thanks. So many voices at once. The angel disappears with a flash of white light.

And then, once again, all I can see is white emptiness too. It's nothing, and yet it's everything, filling every space imaginable, seeping into my very soul. And then it's gone, and I'm watching time play out over the centuries, battles between the nephilim and supernaturals—all kinds of supernaturals. Werewolves. Dragons. Shifters. Fae. So many others that I've never believed in or expected or even recognize from fiction.

And vampires.

So many vampires. They multiply the fastest of all.

One by one, I witness the supernatural races fall, but the vampires are harder to kill, and they're so much stronger than the nephilim.

Generation after generation, the vampires remain.

I blink, and then I'm back in the dining room with the De Luca family.

"I think I understand now." My voice is a hoarse whisper, and my cheeks redden. How have I gotten it so wrong? Here I thought they were the bad guys, and they're the ones doing the exact thing I've been praying for all my life––ridding the earth of vampires.

Chloe releases my hand and smiles broadly.

"There is only one record keeper for our people alive at a time," Camilla says, "and we're lucky enough to have Chloe in the family." There's an undercurrent to her words, something I can't define, but it's clear how happy she is that Chloe is theirs.

I glanced over at Chloe who's now returned to her seat. "So you can travel back in time?"

"Not really travel, but I can look, and I can take other people with me to look as well."

I turn to the others. "Do you all have powers like that?" I already know Tate can manipulate people's memories and make them trust him, that Camilla can actually peer into someone's mind and riffle around as if sorting through files. I'm pretty sure Remi was trying to sway my emotions yesterday when she kept grabbing my hands. What else can these people do to me?

"Every nephilim has a special gift," Tate says. "Each gift is tied to that individual's mission here on earth."

"We're not angels, though." Greyson speaks so loudly that I nearly jump. "We're humans with some of their blood, that's all. And with every generation, we're weaker and weaker. So don't get any ideas into your head about what you can do."

"I'm not sure what ideas those would be," I shoot back.

"That's enough," Camilla cuts him off. "What matters is that Evangeline is part of the family now. This is what we do here. We find those with angelic blood, bring them in, and teach them how to protect themselves from evil, and if they choose, how to hunt that evil down and kill it."

I'm definitely interested in hunting, but this whole thing has me a little confused and unsettled. I still can't believe it's real, but then again, I can. It explains so much. "I would know if my mother was some kind of angel, and believe me, she's not." They laugh awkwardly, but I wasn't joking. "My father was killed when I was a baby," I go on. "So I must have gotten this gene from him."

"It stands to reason," Dario says dryly. I shoot him a scathing glare. What does he expect from me? This is all new, and it's not like I have any answers about my heritage. "Did you know him? He was Italian. Maybe he went to this school? His name was Carlos Russo. My mother gave me her last name."

They shake their heads, everyone claiming not to have known him. Fredrico explains, "Most with our blood will live perfectly normal human lives without ever knowing what they really are."

"But what about the gifts?" I can hardly imagine that someone with special gifts like these would not suspect something was different about them.

"Most people never live the purpose they were here to live. And if they don't live their purpose," Tate picks up the explanation, "then those gifts will never surface." He rubs his hands together. "Unfortunately, that's that."

"We can sense those who are like us, and we look for them, bringing them here when we find them. It's not enough to slow the vampiric scourge though, which is why we started recruiting the younger humans to help us with our cause," Camilla says.

I'm angry about that, but I get it. The vampires keep growing in number. It's not like these nephilim can bite someone and turn them into part-angel. It's something a person has to be born with. It would also explain why this family is large. They'd want to have as many children as they could to recruit into their little army. I'm actually surprised there aren't more of them.

"Tell them about Queen Brisa," Camilla says, her eyes gleaming with triumph. "Tell them what happened, what I saw."

I take a deep breath, not used to giving away so much information but deciding it needs to be done. "You already know she tried to turn me, and I think that's when my gift surfaced because my hands started to glow and then light exploded out. I'm pretty sure it killed her."

Adrian already confirmed it, but Camilla didn't get that far with my memories. She stopped after that moment. She takes my hand again, and all the roughness from before is gone. She's soft edges and brimming with child-like excitement. Everyone is looking at me the same way. Whatever the light thing is, they must think it's cool, and suddenly they're not so distrustful of me.

"It's the miracle we've been praying for," she says, and then everyone is talking at once.

"The blood bonds will be severed," Enzo says to Nicco. "We need to get out there!"

"She couldn't have killed her," Dario adds. "We would've heard word of it. It would be all over the news."

"They'll try and keep it a secret," Lainey says.

"There have been increased vampire attacks," her husband agrees.

"We should alert the other families," Tate says, "all nephilim need to be in on this."

"Not until we know for sure," Dario cuts him off. "We haven't confirmed."

"He's right," Lainey argues. "They deserve to know. Everyone does. The humans too."

"Enough!" Camilla bursts out, and we all turn to her. She really does know how to command respect. She accepts nothing less. "We will proceed with business as usual until we can confirm the death. But I suspect what Eva believes happened, did indeed happen because I saw it too. I didn't see her burn, the light was too bright, but it makes sense."

We talk for a while, but I'm sent to bed without most of my questions being answered. All I know is these people truly believe they were put on the earth by God to rid it of supernaturals, and they've done a pretty good job at eradicating them all except for vampires. There are families of neph all over the world who have known about this mission for generations, and the De Lucas are the oldest and wealthiest. They claim to be training others to further their cause, that they only take energy from humans that are close to death, and that they're the good guys.

But how much of that is actually true? How long until I figure out they're lying to me, too? It's hard for me to trust anyone, and I don't know if that's because I'm being smart or because my trust has been broken so many times before that I no longer know what it feels like. The information they gave me tonight is all I have to go on, so I choose to assume the others I saw stealing energy from perfectly healthy humans at the Neon club were not from this family. I'm hoping for the best here, but also preparing for the worst.

Seventeen

꧁꧂

T he De Lucas welcome me into their fold. The next day they
introduce me to the other students and get me started with classes.
We're a small group, but we spend time with the teachers and the
older family members. We're here to learn everything there is to know about
supernatural history and nephilim ancestry, and we work on our physical
training constantly, similar to what I did back home with the hunters. And
each afternoon the others go off to hone their unique gift, but the light still
hasn't returned to my hands. I don't know how to get it back, and neither
does anyone else.

"Everyone's gifts are as unique as the individual," Remi says to me one
day when she finds me sitting in the courtyard alone. "Don't worry, yours
will come back when you're ready."

I scoff. "And when will that be?"

She shrugs. "When God needs you."

All this talk of God leaves me even more confused. I still don't know
what I believe or how heaven is supposed to work. And honestly? I don't
think the others really know either. Not truly. They have faith--something
I've always lacked.

The sun is strong today, making this the warmest room in the house, and
I've been pretending I'm back home for the last hour. Remi must see the
pain in my eyes because she sits next to me, our backs to one of the huge
potted plants, and gives me a small smile. "Can I help? I can make you feel
better."

Normally I would say no, but today feels especially bleak, so I take her hand and she instantly floods me with a peaceful calm. I drift away on that blissed-out feeling, like a fluffy little cloud in the middle of a summer's afternoon sky. *Everything will be alright. It always is. One way or another.*

But that's not true. It wasn't for Kenton. It wasn't for my father who died when I was an infant. It wasn't for Grammy when she died of cancer in her sixties, and it wasn't for my mom when she got addicted to gambling.

I drop Remi's hand. "Sorry," I say, "I just can't lie to myself."

"It's not a lie," Remi insists. "You have access to these feelings at any time, I'm just helping you along is all."

I stand and brush myself off. "Thanks, but I know what I have to do."

Despite the vampire venom making it so much easier to see, feel, and do whatever I want, there's one thing I've been needing that I can't get. And no, it has nothing to do with the light tucked away in my body.

I go find Camilla in her office. It's more of a sitting room, and she's there often, handling the business of running the household, her family, and more importantly, hunting down the bad guys. She peers up at me over her laptop and shuts it as I pad inside the room.

"I'd like to call home," I say, "it's really important."

I expect an argument, but she immediately hands me a cell phone. I wander into the corner of the room and dial mom's number. An answering machine tells me that the number has been disconnected. Tears well in my eyes as I return the phone to Camilla. "I haven't talked to her in almost two months," I say, my voice cracking helplessly. "This has never happened before."

"Why don't you email her?" Camilla offers, patting her computer chair. I slide onto the chair, typing out an email to my mom, letting her know I'm safe but not saying where I am, and asking her to please email me back.

"Thank you," I whisper when I finish. "I don't know what else to do."

"We'll help you look for her," Camilla responds with a grandmotherly smile. There's a warmth in her that's usually missing, and I hope I can trust it to be real. "We have a lot of resources and contacts at our disposal. We'll do our best."

I thank her and leave. I know I should feel better, but I don't.

I'm RUNNING on a treadmill a few weeks later, my mind moving faster than my feet. I keep thinking about what it would feel like to take energy from a human. I don't want to, but if I did, would it bring the light back? The longer I'm here without my gift resurfacing, the more I worry about my future. Sure, my senses are heightened, and I've grown used to it. It's like the

438

lights have been turned on after a lifetime of living in the dark. I can see and feel and *do* so much more. And yet, there's even more waiting to be unlocked.

And it's tempting––all this power is like a drug. How easy would it be to slip into bad habits and end up hurting someone? I can't risk it, so I vow never to do so.

"I have a surprise for you, child." Camilla finds me, gliding into the gym. Her voice is a calming presence to the thumping of hip-hop music the other students like to work out to. Several of them turn to eavesdrop on our conversation.

My heart leaps. "Did you find my mother?" I've been worried sick about where she could be. So far, there haven't been any updates. I stop the treadmill and rub a towel at my hands and neck, following Camilla from the gym. My skin feels flushed and my limbs loose, which is about the only thing that feels good right now.

She doesn't answer my question, and I don't know if that's a good thing or not. She takes my hand and leads me into the center courtyard with the greenhouse roof. New flowers bloomed recently, and it's probably my favorite place in the Casa these days. Autumn has lost its battle to winter, and I miss being outside.

Someone is waiting for me next to a row of orchids. It's not my mom standing there, but it is Felix. I haven't seen him since that horrible experience in the castle. My heart thuds, and my cheeks warm.

"I'll leave you two to talk," Camilla says, then flits from the room.

"I wondered where they took you," he says cautiously. "You look well. I see you didn't turn into a vampire after all."

"You look well, too." I smile at him because it's good to see him healthy and alive, even though he does look tired and a little rough around the edges.

He shakes his head. "Not really. We've been so busy hunting. Haven't gotten very many suckers, though."

My mouth pops open, and I take a step toward him. "I didn't know you guys were actually out hunting now." So much has changed. When we were all together, we had still been in training, and it had seemed like it would be a while until we'd be able to actually get out there and hunt. But then Tate decided we should attack the meeting at the casino, and everything went downhill from there. "I thought you would have returned home by now," I add.

"We haven't left Europe. There are a lot of vampires here that we're trying to get under control, and then we'll go home." He shrugs like it makes perfect sense.

It's not what I want to hear. In New Orleans, the guys were only hunting on the side. School and lacrosse were still the main things in their lives. But now they're here, and I'm sure their whole semester is shot. I wonder what the Moreno parents must think of Felix's whereabouts. First, their daughter drops out of school after a few weeks of freshman year, and now their son has run off to the other side of the globe.

"Do your parents know why you're out here?"

His eyes narrow, as if considering how much he wants to say. "They think I'm studying abroad right now."

So they don't know what he's doing or they'd have dragged him home by now. That family is good at staying out of trouble. They're the sort of people I aspire to be someday, even though I accepted long ago that it will never happen. It's one thing to daydream about nursing or police work, but it's quite another to do something about it. I'm a hunted woman, and until I can get control of my neph gift, I'm stuck in the Casa.

"Listen, I'm really sorry about all the horrible things I said to you back at that castle," my voice drops.

His lips thin, and he nods. "I've had a lot of time to think about it over and I see now that none of it was you."

"It wasn't. The venom made me into a different person."

He nods once. "But what you said still hurt me, Eva." I think of how I rubbed my relationship with Adrian in his face and wince. "But I'm not mad at you anymore. I want to be your friend, but I'll never be able to try again with you." He clears his throat awkwardly. "Romantically, that is."

I don't blame him, but I'm suddenly filled with so much regret that it's physically painful. I'd kneel down and cry right now if I could, but I don't want to embarrass myself, so I reach out to offer a handshake instead. "Friends?"

"Always." We shake, and he smiles, but it doesn't quite reach his eyes. I realize I'm smiling too, and like him, my smile feels forced.

We step away from each other and begin to circle the courtyard, admiring the plants because that's easier to talk about than everything that hangs between us. I'm especially taken by the lilies. I lean down to smell one, savoring the floral scent, and notice the flower next to it as one I recognize from my studies.

"Wolfsbane," I mutter.

The plant is used to poison werewolves, but since the wolves have been hunted to extinction, there's no need for it save for its pretty lavender petals that are nice to look at.

"Maybe the family keeps it around just in case it's ever needed again?" Felix offers, and I shudder at the idea–vampires are scary enough. All I know of werewolves comes from television, and I can't imagine adding those monsters into the mix.

"So what are you on to next?" I ask.

"Seth and I have joined up with some of Tate's other hunters here. They're a good group of people. I think we'd like to stay and work with them for a while."

"How long is a while?" What I'm really wanting to ask is when is he going to go home. I want to press him on his studies again, but I don't. He must know what I'm thinking, though, because he turns me to him and squeezes my shoulders, peering down into my eyes with a serious expression.

"A while would be until I'm twenty-four if I can help it. This mission is more important than my education. You see that, right?"

But why does he have to be the one to hunt? Why does he have to give up so much of his future when most humans willingly donate their blood? Then again, now that Brisa is dead, many vampires are going to go rogue and start killing their prey. If there was ever a time to squash them, right now would be it. I'm tempted to convince him to harvest some vampire venom for himself since it will make him a better hunter, but I don't say anything because the idea of trying to extract venom is terrifying, and I know Felix would want to try. Maybe he's already working on it. Felix and Seth know a little about this stuff already, thanks to me.

"So when do you go back out?" I ask.

"Actually, for the time being, we're staying here," Seth's voice interrupts us, and I turn to find him striding toward us with his hands in his pockets and his hard eyes fixed on me. I can instantly tell he's still pissed off at me. He doesn't have the same forgiveness that Felix does, but I can't blame him for that. Seth and I don't have the best history, and we've only known each other since August. Not to mention, Seth is secretly in love with Felix. As far as I know, he still hasn't come out of the closet. He hates that I figured it out. It makes him uneasy around me, but his sexuality is something I'll never break his confidence on.

"I just spoke with Camilla," Seth explains, looking at Felix and not me. The lack of eye contact isn't lost on me. "They want to up their security around here, so she's asked our team to stay on for the time being."

Felix's reaction is unreadable. I can't tell if this is good or bad news when he nods and says, "Alright, then."

Is it alright?

Not to me. Sure, it's nice to see them again, but everyone here is a nephilim. I don't think they all have strong abilities or are built to be fighters, but none of them have auras, so I know they're not regular humans. And what does that mean? They'll be tempted to feed on my friends!

Right now, Felix's aura is swirling in shades of purple, and Seth's is a stormy blue, but I have no idea what those colors even mean. When I asked about aura colors during one of the lessons, I was told the others can't see them. I didn't reveal that they could if they used blacklights, but I'm sure they know all about that. Apparently, Greyson is the only one that can see them like I can, but his sight has something to do with his gift, not venom, and that guy is a Grump with a capital G.

"So we'll be seeing a lot more of you," Seth finally addresses me. "And the others like you."

I blink as his words settle in. "Wait, so you know what I am?"

They nod in unison. "Tate told us a few days before bringing us here. You've got angelic blood," Felix says. "That's pretty cool, Eva."

I bet Tate did more than just tell them about me, he probably used his Jedi-mind-tricks to make them think the nephilim are worthy of protection no matter the costs.

The conversation moves to sleeping accommodations and schedules, but I'm distracted by their swirling auras. The colors are truly magnificent. A longing burns through me, something I haven't allowed myself to feel before now. I'm like a magnet being pulled toward these men because of their energy.

I could try sucking up some of their energy, just a little bit so that nobody would know. And why shouldn't I? They are here to help us, and I think Felix would do just about anything for me. If taking a bit of his energy unlocked my gift, then he would want me to try.

"Are you even listening?" Seth asks with a dark scowl.

"You look a little pale," Felix adds. He leans down and peers into my eyes while pressing his palm to my forehead. "Are you okay?"

He's all up in my space now––that purple aura swirling around me and calling out to my base instincts. It would be so easy.

No.

I step back. "I've got to go," I sputter. "I'll see you around, okay?" Before he can respond, I take off, practically sprinting from the courtyard. My tennis shoes smack against the stone floor, and plants brush my elbows as I run past them. I can hear Seth questioning Felix about my behavior, but I don't allow myself to turn back.

It's not good that they're here. It's actually very, very bad. Because they're going to be hurt. *Used.* If not by me, then by one of the many other neph roaming these halls. Surely, the others will desire their energy the way I just did?

This is not okay.

The farther I get away from them, the more I can relax and gather myself together. I decide to steer clear of my friends, but in the meantime, I've got to get a handle on this darker side of myself because if I don't learn to control it, it will control me.

Eighteen

ADRIAN

We're gathered in the palace ballroom, the garden terrace doors thrown open to let the cold air fill the space. Winter is upon us, it's a new moon, and the cloud cover is heavy. The darkness is thicker than usual, and I find myself sinking into it, letting it soothe me. I've spent so many years hiding from the sun that dark places have become a comfort zone.

I'm currently standing in one of the doorways as I observe the others mingle and find their seats. Above them, the chandeliers drip with long rivers of creamy wax from the candles Brisa had insisted replace the modern lights. Sebastian flits from group to group, his charismatic smile never once faltering as he networks through the crowd. Most of the guests are dressed in contemporary clothing, but he's still wearing the same ridiculous renaissance outfit Brisa had picked for him. It doesn't surprise me. Seb has always cared about appearing traditional, and tonight is especially important for his cause. If only he'd died with Brisa and the others, this would be so much easier.

I'm unmoving as I focus my hearing on the conversations, hoping for a sense of which vampires voted for which plan––mine and Mangus's, or Sebastian's. A few vamps are open with their opinions, but most have enough sense to keep their opinions to themselves. Tonight proves to be more of the same, though I can't say I blame anyone for skirting around the true reason we're all here. One never knows when an enemy could be plotting, and even friends can't be trusted when they have too much time on their hands. Even my own coven back home is growing restless without me.

I've been in contact with them daily, but if I don't return soon, they'll find reasons to doubt my leadership.

"Are you ready for this?" Mangus slides up next to me. He's one of several who were tasked with making sure the votes were properly counted, and the man looks exhausted. If only vampires could sleep, I'd send him away for a week's worth of slumber, but perhaps the dark circles under his eyes have more to do with grief and less to do with the election.

I nod once. "The courtiers aren't going to let this go if they lose tonight," I say. "Are you prepared to fight for this, Mangus?"

He nods. "I couldn't care less about the court. At this point, they can all burn in hell. Most of them are lazy, entitled leeches."

"Tell me how you really feel."

He's right, of course. Everyone from Brisa's court has attended the meetings that we've held over the last two days. We've debated about how to proceed since her death, and the courtiers have been the most vocal about clinging to a royal system. They hate that we're putting this to a vote that includes all coven leaders. If they had it their way, they'd be the only ones who get a say. And then, of course, there are the vampires who want to break away––coven leaders who see no reason to be governed by others.

Mangus snorts. "Do you know how long I've spent pretending to like these people?" He points to a group of courtiers dressed in the same regalia as Sebastian. They're grouped up together, their noses held high.

I shoot him a hard look because, for one thing, I do know how that feels, but more importantly, he needs to keep his mouth shut. Especially now that we're so close to an uprising.

"Okay, yeah, yeah, I get it," he relents. "I'll hold on a little longer."

"There are many here I don't recognize." I nod to some of the coven leaders. They've traveled from all around the globe, a mix of ages, genders, shapes, sizes, and ethnicities. I haven't admitted it to Mangus, but the diversity has given me a measure of hope. Mangus knows many of them since he was always on the move at Brisa's bidding. His contacts have served us well throughout the debates, but it's become clear that most of the queenless court will do anything to keep their status. There's no vampire court if there's no king or queen, so they see a vampiric council as a threat, especially the ones who aren't coven leaders.

Mangus saunters off to the drinks table, snatching up an entire bottle of bloody wine. When Mangus turned out to be alive, Sebastian had been utterly floored that he'd been so wrong about everything. Mangus, on the other hand, had nearly ripped Seb's head off. Katerina is dead because Sebastian had insisted she was responsible for the princes being killed off. But everyone had gotten it wrong, and none of us have been able to figure out what really happened. It was probably hunters, but we can't know for sure, and without Brisa to investigate, we may never know the truth.

A human fledgling scurries up to me and bows low, her sheath of perfect hair shining like glass under the candlelight. She's Sebastian's, and I'm surprised he hasn't turned her by now. "The live feed is all set up," she says in a sultry voice. "We're ready to go."

"Thank you." I peel myself from the doorframe and stride to the front of the room, eyeing the camera on the tripod.

Sometimes technology amazes me, sometimes it feels like we've always had it, and sometimes I want nothing to do with it. Tonight, I'm grateful. While many coven leaders traveled here, most had downright refused. There are over two thousand covens, and many leaders worry about their safety, refusing to venture from home. They're smart to stay back. With so many of us in one place, we're primed for an attack. But it's not hunters that worry me. Whichever way the vote goes, a lot of vampires will be unhappy.

Someone scurries forward and hands me a microphone. I tap on it, and the sound thumps through the room. I hope whatever I say will bring our kind closer together instead of splintering us further apart. The solution Mangus and I have proposed is so simple. One governing system with universal laws, covens operating as they are now, and all vampire-run businesses paying fair share in taxes and blood donations so we can keep our people healthy and a strong Vampire Enforcement Coalition tasked with enforcement. But with so many egos involved, egos who want a royal family to run things, there's a good chance none of this will happen.

And Sebastian has the biggest ego of them all.

He claims the three of us princes should take over, but I'm sure he'd just kill us and instate himself as king. I've been around long enough to know how royal families actually work.

I clear my throat as someone hands me a sealed envelope. The crowd quiets and watches in anticipation as I tear it open and read the contents, careful to keep my face a mask of indifference.

"Thank you all for being here and for your votes. We polled all the courtiers and every coven leader to come to this agreement, and we demand that you respect the outcome." Some nod their heads while others do nothing. The energy in the room grows impossibly tense. "Let it be known that a majority vote has been reached. With a vote of seventy percent, you have chosen a democratic vampiric council to replace the monarchy."

A few people voice their dissent, but many more cheer their approval. I have to fight back a grin. "The council will consist of Brisa's three remaining princes––me, and my brothers, Mangus and Sebastian. We will be joined by six other leaders representing the six continents." Vampires don't live on

Antarctica, but everywhere else in the world has thousands, and the amounts are roughly the same from continent to continent. "The leaders of each continent will be voted into power by the coven leaders presiding over their respective continent. Elections will be held every ten years, and council leaders can be reelected."

"What happens if one of the princes dies?" a courtier calls out.

"If one of the princes were to perish, then the seat would remain vacant. However, if there isn't an odd number of council seats, then the council may bring in a new member but only if all council members agree on who that vampire will be."

Silence . . . because this effectively *ends* the monarchy.

"This isn't our way!" someone shouts, and then another vamp responds, "Times have changed, you old git!"

"Enough," I roar into the microphone and glare out at the crowd. "It has also been voted that if you choose to leave the protection of the council at any time, you will be hunted down by the VEC and brought before a tribunal." The room falls to silence, and several vampires send me death-glares. "The VEC is hereby instructed to enforce our laws by any means necessary."

A few more people grumble, and I drop the paper, speaking to them now as a man. "These results should come as no shock. Many have wanted to create a different system for years. We loved our queen, but she is gone now, and her royal blood bond is irreplaceable. It's time we step forward into the future. We did it eighteen years ago, and we do it again today."

I get a few cheers from that. I clear my throat and continue. "It's also been voted by a margin of sixty percent that all of Brisa's laws will stay in effect until the first council meeting, at which time they'll be voted on by your elected leaders and princes. Elections are to be held by January first, and the council's official commencement meeting will take place at an undisclosed time and location shortly after."

People start talking again, throwing names around about who should represent their continents. Most of the courtiers are European, and they're the loudest of them all. Several are standing and throwing their arms about, making claims and nominations.

"I'm not done," I roar, and the crowd reluctantly quiets. "Let it be known that anyone convicted of attempting to usurp the council and stage a coup will be given true death by way of the sun."

Silence . . . *finally.*

"That is all." I put the microphone down, and the buzz returns. I nod to Mangus in the back of the room and start toward the exit. We need to talk in private about Eva. Now that this has been taken care of, I need to get to her.

Using Brisa's access to video surveillance and radar logs, Mangus was able to track her to the Italian coast. He's agreed to help me get her back. In a way, I think this has become a means for him to process what happened to his wife. He couldn't save Kat, but Eva still has a chance.

A throat clears, and I swing back to find Sebastian with the microphone. I narrow my eyes at the man who's always been a thorn in my side.

"There is one last thing that needs to be brought up before we end this proceeding," he says, voice sweeping through the crowd. They quiet for him in a way that they didn't for me and it makes me want to scream. "There's still the unfortunate matter of *how* our beloved queen lost her life."

I go utterly still. Mangus appears next to me and tugs me closer to the edge of the room. "We don't need to be the center of attention right now," he whispers under his breath, but I want nothing more than to storm up there and knock the microphone from Seb's greedy fingers.

"As some of you may know, but many do not, I was there when it happened," he goes on, pressing a hand to his chest as if the memory pains him. "It took me a week to heal my wounds, and I'm lucky to be alive. My poor prodigy was able to get me out, though, and I owe her my life."

He nods toward the pretty human woman who'd helped me earlier, then finds my gaze and smiles cruelly. "As you know, many were not so lucky as I, our beloved queen among them."

Beloved? No. Feared and respected, but never loved.

"I wouldn't have believed it if I hadn't seen it myself," he goes on. "But Brisa wasn't staked, she was burned by sunlight." Whispers erupt, and I'm seconds away from ripping the man's head off. But in such a public setting, there's nothing I can do to stop him now. "You see, Brisa was in the middle of creating a new child. Her first in centuries and the only daughter she ever wanted."

My throat goes dry. "No," I whisper and Mangus shakes his head once.

"The human girl that Brisa was attempting to change was part nephilim." More murmurs. Those with angelic blood are not always easy to spot, but I had sensed something different in Eva the moment I'd met her, and had confirmed it when I'd tasted her blood during our first kiss. It was a big part of why I chose her to spy on Tate for me. She wasn't just another one of his human pawns, she was something more, even if she didn't know it. Of course, Brisa had confirmed everything and then tried to take Eva for herself.

Sebastian wipes a tear from his eye. An actual tear!

"Oh hell, what a load of crap," I mutter.

"It was during the middle of the ritual when blood had already been exchanged that the nephilim's hands began to glow."

448

I knew something would happen when she tried to turn a neph, but didn't know what exactly. My stomach hardens at Sebastian's description of the events. This is not good for Eva. It changes everything.

"Evangeline Blackwood is her name. And her angelic power replicated that of the sun. She used it to attack and kill our queen."

People are talking now. Some don't believe it, but most do. Some are afraid, but most are angry. I still don't know how to feel.

"I've never heard of such a thing," I speak up, striding toward my brother against my better judgment. Mangus winces but follows after me. "How can you be sure it was the sun?"

"Are you questioning me?" He laughs bitterly. "I'm not surprised. Ladies and gentlemen, Eva was supposed to be Adrian's child, but Brisa took her from him. He's only defending her because he wants her for himself."

I won't deny it, but I won't admit it either. "If you're mistaken, then you would be hunting down an innocent. And how do we know that's what really happened when you were the only witness? It's her word against yours."

"My fledgling survived," he challenges. "She's a witness."

"She's your witness! She's your fledgling! We all know they'll do anything to please us."

"So you're claiming Eva is innocent? She's hardly innocent! She's a neph with the sun in her fingers, and she needs to be brought to justice."

"And she's very much alive!" Someone comes striding into the room, and I turn to find the vampire I threw into a lake instead of killing. She skips up to Sebastian and kisses his cheek. "I saw her alive, and so did you." She glares at me. I'm waiting for her to call me out on what happened that night at the castle, but she doesn't say anything. Sebastian had sent his minion after my girl, and he needs to pay for it.

"I felt her power," the woman continues, addressing the crowd. "My father speaks the truth."

"There hasn't been a light-bearer in generations," Sebastian says. "If she is what I think she is, then this could change everything." The term light-bearer presses at me like a knife. It's a legacy among the neph, and if Eva really is one, she'll never rest another day in her life. Everyone will want a piece of her. "Evangeline Blackwood is one of two things to us. She's either our greatest enemy, in need of snuffing out," the crowd likes that idea, "or she's our greatest weapon that we must possess."

"And what would you do with her?" someone calls out.

"Trust me with her and I'll give you the one thing our queen never could." His grin spreads like an ink stain. "I'll harvest her power for ourselves, and together, we will once again walk in the sunlight."

Nineteen

Staying away from Felix and Seth proves to be impossible because they're swapped out for my current guards. Tate insists it's to make me feel more comfortable, but I don't believe that for a second. He's trying to tempt me into taking their energy. They sold me on this idea that they only "help" the humans who are ready to pass, but that's got to be a lie. I've reiterated that I won't do it, even on those humans who are dying, so what better way than to force it on me through sheer proximity?

If I don't give in, I'll eventually do it by accident, and I won't be able to directly blame anyone but myself. And then what? Will I be hooked on human energy? Will I want to do it more—trading one form of vampirism for another? Something terrible was unlocked within me when my hands glowed, and I want nothing more than to go back in time and undo all of this from ever happening. If only I could be like the nephilim whose gifts never emerge, living life thinking about ordinary stuff instead of worrying about sucking my friends dry. The De Luca family must really want my gift to come back, enough for them to force the issue.

"Hey, I need to talk to you guys about something in private," I whisper to Felix and Seth as we finish up dinner a week into their new assignment.

We're given free time most evenings which the three of us use to hang out in my room and watch movies. I've even tried to keep my distance from the other nephilim, but Remi keeps showing up. She's crashed most of our movie nights, so I need to take my friends somewhere she won't check right away.

"Is everything okay?" Felix's voice is brimming with concern as he slings an arm around my shoulder. He might not be so kind after I tell him the truth, and I savor the friendly gesture while I can. It was a little strained at first, but after a few days, things between us went back to how they were before we dated. It's nice to have my friend back, and I want to keep it that way.

But a week of having them as my constant companions has made this secret unbearable. A primal need is building, urging me to taste their energy. My instinct says it'll be as easy as breathing, not something I'll have to practice or study. Something that will happen the second I let the floodgates down. They deserve to know the risks.

"Not here." I feel like everywhere I go in the Casa someone is watching me. Listening in. Waiting for the moment to strike. The De Luca family lives all over the world, but this is their home base, and Camilla called them all here only recently. They won't confess why, but from their lingering stares, I suspect it has something to do with me and my power.

"Let's go swimming," I offer. "It'll be the perfect place to talk." The weather has grown bitter over the last few weeks, turning most people off from wanting to swim in the cool pool water. If Remi comes looking for us, she probably won't check there first.

"Sure," Seth says in an agreeable tone that surprises me. The guy still hasn't warmed up to me. He's here for the job and for Felix. Not me.

I eye his blushing cheeks and fight back a smile. I know exactly why he's keen on the idea of swimming. Witnessing Felix in swim trunks is a real treat; I used to melt every time the Moreno's would take me along to the pool.

We go back to our rooms and then head down to the pool twenty minutes later. I smile at the empty room. I love being right. It's just us tonight. Nobody to pry, nobody to tattle. I slide into the cool water, and Felix cannonballs in. Seth chuckles and jumps in after him. We swim for a few minutes, and before I know it, I'm making unnecessary waves again.

"You okay there?" Seth stops me. "Is this an angel blood thing?"

I shake my head. "I actually think it's a vampire venom thing." I quickly change the subject to why I brought them here. "I wanted to talk to you guys about something important. Something that you won't like." I swallow hard, and the three of us swim to the edge of the pool. I lean against the side and let my legs drift up. I can't bring myself to look them in the eye, so I gaze off toward the closed door.

"So what is it?" Seth prods.

Now or never. "Do you remember the energy demon things? I know we talked about this before, but then Tate tampered with things, so I'm not really sure--"

"The what?" Felix questions.

"The energy demons?"

They stare at me, and I get the confirmation I need. Tate really did clear so much from their minds.

"Let me back up and explain," I say timidly. "Cameron Scout was the first one to alert me to them. They're people who steal energy from human auras, similar to how vampires take our blood."

"Auras?" Seth questions. "You mean the energy color things people are supposed to have around them? I didn't think those were real."

Felix's lips twist as he ponders.

"Okay, let me explain." I swim out to the middle of the pool and turn on them, "Auras are real, people can even take pictures of them, so let's not try to contest that, okay? An aura is like this energy field of color around a human. They change throughout the day depending on what's going on with someone, but the core colors tend to stay the same." I swallow hard, afraid I'm going to lose them. "Long story short, supernaturals don't have auras, and neither do the nephilim." I shrug. "I don't have one. I thought it was just that I couldn't see my own, but it turns out that it's because of the whole neph thing."

"You can see these auras?" Felix's eyes widen. I've got him curious. "Can you see mine right now?"

"If I think about it, yes, I can."

"What color is it?"

"Right now? Mainly blue. But that's not the point," I rush on. "Just let me explain. It turns out that nephilim can take energy from these auras."

Seth frowns. He's not sure about all this.

"I promise, they can. They do it to strengthen their gifts, but when they do it, it hurts the human."

"Have you done it?" Seth asks.

"No, not yet, and I don't want to, but there's this voice inside screaming at me to try. This is why I wanted to bring you somewhere private to talk. I think Tate brought you here to tempt me. He wants me to get a taste of your energies."

Felix shakes his head. "No, Tate wouldn't do anything to hurt us."

"He's right. Tate is on our side."

I scoff. "Are you kidding me? You're in constant danger because of him. Why do you trust someone who––"

"You're wrong," Seth's interruption is harsh. "We don't have anything to worry about, and you shouldn't either."

"Come on, let's go. It's getting too cold in here anyway," Felix sounds almost robotic, but sure enough, they climb out of the pool, going for the towels like our conversation didn't happen.

452

They shift from being stiff and defensive to relaxed and their normal selves in a matter of seconds, then turn to wait for me. I'm flabbergasted, and anger burns through me as realization dawns. Of course, this was always going to happen. I should've realized it sooner. Tate has used his memory manipulation and persuasion ability on my friends as he's done time and time again. They're never going to believe me. And if they do, it won't be long until he's back, whispering things in their ears.

As I climb from the pool, tears splash down my cheeks, mixing with the pool water. Nobody says a word. And then I'm struck with a heartbreaking thought--do they actually care about me? When they first came here, they didn't seem all that happy to see me, especially not Seth. Their forgiveness came quickly and easily. What if everything has been against their free will? Suddenly, their friendship feels like another one of Tate's lies. They're here because of him, not because of me, and I have no idea how to make it stop.

Twenty

"We have a surprise for you," Remi beams, taking my hand and leading me outside after dinner.

It's officially been three weeks since I arrived at the Casa, and I'm no closer to figuring out how to access my power, let alone finding my mom or helping my human friends break free of Tate's hold. I'm caught in an endless loop, waiting for something to happen, and I can't keep up the charade much longer.

Warm happiness pulses through me with the squeeze of her hand, and I push the emotion away. She frowns. "I just want to help you to relax. You've been so uptight lately, Eva."

I drop her hand and sigh, gazing up at the night sky sprinkled with stars, but the winter wind whips my hair back and brandishes my skin with goose-bumps. Even though I'm wearing a coat, it's not enough to combat the cold. The burn of venom is still strong but I only enjoyed the cold during those three awful days and nights. I fight the urge to tell Remi off and run back inside. "I know you do, and while I appreciate you wanting to help me feel more comfortable, I need to be the one in charge of my emotions."

"Alright, I get that." She sounds dejected.

"What's the surprise?" I try to make my voice honey-sweet, but I'm pretty sure it comes out as bitter as vinegar. "I promise I'm excited," I go on, "I'm just not used to this cold and I'm being a baby about it."

That, and she's right, I *am* uptight. Who wouldn't be in this situation?

"It will be worth the crappy weather, I promise." She grins and turns to motion Felix and Seth closer. They're always nearby since guarding me is their job now, and I hate that I can't call Tate out on it. Not yet anyway. But soon enough, I will. I just have to find leverage first, a reason to get him to do what I want. There's got to be something I can use against Tate. Nobody's innocent, and I'm sure Tate has more secrets than most in this house.

Remi leads us out on the big lawn in the back of the Casa where a crowd is gathering. All the students and most of the household staff mingle in tight-knit groups, all dressed in lush winter attire. There are generations of wealth here, and I'd stick out like a sore thumb if it weren't for the fact that Camilla had my closet outfitted with the same luxurious clothing. Tonight, I'm dressed in thick tights, a soft camel-colored cable-knit sweater dress, matching boots, and a black peacoat. My outfit isn't half as extravagant as my peers' but I feel more put together than I ever used to back home.

Gentry gives our group a little wave, his eyes landing on Seth and a dimpled smile lighting his face. He's with his crew, and Bella swats his arm down, hissing something I can't hear. There are not many students here, but most seem indifferent to my presence, and the De Luca family is a mixed bag of kindness and distrust. Besides Remi, Gentry is the nicest person I've met, and Bella and her brother Greyson are the worst.

"Are you ready for this?" Remi giggles, pointing back to the Casa. Just as she does, the entire building lights up with twinkling gold holiday lights. Everyone cheers, and I admit it makes me smile too. It's beautiful. Orchestra music starts playing over outdoor speakers, and something else lights up behind me––a towering Christmas tree, glittering with red and green orna-ments, and more gold lights.

"Wow, this is amazing," I gush, filled with awe and longing all at once.

"Isn't it?" She squeezes my hand. "Camilla loves the holidays and deco-rates to the nines every year."

Sure enough, the crowd splits, and Camilla stands at the base of the tree. Her family goes to her first, offering congratulations and kisses. I don't want to be rude, so I follow Remi over. Truth be told, I've avoided Camilla as often as possible except for getting help with my mom's whereabouts. Ever since that woman peered into my mind and sifted through my memories, it's hard to want to be around her. Great hospitality only goes so far when you're sure you're being manipulated. I've tried to trust everything they're teaching me here, to lean into this new role in my life, but it's been hard. I still have my walls up.

"How are you enjoying your time here?" Camilla asks after I compliment her on her beautiful decorating.

"It's been great," I say, not trusting her with the truth that I'm still both-ered by a lot of things. "Thanks again for allowing me to stay here."

Her eyes slide over my face and a bit of that kindness dissolves into a sharp stare, confirming my intuition about her. "I've been following your progress. No light has come back into your hands, not even when you're on your own? Or perhaps by accident?"

I shake my head. "Sorry to disappoint."

"You know what you need to do, do you not?" Her eyes flick to where Felix and Seth are standing, and my stomach hardens.

"If you're asking me to hurt anyone, I won't do it." I fold my arms over my chest and glare. "Besides, you insisted that you only take from those who are already terminal. Are you telling me that was a lie?"

Her face hardens. "That's how we usually replenish our energy stores, but every once in a while we do what's necessary. Humans are far more resilient that you might think, Eva. They bounce back quickly. A little siphoned energy here and there hardly hurts them. And wouldn't you agree that the good of humanity outweighs the experience of a few individuals?"

My stomach twists. So they were lying.

"Anyway, dear, nobody is going to make you do it." She tilts her head and smiles sweetly. "But if you would like a lesson, I'd be happy to be of service. We could even take you to the local hospital. In fact, Greyson is going tomorrow, I'm sure he'd show you the ropes."

I shake my head and stomp away, perhaps making an ass of myself, and definitely being rude to the hostess, but I don't care. Cat's out of the bag—they want my power and want me to be willing to do whatever it takes to get it, even going against their own supposed code of ethics.

"You think you're better than us?" I turn to find Tate's bratty children glowering at me. Bella is full-on glaring, and of course it's Greyson standing there with his typical judgmental sneer. His hands are stuffed into his pockets, and his black curls hang around sunken cheeks. Something about him isn't right, and I realize he might be ill. Maybe that's why he's going to the hospital tomorrow and the others aren't. There's more going on with him than anyone has let on, and I want to figure out what it is.

"I don't think I'm better than anyone," I reply. "But I'm nobody's pawn either."

Bella's laugh is bitter. "Everyone is a pawn, but that's the point. Don't you get that? We work together to win the bigger game, and the sooner you do your part to help out, the sooner—"

"Let's go," Greyson interrupts, his eyes zeroing in on his sister. "Eva's not going to change her mind."

He grabs her and drags her away to their father across the lawn, who whispers something harsh into her ear by the way she stiffens. All three turn to look at me, and I force myself to continue inside. I'm so angry, I could scream. I open and close my fists, something warm tingling between my fingers.

Light. It streams from my fingertips like golden laser beams. I squeal, and then it flashes to darkness seconds later. I almost run back out to tell Camilla, but I don't. She doesn't deserve to know.

"Woah, what's wrong with you?" Felix stops me, and Seth's mouth flattens into a thin line. I quickly close my hands and open them again, but the light is still gone. I don't have control over it, but my heart is bursting with excitement.

"I did it," I breathe out, hardly believing it myself. "You saw that, right?"

"Oh, we saw that," Seth says. He blinks, almost like he's coming out of a stupor. "This place is something else, isn't it?"

"This is what I've been trying to tell you." I widen my eyes at them. "I don't think you guys are here by your own free will and choice. I don't think it's safe for you."

Blank faces––*once again* I'm met with blank faces. I want to scream, but I force a steadying breath instead. Both of their auras have grown brighter and larger, a mix of colors swirling around the three of us.

"If you feed on the energy, you will be more powerful." Chloe appears next to me, seemingly out of nowhere. I jump and turn on her.

"I'm not going to do that," I rush out. Felix and Seth look on, confused.

"You sure? There's ways we can do it that doesn't cause much harm. I can show you how."

"No," I insist.

"I understand where you're coming from." She twists her lips and nods toward my hands. "But I saw that too, you know. That's a good sign."

"What does it mean?"

But she doesn't say. Her face falls, a flash of concern in her eyes, and then she scrambles off before I can get another question in. I make a mental note to look for her tomorrow and demand answers, but the next day comes, and Chloe is nowhere to be found. And when I ask after her, nobody will tell me a thing.

Twenty-One

6∿

We're finishing a decadent Christmas dinner, and I'm grateful to be safe, but I'm sick with worry for my mom and friends, and in the back of my mind I know vampires are out there looking for me. I'm tired of living like this, days spent exercising, trying to find ways to pass the time, with most of the lessons being interesting but not all that helpful. The holidays have deepened my homesickness, and I'm ready for things to be different.

"Merry Christmas," Camilla calls down the long dining table, raising her glass. We all raise ours in kind, saying cheers to new year's wishes coming true. The bubbly champagne does nothing to lift my spirits.

"Now, are you ready for your gift?" Camilla continues, her eyes sparkling with yuletide mischief. "We've arranged to leave the Casa and travel to a party tonight." The room erupts into excited whispers, and I have no idea what this could mean, but I'll admit my curiosity is piqued.

I can hardly eat a bite as my stomach twists in knots. Everyone else must feel the same way because a lot of half-eaten meals are left behind as we flounce off to get ready for the party and congregate at the front of the house. It's a semi-formal event, and I've chosen an emerald green velour gown that hugs my curves perfectly but still covers me enough to keep me warm. The family stylist piled my hair atop my head, and went extra smoky with the makeup. I feel beautiful as I slip into one of the SUVs waiting in the drive and hope the party can cheer me up.

The second we leave the Casa gates behind, I breathe a sigh of relief. I'm acutely aware that I should be feeling the opposite. We're leaving the safety of the family estate *in the dark*, but I can't help but feel better. I know I'm not a prisoner, but sometimes it feels that way, and the cabin fever has been bad lately.

The roads are windy and steep, bordered on either side by beautiful Italian homes all lit up and sea-weathered stone walls shadowed by lush greenery. Even on a dark winter's night, this city is gorgeous. I'm hit with a pang of longing in my chest, a need to explore the world, to experience more than I've been allowed.

We pull up to a large ornate burnt-orange building with a stream of stylish cars already parked in the drive. Ivy climbs up one side, and lights flicker from the many windows. It's warm and welcoming, and I can't wait to get inside. Climbing from the SUV, I spot Remi and hurry over to her, Felix and Seth on my heels.

"What kind of party is this?" I ask. "Is there going to be dancing?"

Her smile falters, and my heart falls. There's something more going on here, something she knows I'm not going to like. "You'll see," is all she says, and then we're ushered up the stone steps and into the warm building.

There are humans everywhere, all immaculately dressed, partying in a huge ballroom. My fingers itch, and my heart thuds as I take it all in. Everyone is so stylish, milling about with champagne flutes in their hands as if they haven't a care in the world. A few rosy-cheeked children are running amok between the adults, most likely high on Christmas cheer and sugar. A string orchestra is set up in the far corner, and couples are dancing nearby. A buffet that could feed an army sits opposite the orchestra. And everything is tied together with decorations of green and red. I catch the scent of pine trees and sugar cookies, and breathe it in deeply, savoring the moment.

The others don't hold back. They join the party seamlessly, mixing with the humans, many of them talking like they're old friends. I stand back to survey the auras. Everyone is practically glowing, they're so happy, so vibrant, so alive. I don't think I've ever seen so many people in one place. And then the colors begin to shift and change as the nephilim feed.

"I'm sorry. This is just the way it's done," Remi says, still at my side and practically reading my mind. Seth and Felix are a few paces off, but I'm sure they can hear our conversation. I'm not sure it will matter.

"Camilla lied to me." I clear my throat, my cheeks going hot. "Tate lied to me. They all did."

"If it's any consolation, they weren't totally lying. We don't normally do things this way," Remi continues.

"It's not," I huff.

Chloe floats up next to us. She came back on Christmas Eve from wherever she was, but I haven't had a chance to talk to her yet. "Good to have you back," I say. "Where did you go?"

She shrugs. "I had an assignment for my grandmother. No big deal."

"You left Italy?"

Her eyes flash and she laughs. "You're nosy tonight. If you must know, I was in New York City. Some of our friends needed my help with new recruits."

I can only imagine what that means.

Of all the De Luca grandchildren, Chloe's my favorite, but I still can't trust her as far as I can throw her. She turns her button-lipped smile on me. "But like I told you before I left, I can teach you ways of feeding on the humans' energy that won't hurt them that bad."

Remi goes red and looks away, which only confirms what I already think.

"Does it hurt them or not? Because hurting someone innocent without their consent is still messed up."

Chloe frowns, but doesn't say anything more, and that's all the answer I need. She may have found some tricks, but the fact still remains that they're stealing the life-force right out of people to help fuel themselves.

And part of me longs to do the same.

Fists clenched, I march over to Camilla, ready to give her a piece of my mind, when Tate intercepts me. He grabs me by the elbow and pulls me to the edge of the party. "This was all for you. Don't look so ungrateful," he hisses.

"I never asked for this," I snap back.

"If you don't feed soon, do you know what's going to happen to you?"

"Guess I'll find out, because I'm never going to feed." I rip my arm from his grasp.

He mutters something in Italian before locking me in with his stare. His whole demeanor has changed––gone is the charismatic father figure that I'd so foolishly trusted. A manipulative liar stands over me, but I refuse to shrink or back down.

"You need to build your strength and get control of your power. Don't you want to do as God intended?"

"Oh, so you have proof that God intended for me to hurt people?" I glare, throwing up my hands. "News flash, Leslie, I don't see God anywhere around here."

"The humans hardly notice their energy leaving them, and they have more than enough to spare. And what we're doing by ridding the world of evil? It's for them."

I motion to the crowd, raising an eyebrow. The energy in the room has started to shift, and already the merriment is being siphoned away. The nephilim are sure getting their fill, though; they look great. "You're not going to convince me."

He bares his teeth. "If I could make you do it, I would. But I can't, so I'll continue to give you opportunity after opportunity until eventually your body wears down enough for you to feed. Don't you see, Eva? You need this. You need the energy, the fuel for your gift. And you have no idea what you're missing."

"Stop lying to me, then." That gets his attention. He goes eerily still as I continue, "Why can't I get ahold of my mother?"

He blinks, startled by my sudden change in conversation. "We're not lying about that," he says defiantly. "We don't know where she is. Believe me, if we did, you'd be the first to know." There's an undercurrent of threat to his tone that sets me on edge. Goosebumps prickle across my flesh.

"What's all this about?" Dario De Luca appears next to us, oozing his typical sliminess. There's something about him that sets me the most on edge, even more so than what I feel around Tate and Camilla. Fortunately, he's kept his distance since our first introduction, but now he's standing too close with probing questions in his gaze. He pats Tate on the back. "What? Is my mother putting pressure on you to get your newest acquisition in line?" He chuckles low.

Tate brushes him off and shoots me another scathing look. "Don't forget, you need our help. Do as you are asked or find someone else to keep you alive."

He stalks off, and Dario laughs again. His stare is just as cold as the others, and his creep factor hasn't eased in the slightest, but at least he's upfront about his feelings toward me. It's obvious he'd rather see me dead than in the Casa. He's never once smiled at me or pretended to want me around, and the few times we do make eye contact, his are glaring daggers. It's so strange that many of these people hate me, and I still haven't figured out why.

"Tell me, Eva, have you learned about the angelic-factions yet?" He takes a casual sip of his champagne.

"Factions?" This is news.

"Figures," he snorts. "Okay, let me be the one to clue you in. We nephilim aren't the most agreeable bunch. We fight amongst ourselves almost as much as we fight the supernaturals. Ironic, isn't it?"

My mouth pops open.

"Nothing to say?" He takes another long swig of his drink. "And you *just so happened* to be picked up by the most powerful faction in Europe, and I'd argue the most powerful in the world, though, some other factions would disagree."

The way he said "just so happened" makes it sound like it was anything but a coincidence. "Why are you telling me this?"

"Because the truth is, if you don't get in line here, my mother will send you off to one of our allied families to be dealt with, and let me tell you, none of them are going to put you up in a nice house, educate you, and take you to parties." He raises his glass out to the people around us, and my eyes land on Seth and Felix. They're dancing with a couple of others, no longer worried about me. "Your gift will be *forced* out, and while my brother-in-law is a brown-nosing pain in my ass, he's also right." He steers me into the crowd, hand firmly on my back. "Now, be a good little girl and do as you're told, or we'll stop asking nicely."

"Did you ever stop to think that maybe the reason your factions fight is because you're doing something wrong here? Maybe the power is corrupting you."

That makes him laugh. "You could be right, but it doesn't change anything."

Felix turns from his dance partner, and Dario shoves me into his arms. Felix's eyes are glossy as my childhood crush looks down at me, his mouth slack. He leads me in a dance, oblivious to what's really going on here. Tears prick at my eyes, and an inferno burns in my chest. I don't want to do this, any of it, and they're going to make me do it to one of my oldest friends.

I can't.

I rip away from Felix and fall into the arms of a human I don't recognize. The handsome man smiles ruefully down at me and begins speaking in Italian. I tell him I don't understand, and he laughs, but continues to speak so quickly it all blends together. His grip on me is tight as he spins me across the dance floor. I grow dizzy, my chest burning with a primal need to feed on him. His turquoise aura surrounds me, and I can feel the electric pulse of it tickling my senses. I don't want this, I don't, I don't . . . but I do. And before I can stop myself, I'm letting the turquoise flood me, like diving into the sea. The energy fills me up quickly, endorphins bursting with exuberance and life.

I want more, but my guilt is instant, and I rip away from the young man, rushing from the ballroom.

Someone laughs as I go, but I don't look to see who. It doesn't matter. They won. I did it. I did it, and it felt amazing, and I hate myself for it. I may not be a vampire, but I've become just like the very monsters I hate the most. And still, even now, the longing to go take more of that sparkly turquoise energy is stronger than ever. It whispers assurances that I'll eventually go back for more.

I search for an exit, needing fresh air, to be alone, but I can't find one that isn't surrounded by people, so I run to a stairwell instead, climbing up, up, up. My legs don't burn like they used to before everything happened. I'm so full of venom and that energy that I don't know if I'll ever feel pain again, save for my own hurt pride. I slam through a door and stumble out onto a bare rooftop. The cool air is instant salvation, and I lap it in, praying it will calm my nerves.

I drop my head between my knees, panting, crying, about to scream. What have I done?

Twenty-Two

ADRIAN

For weeks I've been trying to get her back, and now here she is, a goddess with the warm light of the opened door illuminating her silhouette. I swallow hard at the stark thought that she's the most gorgeous creature I've ever seen, that I'd kneel down and worship her right now if I could. And then she doubles over, a cry strangling her body, and I'm frozen. I don't know what to do––I *never* don't know what to do.

She can't see me, and I want nothing more than to go to her. I don't. I stay hidden in the shadows, watching. Waiting. The door slams, light disappearing, and then I can see all of her. Her cheeks are wet with tears, and she's clenching her chest like she's been shattered and is clinging onto the broken pieces. I've never seen her like this. I'm momentarily stunned.

The desire to save her slams through me. I could grab her and leave, even if she fights me. It wouldn't be easy, but I'd do it for her. To get her away from these people who are clearly using her––harming her. But I know Eva too well. She'd fight me every step of the way, and I need her to come with me willingly.

In the time it took me to find out where she was and get to her, I realized that taking her against her will won't give me the results I want. She needs to trust me––to believe me. She'll never do either if I force her.

She strides to the edge of the roof and stares out over the city. We're five stories up, and the vast lawn below sweeps out to the glittering lights of more buildings and then the darkness of the sea beyond. I wish I could go there with her. Take her someplace where there's nobody but us for miles. I rather like the ocean at night with its high tides and pounding waves. It doesn't scare me like it did when I was a boy. Would it frighten her? Or would she find solace in it like I do? We could find a secluded beach, lay in the cool sand and watch the clouds roll by, waiting for a glimpse of the stars, and then we could fly away.

She breaks out in a sob and it's like being shaken awake. I can't wait any longer. This may be my only chance to get her alone.

I step from the shadows, making sure my shoes rub against the concrete. She turns and gasps, eyes wide and face full of surprise. And then it falls and anger takes over. "Adrian," she says coolly, "what are you doing here?"

"I came to give you something."

She extends her hand, her features going hard, but I can hear the thumping of her heart as it accelerates. Her blood is hot and ready for the taking, but that's no longer what I want from her. "Hand it over then."

I cock my head. "So that's it, then?" I say cockily. "You're not going to ask me how I've been? No catching up for old time's sake?"

She narrows her eyes. "I think we're past fake pleasantries. If you're not here to kill me, then give me whatever it is you want to give me and leave."

"Don't you want to know about the vampires? Aren't you curious what's happened since you ran off with *them*?"

"Them?" she scoffs. "You mean the nephilim––of which you failed to tell me I was one of?"

"Brisa forbade us to speak of them or I would've told you." I step closer, and she steps back, the push and pull between us tugs at unseen wounds. But what was I expecting? She hates me, as she should. I hurt her. I made things so much worse for her. Omitted the truth. Lied at times.

She hates me.

"Fine. Whatever," she says. "I know the truth now. They've told me all about it. I've even been taking lessons."

I laugh bitterly. "Lessons, huh? You can't trust them or their lessons." To see her defend them so readily sets me off my axis. I wasn't expecting this, and now I'm spiraling out of control, seconds away from making her leave with me, the plan be damned.

"At least they told me what I am."

"I hardly doubt they told you everything you need to know." I stride to her in two long steps, no longer able to keep my distance. I pull her up against me and she yelps, but doesn't push me away. Our bodies are flush, and her intoxicating scent calls to me like a drug. "Come with me, and I'll tell you everything," I promise. "I'll answer any question, every question. Anything at all."

"No more secrets?" Her mouth parts, and I'm distracted by her blushing lips. I need to kiss her.

"No more secrets." I lean down to taste my angel, slowly so she has time to meet me halfway.

She shoves me back. Her strength has grown tenfold, and it sends me flying back. I catch myself and raise my hands in surrender. She's glaring daggers at me now, her face drawn in anger.

"Please," I growl. "Don't make me beg." A stab at my pride because I know I'll do it.

"I'll never trust you again, but I'm not stupid enough to trust the neph either. I don't think I'll trust another soul on this earth ever again, come to think of it. You should know me better than that, Adrian."

She's right. I should. *I do.* And it's my fault she's turning out this way. Me and my kind have done this to her.

I slip the little burner phone from my pocket and hold it out to her. She eyes it skeptically. "This isn't a trick. Take the phone. Call your mother. She knows the truth. She knows everything."

Her stoic mask slips, and the worry she's been harboring mars her pretty face. Part of me feels guilty for using Eva's love for her mother against her like this. She's already been through so much with that woman. But the other part of me knows this will work. If I can't get through to her, Virginia can.

"Let me guess, they can't find her?" I prod. "They've been trying for weeks, but she's nowhere to be found?"

She shakes her head and snatches the phone from my hand. Her voice cracks, "Thank you for finding her."

"You really don't get it, do you?" I say. "I didn't find her, Eva. I've been hiding her, keeping her safe."

"What?" Her mouth falls open.

"Right before we left for New Orleans she came to me, asking for my protection. I gave it to her," I shrug. "I should've told you before. It wasn't your fault you had to come to Versailles with me. I've made sure to keep your mom safe and your apartment rent paid. As for your job, that was a little trickier, but it's promised to you if you're ever able to return."

I don't have the heart to tell her things will never go back to what they were before. Now that Sebastian has every vampire in the world after her, Eva's chances at a normal life are all but decimated. But I'm holding onto her old life for her anyway, just in case. "Call her," I urge. "Call her when you're alone. Don't let anyone know you have that phone. And then call me. My number's in there too."

I hope it will be enough. And I hope she calls soon, because it's only a matter of time before the others track her here, and when that happens, I don't think the nephilim have enough precautions in the world to protect her. She's too valuable. The other vampires think they can use her ability to somehow get us back in the sun. It's enough to make the vampires do anything to get her, even attack one of our enemy's strongholds.

Before she can answer, I slip away, stepping off the edge of the roof and floating down to the lawn. I walk out into the quiet street, my mind a whirl at what just happened and my heart screaming at me to go back to her. I forgot I had a heart, to be honest, but here I am, willing to trade anything-- even the sun--for that woman.

But I must be patient. I've waited this long, haven't I? What's a few more days? Hell, she may even be calling me in a few hours. My number is one of the three programmed into that phone. And I'm not scared of their compound. I'll get her out of there one way or another. And then we'll go--

Something grabs me from all sides. Seering white-hot fire sizzles my flesh as silver ropes wrap around my entire body. I grapple for an escape, but they're heavy, and when I push on them they burn even harder. I blink against the netting, realizing what's happening. I drop to my knees and try to dig, but the street is solid frozen concrete, and my muscles are growing weak.

This can't be happening . . .

This . . .

"I thought perhaps you'd follow her here," a man says, and I blink up to see my nemesis, Leslie Tate, boasting over me. "Glad to see I was right."

"What do you want?" I gasp up at the man I've been hunting for the better part of three decades. He did me wrong, killing the last prodigy I had before Kelli, and I've been trying to enact my revenge ever since but he's kept himself well-protected. The irony that he's the one who's caught me isn't lost on me. I'm so angry I want to scream obscenities, but I don't have the strength. The silver even burns through my clothes, and the searing pain is so intense I can hardly breathe, let alone scream.

No answer.

The question dies off as my body succumbs, a darkness thicker than I've known taking me out to sea.

Twenty-Three

I stay up there for a few minutes, holding the phone in an iron-tight grip. Screw what Adrian said about waiting to call her, this is my lifeline, and I'm going to use it while I have the chance. The phone is one of those cheap burners, and I flip it open, finding three contacts listed—— Virginia, Adrian, and one cryptically titled "*In Case of Emergency.*"

The phone is fully charged, but I don't know enough about these kinds of phones to gauge how long I have before it dies. Could be days or hours, and I'm not in the habit of being patient. I click on all three contacts and commit the numbers to memory. It's surprisingly easy. I never had this kind of mental aptitude before the venom, and I'm thrilled with the results.

I toggle to my mom's contact and tap the call button. She answers on the first ring.

"Evangeline, is that you?" Her voice is more panicked than I've ever heard before, and my heart drops to my stomach.

"Yes," I gush, instantly in tears again. "It's me."

"Oh, thank God," her accent comes out thicker than usual through the tears that are surely rolling down her face. "I was so worried. Are you okay? Where are you?"

I turn around to face the door of the building, surveying the rooftop. I'm still alone out here. Edging as far from the door as I can, I start to whisper. "I'm in Italy. I'm staying with some people here who are keeping me safe from the vampires." I don't tell her that I'm okay because I don't have it in me to lie. I'm far from okay, but she sounds frantic, and I don't need to make it worse.

"What people in Italy?" she presses, voice dropping an octave.

"Didn't Adrian tell you?"

"I haven't talked to Adrian in weeks. He got me out in time and found me a safe place to hide out."

"Hide from what? What's going on, Mom? What aren't you telling me?"

She's quiet for a long moment. "Your father didn't die in a car accident, honey. He was murdered."

If the ground opened up and swallowed me whole, I'd be less surprised than this. "What?" I squeak out. My heartbeat pounds in my ears.

Her confession crashes over me like a tidal wave. I've never known much about my dad because it hurt her too much to talk about, but the one thing I did know for sure was that my father was killed in a car accident when I was a baby. "It wasn't safe to tell you," she continues. "The only one who knew the whole story was Gram."

"What's the story, Mom? Tell me!" My face is burning, and my body is floating. I'm about to drift away.

"Listen carefully," she says, growing serious. "When I met him, he told me his family was mafia and he'd gotten out, that he'd come to America because he wanted a fresh start away from all that. I fell hard for him, and I believed him, but he wasn't the man he said he was. He wasn't a bad man, but he wasn't mafia either."

"This doesn't make any sense. Why would someone lie about something like that?"

And then my mind catches on that word, and I think of my conversation with Tate that first day in his car.

"Because his family may as well have been the mafia for all the things they were mixed up in and all the pressure they put on him to carry on their legacy," she says bitterly. "They're nephilim, honey. Do you know what that means? It means they have angelic blood. I know it sounds crazy, but it's not. And you're a nephilim too, baby. He only ever told me the truth because I got pregnant and he wanted me to know what I was getting myself into with you."

"So all this time, you knew and you said nothing?" My heart drops.

"We wanted to protect you from it," she rushes on, "and it wouldn't have affected you until you got older when I thought I'd have him there to guide you through everything. When he died, my mother got a special talisman made. She gave it to you when we feared you'd come of age soon. It was meant to keep you from ever knowing what you are and from them ever finding you."

"The necklace?" It's back in a safe somewhere in Adrian's suite. I haven't

469

worn it since I left the country. "I figured out what it was, but not what it was supposed to protect me from." I never would've guessed.

"The witch she bought it from asked for a great price," Mom continues. "Something money couldn't buy."

Fear settles through me. "Just tell me."

"Gram's cancer wasn't just cancer," her voice cracks. "The witch got the last twenty years of her life in exchange for that talisman."

My heart sinks. And to think, I don't even have the necklace anymore. Her and Gram always insisted I wear it, and I usually did, but I didn't even fight Adrian when he took it away from me. Because it was shaped like a cross and would offend Brisa, I'd given up the protection. Did Adrian know what it really was?

"The crossing feathers on the back of the crucifix? Is that the talisman?"

"Yes," Mom continues. "It was magicked by the witch. But that doesn't matter now. What matters is you need to know the truth. You need to be safe."

"I don't necessarily like it here, but I'm pretty sure I'm safe. I don't want you to worry about me. I want you to worry about your own safety."

"I'm fine. But, honey, remember what I said about your father being murdered?"

"It was vampires wasn't it?" This time, my voice cracks. Another thing vampires took away from me.

"No," she replies. "It wasn't vampires. It was nephilim. I don't know a whole lot about them, but I do know most of them are bad. And his family were the worst of them all." She goes quiet for a minute, and I stand still, lost and frightened and missing my mom. "Honey, your father had a unique gift, and when he refused to use it any longer, his own family had him killed."

"What?" My mind spins. "What gift? Why kill him over something like that?"

"Because sometimes these gifts can only go to one person at a time. One dies with it and another is born with it."

My voice starts to shake, fear at what this gift could be. "Tell me. What was his gift?"

She sighs heavily. "Something to do with memory."

My head spins. I don't know what any of this means. "Mom, this sounds crazy. Are you sure he was murdered? Did you see it?"

"In a way," her voice is thick with tears. "It was a car, but it wasn't an accident. I was there, honey. He saved me, and then he held my hands as he was dying and took me to this place where he could show me the past."

Realization dawns on me, and my stomach twists. "Like--he took your hands and showed you the memories? Was it a white room, and then it was like you were standing there watching something happen in real time?"

"Yes, it was exactly like that."

I swallow hard, and my fingers go numb. I'm holding the phone too tight. "Oh no," I whisper slowly, dread building in my chest. "Mom, one of the people I'm staying with can do that exact same thing. They call her the record keeper." I think of beautiful Chloe. She's about my age, but almost a year younger. Could she have been born soon after my father passed away? Was she given his ability because he refused it?

I don't want to believe it, but it must be true.

"Who are you with?" Mom presses. "What are their names?"

"De Luca."

But that's not my father's last name . . .

So was it simply fate that Chloe was the one who got my father's ability when he died? Maybe it goes to the next nephilim child to be born, and she was that one. But then why have him killed for not helping? The way I see it, someone on the brink of childbirth could have had my dad killed with the hope that their son or daughter would get the record keeper gift next. Is that something the De Luca family would do? Would they kill their own son—my father—just to get their hands on this gift and keep it within their bloodline?

I get the answer with the sound of deafening silence on the other end of the phone. Mom's panic is palpable, and fear slices through me like a hot knife. "Mom—" I press on, "don't tell me it's the same family."

I'm staring out into the darkness, watching the lights twinkle from the city below. They blur behind my eyes, and my knees go weak. I need to sit down.

"We gave you a fake name," she whispers. "Your father was the oldest De Luca son, and he insisted we change our names, that we start fresh." All at once, she erupts. No more whispering, she's screaming. "You have to get out of there! Get away from them! They'll hurt you! They'll—"

Hands push me from behind. My waist hits the edge of the railing, but I'm not fast enough to catch myself. I careen over the edge, phone flying from my grip. And then I'm falling. So fast. The night swallowing me whole, and the ground reaching up to grant me death.

Twenty-Four

The impact never comes. I'm hovering a few feet off the ground, levitating like a certain blood-sucking vamp . . .

A stunned second after I realize what's happening, I lose control and plummet the rest of the way, hitting the ground with a smack. I groan, roll over, and sit up, frowning at the broken cell phone parts scattered around me. Thank heavens I memorized those numbers, but now I don't have a way to call anyone, and Mom has to be more worried than ever.

But at least I know the truth.

I peer up at the rooftop, searching for whoever just tried to kill me, but of course there's nothing to see but empty skyline and winking stars. I could try levitating up there, maybe catch whoever it was on their way down the stairs, but there's no chance I'm going to attempt to levitate again so quickly, and they're probably long gone. The best thing I can do is rejoin the party and see if anyone acts surprised to see me alive.

And then I have to figure out how to get away from the people who killed my father. One of their own. Flesh and blood. How could someone do that?

And to think, I'm one of them too. This is my long lost family, the family that put so much pressure on my parents to move back home when Mom was pregnant. The family that she's been hiding me from, that I thought had written us off. And here I've been staying with them for over a month with absolutely no idea of the connection.

But they must have known.

I growl under my breath and stand, brushing myself off with quick, angry swipes. I lift my hands to my eyeline, they're shaking, then I shove them to my sides and inhale a deep breath. I need to get it together.

But someone just tried to kill me! How can I possibly go back into that ballroom?

And of course, they know who I am. How could they not? And they've been trying to find my mother for me, a woman who has been hiding from these people for nearly half of her life. My memory flits back to the talisman and how I wore it around Tate at the hunting gym. He only saw a common enough crucifix since the feathers were on the back of the metal. He probably didn't think much of it considering a lot of humans wear crosses, and at least half the hunters in that gym did the same. Did he ever figure out what it was? And Gram. Was she ashamed of me? Did she resent me for what happened? If I got the talisman back, would it make any difference for me whatsoever?

No. The truth is out there. The necklace is gone, and so is my ability to hide my true identity. The nephilim and vampires already know all about me, and I'll never be able to live a normal life again. Maybe I never was meant for normality––it's not like I'm fully human. There's no going back. Not anymore.

With a shivering breath, I stride back into the party. People aren't really dancing anymore. The humans look tired, some have already cleared out, and others look like they're in the middle of goodbyes. The nephilim, however, are energized and smiling satisfied grins. I search for the man I stole energy from so I can avoid him, but he's nowhere to be seen. So I watch the neph instead, waiting for someone to see me and act like they just pushed me off the roof.

Of course, that never happens.

Camilla is completely unruffled, and same goes for the rest of the De Luca family. None of the others seem to even notice me. Or if they do, they don't care. They're too busy buzzing off the energy they just ripped away from innocent people. I want to scream at them, to demand they do better, to confess everything that just happened to me and everything I know.

But I don't. Instead, I plaster a fake smile to my face and circulate the room, flitting from group to group to chat as if I don't have a care in the world and life is all bon-bons and roses. As if I wasn't just pushed off the roof!

Bella and Greyson saunter over with smug expressions on their faces. "My father caught your little friend. You're welcome, by the way."

I frown. What friend? "Felix? Is he okay?"

She raises an eyebrow. "Nice try."

"The bloodsucker," Greyson quips.

My mouth pops open, and my voice comes out hoarse. "Adrian?"

She grins. "That's the one. Though, I thought his name was Adrianos? Leave it to you to call him by his nickname. Mother said you're probably his lover, but none of us wanted to believe you would stoop so low."

"You don't know what you're talking about," I whisper.

She shrugs, but her eyes are glittering, and Greyson looks more awake than I've ever seen him. He also looks much healthier than he did a few hours ago. He's probably been feeding non-stop. "Well, be that as it may, my father is taking him back to the Casa and throwing him in the dungeons below the house," she continues.

"Dungeons?" I had no idea the house even had a basement.

"Of course," she speaks as if we're discussing the latest drama on a reality television show, not the fate of someone's life. "I say give him a true death."

"I'm sure you'd be happy to do the honors," Greyson chuckles darkly at his sister.

She bats her eyelashes at me. "Oh, you still don't know what my gift is yet, do you? Would you care for a demonstration?"

I couldn't care less. I'm too caught up on the whole "they caught Adrian" thing. They're going to kill him, and I may not trust him anymore, but he helped my mom and he gave me the phone. He's more on my side than these people are.

I leave the Tate children standing there, marching straight over to Camilla. She's with a group of humans and breaks away from them when she sees me coming. We meet in the middle of the dance floor, bodies swaying around us as we stare off.

"You got Adrian?" I breathe.

Her knowing eyes travel me up and down slowly, and the hairs on the back of my neck stand on end. All it would take is one touch and the woman could jump right into my memories of tonight, learning everything I know now. That would be disastrous. What was I thinking coming to her so hastily? I backpedal, dropping my voice into a grateful whisper. "What I mean is, your grandkids just told me Tate captured him. Where is he? You know he betrayed me, right?"

Her mouth flickers into a small smile. "I do know. I saw it, remember, dear?"

Of course. She saw everything that happened with him right up until Brisa died. My cheeks blush at some of those memories.

"Don't be embarrassed." She catches on immediately. "I don't think any less of you considering what little information you had at the time. And he is rather handsome, isn't he? You wouldn't be the first to fall for a vampire's tricks."

I nod numbly.

"We have some questions for him. Important questions. Perhaps you would be persuaded to help us interrogate him?" Her eyes sparkle with dangerous fantasies, and I have to fight to keep myself from giving away my true feelings.

"Absolutely," I smile and nod, hoping I look eager and not desperate.

"Good. First thing tomorrow, then. Now, go enjoy the party. Be young. Have fun. Indulge yourself." She lifts her brows, and I know she's talking about the energy transference I never hope to experience again.

"Thank you, Camilla. For everything."

"Oh, and, Eva, one last thing."

I squeeze my hands behind my back and will myself to stay calm and my heartbeat to slow. Is this it? Is this when she grabs me and infiltrates my mind again, searching for more of Adrian? Is this when she figures out what I know? Maybe she'll throw me into the dungeon next to him.

"Merry Christmas."

So I'm some kind of freakish mutant. Memories of falling and then levitating a few feet from the ground sweep through my mind on repeat. I'm certain that's from the vamp venom, not the neph blood, and I wonder what else I can do. How much of my potential is still untapped? Maybe I should embrace this new life.

I barely sleep a wink and end up staring at the ceiling as golden morning light crawls up my bedroom walls. When I can't stand my thoughts any longer, I peel myself from the warm bed and get dressed. I'm supposed to get Felix and Seth before I go anywhere--they're staying just down the hall-- but I really don't care about this family's rules anymore.

This family . . . *my* family.

They're technically mine, but if they really cared about me, they wouldn't have killed my father. They took something that I'll never get back and broke my mother's heart in the process. And this whole time they've pretended that Camilla had three children, conveniently omitting the fourth. Nobody has even remarked on my appearance resembling theirs, something I'd chalked up to being part Italian. Their silence has spoken volumes--they never wanted me to find out the truth. I may have a place in the Casa, but I don't have a place with them.

I pad downstairs in search of a stairwell that could lead me down to Adrian. I think of that first day here and how my guards had seemed perturbed when I made a wrong turn on the way to the pool. I retrace my steps to find that area, then head down the quiet corridor toward what I've since learned are the staff quarters. It's not long before I find the tiny stair-well. I don't let myself think, I just act. Hurrying down the steps, my mind is set on Adrian. The temperature turns cold and the light dims, and then I'm standing in a hallway.

And I'm not alone.

"There you are," Camilla says, turning on me like she expected to see me here all along. "Good. Now we can get started."

Blood drains from my face. Did I just walk into a trap? The entire De Luca family stands behind Camilla, even the older twins, Enzo and Nicco, who are usually absent.

"You're all looking bright-eyed this morning," I smile and keep my voice chipper. "Guess you got more sleep than I did."

"I didn't sleep a wink," Chloe sighs, but there's a happiness about her that never seems to go away, even without proper sleep.

Of all the De Lucas, she and her mother, Lainey, are the only ones I kind of like. But that might be because they seem kind of clueless. I wonder how much they know about the matriarch they've let control their lives. Does Chloe know my father was the last to hold her gift? Does she even know about his existence or have they kept that from her as well? I am overflowing with questions that are far too dangerous to ask.

"Isn't this so exciting?" She slides over to me and threads her arm through mine. "Uncle Tate has been hunting this guy down for ages. Apparently he's one of the worst. And a prince! Can you believe it? We caught a prince."

"Sounds dangerous," I deadpan, and Chloe's face scrunches up as she nods.

Tate has been standing at the back of the group, but he strides forward now with his eyes pinned on me. "Yes, and we couldn't have done it without Eva."

My body goes cold, and I'm very aware that Tate knows I met with Adrian last night. Was Tate the one to push me off the roof? But why would he do that? He's worked tirelessly to keep me alive. If he wanted me dead, he's had ample opportunities to make it happen.

"Let's get this over with," Dario drawls, smirking right at me. His eyes twinkle as if he can read my mind, and I'm suddenly more suspicious of him than anyone else here. But again, I don't know what he could possibly have against me. "We all have a job to do, little girl," he says. "And if you don't do yours right, then I'll do it for you."

Bella giggles, and Bianca smirks at the back of her brother's head. "What's that supposed to mean?" I question. I still don't know what Dario's gift is. In fact, I don't know what most of them are capable of.

Dario simply chuckles as a glittering light passes over him in the blink of an eye. I stumble back with a yelp. He's no longer Dario. He's *me!* At least, he looks just like me. From my stick-straight hair to the jeans and t-shirt I threw on only a few minutes ago, it's like looking in a mirror. I've never felt more violated. That's my body. That's my face. I open my mouth to scream but no words make it out.

"Shapeshifter," he snorts, the voice that comes out sounds like Dario at least. It's jarring, but it's a chink in the armour. "I can't talk to Adrian, but I can get him to believe I'm you if the need arises."

Then all at once, he shifts back to his usual slimy self. It's no wonder I always got the ick-factor from the guy.

"And not all of our gifts can be used on vampires, so some of us will just be observing today," Camilla says, motioning for the group to follow her.

And that makes sense considering the things I've been through with Tate. I wonder about the rest of them. I know Camilla can read memories, and Chloe is the record keeper that replaced my father. Both of them have been able to impose their gifts on me. And while Tate manipulates minds, he's no longer a threat to mine. Shortly after arriving here, some of the other students told me the hulk-like twins have super tracking abilities, which doesn't affect me. Dario is a creepy shapeshifter, but what about Tate's kids, Bella and Greyson, or his wife Bianca? And what about the third De Luca son, Fredrico, and his wife Lainey? There are still so many things I don't know, things they're withholding.

The hallway is made of misshapen stones, and the floors are damp. There's no electricity down here, but someone's lit sconces along the walls. We pass by several cells with silver bars at the doors. Is Adrian the only one down here? I glance into the cells as we pass, but I don't see another soul. That doesn't mean anything. We stop at two doors next to each other. The first is a normal oak door, and the other is completely made of silver. Camilla opens the oak and ushers us inside. The sconces have been lit in here as well, and rows of arm chairs are set up facing a glass wall.

"It's a two way mirror," Lainey explains to me, patting me gently on the back. "He can't hear us, don't worry."

I blink as the others take their seats, staring through the mirror at the man on the other side. Adrian is chained to a wall with silver shackles at his arms and feet. Even in the dim light, I can see that the flesh around the shackles festers with angry red blisters. But it's the look in his eyes that haunts me. I expect him to be angry, or maybe even defeated, but he is afraid. The fear is unmistakable and raw on his usually unreadable face.

"I know you're there," he calls out, eyes trained on the glass. "I can't see you, but I can hear your heartbeats. All of them."

Bella snorts, and Camilla tells her to hush.

My stomach twists into awful barbed wire knots as I force myself to sit down and keep calm. But I'm anything but calm. Adrian isn't afraid for his own life, he's afraid for mine. And suddenly, his fear envelops me as well. Should I be afraid? What does he know about them that I haven't learned already? Mom's frantic voice comes to mind, and I wish I could be anywhere but here right now.

"Sit tight," Tate instructs the group, then he and Camilla leave the way we came and a few seconds later stride into Adrian's interrogation room.

Adrian gazes at them with a disgusted grimace. "I know what you're here to do," he snarls, "so why don't you just kill me and get it over with."

Bella clicks her tongue in disappointment. "A vampire with a death wish? Well, that's no fun."

I shoot her a dirty look, and she laughs. "Careful, Eva," she taunts, "you don't want to give yourself away. Your precious boyfriend would die for nothing."

Twenty-Five

I ignore Bella and focus on the three people in the cell. Tate tilts his head, assessing Adrian's words. "I'm not here to kill you," he says with a sly grin. "Well, not yet anyway."

"Stop wasting my time," Adrian replies.

"Oh, did we interrupt a pressing engagement?" Tate asks. "Because as I recall, you were hanging around our party last night. You came to us, not the other way around."

Adrian glowers at Tate. "I've been hunting you for ages, don't act so surprised."

"But you weren't hunting me last night," Tate chuckles. "You were trying to get to Eva. What's your plan then? Kill her? Take her for yourself?"

Adrian says nothing, but I'll admit, I'm conflicted. I don't want them to hurt Adrian, and I don't want him to give in to them, but I'm curious about the answers as well.

"Where is the Gateway?" Camilla snaps.

"There you go. See, that wasn't so hard, was it?" Adrian laughs. "That's what you're really after. The elusive Gateway. You know we found it, and you want me to tell you where it is?"

"Of course!"

They fall silent, eager for his answer. I've never heard of this Gateway before, and have absolutely no clue what it could be. In my lessons at the Casa, nobody has mentioned that word to me. I peer around at the others, and they're all eagerly on the edge of their seats. So I guess I'm the odd one out.

479

"Okay, I'll tell you. . ." he pauses for dramatic effect, "nothing."

"You don't want to do that," Camilla seethes.

"Oh, believe me, I do."

"Did you forget that you're at our mercy now?"

"What mercy?" he scoffs. "You neph think you're so high and mighty, but you're no better than the monsters you hunt."

Tate steps forward. "If you're so quick to call yourself a monster, then why shouldn't we kill you after all?"

"Because I've got the answers you seek." Adrian's eyes grow dark, and his voice raspy. "You're right, Tate, I'm a monster. And when I get out of here, I am going to show you just how evil I can be. That wife of yours? Bianca? Oh, I'll start with her, but I won't stop there. Your children? Bella and Greyson? I'll hunt them down too. And when I do, I'll make sure they know their father is responsible for their deaths."

"Sick bastard," Bella mutters from beside me, growing agitated.

"Let's kill him now and get this over with," Greyson agrees. There's a rattle to his voice I've never heard before. He's afraid. And he should be.

"Trust your father and your Nana," Bianca whispers to her children. "They know what they're doing. Adrianos can't die until he gives us the information we need, but once he does, we'll take him out."

"What's the Gateway?" I ask, and they all turn on me with closed expressions.

"Have it your way," Camilla's tone is clipped as she leaves Tate there with Adrian and returns to our viewing room seconds later. She points to me. "Don't go anywhere. We'll get to you once we wear him down." And then she points to Bianca and Bella. "One of you. Bella, I think you're ready, but if you'd rather have your mother––"

"I can do it!" Bella jumps up eagerly and follows her grandmother out the door.

"You really think she's ready?" Fredrico asks his sister, and she nods reluctantly. Then everyone grows quiet as Bella and Camilla join Tate.

I don't know what I'm supposed to be seeing, but nothing happens. Bella's smug expression makes me think something is going on, but maybe it's meant for Adrian's eyes only?

"Ah, the infamous Bella De Luca-Tate," Adrian says, "Good to get a visual on you again."

"Shut your mouth," Tate snaps.

Bella turns to her father. "Daddy, it's not working."

"Vision-warps don't work on me, *Daddy*," Adrian laughs. "Don't you know I'm not your typical vampire? It'll take more than party tricks to get into my head. But maybe you ought to get your wife to come play. I hear she's quite skilled. Maybe she'll succeed where your daughter has failed."

Bella screams violently and storms from the room, and Bianca jumps up to meet her out in the hallway. I want to laugh, but I don't have a death wish. Vision-warp, huh? If I had to guess, that would be making people see things that aren't really there. My skin chills at that, and I hope that if it doesn't work on Adrian then it doesn't work on me either. I've certainly got enough vampire venom in me.

The others go next. The twins beat him up, and I have to look above them instead of directly at them as they pummel his body over and over. They punch and kick, and the more they do it, the more Adrian seems to grow stronger somehow. He's laughing hysterically by the end of it, even as blood runs down his face and mixes with his teeth. After what feels like ages, they give it up, and Lainey goes next. I don't know what she does, but the twins hold Adrian back and she touches his wounds.

I stand, face pressed to the glass as Adrian heals, his cuts stitching themselves back together as if everything is happening in reverse.

"Oh my gosh," I whisper. Something like this is a dream come true. If I could go back and wish for any gift, this would be it.

"I know, right?" Chloe laughs.

And then Lainey steps away, and the twins begin their beating all over again. I fall back into my seat, staring at my feet. I can't watch this. Vampires can heal on their own, but what Lainey does is remarkable, and they're using it so they can beat him over and over. Again. And Again.

And again.

This continues in a cycle for hours. My stomach rolls, and I want to leave and I want to stay all at once. Deciding to take a break, I go for the door, but rough hands drag me back to my seat. I turn to glare at Fredrico. "My power will work on you, so don't make me use it," he says dryly.

"What's your power?" I raise an eyebrow.

"Sedation," Greyson says wryly. "Could've used some of that last night, Uncle. I'm exhausted. How much longer until I can go in there and finish this?"

I turn on the sour-faced boy with the chip on his shoulder. *My cousin.* "And what's your thing then, if you're so confident you can get Adrian to talk?"

He pins me with a hard stare. "How often do you have nightmares?"

The others eye Greyson with frustration. Do they not want him to tell me?

"Never," I respond instantly, though it's a lie. I don't dream that often, but when I do they're often unsettling, and sometimes they're nightmares.

Worse than nightmares. Terrors. "And anyway, that stuff isn't real. Even if I have a bad dream, I wake up and it's gone. Big deal."

"Oh, but some nightmares are real, Eva. And what I can show you has nothing to do with dreaming. Have you ever wondered what lurks in the unseen dark places? Have you ever seen something that wasn't really there, only to wonder if perhaps it was?"

I roll my eyes. "Care to be any less cryptic?"

He leans back in his seat with an exasperated sigh. "You really are dense, aren't you?"

"And I really don't understand why you hate me. What did I ever do to you? Absolutely nothing. Are you threatened or something?"

Greyson doesn't respond.

"The kid has the shadow-sight," Dario says dryly. "It means he can see the other realms. Angels. Demons. Ghosts. All that shit." He turns on his nephew with a laugh. "And he thinks he's so damn mysterious now."

I frown. "That stuff is real?"

Greyson throws up his hands. "Asks the nephilim in the middle of an interrogation with a vampire."

"Sorry," I mutter, "these things aren't widely known."

"Didn't your mother ever take you to church?" Dario asks.

"That's enough, all of you," Chloe speaks up. "I'm trying to watch. You should too. What if he reveals something? We need to find that Gateway if we're going to ever complete our mission on Earth."

"Spoken like a true radical," Greyson rolls his eyes.

This is all so confusing to me. "What's the Gateway?"

"Can't tell you that yet," he shrugs.

"This is all a bunch of bullshit," I snap, jumping up from my seat and storming out the door and into the hallway. The others yell after me, but nobody stops me, so whatever. I'd like to see them try anyway. Never mess with an angry woman.

I push open the door to Adrian's interrogation room and stride inside. Six heads snap in my direction. Lainey's eyes are filled with relief. She's standing next to Adrian, healing him for the gazillionth time. The twins glare over all their hulking muscles. Tate raises an eyebrow, and Camilla doesn't look the least bit surprised to see me. Did they want me to interrupt like this? Well, if they did, then they just got what they wanted.

"Are you okay?" I ask Adrian.

"Leave us," he growls. "Get out of here, Eva."

"Uh, no, I don't think I'll be doing that." I've been through so much with this man, and I'm not going to let him boss me around anymore. In fact, I'm not going to let anyone.

"If you don't, they're going to kill you," I continue, hoping to surprise them all for real this time.

His eyes narrow. "You don't know what you're asking of me."

"Whatever this Gateway is, it can't be worth more than your life."

"They're going to kill me either way. And it is worth more than my life. It's worth the lives of millions."

I step back, more confused than ever. "Will someone please tell me exactly what is going on here?"

Adrian begins to speak but his words are lost the moment that Greyson strides into the room.

Twenty-Six

ADRIAN

The boy points at Eva, and then she screams like the weight of eternity is crushing her soul. That noise splits me open, making me question everything. The Gateway has been a guarded secret for centuries that many supernaturals have sought to find. It was only recently discovered by Brisa. Not many of us even know about it, and I've never traveled there myself, though I know Mangus has been there at least twice. The neph have gone to great lengths to get to it, and Eva's pain is the only reason I'd break.

But I won't. I can't. *I can't* be responsible for the genocide that will happen if they find it.

"Torturing an innocent? You will pay for this," I say to the De Lucas and Leslie Tate. "I will not forget what you've done here."

And what they did to my prodigy before Kelli, as well as Kelli herself because it was one of their hunters who killed her. And now they're going after Eva? I'll never let them get away with it.

My voice is barely audible over the agonized screech of Eva's crying. She's babbling something about her mother being hurt, about the demons, about the darkness. They're going to break her. This is what they want. Break her so they can break me.

Camilla stalks in close, her eyes blazing. "Tell us where it is before she loses her mind. The darkness will not be kind to her."

"She's weaker than I thought," Tate adds, frowning down at her writhing form.

"They feed off of pain," the boy, Greyson, explains like it's something to be proud of. His eyes are wild with excitement as he watches, as if he's also feeding too. "And I think they also like her light. It's new for them."

They? I don't know what he has at his command, but whatever it is, it's dark. Evil. Of all the De Lucas this child is the one to fear most.

I need to think. I need to do something to stop her pain. I'm stronger than this, than them, I'm better, faster, more cunning. I've lived a thousand lifetimes, and they have but one. They can't best me. If only Camilla were inches closer, I'd be able to rip her throat out with my teeth. It would be so quick, so brutal, that even their healer wouldn't be able to do a thing to stop her death. I eye her aged skin, reminded of tissue paper. It would be so easy . . . And then the others would lose their tempers and kill me. Or kill Eva. Maybe both. But they wouldn't have the information they wanted, and their matriarch would be gone.

"You kill her, and you do my kind a favor," I spit. "We know what she is. She killed our queen."

But they don't know what Sebastian wants to do with her. If they did, then surely they'd cut her down immediately.

"I think you do care." Tate strides forward. "I think you care very, very much. If you didn't, you'd have given up the location already."

"How do you figure that?"

Eva crawls to her hands and knees now, heaving. Her body is in a fight or flight response. She started in fight mode, but is now caving in on herself, as if trying to chase away shadows. I will her to be strong, to use what she has to defend herself. She has light in her somewhere. Light that might kill me, but if she were to unleash it, it might destroy those shadows. It might stop this. Save her.

But her hands don't glow. And her body stays rigid. And her cries only get louder.

"You care because you love her," Tate laughs. "You care because you know what we're going to do once we find the Gateway. And mind you, we will find it. For a vampire, it's pretty funny that you're acting like you don't want blood on your hands. Such a hypocrite. You'll always have blood on your hands. And soon you'll rot hell with blood on your hands."

"And so will you."

He rolls his eyes. "You can help us or you can die, but either way we're going to find the Gateway. Might as well save Eva first."

I look him square in the eye. "Fine. I choose death."

He steps back and kicks Eva lightly. She doesn't seem to process it, or even that any of us are here talking about her. "So you'd choose her death?"

"You can't put that on me." I press my arms up where the chains snag against my flesh, burning me further. I don't care––I press harder, trying to break free. It's useless. "I'm not the one hurting her, you are!"

"So you do love her," Tate roars. "And you're going to let us drive her mad? Kill her right in front of you? You're more vile than I thought."

My fangs extend, and I cackle. "You aren't going to kill your greatest weapon. This is a bluff. A sick and twisted game that I'm not playing."

I close my mouth and look away, concentrating on the cracks in the walls and shutting my mind away. I've had great practice in putting my emotions aside, and this will be no different.

Someone else enters the room then, and whatever Greyson is doing stops because Eva's cries peter out and turn to muffled sobs. I blink at Fredrico, one of the other De Luca sons, and one of the few whose gift I wasn't able to learn during my years of keeping tabs on the family. Brisa made sure all the nephilim factions were under constant surveillance and had given the De Lucas to me after my unfortunate run-in with Tate years ago. I'm still not sure if she did that to punish me for failing my prodigy or as a way to stoke my desire for revenge.

"One touch from me, and you'll be sedated," Fredrico says, strolling up to me and giving away his play. "And do you know what happens next?"

"You're not supposed to tell me what you're going to do before you do it," I mock. "Where's the fun in that?"

I've never met a sedator before, but they're dangerous. My fangs pang in protest.

"I'll sedate you, and then I'll extract your venom." His eyes are cold. "Venom isn't always easy to come by, and yours must be quite strong. We could use it in our war efforts, don't you think?"

So they know about the venom. I'd suspected it, but couldn't get confirmation. Well, here it is, and it makes me sick.

"Touch me and die," I glare at the lanky man. "Go ahead. See if it works. Most of you can't affect me. Not even ghost-boy over here can hurt me."

I don't actually know if Greyson sees ghosts, but it's a close enough guess. The kid glares, and I swear Eva holds in a laugh. She must be feeling much better. Nobody moves.

"Well, are you going to do it or not? I haven't got all day. The sun will be setting soon. Better get moving if you think you're going to extract my venom and then throw me out for the sun to burn."

"We could always stake you," Fredrico quips.

"But you won't. Where's the fanfare in that when you can watch your enemy go up in flames? Ah, don't feel bad, I'd do the same thing to you in a heartbeat."

"You don't have a heartbeat."

"Good point."

Fredrico's ego gets the best of him, just as I'd hoped. He reaches out to touch me, and I'm wagering on one thing: that his power won't be stronger than I am. Because I'm fast, I'm old, and I've been through enough close-encounters over the centuries to know how to survive.

My wager pays off. His touch sends a wave of drowsiness through me, but not enough to put me to sleep. I'm all out of patience. All out of good ideas. All out of mercy.

There's nothing left. Not for these people.

Still manacled, I snatch Fredrico's wrist in my hand and tug him to me, making good on my promise. It's so quick. The flesh of his throat is warm and soft under my razor fangs. I slice him right open, his blood splattering across the room, and drink him in before biting deeper, ripping his throat out.

So much glorious blood.

It pours down me, and then I'm dropping his body at my feet, rivers of red slipping down my chin. "Who's next?"

More screaming––more for me to feed on.

Now they'll stake me. It's over. But they'll have to be brave enough to get near me first.

"You!" I growl at Greyson. "You're next. Come join your uncle."

Tate pushes his son out the door while the healer screams, grabbing onto Fredrico's body and hollering about her husband. Even now, she's trying to heal him. It won't work. And if she gets any closer, I'll kill her too. I'll kill every last one of them if given the chance.

Camilla is saying something to me in Italian that I hardly care to listen to. Something along the lines of comply or die, but I drown it out.

I expect to deal with a stake at any moment, but I don't get one. They all leave, dragging the body out with them, a smear of crimson marking the floor. Tate picks Eva up and carries her away. Just as they're closing the door, I catch her eyes. They hold onto my gaze, possessive and strong. She's no longer crying.

Is she on their side or mine?

Night must come because hours inch by, but there's no way for me to know for sure. They keep me locked up. Isolated. Waiting.

At least I fed. I feel amazing, and I don't regret what I did. Maybe I should. But I never pretended to be anything other than what I am. I've killed before, and I'll kill again. They're the fools for thinking they could expect anything else from me.

Anything less.

Hours pass. Days? Minutes? I don't know anymore, until the door swings open again. Four pairs of legs walk toward me. I gaze up, assuming the De Lucas are back, but it's Evangeline standing before me with a grim expression on her pretty face. At her sides are her two hunter friends, Felix and Seth. I'm surprised to see them. But not as surprised as I am to see the fourth person.

"Mangus," I breathe. "You came."

Eva must have used the "In Case of Emergency" number that I'd programmed into the phone. Does that mean she trusts me again? Will she leave with me? I don't know what I'll do if she breaks me out of here but refuses to come along.

"At your service, brother." Mangus nods. "Now let's go. We've got things to do. People to see."

He's got nothing to do or see, but leave it to Mangus to keep things light. Eva gets to work on my chains, producing a key to attack the locks. I have no idea how she managed to get a key, and I want to kiss her in gratitude. Felix and Seth stand in the corner, apprehension evident on their faces, but here nonetheless. I guess I'll let the fact that they're vampire hunters slide for the moment considering they're here to save my ass.

"And where are we going then?" I ask Mangus just as Eva manages to get me unshackled. The relief is palpable.

"Don't you know?" Mangus laughs. "There's this Gateway that everyone is fighting over. Guess we'd better get there and make sure the wards are still strong. You're in luck because I know just where to go."

Twenty-Seven

"How did you manage to get to me?" Adrian asks, bewildered. His hair is a bloodied halo around his face, rings of exhaustion circling shallow eyes. But at least he's still alive. The Gateway must be important. I thought for sure they would have staked him after he killed Fredrico.

I'm still angry with Adrian, but I'm also proud of myself for coming this far. The fact that I'm here is nothing short of a miracle. "It was the hardest thing I've ever had to pull off. Now hurry up, let's go, and I'll explain on the way."

We sneak back out into the hallway, and I handle any silver in our path, grateful that only bothered me during the three nights of transition. Adrian is weak so Mangus holds him up under an arm as they shuffle along. "I've never heard vampires make so much noise," I hiss, and they stop.

"Is she always this pleasant?" Mangus asks Adrian.

"Only in the mornings," Adrian replies dryly, and my cheeks burn. Felix and Seth exchange a disgusted look that makes me want to slap them both, but there's no time for that. And I shouldn't be so smug because we could be caught at any moment.

"Follow me," I whisper-yell.

The house has silver bars on the windows and doors, but Mangus got in, so I'm determined to get out. The best route won't be through any of those doors or windows, and that's because it won't be what the De Luca family will expect. I quickly lead them out of the dungeon and up to the center atrium on the main floor, passing the guards the four of us gagged and bound on the way.

Just as we sweep into the muggy room with the overgrown plants, unseen alarms blare, and my heart drops.

"You can levitate, right?" I ask Mangus, and he snorts.

"What do you take me for?" he says, "Of course, I can levitate."

"Well, Hugo couldn't, so it's not an unreasonable question."

Mangus turns on Adrian. "What does she know of Hugo?"

My cheeks warm. "Later. What about you, Adrian? Do you have enough strength?"

"Yes, and I'll carry you." He's mighty confident for having just been tortured, beaten, and held captive for the last forty-eight hours.

"Adrian, you carry Seth. Mangus, you carry Felix. And I'll worry about myself."

All four men stare at me, and before I can address their obvious lack of faith in me, I'm floating in midair.

Mangus whistles low. "Impressive. How much venom did you get?"

"Enough to do that," Adrian says.

Felix and Seth's jaws drop, and Mangus mutters something about having seen it all now. Then he throws Felix over his shoulder, and I almost laugh at my large Cuban-American friend's protests.

"They're in here!" a man yells, and footsteps sound from the hallway outside the atrium.

"We've got to move!" I hiss. "They've got silver bullets!"

Adrian scoops Seth up, and then we're all flying for the ceiling. I curl in on myself, my back a battering ram as I fly through the glass. I hit it hard, shattering the pane around me, shards raining down. I press on, concentrating. I'd practiced in a room a bunch over the last few days but figured that all it really took was concentration, otherwise it was easy. But that was a few feet off the ground, and this is entirely different. We continue up into the sweeping blackness, and my gut clenches. I try not to think about falling, so instead, I focus on the cool, still night to distract me. The moon hangs bright and full in the sky, and with the added benefit of the venom, the world is illuminated to near daylight.

We zip up and away from the Casa, and I allow myself to relax. And then giggle, thrilled that levitating has come so easily. Just as that thought hits me, I plummet and yelp, the ground coming at me fast. Someone swoops ahead of me, catching me in his other arm. Mangus.

I cry out with relief. "Don't get cocky," he says, "that's how people get killed."

"Thank you for catching me," I say through ragged breaths. "I always thought you didn't like me."

"I didn't," Mangus responds, "but I like Adrian, and he likes you."

"Can we not have this conversation right now?" Felix groans from Mangus's other arm. His eyes are round saucers taking in the blur of landscape as Mangus flies us over the city and out toward the sea. "I think I'm going to be sick."

"Get sick, and I'll drop you," Mangus warns.

"You wouldn't," I snap. To Felix I add, "He wouldn't."

Mangus only growls, indicating that he, in fact, would. It doesn't matter though, because Felix doesn't get sick, and soon we're flying over lapping ocean waves and toward a small island off the coast. Adrian isn't far behind us, and even over the rushing wind, I can hear Seth saying something about not being a good swimmer.

We land on the island, which is nothing more than a big rock with an old lighthouse and a dock with a couple of boats tied up.

"Our ride will be here soon," Mangus says. "Hang tight everybody."

"How did you do it?" Adrian turns on us. "You saved me."

"You could've gotten out," Mangus argues. "You always do. How many times have you been in situations like this before?"

Adrian shakes his head. "This time was different. I lost my temper, I killed one of the higher-ups. They would've kept trying their powers on me until I grew weak enough for them to actually work. They wouldn't have let me live much longer."

So supernaturals aren't entirely immune to angelic gifts, which explains a lot of what I saw two days ago during the interrogation. I tuck that information away for later.

I think he's right about them killing him, but I don't say it. The De Luca family has been a mess since Fredrico died, and their anger has been as thick as smoke. "I faked Greyson's little torture bit," I explain. "It worked at first, but I was quick to fight it off. I already knew that was his thing, so I pretended the shadows were still after me, and everyone bought it."

Adrian nods, leveling me with a stare that makes my insides twist. "You're a good actress, Angel."

Angel . . . I'm not sure I like that nickname anymore. I shrug. "When I need to be."

Once Adrian had killed Fredrico, the entire Casa fell to pieces. People were crying, whispering in corridors, there was even some wailing behind closed doors from a few of the family members. All those emotions hitting the house at once made it easy for me to do what I needed to get Adrian out of there. It was the perfect distraction.

"They expected me to be out of it as I recovered from his attack on me. So I walked around like a zombie, and nobody talked to me for a while. The first thing I did was lift a phone off a staff member and called that 'In Case of Emergency' number you left for me."

"You lost the phone I gave you?" Adrian raises an eyebrow.

"You gave her a phone?" Seth interrupts. "When did that happen?"

I snap my fingers. "None of that matters anymore. Listen. I called it, and your pal Mangus here answered. When I told him you were in trouble, he immediately offered to rescue you, and we worked out a plan."

Truth be told, I was floored when Mangus answered and so quickly offered his help. The guy never liked me, but this wasn't about me, it was about Adrian, which showed me how much he cared for him. It gave me hope and a reason to do the risky thing I did next. "Getting the keys off Camilla had been a lot harder."

"Yeah, that woman doesn't seem like the type you could pull one over on," Felix admits.

"And she's scary as hell," I let out a laugh.

"She's not so bad," Seth argues. "Remember what Tate said? She can be trusted." He turns and gazes out at the water. "Maybe we should go back. They're not that bad."

The vampires scrunch up their faces, and I quickly explain how my friends have been continually manipulated by Tate's mind tricks. Not that either of these guys have room to talk, considering vampires compel humans. It's almost the same thing.

"Go on about the keys," Mangus interrupts, gazing at me with new eyes. "I want to hear this part. You're more interesting than I gave you credit for, Angel."

"Don't call her that," Adrian hisses, "Only I can call her that."

"The only person who has permission to call me that is my mother." I roll my eyes and go on. "Anyway, I went to visit her in her study to offer my condolences. She'd been an emotional wreck, not like herself at all, and I hate to say it, but I took advantage of that and snagged the ring of keys when she wasn't looking."

I pull them from my pocket now and toss them out to sea, my super-human strength sending them whizzing ridiculously far. I still feel a little bad about taking advantage of Camilla, but I'd realized that these people weren't on my side the moment they'd taken me to that party to feed on human auras. Everything had gotten so complicated since walking into the casino that day back in August. I'd always seen the world in black and white, and both the vampires and the nephilim had me questioning that, making me feel like everyone was a solid mix of gray.

I don't want to be gray.

There have to be good guys out there, and I'm going to be one of them. I have a choice of doing right or wrong, and I'm going to do what's right, and if I end up making a wrong choice, then I'm going to correct it. Staying with the De Luca family would've turned me into someone I'm not. I think of my dad. How hard it must have been for him to get away from them. That choice ended up costing him his life. I'm following in his footsteps, and just have to hope I get a better ending to my story.

Felix breaks the silence next. "I'm pretty sure that's when Eva came and got us," he says to the vampires, "she asked us to come with her, and since we swore to Tate that we wouldn't leave her and that we'd protect her no matter what, we had no choice but to agree to her terms."

Mangus's nostrils flare, and his pupils dilate. "You're hunters, though? And you've made promises to Tate?"

My friends nod slowly and it's like an invisible goes up between them and the vampires.

"You're lucky you're not dead," Mangus says. "That I didn't kill you the second I saw you."

True to his word, the viking vampire prince had shown up at my door an hour ago. He'd broken into the house, claiming that he was stronger than most vampires and therefore had no trouble getting into homes, even if they were inhabited by neph. I hadn't questioned him––the older the vamp, the more powerful and skilled they can be. I don't know when vikings were around, but Mangus is as old as them.

My friends are clearly uncomfortable and inching away from the vampires. They don't have stakes or guns on them. They've got no defense, and the sun is still hours from rising. At any moment the vampires could kill them for being hunters.

"They can be trusted," I say to Mangus, trying to comfort my friends, although a thread of fear weaves down my spine. "The fact that they're here and didn't cause any issues getting Adrian out is proof enough."

Mangus doesn't seem convinced. "One mistake, and I'll kill them."

I gape at him, then at Adrian. He shrugs. "You're my priority, Eva. If they attempt to double-cross us, then I'll kill them if Mangus doesn't beat me to it."

And I know he will. These men mean every word, which is exactly why my friends *must* go home.

Twenty-Eight

❧

"Do you guys have your passports, money, things like that?" I turn on Seth and Felix. When they nod, I muster up the courage I need to do the right thing, even though it's going to hurt the relationships I've spent weeks rebuilding. "Then you should go." I point to the boats bobbing at the docks. "Take one of those and get out of here. Go back home and return to your lives."

"We're not leaving you," Seth replies first, surprising me.

"Yeah, Eva, whatever this is, we're in it." Felix nods, eyes earnest.

"Eva is right," Mangus says, "it's not safe for you."

"It's not safe for any one of us," Felix argues, jabbing his fingers at the vampires. "You just don't want hunters around, but guess what? I don't trust you with Eva any more than you trust me with her."

"We could make you go," Mangus snarls. His temper flares, and it might be the first time I've seen him like this. He's usually so cold and aloof. He's different than he used to be, but that was when his wife was still alive. I know she died being blamed for his death, which is part of why I was so stunned when he'd been the one on the other end of that "In Case of Emergency" phone number.

Seth stands taller. "We're not old enough to be compelled. So what are you going to do about it?"

The tension between our little ragtag group is as dangerous as a taut wire about to snap, and whoever pulls on it next will likely end up getting hit. "That's enough." I hold up my hands in surrender and turn on my friends. "I appreciate everything you've done for me. I love you guys, but the people who are after me could hurt you, and you're not going to be able to fight them off."

Because now I'll have vampires *and* nephilim on my tail.

"When are you going to get it?" Felix rakes a hand through his dark curls and levels me with an exasperated look. "We're here by choice. Sure, we made a promise to Tate but that was only because we care about you. Protecting you is what we wanted, too. Don't treat us like a liability."

But that's exactly what they are.

"I'm sorry," my voice cracks, and their faces fall, but I can't give up on them. Not yet. "I've tried to tell you multiple times, but every time I do, you just gloss over it like it's nothing. The truth is that Tate is the reason you care so much about my safety. He used his mind manipulation to get you to trade in your normal lives to be here for me. I mean, just think about what you've been saying tonight. Don't you see that I'm right?"

It seems so obvious. He even said himself that Tate made them promise.

Felix shakes his head and steps forward. "You're wrong, Eva. You're my sister's best friend and have been a part of my family for years. It wouldn't matter what Tate did or didn't do, I'd still be here."

Is that true, though? Because while he always treated me well, it was never like this. Our relationship has been a rollercoaster since August, and I need to get him out, for his own sake more than anything. "I'm no good for you," I say, reaching out and squeezing his hand. He squeezes back. "You had such a bright future until all this happened. Think of your family. They're probably worried sick about you. And think of Ayla." Last I saw her, she'd gone into an agoraphobic depression and locked herself in her room and everyone out of her life. "She needs you now more than ever. She's your family, not me."

The unmistakable humming pulse of helicopter blades slices through the night, weak at first and growing stronger. Buzzy adrenaline shoots through me. "That will be the De Luca family," I hiss. "They have a helicopter. We need to take cover."

"You think the De Lucas are the only ones with deep pockets?" Mangus chuckles darkly. "That's our ride, honey. Right on time."

"And we're going with you," Felix adds. "That's final."

Mangus and Adrian catch each other's eyes, and I wonder what they're thinking.

The noise grows, and a couple of minutes later the wind wraps around us as the helicopter lands. The five of us run to it, and Adrian lifts me up to get in first. I turn back to a blur of movement so fast I almost miss it. But apparently my friends don't see it in time because a second later Mangus and Adrain are dropping them off at the distant docks. A second later, the vampires are back, climbing in next to me, and we're lifting into the air while my friends are sprinting toward us up the pier. But they're not fast enough—nobody is as fast as the vampires, and the chopper is quick.

"I'm sorry," I yell out the door, hoping my voice isn't lost to the noise. "Be safe!"

They're hollering something back, but I can't hear them, and then Mangus is sliding the door shut and falling back into the seat beside me. The chopper veers to the right, and we're zipping off over the sea. I've yet to decide if we're running to or from the greater danger, but at least I'm leaving the Casa.

"We've got a private jet waiting for us in Geneva. Then it's a three hour flight to where we're going," Mangus says. "We'll get there before sunrise. Get some rest."

"I don't need any rest. I'm fine."

Mangus clicks his tongue but doesn't say anything more. The viking is sitting next to me, and across from us, Adrian is slumped over the seat. His normally vibrant blue eyes are pale, there's blood turning his hair copper, and his cheeks are sunken in. "You need to feed." I eye him with a frown.

"I'm fine," he mumbles.

Mangus leans over Adrian to say something to the human in the cockpit, and we start to descend.

"What are you doing?" Adrian asks at the same time I say, "Where are we going?"

"Adrian needs to eat sooner rather than later, so we're making a quick pit stop in Rome," Mangus replies gruffly.

"No!" Adrian roars, forcing his body up and glaring at Mangus. "The priority is getting Eva out of here. Rome will slow us down, plus it's not our territory. I can eat later."

I must admit, I also really want to get out of Italy.

"The priority is getting all of us safely to the Gateway." Mangus levels Adrian with a hard stare. "We do what I say, and then we'll do what you say, brother."

"What's the Gateway?" I demand, then sigh. "Actually, hold that thought, first, Adrian does need to eat." I can't believe I'm doing this, but seeing him this exhausted has me panicked. I'm still angry with him, but I don't like this weak side of him, not when I can do something about it. I extend my wrist. "Drink."

Both men flash me strange looks.

"Absolutely not," Adrian hisses. "It's forbidden anyway."

"Says who?" I press. "I don't see Brisa around to enforce anything, do you? You need blood, and I need to get out of Italy as quickly as possible, so it's a win-win."

Mangus gives me a hard look. "And how do we know you're not becoming addicted to the venom?"

Maybe I am, but this truly isn't about that. "Look, do you want to get out of here faster or do you want to stop and waste time?"

They both stare at my wrist, and then Mangus nods to Adrian before leaning over to instruct the pilot to get back on course. Adrian grabs my wrist and yanks me into his lap. I expect him to bite the delicate flesh there, but he doesn't.

"Make me stop," Adrian says to his brother. "Don't you dare let me kill her."

"I wouldn't dream of it," Mangus winks.

Before I can process how their conversation makes me feel, Adrian is shifting in closer, his body pressing to mine. He runs his nose along my cheek and down my jaw, inhaling my scent. "I can't say no to you," he whispers. "Do you understand what that means, Angel?"

"I hardly doubt that's true." One thing I know about Adrian is he'll do anything to get his way. Even if it means waiting a century, he'll wait . . . and then he'll strike. His mouth inches toward mine, that intoxicating scent wafting over me, and my insides flip. Memories of being with him and then being left by him pummel me, and I shift back. I can't kiss those lips again. I'll be lost if I do.

So I lift my wrist to him again. "Take what you need." There's a long pause, and then he's moving my wrist out of the way and going for my neck. I arch into him, letting him, the anticipation blushing through me. The bite stings at first, like the cut of a razor, but the venom slides into my veins, and I'm soon flooded with bliss. A vulnerability I haven't felt with him since we slept together blossoms within, closeness and openness all at once. I want to cry, to scream, to laugh, to do everything and nothing all at once. I'm so overcome with emotion that it's peacefully paralyzing, and my entire body relaxes into his grip.

With Hugo and Brisa this experience had been horrifying, but with Adrian it's wonderful, and I suddenly know what Mangus said about it being possible to get addicted to this. How could I not? I could go on and on like this forever. I moan and lean into him, his fangs pushing in deeper. And then he's rearing back with a hiss, and I feel lost. Our eyes meet over shared gasps. His are rimmed in red and hungry with desire.

"Have you had enough?" I rasp out, inching back.

His entire demeanor changes from feral animal to chastised puppy, and his eyes drop, fangs retreating. "Yes, thank you." He carefully lifts me from his lap, putting me back in the seat next to Mangus who's watching us with an equal mix of interest and heartbreak. I've always had a hard time getting a read on Mangus, but now his emotions are plain on his face. He misses his wife. He's angry, hurt, and most of all, heartbroken.

The moment is too much, and we turn away to stare out the windows. There's nothing to see but dark sky, clouds, and night. *So much night.* They're used to living this way, but I'm not. I can't ever become like them, it would ruin me.

"Alright, guys," I gather up my courage and start the conversation that needs to be had. "It's time to answer some of my questions."

Adrian's lips thin, and Mangus bristles, but I don't back down.

Twenty-Nine

ADRIAN

What will happen if Mangus realizes the truth about Eva? If he figures out just how much power she's acquired, he may kill her or side with Sebastian's way of thinking. So even though my vampire brother has more answers than I currently do, I take the lead. I gaze at Eva, unable to take my eyes off her. Her blood has given me a new sense of purpose. I've never tasted anyone so sweet––and with so much potential. I can't let anyone else have her. I have to keep her safe, and that means telling her as much truth as I can in front of Mangus.

"I've wanted to be honest with you for a long time, Angel," I say, careful to keep my voice steady. "I hope you know that."

She raises a skeptical eyebrow, and it's the most Eva-like thing she's done all night that I have to fight back a grin. There's my girl. "What I know is your words and your actions don't always line up, so you'll excuse me if I'm a little apprehensive."

"That's fair, but I could only say and do so much without my maker stopping me." Surely she understands that about vampires by now.

"You're saying Brisa is to blame for your shortcomings?" she snorts.

I sit up, my patience beginning to wear thin, but I'm also desperate. I can't lose her again. "That's exactly what I'm saying. So many times back at that palace I wanted to tell you exactly what was going on, but my maker refused me. I've done the best I could to keep you safe. But I see now how badly I failed you, and I'll never forgive myself."

"Since when are you so dramatic?" Mangus scoffs, interrupting me. His eyes are rimmed with disdain, and I worry where this conversation could be headed. "Come on, enough with this pathetic lovers' quarrel." He turns on Eva. "You can forgive Adrian later or not, but enough about that. You want to know about the Gateway, correct? Let's talk about the important matters."

I'd argue that our "lovers' quarrel" is the important matter.

She breaks our gaze to glare at Mangus. "Yes, but I'd also love to know why Brisa believed you died. Or are you going to blame everything on your maker as well?" She shoots me a quick roll of her eyes. "Being unaccountable for your actions is so unattractive."

Ouch. I can't help but laugh, and Mangus does the same. "I didn't realize you were so feisty," he says to her, and then to me, "I can see why you like her."

"Enough," she waves her hands, her cheeks going slightly pink. "Just tell me about your supposed death, and then let's talk about the Gateway."

"Very well," Mangus sighs and leans back in his chair. I'll admit I'm interested as well. I've only heard bits and pieces, but I'd like to know the whole story. "It actually starts with the Gateway, so I can tell you both in one story. Have you heard of the Gateway before, Eva?"

She shakes her head. "The only Gateway I know is a run-down shopping mall."

Mangus snorts. "No, not a shopping mall. The Gateway is a hidden portal to the fae realm," he explains. "The fae have kept its location a well-hidden secret until Brisa's agents recently tracked it down. I lead the team that found it."

Eva is statue-still. I'm not sure if she believes him or not, but he's not lying. Fae are real, but since they stopped coming to the human realm long ago, they haven't been on our radar.

"You're confirming that faeries are real?" she questions, but there's something in her eyes that's not completely honest. Maybe she already knew about them. Considering where she's been lately, I wouldn't be surprised if she already hates them.

"How much did the nephilim teach you?" He shakes his head. "Yes, of course, they're real. Fae is the term we use for magical creatures that are connected to Earth's elements. Faeries, trolls, elves, mermaids, leprechauns, boggarts, dryads, and so on and so forth. You know what I'm talking about, right?"

She lets out a strangled laugh. "I guess so."

"There are three Earthly realms––the human realm where we're all living, the fae realm where they live, and then the spirit realm, but we don't know much about that."

I think of Greyson and wonder what he could tell us about spirits.

"Many of the fae used to travel between human and fae realms, but when vampires, nephilim, and werewolves grew in number, they retreated to their realm and stayed there. The Gateway is the only known portal between those realms that hasn't already been destroyed."

"So why did Brisa want to find it?" she asks.

"There are rumors of fae witches who will grant wishes to those who find them," I pipe up. "Is that what happened to you, Mangus?"

He gives me a slow grimace, probably because I'm going to make him reveal more than he'd intended. "Well, it turns out fae witches don't grant wishes, but they do make bargains."

I swallow. Of course, it's not that easy. Nothing ever is.

"So that's why you're alive when Brisa said you were dead?" Eva breathes out slowly, her mind at work.

I don't know how much more he'll divulge, but he gives in to her easily, which only causes my suspicions about her abilities to grow. This isn't good.

I keep a close eye on Mangus.

Does he realize what's happening? Will he kill her if he figures it out?

"I made a deal to break the blood bond with Brisa," he confesses. "It was all set to go through on the final day of October. She would assume me dead, and Katerina and I would be free to live out eternity without her ruling over us anymore."

If I'd known a fae witch could do such a thing, I'd have gone looking for one long ago, and I haven't been treated nearly as poorly as Mangus has. When he got engaged to Katerina, Brisa was threatened and angry. She'd allowed them to be together but had made their lives hell, stripping them of a coven and not allowing them to make any prodigy.

They'd spent decades on the move, slaves to Brisa's errands, enforcing her rule of law whether they liked it or not. It's no wonder he found a way out of that, but I can see the torture in his eyes now. It's worse than the days of Brisa because at least before he still had his wife. Now he faces an eternity without her, and little to show for it.

"What was the bargain? What did you give up?" Eva asks, and his face crumples.

"I think that's enough," I interrupt. Mangus doesn't normally answer questions like this, and I can't have him figuring out what's going on here—— just how much power Eva has over us. I first realized it when she insisted her friends not come along with us back on that island. I'd been overcome with the need to make her wishes a reality.

But Mangus ignores me. Further proof. "I owe her a favor," he says. "Any favor that she can call upon at any time. Considering the fae never travel to our realm, I figure it won't be a problem."

Oh, brother, you're smarter than this.

Eva's face softens, and she pats his shoulder. Mangus has always been so hard to read, his emotions a glacier with very little on the surface, but right now he's entirely on display. He doesn't even flinch when Eva touches him, which wouldn't have happened with the old Mangus. The old Mangus was like the rest of the princes––stoic, professional, lethal, and no-nonsense.

Timing is a cruel mistress sometimes. If he hadn't made that bargain, Katerina would still be here. And Eva would've still killed Brisa, so he'd have been free of the blood bond either way. But things rarely work out the way they should, a lesson I've had to learn repeatedly since my human death. It's better to plan for the worst, especially if you want to stay alive.

"So why are we going to the Gateway?" Eva asks.

I think I already know. Mangus has figured things out. He wants to make another bargain.

"Sebastian wants to take the throne," Mangus says. It's no surprise that Seb is a greedy bastard, but I was expecting him to do something else. "We're going to make sure that doesn't happen." He turns to me. "It's time to tell her about the council."

My energy stores were so weak when they broke me out of the De Luca's place that I wasn't paying too much attention to where we were heading or why. But now we're in the air, and Eva is here, and all I want is to get her to safety. I'm not sure why she needs to know about the council, it might put her in danger to know too much.

"Go on," he prompts. "She's along for the ride now, might as well tell her what she's getting herself into."

But even I'm not sure what that is.

I narrow my eyes, but do as I'm asked and explain. Eva nods along, and when I'm finished, she doesn't say anything for a long time.

"On the one hand, I think the world would be better off without vampires, but I'm not as radical as I used to be, and I'm not like the other nephilim." Eva very well could be bluffing. She's hated vampires from the moment I met her, but I don't doubt her out loud. I can't risk what Mangus will do. "But on the other hand, that sounds like a better idea than a crazy monarch who has all the control. Brisa was awful, and Sebastian would be too."

"It's done. There will be no monarchy. The elections are almost finished, and then our council will be meeting soon."

"Do you really think voting is going to be enough?" Mangus deadpans. "How long have you been alive? How many monarchies and governments have we seen fall in our time on Earth?"

"Voting is all we have."

"Well, we need more than that, we need another blood bond, not a royal one, a council one, and that's why we're going to the Gateway."

My mouth pops open. It's brilliant. But it's also terribly dangerous. "You'd be willing to risk the future of our kind on the mercy of fae?"

"If we don't, there will be constant strife among the vampires, and Sebastian will never give up." Then he turns to Eva and drops the bomb. "He wants you, and he's got thousands of vampires looking for you. A council is in your benefit as much as ours."

Her face has gone ashen, and she doesn't move for several long seconds before nodding. "So what am I supposed to do? I'll do anything to get back to a normal life."

Mangus laughs bitterly. "Wouldn't we all. That's not how it works for people like us. Not anymore. Might I make a suggestion? Make your own bargain with the fae witch while you've got the chance."

"No," I snap. "She will do no such thing."

Eva slinks down in her seat and glares at me. "Do you have any better ideas?"

Not really, and she's stubborn as hell. If she's got an idea in her head, then she's going to act on it. So much for her just being along for the ride.

Thirty

᠀

"**W**elcome to Ireland," Mangus says when our jet lands an hour before sunrise. Rolling hills stretch in every direction around us, and I wish I could see the colors a bit better at night. We're being dropped off in the middle of nowhere, the adrenaline is gone, and I'm so exhausted that it's hard to muster up any excitement. We're in a country I've always wanted to visit, but once again, I'm no tourist.

Luckily the switch over from helicopter to private jet in Geneva was uneventful. And on our way off of the airplane, Mangus compelled the human pilots to forget all about us.

"There are not a lot of safe houses for vampires in Ireland," Adrian remarks as we watch the jet turn and taxi up the runway. It's a tiny airport and I'm sure those pilots will be out of here as soon as they gas up.

I spin in a slow circle, frowning at the structure-less land, and worry Adrian might be on to something. There's only the tiny airport but it's got lights on and humans inside. They need somewhere safe and private to hide from the sun that won't be tracked by hunters, but I have faith in their instincts to find just the place.

"Let's go," Mangus rises into the air, and Adrian lifts me into his arms.

"You're tired," he whispers against my ear as we take flight. "You rest, and I'll fly."

Maybe he's right, but I should probably fly myself since I'm still grappling with the idea of forgiving him. I'm still mad. I'm still hurt. But the truth is, bearing witness to that beating changed my perspective on our situation. I've realized how much he matters to me. I shouldn't want him anymore, but I do. I shouldn't forgive him, but I feel myself already starting to. And I've missed him. I've missed him so badly that it carved out my stomach and slowed my heart and fuzzied my head.

A few minutes later, we land on the grassy lawn of an old stone building with a few crumbling outbuildings. There's nothing else here.

"What is this place?" Adrian asks. "An abandoned farm?"

From the overgrown garden of dead brambles, the falling-down fences, and the fields beyond, I'd guess the same thing. "If nobody owns it, you won't have to get permission to enter."

Adrian scoffs. "Permission to enter is one of our flimsiest weaknesses anyway. I'm not worried about that." He sighs and heads toward the front door.

"Your boyfriend is a bit of an elitist." Mangus winks at me. "Poor guy is used to penthouse suites and palaces."

My heart skips at the word *boyfriend*, and I'm suddenly not sure what to do with my hands.

Adrian laughs, motioning to the decrepit house. "And you're telling me that with our global network and endless resources, this is the best you could do?"

"Beggars can't be choosers."

Their teasing allows me to relax.

"The vampire network is vast," Mangus explains. "We hacked into Brisa's accounts after her passing and were able to access them in their entirety: every coven, every property, every ally, all of it. But if I could hack that information, then it's possible others could as well, so it's best if we stay off the grid the closer we get to the Gateway. It's location is one she didn't record anywhere, and it's best that others don't find it."

Adrian pulls open the door and the entire thing comes off its hinges. He tosses it to the grass. "I hope you know what you're doing."

Mangus grins. "Worst case scenario, we dig like the old days."

I wonder about how many worst-case scenarios these men have been in, guessing that their stories would be more entertaining than anything I could dream up.

"You're talking to someone who was recently captured by the De Lucas, so you'll excuse me if I don't feel confident right now."

Mangus points to me. "Because she's your weak spot, and they knew it."

The guilt follows me into the old house with all its dust bunnies, peeling paint, and graffitied walls. I bet it has seen its fair share of squatters and bored teenagers looking for a place to party. But is it empty? I listen quietly, focusing on my heightened hearing, and don't find a beating heart or slow exhale other than my own. Unless a vampire is lying in wait, nobody is here.

We find an old staircase and head to the basement. There's not much down here. The floors are dirt, the ceiling is low, and there's no furniture. It's nothing like the opulence these vampires have grown accustomed to. But there are three rooms at the back of the basement without any windows, which is all the vamps need to hide.

"This is the exact opposite of what I had in mind," Adrian says ruefully to Mangus, who laughs. "But thank you for saving my life."

Mangus claps him on the back. "You would've done the same for me." Then he wanders off to check out the other rooms, and I'm left alone with Adrian.

"You too," he says. "I'd be gone if it weren't for you."

"Or because of me," I point out. "Mangus thinks I'm the reason you got caught. And honestly, his reasoning makes sense."

He brushes the comment off.

"I'm serious. You came to help me. You didn't have to do that." He wouldn't have been near the De Luca family if he hadn't been trying to get me that phone. I shudder to think what would've happened if he hadn't programmed it with Mangus's number. And it's only because he killed Fredrico that the family was shocked enough for us to break him free.

"I got caught because of me, not you," he says in a low rumble. "Stop blaming yourself."

A wave of exhaustion passes over me, and I yawn despite wanting to stay awake. My vision goes a little blurry, and I want nothing more than a bed. Looking at the dirt floor almost makes me want to cry.

"Come on, sleepyhead." He takes my hand and leads me into one of the dark rooms.

I'm slightly jealous that he doesn't have to sleep because I'd love to stay up and talk about things between us, but I'm beat. He sits down with his back to the wall and tugs me down into the dirt next to him. "Not exactly the Ritz Carlton," he teases.

"Ah, that's too rich for my blood anyway." I settle in and lay my head on his shoulder. Despite the cold, the closeness, and the hard planes of his body, I find myself relaxing and drifting off to sleep.

I wake reluctantly, teetering on the edge of falling back under.

"How are you feeling?" Adrian's raspy voice pulls me from the lapping waves of slumber.

His voice is pained, and I sit up, my eyes adjusting. There's not much light to go by, but with the added abilities from the venom, I can see everything. "I'm doing okay. What about you?"

He's still sitting in the same position he was when I fell asleep against him. Did he stay that way while I slept? Unmoving with nothing but his own thoughts?

"I owe you an apology," he says softly, and I study his face. He's serious––appearing like he hates himself, and I want to shake it away. This isn't the Adrian I'm used to. "I never should've involved you with my kind. I made that fake blood vow with you out of pure selfishness, and if I could go back I never would've done that."

I know where he's coming from, but I can't help the pang that hits my chest. Is he saying he wishes we'd never been together? Does he regret everything? My face falls, and he cups my cheeks with his hands.

"Please don't mistake me. I don't regret being with you, but I do regret hurting you. I've ruined your life."

"You haven't," I sigh, angling back to get a better look at him.

"If it weren't for me, you'd be back in New Orleans and none of this would've happened." He shakes his head, and a thick strand of golden hair topples to cover one eye. I push it back, and he winces.

"We can't speculate on what would or wouldn't have happened."

"Hugo wouldn't have targeted you."

"I'd killed his new prodigy, though," I press. "I did that. Me. That was my choice and had nothing to do with you."

"He wouldn't have known it was you if you weren't staying with me at the Alabaster and came in bleeding that night. Think of where you are." He motions around to the dilapidated basement. "You're hiding out here because of me. I've made your life infinitely worse, and I'm so sorry."

"What about my mom?" I argue. "You compelled her to give up her addiction. She never would've gotten better if I hadn't met you."

He sighs and leans back into the wall again, staring at the ceiling. "Addiction isn't that simple, Angel. I did what I could, but who's to say she won't wake up one day and make a different choice? Find a new vice? Compulsion can only go so far."

"Well, I'm still glad you did it." Does he not understand what that means to me? What anyone with a family member struggling with addiction would give to have the same offer? I'll take all the bad with Adrian if it means I get the good sometimes too.

"I did it because I owed you. Again, purely selfish on my part."

And now I know he's lying. He never owed me that. "No, Adrian, you did that because you care about me." I take his cold hands in mine and squeeze. "Don't try to deny it. I've been angry with you for so long, but only because I didn't want to admit the truth."

His eyes snap to mine. "And what's the truth?"

"That you're my ally and my friend," I swallow hard, "and more."

"I'm going to find a way to make you safe again," he growls, leaning forward to kiss my knuckles. "I'm going to give you your life back. I swear it."

"Stop--"

"And when I do, I'm going to leave you alone."

That's not what I want. His eyes are so earnest. He means every word, but those words are killing me. This isn't what I want. I see now how bad things have been for him. He's not a "good" man, but he's not a "bad" one either. He's like everyone else, living in the middle, doing the best he can with the crappy hand he was dealt.

"I said stop." I crawl into his lap and run my hands up his arms, then up his neck to thread my fingers into his hair. I press my forehead to his. "I forgive you, but it's you who needs to forgive yourself." My voice trembles as I say what's been on my mind ever since he told me about his past back in Versailles. "And you need to forgive yourself for what happened to your wife and unborn child all those years ago."

He's completely frozen, and I can't tell if he's processing or locking down. But then his eyes are on my mouth and his lips follow, and I lose all thought. His mouth is healing me, or maybe mine is healing him, because something unlocks between us. I'm overcome with a new level of vulnerability I haven't felt with anyone before, not even him when we were back at the palace. Warmth spreads from my heart and out into my chest. So perfect. So natural. I deepen the kiss and the warmth continues to grow.

Abruptly, Adrian sets me on my butt. He's up and backed into the corner of the room before I can blink. "Eva," he whispers, but he doesn't have to say more because I see it.

My hands are glowing again.

Not just my hands. My whole body. I'm lit up from the inside out with golden light--a light that is about to kill him.

Thirty-One

※

I jump up, about to scramble from the room, when Adrian speaks, "It doesn't hurt."

I turn back, and he's staring at me with utter amazement. He takes a step forward, and light reflects off his smooth skin. I flinch back toward the door. "It's okay," he continues, "it already got me. I should be ash by now, but I'm not."

"I don't understand," I mumble. "I killed all those vampires." I look down at my hands, my arms--they're still lit up. The light emitting from them is a soft golden glow that fills the room. "This doesn't make sense."

"You could probably kill me if you wanted to, but you don't want to kill me." He steps closer still. "So maybe that's the difference."

I mull that over in my mind. "It's about intention?"

He shrugs, and a smile stretches across his face.

When it happened the first time, I'd been under attack and the light had been a brighter white, blasting from my hands. It had come from a place of fear and desperation. But this? This is different. This is a lovely golden warmth that emerged from my heart and spread through my body when he kissed me. Adrian must be right, which means I have access to different kinds of light. Or maybe it's the same light, but I can use it in different ways. Either way, this news is revolutionary.

And dangerous.

"Nobody can know," I whisper.

He nods, and then he's back, wrapping his arms around me. "Your secrets are safe with me from now on. I promise you."

509

I shouldn't, but I believe him. "This doesn't hurt?" My light is wrapping around his body in a gentle caress.

"Not at all. It actually feels really nice." His voice goes hoarse. "I haven't felt this kind of warmth on my skin since I was human. I'd forgotten what it was like." He steps back and marvels at me. "You're like the sun, Angel."

He's right. That's exactly what this light reminds me of––like the golden hour when the sun is setting and the world goes fuzzy and warm. The light fades from my body as my excitement slows. It soon retreats, and I'm back to normal.

"What do you think it means?"

He stares at me for a long minute before speaking. "That you're a gift." His smile falters. "And that you're right. We can't tell anyone about this."

The rest is unspoken. Vampires have been trying to find a way to return to the daylight for centuries. This quest could be exactly why Brisa had wanted to find the fae so badly. She probably thought they could help her. What if they could use my gift to do it? My very existence could end human civilization as it is today. Everything would change.

"Do you think Mangus saw?" I whisper.

Adrian shrugs.

"Saw what?" Mangus's voice booms into our space as he opens the door. "Saw you kissing? Don't worry, I heard you making out and, no offense, but I don't need that lovey-dovey stuff right now. I went to check the perimeter. The sun set an hour ago; it's time for us to get moving."

I have no way to tell if he's lying, and I pray he isn't.

Adrian looks me up and down as if checking for any residual light, and then takes my hand and leads me from the room. We head outside, and nobody speaks. We take flight immediately, following Mangus into the darkness.

This time, I do fly myself, and it's relatively easy. It's like walking, once you get it, you get it. And I've got it. We're about ten feet up, gliding quickly over fields of green. There's no wind tonight. The outside world is quiet and peaceful, but my inner world is a jumbled mess. I don't know what's going to happen, and I'm afraid I've lost control. And now we're headed to a fae portal, which seems so unbelievable I'd laugh if I didn't know this was really happening.

It doesn't take long. We stop just outside of an ancient-looking grave-yard, and I can't help but shiver. This would be beautiful if the energy here didn't give me the creeps. Everything inside is screaming for me to get away. I step back, unable to proceed.

"Are you guys sure about this?" My voice comes out strained, but I don't even care. I just want to get out of here.

"That's the wards," Mangus says. He grabs my hand so I can't run off, but I'm willing to fight him if I have to. "They've made it so that anyone who comes here will immediately want to leave, supernatural or human or otherwise, everyone gets hit with that same feeling of dread."

"That's exactly what this is," Adrian's voice shakes. "Dread."

"You have to fight it."

Mangus's words are making sense, but my intuition is still screaming at me to run. I force those feelings into the background and hold onto Mangus and Adrian. The three of us walk together into the graveyard, a line of power against the wards. I feel stronger with them at my side. They give me the inner strength I need to get through this.

We weave between moss-covered graves so old and dilapidated that the inscriptions are unreadable. It's darker here than it was outside of the graveyard, perhaps that's one of the wards as well. A fog rolls in so fast and thick that I lose most of my visibility.

"We got you," Adrian says, squeezing my hand. I squeeze back.

"This way." Mangus leads us toward what I assume is the center of the graveyard. The fog clears, inking away on an ethereal breeze, and a massive tree looms above us. Its trunk is as wide as a house with gnarled branches growing in every direction like thick outstretched arms. The tree isn't of this world. Every season is present at once––caterpillar-green leaves the size of my face on some branches, buds of pink and white on others, some are covered with crumpled leaves of every autumn color, and several bare branches glitter with winter frost.

I'm drawn to it like a moth to a flame. I can't help but want to touch it. I reach my hands out, but Mangus yanks me back. "We go together."

I blink, perplexed by the sudden need to touch the tree, a need that hasn't diminished by Mangus's outburst. Wordlessly, the three of us link arms and Mangus is the first to touch the tree's ruddy bark. The world flashes and then goes dark as we're thrust forward. I hang on for dear life and squeeze my eyes shut as my body spins. It's as if we're being thrust through time and space, or something very near to it.

We stop abruptly. I blink, taking it all in, first amazed that we're still standing and hanging onto each other, but then amazed by the new world that has materialized around us. The tree is still in front of us, but the Irish graveyard is gone. A forest of crystalline trees of pure silver and gold and a blanket of black night still overhead are in its place. Long strings of purple mist weave through the trees like ribbons. One stops at our feet and then rushes away as if it's got a mind of its own. Maybe it does.

"What was that?" Adrian asks.

"A messenger to let the guardian know we're here," Mangus says. "Now don't touch anything. And I mean *anything*. This is not our realm, and we're not meant to be here."

"Oh joy," Adrian mutters.

Truth be told, I'm still in awe even though my gut says he's right. "This is the most stunning place I've ever seen," I whisper, "it's straight out of a fairytale."

"No, Eva. This isn't a fairytale, and you're no princess," Mangus corrects. "One mistake here and you're dead, so let me do the talking."

I nod once.

"And for God's sake, whatever you do, don't eat anything."

The ground shakes. I've never experienced an earthquake before, but this is exactly what I imagine it would feel like. Adrenaline strikes through my veins and my knees weaken as I try to keep steady. Something shoots out of the ground a few paces away from us, rising up like a small mountain. The ground calms, and upon further inspection, I gasp. It's a cottage. Exactly like one you would see in a fairytale.

"Isadora is an earth fae witch," Mangus explains. "She's also a guardian of the portal, making sure people like us turn back if we do happen to make it this far."

Adrian frowns. I can tell he wants to say something, but he stays silent.

The front door to the house creaks open. "Back so soon?" A wispy voice floats from inside. "And you brought company this time."

I swallow hard.

"Please, come inside."

"We're good out here," Mangus says, shooting us a look that says do not go in that house under any circumstance.

The voice sighs. "Very well, I'll come to you." The woman is not what I'm expecting. In my mind, an old crone would step from the earthen hobble to make deals with us, but in reality, it's a gorgeous fae who glides toward us. She's petite and pointy, with a slender waist and sharp shoulders, cheek-bones, and of course, pointed ears. Her white-blonde hair flows in tight curls all the way down to her knees, and her olive skin glistens with emerald green undertones. She wears a tight gown resembling moss, and as she moves closer, I realize it actually is moss that's clinging to her body. She's gorgeous and earthly and terrifying all at once, and bright amber eyes flash to me as if sensing my fear.

"We've come to strike three deals with you," Mangus says.

"One deal," Adrian quips, glaring at his brother.

"Three deals," Mangus repeats, and I'm confused. We're here to make a bargain for magic to seal the council into a blood bond and force the vampires to follow the rule of law. That's what I agreed to. And it's a great plan that will take one bargain with the fae witch, *not three*.

What is Mangus up to?

"Did you not appreciate the last bargain, vampire?" Isadora's smile spreads across her face like a sunbeam, her beauty amplifying tenfold. I don't trust it, even though it draws me in. Glancing at my companions, I suspect they're feeling the same way. Their eyes are pinned to the fae, their faces are soft, and their bodies are unnaturally relaxed.

"Your spell to release me from my maker's blood bond worked, but had unintended consequences," Mangus says darkly. "My wife was killed in the process."

Isadora pouts and traces pointy fingers along Mangus's cheek. "You poor thing. Do you need consoling?"

"Enough––" Adrian cuts in. "We're here because we need you to recreate a vampiric blood bond similar to a master and a prodigy." All eyes turn on him as he explains what's needed. It's an intricate plan, but a good one, and by the end of it, Isadora seems impressed with the ingenuity.

"I can do it." Isadora's amber eyes flash gold with mischief. "But it's going to cost you a great deal."

"Name your price," Adrian says.

She turns and grins in my direction. "I'll take the girl."

Thirty-Two

I freeze, readying my stance. If I have to fight this woman, I will, but I don't know what kind of magic she possesses besides the earthquakes, so I doubt I'll win. The tree from the graveyard is several paces behind us, and I prepare to make a run for it. If it doesn't send me back through the portal, I don't know what I'll do.

"You're not touching her." Adrian glowers at the witch. His rage is a growing inferno, and he has no problem putting himself between me and Isadora.

"Oh, relax," Mangus drawls, "nobody is going to hurt your little angel." He smiles at Isadora. "As I was saying, there are three things I'm here to bargain for."

"Mangus––" Adrian hisses.

"There are actually two blood bonds that need addressing," Mangus continues unperturbed, "the one Adrian described, and the one that strips Eva here from having any control over my kind."

I frown, questions spinning me to dizziness. What is he talking about? Does he mean he doesn't want me to have power from the venom anymore? But that has nothing to do with control over his kind. "I don't know what you're talking about," I say, "but I don't consent to whatever the hell it is you think you're doing, Mangus."

Both men turn on me. "So you really don't know?" Adrian asks.

"Of course she knows," Mangus snorts. "It's quite obvious."

Know what? I know that the venom has made me strong enough to survive their kind, but that's about it.

"Let's get this done. We don't need her consent for this anyway." My breath hitches, and he shoots a sly grin at the witch. "What else do you want?"

Isadora's eyes squint as she looks me over, but I'm more confused than ever. I don't understand what I'm missing. Everyone knows about the venom already, so what else could they be talking about? "I already gave my terms. I want the girl."

"I'm not for sale." I glare and step back.

"Nobody is touching Eva," Adrian agrees.

"Fine," the witch huffs. "Then I'll take the next best thing." Her bottomless eyes pin me in place. "Her blood."

I shake my head.

"Only a thimble-full. You won't miss it."

"Can't you take something else?" Adrian growls. "You can have my blood. As much as you want."

The witch hisses. "I don't want your dirty blood, vampire. I will change the blood bonds, but this is my payment. Take it or leave."

My heart thuds in my chest. I don't want to give her my blood, but I want the vampires secured under Adrian's new government. It will save countless lives.

"Let's not forget the third request." Mangus steps forward, voice growing desperate. "Bring my wife back. She was wrongly accused of my death because of your spell."

That's new information . . .

"Even if I could bring a vampire back, I wouldn't," the earth witch hisses. "Don't ask for that abomination."

"Please, I'll do anything." His eyes flash violently to me, and I'm certain he's about to offer me over, but when our gazes meet, something inside of him crumbles. Can he do it? Will he? Would I do the same if I were in his position?

"Enough," the witch's booming voice breaks through the forest like a crack of thunder. "I will spell your blood magic, but I will not perform necromancy." She points to Mangus. "And you will give this up. Even if you were to find a fae dark enough to bring your wife back, she wouldn't be the same. She'd be a shadow of herself, and she would hate you for it."

His head falls, but he nods solemnly. I feel bad for him except for the part where he seemed mighty willing to hand my life over in exchange for Katerina's.

I turn on the vampires. "I'll do it, okay. I'll give a thimble of my blood to your witch, but I have some terms of my own."

"Don't do it." Adrian surprises me. "Let's go. We'll find another way. Your blood is not worth what--"

"Let her speak," Mangus cuts him off. "We came this far."

I take a deep breath and draw on my desire to do the right thing, even if it costs me. "I'll help with the blood bonds if you promise that you'll do everything in your power to keep me and my friends and family safe from vampires." My heart aches to think of what this will mean for my romance with Adrian. As much as I want him, I think of Mom and Felix, Ayla and Seth, and I know it's for the best if we part ways before this goes any further. "You have to promise to make sure vampires leave us alone."

They're going to make up two of the council members and have more control over their own kind than they ever before. It's the least they can do for me.

"Is that really what you want?" Adrian's throat bobs, and his eyebrows furrow.

The truth is, my head and my heart want completely different things, but this isn't about what I want anymore. This is about what I need. "Yes," I whisper.

He takes my hand, squeezes it, and then drops it. "Alright then."

"Done," Mangus promises. "You have our word."

I peer down at my shoes and then up at the witch before I lose my nerve. "Do it."

Her mouth quirks. "You know, most people wouldn't give up the kind of control you currently possess," she says, "which leads me to believe you don't know what you have."

"Control?" My mind reels. "I've never had control. Not once. Not in all my life."

"Well, you did, but it's too late now," she laughs, snatching my hand in hers so fast I almost don't see it happening. Her fingernails are long, pointed, and the same color as her mossy gown. She drags one along the top of my index finger, slicing a small incision into the skin. A crimson bead rises to the surface and she squeezes.

Part of me wants to pull away, to go back on my word, but I can't move. And it's not because I'm afraid, although I am, it's because I've become immobilized by her power. I gasp as earthy roots wrap around my arms and limbs, they move just as fast as she does.

"Almost done," she whispers, "Don't worry your pretty little head. It'll all be over soon."

"What do you want my blood for, anyway?" I whisper back, but she doesn't answer. Whatever it is, it can't be good, and maybe Adrian was right. But if doing this gets the vampires off my back and allows me to live a somewhat normal life and keep my loved ones protected, then it'll be worth any cost. "What did you mean about giving up control?" I ask instead.

This question, she does answer--an answer that guts me down my center.

"Looks like you took possession of the royal bond from Brisa," she says with a little cackle. My ears ring, and my throat itches. I can hardly believe what I'm hearing. "Your friends figured it out. Too bad they didn't tell you."

If they'd told me, everything would've been different.

"Of course, I sensed it the moment the three of you broke into my domain. And to think, you could've bossed around these princes. Ha! Wouldn't that have made you queen?"

"Stop talking, witch," Mangus growls from behind me. "You've done enough already."

And Adrian says nothing.

I try to look over at the men, but the vines hold my head in place. I can hear them, but I can't see them. The night goes eerily silent as Isadora's confession sinks into me like a knife--a blade of betrayal that I can hardly believe, but that I can't deny has sliced me clean open.

"How long?" I whisper.

She smiles. "Long enough."

It definitely wasn't a thing when I was at risk for being turned because Adrian didn't help me, so it must have solidified later. I revisit the interactions I've had with vamps over the last twenty four hours and realize they've done everything I've asked. But how was I to know? I've been running from vampires and hiding out alongside nephilim with so few opportunities to tell a vampire to do anything. Did Tate know? Did Camilla? I don't think so. If they had, they would've been much more forceful with me. Or maybe they did know, maybe that was why they were trying so adamantly to get me on their side. *No.* Because they would've made me ask Adrian about the Gateway outright, which I never did.

"Don't worry, little angel, I'll make sure they stick to their agreement with you." The witch pouts, but she's not sorry at all. Her eyes gleam with delight. "I do feel a little bad about this, you know. I'm no dark witch, I do have a heart."

I glare. "Could've fooled me."

She dramatically clasps her hands to her chest. "No really, I have a heart. Only dark fae give up their hearts for power."

She rattles on, but my mind drowns her out, the revelations spinning through my head. I had everything I needed to change the entire world, and now it's all gone.

She finishes squeezing the last of the blood into her thimble and caps it off with a lid, tucking it into the moss of her gown. I expect her to release me from the vines, but she doesn't. I'm stuck, and panic begins to bubble. I suck in quick gasps of air as my eyes fill with hot tears.

She begins to speak in a language I don't know, the consonants longer than anything I've heard before. A wash of peaceful warmth trickles through me, allowing me to relax just a little, but it's quickly replaced with an empty nothingness.

They're talking now. Somewhere behind me. They're talking. She's telling them that I have no more power over them. She's saying that the binding of the vampire council's bond is temporary until they complete her spell. She's saying that her magic only goes so far and will require some work on their part. I'm too overwhelmed to catch much of their conversation, and the harder I try, the harder it is to listen.

"Breathe," I say softly to myself. "Just breathe, Eva." This is important. Somehow I know I need to be listening in, catching every last detail.

"And when do we do the ritual?" Mangus asks.

"The next full moon." If the new moon was yesterday, then the full moon will be here in a few weeks. I want to scream at Adrian for the position I'm in, but I keep my mouth shut. It's almost like I'm forgotten by all of them, trapped in these blasted vines, facing a gold and silver forest while they chatter like I don't exist.

The gold . . .

It calls to me, a reminder of who I am and what I can do. If I can just pull my angelic light to the surface, I can get out of here. I can break free, and they'll wish they'd never underestimated me when I turn that light on them. All of them.

"You're not the only vampires to have found me," Isadora says, knocking my focus away from golden light to what she's saying instead. "But I do hope you'll be the last. We don't care for your kind here. If you fail to complete the spell, don't come back. There will be no second chances."

The vines snap away, and I fall to my hands and knees. I expect pain, but the earth is soft, as if it's caressing me. Consoling me. Is this Isadora's doing? Maybe she doesn't hate me like she hates the vampires. Maybe she really does feel sorry for me. Before I can question her, Adrian's familiar arms are lifting me, and his mouth is whispering against my ear, "Thank you."

Thirty-Three

〜◯〜

We leave the same way we came, hurtled through time and space, returned to our realm in the blink of an eye. The magical forest is gone, replaced by the foggy graveyard. We land next to each other among the tombstones. This time, the ground is not so forgiving. I hit it hard. It knocks the wind from my lungs and rattles my bones.

Get up, get up, get up . . .

But my body doesn't want to comply. My thoughts are a riot. My heart is numb. I'm still floating in that awful emotionless void, still stunned by everything that just happened. Adrian lifts me into his arms again, and then we're flying, up and away. The night is pitch-black, but he seems to be in a hurry anyway. I blink through watery eyes, noticing that Mangus is flying right next to us. He looks the same as I feel––utterly broken. He really must have thought he'd be able to get his wife back.

We don't go back to the old farmhouse. We fly over a city and land on the roof of one of the tallest buildings in the city's center.

Where are we? I think, but when Adrian answers, I realize I've spoken aloud. I hadn't meant to. My thoughts and my words are mixed together, and I wonder what else I've been saying during our flight here.

"We're in Dublin," he says. "The coven here are our friends. They'll house us for a day or two until we can get back home."

Back home. It doesn't seem real.

Mangus drops his face into his hands. "And where's your home?" I ask him boldly. A fire has reignited within––he'd *used* me tonight.

But Mangus turns away, and Adrian is the one to answer. "Mangus doesn't have a coven, so he's coming back to New Orleans until he figures out his next step."

So that's it then. They got what they wanted. At least I'll be able to return home, but it won't change the fact that the De Lucas will be waiting for me. Everything that happened with them still stings. It hurts that I can't trust them. My own family.

My own family...

Something about that rings alarm bells in my head, but then it slips away as Adrian stands me upright and I take in the glittering city lights and the beautiful Georgian-era buildings. I have no trouble with my vision, so at least I didn't lose the abilities the venom gave me.

"I haven't been here in over a hundred years," Adrian breathes. "So much has changed, and then some things look exactly as I remembered."

Mangus nods.

"But what I do remember is that the coven here is ruthless. Has that not changed? Are you sure they're our allies in this?"

"They voted for our plan," Mangus says.

They discuss their plans while I walk to the edge of the rooftop to admire the view. It's truly spectacular, and I'd give anything to be here under different circumstances. "Another bucket list item to check off," I grumble. But I won't. This doesn't count.

I hear mention of the full moon and Isadora's name, and a shiver runs down my body. What will she do with my blood? I don't know anything about fae, and I have no idea what to expect, but since they seem to stay in their realm and we stay in ours, I hope that whatever she does won't affect me here.

I swing around to say something to the men, but they're already strolling toward the rooftop doorway without me. Mangus swings the door open and Adrian walks through. I'm so startled, I almost let them go. "Hey, wait," I call. "You're just going to leave me here?"

They look back, squinting at me for a long second, and then Mangus says. "Come on then."

I step forward just as a loud crack hits the rooftop, followed by a couple of shadowy figures falling from the sky and several more crawling over the edges of the roof. The shadows stop moving, and I realize they're not shadows, they're vampires dressed in black.

"We've been looking for you," Sebastian says with a sharp-toothed grin, his focus zeroing in on me. His trenchcoat swooshes around his ankles as he takes a step closer and my nerves turn to ice. They're surrounding me on all sides, more vampires than I can comprehend, and far more than I can fight.

I call upon my light magic, willing it to the surface, but nothing happens. I glance at my hands, shaking them out.

Someone tackles me to the ground, and my hands are quickly tied behind my back. I don't understand the different kinds of light yet, but the one I'd killed Brisa with had sprung from my hands. It was nothing like the golden all-over light I'd conjured from kissing Adrian. My face is pressed into the hard surface of the rooftop as someone sits on top of me, keeping my hands restrained and my body pinned tight. The ligaments of my shoulders burn, and I muffle a cry.

"What do you want?" I crane my neck up. Where is Adrian? Mangus? Surely, they'll stop this. But then I see they've also been restrained, and even though they're impossibly strong, there's an entire coven's worth of suckers here to keep them in line.

"You betrayed me," Mangus growls at one of the Irish-looking vampires, but the burly man only shrugs and says that had he known about me, he would've sided with Sebastian.

So what do they know about me then?

Sebastian kneels down to get a better look at me. Is this it? Is this the end of my life? So many times I'd told myself I'd rather die than become one of them, but now faced with death, I'm not sure I'm that brave. It's all too much, and I almost beg him to turn me.

No. I won't do that. I'll never do that.

"Stand her up, Kenton," Sebastian motions to the fanger with their knee currently jammed into my spinal cord. "I want a better look at her."

My heart races. "Kenton?" I gasp as the man hauls me up. I crane my neck back, and sure enough, it's my old friend holding my arms.

I'm reminded of the first time I met him. It was in that graveyard and he'd handed me the stake that had ended up saving my life. "You were dead," my voice cracks. "I saw you. You were dead."

His eyes flash to me, red-rimmed and glowing with bloodlust. "Oh, I remember, Eva. How could I forget dying for you?"

Guilt wracks my chest because he's right. He died in battle for my life. Or at least, I thought he'd died. He must have still been alive, clinging onto the last shreds of life, and then one of them found him.

"She brought me back," he explains, his voice a low rumble against my ear. "And she made me so much stronger."

"I'm so sorry," I whisper. The tears break through and leak down my face. I'd give anything to go back and save him from this fate.

"Don't be," he sneers, shoving me toward Sebastian.

Sebastian's grin is ruthless when he grabs hold of me. He looks so much like his twin, Hugo, that I'm momentarily speechless. "Tell her," he nods to

Kenton. "What is life like as a vampire? Is it really as bad as you believed it to be?"

I stare at my friend as his old familiar smile lights his face and then fangs slip out of his gums. "Being a vampire is incredible," Kenton steps forward, and his harsh voice softens. "When it's your turn, you're going to love it. I promise."

"When it's my turn?" I squeak. He sounds so much like the old, caring Kenton. My stomach twists. This was his worst nightmare.

"Don't worry," Sebastian says. "That won't happen for a long time, and when it does, you'll be begging for it."

"Wait, who is 'she'?" I question my old friend. "Who found you?"

Kenton's smile is genuine, and my heart drops for the boy I loved deeply. The boy who fought alongside me for all that is supposed to be good and right in the world. "I'm one of the princes now," he says. "Isn't it wonderful?"

"I--I don't understand."

His eyes glitter with possibility. "Brisa is my maker."

"That's a lie," Adrian growls from over Sebastian's shoulder. "Brisa is dead."

"We felt the bond break," Mangus adds. "Sebastian, you did too. Don't lie to these people." He looks around at the coven of vampires. "Well, are you going to just sit here and let him lie to you?"

"Did you feel the bond break, though?" Sebastian asks his brothers. "Or did you feel the bond transfer? Because you see, it turns out there's a big difference."

That's when the truth of it hits me.

I took Brisa's royal blood bond, but I didn't actually kill her. And it's not as if I saw her die. Nobody did. There was light and there was screaming and then there was nothing.

The crowd of shadows parts, and the vampire queen steps through, her glowing amber eyes right on me. She's as beautiful as ever, and radiant in her rage. "Hello, Evangeline," she says, "I believe you have something that belongs to me."

Thirty-Four

⁂

"Actually, she doesn't. There is no more royal blood bond." Adrian pushes his captors off him with the force of a hurricane and strides right up to Brisa. He's a man possessed by revenge and without an ounce of fear. The way he is toward her now is a complete one-eighty to how he was with her before.

Brisa's eyes go dark. A breeze catches her honey hair on the wind, and it whips behind her as she snarls. "You dare to betray me? Oh, I know all about your pathetic council."

Adrian's laugh is maniacal. I've never seen him like this. "Betray you? We thought you were dead. How can I betray a ghost?"

"You didn't even try to find me! I went into hiding and was right to assume Sebastian is the only one of my children left who is worth anything, considering your and Mangus's disgusting behavior."

"What would you have had us do?" Adrian throws up his hands. "Try to have three princes rule together without a royal blood bond to make sure our laws are actually imposed? We'd have been assassinated." He points to Sebastian. "By your *oh-so-worthy* son."

"It doesn't matter now," she says in a clipped tone, "I'm back. And I will forgive you if you help me, but if you get in my way, I will kill you." They stare off, neither willing to break. Mangus drops his head.

No. This can't be. Things can't go back to the way they were.

"She was always going to kill you," I burst out. "She told me." I look at the three brothers. "All of you. She said she was going to start a new line of heirs, starting with me."

The men don't react at all. Had they known, or is this news? Brisa turns those killer eyes on me, strides forward, and slaps me clean across the face, her sharp nails cutting the skin. It burns hot, but I refuse to back down. "You would be wise to keep that mouth shut. Have you forgotten with whom you're speaking? I am the queen of all vampires."

"Not anymore," I hiss back. "There's no royal blood bond, remember?"

Her pupils dilate as long, thin fangs extend. "With or without the blood bond, I am still queen. I'm taking the bond back, and then we shall see what becomes of you after we are through with your gift."

I swallow hard. Of course, she wants my gift. She saw it, she survived it. And now she wants to do something with it. And when she's done, there's no doubt she'll kill me. The hatred burning through her eyes is great and terrible––and directed entirely at me. But strangely, I'm not afraid. A sense of calm takes control of my body, and everything becomes crystal clear.

"And how exactly are you going to take it back?" I tilt my head, looking her up and down. She needs me, which means she needs me alive.

"It transferred with our exchange of blood the first time," she says, "so we'll exchange blood again to transfer it back."

Except that it's gone, done away by fae magic. I open my mouth to argue, but she's too fast. Like a bullet leaving its chamber, she's on me, sinking her teeth deep into my neck. I scream out as pain slices through me and venom pours into my veins. "Last time you did this I almost killed you," I say between gasping breaths. "How can you be so sure it will work this time?"

But my hands are bound, and everything feels different than before. Worse. I start to fade. She's drinking so much so fast. My knees go weak. Then Brisa is being ripped away from me, Adrian the one pulling her off.

"There is no more royal bond!" he booms, and the world goes silent. "You're going to kill the only asset you have left."

The only asset she has left . . . I fall to my knees, trying to breathe, trying to stop my heart from breaking at his words. Everyone turns to look at him, half the group curious and half the group gearing to rip his head off.

"We didn't know you were alive," he says carefully, "so we took Eva to the Gateway."

Brisa's eyes go wide, and Mangus laughs from where he's being held by the door. "Why did you think we came to Ireland, Mother?" he calls out. "Wow, you've really lost your edge, haven't you?"

"What did you do?" she growls, and Mangus is thrown at her feet. "What did you do!"

"You killed Katerina," he glares up at her. "You blamed her for deaths that were your own doing. All the princes? Is Eva telling the truth, *Mother*? Were you killing off your children one by one only to pin the blame on Kat?"

She glares right back. "I did as I saw fit. Those who are weak are culled. This is our way, don't act so surprised."

He rolls onto his back and laughs. "So she admits it, ladies and gentlemen."

"What did you do, Mangus?" She drags him to standing. "What happened at the Gateway?"

He spits in her face, and she rears back, horrified.

"Guess what, mommy-dearest? I don't have to tell you shit anymore."

They're about to fight, and it's one Mangus won't win, but he doesn't seem to care. I do, though, and I care about Adrian and Kenton who might get caught up in the fray.

"They made a bargain with a fae witch!" I yell.

"Eva, don't," Adrian growls.

It doesn't stop me. "The effects of your precious royal blood bond have been transferred to the vampiric council." Satisfaction sweeps through me as the crowd murmurs, and Brisa's face falls. "So yeah, I don't have it anymore. I never even knew I did, or believe me, most of you bloodsuckers would be dead by now."

Brisa screams--and maybe I shouldn't have added that last part. Sebastian goes for Adrian, and Mangus is jumped by several vampires at once just as Brisa dives for me. I'm on the ground in an instant, my head pounding against the stone. I'm going to die. There's no doubt in my mind that she intends to kill me. I'm no use to anyone now, and I'm a liability to the vampires if I'm alive. But at least I beat her in this one thing.

"Leave me alone," I cry when her fangs catch my neck again. She'll tear me apart in seconds. "Stop! Leave me alone! All of you, please--" the last part is a choked sob.

She's there, uncaring, violent--and then she's gone.

I blink and sit up, trying to catch my breath. Inexplicably, they're all being dragged away as if by some invisible force. *What in the world?* I don't understand it. I reach out toward Adrian, trying to catch his hand as it reaches toward me. His eyes are panicked as he yells, "This is the condition you made. It's the fae magic!"

And then they're being pushed off the rooftop and are lost to the darkness.

Every last one of them.

I jump up and run to the edge of the building, searching the streets below, but there's no sign of them. It's just a quiet, beautiful city in the middle of the night. Not a soul to be seen--not even the soulless.

I press my hands to my neck. It's slick with blood. I've already lost a lot, and my mind is hazy and light. My fingers search out the wounds, but I find that they're already knitted back together. There's so much powerful venom in my blood now that I healed as quickly as a vampire would have.

But I'm in no danger of becoming a vampire because I didn't take any blood from her tonight. We didn't get that far. No locking myself up for three nights.

I blink, the realization of Adrian's final words hitting me--it was the fae magic. I yelled at Brisa to leave, demanded they all go, and they did. Not by choice, they were forced away, as if by magic.

The fae said that she'd make the vampires hold up their end of the deal with me, and boy did she honor that. She got a thimble of my blood, they got their spell for the council blood bond, and I got my wish, that the vampires would leave me and my friends and family alone.

And when I demanded it, all of them were forced away.

I want to cry, to scream, to laugh, to smile, to rage . . . but I do none of those things. Instead, I walk to the edge of the building and jump, levitating down to the street without issues. I need to get out of here. Not just out of Dublin, but out of Ireland.

It's time to go home.

Thirty-Five

Turns out fleeing a foreign country without any money or identification is no walk in the park. I wander around the streets for a few hours attempting to come up with a plan. I'm shivering and have no clue where I am, and I'm not as smart as I thought I was because I've literally got nothing. When the sun finally rises, I feel as if I can breathe fully again. The light bathes the city in warmth and calms my nerves.

I sit down on a bench and close my eyes. *You can figure this out.*

It's not like when I was in Paris and had a countdown clock hanging over my head. At least now the vampires can't come after me. The nephilim are another story, but they won't know where I am, and by the time I get back to New Orleans, I'll have come up with a better plan to avoid them, even if it means getting Mom and going on the run. Adrian made sure my rent was paid and had worked out a deal with Pops so I can return to my old life, but I know that's not in the cards anymore. Mom and I will have to go start a new life somewhere else. We can get new talismans to take with us.

It seems too simple and too impossible all at once, but it's the only plan I've got, so I cling to it. First things first, I need safe passage out of Ireland. I frown down at my tattered clothing. I'm in all black, which helps hide the blood, but I'm also filthy and need to find something presentable to wear. I'll have to convince someone to let me use their shower and give me new clothes or access to a washing machine. While they're at it, some food and water would be nice, but I'm not going to count on that.

The thought makes my stomach grumble. What do vampires do when they're in situations like these? Oh, that's right, they just compel humans to get whatever they need. I obviously can't do that, but I'm as fast and as quiet as a vamp. Maybe I can sneak into someone's flat while they're at work, and then once I've gotten myself cleaned up, I can find the U.S. Embassy. This is the capital of Ireland, so there should be one, and if anyone can help me get back home, they're my best bet.

I find an apartment building that doesn't look nice enough to have good security and peer up at the windows. The sun reflects off of them, so I have to go around the corner to look from a different angle. I feel icky, but I don't know what else to do. Most of the windows are covered with curtains or blinds, but a few aren't, and I can see right into several living rooms.

A car screeches to a stop right in front of me. I slink back against the brick building just as a door is thrown open. My immediate instinct is to run, and that instinct is confirmed when Leslie Tate glares up at me as he climbs from the vehicle. He's quickly followed by Camilla and the twins, Enzo and Nicco. The twins are fast, splitting to either side of me, boxing me in.

"How did you find me?" My fingers clench, and I glance up. I could fly, but we're in broad daylight and there are people around. Right now though, I'm not sure that will stop me.

"A lot of people care about you, Eva," Tate says. "We're here to help."

Another door opens and a rumpled-looking Felix and Seth climb out. I gape at them, wanting to tell them off, but they shoot me sharp warning looks that make the hairs on the back of my neck stand. Something isn't right, and now isn't the time or place to interrogate my friends. I just hope they hadn't gone running back to the nephilim. I don't think I can take another betrayal.

"They didn't know I was coming to Ireland," I challenge. "So why don't you tell me how you really found me."

Camilla smiles and smooths out her already perfect silver hair. "You're a smart girl. Think on it for a while, and it'll come to you."

I have thought about this––how Tate knew to find me outside the cata-combs and how he's conveniently known about some of the vampire's whereabouts. Even back in New Orleans, he came to Adrian's suite when I was locked up there, not to retrieve me but to do something else, something I still haven't figured out.

"Well, I know your boys here are trackers," I nod to the twins, "but that doesn't fully explain how you keep finding me, especially back in Paris. If I had to guess, I'd say you have a mole somewhere in the vampire's orga-nization."

"Ah, very good," Camilla winks. I know she won't outright give up her source, but I'm dying to know who it could be. All the vampires I've met seem pretty keen on staying alive, so an alliance with the neph doesn't make sense.

"Why can't you let them go home?" I point to my friends. "They're good people with bright futures that you're ruining."

"How many times do we have to tell you, Eva?" Felix pipes up. "We want to be here. We want to hunt and protect. School and everything else can wait." I'm not sure he believes the rhetoric he's spewing. How can I know if that's the real him or the one manipulated by Tate's mind-tricks?

I'm preparing to make a run for it when Camilla pounces. For an old lady, she's fast as a whip, grabbing hold of me and hanging on tight. I scream and push her away, but then Tate is on me too, holding me still while his mother-in-law slides into my mind. Her attack is violent and thorough, riffling through memories and ripping them to shreds in the process. It burns like an instant headache, and I gasp in horror.

Just when I think I'll pass out, she releases me, and I stumble to my knees. I glare up at her through strands of dirty hair, hoping she can see the vitriol in my eyes. "You are a murderer," I seethe. "I know what you did to my father––to your own child. You make me sick."

She stomps her foot, and I jump. "You don't know the whole story."

"I know enough."

"Sacrifices have to be made. This is a war. And we'll continue to make sacrifices to win it."

My eyes flick to my friends, and I know this is a veiled threat. She'll kill them if I don't cooperate. For the first time, I'm pretty sure they know it, too.

"Get in the car or see what further sacrifices I'm willing to make," she demands.

I have no choice but to get in, I'm not going to risk my friends. They slide in after me, and I buckle up. I'm exhausted and angry, but most of all I'm frustrated. I feel so hopeless. There's nothing I can do. Getting away from the De Lucas the first time was hard enough, but now Camilla knows everything. She knows I can levitate, she knows about the blood bond, she saw me go to the Gateway. She has *everything*.

"I'm not happy about the blood bond," Camilla says. "I can't believe we missed that."

"Sorry to disappoint," I snort.

"And that blood you gave to the fae," she continues, exasperated. "Do you know what you've done? Do you know what a fae can do with a nephilim's blood freely given like that? They can't just take it, they have to have it given, and you barely put up a fight."

I scoff, "But you saw exactly why . . ."

"To help the vampires," she lifts a brow. "Oh, I saw enough."

I fold my arms over my chest and glare out the window. It's not like she's going to answer my questions about the fae anyway. And what does she expect here? I did the best I could in a crappy situation.

"But I do have to thank you for something marvelous you did on your little adventure."

I turn back. The car is one of those limousines that seat a bunch of people, and they're all staring at me now. "And what's that?"

"You're smarter than I gave you credit for."

"What did she do?" Tate asks.

"The fae cast a spell, and Eva made sure the spell included something valuable." My throat goes dry, but I let her finish. "The vampires are not to hurt her friends and family. Isn't that sweet?" She taps her fingers together in excitement. "And they're to leave them alone."

I roll my eyes. This isn't her business.

Tate and Camilla smirk as if they've just won the lottery but can't let anyone know until they've secured a good lawyer.

"What?" I give in, curiosity getting the best of me.

"You already know," Camilla taunts.

"I don't--"

And then it hits me . . . *family*. At the time I'd been thinking of Mom's well-being, but she's not the only family I have. The De Lucas are my family too. I've unwittingly made it so vampires can't harm them.

"Congratulations," Tate deadpans. "You figured it out."

I sink back into my seat, the gravity of the situation dropping a million pounds of weight onto me. I can't believe I was so foolish. If the De Lucas can't be harmed, then they'll be free to hunt vampires as they see fit. Months ago it would have been great news, but I feel differently now. I still hate most vampires, but they're not all bad, and I have friends who are vampires now. Mangus helped me, I'm still in love with Adrian, and Kenton got a second chance.

"We'll start with the princes." Camilla turns from me to direct orders to Tate. "Take them out, and then we'll work our way down the ranks."

I shake my head. "No!"

"Hush, girl. Let the grown-ups talk."

"Adrian and Mangus aren't bad. They're not the ones you want."

That does it. All the De Lucas glare daggers at me as Tate sneers, "Believe me, they're the ones I want to kill first, especially Adrian. And how can you say he's not bad when you saw him murder Fredrico?"

Were we not in the same room? They were torturing Adrian when he did that. They're the ones who forced it out of him, they're the ones who put

Fredrico in that position to begin with. But they don't care, they've got an opportunity to strike at the vampires, and they're going to seize it.

"Wait," I interrupt, heart hammering in my ribcage. "Brisa is still alive. Camilla saw that, too. Take her out first. She's the worst of all of them."

"She's powerless now," Camilla grins wickedly, "thanks to you, my dear." She studies me for a long minute, and I don't know what to say. For once I'm completely speechless and out of ideas. There's nothing I can do. I don't even know who my enemies are anymore because everything has gotten so convoluted. I've made a mess of it all, but the one thing I know for sure is I don't want Adrian,Kenton, and Mangus to die. Not even for a bigger cause. Not even if it's the "right" thing to do.

"You can be a team player or you can be locked up," Camilla offers. "Your choice."

What choice is that?

"I'm a team player," I lie because being locked up isn't going to help anyone. I have no intention of hurting the vampire princes unless we're talking about Sebastian, but if I can be part of the team to hunt them down, then maybe I can warn them before it's too late.

"Good." Her eyes flick to Felix and Seth, and I know the threat is there again. Do what she wants, or watch the ones I love pay the price. "First things first, take us to the Gateway."

My mouth pops open. The last place I want to go is back to that fae portal, and I certainly don't want to see the witch again. She even said she didn't want us to return. I can't go back there. "Why?" my voice cracks, and I swallow my fear.

"Because we've been looking for it, and you can get us there," Tate states the obvious while simultaneously avoiding my question, but Camilla can tell I'm not satisfied with his answer. She sighs heavily.

"As long as there are abominations walking this earth, then it is our duty to see them destroyed," she says. "It's why we've been placed here. It's what we're meant to do." She leans forward and pins me with her dark crinkled eyes. "It's what you were made for. Stop denying who you are, embrace your destiny, and watch as your gifts flourish."

Embrace my destiny? One where I kill anything that isn't nephilim or human? One where I feed off of human energy?

No, I can't. I won't. Not ever.

But I'm smart enough to nod my head and tell her exactly what she wants to hear. "You're right. I'll take you to the Gateway."

"You're doing the right thing," Tate says.

But I'm not. I know that. No matter what I choose, someone is going to be hurt. There are no clear choices, no right or wrong answers. The world is not black and white. It's gray. It's a series of maybes and what-ifs and trying to stay alive. And I'm no better than the rest of them because here I am playing along, joining in their games.

I can't be better than them, I've tried to take the moral high ground so many times and failed to the point of making things so much worse. I have to accept it.

I'm not better than vampires.

I'm not better than the other nephilim.

Or the fae.

Or *anyone*.

I've wanted to believe I was, but the truth is I'm not, and the only way I'm going to beat them is if I play on their level. I remember enough to direct the De Lucas in the general direction of the Gateway. Once we find the graveyard, the rest will be easy. In the meantime, I make a conscious decision to embrace my dark side.

I'm tired of playing by a set of rules that are constantly changing. It's impossible to win, and I'm done. Maybe I wasn't meant to be the hero of my story. Maybe I was meant to be the villain. In storybooks, the good guys always prosper, the light always trumps the darkness, and the impossible odds win out. But this isn't a storybook. This is a real-life war, one that has spanned for centuries and claimed millions of lives. I refuse to be another casualty, not notable enough to mention by name. Just another statistic. Another failure. Another sad story forgotten by time.

If you can't beat them, join them—and make them suffer.

Felix

USA TODAY BESTSELLING AUTHOR

NINA WALKER

GOOD THINGS COME
TO THOSE WHO STAKE

TRUE
DEATH

VAMPIRES & VICES, NO. 4

For the book girlies
and the villains we can't help but love.

One

ADRIAN

Wh, when you live as long as vampires do, time almost becomes irrelevant. *Almost*, because our existence is chained to an endless countdown. Sunrise is our constant reckoning, a reminder that we were made for the darker halves of this world. Trying to change that is like trying to change the speed of light. Impossible.

"Two weeks," Mangus grumbles. "How are we supposed to round them up in only two weeks?" My vampiric brother and I are hiding out in a decrepit basement somewhere in rural Ireland, waiting for the sun to set so that we can run.

Mangus isn't my real brother, but we have the same maker and he's the only other prince I've ever considered a true friend. Now that I don't know how much longer I'll have him, I'm finally allowing myself to accept him as the brother I never had. He's not doing well since Kat's death. The man doesn't want to be here anymore. I understand that because I felt the same way for ages after I killed Eleni. I wanted to crawl into the grave with her, to find her in the afterlife and beg her forgiveness, and then to burn in hell for what I'd done.

But mostly, I wanted to kill Brisa for what she'd let happen to us.

And that's the other thing about being undead––we learn to be patient. Even when we don't want to be, it's forced upon us. Days. Months. Years. Centuries. Eventually the patience runs out, and when it does, someone always ends up dead.

"Two weeks is not a lot of time, but it's almost too much." I hate to point out the obvious, but we're in trouble if Isadora's spell doesn't work,

539

and there are plenty of vamps who would love for the spell to fail. We can't forget that the council wasn't voted in unanimously.

"It's not going to be easy to contact the right people without leaking the location to the wrong ones," he agrees. "Or to tip them off as to why we're meeting in the first place."

That's the other thing I'm worried about.

Isadora said that we need to meet with the rest of the vampiric council under the full moon to complete her spell. That only gives us two weeks. The royal blood bond has already been transferred to the council, but the magic containing it is still unstable. If we fail to heed that fae witch's instructions, the bond could be stolen or destroyed completely.

That can't happen.

If anyone stole it—namely Brisa—I'm as good as dead. And God forbid it's destroyed because then the only thing we will be able to rely on for some semblance of rule is the Vampire Enforcement Coalition, and there's no way the VEC is strong enough to keep so many vampires under control. An inevitable bloodbath would follow, and with it, far too much death. The humans have more weapons and people than ever before. They'll regroup and fight back, and the resulting war will be catastrophic for both of our kinds.

"What are we going to do about Sebastian?" Mangus asks.

I lean back against the stone wall and drag my boot along the dirt floor, casting up the stench of mildew. "Ah, the question of the day." I curl my lip. Hugo used to be the thorn in my side, and now that Seb has shown his hand, he's no better than his dead twin. "We don't tell Sebastian about the meeting until a couple of days before. That way, if he's still helping Brisa, they won't have a lot of time to prepare an attack."

Mangus goes quiet, and I know what he's thinking. He doesn't want to tell Sebastian at all. But we have to, the entire council needs to be there. That, and even though we hate our brother, he was still voted into this position. He has a right to it, and to undermine that now would be to undermine the council as a whole.

"We should wait to tell the others until a few days before. This is on a need to know basis." Mangus is lying on his back on the dusty floor. He's so still, he'd look dead if his mouth wasn't moving. I know he's still angry about what happened in Dublin. The coven was supposed to be our ally, but it turned on us for Brisa's sake. We don't know who to trust, but we never did. It gets old.

I begin to pace like a damn dog. I'm so full of anxious energy that I can't stop moving. Even my hands are flexing and unflexing, a habit from my human life that I thought I'd long since broken.

Nine council members. The three remaining princes, and the other six council members, have all been elected with a seventy percent majority. The first official vampire council is here and primed for success, but Brisa will try to stop us. That's exactly why we must get this spell solidified. The bond has to be untouchable. There can be no question about who's in power. Not from Brisa herself and not even from the lowest level fledgling belonging to the smallest coven.

"Brisa will never back down," Mangus says, as if reading my mind.

"Brisa doesn't have any power anymore, and in two weeks she never will again," I spit.

I hate Brisa. Always have. Always will. Seeing her fall from grace has been the greatest joy of my afterlife.

But even as I think that, I question if it's true. Aren't I forgetting something?

Mangus sits up, raking a hand through his tangled bronzy hair and nods, a satisfied grin tugging at his lips. He hates our maker just as much as I do. She's the reason both of our wives are dead. It's not something I would ever wish we had in common, but we do and we always will. So the question remains, what are we going to do about it?

"Where do you want to do this ritual anyway?" Mangus asks.

The witch didn't specify where it needed to be done, just when and how, so wherever we go, I want people I can trust nearby. I need to get back to my own territory.

"New Orleans," I say with finality. My coven needs me, and I need them. I can't imagine doing the ritual anywhere else. "We'll meet on the roof of The Alabaster Heart."

"That works for me. I haven't been there in years."

And I've been gone for over three months, which is far too long. As the coven leader it's unacceptable, but I didn't have much choice.

Mangus nods and hands me his cell phone. "Make the call."

I turn it over in my hand, amazed it still has juice after the last thirty-six hours we just had. I dial into my coven and my new number two, William, picks up on the first ring. He's no Kelli and he's not bonded to me, but his master is long gone and he's loyal to our coven. He'll do what I ask of him, no questions asked.

"It's me," I say. "I'm flying home tonight. Is everything okay there?"

"Everything is fine," William answers tentatively. His voice is different than it normally is. He's usually so cool and collected, but right now he sounds worried. "Something strange happened last night. I can't quite explain it."

"Try anyway," I reply carefully.

"That woman we were supposed to be protecting? Virginia? Well, she's gone. She and I were in the lobby talking and it was as if some unseen force picked her up and took her right out of the casino. I've never seen anything like it before."

I blink, my mind trying to grab onto something slippery. "What woman?"

"Virginia Black––something."

Blackwood.

My mouth goes dry.

Why do I know that name?

I turn to Mangus. "What are we forgetting?"

He blinks up at me and shrugs.

"Does the name Virginia Blackwood ring any bells?"

He squints. "No, should it?"

It should––I know it should, but I can't remember why. Worry floods my system, and I return to the phone. "Thanks, William, we'll look into it more when I get back. Until then, prepare the coven for my return."

I hang up and hand the phone back to Mangus. He calls the helicopter for our pickup, and I keep pacing. I can't stop thinking about that name, *Blackwood*, but it's also as if the more I think about it, the more I lose track as to why it even mattered in the first place. More prickling unease washes over me. Something isn't right.

"How did we get here?" I turn to Mangus, suddenly feeling very disoriented at our surroundings: the dank basement, the old stone walls, even the fact that we're in Ireland in the first place. None of it feels right to me.

Mangus glowers up at me like I've lost my mind, and maybe I have. How is it that I'm feeling this so strongly and he's not? "We came to Ireland to secure the blood bond by making a deal with the fae witch, Isadora."

Yes, I remember that. "What was our side of the deal?"

He frowns and thinks for a long moment. "That's strange. I can't remember."

"Something with blood?" I question, raising my eyebrows. It's always blood with vampires.

He nods once. "Yeah, that sounds right."

"Who's blood?" A girl. There was a girl.

"I don't know," his voice trails off, but less in confusion and more in apathy.

No. No, this is definitely wrong. I should know the answer to this question. I was there. So why can't I remember? What did that witch do to us? "And what happened after we left?"

Memory sparks behind his eyes, and he jumps to his feet, anger seeming to overtake him. "We were seeking refuge with the Dublin coven, but they were housing Brisa and they turned us over to her. We didn't know she was still alive. We fought. Then we . . ."

"Then we?" Only bits and pieces of memory will come to me, along with the sick feeling of panic. I was forced away from someone. All the vampires were blown off the rooftop of the Dublin coven's headquarters. It was as if the unseen hand of God had reached down and plucked us up all at once, flinging us away from that girl.

What girl?

And why? Why did that happen?

"Angel," I blurt out, the word coming at me fast. "What does Angel mean in all this?"

"Nephilim?"

"Maybe?"

"No idea, brother. I can't remember the details either." He shrugs, his eyebrows drawing together in frustration, and I know exactly how he feels.

Because I can't recall the details either, nor can I recall anything about the girl who we were being forced away from. It feels important that I remember her, that I remember what happened on that rooftop, but by the time the helicopter arrives, I've not only forgotten all about her . . . I've forgotten why I should care.

Two

"**I**s this the right one?" Camilla demands as we pull up to yet another graveyard. She rolls down the window for me to take in the scene.

We've been traveling the countryside all day looking for The Gateway and haven't found it yet. More cars have joined up with us; the group is bigger than I thought. And everyone is acting like I'm purposely messing with them, as if I'm somehow to blame for the abundance of graveyards in Ireland.

When Camilla went into my head, she wanted a detailed map of the location, but that's not what she found. My mind only held onto what I thought was important at the time, and didn't include the exact details of getting there, just what it looked and felt like. She saw what I saw, but I had only followed Mangus. He's the one with the map, not me.

And I was hoping that without him, we'd never find The Gateway.

But as I catalog the newest graveyard, I'm filled with dread. This is it; I recognize it immediately. I can't undo the last day of my life, I can't make this not happen. We're here now, and the fae realm on the other side of that portal is the absolute last place I want to be.

"Not it. Sorry." The lie rolls off my tongue, and the other passengers exchange frustrated glances. Camilla grabs me, her bony hands circling my wrists in an iron grip.

"Do not lie."

"Ouch, you're hurting me," I sputter, not that she cares.

"Hush." She pushes her gift past my barriers and into my unwilling mind.

Her intrusion is a sickening violation, so I close my eyes and fight back, willing her out. Already, I can feel her sifting through yesterday's events, peeling back the layered memories one by one. She may think she has control over this, but I'm done playing these games. She's supposed to be my family, my own grandmother, but none of the De Lucas care about my well-being. I'm a tool to be used, and if I don't participate willingly, then they'll force their gifts on me. And if they can kill my father for defying them--if Camilla can order the hit on her own son--then there's no doubt they'd do the same to me.

My stomach hardens as the aged matriarch peers into my private moment with Adrian in the farmhouse basement and the hungry kisses we shared.

"Out!" I hiss, wishing her from my mind. I imagine my memories to be a photobook, and I firmly slam it shut. She drops my wrists, and I open my watery eyes to find her glare hot and enraged.

"How did you do that?" she demands.

An undercurrent of worry accompanies her question, and a wicked smile curls up my lips. "Maybe I'm stronger than you think."

And I am strong. Brisa bit me again last night, so now with more venom than I've ever had before, it stands to reason I will have even stronger capabilities. The nephilim know all about the venom's abilities and have killed vampires to get it, but do they have Brisa's? Adrian's? Hugo's?

No--they don't.

My blood is ripe with royal venom. It's the oldest and strongest in the world, and it's made me powerful enough to make even Camilla De Luca feel threatened.

Fortunately, as long as I don't exchange actual blood with a vampire, then I don't have to worry about becoming one of them. I'm thankful to whatever God that could be out there that it didn't happen last night, as was Brisa's intention. I never ever want to go through fighting off the vampiric transition again. I'm so lucky to have survived it the first time; I'm not sure I could survive it again. Just the thought of it makes my skin crawl.

"Yes, you are strong," Camilla says slowly. "But so am I. And I still saw enough." She turns to the others, a calculated smile playing at her overly-lined lips. Everything about her is too much, too intense, too fanatical, too controlling. Since she's old, it's almost like she's bound and determined to get her way before she dies, growing more dangerous with each day. "We're here," she announces.

I let out a groan. There's no denying this is the correct graveyard.

"I'll stay in the car," I try.

They don't bother to reply to that.

The other vehicles join us, and a wave of excitement courses through the group as we all climb out of the cars. The entire De Luca family is here now. Enzo and Nicco tuck me between their hulking forms, becoming my prison guards or bodyguards, I'm still not sure which. Others go to the trunks and retrieve medieval-looking weapons. Swords and daggers and little balls with spikes, all shining from recent polish despite the lack of afternoon sun.

"Iron," Nicco says wickedly. "It's deadly to the fae."

I fight back tears as I take the weapons in––this isn't going to end well. War never does.

I nod to my friends Felix and Seth. They are also outfitting themselves with the weapons, but they don't have angelic gifts. They shouldn't be putting themselves in this kind of danger. "Okay, but the humans don't have to come, do they? They don't know anything about the fae, and they're not equipped for this."

They both stare at me with their eyes glazed over, and I know Tate has been in their minds again. How many times until it's too many? Until he breaks them entirely?

"The humans will do as I say," Tate replies. "And I say they come and fight with us."

For as much as I hate Camilla, I think I hate Leslie Tate more.

He's not even blood-related, he married into the family, and yet he's bound and determined to be Camilla's iron fist, as if that will ensure his wife, Bianca, and his children, Bella and Greyson, are the favorites. But at what cost? Is manipulating human minds really worth it? I scowl at him with my nastiest glare, wishing that looks really could kill. That would certainly be more useful than the unreliable light I have hidden somewhere within me.

"How are you so sure that God will forgive you for hurting humans?" I challenge Tate. "You think God wants you to protect them, and yet you're willing to put them in harm's way? It's hypocritical."

He doesn't even deign to give me an answer, but his children sure do. They both stalk up to me, vitriol in their hateful expression. "Keep your mouth shut about things you don't know," Bella threatens. But she doesn't scare me, not even a little bit.

"Or what?" I prod.

"You don't want to know." Greyson offers a cruel grimace. "But trust me, your friends here will be the first to find out."

Felix and Seth step back from me, and I force myself to shut up despite my white-hot anger. Greyson just got added to the top of my shit-list.

The sky has dimmed to an ominous swath of thick gray clouds, and the sun will be setting soon. We should be worried about that considering the vampires will be out, but we're not, thanks to me. Thanks to my messed up agreement with Isadora. I still can't believe I made sure that the vampires have to leave me and my friends and family alone. I should've been more specific because now the entire De Luca family has an advantage and are under the protection of that spell. Do I consider them my family? No. Does the spell know that? Also, no.

"Now what?" I say, wondering how I can stall because Faerie is the last place I want to be. We only visited one tiny corner of it, and I was held down by vines. I don't want to find out what else the realm has to offer.

"What do you think?" Nicco asks under his breath, and I'm almost surprised he's even addressing me at all. When I was in the car with him and the others, he kept his mouth shut and barely even looked at me.

"I think we're all about to die if we go in there." He doesn't reply to that, so I speak louder. "And we don't have a lot of time before the vampires will be out again, hunting us down." It's a long shot, but maybe someone in this group will fall for it.

Tate shoots me an incredulous smile. "We're not worried about the vampires anymore."

"Thanks for that," Enzo adds.

"Thank the *fae* magic," I grumble, making sure to accentuate the fae part because hello, if they kill off the fae then it stands to reason the magic protecting this family from the vampires will be gone too. "No more fae magic, no more vampire protection."

"Fae are immortal beings, and so their magic is immortal too. Even if they are all killed, the protection from that spell will last forever."

"You really believe that?" I snort.

"Blood is blood," he says. "You cannot change your bloodlines, so yes, I really believe that the De Luca line is protected."

My stomach hardens––I really hope he's wrong.

"But *we* don't share blood, Leslie. You're only my uncle through marriage."

He laughs. "And through marriage, I am your family. I am still protected. In fact, I'm pretty sure all nephilim are protected, not just this family, but time will tell."

"Enough," Camilla announces, surveying the group. Save for Seth and Felix, all of these people are related to me in one way or another. I wish I could change it, but that's impossible. Tate is right, they're all protected. "We don't have time for bickering. We need to move."

As we set out on foot, I study the familiar graveyard, noting that something about it has changed. It doesn't look any different, but it feels different. It's the same Irish graveyard that I journeyed to just last night with Mangus and Adrian, but it feels brand new. Has something changed so quickly, or is my mind playing tricks?

I shake my head. No, it's not my mind playing the trick, it's the fae. They are known for their tricks, and right now they have every right to play them considering the evil intentions of my companions.

"I can feel the wards," Bella points out, sounding sinister and gleeful at once. It's completely unsettling.

Camilla smiles. "Me too, even now I have the urge to turn back."

"Good idea," I try. "Let's go back."

Enzo glowers down at me. "Do you need me to get the duct tape, cousin?"

I roll my eyes. "Don't call me cousin. I don't claim you."

Nicco just laughs.

Tate shoots the three of us a sharp-toothed grin, and my stomach lurches. These people are excited to gain access to the fae realm because they're zealots who believe they were put on the earth to kill everyone besides the nephilim and the humans. They've already obliterated so many innocent creatures, and gaining access to this realm will help them continue their mission. A mission they believe comes from God, but I know couldn't possibly come from a higher power. I don't care that Chloe showed me the avenging angel in her records; I still don't trust it. Because how could a god want to kill his own innocent creations?

"This is wrong," I plead, bypassing Tate and Camilla, and looking instead to everyone else in the family. Uncle Dario shoots me a pathetic look while Aunt Lainey completely ignores me. I turn to Felix and Seth, wishing I could reach out and stop them myself. "You don't have to do this."

"I mean it about the duct tape," Enzo snaps. "You don't know what you're talking about, and I can't stand hearing your crap for another second."

"She's already proven her loyalty isn't to her own kind," Camilla says. "Please, everyone, you would be wise to ignore her."

"Don't you dare talk to me about loyalty! Tell me, were you there when my father died? Did you kill your own son, or did you send one of his brothers to do it for you?"

"Enough!" Camilla strides right up and slaps me across the face. Pain erupts on my cheek, and I stumble back. My face is all tingles, and hers is all rage. "Don't you dare speak again. You are to be quiet, or I will make you be quiet."

I keep my lips sealed after that, not because she deserves any kind of reprieve from her wrongdoings, but because I'm in a weak position and I really don't want that threat of duct tape to become a reality. But I do make a vow right then and there--as soon as I get the chance, I'm fighting back against the De Luca's. I'm going to stop their madness. And then I'm going to avenge my father's death.

"It's this way." Tate leads everyone forward, weaving between the headstones without a care to the actual graves themselves. It's disrespectful, but these people are only focused on one thing, and respect certainly ain't it.

"What are we allowed to do when we get in there?" Enzo questions. He wants blood, I can tell.

"We're going to scope it out, make sure the portal works, then come back with a nephilim and human army, killing anything living in Faerie." Tate makes it sound like it's going to be easy, like it's inevitable, and like it's not vile.

They're sick.

And they're complete fools. The fae will fight back, and they have strong elemental magic, not to mention they also deal in blood magic. When it comes to supernaturals, it's not an even playing field. We're not even in the same league.

"We won't fail," Tate reassures the group. "We've been prophesied to be successful. Have faith."

"What a load of crock," I mutter under my breath.

For the first time since we got out of the cars, Chloe catches my eye. She's not like the others--her face is ashen, and her demeanor is uncertain. Maybe she doesn't want to do this either, and that gives me a small flicker of hope.

Sure, I saw the history being stored away in her head when she took me back in time to show me the records, but does one memory of an angel telling our people to kill supernaturals make me want to actually go out and do it? Hell no. The nephilim are part angel, and so they believed this angel without question, trusting that he was a messenger from God. But what if they were wrong? Or if they were right, then what if God was wrong? Because this is evil.

I don't voice the things I'm thinking out of self-preservation, but also because I've been thinking about something Dario said to me at the Christmas party. He'd asked me if I knew about the different factions of nephilim, and then he said that the neph fight amongst themselves almost as much as they fight supernatural races. That information didn't make me trust him, but it did make me start to think more about my history.

There must be good nephilim out there, people who think the way I think. Maybe those people can help me gain control over my gift without having to feed on human emotions to do it. Chloe sure made it seem like there was another way. And after being forced to feed on a human's emotions at Christmas, I never ever want to do it again unless I know for certain it won't hurt them.

As we approach our destination, the graveyard grows thick with fog. An eerie sense of foreboding surrounds me, seeping into my skin and tightening my lungs. My heart races. My fingers flex.

The urge to run is all-consuming.

"There it is." Camilla points, and my heart drops because she's found the tree with every season clinging to its branches.

It's still as ethereal and otherworldly as it was before with its massive trunk and gnarled outstretched branches, and just seeing it makes me feel ill. Because I know that nothing is ever going to be the same after what we're about to do. And it's all because of me, all because I led them here, because I couldn't protect my mind from Camilla, because I made a mistake and magically distanced myself from the vampires who were protecting me.

"When we touch the trunk, we'll be sent through the portal. Kill anything you see." Camilla smiles at me. "You're the answer to our prayers, Evangeline."

My stomach twists. "You're delusional if you think you're going to make it back out of Faerie alive. You can't just go in there and kill without retaliation."

Enzo unsheathes his sword with a metallic whoosh, as if to rebut my warning.

"All together," Camilla instructs, and the group links hands.

Nicco grips one of my hands in his free one, and Enzo takes the other. "You're not getting out of this," Enzo says. The twins are so strong from their angelic gift that I can't break away from them, even with the vampire venom.

I shake my head violently. I can't keep silent. "But I don't want to go. I don't want to hurt anyone. This is wrong."

"Now," Camilla commands, and against my will, the twins press my hands to the rough bark.

Nothing happens.

Camilla growls, turning her vitriol in my direction. "Why isn't it working?"

I smile prepared to gloat, thinking that maybe the magic has changed and the portal is closed, when I'm yanked through time and space.

The world ignites into shimmers of silver and gold.

Three

"**D**id it work?" A gruff male voice sweeps through my mind, tugging me back to consciousness.

I'm surrounded by rich scents of earthen moss, a wood-burning fireplace, and warm cedar. I could stay cocooned here forever, safely sleeping my life away on this wonderful bed. Too bad that's not how life works.

"I think so," a softer female voice returns, and a prickle of familiarity courses through me. I know her voice from somewhere, somewhere that doesn't make me feel so safe anymore.

"You think so or you know so?" the man returns harshly.

"I know so, Your Highness." Her words come out rushed, a bit fearful and a bit annoyed.

My mind catches on the way she addresses him, noting that this man must be some kind of royalty. I can't remember if "Your Highness" is used for kings or princes, but my head throbs so violently that I can hardly hold onto the question for long. My eyelids are a million pounds as I fight against the impossible weight to blink them open.

Gazing around, I find myself lying on a soft bed in a dim room. It's not like any room back home. The walls are made from river rock, and the roof looks like thatched straw. Lining the walls are knobby wooden shelves with countless glass jars, each filled with a different substance. There are butterfly wings, plants, stones, powders, and all kinds of dead insects. I spot one that looks like it's filled with inky crusted blood, and I wince.

Isadora.

This is her home—the place Mangus told us never to enter.

"I see you're awake," Isadora says calmly, kneeling down in front of me. She brushes her calloused palm over my forehead and holds it there. "You're no longer feverish. That's good."

"So she'll live?" That man's voice speaks again, and I nearly jump out of my skin. I'd forgotten he was here.

I turn toward his voice and forget to breathe. I'd always heard fae were otherworldly, that they were beautiful, that they could make people do unimaginable things. And obviously Isadora looks like she belongs to the forest with her emerald skin, bright amber eyes, and white-blonde hair. But this man is the most fae-looking creature ever. Not even my imagination could have created him and come close to getting it right.

He appears to be in his late twenties, but I suspect he's much older than that considering fae are immortal beings. His hair is inky black, seeming to absorb light completely. It's tied back behind long pointed ears, each with several jewels pierced along the shells. His skin has a soft pale blue hue to it, and his eyes are like liquid silver around two black all-seeing pupils. He's tall and broad-shouldered, dressed in a black tunic and breeches, complete with a black cloak. He's gripping the hilt of a wicked-looking sword, and I hope to never see the sharp end of that thing.

It's like he stepped off the set of a movie, and he's glowering at me as if he wants to kill me simply for existing.

I raise my hands and utter the words, "I mean no harm," just as he unsheathes that damned sword and presses the tip to my throat. I freeze, fear icing through my veins.

"Do not speak, nephilim," he commands.

He says nephilim like it's a sin.

This is it. This is how I'm going to die. I always figured it would be at the hands of a vampire. Never in a million years did I imagine a fae would be the one to do the deed, let alone in another realm, and certainly not like this.

"Stop it, Prince Casimir," Isadora hisses, confirming my earlier suspicions that he's royalty. "The girl is telling the truth. She wouldn't have been able to make it through The Gateway if her intentions were ill toward any of the fae, and you know it."

Casimir continues to glare, but after a tense moment, returns his sword to its sheath with a metallic clang and steps back. "Make no mistake, demon," he threatens, staring me down. "I will kill you at the first sign of obstinance."

"Fine, but just so we're clear, I'm not a demon. I'm actually part angel." I rub at my neck and sit up. My body feels as if it's been asleep for years, and my head is already starting to ache again.

"That's debatable," Casimir spits, and I have to fight not to roll my eyes. He's still the one with the sword.

"Where is everyone else?" My voice croaks, hoarse from disuse.

"You're the only nephilim who made it through." Isadora sounds pleased, like she expected this to happen and now she has bragging rights.

"How long was I out?"

"Three days."

My stomach drops. Three days is enough time for my wicked grandmother to assemble her army. She'll come back. She'll keep trying. There's no way they're going to give up so easily. I close my eyes for a second, wanting to get a sense of what to do about it, when an idea comes to me. "But three days here isn't as long in the human world, right?" I ask, hopeful.

Casimir's laugh is bitter. "Been reading fairy tales, have you?"

I shrug at the prince. "You've been cut off from humans for so long that most humans don't know you actually exist. So how are we supposed to know what's true and what's not about the fae?"

"Ah, but you are *not* human." The venom dripping from his voice is so toxic that I have to look away.

I turn to Isadora instead. She scares me too, especially because I know what she can do with her earthen magic, not to mention blood magic, but at this moment, she's giving me answers and helping me. I'm certain she doesn't want me dead, but I can't say the same for Casimir. She's sitting on the edge of the bed now, watching me as if she's looking for something dark to uncover, some buried secret that she must unearth. "My family will come back for you. They're not going to give up."

"As if we'll let them touch us," Casimir barks. "We can kill any threat easily. We're the *fae,* and nephilim are no match for us."

He says that, but I know for a fact that nephilim killed so many of the fae that they retreated to their realm ages ago, sealing off every single portal except for one, which they managed to keep hidden for years. It's only recently been discovered, and if they seal off The Gateway before I get out of here, I'll never make it home.

Isadora's smile quirks as if she's thinking the exact same thing that I am. She looks to the haughty prince and then back to me. "I'm good at my job, and my job is to protect The Gateway. Rest assured, your family members didn't get through, and they won't get through. We have no plans to seal it off completely. The wards will hold."

I swallow my relief, not because I actually consider those people my family and care about their well-being, but because I don't want innocent blood on my hands. And because I'd really like to make it home. "Okay, but that doesn't explain why I'm here and the others are not."

"Your blood links you to *all* nephilim," she supplies. "Blood given willingly can be used in our spells, so I used yours to strengthen the wards here. Now anyone with ill-intent toward the fae who are also linked to a nephilim bloodline cannot use The Gateway to cross into Faerie."

Her answer sinks in slowly at first, and then all at once it floods me with the truth.

"You're brilliant!" I lunge for her before I can think, wrapping her in a tight hug. With the strengthened wards, I no longer have to worry about a war between my people and the fae. Isadora has done a wonderful thing here. When I gave her a thimble of my blood in exchange for helping Mangus and Adrian, I imagined all the ways she could use my blood against me. Never did I imagine she'd use it for good and not evil.

"Would you like me to remove her?" Casimir deadpans to Isadora, the sound of his broadsword being unsheathed yet again.

"Are all the fae men like this?" I ask her, and she chuckles, the sound reminding me of aspen tree leaves blowing on a warm summer's day.

Maybe she's not so bad. Maybe I even like her.

"Yes," she confirms, "especially the princes."

How many fae princes are there? From what I do understand of Faerie, there are multiple courts, and the kings here have oodles of immortal children. Casimir is probably one of a dozen or more. But he's still threatening, still standing there with his sword ready to lob my head off.

"I'm fine, Casimir. Not all of us hate humans," Isadora tuts. Her hug feels so good that I nearly melt right into her. If someone would've told me I'd be hugging this woman when I first met her, I wouldn't have believed it. She terrified me, holding me down with vines, asking for my blood, spelling me . . . and now we're hugging.

"As I've said before," Casimir cuts in, "Eva is *not* a human. And all fae should hate all the nephilim. Do you not forget what they did to our people? To your own parents all those years ago?"

Her body stiffens, and I take that as my cue to release her. I sit back on my haunches and frown up at Casimir. "I don't claim the neph as my people, just so we're clear. I only recently learned I'm one of them, and I don't buy into the whole righteous-genocide stuff. Besides that, I've recently learned that only some of the nephilim factions want to hunt you guys. We're not all bad, you know."

He tilts his head at me, eyes blazing in disbelief.

"If she was lying, she wouldn't have been able to come through the portal." Isadora backs me up, and once again I want to hug the witchy woman. She pats my back and gives me a wry grin. "Intention is a bigger part of that spell than you realize."

Casimir cuts her off. "Be that as it may, orders are orders." He steps forward, his silver eyes pinning me down as he addresses Isadora. "Now that the aftereffects of your spell have worn off and she's awake and well enough to travel, the neph is coming with me."

My mouth pops open. "Where?"

Because I don't want to go anywhere but home.

I miss my bed, the Moreno family, my old job at Pops, and even my roommates who I barely got the chance to know. It's been months since I've been home, and I have a good life in New Orleans that I intend to return to, a life that has nothing to do with this place.

But then there's Adrian––we had just gotten together when we were separated, and I need to figure out how to undo that part of Isadora's spell. I still hate most of the vampires, but I don't hate him––I might actually love him. Her spell needs to be amended enough so I can actually be with the man I want to be with, the man I want to choose if fate would stop messing things up for us. Yeah, it's a little insane that I want to try to date a vampire, but the heart wants what the heart wants, and my heart yearns for Adrian.

Isadora is the only one who can help me get back to him.

I turn to her. "I need your help with the spell––"

Casimir interjects, "You're a prisoner of my father's. You are to be brought to him at once."

"Who's your father?" I'm stalling. Of course I already know. If Casimir is a prince, that would make his father . . .

"The High King of the Unseelie court."

My mind races. "Yeah, I don't know enough about Faerie to know what Unseelie even means," I blurt out.

"The dark fae," Isadora answers, squeezing my hand once. "Remember what I said about intention," she adds with a cryptic whisper.

Casimir chuckles wickedly, and then all at once he's surrounded by thick billowing shadows. They materialize into my worst nightmares, physically lifting me from the bed and carrying me away.

Four

Casimir strides from Isadora's hut, the shadows dragging me close behind. I expect to be thrown into a carriage or onto a horse, but there's nothing out here except for the sparkling gold and silver forest. I briefly register how pretty it looks during the day compared to when I was here during the night, admiring the way the sun reflects off everything, turning it to glitter, and how a flock of birds match the silver trees, their wings bright as mirrors.

I've never seen birds like that. They swoop in my direction, zooming straight toward us. Something unseen cracks as loud as a bolt of lightning, but I don't see where it came from. I squeal when Casimir grabs my hand and tightens his grip, those terrifying shadows surrounding us growing even thicker, and the birds dive in, circling us like we're their next meal.

I try to scream again, but I can't. It's as if the oxygen has been ripped from my throat. And then all at once, the light returns and the air with it. I cough, my eyes watering, and the clouds in my vision clearing as I take in my new surroundings.

We're no longer in a forest. The scenic trees and great blue sky have been replaced by the wide courtyard of a literal stone castle. The birds are still there. They take off into the sky, disappearing over the massive castle walls.

"How did you do that?" I rasp. "I thought teleportation was science fiction."

"Do not ask me about my magic again," Casimir responds harshly, then his shadows drop me on my ass right there on the cobblestone floors. Pain shoots up my backside, and I groan.

"Really? Thanks for the warm welcome."

Ugh . . . why don't I know more about these people? Ayla would have an inkling of what to do around someone like Casimir considering she's obsessed with the fairy romance books everyone raves about on social media. I, on the other hand, never got into the fantasy romance thing and know nothing about this new world. Then again, that's all fiction anyway, the strange imaginings of authors tucked away in their home offices. This is the real deal, and I'm completely out of my element.

At least Mangus's voice comes to mind, reminding me not to eat or drink anything. And also not to enter Isadora's hut. The second one happened while I was unconscious, so I can't be blamed for it, but the first one I can still work on. As if on cue, my stomach releases a painful growl. I hope I'm not here for long because I really don't want to starve.

I know me, I like food too much. I'll give in before I get too hungry.

"Follow me," Casimir instructs, stomping off in the direction of a large oak door. We're alone in this courtyard, but I have a feeling that wherever we're going, we're not going to be alone for much longer. My stomach begins to claw at itself for reasons beyond hunger, but I'm not stupid enough to hang back.

I scramble to my feet and take off after Casimir. He's so tall that he has at least a foot on me. His stride is long, and he definitely doesn't have the patience to wait for me to keep up with him. I practically have to run to match his speed as I cut across the courtyard and slip through the oak door moments before it shuts. I find myself in an arched hallway but don't have a lot of time to take it in because I'm too busy chasing after the prince. I quickly follow him into what is obviously a throne room.

It's not the first time I've been in one of these, but it's definitely the most terrifying. Brisa's throne doesn't hold a candle to the throne made of actual *bones* laid out before me.

Really, does it have to be bones?

Unseelie means dark, so I shouldn't be surprised. But it's not the bones that are the most terrifying thing about this place—it's the people. The room is filled with human-like creatures of all shapes, sizes, and colors. Some even have wings. Intermixed with the creatures are loads of beautiful fae elves. Many here have pointed ears, and every single person is dressed like they not only belong in this medieval castle, but like they belong to its court. There's not a stitch of modern human clothing here, and I stick out like a sore thumb in my days-old jeans and t-shirt.

They hiss and glare, already targeting me as their enemy, malice burning behind their strange eyes. My gaze locks with the king sitting upon the bone throne, and my breath catches. The king sits alone, no queen at his side—power emanating from him as if he were his own sun.

He's an older version of Casimir with thick black hair hanging around his shoulders and sharp features. Unlike his son, he doesn't have pale blue skin, but skin of blue-black midnight. And his eyes are so light, they're almost white. They shine like moonstone, not even looking real. If we were in my world, I'd assume he was wearing contacts.

Questions begin to fill my mind as we stare at each other. How many children does he have? How much power? How long has he been king? Was he born royal or did he have to kill for the title? And most importantly—what does he want with me?

As if reading my mind, his eyes flash, and it almost feels as if he can see beyond the physical, like he can see me at my basest layer. My fears. My hopes. What makes me different and what makes me the same. He *knows* me.

A shiver jolts through my body.

If this man wants me dead, I'm dead. If he wants to keep me as his prisoner for eternity, I'll rot in the realm and never be able to leave. Because whatever he wants, he gets.

It doesn't matter how quick I am. How cunning. How powerful.

He's so much more.

Do I bow to him? Do I speak?

Casimir shoves me forward before I get a chance to decide. "Father, as requested, I've brought you Isadora's nephilim girl."

More hissing from the spectators, their hatred of me becoming this palpable thing that could easily kill me if the king allows it. I decide right then and there that I value my life more than pride, and I offer the king a deep bow.

He begins to speak, his voice holding depths unheard of in my world. "I'm King Orlyc, the High-King of the Unseelie Court of Faerie and you are . . ." This is my time to say something, but my mouth is as dry as dirt. "Not what I expected," he finishes with disappointment. "But I guess you'll have to do."

I'm not sure what to do with the insult, and I'm almost too scared to ask, but I have to speak. "I'm Eva Blackwood. And I'm wondering . . . why am I here?" I stand tall and force my voice to come out much stronger than I feel inside. If there was one thing I learned from Brisa's court of nightmares, it was to never show weakness. Of course we all know I'm weak compared to them, but if I show it, they'll take advantage, and they definitely won't respect me. And I'll need some semblance of respect to survive this place.

"You'll see soon enough." His response is cryptic, which feels very fae to me. I remind myself not to think of these people as humans. They're not going to act how humans act. They won't value the same things or do what I expect a human would do. If I want to survive their games, I have to play to their level. I have to be more cunning. And maybe even more wicked.

"Now about your magic," he continues. "Tell me, what can you do?" I hesitate, unsure how to answer or if I should. "I know that all nephilim have gifts, so what's yours?"

He stands from his throne of bones and stalks toward me. He's slightly shorter than his son, but still towers over me. I'm not used to looking up so much to talk to a man, and I don't like it. "Do I need to pry answers from that mouth of yours?"

I narrow my eyes and shake my head. "It's not that I don't want to answer you, it's that I'm not entirely sure how to. I just found out what I am two months ago, and I've barely scratched the surface of my gift."

He holds up a hand encrusted in golden rings, several with inlaid gems glimmering like hard candies. A few stick out and look sharp enough to cut, and I take note to avoid the back of that hand. "Excuses, excuses."

I shake my head carefully. "I'm not lying, Your Majesty. I mean no harm to you or your people, I swear on my life."

He raises an eyebrow. "Ah, but don't you know not to swear on anything in Faerie?"

To that, I have nothing to say. Did I just unwittingly bind myself to something?

"I know you're safe to us," he says slowly, narrowing his eyes as he steps closer. I catch the scent of something sweet and cosmic, as if cotton candy were made of stars instead of sugar. My mind grows fuzzy. Intoxicated. He hardly notices as he continues to speak. "You wouldn't have been able to come through The Gateway if your intentions were impure toward my kind, but the fact remains you are still the child of nephilim, and therefore the spawn of our great enemy."

"I wasn't raised by them," I argue, blinking several times to shake myself from that intoxicated feeling. It isn't easy, but I somehow manage. "I don't claim them, and I don't agree with them. You have my word that I won't defend their prejudices."

He holds my gaze for a long moment. "And for that I should spare your life?"

"Yes." It's the only thing I can say, but it hardly feels good enough.

"So far, you are innocent, but that could change."

"Okay, but as far as I understand it, my blood is now tied to your wards protecting The Gateway. Don't you need me alive? If you kill me, won't you kill the added protection that you need there now that the portal has been discovered?"

I'm stalling.

I know I'm stalling, but at least my headache is gone, and I no longer feel intoxicated. I feel terrified. I feel foolish. Lost. Alone. Out of my element. But I have my mind and my thoughts. I can find a way to get out of here, even if it takes a bargain.

"Our spell will be forged by the upcoming full moon, and then nothing can break it, not even your death. In ten more days we will no longer have any need of you."

I have no idea what any of that means, but it doesn't bode well for me.

Casimir stirs, and I almost forgot he was standing beside me. "She's stalling the inevitable, Father. You may as well lock her up and let me do the honors when the time comes."

I inch farther from Casimir, but his shadows reach out and drag me back so fast that I don't even see it happen.

This is it.

Even if I try--and I will try--I won't be able to fight all of them off. There are just too many fae here, and every single one of them looks like they're out for blood. I know very little about these creatures except that they're immortals, that they're strong, and that they're ruthless. They have grudges that reach all the way back to ancestors I'll never know a thing about but whom they'll never forget. Their memories are just as immortal as they are. They still hate my kind for starting a war and pushing them out of the human world, not to mention all their friends and family that were killed in the process. My death is their revenge.

But maybe they'll play with me first, and if I'm smart enough, I'll find a way to play them right back.

King Orlyc tilts his head and looks me up and down. "Do you know what power my throne gives me?"

I blink rapidly. Of course I don't know, but considering it's made of bones, it can't be anything good.

"I can manipulate any and all magical gifts, can see what's beneath the surface of a person, can even change your very DNA," he says cryptically. "So if you won't reveal your gift to me, I'll take the answer by force."

Quick as a whip, he reaches out and places his hand on my forehead, practically palming my skull like a basketball. Before I can pull back, icy magic zips through my entire body, rooting me in place. I can't move. I'm completely at his mercy.

I can't even speak.

That's when the light erupts from my hands, bright white and violent.

But it doesn't hurt them. They're either immune to it or I don't know what I'm doing. Or both. Either way, it doesn't matter because the crowd erupts in mocking laughter. Shame burns me to the core. What do they care about? I haven't impressed them. I've become the entertainment.

"That's it?" Someone cackles from a group of gorgeous elvin women standing nearest to the throne. "What's she to do with that?"

"Be nice," Casimir teases back, but he's laughing right along with the crowd.

"I'm not ashamed," I lie, spitting at the prince. And then I speak my truth. "I don't want to hurt people, but I could. With this light I could, and I have."

Casimir sneers, and the king raises his hand to quiet the crowd, before turning back to me. "You mean vampires?"

I swallow and nod, not saying anything else. My mind races to Adrian, and my heart does a little squeeze. I feel like everytime we have a chance to make something work it's taken away from us. I don't even know where he is or if he's okay. And now that I'm here in Faerie, I don't know when I'll see him again. If ever.

"Very interesting," the king speaks, and the laughter dies down. "I wonder what we could get for trading you to them. There are vampires who would probably do anything to get their hands on you."

Brisa comes to mind . . .

"No, they can't get their hands on me," I point out. "Thanks to Isadora's spell, the one that you need right now, they've been forced to leave me alone."

His eyes sparkle, and he barks out a laugh. "Alright, you can stay."

What did he just say? I'm taken aback and have to fight not to get upset that he doesn't see how much I want to leave. "I don't want to stay here. I want to go home to New Orleans."

His gaze turns hard, the ice in his white eyes nearly burning me. "You will leave when I say you can leave."

"Am I your prisoner then?" The words are bold, maybe even too bold.

He smiles wickedly, lifting his arms out wide. "You're my guest." A guest who is forced to be here? No, that's a prisoner, and I won't be anyone's prisoner. "Besides, I have a feeling you won't be here longer than ten whole days."

He winks at his son, and I'm clearly missing something here. Something important. Something about the forging of the spell happening in ten days.

Even though ten feels like ten days too long, at least I have a date I can count on. I'm so tired of being at other people's command, stuck under their roofs, made to pretend to go along with things I don't agree with. First it was the bloodsuckers, then the nephilim, and now the fae. It needs to stop, but it's only ten more days . . .

"Don't be so ungrateful, nephilim," Casimir says. "Don't you know we have the most fun in Faerie? You should be so lucky to enjoy our company."

More peals of laughter.

"My son is correct. This is a great privilege. Your kind has never been invited into my home before, and if you're very lucky, you will get to meet my consorts, maybe even my other children. One may take a liking to you."

Dread fills my body, pooling in my belly and turning it sour. I don't want anyone to "take a liking" to me so I can become some kind of nephilim plaything. How much trouble do these fae get up to? I'm afraid I'm about to find out they're even more wild and dangerous than the vampires ever were, and the vampires wanted to drink me dry. Worst of all, in this court, I don't have Adrian's protection. I'm completely on my own.

The king nods toward the corner of the room where a string quartet is waiting. I don't recognize most of the instruments, but when they begin to play, weaving together their earthy tune in a perfect melody, I find I no longer care. I just want to keep listening, for their gorgeous music to last forever.

Before I can protest, Prince Casimir draws me into his arms and begins to lead us in a waltz, dragging my feet along with him whenever I miss a step. He laughs when I ask him to slow down, and he's so much stronger than I that I can't force him to. Even with my vampire venom, he keeps me locked in an extreme grip, shadows nipping at our heels.

A flash catches my eye, and one of those silver birds lands on his shoulder. The little monster's eyes sparkle like precious rubies. It stares at me like it can see into my soul. Maybe it can.

"What is that thing?" I ask, grimacing at it. It squawks right in my face.

"I told you not to ask about my magic."

So they're *his* birds . . .

I roll my eyes. "I wasn't born yesterday. I can already tell it's some kind of magic bird, but I didn't realize it was yours until you gave that away. So what do they do? Spy for you? And how many do you have?"

I've never liked birds. Always thought they were kinda gross, pooping all over, eating worms, throwing up into their youngs' mouths. Not to mention their sharp beaks and beady little eyes and avian flus and who knows how many parasites.

"You reek of vampire venom," Casimir hisses into my ear, moving in closer and changing the subject completely. "I hate the smell of vampire venom almost as much as I hate the stench of nephilim. But lucky for you, my sister Cressida adores vampire venom. She was in love with a bloodsucker once, though, that was many years ago, and that vamp is long dead. Poor thing got drunk on faerie wine and accidently walked into the sunlight."

He laughs and passes me to the woman called Cressida. Tall and beautiful, she also forces me to dance. A few minutes later Cressida passes me to a different woman, and then she throws me into the arms of a different man. I'm tossed through the ballroom for what feels like hours, from prince to princess and courtesans alike. It reminds me of when the vampires made me dance, but it's also different. There's magic here, which makes it so much worse––because I like it.

I can't help myself.

There's something to the otherworldly music. The strange magic weaves through the air like secret whispers. And that wonderful smell has returned, all sugary and ethereal and cruel. It makes my thoughts go soft and hazy.

Soon, I find myself enjoying the endless dancing. I laugh so hard I cry. I can't remember the last time I did something like that. At one point, the king has me in his clutches again, his arms holding me up as we twirl around the room. He says something I don't catch, and once again, the light is emitting from my hands. White. Bright. Ageless. Boundless.

"That's good," he whispers in my ear. "Keep practicing."

I do.

"That's good," he breathes in the other ear. "What else can you do?"

And then I'm glowing with the golden light. It's so warm and wonderful. It feels like coming home to myself. It's pure. Sweet.

And then he's passing me off to someone else. Someone with gossamer wings this time. I can't tell if it's a man or a woman. "They're so beautiful," I say, reaching out to touch them, but my hand is slapped away.

"Never touch our wings without permission," they are telling me.

I should feel ashamed, but I don't. I can't feel anything but happiness.

And then someone else is saying something about my soul. Asking if it's strong enough to handle the vampires, to forge with the bonds. Is it strong enough for immortality? For magic? I don't know what to think about that––*I can't think.*

I don't know what's happening, don't *care* what's happening. My mind comes back to me and goes out again like breathing, easy in and easy out. Like the ocean waves crashing on the shore. And the party continues. The dancing lasts forever. The food is delicious. The wine is heaven.

What did Mangus say? *Whatever you do, don't eat or drink anything in Faerie.*

I stare down at the goblet of crimson fairy wine in my hands, tasting the sweet nectar on my lips, and wonder how much I've already had to drink tonight.

Five

ADRIAN

Everyone is here. All nine of us council members are now standing in a circle on the roof of The Alabaster Heart, the sky dark and the full moon almost in position for the spell to be forged. The time has finally come, but now that it's here, I don't trust it. Something feels off. Even though everyone knows that attempting to usurp the council is an automatic true death, there's still a very real possibility someone is going to try.

"It's always circles with witches," Mangus grumbles, looking around at the lot of us. We represent the three remaining princes and six continents where vampires reside––four women and five men.

Each of us is old.

Everyone is powerful.

All of us are deadly.

"Circles mean infinite possibilities." Sebastian smirks from his position across the group.

I watch him intently because as far as I'm concerned he earned the true death when he allied with Brisa and tried to attack us two weeks ago. But Mangus and I already decided that it would be Seb's word against ours, and Sebastian's got way too much sway with the others here for us to deal with that right now. What the rest of them don't know is that our dear brother is back in Brisa's good graces, and I plan to hold that information over his head. If the other council members knew she was still alive, they would see her threat to our power and want her as dead as I do.

And I plan to do just that after the spell is forged tonight.

"I wasn't talking to you," Mangus snaps at Sebastian, and the other council members exchange annoyed glances.

Since the moment Seb showed up here an hour ago to complete the ritual, he and Mangus have been at each other's throats. It's growing tiresome. I can't say I blame Mangus because I hate Sebastian too, but at least Brisa is nowhere to be seen, so that part of the plan is working. She will want to take the blood bonds for herself, but she's still weak and won't be able to fight all of us. We're the strongest vampires in the world.

She would know.

"I think you and I are in agreement about fae witches." I turn to Mangus, who's standing directly at my side. "Avoid them at all costs after this?"

Because something is wrong and has felt wrong for two weeks. I still can't put my finger on it, but I know Isadora meddled with my memories.

Mangus curls his lip, his voice going low. "I never cared for magic."

"Unless you really need a witch, and then you do whatever it takes to find one, isn't that right, boys?" Seb cuts in, his eyes narrowing in on us, and a few of the other council members nod their agreement.

He's not wrong, but that doesn't mean I have to like agreeing with him. The fae witches are the strongest and most stable who deal in spellcraft, naturally deriving their magic from the earth herself. However, this spell wasn't only derived from the elements, but also from the moon, and it's about to be forged in our blood. Considering we're vampires, it makes sense that she would have us use blood, but it still makes me uneasy. I can't remember the last time I felt this nervous. And I can't stand the tickle at the back of my mind telling me there's something else I'm forgetting, something that I should be even more nervous about. But that's the problem, I can't just force a memory when I don't know where to start.

Shaking the infuriating feeling away, I retrieve the steel knife from its sheath under my shirt. The blade shines in the moonlight, slate gray and razor sharp. This is the part that Mangus and I didn't tell the others about, and they gaze upon the blade with mistrust.

"What is that for?" Nadia asks. She's the newly elected councilwoman from Russia. I've always liked her, and I don't blame her for questioning things. Her eyes thin into mistrustful slits as she stares at me. "You said no weapons, Adrianos. Explain yourself."

"Relax, Nadia. We're all weapons," I reply casually, holding up the knife. "Your fangs are sharper than this blade, and it's not silver, it's only steel."

Except for the gusty wind that's rattling the trees below, for the rumble of the Mississippi river a few blocks away, and for the few humans still out in the streets at this early hour, everything is eerily quiet. Nobody speaks, and Nadia finally nods her head and relaxes her shoulders.

I point the blade into my fleshy palm and cut deep, the cool blood dripping down my fingertips. "We are here because the royal blood bonds have been transferred to our council by a fae witch. She has called us here tonight to forge her spell in our blood," I explain, knowing that this news is probably hard to believe for most of them. "We must be quick. The wounds will heal themselves within five minutes, but the moon will be at its peak within three." I cut the other hand, then pass the blade to Mangus. He doesn't hesitate, cutting with calm precision and then passing the knife to the next person who quickly does the same.

"Fae blood magic?" Sebastian questions when the knife gets to him. He holds it for a moment, hesitating to make the cut.

"We're vampires, so of course she chose blood," I say harshly, but only because it's Seb and I'm tired of him. He can step out of the council for all I care.

"And we're just supposed to take your word for it?"

A few of the others go stiff, and Mangus smirks. I'm sure he'd love nothing more than to exclude Sebastian from our circle, but he was elected to be here, same as we were.

"As far as we know, blood magic dates back to our origins. What are vampires if not magicked to live our eternal lives at the mercy of blood?"

Live by the blood . . . and die by the sun.

"This is the only way to ensure we'll be bound together," Mangus adds with a bitter hiss. It's no secret that the last person Mangus wants to be bound to is Sebastian, especially after what happened to Katerina. "It's the only way our council bond over the covens will be as strong as the royal blood bond once was. Keeping our covens in line is the only way to ensure that our empire doesn't fall."

Sebastian scowls, but he makes the cuts.

I wish I knew what Seb was thinking. He wants power, so does he really still want Brisa now that she's lost everything? Now that he knows the truth, that our mother was planning to kill her princes and that she was behind the murders all along, have his feelings toward her changed at all? She wanted to make a new generation of royals that didn't include him—it's not often that someone like Sebastian forgives such a betrayal.

The knife returns to me, all the cuts have been made, and eight pairs of expectant eyes scrutinize me. I return the knife to its sheath and continue. "Now we clasp hands, sharing our blood, until the moon passes directly overhead. The magic is already in play, but this will forge it, making it untouchable. After tonight, the blood bond can never be lost."

That's the thing about magic. It's unstable. This final part of Isadora's spell is supposed to rectify that, to make it so nobody can ever come after the blood bonds again. But just as we clasp hands, the rooftop door flies open, and a young vampire races out. Recognition hits me like a freight train.

It's Kenton--but how do I know Kenton?

"I'm here to join the council," the young man announces boldly, his voice echoing into the night. "I am also Brisa's child, so I have just as much right to the council as the other three remaining princes."

"Don't let go!" I demand of the others. "Kenton, you need to leave."

"But it's true, isn't it? Kenton is a prince too." Sebastian smirks when the other council members murmur their disbelief. "This young vampire is Brisa's newest child. I saw the transformation happen with my own eyes."

Of course he did, always Brisa's loyal puppet.

Mangus swears under his breath. He must be thinking exactly what I'm thinking. With Kenton on the council, the numbers won't be odd anymore. Even numbers will create imbalances, and it will give Seb sway to have someone like Kenton in his pocket when it comes to voting power. Not to mention, it will give Brisa sway for whatever she's planning, because there's no way she's going to hide in the shadows for the rest of eternity.

"You can't be a prince. Brisa is dead," Santino argues. He's the councilman elected to represent the South American covens, and a man whom I know little about. I still haven't been able to peg him as reasonable or a zealot. I only know that he comes from Brazil and that his maker died many years ago.

"And yet, he is a prince." Sebastian laughs. "Come, Kenton. Join us."

Employing my telekinesis, I lift the knife from its sheath, spin the blade toward Kenton, and aim it straight for his throat. In all of a second, it's tipped right against his dark skin. One more inch and it'll be lodged into his jugular. "I'll rip your head clear off before you step foot in this sacred circle."

Kenton turns on me then, and those familiar eyes of his spark something within my soul. Something deep.

A memory.

And then another. And another.

The knife falls to the pavement with a clatter. I am frozen. Undone.

Kenton quickly snatches the knife, slicing open his palms, but I don't even care--all I can think of is these memories as they fill my mind.

Memories of her.

And all I can see is her face, all I can feel is her hand in mine, all I can hear is her voice teasing me. Challenging me. Hating me. Loving me.

Eva.

Eva is all that matters. Eva is how I know Kenton, because he belongs to her. He's not Brisa's, he's Evangeline's. And she's mine.

She's mine.

The memories fall into place, completing the puzzle of Isadora's treachery. Separately, each memory doesn't reveal the whole picture, but putting them together now, I can see it all so clearly. I remember everything that happened, how Eva and I got to this moment, but most of all, I remember how I lost her.

And how I forgot her.

Kenton steps into the circle, clasping hands with Sebastian on his left and Nadia on his right. Any minute the moon will slide into position and this spell will be immortalized, and I'll never be able to step foot near Eva again.

Because that was her end of the deal. The vampires had to leave her friends and family alone. We had to leave *her* alone.

And so we will forget her entirely.

I drop my hands.

"What are you doing?" Mangus hisses.

"Leave him," Sebastian says, his lip curling in a smug smile. "If he doesn't want to be a part of the council then he shouldn't be."

"I never said that," I mumble, my mind racing for a way to make this work.

Sebastian looks pointedly to my hands, unclasped from the group, because my dropped hands certainly say something different.

I don't know what to do.

I don't know how to save the human and vampire races if I don't go through with forging the spell. If there's no vampire council, then the covens will have carte blanche to do whatever they want. War will surely be the result. War and death.

I've lived through too many wars already, and this is one I don't want to experience, but if I do go through with the spell, I'll lose Evangeline forever. I've had countless lovers over the centuries, and I've fathered vampiric children that I deeply cared for, but there's only been one other woman that I actually loved with true romantic affection. I lost her in the most horrific way imaginable, and I can't stand to lose Eva too. Not like this. Not now, not before we've even had a chance to really be together, to see what we could become.

"When did you turn?" I address Kenton, trying to buy a little time before the group cuts me off and proceeds without me.

His face stills, and Sebastian straightens.

"What does that matter?" Kenton asks.

My mind races back to what I thought was Brisa's demise but had actually turned out to be the royal blood bond being transferred to Eva. I narrow my eyes on Kenton, and the kid turns fidgety. He's out of place with us, and he knows it. "Brisa lost the royal bond, so if you didn't become a vampire while Brisa was still queen, then you're not actually a prince."

"What are you talking about?" Santino demands. The other council members are growing restless, but I am the only one who has unclasped their hands from the circle.

"Now is not the time," Mangus is seething, his chest rising and falling as he stares up at the moon. He's right. I need to move this along quickly, but I definitely don't want Kenton to be part of the council if he's Brisa's pawn and Sebastian's friend.

"Brisa is still alive," I announce, hedging my bets.

Mangus freezes, Seb smirks, and the silence from the rest of the council grows palpable. Nobody knows what to believe or who to trust, but Brisa being alive is not a good thing for our council. She never wanted such an organization to exist. She's a threat to our success. She's got enemies all over the planet, but she has allies too.

"Explain yourself," Antara, the council representative from India, asks with cool disdain.

"Brisa lost the royal blood bond, but she never died. She's still alive, Sebastian can tell you all about it."

Everyone turns on Seb, but he keeps his mouth shut. He turns his hateful gaze on me, and I'm certain that he'd love nothing more than to kill me right now. He would if he could, but I'm an equal match and he knows it.

"Is this true? Is she alive?" Santino asks Sebastian, and Sebastian nods once.

I continue my point, "Brisa didn't turn Kenton until after she'd already lost her royal blood bond, so that means he's not a prince. He's just a young vampire, nothing else."

Nadia tosses Kenton's hand away like it's made of rotting meat.

The moon is approaching its perfect position, shining its full light right down on us, and I feel like I'm standing on the edge of a cliff, one that's on either side of me. No matter what step I take, no matter which direction I go, I'm doomed to fall.

"Now," Mangus roars, looking up to the moon. "We do it now or else we face Brisa's wrath."

And somehow, that's enough for the rest of them. They all clasp hands again, except for Kenton, who's stumbling back toward the exit. That's fine, he should go, he doesn't belong in the council.

But I do.

If I don't enter into the council at this moment, I'll be without power, and whether I want this spell to happen or not, it's happening. There's no turning back. I can either be a part of the council without Eva or I can not be a part of the council and still be without her. There is no easy choice because there is no solution I can live with.

I'm sorry, Eva.

I hate myself for doing it, for not being able to find a better way, and for losing Eva in the process, but I've run out of time. So I take their hands, mixing our blood, and bury my pain down deep with all the other ghosts.

The moon slides into its exact position.

The magic is undeniable. It zaps through us like an electric current, racing from one body to the next and to the next and to the next. The wind picks up, swirling around us like we're the center of the universe. Shadows descend. Thick and otherworldly.

Everything goes dark.

I hold on even tighter, and the world becomes bright with lightning and the sound of cracking thunder. A flock of silver birds flies through my periphery. There one second and gone the next.

I hold on even tighter still.

And then all at once, the magic ceases to exist. The night returns to exactly how it was only a minute before. The moon shines as it always does. The wind blows at the same strength. Even the sweet electric smell of magic has dissipated.

It's all as it was, save for one very important detail.

In the center of our sacred circle, with her brown eyes gaping up at me, lies the body of a young woman.

And not just any woman.

My woman.

Six

I blink up into the night and questions come at me so quickly I can barely grab hold of them. Where am I? How did I get here? How long was I in the fae realm? Am I still in it? They swirl through my head until I catch sight of Adrian towering above me like an avenging angel.

My thoughts disappear.

His golden hair spiderwebs across his forehead in the wind, and his black trenchcoat flutters about his boots. Hot tears fill my vision, and my heart swells with relief—I never thought I'd see him again. But here he is, beautiful and terrible and very much real.

I glance down at myself, my fingers splaying over a strange velvet green dress. I've never seen this dress before, and I have no recollection of putting it on. Then I peer up at the circle of vampires standing around me, and my insides flip. I may be stronger than I've ever been, but there are nine of them. They could end my life in a millisecond.

I look back to Adrian and then to the viking, Mangus, at his side. At least I can trust two to have my back.

Can I, though? Adrian and Mangus tricked me into surrendering the royal blood bond. I unknowingly had it for almost two months. It could've changed everything, *and they lied to take it back.*

Blinking up at the silvery full moon, I feel ensnared by its pearlescent light. Something about it looks different tonight, as if it's holding in a secret.

As if I'm that secret.

Fear chases the confusion straight from my lungs in a painful gasp. I'm hardly myself right now. And Adrian . . . Adrian's looking at me like I'm a ghost.

"What happened to me?" I ask. My voice is raw and raspy, as if I've been screaming at the top of my lungs, but my mind is too foggy to remember how it got that way. What did the fae do to me?

Adrian doesn't answer my question.

"Nephilim." Sebastian's single word announcement comes out like an accusation. "Now I remember you. How did you make me forget?" He steps closer.

Fae magic . . . but he remembers me now. I don't understand what changed.

"I've been looking for you," he breathes, his fangs beginning to extend.

"Sebastian," Adrian warns. "Don't."

But it's too late. I already know it's too late. They've got me right where they want me. If Brisa is nearby, she'll be turning me into her little blood princess. Either that or she'll kill me. And if she's not nearby, surely Sebastian will do it for her.

Sebastian directs his next statement to the others in the circle, bypassing Adrian completely. "This is the girl I was telling you about, the one who we thought had killed Brisa, the nephilim with the gift of light."

Several vampires step closer, unbridled hunger shining in their dead eyes. A woman reaches her hand out, her smile turning wicked.

"Don't," I command, and she stops––they all stop. Maybe there's something left from Isadora afterall? But I still don't know the extent of it, and I'm not willing to test it and lose Adrian again.

"Eva, do you remember what happened in Ireland?" Adrian asks carefully. Fear is etched into his features, it's not a look I've often seen on the man.

I rake through the memories of Ireland, but all I can think is he wants me to remember my deal with Isadroa. I can make it so vampires have to leave me and my friends and family alone. If it's still in play, it would be so easy to demand it now, to send them all away. But what had Isadora said to remember? Something about intention . . . I don't remember a whole lot of what happened after that.

So if I really want the vampires gone, they'll be gone. And if I don't, then they won't be. But right now, I'm just so happy to see Adrian. I'm not going to dare mess this up for us.

"Can I?" he asks.

I nod, and slowly, he kneels at my side.

"Do you remember?" he asks again. All I want to do is crawl into his lap. To get away from these other people. For it to be just him and I here and nobody else. But I don't dare speak anything of the sort because Adrian is one of them, and I can never forget it.

"I remember most of it," I answer.

"What's this about?" a man demands, but Adrian ignores the question. Instead, he asks me if he can touch me, and when I nod, he scoops me into his arms and turns to the others, many of whom are still staring at me like I'm their meal ticket.

"She's mine," Adrian growls at the others. "Do you understand that? Mine."

"She's not just yours, Adrian," Sebastian argues. "Looks like the fae brought her for all of us to enjoy."

Part of me wants to stay tucked in Adrian's arms, but I've never been the damsel in distress, and I'll be damned if I start now. I shimmy myself out of his grip, but still stay close. His hands rest on my hips, and I don't remove them. He's behind me now, backing me up, no longer in front of me like I need saving, but behind me like he knows I can handle myself. With the familiar skyline surrounding us, I can see now that we're on top of the casino. Being back in New Orleans is a comfort, at least. I've missed this city so much, but I don't have time to process how it makes me feel to be back.

"You landed in our circle." Sebastian continues scowling at me. "You belong to all of us now."

"I belong to no one," I say boldly.

"The vampire council is all here. Shall we put it to a vote?" He motions to the others in the circle.

I turn to Adrian. His expression has grown murderous. "I said, she's *mine*. There is nothing to vote on."

"The vampiric council is set? The blood bonds have been transferred? Is that what was happening tonight?" I ask him. Suddenly I remember the circle of vampires that I woke up in––the blood on their palms, the full moon shining above them, and the electrical charge of fae magic sizzling through the air.

When Isadora had cast the spell the first time she'd been giving them instructions, but I hadn't listened. This meeting must have been part of that.

"Yes, it's done," Adrian confirms.

"So what does that mean for me?" I search his eyes, hoping for good news but expecting the worst.

"That remains to be seen, Angel." His reply is crisp. Succinct. Careful.

"We don't know yet," Mangus drawls with a pat on my shoulder.

Sebastian adds, "We don't, but we will."

"Enough," Adrian growls. "Touch her and die."

"You can't kill me now," Sebastian cackles. "The magic of our bond won't allow it, remember? No members of our council can kill the others. Those were your rules, and now we get to play with them."

"I'll kill you myself," I challenge, and the others laugh.

"That would be fun to watch." Mangus winks playfully, but I know him, and he'd probably love to watch me kill some of these people.

I find their "no council members can kill each other" edict pointless. These men and women are powerful enough that they could plot around that magic, using their covens and progeny to do their dirty work for them. Adrian leads the coven here, but he doesn't have any progeny, so he's already at a disadvantage. And as far as I remember, Mangus has nobody. I can't speak for the others, but I'm certain that Sebastian has powerful resources up his sleeve.

"The spell is complete, and that's what matters," Adrian addresses the others, all of whom have inched closer to me throughout this conversation.

It seems that when I gave Adrian permission to come closer, I gave all the other vampires license to do the same. A prickle of unease goosebumps over my skin. What are they going to do to me? I'm still not even sure why or how I ended up here, except that the fae are the ones responsible for it. But if I have to, I'll command them away again. It's my last option, but at least there is one.

"We are a council now," Adrian continues. "There is much work to be done."

Mangus claps sardonically. Everything about that man drips sarcasm and resentment, and right now it's aimed at the other council members. There was a time when it used to be aimed at me. I'm glad we've moved past that. "Go team," he deadpans. "Now can we go have a meal please? We can talk all about our plans for world domination at our first council meeting tomorrow night."

A few of the others nod, but most are still watching me with distrust.

And a few stare with hunger. They don't even try to hide it.

"The girl stays close," a woman instructs, and the others nod. I expect Adrian to tell them all to stick it where the sun don't shine, but he agrees.

"That's not going to be a problem. Eva's staying with me."

Um--what now?

I want to tell him off, but I also have to remember what happened in Ireland. If I say the wrong thing, we'll be separated again. I don't want that to keep happening. So I pin him with a knowing glare instead, one that says he and I need to talk. And with that, he grabs my hand and pulls me after him, through the rooftop door, down the little hallway, and into the elevator.

It's only once the elevator doors close, once we're blissfully alone, that he wraps me into a tight hug. My body melts like butter under his touch, and my breathing slows.

The nephilim and the vampire. Who would've thought?

"You are not to leave my sight ever again," he growls into my hair.

I inch back to peer up at him. "Yeah, I don't think my staying here is a reasonable request. Did you see those people? They want me, and not in the way you want me."

"I don't care." His eyes are wild as they search me over. "I can't lose you again. I won't let you out of my sight."

There's a fear within him that I've never experienced before. In fact, I didn't even know it was possible for a creature like him to have so much fear. He's the scary one in every situation he walks into.

"You won't lose me again," I assure him, but even as I say it, I know it's an empty promise. I can't guarantee anything. Neither can he.

The elevator doors slide open and we're in the beautiful art deco lobby of the hotel, the sounds from the casino are not far off. I'm not sure where we're going next, but I'd love to see my mother. It's been too long, and my heart can't take another minute. I know we have our differences, that I've played more of the parental role in the last few years, but she's irreplaceable. And sometimes a girl just needs her mother.

"Where's my mom?" I ask. "Please take me to her."

He doesn't say a word, but his eyes flash meaningfully.

The penthouse elevator whisks us up, and then we're in the hotel hallway. One of these two suites belonged to Hugo and the other is all Adrian's. Could my mother be staying in the second penthouse? Adrian said he was protecting her for me, and it makes sense that she'd be hiding out there.

The familiarity of this hallway is unsettling. Something about being up here this time feels so different than all the other times before. So much has happened between us. For one, I don't hate Adrian anymore. I love him. I've accepted it to be true; despite all the odds, I love him. And I need to tell him that.

After I check-in with my mother.

"Where is she?" I ask as we approach the two front doors. He opens his, ignoring the other, and unease spreads through my system. "Is she staying in your place?" Maybe she's in my old bedroom?

We step into his suite, the door closing behind us. He wraps me into another hug before falling to his knees. As if in prayer, my body becomes his altar as he holds my waist and presses his face to my stomach. He clasps my hands and peers up at me. The scent of night still clings to his windswept hair. And his eyes . . . his eyes are filled with torment. "Please, forgive me," he whispers.

Seven

❧

"Where is she?" I breathe.

He doesn't respond right away. I try to shake him off me, but he won't budge. I'm stronger than I've ever been before, though, and I know I could push him away if I really wanted to, but all my energy is depleted. It's like I can't even move. "Where is she?" I repeat again. Tears burn my eyes as my mind is pelted with visions of worst case scenarios.

He's still staring up at me when he tells me the truth. "I don't know. I forgot about her."

Those words break me from my trance, and I yank away from his hold, stalking into the living room and whirling around to face him. "You forgot about her?"

"It's not what you think. I lost her," he says. "I lost you, too."

My eyes narrow, the tears thickening. "Explain."

"Do you remember what you asked for as part of that spell?"

How could I forget? "I can't repeat it," I say. "Because even though I'm mad as hell at you right now, I don't want to go through losing you again, and I'm pretty sure if I say it, it'll happen all over again."

He nods once. "It looks like you have some control over that part."

I nod. When Isadora told me about intention, she was referring to exactly this thing. I can't control the vampires, but if I tell them to leave me alone, they will. "It seems that's the case. And that's how you lost my mother?"

And me.

He said he lost me too.

His eyes search me up and down, like he can't believe I'm here or even real. He stands. Steps closer. I step back. He stops, staring at me. Tormented. My fears double.

"I forgot that you existed," he confirms.

Those words are hard to believe at first. I have to sit with them for a few seconds to fully let them in. Never in a million years could I forget Adrian, but he forgot me?

He forgot me.

It hurts, more than anything else. My heart has already been through so much. And now I have to live with this fear that I will mess up and he'll forget all about me. Even though my logical side understands this happened because of Isadora's spell and my own bargain with her, the illogical part of me, the messy and human part of me, is overcome with complete and utter devastation.

"And I forgot your mother," he goes on. "She was ejected from the coven that night. I only just remembered her––remembered you––a few minutes ago."

A tear breaks free, hot rejection splashing down my cheek.

I know I shouldn't blame him.

And I don't.

. . . but I do.

Again, it's my stupid illogical heart. I don't care if I'm nephilim now, I'll always consider myself a human too. I was raised by humans, and at my base I relate to them the most. And this feeling is all human.

"And you're certain that you remember me now?" I chew my bottom lip, the nerves starting to get to me now. "Do you remember us?"

He answers by pulling me into his arms and crushing his lips to mine. I'm frozen at first, still hurt, still disbelieving, still angry at him and angry at myself, but then his lips do what they've always done to me. They open me up to a level of vulnerability I've only experienced with him. Even though they're cool, they warm me from the inside out. Even though they're hard, they're just the softness I need. Only his unforgiving lips can strip away all my defenses and tear down my walls.

I kiss him back with equal hunger, my fears disappearing. I'm not thinking about the fae or the vampires. I'm not wondering about where the nephilim are or what they're doing. And even the worries for my mother are put to the side, just for this moment.

Just for him.

For us.

He deepens the kiss and lifts me into his arms. My legs wrap around his torso and I press my body into his. This reunion feels like a homecoming and a confession. It feels like everything I've ever wanted.

His spicy male scent is intoxicating as he walks us into his bedroom and lays me down on the bed, looking down on me like I'm a present he can't believe he gets to unwrap. And when he joins me, my mind clears in the most peaceful way, and then that same mind is gone entirely as our bodies take over.

I've only done this once before. Last time he showed me what to do and how to trust myself. This time, I'm bold enough to take the lead for as long as he'll let me. And for a while he does, but eventually his possessiveness takes over and he can't let me have control for another second. And somehow, that's even better.

"You know how to make me feel things I didn't know were possible," I confess, and he chuckles darkly.

"Good girl. Tell me all about it."

We continue like that, him praising me, urging me to speak more freely about what I want, to tell him everything I'm feeling. And so I do as we spend the next hours reacquainting ourselves and making up for lost time. And even when I start to glow, my body emitting my warm golden light from the inside out, we don't stop.

"You're gorgeous," Adrian whispers into my ear.

After spending the entire day in bed with him, only sometimes sleeping, I'm dressed for the coven meeting tonight. The vampires dress up for these things in luxury designer clothing, and though I'm no vampire and never plan to be, I still want to fit in just enough to be comfortable. I don't want to be the thorn among roses tonight.

"Thanks." I place a soft kiss on his lips, and he groans regretfully.

"As much as I want to take you back to bed, we have to go to this."

"I'm not looking forward to it, are you sure I have to go?"

The last place I want to be is in the basement hotel ballroom with all the bloodsuckers. Even if my opinion has changed about certain vampires, I still distrust most of them. Adrian is the coven leader, so he won't let anything happen to me. And Brisa holds no power, so she can't demand things. But I can't get the images out of my mind of the first time I sat in for one of those meetings, of the woman that had been killed, and how Adrian had been forced to take part in it.

"I'm not ready to let you out of my sight," Adrian repeats the same thing he's been saying since he brought up the coven meeting and I said I wanted to stay back in the room. Eventually he's going to have to let me out of his sight, but I know he's not ready. And honestly, I might not be either.

"Fine." A smile crosses my face. "But can I bring a stake?"

"Very funny," he deadpans, and I snort.

He knows by now that I carry a stake as often as I can. It's rather unfortunate that I haven't been able to get my hands on one today. I hate knowing I don't have a weapon right now. Even if I don't plan to use it, it still acts as a security blanket for me, and it has saved my ass on more than one occasion.

But things are different now. First of all, Adrian would never let any of those vampires touch me. And secondly, I've been bitten enough times that the venom in my blood has made me nearly as strong as the vampires themselves. I'm not powerless, and I'm not weak.

And I have angelic light––though I still haven't gotten a complete handle on it.

Except . . . the golden light was easy for me to control while Adrian and I were together earlier. I let it come to me, and when I wanted it to go away, it did. I still don't know what it does or what it means, but I'm no longer afraid of it, and neither is Adrian.

It's the white light that he should be afraid of, and that doesn't come from love. That's my weapon, and it's just as powerful as a stake anyway.

"Have you heard any news about my mom, yet?" I ask, changing the subject.

He shakes his head. "Give it some time. We'll find her. I promise."

I nod, and try to put her from my mind, though it's not easy. I'm so worried, but she's a grown woman, and I know she can take care of herself. That is––if the De Lucas don't find her first.

He drops a kiss to my forehead. "Are you ready to go?"

I nod and clasping hands, we head down to the coven meeting together.

"What's that smile for?" he teases.

"I'm happy," I admit with a shrug. And it's true, even though I feel guilty that my mom could be in danger somewhere, I'm still happy right now. I'm finally seeing myself for exactly what I've always thought was there––a strong woman. I can take care of myself. I know what I want. I have a strong sense of right and wrong. And I'm not going to back down from a worthy fight.

"I'm happy too," he says, pulling me against the elevator wall and kissing me with reckless abandon.

"I've never liked elevators before, but I think I might love this one," I tease between our kisses, and he laughs wickedly.

"Note to self, get trapped in an elevator with Eva."

But that doesn't happen, and all too soon we're out of this one and waiting for the one that goes exclusively downstairs to the coven head-quarters.

When we step inside, we're not alone. "Prince Adrianos," a group of four equally gorgeous vampires address Adrian, bowing their heads low in unison.

He nods a hello, engaging them in conversation while simultaneously running the pad of his thumb up and down the side of my hand.

It's not lost on the others--they shoot quick glances at our clasped hands.

And it's not lost on me either.

This is more than an announcement--it's a claim.

I'm his and he's mine.

They know it, Adrian knows it, but most importantly, I know it.

I squeeze his hand tighter. Three times. *I. Love. You.*

He squeezes back. *I. Love. You. Too.*

The elevator doors open, and we stroll into the foyer and then the coven ballroom--soon, everyone else will know we're together.

My heart speeds as the many vampires turn to look at us. They can hear my heartbeat, and from the looks of it, they weren't expecting me to be here tonight. There are more vampires here than ever before, reminding me of Brisa's court. But looking around, I don't see a single human fledgling or servant.

Not tonight.

Maybe I am a thorn among roses afterall. But who said being a thorn was such a bad thing anyway? Someone's got to be the prickly one.

"The council is here, and they brought many of their own coven members for added security," Adrian reassures me, but he doesn't say more, probably because of all the listening ears.

I press my shoulders back and stride into the room with him, proud to be at his side. I know I'm safe, protected by more than just Adrian's feelings for me. I'm protected by an angelic gift. And by fae magic.

Fae magic that threw me into the center of their council's sacred circle.

I still don't know why, but I'm starting to have an inkling of what their reasoning was for doing that. Tonight is the perfect opportunity to confirm my suspicions.

A slow smile forms on my face.

"Be good," Adrian says in a low tone, raising an eyebrow at my smile.

"I was your good girl upstairs, Adrian, but down here, I get to be as bad as I want."

Eight

The blood is always the worst part at these things. The vampires like to keep it flowing, stocking the bar with loads of blood bags that they can pour into their wine glasses. The distinct coppery smell is undeniable to any human, let alone to a nephilim like me with an incredible sense of smell thanks to both venom and my angelic bloodline. As we mingle, I keep having to hold my breath.

"And who is she to you anyway?" One of the vampires I recognize from the rooftop last night approaches us. She's a stunning Indian woman with black wavy hair, a petite frame, and dark winged eyes—but her voice is dripping in cruelty.

She hates me.

Probably because she knows I'm nephilim, but maybe for more reasons than just that. Showing up in the middle of their sacred ceremony probably didn't earn me any brownie points. But she doesn't know me either, and maybe that's a good thing. She doesn't know what I'm capable of and what I'll do to make sure the people I love are safe. Especially my mother, whom Adrain has people looking for at this very moment.

"Antara, good to see you again. This is Eva," Adrian introduces me. "And she's my girlfriend."

Several of the nearby vampires––all clearly eavesdropping while pretending to have conversations––go quiet. My cheeks warm.

"Have you ever had a girlfriend before?" Mangus approaches, a wicked glint in his eyes.

"No, not since I was a human," Adrian answers, not an ounce of embarrassment or regret in his tone. It's the opposite. He's proud we're together.

So I'm his girlfriend? And his first one? I mean, obviously the man has taken lovers, he certainly knows how to perform in the bedroom, but this? This is vulnerable and real in a way that I wasn't expecting tonight. Anyone who wants to touch me will have to go through him, I already knew that. But now they all know it too.

He's the oldest prince, and the second oldest vampire alive. And most of these people don't know Brisa is still kicking it somewhere, so they consider him the oldest.

He's a founding member of the first ever vampiric council.

He's the coven leader here in New Orleans, but his power and influence reach much farther than just this city, in fact he has authority over the entire continent.

And he's all mine.

And as wonderful as that feels, it also puts a target on my back. I'm not stupid, but I'm also not stupid enough to let go of his hand right now.

"Cute," Antara replies curtly, her tone implying that she thinks our relationship is anything but cute. Do I even blame her? I remember what my cousin Chloe, the nephilim record keeper, showed me back in Italy. My kind and the vampires have been at war for centuries. Hundreds have died on both sides. Maybe even thousands.

And now here I am, Adrian's girlfriend, crashing a coven meeting. Holding his hand. Under his protection. We're like Romeo and Juliet, and we all know how that story ended.

"It's nice to meet you," I pretend, and she pretends too. They all do. The only ones I can trust here are Adrian and maybe Mangus. Suddenly, I miss Kelli. We weren't friends, but I still think we could've been, and I know she would've had Adrian's back no matter what. It would've been nice to have another ally. These vampires have so many children at their beck and call, and Adrian has none. I get his reasoning because if I were a vampire, I wouldn't want to turn anyone either, but the political ramifications might be deadly for us both.

Finally, the conversation dwindles and it's time to get to council business.

Everyone takes their chairs, and the nine council members stand at the front of the room. Cameras have been set up to broadcast this meeting to covens all over the world, and I wonder how many are watching right now. Just thinking about it makes me nervous. Adrian sits me down in the first row, only a few paces from where he's standing with the others.

"When you said you didn't want to let me out of your sight, you really meant it, huh?" I raise an eyebrow.

He drops a kiss to my forehead. "I really meant it."

Sebastian speaks first, and I have to fight to keep my face void of the disgust I feel for that man.

"It is done," he announces, throwing his hands up in celebration, and everyone cheers. He's so sanctimonious and self-satisfied, as if he wasn't trying to take the blood bond back for Brisa just two weeks ago. I still can't believe I was in Faerie for two weeks, but Adrian confirmed it to me earlier. I only remember bits and pieces of the first night, and when we talked about it today, there wasn't a whole lot I could tell him.

Which is killing me because there's got to be something I'm missing. Something important. And it's just beyond my reach . . .

Sebastian bows to the applause coming from both the crowd and the livestream. The other council members do as well, and Adrian's bow is so short lived I have to fight back a snort. He hates this crap. He's not here for applause, he's here to make sure his people are okay.

And all I can think is that somewhere out there, Brisa is probably watching along with the rest of the vampires.

Watching and plotting.

"Your council has been selected through a democratic process, and the blood bonds have been forged by the moon," Sebastian continues.

The crowd grows even more enthusiastic, and I clap along, though it nearly kills me to be clapping for anything to do with vampires. My prejudices run deep . . . something I might need to work on now that I'm dating one of them.

Logically, I get why the vampiric council is a good thing for humans, that they'll be able to govern and keep suckers in check this way, but emotionally, I can't help but hate the power these creatures hold. No, they're not *all* bad, but so many of them are still monsters and would enslave us if they could. I see the way I'm being watched in here, some of these people would happily rip me to shreds and feast on my blood if given the opportunity.

And of all the suckers here, I think Sebastian would love that opportunity the most. Who else on that council would do the same? If enough of them vote, they could change everything. They could decree that vampires can go out this very night and start killing.

"Our first order of business is to put the current laws to a vote." He turns to the other members. "Are there any that you would like to challenge?"

I don't know what I am expecting exactly, but it's not the silence that follows. None of the council members want to challenge the status quo? I find that extremely hard to believe, but maybe I underestimated them.

"Now is the time," he presses. "The next council meeting won't be until quarter two."

Again, silence.

"Nobody wants to show their true colors, huh?" Mangus laughs bitterly, looking them each in the eye. "Very well. We set the rules, the VEC enforces the rules, and the blood bonds will keep those rules from being easily broken to begin with. How very special."

"Things will go on as they have," Adrian agrees, patting Mangus on the back. "It's not so bad, brother. There's always next time." He says it with a teasing wink.

Not so bad, huh?

The vampires will get to keep their fingers in human vices, exchanging blood for everything from gambling to alcohol to drugs and prostitution. I hate it, but I understand their logic. This is the best way they have found to get as much of the sustenance they need without biting humans directly and making them stronger with venom.

Couldn't you just just *pay* for that blood instead?

As everyone turns to look at me, I realize that I blurted that question out loud.

Nine

"**A**drian, muzzle your pet," Antara spits. She and several other council members look like they're seconds away from ripping my head off.

"Eva has a point. We have plenty of money. We could easily pay for blood." I blink at Adrian's words. They're the last thing I ever expected.

"Are you putting it to a vote?" Sebastian cackles. "Please do, brother. I would love to see your first proposal fail miserably."

"What do you think, Eva?" Adrian shoots me a smirk. "Should I propose this idea of yours?"

Everyone else is staring at me.

Shocked?

Disgusted?

Rageful?

All of the above . . .

Adrian turns back to the others with a long sigh. "No, I'm not putting this up for a vote. I was simply pointing out that it's not the worst idea. In fact, paying for blood instead of trading for it has been discussed before, as some of you might recall."

"Right!" I can't help but butt in. "Humans *love* money, and if you got all your blood that way instead of how you're doing it now, you wouldn't have to promote human addiction at all." I'm sitting up taller in my seat, my voice turning passionate. "Do any of you know what it feels like to have the person you love the very most in the world love their vices more than you? Because I do, and it sucks. It doesn't paint y'all in the best light, no offense."

"You dare speak to us in this manner?" one of the councilmen snarls. "You don't even belong here!"

"That's enough," Adrian snaps, though, I'm not one hundred percent sure whom he is telling to shut up. Probably me.

I sink back into my padded seat, pretending to be chastised by the council and Adrian, when really I want nothing more than to continue making my point. But I know better, anything I have to say about blood donation is going to fall on deaf ears here. It has to––because they could pay for blood, but why would they? What they have going has provided them with more blood than they could ever dream of, and they're not willing to risk losing that.

At least they don't go around killing for it anymore. And for the millionth time in my life, I praise the sun for making sure these suckers can't roam around during the day like they can at night. At least the daylight is still a safe space for humans.

Well, it's safe from vamps, but it's certainly not safe from all the other supernaturals out there.

My face continues to burn, and I sit on my hands, trying not to feel so helpless for the next few minutes as the council finishes up their meeting. I seriously feel like everyone in this damn ballroom and all the viewers the world over are staring daggers at me and planning my bloody demise. I should've kept my mouth shut, but that's not really me, now is it?

"If that's all, we can adjourn this meeting," Adrian concludes.

The gorgeous Indian woman, Antara, juts her chin. "Actually, I have a little something I would like to propose to the council."

"You have our ears, Antara," Sebastian replies smoothly, and there's something conspiratorial in his tone that rubs me the wrong way. He was expecting Antara's interruption this whole time.

I swallow a hard lump in my throat and sit up straighter, catching Adrian's ever-watchful gaze. He's even more alert than I am, and I wonder if he expected this to happen or if Antara waited for the perfect timing to spring this little request on us.

Her little request turns out to be not so little.

"Nephilim Girl," she points to me, "Stand up, please."

"Her name is Eva," Adrian barks. He's already told her this, she knows my name, but that's not the point. The point is that she's purposely calling me by what I am because everyone here is enemies with the nephilim.

And I'm guilty by association.

"I thought it was Evangeline?" She bats her eyelashes, and my body goes cold.

This is all a game to her, and I don't know what rules she's playing by, if any.

"She prefers Eva," Adrian corrects, and my heart does a momentary happy dance. It's silly, but I love that he calls me the pet name Angel or the name I prefer and not by the legal name I don't relate to. The name I *never* related to.

But to everyone here, I'm Eva. I know how to be Eva. Eva doesn't back down from a challenge, and she sure as shit isn't going to let these vampires scare her.

"That's right," I say, standing from my seat and walking forward to Antara. "It's Eva, not Evangeline, and not Nephilim Girl."

Antara grins slyly. "Ah, but you are a nephilim, aren't you?"

I shrug. "So? I didn't know I was one until very recently, and I don't align myself with those who seek to kill off innocent supernaturals, nor am I willing to feed on human emotions."

Although that last bit makes me wonder why I was able to control the golden light so easily last night. It's never been that easy before. What really happened in Faerie?

"So you think you're special?" She raises an eyebrow, and several in the crowd laugh.

Adrian is fuming, and I know he's taking notes on exactly who is laughing at my expense. Knowing him, they'll pay later, and knowing me, I'll help him.

"I know I'm special," I respond sharply. "And I think you do too. Why else would you single me out? So tell me, what do you want?"

"You're the first nephilim light-bearer in well over a century," she snaps. "Don't try to deny it."

"I never did," I snap back, "but as I said before, I'm not willing to feed on humans, so my gift is weak, and that's fine by me. You don't need to fear my light."

But she does.

They all do.

I can sense it the way one can sense when a storm is brewing. Something happened to my gift in Faerie, something for my benefit. I can't remember what they did with me for those two weeks, but whatever it was, I'm suddenly able to control my gift in a way I never could before.

That can't be a coincidence.

I can feel it right there below my skin. It's mine for the taking. As if clouds are gathering, the pressure is becoming more dense within me, and it's only a matter of time before the skies open and my gift comes pouring out. I'm the storm standing here right now, and I don't fear it anymore. Let it pour down on all of us because I'm strong enough to handle it.

Antara keeps her eyes pinned on me, as do all the others, when she makes her statement. "I propose that Evangeline Blackwood becomes our prisoner until such time that we can harness her light to help us walk freely in the sun once again."

I blink at her, stunned and horrified that we're doing this right now.

The crowd is silent, but only for the briefest of moments, and then cheers erupt.

Antara turns to her other council members. "Who is with me?"

"You do this and you'll lose her forever," Adrian roars. "You know what happened in Ireland. Are you really so foolish?"

Except for me to push them away would be to break my own heart.

"Let's vote!" Antara calls.

Half of the council raises their hands, the dissenters being Adrian, Mangus, and two others whom I make note to thank later. But the four who are on my side are outnumbered by the others. It's five to four––and I'm the one who will face the consequences.

"No," Adrian sneers, pulling me into his arms for protection. "She belongs to nobody."

"Oh, because you've claimed her?" Sebastian challenges, stepping forward and turning his lip up at us. "Because you think she already belongs to you? Isn't that what you told us last night, *brother*?"

"It's not like that," he argues. "I'm not using her for her light. She's my girlfriend."

Seb cackles. "Save it. Since when have you had a girlfriend? Since never. We all know you really just want her light for yourself. Let me guess, you've already experienced some of it, haven't you?"

They're twisting everything, they're twisting us. But in the back of my mind, I can't help but wonder if they could be right. Is it possible that Adrian is using me? That he found out what I could do and that's what changed his mind about me?

"I belong to myself and nobody else," I bark, peeling myself from Adrian's arms. I stand tall all on my own and glare at the council. Antara and Sebastian my main targets.

"Sorry, it doesn't work that way." Antara flashes her fangs as she laughs. "We've already voted, and you're ours now."

This is it. This is my chance to test why I was thrown into that sacred circle last night. And I have to, don't I? I'm all out of options, and not even Adrian can protect me now. I'm going to have to protect myself.

I'm going to have to become the storm.

Raising my hands, I point one at Antara and one at Sebastian, careful to keep my back to the crowd so I'm only facing the other council members.

"Have you stopped to ask yourselves why I was placed into your sacred circle last night? Haven't you wondered who did it?" I question, mustering up as much courage as I can for this. It's not a lot, but it's enough.

"We already know it has something to do with the fae," Sebastian glares, "They gave you to us as a gift. Maybe they want to repair our poor relationship." He doesn't believe a word he just said, I can hear it in his voice. But I can also hear that he doesn't care so long as he gets what he wants. "Now put your hands down."

"No," I say between gritted teeth. My hands begin to warm.

"What do you think you're doing? Are you asking to die? I said, put your hands down!" Sebastian's eyes are ablaze, but my hands are only getting hotter.

I ignore his threat because I am not afraid.

If they kill me, they kill me. I won't just let them take me as their prisoner––their experiment––and I won't let them force me apart from Adrian either. "The fae had me in Faerie for the past two weeks. That was two weeks to weave their magic into me. And what do you think they did with me during that time?"

Mangus and Adrian are at my side now. I've got back up, but I don't need it because I'm not putting down my hands. I'm not stopping this.

"I'll tell you," I continue, bluffing a little bit here because I don't actually know what they did, but I've got a pretty good guess based on how I feel right now. "They forced my angelic gift to surface and then taught me how best to use it."

"So you were lying about your gift being weak?" Sebastian challenges.

"You, of all people, should know how to spot a liar."

My hands are growing hotter now. This is it.

"You wouldn't dare," Antara shrieks. For the first time tonight, her voice wavers, and her eyes dart to the sides. She's planning her escape. "You're just proving my point. You need to be tamed and controlled, and we're the ones tasked to do it."

Just like I ignored Sebastian, I ignore Antara. I speak to the council as a whole, loud enough for everyone to hear whether they're in the room or streaming from a coven far away. "Let it be known that the fae threw me into your sacred circle at precisely the right moment when the moon was forging the spell. I would wager that they have big plans for me, plans that made me part of your council."

"Impossible!"

"It was the fae who forged the blood bonds, and it was the fae who placed me in your circle at the perfect moment. You say it's impossible, but I say it's more than possible, it's obvious that I'm part of your council now."

"You're not one of us," Sebastian growls. "Is that what you want? Do you want me to turn you tonight? Do not tempt me."

"I'm not a vampire, and I never will be, but I have an idea as to how I can test my theory." I tilt my head toward Adrian. "Adrian, the vampiric council members are protected from killing each other, is that right?"

"That's right," he confirms in a low voice. He's prepared to jump into action at any second, his entire body tense with anticipation. But he's letting me have this because he trusts me, because we're finally on the same team.

I pin my eyes on Sebastian and Antara, though I wish I could glare at each and every one of those vampires who just voted to lock me up and turn me into an experiment. "The way I see it, I have two options. Either I kill you, and your vampire council doesn't have enough votes to sustain hurting me. Or I don't kill you, thereby proving that I am now a part of your council, in which case I'll tie up your vote."

"That's ludicrous," Sebastian says. "You dare to threaten us?"

He's about to attack. I can feel it, but I can feel my own gift more.

My smile splits the sky. "Either way, I win."

With that, I take a chance. My gift explodes from my palms, white and ungodly bright light––a reckoning unlike anything the vampires have ever seen.

Ten

H aving a gambling addict for a mother comes with a lot of wisdom that I didn't ask for, but there are a few things that have stuck with me. They're like peanut butter on the roof of my mouth, not always easy to swallow and impossible to ignore. And right now, it's my mother's voice telling me to bet on myself, reminding me that I can't win if I don't play the game. It's her voice that is giving me the strength to fight back.

Sebastian and Antara don't move fast enough to shield themselves from the stream of blinding light because nothing, not even a vampire, is faster than the speed of light. It shoots at them like a laser, and one of two things is about to happen. They're either going to burn alive and all hell is going to break loose, or nothing is going to happen at all. And if that's the case, which I'm hoping it is, then I'll have figured out that the fae really did bind me into the vampiric council.

People scream while Adrian and Mangus move in closer to my sides, offering their protection. The light is as bright as a bolt of lightning, but it's not a flash. It's a steady stream exploding from my palms and going right into the two vampires. It lasts for a solid ten seconds before I let it drop, blinking rapidly as my vision adjusts to the lack of light.

The screaming fades as everyone takes in the scene. Sebastian and Antara are cowering on the floor, but they're not dead. They're not even injured.

"Angel, it looks like you're going to have to explain yourself," Adrian says loudly, but there's a sweetness to his tone that's bordering on amused. He's obviously fighting back a laugh. A laugh that Mangus lets out without a care in the world.

Sebastian is the first one back to his feet, immediately coming at me, but Mangus cuts him off. Antara isn't far behind, but Adrian doesn't give a shit about hurting a woman apparently because he lifts her up and throws her against the wall. She's tough, so she gets to her feet quickly, but she doesn't attack a second time.

I sigh, prepared to explain myself to everyone in the room. Let them hate me, but let them fear me too. It's the only way I'm going to survive. "I don't know why the fae wanted me in your council and I didn't know it was coming, but I swear to you this is the truth of our situation." Mangus continues laughing maniacally while everyone else stays silent, half of them staring at him like he's lost his mind.

"Make no mistake that the light from my palms can kill vampires," I threaten. "But it couldn't kill Sebastian and Antara because the magic forged in our council bond is even stronger than my angelic gift. The council magic forbids me from killing anyone else on the council, same as it forbids them from killing me. And that right there is all the proof you need that I am now a part of this vampiric council."

I don't mention that I could also tell them to leave me alone and they'd have to, that they might even forget me entirely, simply because I don't want to risk losing Adrian. But if it comes down to it, if they try to take my life or my gift, then I'll take that risk. I wouldn't have another choice.

"It can't be true," one of the council women gasps in a thick Russian accent. She didn't vote for me, so I don't really care what she has to say. "This nephilim is not a vampire. She cannot belong with us."

"She just proved to you it is true, Nadia," Mangus sighs. "Don't underestimate fae magic. Or haven't you learned that lesson yet? Remind me, how old are you? A hundred years? Sometimes I forget how young most vampires are these days."

That comment earns him a death glare from just about everyone in the room. They're all pretty young compared to the princes, and I think it has something to do with the earlier nephilim wars and the sheer number of vamps who were killed.

The council stands divided as they take in my news. With me as part of the group now, we're an even split. There are ten of us to vote on matters. Ten of us to vote on my future.

"You can't have me," I announce boldly. I make sure to look each of them dead on so they can see how serious I'm being about this. "With nine votes there was a split, but with ten there's a tie. And I vote for my freedom." I turn to Mangus, Adrian, and the two vampires who also voted for my side. "Thank you for helping me keep my freedom. I won't forget this kindness."

Mangus and Adrian nod. The others don't look so sure, but they eventually nod as well.

"So it's settled," Adrian is quick to say. "We'll meet again at the next council meeting scheduled to take place at Santino's coven headquarters in Rio De Janeiro in three months' time."

"This isn't over," Sebastian says darkly.

And then he turns and leaves, his entourage following him out the door. I recognize his new child, Fiona, who was a fledgling not that long ago. And I remember how she tried to help turn me back in Italy. At the time I'd considered her my savior, but I was under the influence of vampirism and not in my right mind. Now I can only see her as the demon working overtime for the devil that is Sebastian. She gives me a little wave on her way out, her eyes mocking.

"Sebastian always did have to have the last word," Mangus grunts.

I sigh and press my forehead into Adrian's chest. I'm so ready to get out of here. I feel depleted but also so full at the same time. Even though I can't remember it, I'm now certain that the fae king Orlyc forced my gift to surface and, in the two weeks I was with the fae, they taught me how to use it without needing human emotion to feed it.

But how? I thought nephilim had to feed on humans.

Part of me would love to thank him, part of me wants to demand answers, and the biggest part never wants to step foot in his realm again.

"Games are afoot, eh?" Mangus nudges me. "Fae don't just help nephilim for no reason. They hate nephilim even more than we do, no offense."

"I know . . ." I bite the inside of my cheek and try not to freak out. "It's clear they want something from me, but the question is, what?"

Adrian keeps me tucked under his arm as we leave the ballroom. It's not until we're alone in his penthouse that he relaxes a fraction, but he's still roiling with anger. He looks like he wants to kill someone. Probably five someones.

"I'll kill them before they ever lay a hand on you, Angel," he growls the second the door closes us in the penthouse, proving my point.

"You can't kill them. The magic won't let you," I point out.

"Then I'll make someone else do it."

I sigh, taking his hands in mine and kissing his knuckles one by one. He goes still as he watches me. "Obviously, I want them dead, too. They're dangerous to me. And if it's between me or them, well, I choose me. But we can't just start a council war over what happened tonight, at least not right now."

He shakes his head and a golden lock falls across his troubled eyes.

"Nobody said anything about torture, though. I'll start with Sebastian. Peel his fingernails off one by one."

I snort. "You can't do that. He has his entourage here to protect him."

"And I have my coven. They'll back me up." He's seething. I don't know if I've ever seen him so angry. "I know he was the one who convinced the other council members to try and get to your gift. I'm sure he asked Antara to propose the idea just to piss me off. He's so much like his twin, Hugo. Always playing games with everyone, always making deals and scheming."

At least Hugo is dead, but Sebastian isn't going anywhere any time soon, especially with the protections now in place. But we're not going anywhere either. After losing Adrian on that rooftop in Ireland, then getting him back and spending the night with him, I couldn't care less about Sebastian right now.

Because I know exactly how I feel in my heart, and I can't wait another second to tell him. I take his hand in mine and squeeze gently––three times for I love you. But I haven't said it out loud yet. "Hey, look at me."

His breathing is heavy. He only does that when he's upset. The man doesn't even need to breathe at all, but when his emotions get away from him, he starts to breathe like that, just a human man. His emotions are right here for me to see, they're plain on his face, and yet his mind is far away. With my other hand, I trace my fingertips along his neck, up his jawline, to cup his cheek.

"Adrian, look at me." He does, and there's so much worry and pain behind the glacial blue that it nearly breaks me.

"I love you," I whisper the three words that I've never said to a man before.

His eyes narrow as they search mine. They're so electric blue right now that they would be frightening if I didn't love him so much. He doesn't have kind or soft eyes, and nothing about him is approachable, but that doesn't matter because right now he's looking at me like I'm the only woman in the world.

I am mad with love.

"I would kill them all for you, Eva," he confesses. "Do you know what kind of monster you have fallen in love with?"

It's not what I expected him to say. It hurts. Not because he didn't tell me he loves me back, but because he thinks so low of himself.

"You're not a monster."

"But I am," he growls, dropping my hand and gripping the back of my neck instead, pulling me in closer. "I've killed so many people. I killed my own wife. My unborn child. And I know that I don't deserve your love, but

594

I'm a selfish man, and I'm going to accept it anyway because it's the best thing that has ever happened to me in this morbid existence."

I can't help it. I giggle. "God, you're dramatic. Did anyone ever tell you that?"

His smile quirks, the intense energy loosening, and those wicked eyes transform with happiness. It might be the first time I've ever truly seen him allow happiness in. "I love you too, Angel," he says firmly. "I love you, and I swear to you, I will kill anyone who dares to harm you."

"Again with the theatrics," I tease.

But I love it. I love every second of this moment, theatrics and all. "I don't know if anyone's ever loved me back as much as I've loved them," I confess, suddenly more vulnerable than I've ever been. Being naked with him is not nearly as vulnerable as telling him these deep dark insecurities. It makes me feel weak even though I know it's actually making me stronger. "I'm not even sure my own family could love me fully. I didn't get a chance to know my father, and my mother and grandmother were probably afraid of me to an extent. But this? And you? You're what I've been searching for, Adrian." I press his hand to my heart. "Feel it beating?"

He nods, dropping his forehead to mine with a soft groan.

"It's all for you. I'm yours. My heart is yours."

Finally, I've found someone who will love me enough to put me first and fight for me. I saw it tonight during the council meeting, and it's given me the strength to do this.

He presses a kiss to my lips once. Twice. But then he pulls back. "There's something I have to tell you."

I don't like those words. Those words scare me. But I nod, forcing myself to be strong. "Okay."

He leads me to his sofa, and my mind races with the possibilities of what he's going to say. Does he not want this like I do? Is there something he's been hiding? Is he going to try to let me down easily? Whatever it is, he thinks it's bad enough that I need to be sitting for this conversation.

"I have responsibilities to my coven and to my people," he says.

"I know, and I wouldn't ask you to give those up." But is that really true? If it came down to it--them or me--what would I want? I'm not entirely sure I have the answer to that right now, because I just want us to stand a chance.

"When Isadora's spell was being forged last night, I was faced with an impossible choice." He stares at me expectantly, like I should get this, but I don't understand what he's trying to say.

"Just tell me, Adrian. Whatever you have to say isn't going to scare me off."

He scratches his jaw, a pained expression overtaking his face. "I love you, but at that moment, I knew that if I didn't join the council, I wouldn't be able to protect my coven, let alone protect the humans from the worst of my kind. It killed me to do it, but I decided to move forward with the council bond." He swallows hard, and his words start to make sense to me. My face burns hot. I hold my breath. "I chose them over remembering you because I couldn't live with myself if I allowed the council to forge without me or not at all. And I'm so sorry."

He drops his head, and I expect to feel betrayed or disappointed.

But I don't.

"I'm proud of you," I say, surprising both of us. "You made the right choice. I would've done the same thing."

His head pops back up. "What?"

"You heard me. I wouldn't have wanted you to choose me over the billions of humans on this planet that need protecting, and I wouldn't have wanted your coven to be in danger either. You understand what's important, and that's why I love you."

"But *you* are important," he growls, pulling me into his lap. His hands roam under my skirt to grip my thighs. "You deserve more than I'll ever be able to give you. You deserve a full life, and you can never have that with a vampire."

"Stop. Don't say that."

"But it's true."

I kiss him hungrily, losing myself in his embrace and in this safe space we've created tonight. I don't want to lose him. Not like this. It feels like we're building ourselves up and breaking ourselves down at the same moment. I don't know how to stop it before we crumble.

Pulling away, I stare into his eyes. "Listen to me carefully. I get to say what I deserve in my life. And what I want is for us to be together." I take his hand and place it over my heart again. "This is yours. Don't forget it." My heart pounds against my chest, and I know that he can feel and hear it. Finally he nods, relief plain on his face. Mine is probably mirroring back the same thing. "As long as that damn thing is in my chest, it belongs to you."

"My heart belongs to you too, but what need do you have with a heart that's been dead for centuries?" He means it, he really does look down on himself. He's always been so calm and collected, so confident and cold. To see him like this kills me.

"If it's yours, then I want it."

He smiles.

And when he smiles, the golden soft glow emits from my skin, lighting the darkness between us. I run my fingers over his face, his arms, his body. Everywhere. He does the same.

I know what he's thinking. That I should have a normal life, one with a human or even a nephilim man at my side, one with children and motherhood and everything that a human life has to offer someone like me.

A life without vampires.

And before I fell in love with him, I would've agreed. I never wanted a vampire, but I also never thought I would feel the way I do right now. I'm in love, and anything else would be second best. Adrian is the only one I want. I'll gladly give the rest of it away, give it all up, because having him is better.

Just as he's peeling off my dress, pounding booms on the door. Adrian groans into my mouth, and I do the same to him, my hands gripping his white shirt.

"Go away," he calls out.

"Your Highness," a male voice calls back, muffled by the door but still audible enough to send alarm bells through my system. "Please, we need you to hurry. There's been an incident in the casino. You're going to want to see this."

Eleven

"**S**tay here," Adrian commands, putting me gently on the couch like I'm made of glass. He stands and goes for the door.

"Don't you know me better than that?" I scoff, jumping up and adjusting my dress. "I'm coming with you."

His mouth lifts on one side. "You're right. What am I going to do with you?"

I waggle my eyebrows. "I can think of a few things."

"And we will do all those things later." He takes my hand and leads me to the door. "Come along. Let's get this over with."

A vampire stands waiting in the hallway. I immediately recognize the pit boss from the first night I met Adrian. I don't like this man. "William, this is Eva. Eva, this is William. He's my right-hand man on the casino floor."

"We've met," I say smoothly, pinning William down with a nasty glare.

He sighs heavily and turns back toward the elevator. "You really need to answer your phone, Adrian. I shouldn't have to come all the way up here to drag you away from your new toy."

Adrian moves lightning quick, pinning the man against the elevator doors. "Speak one sour word against Eva again and I will rip your intestines out and feed them back to you, is that clear?"

William blinks rapidly and nods.

"Now apologize."

"I'm sorry, Eva," he gets out just as the elevator doors open. He steps back into the box, and we follow.

Adrian is busy straightening out his suit and tie as he finishes with

William. "You know, sometimes I think I'm too soft on the coven. Do you forget who I am? What I can do? Do I need to remind you?" He says it all casual and smooth, as if this is a conversation about the weather. It's terrifying and hot as hell.

"You're right. I'll do better," William replies. "You know I am loyal to only you."

Adrian stares at him for a long time before sighing. "Your maker is long gone. I took you in because I saw potential in you. And I still do."

"You're right," William offers. "Forgive me."

"You're forgiven." Adrian pats him on the shoulder. It's so strange seeing them together because William appears to have a decade on Adrian, but Adrian is actually much, much older. "I apologize for the outburst, William. I'm very protective of Eva, but I can do better, too."

Okay, that was also very hot.

He pulls me into his arms, kisses me on the top of my head, then continues his conversation with his number two. "Now, tell me what we're dealing with."

William swallows hard, his lips going thin. "The night was going just fine until a new vampire arrived. He attacked a group playing roulette on the casino floor. He drained one of our regulars before we could pry him off the guy."

"Who did he drain?"

"Raymond. He's one of our elderly player's club members. Comes in every day except Sundays because he says Sundays are for God."

Adrian's holding me tighter now, his muscles straining. I can feel the anger rolling off him and wouldn't want to be that baby vampire right now. Whoever it is, they're dead. For real this time. And they should be because that's messed up. Killing an old guy for no reason? I'm sick just thinking about it.

"Did you call the VEC?" Adrian asks.

"Not yet. I knew you would want to deal with the issue first."

Not to mention, Adrian is one of the primary members of the VEC. He nods and rolls back his shoulders, his neck popping in the process. "Thank you, William. You did good. Did any of the other council members see it? Or their guests?"

William shakes his head. "No, they all think they're too good for the casino."

Adrian chuckles darkly. "They're not too good to drink the blood it provides."

My stomach churns at that not only because he's got a point, but also because the thought of the blood casino still makes me want to vomit.

My feelings are all jumbled up about this. Yes, I'm upset that a vampire killed someone, and yes, I think it should be reported. But I also know the VEC is in the pockets of the vamps anyway. And I trust Adrian. Back when I first met him, he killed a man in front of me as an intimidation tactic, but I later learned the guy was a gangster who deserved it. Adrian may call himself a monster, but he's the kind that takes care of the other monsters.

We head through the casino floor, to the roulette table where this apparently happened. But from the looks of it, you'd never know. The blood has been mopped up and there's a group of humans standing around gambling. They were probably compelled to forget what they saw. I catch sight of a woman with a small splatter of blood on her white dress and have to look away.

It's triggering. Makes my skin crawl. I'd still rather be anywhere else than this place. Up in the hotel I can almost forget this is here, but then I have to walk through the casino, and I'm affronted by the overstimulation. The dinging of the slot machines, the desperate patrons hoping for another hit, the stench of stale cigarette smoke, and especially the people with blood bags slowly dripping while they play. That's the worst part, and it's for show. They could just have people donate in the nurses station, but the vamps like the novelty of it all.

Even though The Alabaster Heart is a luxury hotel and casino, even though a lot of people in this city think it's a nice place, I still hate it.

The memories will haunt me forever.

I can almost see my mother there at that Texas Hold'em table. Her sparkly red purse slung over the back of the chair while she plays her games and loses herself. There's a woman there right now that looks so much like her with that curly auburn hair hanging down around her slim waist.

Wait . . . I squint, and my heart drops to the floor.

No. It can't be.

But it is.

The woman *is* my mother.

I stop dead in my tracks and just stare. Time crawls, and my vision narrows. My hands begin to shake. My mind races far too fast for my emotions to match. What is she doing here? I'm happy to see she's alive, but this is the last place I ever wanted to see her again. She's supposed to have been cured from her addiction. Adrian compelled her to give up gambling. But there she is——gambling once again.

I don't understand.

Adrian is saying something to me and then to William, but I don't pay attention. I can't. His words are like sand streaming through my fingers.

Without thinking, I run to her. "Mom!"

Her back stills, and then I call her by her name. She turns to me, standing, taking me in her arms, an IV line tugging at her hand.

"No," I say. "No." I can't believe it. I won't.

But I have to because the proof is right there. She's donating blood in exchange for chips, just like she used to do. Her blood is a red line in a tube of plastic leading to a plump bag, but it might as well be a knife to my heart. She was never supposed to donate to the vampires again, and especially not in this manner. Suddenly, all I want is to command the vampires to get away from her, to demand the deal I made with Isadora be enforced.

But at what cost?

It won't save her from her addiction, and I'd lose Adrian.

So I don't say a word about it, I don't, but I'm speechless to say anything else.

"Oh, honey," her voice wobbles, "It's so good to see you. I've been worried."

"What's going on?" I finally whisper, my voice breaking. "I thought you never wanted to gamble again?"

Her eyes well with tears, mirroring my own, and then she shrugs. "That feeling faded and the old one came back. I'm so sorry, Eva. I missed you so much, and then I was hiding out here, and being close to the casino wasn't easy, but I swear I never gambled." She swallows hard. "And then a few weeks ago I was in the lobby and something terrible happened. It was too fast for me to even see who did it, but the vampires threw me out on the streets. Adrian wasn't here to help me. Nobody wanted to help me. I had nowhere else to turn."

"What does that even mean?" I don't understand why that explains her coming back here to gamble. None of this makes sense––but I also don't want it to make sense because then I would have to accept that it's real, that she relapsed.

The man next to her swivels in his chair, a smug grin coming over his familiar pockmarked face, and things become ten times worse.

Armondo.

He's the mafia boss with the sinister grin and the deep scar in his left eyebrow, the one who nearly killed her in September. He gives me and Adrian the smuggest grin that I want to claw off his face. I outplayed him once before with Adrian's help, but he's back for more.

"Nice to see you again, Evangeline. And you too, Adrianos." His eyes flash to Adrian, and I know this has more to do with him than with me. Powerful men are like that sometimes, they underestimate the women, only ever looking to the men as worthy adversaries. "Eva, your lovely mother needed a place to stay while she got back on her feet. What kind of man would I have been to refuse a beautiful woman in need?"

"I know exactly what kind of man you are," I hiss between gritted teeth. I grab her arm. "But thank you, she is safe with me now."

He snakes his slimy hand around her waist and actually pulls her into his large lap, then he peels my hand off of her arm and kisses her neck as if he's done it a thousand times before. "Your mother and I came to an arrangement. She lives with me now."

He grins up at me with a mocking wink, and she shoots me a warning look. I don't know what to do. I truly don't.

Adrian steps closer. "Armondo, what are you playing at?"

Armondo laughs. "I thought I was playing Texas Hold'em. Is there another game I should be betting on right now? Maybe something with better odds?"

He winks.

He's taunting us.

And silence stretches between the group because we all know there's definitely another game going on here. A game of egos and power and the women who get caught in the middle. The dealer finishes distributing the current hand and the gamblers on either side of Armondo and my mother prepare their bets.

"Mom, you don't have to stay with him. Come with us. Right now, come with us, and we'll pay him back however we have to."

"She's mine." Armondo squeezes her closer to his body, but I force myself to ignore it and will my mother to stand instead. "And if you'll excuse us, we have a hand to play."

She doesn't move, just stares at me with big sorrowful eyes. "I assure you, Eva. We're okay. We're enjoying ourselves. You don't need to worry about us. I'm happy with Armondo."

It's a lie. I know it's a lie.

How are we back here? After everything we've been through, is this really what she wants? Because not only is she in the clutches of this mobster again, but she's out in the open where the nephilim can track her and hurt her, and she's gambling. She's giving in to the thing that hurt her the most, the thing that she loves but that doesn't love her back.

It's all my fault––if I hadn't made that stupid deal with Isadora none of this would have happened. Mom would've stayed hidden by Adrian's coven. Protected and cared for until we could've found a way for her to live her life without the fear of the De Luca family. Once things were safe, we could've gotten her away from here forever.

"We'll see you around," Mom says gently, and then she turns her back on me, placing her bet. And even though I can tell she's sad, I can also tell she likes this, that this is also her choice. Armondo isn't making her do this, he's just enabling her.

And me?

I'm lost at sea, swallowed up by crashing waves of emotion. I'm falling through space with nowhere to land. I'm crawling through the barren desert, reaching out toward an oasis that isn't real, that was never real.

It. Was. Never. Real.

My mother was never really cured of her addiction. She was in a forced remission, but she was never cured, and now I'm going to lose her to it. In the pit of my stomach, I know it to be true. All my worst fears are happening, and I can't stop them.

"Eva." Adrian cups my elbow and guides me from the casino floor. I shuffle along aimlessly, not caring that people are staring at us, that vampires are glaring at me, or that my emotions are exposed for the whole world to see.

He pulls me into a dark side room and flips on a fluorescent light. I wince because it's too bright and too sterile in here. It's only when he wraps me in a tight hug that the floodgates burst open and I sob into his chest. "Shh," he whispers into my hair, and then he mumbles something in another language.

I don't know how long I stay like that. Minutes? Hours? But eventually, I peel away from his embrace and look up into his eyes. I find pity staring right back, and I hate it. I don't want his pity. What I want is action.

"Please," my voice hitches. "Compel her again. Make her stop. Make her better."

He shakes his head regretfully.

"Why not?" My hands fist, and I press them to his chest. "You say you love me, then prove it."

He grabs my fisted hands and holds them still, kissing the knuckles one by one. Eventually, I deflate.

"I will compel her if that's what you really want, but I have to warn you, compulsion can be dangerous if used over again on something as strong as this. She just proved her addiction is stronger than my first compulsion. If I do it again, I could scramble her mind. You could lose her forever."

Twelve

—∞—

"How can an addiction be stronger than a centuries old vampire? You're the strongest vampire in the world. If anyone can help her, it's you."

At least my tears have dried up, but it still feels so unfair. I never thought I'd have to cry about this again. I didn't even get a chance to spend time with her while she was better.

"I will try. If that's what you want, I will try, but I can't promise that it won't hurt her."

My mind reels with the implications of his warnings. "And what happens if it does? What do we do then?"

"I can't undo a traumatic brain injury," he explains regretfully. "If her mind was strong enough to fight my compulsion, then I'll have to use even stronger compulsion to get her to stop gambling again."

"So you shouldn't do it . . ."

"Right now, we should be most concerned about Armondo. Would you like me to kill him?"

I snort and wipe away my remaining tears, but Adrian doesn't laugh. "Oh, you're being serious."

"Just say the word."

It's incredibly tempting. "What happens if we kill him?"

"First we have to get your mother away from him, but we kill him and wait for retaliation. That's if they know it's us. We've had a bad relationship with them for years. It won't be pretty, but I'll do it for you."

"Is there another way to get her away from him? Can we negotiate?"

He smiles. "If there's one thing I've learned in my time, it's that negotiating with guys like Armondo doesn't work."

Am I really going to put a hit on Armondo? Is this what it has come to?

It won't solve her gambling addiction, but getting her away from him will help. That slimeball brought her here to goad us, which means that word must have gotten out about Adrian and me being together and back in New Orleans.

Who else knows? My mind flits to the De Luca's. I just know they're lying in wait somewhere, wanting me to answer questions about what happened at The Gateway. But right now, Armondo is my biggest concern. He feels manageable. A bug I can squash. My awful relatives do not. They're more like an infestation.

"Whatever it takes to get my mom back, I want to do it."

Adrian gives me a quick nod and another hug and then leads me to a private bathroom to get cleaned up. I go in alone and glare at myself in the mirror, rubbing off the black mascara tracks that have stained my cheeks. My brown eyes are bright from crying, almost golden, but they're rimmed in red. Proof of my vulnerability. I really hate crying, especially in front of other people. Falling apart in Adrian's arms like that wasn't ideal, but somehow I'm not mortified by it. He's my person now.

I haven't had a person since Ayla broke off our friendship. I miss Ayla, and I'll always love her, but she hurt me. Yes, I made mistakes too. I never should've kept things from her, and I should've listened to her more when she shared her feelings about me dating her brother. I want her friendship back, but only if we're both fair to each other. It's been months, and I just hope that whatever she's doing, she's healthy and no longer hiding in her bedroom. If anyone deserves to live a wonderful life, it's that girl.

Adrian knocks on the door. "Are you ready?"

I shake my thoughts clear and head out to meet him. The detour with my mom wasn't expected, she could've been the one killed in that attack, and we still have to deal with the issue at hand. A new vampire killing a human means true death. That's the rules, and honestly, I'm all for it. If a vampire can't control their urges and kills an innocent, resisting strong blood bonds, then they're too dangerous.

Hell, I'll kill the vampire myself. That might make me feel a little better.

"Will it be a true death?"

"Yes, he's being held right now."

"Can I have the honors?"

"Would that make you feel better, Angel?" he asks. I expect him to tease, but he doesn't. He knows I hate vampires. Not all of them anymore, obviously, but vampires in general, and especially ones who break the rules and kill innocent humans.

Would it make me feel better? That's a good question. And an easy answer. "Absolutely."

A small smile flickers across his otherwise unreadable face. He's already so beautiful when he doesn't smile, that when he does it's like Christmas. "Then yes, you can kill him, but first we need to have a discussion with the vampire, and I need to talk to his maker. There's a proper way that we deal with these situations."

"Proper? Like when Hugo's vampire attacked me in the lobby, so you ripped his head off? Something proper like that?"

"Something like that, yes."

Our banter is making me feel better, and I couldn't be more grateful. I need to get my mind off everything. My life is a mess, and so many of the people I love are also caught up in messes that I can't clean up for them. I wish I could. It would be so much easier that way, but that's not how it works. I can't make my mom better, and I can't just force Ayla to be my friend again. I can't go back in time and stop myself from making mistakes.

I take Adrian's hand as we go back out to the casino floor. The sucker is being held on the opposite end of the casino from the hotel, so we have to walk the whole property. I can't help but notice how Adrian steers me well away from the Texas Hold'em tables. And I can't help but look in that direction anyway.

She's still there, but her blood bag has been removed. At least there's that.

It turns out that the casino has a row of jail cells hidden behind a massive locked door near the cashiers. It's incredibly secure, almost like a second bank vault, and we go from the lavish interior design of the casino to gray everything. That feels like a metaphor for my life lately, but I'm too exhausted to dissect it.

William is waiting for us. "He's in the last cell." He points us down the wide hallway. "He's the only one here."

There are several normal looking cells that must be for humans, a few with what I think are made of iron, and then there are several silver cell doors at the very back. Just seeing the silver takes me back to what it was like seeing Adrian locked up at the Casa. I inwardly shiver, wishing those memories could be erased forever. For both our sakes.

We walk up to the cell door made of solid silver. It has a small window with silver bars at eye level. Adrian peers through first. His shoulders tense, and he goes completely still.

"What?" I ask, already figuring whoever is in there can't be good news.

He turns to me, and his usually stoic face is filled with regret. My heart clenches.

"Let me see." I try to push him aside, but he doesn't budge.

"Maybe it's best if you didn't."

"You and I both know that's not going to happen."

He sighs and inches away, so I look through the little window.

"Kenton." My voice cracks on his name.

My friend is sitting on a bare mattress, and when he turns to look at me, his vampire-bloodshot eyes widen.

"Eva," he croaks. "I'm so glad you're here. You've got to help me."

"What did you do, Kenton?" I ask carefully, trying to remind myself that he's not the same Kenton that he used to be. This isn't the sweet Kenton who cracked jokes and rode around with me in Adrian's Porsche singing at the top of our lungs. This isn't the Kenton who handed me my first stake and stood up for me. This is the Kenton that was attacked in Versailles, that I witnessed die. The Kenton who wasn't actually dead because he was turned by Brisa. He's the man that helped ambush me in Ireland, telling me all about how great being a vampire is, and how much he loves drinking blood.

This is the Kenton who murdered an innocent elderly man earlier tonight.

This is Brisa's Kenton.

Mine is gone.

"Can you come in here so I can talk to you?" he pleads.

My mouth turns to ash. I don't know what to say . . .

"No," Adrian snaps.

I rest my hand on the door handle, trying to remember the friend I used to have. Could he still be in there somewhere? Maybe there's still a chance for him.

"It's okay," I say slowly, my eyes never leaving Kenton. "He won't hurt me."

At least, I hope he won't. I don't really know him anymore.

Adrian growls, "You don't know what he's capable of, Angel. He's not the friend you used to know. He's a soulless killer now."

Kenton starts to cry. I've never seen him cry, he was always the happiest person I knew. And something about the way his shoulders bob up and down and the pain in his voice breaks me.

I turn on Adrian. "You were a killer when you first transitioned. It doesn't make it right, but he has the same maker as you, so shouldn't you of all people have some compassion for what he's going through?"

Adrian rakes a hand through his hair, shaking it out as he thinks of what to say. Finally, he speaks, careful with each word. "You're only saying that because you care about him. If he was any other vampire, you'd have killed him by now."

"You're going to kill me?" Kenton jumps up, flashing forward to the door, only inches from us on the other side of the bars. "For what? For feeding?"

"For killing," Adrian growls. "We have rules for a reason."

And while I know that's the truth, I also know that my Kenton could still exist underneath all the death and destruction. For all we know, Brisa told him to kill in order to gain Adrian's attention.

I turn on Kenton. "Did Brisa make you kill that human?"

Kenton's dark eyes shift away and he steps back. "No, I wanted to feed, and I didn't want to stop."

I can't tell if he's lying, but my gut says he is.

"Brisa is trying to use you, and probably others, to get to the council," Adrian states. "Don't deny it."

Kenton shrugs. "So what? She failed. And now I'm here."

"And now you're here . . . which is a problem. Eva may wish to save you from true death, but I can't let you live. You belong to Brisa, and you operate outside the council's bond. It's only a matter of time before you kill again. You're a liability."

Kenton hangs his head. "You're right. Kill me. I never wanted this to happen, and I never would've asked for it. Just do me a favor and make it quick."

Adrian watches Kenton with interest, his eyes narrowing, and I don't know what I expect, but it's not what comes next. "No," Adrian states.

"No?" Kenton laughs bitterly. "Why not? Seconds ago you were listing the reasons I should die."

Adrian turns to William. "Keep this area well guarded. Nobody comes in here or leaves without my permission first."

William nods.

"You're just going to keep him locked up?" I cry.

"For now, yes."

"Is that your master plan?" Kenton growls, his tone becoming murderous. "Just drag it out, maybe starve me while you're at it? Or do you want me to sit here and think about how I've become the very thing I hated?"

Adrian doesn't reply. Instead, he takes my hand and tugs me after him. I look back at Kenton, but he's already gone from the cell door window. Kenton's right, I wouldn't want to live that way either, especially knowing I'd killed someone. But despite all that, I can't seem to part with the idea that he could become a good man again. Not the same one, not with the yummy goodness of his human self, but still someone worth saving despite the flaws.

As soon as we're out the door, Adrian turns on me. Taking my face in his cool hands, our gazes lock. "Brisa did this to your friend. Don't be angry at me. Don't be upset with Kenton. It's Brisa we need to stop."

I nod as tears blur my vision. I'm so tired of crying tonight, but at least I've washed off all the mascara during my last cry. "I hate her."

"Me too," he says with conviction. "And I promise you, Angel, I'm going to kill her."

He thumbs away my tears, and suddenly I'm red hot with anger. Screw crying, I want to punch something, preferably Brisa's face. I wish I could do that right now, but she's in hiding and could be anywhere. "So what's the plan?"

"Your friend just became our plan."

Thirteen

By the time we make it back upstairs to the penthouse, I'm so tired that I fall into Adrian's bed without doing more than removing my shoes. I'm vaguely aware of him tucking the covers in around me and kissing my forehead, whispering something lovingly in that language I don't understand but am pretty sure belonged to the ancient Greeks. I don't spend much time worrying about it because sleep is the break I desperately need. I just want to shut my mind off for the next six to eight hours.

And that's exactly what would happen if I didn't dream.

But I do, and the one that comes for me tonight is lucid and exhausting.

I'm in an old playground that I used to frequent as a child. I'm also keenly aware that this is a dream. I'm alone, and everything is slightly off somehow. The colors are muted into creamy pastels instead of the bright primary colors I remember. The slide should be red, but it looks like a tube of tacky pink lipstick. The grass isn't green, it's gray.

"Wake up," I tell myself, but nothing happens.

I stroll over to the swingset and plop down in the plastic seat, slowly rocking myself back and forth, the tips of my bare feet rubbing against the gravel. I'm wearing the dress I fell asleep in, and find that particularly odd. Kicking up a spray of the gravel, I will myself to wake up again, or at least to move on into a dreamless sleep.

A flash of silver flutters past my periphery, and a metallic dove lands on the swing next to me. My stomach fills with dread––I've seen a bird like that before.

"You can come out now, Casimir," I call, my voice echoing into nowhere.

I stand and turn around in a quick circle. He's nearby, he has to be, because those silver doves are some kind of extension of his shadow magic. Shadow magic that can also somehow be used to worm its way into my mind while I'm sleeping, which explains this lucid dream.

"Seriously, Casimir, this is not what I had planned for tonight. I'm exhausted and need restful sleep."

"Evangeline Blackwood." He addresses me by my full name, and I whip around to face him. "You can rest later. We need to talk."

He's garbed in a long midnight black cloak, and his inky hair falls around his startling silver eyes. He's watching me like he expects me to try to run. He's terrifying, maybe he's used to women running from him, though, I doubt that's the case. Because he's also beautiful.

"How are you doing?" His cruel mouth grimaces, and I'm pretty sure he couldn't care less how I'm doing.

I raise an eyebrow and scoff. "Really? That's what you're going to ask? This isn't a social visit. What do you want, Casimir?"

"You're right," he steps forward, his suede boots crunching against the gravel, "But I've been instructed to check on your well-being . . ."

I shrug. Might as well tell him the truth. "Well, if you must know, everything is shit, but your plan worked."

"What plan?" he tries, and I laugh.

"The one where you threw me into the vampire's sacred circle and bonded me to their council? Yeah, that one. We confirmed it tonight. I hope you're happy."

His grin is vicious. "Excellent."

The dream begins to fade, the scenery curling into wisps of inky smoke and liquid silver. But as much as I want this to be over, I didn't get anything out of this, and I'm not leaving empty-handed.

"Wait," I yell. "Don't leave yet."

The landscape seems to pause––not disintegrating anymore but not returning to how it was either. The fae stares at me expectantly, shadows pooling at his feet.

"Why did you bond me to the vampires?" His silence causes me to continue. "The fae are incredibly secretive and protective. They keep to themselves. Why meddle in nephilim and vampire affairs?"

"Why would I tell you that?" he asks coldly.

"Because maybe I can help you," I prod. "We might agree, you never know until you give me a chance."

Again, he's quiet, and a dark thought pops into my mind. I blurt it out instantly. "Unless you're planning to sacrifice me for something."

His eyes flicker, as if I just caught him, and my heart skips.

Oh shit.

I keep my mouth shut. As stupid as he thinks I am, I'm definitely not stupid enough to let him know what I'm thinking right now––that I have to figure out a way to best them or at least gain their mercy.

"You want to help us?" he finally asks, his eyebrow practically crooking into a skeptical question mark.

I shrug, feigning nonchalance, but inside I'm reeling. If the fae have marked me for dead, I'm a goner. Surviving vampires and nephilim is one thing, but surviving the fae is something else entirely. They have elemental magic, the kind that's drawn from the earth and the moon, they know just how to use it to their benefit.

Not to mention they use blood magic.

And didn't Isadora once say something about some fae trading their hearts for endless power?

Out. Of. My. League.

I squeeze my hands, knowing that my angelic gift can't hurt the fae. They have no aversion to light. If I'm going to survive them, I'm going to have to prove my worth, which isn't going to be easy if they value me more dead than they do alive.

"I want to help you stop the nephilim from hurting your kind," I say with conviction.

He studies me for a long minute. "Okay," he says at last. "Then get me your cousin."

Surprised, I frown. "Which one?"

"The record keeper."

"Chloe?"

He smiles cruelly, as if I just accidentally let him in on a nephilim secret. "Yes, Chloe. Get her for me, and I'll make sure you live."

"You really have that kind of power?"

He nods. There's something nefarious going on here, but I can't quite put my finger on it. "I won't let my people kill you. I'll make sure you live."

Right . . . so why does this feel like I'm walking into a trap?

"What do you want with Chloe?" I step closer, meeting his pearly gaze. "She's not a bad person. She's the kindest and most gentle one of the entire family. I'm sorry, but I won't hand her over to you if you're going to slaughter her."

"I doubt she's as kind and gentle as she's led you to believe, but don't worry, we have no intention of slaughtering Chloe. We won't hurt her at all. We simply need access to her gift."

What could they possibly need her records for? Off the top of my head, I can't think of anything, but I'm also sure the Unseelie Prince isn't going to tell me either. "And what happens after you're done with her?"

"Her life goes on," he says.

"Where? Does it go on in Faerie or does she get to return to her life in the mortal world?"

He pauses, clearly growing agitated. "She will return to her regularly scheduled life."

I nod, really hoping I'm not about to make a huge mistake. "You've got a deal."

"Excellent."

"How do I let you know when I've got her? Is there somewhere we're supposed to meet?"

His eyes travel me up and down, taking in my bare feet and dress with the pinch of his lips. "Invite her into a dream, and I'll take it from there."

"How does that work?"

"She already knows."

And that's the last thing he says before he steps back into the shadows, the silver swallowing him up, and the dream disappearing entirely. And then I'm falling. Falling through black nothingness, with nowhere to land.

Two arms catch me as I wake up with a startled scream. I'm gasping for breath, clutching at my chest. Adrian holds me tight.

"It was a dream," he whispers against my ear. "Only a dream."

No, Adrian. It was so much more than a dream.

Immediately, I want to tell him everything that just happened, but I find myself holding back. He might not agree that I should do this. In fact, I'm pretty sure he'll tell me not to trust the fae at all.

But the fae can't lie.

That doesn't mean I can completely trust Casimir, but it does solidify my decision. I need to do this. I just hope Chloe doesn't kill me for it.

I turn over in Adrian's arms, curling up against his cold chest.

I'm hot all over, and his cool body is a comfort to me. It's refreshing, pulling me from the creepy feeling Casimir left behind. Adrian lightly runs his fingers over my back, up and down my spine until my breathing steadies.

"When I asked you how you overcame your nightmares, do you remember what you answered?"

He kisses the top of my head and then inches back to peer down at me. Even in the darkness, I can make out his features. His genuine concern. "Yes, I said that I became the nightmare."

I nod once. "You're not a nightmare, Adrian. Not to me."

He squeezes me tighter. Kisses me again.

"But I think––I think I might be one."

"Why would you say that?" he asks sharply.

"Because I'm willing to be the villain in someone else's story if it means I get to be the hero in my own."

Fourteen

ADRIAN

After Eva falls back asleep, I slip out of bed and head downstairs, double checking that the doors are locked and the security cameras are working. It makes me nervous to leave her here alone, but I have business to attend to, and she needs her rest. If anyone goes into that penthouse hallway, the advanced motion detectors will alert my phone. But even with security measures in place, I can't trust that someone won't try to get to her, so I also enable the elevator security feature. It makes it so that only my thumb print can enter the penthouse floor. I'd had it disabled when Eva stayed with me the first time, but this time she's just going to have to be okay with waiting for me to move about the property.

I can already picture how that conversation is going to go . . .

From the moment I met her, she's been under my protection. At first I lied to myself about why, but I've accepted the truth now. It's because not only is she mine, but I'm hers.

The casino is no longer bustling with evening activity. It's five in the morning, and the place is dead. By now, my vampires have retired to their private rooms and communal spaces. We've outfitted an entire floor for the coven to be able to hang out without humans around. Still, a lot like to gamble during the day and paint the town red at night. That's when they're not working. Everyone has a job, too. We all contribute.

Almost all the humans have gone home, save for a few stragglers hanging out at the twenty-four hour bar or the ones here betting on European sporting events. A few more are slumped at the slot machines, mindlessly pushing the max bet button and watching as their credits dwindle down to nothing.

The feelings of pride I had when I walked through the casino aren't what they used to be. When we first came out into society, I made this place my baby. But now, I'm not so sure I love it like I used to. Since returning from Europe, the casino just doesn't look the same. It used to be the thing I felt had brought me back to life, especially once we added on the luxury hotel and made the historic building what it is today. But now I keep seeing it through Eva's eyes, keep feeling what she feels here, and I'm starting to question everything.

I round a corner and find Mangus there. The guy is looking worse for wear. His hair is a mess and he reeks of alcohol. Drinking doesn't do much to our vampire bodies, our metabolism is too fast, but Mangus likes to indulge anyway. Especially since Katerina died.

"We need to talk," he says, waving me into a quiet corner.

"Now isn't the best time." I have a few things to attend to and then I need to get back upstairs to check on Eva.

He ignores that. "Listen, I want to walk in the sun as much as the next vampire, but I'm not willing to risk Eva like that. Not to mention, you know guys like Seb will use it to try to lord over the humans. We have to protect our food source."

"I'm glad we agree," I say carefully. It's hard to know who to trust. Mangus could be saying these things to get closer to Eva, but my gut says he's not.

His eyes search the near-empty casino. "There's something I need to show you."

I sigh, because I really hate leaving Eva alone. I need to get my errand done so I can go back to her. "Can you be quick?"

"Can you pull your head out of your ass? This is important." His eyebrows draw together. "Do you know about the fae witch coven living in the French Quarter?"

My body stiffens. I know all about them, this is my city.

"They're harmless," I say. "They're half-fae outcasts. They sell voodoo trinkets to tourists and keep to themselves. As long as they don't mess with us, we don't mess with them."

Mangus grimaces. "You're sure they're harmless?"

"Well, they're not full-blooded fae. Their magic is diluted. And besides that, I have a good relationship with their coven leader. We have an agreement. They stay away from us and we stay away from them. As far as I know, they hate all supernaturals. And they hate the full-blooded fae who want nothing to do with them."

He retrieves his phone, swiping open the photos app. I glare down at the picture of Sebastian and Antara entering a French Quarter voodoo shop. Even with the night time shadows and dim streetlights, I know exactly which shop I'm looking at. The very same one belonging to the half-fae witches.

"When was this taken?" I ask.

"A few hours ago. I've been tailing Sebastian."

"Shit," I grumble. I don't know what this means, but it can't be good.

"Shit is right." He deletes the photo and slips his phone back into his pocket. "My guess? They're after Eva's gift and hoping to use that witch coven's magic to get it."

I nod. "Either that or they're hoping to mess with the council blood bond."

"Maybe both."

I groan and thank him, then we part ways. He's going back to his suite, and I continue on to attend to my business. This new information makes what I'm about to do even more important. It's critical that I don't let my feelings get in the way.

Feelings.

Since when did I have so many damn feelings?

I find Kenton standing in the middle of his prison cell, staring up into nothing. Using leather gloves, I let myself inside, locking us in together. He can try to fight me to get out of here, but he won't succeed. I could rip his head off his body or his heart out of his chest in two seconds and it would all be over. I didn't bring a stake because I don't need one to kill him. But killing him is exactly what he might want. And I can sympathize with that feeling. How many times have I wanted my immortality to be over? I lost count ages ago.

"What do you want?" Kenton turns on me with a broken expression.

"Where is Brisa?" I come right out with it.

He shrugs. "Why should I tell you?"

"This isn't a request."

"What's in it for me?"

"Nor is it a negotiation." I push him to the floor, coming down on him hard and digging my knee into his chest. Gloves still on, I retrieve the silver knife from my back pocket. "Do you know what silver does to vampires?"

His eyes flash to the knife. "Do it. Kill me. You'd be doing me a favor."

"I'm not going to kill you," I say, releasing a sinister laugh. "But I am going to make you hurt so badly you'll wish you were dead." And then I drive the blade deep into his abdomen.

He screams, and the stench of burnt flesh chars the air.

"Where is Brisa?" I demand again.

"I don't know." His cries are laced with pain and regret, but I can't stop. I won't stop.

In fact, I twist the knife.

He vomits blood. It splatters all over me in a sickening arc, but I don't let up. I keep twisting the damn knife like Eva's life depends on it.

"Where is Brisa?" I demand again.

"Why are you doing this to me?" he sobs. "You know I can't tell you."

But that's not exactly true.

Because what I know is that although she'll have commanded him to do certain things and to keep her whereabouts and plans protected, he is also a young vampire. He can fight back far more than he realizes. Young vampires are notoriously unreliable like that. And I'm counting on this one to break.

Twist. Twist. Twist.

I don't relent.

Finally, something within him begins to crumble. "She was––she was––" He's trying to say it. He's trying, but he just can't get it out.

He will.

I dig the knife in deeper, the silver sizzling his innards, and his sobs come out in gut-wrenching jerks. Eva thinks she's a monster because she's willing to become the villain when necessary, but she's got nothing on me. If she saw me right now, doing this to her friend, she'd hate me. But I'd do anything to protect her, same as I'd do anything to kill Brisa. In this case, I can do both, and if Kenton is the collateral damage, I'm fine with that.

"Where is your maker?" I demand again.

His eyes roll up into his head, and his body goes limp as he passes out. I know it won't last for long. I pull the knife back out and wipe it clean while watching the wounds in his abdomen stitch themselves back together. Internally, his organs are quickly healing themselves as well. He'll wake up in a few minutes, and then we'll have to start the process all over again.

It could take hours of torture, but eventually, I'll break him.

It's the only way.

I hope that even Kenton can see that this has to happen, but even if he can't, I'm not going to stop. And maybe when all is said and done, he'll want to continue this afterlife. Maybe not. That might depend on how many people he's already killed. I doubt poor old Raymond was the first.

As the boy sleeps, I let my guard drop just enough to be able to see myself in him. I remember all the things I had to go through at Brisa's cruel hands. All the murders. The many betrayals. She even sexually abused me, turned me into a lifelong lover who was never allowed to say no. I was forced to allow it all to happen because my life depended on it. And my revenge did too.

I wanted revenge way more than I ever wanted to live as a vampire.

And now that revenge is at my fingertips, I can practically taste it. And in this moment, it's everything I want.

Just as planned, Kenton wakes up a few minutes later, eyes blinking open and horror dawning. He begins to cry. "I can't tell you where she is." He sounds so young and desperate.

"I feel bad for you, I do, but this is the way it has to go."

"No. Please. You know I can't. Please. Just kill me."

I shake my head slowly, sitting back on my heels and brandishing the silver knife again. There are no surprises this time, he knows exactly what's coming for him. "This is the only way to get the information I need out of you. Did you feel how close we were that time? You almost said it. You almost broke the bond and told me her secrets." He goes silent, just looking at me for a long minute. His eyes slowly widening. "Ah, do you see now? Sometimes it takes pain to get the response needed. Trust me, I know. I taught myself to resist portions of my blood bond with her by doing the same thing."

"Just portions of it?"

"Yes, but now I'm free of her, and it's the best feeling."

"How long did it take?" I don't know if he's stalling or genuinely curious.

"It took me years."

"Years?" His voice cracks.

I nod slowly. "But it's not going to take you years. You're young, and that makes you stronger than you realize. That's something she doesn't want you to know, that I didn't know during my youth. It's also why she didn't turn any new children for so long after she made her princes."

"If I let you do this, what will you do to her?"

"I'm doing it whether you let me or not," I growl. "But I thought the answer to your question was rather obvious. I'm going to kill her."

I watch him carefully, looking for signs of loyalty to his maker. But I see none. I only see a boy who reminds me of who I once was, turned against my will, forced into a murderer. He smiles widely, and the blood on his lips is so painfully familiar to me that just for a second I wish I didn't have to do this at all.

"Did you want her to turn you into a vampire?" I ask. "When you were dying in that garden, did you ask for this?"

Because if he did, we might not be as alike as I think we are.

"Never," he says. "I don't even remember when she did it. I think I had passed out by then. All I remember is waking up starving and clawing my way out of a grave to find her waiting for me. I never wanted this. I'd rather I have died that night." He's no longer crying. The tears have dried up. Maybe he'll never cry again. Something has changed within him, has hardened and calcified.

I know it because it happened to me.

"I've killed six people already."

"Six is a lot, but it could've been much worse."

"Oh really? And how many more will die at my hands? She's told me I can feed on anyone I want, that I can kill as I wish, just so long as I help her."

"Help her do what?"

"I cannot say," he sighs. "Do you know how hard it is to resist killing someone when you're feeding on them?"

I do know, but I'm not focused on that right now. I'm focused on this new development. Brisa never made such commands before. Sure, when I was new we fed and killed all the time, but this is a different century. Vampires can't just go around killing people anymore without serious repercussions.

"Let me ask you this. Are you part of her plan, or were you sent here as a distraction?"

"I don't know," he answers honestly.

"Hmm . . ." I sit back on my heels. "And let me guess, she's commanded that you don't seek true death?"

That's always one of the first things most makers require of their progeny. There's no point in going to the trouble of making a child if they're going to kill themselves within a week of turning.

"Among other things." His dark eyes grow even darker, even more haunted, and I don't ask him to elaborate.

"You and I are brothers now that we have the same maker." I place my hand on his shoulder and squeeze, leveling his gaze so he can see how much I mean this.

"But you're free of her," he whispers. "We're not the same."

"I am free. And I want to help you be free of her too, which is why I need to know where she is and what her plans are."

He grits his teeth, nodding at the knife. "Do it again."

Fifteen

I wake up with a start. I'm covered in a cold sweat. My body is slow and heavy, but my mind is racing. Everything feels wrong.

Adrian's not here to see me freak out this time, which I'm kind of grateful for. Don't get me wrong, I love his support, but being this vulnerable with someone who has my heart is difficult. I've never had someone I could lean on besides Ayla, and we hurt each other. I find I'm still holding back from Adrian. I'm not lacking self-confidence, but he's just so untouchable; he's seen so much of this world, experienced just about everything there is to experience . . . and I'm a messy human.

No, I'm not even human.

I'm a nephilim who glows every time we make out.

Sighing, I fall back into the bed and start a mental checklist.

I have to find Chloe and take her to Casimir so the fae don't sacrifice me. I have to save my mom from not only the mafia, but from a crippling gambling addiction. I have to stop the nephilim from committing genocide, which seems impossible. I need to save Kenton from true death and somehow help him become a better vampire, the very creature he hated most. Brisa needs to die, and Adrian is intent on being the one to do it, putting him in grave danger. The vampires need to stay in line through all of this, but meanwhile half of the council wants to use my light to make themselves ungodly powerful and dangerous. And others probably want me dead or to turn me, who even knows at this point.

Plus, the nephilim know way too much . . . Tate picked me up from the catacombs for heaven's sakes. We can't forget about that. We still need to figure out who in the vampire organization is a mole for the nephilim.

And I still need to check on Ayla.

Just a typical Monday.

I climb from bed and pad over to the shower. The water feels amazing, and I let it stream down my body for so long that my fingers turn to prunes. The emotions spill out, and I end up crying into the water. I seriously hate crying, but I can't hold it in anymore. It's all too overwhelming. But nobody is here in this shower to judge me, and I don't judge me either. I just let everything go free, and when I'm done, a sense of numb acceptance washes me clean. I can't claim it to be peaceful, but it's still so much better than what it was. At least I can breathe again.

As I get ready for the evening, I wonder when my life will get back to normal or if it ever will. I'm starting to accept that maybe things will never be what they were, or what I thought they would be. And maybe that's okay.

But there is one thing I can do to help get things back on track . . .

I stride into Adrian's walk-in closet, to the massive safe in the back that I'm pretty sure has my phone in it as well as the necklace Gram gave me. I press my hand to the lock and the accompanying keypad, willing it to open, but of course it doesn't.

I could try using the white light. Could I melt it?

"What are you looking for?"

I jump.

I whip around to find Adrian standing in the doorway, his sleeves rolled up and his arms folded over his chest. I don't know what I expected to see on his face, maybe frustration, maybe distrust, but I find none of that. He only appears to be curious.

"The necklace my gram gave me and my phone. You locked them up before we left for France. I'll have to borrow your charger, but I'd like to have my things back."

He brushes past me. "Remember when I told you I made sure that your life was still here for you when you got back?" He dials the lock first and then enters in a code. "Well, I meant it. Your bills are all caught up, including your phone bill. Your apartment is waiting for you, although I'd like you to stay with me instead, at least until we're sure it's safe. Even your job at Pops is ready when you are."

The safe swings open, and he points to the shelf where my phone and necklace are waiting. There are other things in here, documents, a few pieces of fine jewelry, stacks of foreign currencies, and even a silver stake, but nothing too surprising.

I retrieve the necklace, almost expecting something to happen when I touch it, but nothing does. The feather talisman stamped on the back of the crucifix kept the nephilim from finding me, as well as my angelic gift from surfacing. Gram bought it from a voodoo witch in exchange for years off her life. And what do I have to show for her great and noble sacrifice? Nothing. I still received my angelic gift, and I was still found by the De Luca's. And now I'm sleeping with a vampire.

What would she think?

Part of me believes she'd be horrified, that she's turning over in her grave, but in my heart of hearts, I know that's not true. Gram loved people, she always saw the best in them, giving everyone the benefit of the doubt. It's because she cared so much for me that she did what she did. She would've liked Adrian, and she'd understand why things have played out as they have. But would she still be proud of me?

I still don't know the answer to that.

"Are you okay in there, Angel?" Adrian runs a hand down my arm but stops short of where I'm clasping the silver chain.

I shake my troubling thoughts free and retrieve my phone. "Yes, I'm okay. Just a lot on my mind."

He closes the safe and leads me back to the bedroom. "I think I can help you with that."

I laugh. "Oh, what did you have in mind?"

"How about a real date?"

I don't know what I was expecting him to say, but asking me out on a date wasn't it. I eye him playfully. "No offense, but you never struck me as the 'romantic date' kind of guy."

"That's fair, but you never struck me as the 'dating a vampire' kind of girl, and look at us now."

"Okay, fine, let's do it. When and where?"

"We're leaving in an hour, after sunset, and where we're going is a surprise." He sweeps a loose strand of hair from his eyes, gazing down on me with careful consideration. "I've had the closet in the other bedroom outfitted for you. I even brought over some of the things from your apartment. I hope that's okay."

"You did what?" I gape at him then sprint across the penthouse to check it out. Sure enough, the guest bedroom closet is filled with new clothing, the tags still attached, but many of my old items are here as well. I stick my face into my favorite fluffy hoodie and sigh. A wave of nostalgia rolls over me. Ayla gave this to me for my sixteenth birthday. It's hard to believe it's over three years old, that so much has happened. That we don't even talk anymore.

"I can have it all moved back if you want," he offers, sensing my sudden change. "But I really do need you to stay here with me until we know it's safe for you to move back into your apartment. Or you could stay here . . ."

"I'd love to stay here with you," I confess.

He smiles. "You're under my protection, and I won't fail you again."

Something about those words makes me feel what the long shower didn't––a sense of peace. I don't know what all is going to happen, and I can't solve everyone's problems, but at least I have someone looking out for me.

I turn, standing on my tiptoes to press a kiss to his cheek. "I'd better get ready then."

WE HAVE SO MUCH ELSE to worry about right now other than a date, but I find myself excited for the first time in months. My very dead phone is charging, and I'll look through it when we get back, but right now, I've got my hair curled and my eyes lined in a reverse cat eye. I've never tried the style before, but I love it. And best of all, I've got Gram's necklace back where it belongs, sitting at the base of my neck.

I don't feel any magic coming off the necklace. I'm sure it's all been voided considering everything that's happened, but I still want to wear it. It's my homage to the girl I once was, the girl who will always love her mother and grandmother most in the world.

It's a little chilly out tonight, so I slip into a red sweater dress and black booties and pick out what is probably the most expensive designer coat I'll ever wear. It's sleek and bright red and not my normal black style, but I'm tired of my normal, and I feel good. Accepting lavish gifts is a foreign concept to me. Adrian had to play games to get me to drive his Porsche, and even then I only agreed to borrow it. I don't expect to get it back, not even now that we're dating. I can take the bus again when I need to get some-where, especially if I'm living here in the center of everything.

"You look gorgeous, but what's that look on your face for?" He peeks into the bathroom at the hour mark. "You look like you're calculating a math problem."

I take in the crease between my eyebrows, just the tip of a very concerned expression on my face, and laugh. "Sorry, I was just wondering if we're dating." My cheeks instantly heat, but I turn and lock my eyes on him.

"I told my coven you're my girlfriend and asked you to live with me." He steps closer, his scent filling the room, eyes roaming my face. "Is this what you want?"

I swallow hard. "Yes, it's what I want."

"Good, because you're mine."

"Good," I repeat.

With a smug smile, he takes my hand and leads me from the penthouse.

THE DATE IS PERFECT. We took a motorcycle to the nicest cajun restaurant in the French Quarter, which was unexpected. I'd thought he was going to bring me to an upscale place with tiny proportioned food I couldn't pronounce. Instead, he booked a private room at the kind of restaurant that makes my favorite foods. He doesn't eat, but he enjoys watching me, and I thoroughly enjoy every morsel.

"It feels like home," I say, swallowing the last bite of buttery pecan pie with a happy groan.

"That's what I was hoping for," he says.

I just stare at him. There's such a big part of me that is waiting for the other shoe to drop. It's only been six months since we met, but we've already been through so many ups and downs. I never thought we'd be sitting here, that we could have come this far, let alone that we'd be dating in the first place.

Or that we'd fall in love.

He pays the bill and takes my hand, leading me outside onto the bustling street. Pulling me back into a darkened alleyway, I expect to start kissing, but instead he holds me in his arms as we levitate, up and up, until we're flying above the city, the dazzling lights far below. I hold on tightly, my nerves flying just as high. I can levitate too, but I'm not well practiced, and this is higher than I've ever gone before.

We finally come to a stop, and I take in the stunning view. The moon isn't full, but it's still large and lighting the night like a silver beacon. That, combined with the venom, allows me to see everything in perfect clarity.

"It's so beautiful," I breathe, emotion catching in my chest.

"You're so beautiful."

I snort. "Is that a line?"

"It's a line, but it's also true. Did it work?"

I grin and press my lips to his. His hands grip me tighter, coming around to lift me up so that I can wrap my legs around his torso and press myself into him further. It feels like we're our own personal sun, and when I begin to glow my familiar warm light, those feelings become a visible thing.

When we're finally done kissing, I'm more than ready to go back to his penthouse and continue sans clothing, but he levels me with an assessing gaze.

"I have another surprise for you."

"Another one?" What else could there possibly be?

"Yes, and I really think you're going to like this one."

"But I don't love surprises," I warn. We're slowly floating back down to earth as we talk, and I suddenly can't wait to get my feet back on the ground. All this lovey-dovey stuff is making me lose my edge. It's so out of my element, and I'm scared that I'm going to lose myself in it.

"You want me to tell you where we're going?" he asks.

I trust him, but I'm also a nosey bitch. "Yes, please."

"Alright," he smiles ruefully, "We're going to get your mother back."

Sixteen

⚬⚬⚬

"Armondo lives in the most stereotypical mafia house imaginable," I say, looking down on the place that could, without question, be used to film a mafia flick. It's a white brick mansion with columns all along the front, a huge sweeping yard surrounds it, and a tall wrought-iron fence secures the perimeter. The place demands attention, and even at night, they've got it all lit up for the entire community to see.

"Armondo wants everyone to know just how much power and money is at his fingertips," Adrian explains. "His house is an important extension of his identity."

I wonder if Adrian feels the same way about The Alabaster Heart, but I don't ask.

We're hovering well above Armondo's mansion, waiting for the opportunity to go inside. My golden glow has settled back into my chest, and I've left the red coat behind so that we're camouflaged up here in the darkness. The cold winter air pebbles at my exposed arms and legs, but I don't care, getting Mom back will be worth it. I watch the three guards walking the perimeter of the home, each with automatic rifles strapped to their backs. Each looking for a weak link, just as I'm watching them to see who in their party is the weak link I can break.

"I can't believe my mother is in there, mixed up with these goons."

Adrian is holding me to his chest, my back to his front, and he hugs me tighter. My stomach twists as I remember how Armondo had laid claim to my mother, as if her body belonged to him now. I still feel guilty that I wished vampires away from my friends and family--I still blame myself for

627

what's happened to her. Knowing now that I have control over that aspect of Isadora's spell, I'm going to have to be incredibly intentional about the things I say and do in regards to the vampires.

But I also keep wondering if there's some way I can use that part of the spell to my advantage. I won't know until I talk to Isadora again, and who knows if that will ever happen. Right now, I need to stay focused.

"So what's the plan?" I ask.

Adrian just kisses my jaw in response.

He seems so calm and collected. Meanwhile, I'm a ball of nervous energy. I don't know a lot about the mob, only that they deal in organized crime and they're not to be crossed. They derive their power from using and intimidating and sometimes killing people, and I hate that Mom is with them right now.

"Alright, alright." I shake him off. "We can kiss later. Right now we're getting my mom. What do you need me to do?"

He turns me around, giving me a serious look. "You're staying here and keeping watch. I'm going in to get her."

I scoff. "That's it? That's your master plan?" He really thinks he's just going to walk in and get her, no big deal. "Do you have a backup?"

"I don't need a backup. I've dealt with far worse than these rats."

Good hell. "Okay, but this is a private residence, so how are you getting in there?"

"I've already been invited in before," he says. "On more than one occasion, actually."

"And you think you can just walk in there again?"

"Pretty much," he replies. "Armondo has never verbally rescinded the invitation to me, so until he does, I'm free to do as I please."

I shake my head in disbelief. "Okay, and what if they capture you?"

"They won't." He laughs––he really is that confident.

"The De Lucas did," I point out. "They caught you and tortured you."

"I was being sloppy. I won't let that happen again."

He was being sloppy because I was involved and he had feelings for me. But guess what? He still has feelings for me, and I'm definitely involved with this.

"Those sound like famous last words to me." I fight to roll my eyes. "I'm going in with you."

"Absolutely not." He tightens his hold.

"Absolutely yes," I counter. "She's my mother, and I'm not weak. I've had months of combat training, an angelic gift that can momentarily blind humans, and I'm pumped full of vampire venom." I nod to the guys with guns far below us. "I'm stronger than all those goons put together."

"But can you dodge bullets?" he asks. "No, you can't. If I get shot, I'll heal. If you get shot, you're gone."

I shrug. "I could get shot out here, same as I could get shot in there."

"I knew I shouldn't have brought you with me," he sighs, but his tone is lightened, and I know I've got him.

"And yet, you did." I squeeze his hand and lay another kiss on him. "So what do you know about this place?"

He points to the light in one of the top floor rooms. "That's her bedroom. We're getting her and we're taking her back to The Alabaster Heart."

"You're sure that's where she is?"

He nods. "I'm positive."

"Okay, so we get her out. Then what? Do you really think a casino is the best place for her right now?"

"All problems we can deal with later." He sounds exasperated. "Angel, are we going to save your mother tonight or not?"

"Hell yeah, we are."

He kisses me once. Twice.

And then in a flash, he's gone, and I'm still here, levitating in the darkness, and feeling very exposed.

I told him I was going with him.

But damn, he's fast.

I hover for a while, remembering exactly why I never liked the dark. Bad things happen in darkness. And even being able to see in the dark now doesn't make me feel better. In fact, it makes everything worse, because I'll be able to see if Adrian fails. What if one of the guards shoots him down? Or worse? What if they catch him and stake him?

Nerves fire throughout my body, and I hold my breath as he slowly opens the window, inch by torturous inch. The curtains flutter the second he slips inside--and then he's gone, and everything goes still.

I wait. And wait.

Any minute now he's going to be coming back out with my mother. All I have to do is be patient, but I've never been a wait and watch kind of girl. Adrian knows that, so he shouldn't be surprised when I find myself zooming to the bedroom window and climbing inside.

The stench hits me first.

Cooper and salt. Pungent and strong.

I take in the scene, and my heart catches in my throat. Mom is sitting on the bed in a pink silk nightgown, her red hair smoothed down her back, her face a mask of horror. Next to her is a very dead Armondo. His neck is ripped clear open.

And on Armondo's other side stands Adrian, covered in blood, fangs extended, and eyes bloodshot. In a matter of minutes, he executed the boss of the local Italian mafia, draining him completely.

"What did you do?" I whisper.

He grins at me. "What I should've done the first time he crossed me."

The bedroom door swings open, and a man with a gun sweeps into the room, pointing the barrel straight at us.

Seventeen

I scream, but Adrian moves quickly, grabbing my mother first and then me, and fleeing through the window before the first bullets fly. Shouting and gunfire follow us into the night, but we're moving faster than ever, returning to the casino within minutes.

Adrian's set Mom up in the penthouse across from his own. I figured Mangus or someone else would be living there, but it turns out that's where he had put her when she came to him for help the first time. She was in hiding, and he had everything delivered that she could possibly need. So we're back to that again, but at least this time she has me across the hall. I'm going to make sure she's safe.

Before long, I'm sitting on the end of her bed while she lies back, staring at the ceiling, glassy-eyed. She hasn't said much since we got her away from Armondo and got her cleaned up.

"Mom, say something," I try. "Just tell me what you're thinking."

She sighs, and a tear slips from her eye. "I'm thinking that I've failed as a mother."

My heart breaks at those words. It's never what I wanted her to feel, not in all our time together, not even when it was true. "Because I'm dating a vampire now?"

It's no secret. When we came back here and I told her I was staying with Adrian, I also told her that we're a couple. She didn't even seem surprised. She just told me to be careful.

"Adrian isn't one of the bad guys," she replies. "I never looked down on vampires like you did."

Yeah, because they fed her addiction.

"Adrian isn't all good or all bad. He's complicated." Is Adrian a good guy? Hell no. Is he evil? Not at all. He kills when he needs to kill, but he doesn't do it for sport. He does it when it's necessary and he did it when Brisa commanded him. The memory of him covered in Armondo's blood is still shocking, but I find I don't mind it as much as I thought I would. Because Armondo? He truly was one of the bad guys, and I'm not sorry he's dead. "Mom, you're not a failure, you've just been through a lot. You haven't had as many chances to win as some people."

She shakes her head, her auburn hair tangling against the stark white of the pillowcase. "I couldn't provide for you the way I wanted to, not when you were little and not even when you grew up. I didn't have a lot of family to offer you, only your gram." She pauses for a long minute, the air between us growing thick with the unsaid words. Is she finally going to admit her problem? "And I have an addiction. An addiction that I choose over you too many times."

She hiccups and rolls to her side, then sits up, her feet hanging off the edge of the bed. Our eyes meet, and I fight back the tears. This conversation feels too late, but at least it's happening. Better late than never. "Are you really going to sit there and tell me I haven't failed?"

Okay, that does it. I've already filled my crying quota for the foreseeable future.

I crawl across the bed and wrap her in a hug, then we lie down, and she holds me like she used to do when I was little. We're not the cuddling type, but she needs this right now. And honestly? I think I might need it even more.

"It's okay. What matters is that you're safe now." I take the time to explain everything that's happened to me since I've been gone, going into detail when it's time to explain why she was magically forced from the casino.

"It was terrifying," she recounts, "I had nowhere to go, and I knew that you were in danger too, but I couldn't get to you. I panicked."

"I'm so sorry."

"No, I'm sorry. I should've told you about your dad much sooner. You shouldn't have had to find out about everything the way you did."

We sit in silence for a long time after that, but eventually she speaks again. "I'm going to talk to Adrian tomorrow about moving me out of here."

"Are you sure that's safe?"

"I can't have access to a casino with my mind the way it is, Evangeline." She swallows hard, brushing hair from my face tenderly. "I want to change. It was so wonderful when your boyfriend compelled me not to seek out

632

gambling or any other addictions. I've never felt so free in my life. But it wasn't real. It couldn't possibly last forever if it didn't come from me. Do you see that now, honey?"

I nod reluctantly, trying to ignore the damn frog in my throat.

"I am going to ask him to send me to a rehabilitation center, somewhere that specializes in gambling. It's not going to be an easy addiction to recover from, but I want to do it myself this time." She takes my hand, and hers is shaking. "I want it to be real. Maybe then it will last."

My mother was going to lose everything because of this addiction. It might have killed her. When she was free of it, it was the best thing that had ever happened to me, but it was so short lived. I barely even got to see her like that. I want to hope, to believe that it can happen again.

I understand why the vampires have set things up the way that they have, but it still doesn't make it okay. At the end of it all, people like my mom and their families are getting hurt. I know now that vampires aren't responsible for human vices, humans are going to have those all on their own, but I still firmly believe that manipulating those vices for their blood donation is wrong.

There's got to be a better way.

"I'm proud of you, Mom," I say, pulling her into a hug. "And I'm proud to be your daughter. You're not a failure because you're not giving up."

"You really think so?" She sounds so young, and I can picture her as she was when she met my dad. She was innocent and not that much older than I am now. She had ambitions and was trying to make her way in the world. Vampires had recently come out publicly, and things were uncertain in the world, but she was still so hopeful for her future.

That hope died when he did.

She broke. And I don't know if she ever really healed or if she just pretended for my sake. So it wasn't surprising that Gram dying sent her into a downward spiral. But there's one thing I know about broken people, and it's that even they can be good parents. I know that because she's mine.

"I know so," I repeat my thought out loud, meaning every word.

The next day, we move her out of the casino. She's given an alias and flown to a rehabilitation center in California. One of those fancy places by the ocean we could never have afforded without Adrian's help. I'm not good at accepting gifts, but this one I take without question or an ounce of guilt.

"For the next eight weeks, I can focus on my mental health," she says through the other end of the phone after checking in. "I'll call you twice a week during my visiting hours."

"Sounds perfect." And it really does, I just hope it's not too good to be true. That she gets better for real this time, that it actually lasts.

We hang up, and I scroll over to social media, looking for an update on Ayla.

I've only had my phone back for a day, and I don't know what I was expecting, but it wasn't nothing. She hasn't called. Texted. Messaged me. Tagged me in anything. There are zero notifications from her at all.

The heartbreak is worse than a breakup with some guy because we promised that we'd always be there for each other. Men might come and go throughout our lives, but our friendship was supposed to be forever. I scroll through her posts as a numbness washes over me. From the outside looking in, she's gotten healthy, is out in the world again, and has moved on with her life. She's going out, having fun with new and old friends. She's working at her parent's business. She's even dating a hot new guy I'll never get to meet.

It's like I don't even exist.

But in my gut, I know something is wrong. There's something I'm missing. It's eluding me. It's big. And it's imperative that I figure it out.

Whatever it is.

Eighteen

T he Neon House is exactly as I remember as I weave through the people crowding the dance floor. Adrian wraps his hands around my waist and pulls me against him. We move to the beat, and the man definitely knows what he's doing on the dance floor, but I can't let myself get too distracted.

I also can't let him figure out why I requested to come here tonight, because he'll take me right back to the penthouse.

Now that the human auras are visible to me without the added neon lights, I watch the other dancers carefully. The humans aren't why I'm here tonight. They're just the bait.

The nephilim are my mark.

If Cameron was right, then the energy demons, also known as the nephilim, frequent this nightclub. And if that's true, I'm hoping to find someone who can get me in contact with Chloe. All I need is one conversation with someone in her world who has her phone number. I don't need to see Chloe in person to ask her to visit me in a dream, and I actually would prefer not to.

Adrian and I dance for an hour before I finally catch sight of a nephilim. The woman appears to be in her early twenties, is dressed in a silver halter top and tight jeans, and is dancing between two eager-looking men. She's also siphoning off energy from their auras. It swirls around her in a haze of blues and oranges.

I force myself not to stare, but the confirmation of my time in Faerie hits me upside the head for what feels like the tenth time since I've returned.

They did something.

Because those two weeks went missing from my mind, and I came back here with access to my angelic gift without needing to feed on human emotion. Every time I've been around humans, I haven't felt a desire to steal from their auras, and I think it's because my gift is already well-fed. If I can figure out what the fae did, then maybe I can help the other nephilim do the same.

But what if they already know?

Because Chloe said there was a way to feed without hurting humans. She was going to tell me, but then Camilla sent her away. And then when we were at the Christmas party, Uncle Dario said nephilim have broken into factions, that the most powerful families fight amongst themselves. Could it be because some nephilim know there's a way to feed without hurting humans but they still choose to do it anyway?

My mark breaks away from the two men and heads to the bathroom, giving me my opportunity.

"I have to pee," I yell to Adrian.

He's not necessarily possessive, but he's protective as hell, so I'm not surprised when he walks me off the dance floor and all the way to the bathroom door. Before I go in, he's already casing the hallway, his eyes roaming every corner like he's searching for any possible threats.

"I swear, if you try to follow me into the women's bathroom, I'll scream."

He squeezes my hand. "I'm going to clear it first."

I pin him with a glare. "You asked me what I wanted to do tonight, didn't you? Well, my request includes taking care of myself. I can handle this." I press back on his chest and he lets me walk him to the far wall.

Folding his sexy forearms across his chest, he pins me with a smirk. "Whatever you say, Angel."

I love this man, but he doesn't make it easy to keep secrets. He's got eyes everywhere, and now that we're officially together, he's become my constant shadow. I should hate that, but I kind of love it. Only because I've never had someone care so much. Maybe that makes me pathetic, but I don't let myself think too hard about it. I just want to enjoy where we are in our relationship––outside of the ladies' room.

I head in and find the nephilim girl reapplying her lipstick in the mirror. She's radiant, and I wonder how much of that is from her recent feeding.

"Hi," I say brightly. "Do I know you? You look so familiar."

She turns on me, eyes widening with recognition. "You're Evangeline De Luca," she breathes. "I can't believe it's really you."

The fact that she knows my name and face is unsettling, but I don't have time to worry about it. "Actually, it's Eva Blackwood." I inch closer, getting right to the point. "Do you happen to know my cousin Chloe De Luca?"

She nods, confusion creasing between her perfectly sculpted eyebrows. "Sure. She's younger than I am, so we're more acquaintances than anything else."

"Do you know how to contact her?" I ask, trying not to sound too eager.

She shrugs a shoulder. "Yeah, I have her number from the last time she was in town and we went out together. Why? Do you need it?"

I whip out my phone. "Yes, please."

She eyes my phone while releasing a careful breath, whispering to me so the others in the bathroom can't overhear. "You do realize that half the nephilim world is out looking for you, right?"

"Yeah, tell them I'm in New Orleans, I don't care," I say it as if I really don't care, even though I definitely do. But I also definitely think they've figured it out by now anyway. "Either way, I need to talk to Chloe. We parted ways before I could get her number."

The girl fluffs out her hair and tilts her head at me consideringly. "And why should I help you?"

There are a lot of things I could say here about doing what's right, or I could threaten her with my very scary boyfriend waiting in the hallway, but I don't do any of those things. Instead, I lower my voice, like I'm trying to let her in on a secret. "Because I think she's in trouble."

I'm such a liar. I'll probably burn in nephilim-hell for this.

"Fine." The girl snatches my phone and quickly adds Chloe's number to my contacts. "But you might be in trouble too, your family is a little crazy."

"Tell me about it," I grumble.

"Well, they're offering a reward for information about your whereabouts."

My heart sinks. "And I take it you're going to collect that reward."

"How much?" Adrian's growl echoes through the bathroom, and I would jump if I hadn't expected him to barge in here at some point. The girl takes him in with a mix of agitation and unease, but she doesn't seem afraid. She should be. I've seen what Adrian is capable of.

"We weren't talking to you, bloodsucker." She sticks her nose in the air and turns away from him.

"I asked how much," Adrian snaps. "I'm either going to pay you off or I'm going to kill you and feast on your carcass. Which would you like?"

I roll my eyes, but the poor girl goes ashen, and everyone else left in the bathroom scatters out the door. "I have this under control, Adrian," I chastise him.

He steps closer. "How much? I'm not going to ask again."

"Fifty thousand dollars," she replies quickly, and Adrian practically growls.

She lifts her hands in surrender. "That's how much the De Lucas are offering for information about Eva, and they're willing to triple that if someone can bring her to them." She steps back until she's pressed up against the countertop. "But combat isn't my thing, and neither is kidnapping."

"I'm guessing money is," I say under my breath.

"Everyone has a price," Adrian's reply is silky smooth, but there's a sharp undercurrent there. He's pissed. "Fifty thousand is nothing to me." He retrieves his phone and it's only a matter of minutes before he's transferred the money to her bank account. When it's done, he mocks her with a dark glare. "Eva's worth more than a measly fifty thousand, you should've asked for at least a million."

The girl opens and closes her mouth, her cheeks going pink. "I didn't want to be selfish."

"The audacity to take my money and consider yourself anything but selfish is astounding," he sneers. "If you dare break your word, I will hunt you down and kill you. That's a promise."

She nods, and then she's retreating from the bathroom before I get a chance to ask her about feeding angelic gifts. She'll probably be gone within the minute.

Adrian grabs my hand and drags me from the club and outside into the dark alleyway, pressing me against the brick wall. My breath hitches, and my eyes linger on his full lips. I'm expecting two things. A chastisement and a kiss, both to be filled with the kind of passion that leads to dark and lusty places.

"What aren't you telling me? Why do you need Chloe's number?" he questions.

I try to kiss him, but he pulls back.

"I don't think so. Tell me the truth."

"Do you mean to eavesdrop on my private conversations or does it just come naturally?" I counter.

He laughs, but his mood is still dripping in frustration. "I'm a vampire. My impeccable hearing comes with the territory." Leaning in, he places soft kisses all along my jaw. "Don't you trust me?"

My body melts under his sinful lips, and I sigh. "You've got enough to worry about. I didn't want you to worry about me wanting to keep in touch with my cousin Chloe."

Why am I holding back?

I've told this man so much, but I can't risk him going on a rampage if he believes I'm in danger, and I can't have him getting mixed up with the Unseelie Court either. They're too powerful--even for him.

Besides, all I've got to do is tell Chloe to visit my dreams, and Casimir will take it from there. He's already promised he's not going to hurt her, and if I don't do this, I could end up dead. I just pray that Chloe can find it in herself to forgive me when this is all said and done. As much as I can't stand that side of my family, she's only ever treated me with kindness, and I don't want her to hate me.

I land a quick kiss to his lips, then peer up into his eyes. The storm brewing behind the blue is electrified with worry, and I just want to take it away. I wish I could.

He steps back, and the space between us feels endless. "You can't just call her up. She's your enemy. Or did I just pay off that nephilim tonight for nothing? Promise me you won't call Chloe."

He doesn't understand, and he probably never will. I hate that I'm hurting him, but I can't make promises I have no intention of keeping. "You might have bought me time tonight, Adrian, but I have no doubt that the word is out about my whereabouts. That girl is fifty thousand dollars richer and for what? The De Lucas probably already know where I am by now."

"You don't know that for sure."

"Don't I? There's a mole somewhere in your organization, it's the only explanation for how the nephilim have had so much information on you guys lately." He doesn't try to deny it. "So whoever that mole is will have learned about my whereabouts by now. They probably saw me on your livestream, maybe even talked to me in person. They would've told the De Luca's about me. It's already too late."

He lets out a curse. "Don't you think I know this? Why do you think I can't let you out of my sight? This is why I want to keep you locked up in my bedroom."

I snort. "It's not the only reason why you want to keep me locked up in your bedroom, Adrian."

I'm trying to distract him, it's an obvious move, but it works.

The electricity in his eyes turns molten, and he pushes me up against the wall, breathing me in like I'm his only lifeline. "You smell so good tonight."

Goosebumps erupt over my flesh because I know what he's thinking.

He wants to feed on me.

We only did it that one time on the helicopter, and that was because he needed blood. But now that he's a council member, he's sworn to uphold the vampiric laws. He can't take my blood unless he plans to turn me, kill me, or if he's in grave danger. He may be able to resist the council bond enough to feed on me, but I don't want to cause any trouble. Well, my brain doesn't, but the rest of my body very much does. It felt amazing, the venom unleashing endorphins throughout my entire system, and I can't stop thinking about what it would be like to do it again.

"Are you hungry?" I whisper.

"Let's go." Adrian pulls back, grabbing my hand and marching me from the alleyway to the parking lot where his motorcycle is parked. I climb on behind him, my arms holding tightly to his waist and my body pressed to his muscled back. We zoom back to the casino, pulling into the parking garage, and coming to a stop next to his line of luxury vehicles.

I'm swinging my leg over the back of the bike when his number two, William, approaches.

"What do you need?" Adrian asks. "You're supposed to be on the casino floor."

William tilts his head at us, his eyes narrowing. "Yes, I'm going there now," he says, but his voice sounds off somehow. Something is wrong.

Adrian stiffens. "Go on then."

William nods, turning on his heels and heading toward the elevator. Adrian and I follow, and when William holds the elevator door so his boss can step inside, Adrian only hesitates for a second.

But I can't get into that elevator.

I don't know why——just something in my gut telling me not to.

"What's wrong?" Adrian asks.

My eyes dart to William, and that's the tipping point.

William moves fast, pulling something from his pocket and swinging it at Adrian. At the last second, Adrian moves, and the stake lands in his stomach instead of his heart. Adrian slumps down with a strangled growl, and William steps from the elevator. I jump into action, swinging at him with my bare fists as the elevator doors close behind him.

"Are you going to fight me or are you going to join me?" he questions, and again his voice sounds all wrong.

I answer with a kick to his stomach, just as a blunt object slams into the back of my head. The world goes dark. And I fall.

Nineteen

I'm being hitched painfully up under my armpits, and my body is limp, my feet dragging. I blink my eyes open, confusion washing over me. Fear hits me, and I remember.

I remember.

William was acting strange. Adrian stepped into the elevator, but I didn't. William staked Adrian, narrowingly missing his heart. Then something slammed into the back of my head. Why would William do that? Is he working with the nephilim? Is he the mole? But even as I ask myself those questions, something nags at the back of my mind, something to do with William's voice. It wasn't right.

"She's awake," a man says, and whoever is dragging me stops, setting me upright. My legs feel like jello, but I manage to stand. I turn and find Enzo and Nicco on either side of me.

"I should've known it would be you two brutes." I step back, but Nicco is quick to grab hold. "Don't touch me!"

But they stay silent, glowering down as if I were nothing but a petulant child in the middle of a tantrum and not a woman they bludgeoned over the head and kidnapped.

Footsteps echo through some kind of maintenance hallway. It reminds me of the basement in the casino, the very same one Adrian dragged me down to, where we made the fake blood vow all those months ago.

They don't belong down here. And neither does the man that rounds the nearest corner. Leslie Tate. "I'm glad to see you're awake," he says. "I was worried you'd be out for too long when they hit you that hard, but I should've known you have a thick skull."

I can't even be bothered by the insult. "You probably ordered them to do it."

"That's true, I did." He smiles ruefully. By now he's completely dropped the caring mentor act. He's not even pretending to be a decent uncle. He's just a bad man, through and through.

"I can't believe I used to find you charming and fatherly. You're nothing of the sort."

He waves his hand nonchalantly. "My own children might beg to differ."

"Oh, is that why Greyson and Bella are assholes? Or am I supposed to blame their attitudes on your bitchy wife?"

"Enough with that filth!" He strikes me with the back of his hand, the pain sharp against my cheekbone. He's wearing a family ring, and the damn thing cut my cheek. It hurts like hell, but I refuse to react. Blood fills my mouth, and I nearly choke on the acidic taste. But I don't cry. I don't curse. I don't do anything but glare. "We have questions, and we can get those answers from you now, or we can get the answers after we kill off this coven. You decide, but say one more thing against my family and I will make the decision for you."

He's delusional if he thinks he can kill off an entire coven, not to mention all the council members that are still staying here and the entourages they brought along.

"I don't have to answer your questions." But I have one of my own. "Where's Adrian?" The last time I saw him, he had been bleeding and slumped over in that elevator. But he wasn't dead.

He wasn't dead.

And I cling to that thought like my lungs cling to oxygen.

"Your bloodsucker got away," he glares, "And he also left you to us."

That doesn't make sense. Adrian would never leave me with the enemy, not on purpose.

"I know you two are dating," Tate goes on, saying the words as if dating a vampire is truly disgusting. "But how? The vampires aren't able to come near your friends and family."

"As if I'd tell you anything--"

"I think you forgot to include yourself in that bargain with the fae. Not the smartest thinking, but then again, you never were the brightest in the family." He twists the ring on his finger, smiling at the family emblem for a moment before returning his hateful gaze to me. "It seems that your pathetic mother diluted the bloodline."

642

I grin through the blood between my teeth. "Is that why I'm the first light-bearer in more than a century?"

He goes stone-faced, and I know I've hit a nerve. "Take her to Camilla."

Enzo and Nicco grab me, dragging me between them. My heart bangs against my ribcage for a way out of this. I'm incredibly strong because of the venom, but the twins' angelic gift of strength is too much for me. They've found me, and I can't fight them off.

We approach an unmarked door, and they shove it open, pushing me inside a mechanical room. I'm closely surrounded by a crew of at least forty people, all tucked in like sardines. They're dressed in black tactical gear and are covered head to toe with wooden stakes and guns wielding silver bullets.

They're also staring at me like I'm the embodiment of evil.

There are a few recognizable human vampire hunters, a few people I don't recognize who could be humans or nephilim and I wouldn't know the difference, but the rest of them are the people I spent the last few months with––the nephilim from Italy. Some blood relations and some not. Either way, I won't claim any of them as family. Not after what they've done to me and my real family. Camilla is at their center, pinning me down with her haughty glare.

"Aren't you a little old for all this?" I ask the woman, but the insult rolls right off her back.

"You can answer my questions, or I can get the answers myself."

I push back on the two pairs of vice-like grips holding me in place, but I'm still unable to budge. Frustration floods my system. Resentment too because I don't want her in my mind. She doesn't need to see everything that's happened since Ireland. So much of it is private. And what she would find, she'd most definitely use against me. Against my mom. Against Adrian. Against everybody I love.

"Don't you dare touch me," I warn.

The brightest light ignites from my palms, and even though I'm unable to move my arms, I can still adjust my hands so the light is pointed at her. She covers her face and hisses, and I hope it hurts. I know I can't kill her, if anything it's like the temporary blindness that comes after someone shines a flashlight in your eyes. It's too bad because the old bitch deserves to burn.

"I see you've finally started feeding." Aunt Bianca laughs. "It's about time you accepted your fate."

"My fate? I've been able to access my gift without feeding, so you're dead wrong."

Bianca shakes her head. "Oh, you're still feeding, you just don't know it."

"I'm not," I snap, even as a prickle of doubt surfaces. I ignore it and flash my blinding light directly into her eyes too. She quickly turns away. "But I hope that hurts."

"Come now, Evangeline," Tate says as if he's suddenly the voice of reason when only a few minutes ago he was backhanding me with his gaudy ring. "There's no point in fighting us anymore. We need to know what went wrong at The Gateway, and you're going to show it to us. The more you fight, the harder you're going to make this on yourself."

"You want to know what happened at The Gateway? I didn't want to kill fae, that's what happened."

But those words, as telling as they are, seem to go over their heads . . .

"Bring her to me," Camilla instructs the twins, and just like the good little boys these grown-ass men are, Enzo and Nicco haul me over to their grandmother.

Not mine. Mine was Gram, and she was a saint compared to this snake.

Camilla grabs me, forcing her gift on me like she has every other time, immediately rifling through my memories. She has no real order, no rhyme or reason to where she's looking first. She's reckless, taking zero care with my mind and having no respect for my intimate memories. It's just another day for her.

I cry out when I feel her taking note of my mother's location in California, especially when her own need for revenge poisons the memories of hope I have for Virginia. She still blames my mother for taking her son away from her all those years ago. Even after everything, after she ordered his death, she still refuses to see her part in it.

Then she leaps into the events that happened when I went to Faerie–– she tries to, anyway. But she can't see much, because most of it is still blocked to me. Except for my first day and night there, all the other memories are hazy at best or nonexistent at worst. I'm still not sure if it was the food and drink that did that to me or the king's magic, but I suspect a bit of both. Whatever they did to block the memories, I realize now why they did it. It wasn't to keep me from knowing their plans, it was to keep *her* from knowing them.

Growing agitated, her gift razors in deeper, and the pain of it burns through my brain. It's like the world's worst migraine, and I scream, falling to my knees, begging her to stop.

She doesn't stop.

Twenty

S he fast-forwards to the moment my memories return, to the night I was thrown into the vampiric council. She takes special interest in the sacred circle, replaying those moments over and over again, going through each detail until they begin to bleed and fade together. From there she prys into my most intimate moments with Adrian.

My anger is hot, but her disgust is hotter.

"Those are not for you," I manage between strangled breaths. I want to scream my vitriol, but my voice just sounds like a faraway whisper.

Why can't I push her out this time? I've become impossibly weak. I'm losing the battle and I don't know how much longer I can do this.

But she doesn't care. She continues, ecstatic when she learns that I'm linked into the vampiric council. I can already feel her plotting ways in which she can use that against them. She's trying to figure out how I've been interacting with vampires despite the fae magic, which somehow pops her over to the recent dream with Casimir, and that's my breaking point. Something snaps, and I finally eject her from my mind. She immediately tries to get back in, but she can't. The locks are in place.

I cry in relief.

"You've been a vile girl," she sneers. "And to think, I opened my home to you. You could have had it all, a loyal family, power over your angelic gift, and most of all, you could've lived your purpose and been in God's favor. But you threw it all away, and for one of them."

"What do you know of purpose?" My mind feels shredded, and I press the heels of my palms to my temples. My head hurts so badly. Wetness stains my cheeks, and I realize I've been crying. And I'm so, so tired. It's like she scraped all the energy from my cells.

"God made nephilim so we could rid the earth of unnatural creatures." She reaches out her hand and tugs Chloe to stand above me. I've sunken to my knees at this point. I can't bear to move. "Our sweet Chloe showed you the angel that came down to command it. And yet, despite seeing the truth for yourself, you still choose to partake in such sinful actions. Do you know what that makes you?"

I don't have the energy to respond. And honestly, I'm too exhausted to care anymore. It'll probably have something to do with burning in hell for all eternity.

"It makes you a lost cause." She nods to the others. "Greyson, Chloe, and Enzo, you three stay here and guard her. The rest of you, please follow me upstairs. It's time to do our duty."

"What about me?" The vampire William steps forward, and my stomach sours.

"How could you?" I hiss. I might be tired, but I have enough energy for this bastard. "Adrian trusted you. These are your own covenmates. You're going to slaughter your own people for nephilim? The nephilim will just turn around and kill you too!"

William laughs, and then something strange passes over his face. It's like the cracking of a shell, and for just a moment, I see him for who he really is: Dario De Luca.

My uncle, Camilla's middle son, the shapeshifter.

My mouth falls open.

William never betrayed us because that man wasn't William at all.

They're quick to leave, stakes at the ready, and I'm left with my guards. Chloe sits in the corner of the little basement room, her eyes shut tightly as if in meditation. There's got to be more to her gift than just record keeping or else Casimir wouldn't have said she could join me in my dream. I just need to talk to her. So much for getting her number. That girl from the club is fifty thousand dollars richer for no reason.

My headache finally begins to fade enough that I can think again. I stand, and Enzo stands with me, holding onto my bicep. I give him a seething glare, but he doesn't care. He doesn't even blink twice.

"Chloe, how are you?" I ask.

Her eyes pop open, and she gazes up at me like I'm a ghost.

"Don't talk to her," Greyson sneers.

"You and I should talk privately," I continue, ignoring everyone else. Her pretty brown eyes are as wide as a deer in headlights. Am I really that frightening?

"I said don't talk to her," Greyson tries again. And again, I ignore him.

"You know how to find me privately, don't you, Chloe?" My gaze bores into hers, and she gives me a small nod. It's all I can hope for––I have no idea if it'll be enough. Will she join my dreams before it's too late? Because it seems that the fae need access to her records, and soon. I just wish I knew why.

"You don't listen to instructions, do you?" Greyson steps in close, looking down on me with a nasty glare. "But maybe you'll listen to them?"

His sinister smile grows as he summons his dark otherworldly creatures. He still believes he can hurt me with them, that he can torture me, terrify me, but not all nephilim can use their gifts on each other. Last time he used his gift on me, I faked my terror to make him believe it was working. But this time? This time, I'm not faking shit. Instead, I gather my strength into my center, lean back on my haunches, and kick him dead-center between his legs.

He goes down like a sack of potatoes.

Enzo startles and loosens his grip, and that's all I need. I race to the door before anyone can stop me. Greyson's on the floor holding himself, and Chloe isn't one to fight. Enzo is the one I need to worry about, but I have surprise as my advantage. Swinging open the door, I sprint into the hallway. We're somewhere under the hotel or casino, so the vamps aren't far.

I still don't know what happened to Adrian, but he's probably tearing this place down looking for me. Same as I'm about to do for him.

"You can run, but you can't hide," Enzo yells out. It's just about the most predictable comment the meathead could make, and I would laugh if I wasn't hyped up on adrenaline and scared out of my mind.

Lucky for me, Enzo doesn't know all my tricks, and I levitate through the corridors to not make any noise. An exit sign blinks up ahead, and I want to cry with relief. That's my target.

Just as I near the door, Enzo is on me, tackling me in the center and bringing me down hard. His grip is concrete-tight, but I'm able to wiggle my hands free and shoot my white light into his eyes. It blinds him long enough that I'm able to escape his grip, jump back to my feet, and run for my life. I fling open the door to a stairwell. There typically aren't deep basements in this part of the world, but the vampires have enough resources to defy just about anything, including groundwater. They've built several stories underground, and I don't know how deep I am right now. I levitate through the middle of the stairwell, my mind focused on one thing and one thing only.

Save Adrian.

"There's no point in resisting the inevitable," Enzo calls after me, his footsteps close behind on the metal stairs. "We're going to kill this coven tonight, and then we're going through The Gateway with or without you. We'll find a way, and we have a weapon that will kill the fae when we do."

I whip around at that. I shouldn't--I should keep running--but I have to know what he's talking about. "What's the weapon?" I snarl.

He slows, coming up the stairs one at a time, his black eyebrows drawn together. "Join us, and you'll find out," he offers. "Or don't, and you'll still find out, because it's going to happen."

"How quickly will it kill them?"

"If we infect their entire world with iron and seal them inside the realm, I wouldn't expect it to take longer than a few days."

My stomach hardens, and I shake my head. "It's wrong, what you're doing. You think there's some God out there who wants you to kill an entire race of his people? No God would want that."

"They're not God's people," he snaps back. "They're not even people! They have access to dangerous magic that doesn't belong here. They are an abomination. Same with the vampires who are already dead. We're just finishing the job. You, of all people, should understand that. I know my uncle Leslie trained you, that you came to him begging for a spot with his hunters. He helped you."

"Tate lied to me. And you're all lying to yourselves." He's closer, only a few paces from me. It was foolish to stop. I need to distract him. "Aren't there other nephilim who don't believe the things you believe?"

His lips thin as he considers this. "They're mistaken. Chloe has been making the rounds, showing them the truth. It's all right there in the records. Most of them have come around, and, once we complete our mission and God blesses us, the ones who denied their purpose will see how wrong they were."

He's fanatical.

I'd hoped it was just Camilla and Tate and that the others were falling in line because they wanted access to all the family money and power. But I was wrong. Enzo, at least, buys into this completely. The others probably do too.

My mind races back to when Chloe disappeared for a few weeks before Christmas. She later told me she went to New York to visit the nephilim there and help them with something. Showing them the records must have been why she was there, so she could help Camilla bring more people into their way of thinking.

And if that's true, then it's no wonder the fae want to get their hands on Chloe. Am I really foolish enough to believe they're not going to kill her? Fanatical or not, Chloe is a pawn in this, and I don't want her death on my hands. But it's too late, I already relayed the message to her. She's going to come to my dreams, and when she does, Casimir is going to take her away.

I've drifted too close to him and Enzo lunges for me again. Thank God I'm faster this time, using every ounce of strength I have to get away. I bypass the exit to the street and instead head for the casino floor, pushing through the emergency exit doors and flying into the room. Just as I make it there, loud sirens begin to screech, and the entire floor is bathed in bloodred flashing lights.

Twenty-One

Most of the patrons are confused, but a few scream and scatter for the exits. It's like dominoes how quickly they all turn frantic, stampeding to get away. I return to my feet, and it's chaos for a good minute as I weave through the crowd, trying to find Adrian. Did the nephilim sound the alarms or did the vampires?

I don't see anyone in tactical gear, but I do catch sight of several vampires looking around with discerning expressions. Ever watchful, there's not a whole lot that can get past them. Maybe for the first time ever, I'm extremely grateful for that party trick. I look back at the exit, but I don't see Enzo. I don't think he followed me here.

"There you are." Mangus appears next to me, clasping my elbow and tugging me back from a group of women teetering in high heels as they try to get out of the building. "Adrian is looking everywhere for you."

I rip my hand away. "Are you really Mangus?"

His eyebrows scrunch. "What are you talking about?"

Dario being here makes it hard to trust anyone, but Mangus's voice––it's the same voice I'm used to. The one that's as deep and salty as the ocean.

It's him.

"The nephilim are here, and they have a shapeshifter with them," I explain. "He looked like William and tricked us. I don't know where Adrian is. We got separated when he tried to kill Adrian and I was ambushed."

Mangus's eyes go steely. "He looked like William?"

I nod. "But he didn't sound like him."

Mangus swears under his breath. "Come on. Most of the coven members are downstairs in the ballroom gathering for a meeting. They're in trouble."

We hurry to the elevator, and when it opens, Adrian is inside with another vampire from the council. They're talking in low calculating voices and when they turn to take us in, Adrian's face sags in relief. He pulls me into his arms, crushing me against his bloodied dress shirt. "I'm so sorry," he whispers into my hair. "I thought I'd lost you."

He almost did. "It's not your fault."

"It is, I should've caught on that it was a shapeshifter and not William the second he opened his mouth."

"Where is the real William?" I ask.

Adrian shakes his head. "I don't know, but I'm guessing they may have already killed him."

I don't have time to process that. "We have to get down to the ballroom. The nephilim are here to attack your coven."

"They already know. I was the one who set off those alarms. The red lights mean we're under attack. Trust me, we're prepared to handle something like this."

I can't help but wonder why he isn't already down there with his coven, though, and I ask him as much.

He inches back, staring at me like I'm missing the obvious. "Because I was looking for you. They failed to kill me, but they left me in that elevator before I could get out. When those doors closed, I thought I'd never see you again. I've been in a panic trying to find you. They took out our cameras. They're all down."

"Probably because they got into your basement somehow and are coming at the coven that way." I imagine the trap Adrian could've walked into while he was out blindly looking for me like he was. "Oh my God," I whisper.

"God has nothing to do with those people," Mangus growls. "I don't care if they have angelic blood in them or not. They've always been like this." I wonder how much blood and gore Mangus has seen over the years because of my kind.

"My family might still think the vampires can't hurt them," I confess. "Because of Isadora's spell and what happened in Ireland, they believe they're untouchable, that they can just come in here and slaughter your entire coven." My voice hardens. "But they're not untouchable."

And Camilla may have realized that when she was in my mind, but if she did, she ordered the attack anyway.

Put her family at risk anyway--because that's how much she wants this.

The elevator doors open into the foyer of the coven ballroom. The battle has already started, pouring out in all directions.

Mangus laughs. "No, they're certainly not untouchable."

The first nephilim to catch my eye is my beautifully evil cousin Bella. She's working side by side with her brother Greyson, and both of them are covered in ash. Apparently Greyson didn't waste any time after I took off. It's a sickening visual representation of what they're here for.

We rush from the elevator, and Greyson's dark gaze locks on mine. He's probably mad as hell that I kicked him in the balls, probably even still in pain, and he grins menacingly. The soot smeared on his face makes his teeth whiter and the brights of his eyes stand out. It's a taunt, but I can't think about it for long because there's no time for his shit. I never thought I'd be the one fighting for the vampires instead of against them, but that's exactly what I do. Jumping high, I levitate across the room and catch sight of Dario. He's back to his regular self, dressed in the same combat gear as the other nephilim, probably so he doesn't accidentally get staked by his own people. Regardless, I don't trust him to stay that way for long.

I land on him with a guttural scream, kicking him in the head. He drops, and I yank the silver tipped stake from his hand, breaking it in half and throwing the pieces across the room.

He blinks up at me, dazed and confused, but I don't wait for him to realize what just happened. I kick him in the head again, and he passes out for good. For just a moment I consider killing him, but I decide against it. I won't be killing anyone here unless it's out of self-defense. It might not feel like there's a choice, but there's always a choice. I'm not going to do to them what they did to my father, and what I know they will do to me eventually if they need to and get the chance.

As if to test my thought, Camilla's voice screeches, "Stop!" I whip around to find her in Adrian's clutches. Her eyes are wide with fear and denial, like she can't believe he's able to touch her. It confirms that she didn't see enough of my memories or she never would've put herself in this posi- tion––it's the only explanation as to why she even came here. She usually sends everyone else to do her dirty work, but this time she's the one with blood on her hands, the one who's going to pay the price. She's getting old, she's not a fighter, and she stands zero chance against someone like Adrian.

Someone who doesn't stop, who doesn't even hesitate.

He breaks her neck like it's a twig, and she slumps to the floor.

For a moment, time seems to stand still. She was my grandmother, and maybe in another life she could have actually filled that role. But in this life, she murdered my father, hunted my mother, and imprisoned me. In this life, she was my enemy. And honestly? I'm glad she's dead, but I'm still hit with an immense sense of loss for what could've been.

All at once, the moment breaks, and one of the nephilim calls for their retreat. They stream toward the stairwells, but it's too late. The vampires are out for blood. The attack is merciless, and I'm sure I'm about to witness my entire family line on that side murdered when a black smoke covers the room.

Greyson.

It clouds everyone's visions, but it doesn't do a damn thing to mine. I watch as the vampires keep attacking without their vision, but the nephilim are able to fight them off much better now. They help each other to the exits, even grabbing Dario's unconscious body in the process.

And I'm almost okay with that, with letting them all go free, except for Tate.

Tate's the one I want. He was the one who treated me like a daughter and then manipulated and lied to me. He was the one who recruited humans, took control of their minds, and made them hunt his enemies. Camilla had to die. Tate should have to go too.

But I'm not the only one with a grudge against Tate.

Adrian appears at my side, seemingly unaffected by the black smoke. I know he can't see through it, but he has excellent control over his other senses. He's not going to let a little smoke stop him. Adrian stays true, his eyes fixed on where Leslie is shuffling on a hurt ankle.

"Do you want to take him out or can I?" His voice is that of a predator.

"Can you see him?" I ask.

"I know the man's heartbeat." He nods toward the door where Tate is making his exit. "I don't need to see him."

I'm not going to kill Tate. But I won't judge Adrian for doing it considering Tate was behind Kelli's death and the death of the child Adrian had before her.

"Do what you need to."

Adrian is quick, catching up to Tate in all of two seconds, but Tate is quicker. He swings around, a stake at the ready, and slams it into Adrian's heart.

Twenty-Two

"**N**o!" I scream and stumble in their direction.

Through the fading smoke, Tate catches my gaze for a long second before disappearing into the stairwell. I want to go after him, but I drop to my knees in front of Adrian instead, carefully pulling the stake from his chest. There was already so much blood on his dress shirt that it's hard to tell how much more is being added. His eyes are bloodshot, and the corners of his mouth have turned crimson. In seconds he will become nothing but ash, and my heart might as well turn to ash with him.

"Don't die on me," I plead. "I can't do this life without you."

He smiles, coughing up blood. "Don't be so dramatic. You nephilim really need to work on your aim." He winces, sitting up slowly, and I break out into a relieved sob.

Tate missed.

We stand and assess the damage, looking over the carnage of the battle. It's not as bad as I first thought it would be because vampires can heal so fast. But that's not to say it isn't bad.

"We only have two prisoners," the real William announces, dragging a man and a woman over to Adrian. I'm glad to see William isn't dead, even if I don't like the guy. "A human hunter and a nephilim without an angelic gift as far as I can tell."

Through a mop of blonde hair, Remi stares up at me with her warm hazel eyes. "Please, Eva," she begs me. "Don't let them kill me."

Everyone turns on me. "This is Remi. She can manipulate emotions. But she helped me on more than one occasion, and she doesn't deserve to die."

"She's a hunter and a nephilim," William spits at her feet. "I'll kill her myself if I have to."

Adrian stops him. "Put them in the prison cells."

"What about him?" I point to the human man. "He's just a kid. He doesn't look a day over seventeen. I bet you Leslie Tate was messing with his mind."

Adrian sighs then kneels down in front of the boy, asking him a few questions. It turns out the boy is only fifteen and was picked up on the way in here, convinced to fight because they had gear for one more. Adrian gives the kid a long-suffering sigh. "You will leave here, get cleaned up, and go on with your life as if this day never even happened. You got it?"

The kid nods, looking absolutely terrified, and scampers off. I can practically feel the annoyance of several wounded vampires who are hurting and needing to feed. They can go suck down a blood bag or two, they'll be fine.

"Tate picked that boy off the street. I knew he would stoop low, but I didn't realize he'd go that low."

"I did," Adrian says, his mind far away for a minute. He turns to look down at Camilla's dead body. It's joined by three others, none of which I recognize. I don't know if they're nephilim or human, if they wanted to be here or if they were manipulated to be here. And I'll never know. "Burn them," Adrian instructs.

"Let's go." Adrian is guiding me to the elevator when Antara approaches us, blood splattered all over her face and her normally perfectly styled curls a tangled mess. I didn't even know she was here for the fight.

She steps over a pile of dust and glares at Adrian. "I lost one of my grandchildren, Adrian. I expect you to answer for what happened tonight." He turns on her with a frown, and she continues. "Seeing as this happened under the protection of your coven, you're to blame, are you not?"

He nods once, and I stare at him. "It's not his fault. The nephilim came here under the misguided belief that the vampires wouldn't be able to touch them. They attacked unprovoked."

She raises a perfectly manicured eyebrow, looking upon me as if I were complete scum. "And why would they think vampires wouldn't be able to touch them?"

There's no hiding this anymore. "It was part of the original council spell."

"Eva--" Adrian warns, and Mangus slides up behind me, planting a hand on my shoulder. It seems neither of them want me to speak, but I go on.

"I made a deal with Isadora when the spell was cast. I gave her blood, and in return, the vampires have to leave me and my friends and family alone should I choose it. It seems to be tied to my intention, so I can make it come and go as I want."

"She's telling the truth." Sebastian walks up to us, his voice dripping in resentment. "It's the only explanation to adequately answer so many of the questions I have when it comes to this girl."

I widen my eyes at both of them. "Right, so if I wished you to get away from me right now, the magic would make you leave. And apparently you'd forget me, too."

Her mask slips, uncovering a mountain of rage.

Sebastian inches forward. "Are you threatening us?"

"Of course not." But my answer must be a little bit too sarcastic from the way Adrian tenses and Mangus chuckles. "I'm part of the vampire council now. I want to be your best friend, Seb."

"Don't be so trite."

"We could get mani-pedi's together," I go on. "My treat."

Mangus snorts. "I'll take you up on that, but I'm not letting anyone paint my nails."

"You're childish," Antara hisses at both me and Mangus. "You have no right to a place on our council, it's an affront to vampires everywhere that you're even breathing the air we stand in."

"And yet, she is," Adrian growls. "If you even attempt to break her from the council, or to kill her, you threaten your own power. Is that really what you want?"

Frustration flickers behind her eyes, frustration and something unreadable, but both are gone before I can get clarity on what she's thinking. I already know what she wants: me dead or serving her with my light. There is no alternative in her mind.

The room is divided as more and more people come to join our conversation. The people behind Sebastian and Antara are all those who support them, those who would use my light to give them enough advantages that they could enslave the humans. But there are just as many vampires on my side, backing me up. And best of all, I have Adrian. As long as I have him, I feel like I've got a fighting chance.

"You're lucky the council members sympathetic to your little angel are all still alive," Sebastian says to Adrian and Mangus, as if making easy conversation with his brothers and not threatening death on council members.

He turns on me, looking so much like Hugo that I'm momentarily brought back to what it felt like when I almost died that September night. The fear that burned through my veins as a cold endless forever loomed. "You might not always be so lucky, Evangeline. You should watch your back." He winks, and then he turns away, walking out with Antara.

I'm left with an uneasy feeling whirling through my stomach. The target on my back is starting to feel like a very real thing.

Twenty-Three

T he next few weeks pass without anything big happening. I feel like a coiled spring waiting for something to set me loose, but nothing ever does. Life is just a string of little moments, mostly good and a few bad—my favorites all wrapped up in Adrian.

There's no word about the nephilim. They've gone into hiding, even abandoning some of their strongholds, including the Italian properties.

Most of the council members have returned to their homelands except for Antara, Sebastian, and Mangus, who've stayed in their temporary residences here, even more of their coven members coming out to join them. Mangus doesn't have a coven or a home or plans to leave. But I'm worried that Antara and Sebastian will find a way to entrap me and kill off Adrian. Sometimes it feels like I'm two steps ahead of them. Other times it feels like I just think I'm ahead and they're actually chasing me into a corner.

And despite everything that happened, even the fae have stayed silent.

Chloe hasn't met me in my dreams. She's probably busy mourning her grandmother and planning revenge. I still have her number and consider calling or texting, but I chicken out every time. She probably hates me. And I don't hate her, but I definitely don't trust her.

I'm on a nocturnal sleeping schedule, and without a job or school I have way too much free time to stew and feel useless. Adrian fears for my safety and doesn't want me leaving the casino without him. I have so many questions, but I can't find the answers stuck in his penthouse scrolling social media and reading fanfics on my phone. That's about the only thing I've been doing between our dates. That and visiting with Kenton and Remi.

Remi won't talk to me, but I talk to her anyway. I sit outside her cell door and assure her that I'm doing everything in my power to make sure that things change for the nephilim so she can have a normal life. I explain that my family isn't normal and that she doesn't need to be wrapped up in what they're doing. She ignores me completely, but I keep trying, hoping that one day I'll get through to her. And I promise to keep her alive, even though I'm worried the vampire council will override me on that. If they realize she had been a servant and spy in Brisa's court, they'll definitely want her dead.

On the other hand, Kenton will talk to me. The only problem is that everytime he does, I leave our conversations feeling immensely guilty. He hates himself now, talks nonstop about the people he's killed and how he wants a true death. And all along, I keep thinking about how it's my fault. He wouldn't be a vampire if it wasn't for me because he never would've even come to the Palace of Versailles in the first place.

"What's going on with Kenton?" I corner Adrian one evening over dessert. He already finished drinking his wine glass of blood for dinner, and has been watching me eat my slice of chocolate cake with interest.

"What do you mean?" He begins to clean up the dishes, and I follow him into the kitchen.

"Don't play dumb. I know something's going on. You're keeping him locked up, which I guess I understand since he's dangerous and bonded to Brisa, but there's more to the story that you're not telling me."

Because something is wrong with him. Everytime I visit, he's more depressed. More desperate. More exhausted.

"I'm keeping your friend alive." He turns to me, his eyes going all soft and sweet. I'm not going to fall for it. "He broke the rules, and I should've killed him for it."

"And yet you haven't, even though he keeps asking for it. Why not?"

"I might. He doesn't want to be a vampire. Same as you don't want to be turned into a vampire. Should I keep him alive forever? Make him rot for eternity when he doesn't want it?"

"You're avoiding the question."

"And you're avoiding the very real fact that your friend isn't who he once was."

"I know that."

"Do you? He's not the Kenton you knew. He's a killer now; he's like me."

I want to argue, but I stop myself and really take a moment to think about what Adrian is saying. But is Kenton *really* all that different of a person? At first he was, but all new vampires are blood-thirsty. Once that has worn off, he could be similar to the friend I knew. And what about me? If I were to turn into a vampire, would I really change all that much?

Not once has Adrian pressured me to become one, though I wonder if he thinks about it. I'm going to grow old and die a very human death, and he's going to continue on without me, forever locked in the body of a twenty-five-year-old man. I'm not scared of aging and I'm not scared of death, but maybe those are the words of a nineteen-year-old with life stretched out before her. Will I feel different in ten years? Twenty years?

"If I were a vampire," I choose my words carefully, "I wouldn't want to die like Kenton wants to die. I used to think I would, but I don't know that I feel that way anymore. I think maybe I could be like you and do something with myself."

He steps closer, fangs extending and gaze darkening. "You'd be happy to drink blood and live without the sun? You might lose your angelic gift or it might transform into something else. There's no saying what would happen because your vampire self could snuff out your nephilim the way it snuffs out a human."

I nod slowly, but I don't actually mean it, not in the way other humans do. I'm no fledgling, and I'm not asking to be turned, I'm just saying that I wouldn't want to die because of it. Kenton has made me rethink everything. Because I want Kenton to live. I really do. And wouldn't I want the same for myself?

But no sunshine would feel like no oxygen. I can't even fathom not having the sun in my life. It fills me up in ways that nothing else can. I take note to spend more time outside in daylight, even if it's just going up to the rooftop. I've missed it too much lately. I've missed it, and I need it.

"You couldn't live without the sun," Adrian whispers.

"Yes I could." We both know I'm lying, and he's happy to call me out.

He leans into my neck, sliding his fangs across my sensitive flesh. Goosebumps prickle over my entire body. He's testing me. Maybe I'm testing him right back.

"Shall I bite you right now? Exchange our blood? I could take you to the graveyard tonight."

I say nothing.

"The angel can join her devil," he prods, voice growing agitated.

I shake my head, and he steps back.

"Because you don't want to be a vampire, but I need you to hear this, Eva." He takes my chin in his hand and tilts my head up to lock with his gaze. "I love you just the way you are. I love you for who you were yesterday, who you are today, and who you will be tomorrow. And in none of those scenarios are you a vampire. The truth is, I love you far too much to ever wish my morbid existence on you." He kisses my lips once, then pulls back. "But if something were to happen and you were to become a vampire, I would love you still, but it wouldn't make me love you more than I do now."

My lips part on a soft whimper, my vulnerability on full display. I wasn't expecting it, but he's just soothed so many of the insecurities I've been harboring deep down about our relationship. "I love you too," I say. The words are still the strangest confession to hear from my own mouth, but they're also the most honest.

He retracts his fangs and presses his cool lips to mine, but I've still got that curiosity burning hot in my chest. I liked the way his fangs felt pressing against my neck. The temptation of it courses through my veins like a devilish question mark. He's only fed from me once, and that was when he needed to in order to survive.

"If I asked you to feed from me, would you?" I breathe.

His pupils dilate. "It's against the rules I'm bound to follow." But his body is saying another thing entirely, pressing to mine and flooding us both with lust. "We can only bite if we need it to survive, if we are killing, or if we are turning someone."

This time, I'm the one to groan. I'm not ready to give up so easily. "What if you did it in self-defense? What would happen then?"

He pauses for a long second. "I suppose that might fall under survival."

That's the answer I was looking for––whipping around, I grab a knife from the rack and press it against his throat. A small trickle of blood slips down his pale skin, but the wound is shallow and will heal quickly. "If you don't feed from me, I will kill you," I growl.

He grins, hunger mixing with lust plain on his face. "Are you threatening my life?"

I nod, my own expression mirroring his. "I am."

His fangs extend again, and before I can blink, he's deflected the knife and is picking me up and setting me on the countertop. He sinks his fangs into the warm flesh of my neck and I let out a cry of pain, but it's quickly overshadowed by whimpers of pleasure. The venom burns hot as it mixes into my bloodstream, and my entire body buzzes with activity. Suddenly, everything in the entire universe is centered on this moment and this man.

He laps at my neck, drinking his fill, and I moan with pleasure. All too soon, he retreats before I grow light-headed. I know it will only be seconds before the wounds heal, thanks to the venom, and I wish we could do it again.

But I'm mortal. I'm breakable. And we have to be careful.

He stares at me for just a moment, just long enough for me to see the amazement in his eyes, before he presses his mouth to mine and we're kissing again. Our hands, our tongues, our bodies explore each other with abandon—backlit by the warm golden light that emits from within me. That glow is like a love letter from the angel to the devil. I'm not going to join him, but I am going to love him.

I FINALLY CONVINCED Adrian to let me take the Porsche out by myself today. It's sunny and beautiful and I have somewhere I need to be that's most definitely not The Alabaster Heart. He didn't want to agree, but ultimately he walked me to the parking garage and sent me off. I can't stay cooped up in the penthouse forever, and the nephilim have been quiet ever since the attack. There's just one thing I need to do, and I must go alone.

I step from the car and onto the sidewalk, taking a moment to bask in the glorious sunshine. It fills me up in the most delicious way. I could stand here forever, just letting myself soak in its bright warmth.

But I don't have forever.

Taking a deep breath, I stroll up to the familiar blue front door and knock. I haven't been to the Moreno's home in months, and I can't stand to stay away for another day. If Ayla really is done with me, if she's still sure that she wants nothing to do with me, then I'll respect her boundaries and go. But it's been months since she broke off our friendship, and I can't help but hope that there's still a chance for us to put it back together again.

I expect Mrs. Moreno to open the door, or maybe Mr. Moreno, but when it's Ayla who swings it open wide, my thoughts disappear and emotion takes over.

"Ayla," I whisper, tears burning my vision. "It's so good to see you."

For a long second, she just stands there, staring at me like she's seeing a ghost.

She's going to slam the door in my face. She's going to end this once and for all. She's going to shatter my heart. Years of childhood friendship are going to become nothing but bittersweet memories.

She does none of that.

Instead, she jumps forward and wraps me in a tight hug. "Eva," her voice cracks. "Oh my God, where have you been?"

That's when the tears finally break loose and I hug her back, careful not to hurt her with my newfound strength.

Eventually, we peel apart and she's crying too. "Normally I'm the one who cries. You must have really missed me."

"Of course I've missed you," I hiccup. "I've been lost without you."

She takes my hand and leads me out into the bright midday light to go sit on our favorite porch swing. "We have so much to catch up on, but first, you've got to tell me the truth. Do you know where my brother is?"

I blink rapidly, vision narrowing, breaths stuttering. All as the world comes crashing down. All as the memories return at once. I remember exactly what happened in Faerie, and more importantly, I remember exactly who I was with.

And who I left behind.

Twenty-Four

⟡

The fae used Seth and Felix to teach me how to feed on humans without hurting them. There's a way to cycle the energy, to take and give in the same moment. It doesn't drain the auras. But it's not as strengthening as taking the energy outright, which is why a lot of nephilim choose to feed by taking only. Not to give.

And I've been doing this new way of giving without even realizing it, every single time I walk through that casino. Every single time I'm near a human.

Because it's natural.

Because during those two weeks I was in Faerie, the king of the Unseelie Court forced my gift to surface and then made me practice feeding until it became second nature. That's what he does--he taps into others' gifts. He makes them better. Stronger. Or more dangerous. It's why he's so powerful.

And then when it was time for me to leave, he called in a witch who forced me to forget what happened in Faerie, including all about Felix and Seth being there with me. I didn't forget who they were, but they became a barely-there afterthought. Something I couldn't pull to the forefront of my mind. Casimir took me to New Orleans, but Felix and Seth stayed behind as entertainment for the fae courtesans. Apparently it had been a long time since humans had been to Faerie, and the court treated the boys as a novelty.

The king decided to keep them like pets.

It wasn't until this moment, sitting here with Ayla, that everything became clear. I'm horrified that my friends are still in Faerie, still at the mercy of a dark fae king and his court, and I left them behind.

"What is it?" Ayla demands. "You know something?"

I swallow hard, my throat turning dry as sandpaper. How do I explain this to her?

Her eyes are two round saucers. "He said he was studying abroad in Italy with Seth and Kenton, but none of them have responded to our calls or emails. We haven't heard from Felix since Christmas Day. We've been worried sick. It's been over a month. We talked to the police and filed the reports, but we don't know what else to do." Her eyes narrow, taking in my burning cheeks. "You know something. Please, tell me."

"I'm going to get him back," I whisper hoarsely but with conviction. "I promise."

She stiffens, and the porch swing goes complete still. "What do you mean you're going to get him back?"

I have to explain everything. "First off, he's alive," I reassure her, "but he was never studying abroad." She goes ashen as I attempt to explain the truth. "Kenton is a vampire now."

I start with the bad news, because maybe it will make what I have to say next a little more palatable. "But he's alive. He's with Adrian now. We're helping him adjust."

She says nothing, just stares at me. Unblinking.

I force myself to go on. "Your brother and Seth went to Europe to work as vampire hunters, and they even stayed with me for a time in Italy, but right after Christmas, everything changed."

"No," she whispers. "He told me he was done with all that."

"He lied, but it wasn't his fault. He was being brainwashed."

"How? What happened?"

I have to trust her with the information. Even though I'm so scared she won't be able to take it, that she'll hate me for it, or that it will revert her into old ways of staying locked in her bedroom fearing for her life, I can't keep secrets. Secrets are what broke us in the first place. And I have to trust that she's strong enough to handle this.

"What do you know about the fae?" I try.

"I know they're real," she says immediately.

I'm shocked. "How do you know that?"

She looks away with a shrug. I know that shrug, it's her "I've got a secret" shrug, but it's always followed with her telling me that secret. Not this time. "It doesn't matter right now. What matters is that I did my research and now I know about all the supernaturals. How could I not with everything that's happened?" I guess that makes sense, but I'd still like to know what she means by research. This isn't the kind of thing someone can just Google. "Are you suggesting that the fae have my brother?"

"They have him and Seth." Before I think better of it, I continue, "but I have a plan to get them back."

It's the least thought out plan of all time considering it's coming to me on the fly as we're talking, but I want something to offer her. As I explain what I'm going to do, she goes from hopeful, to skeptical, to hopeful again.

She's twisting her blue strands of hair in her nervous way, and something about that is a comfort to me. It's so Ayla. That and the fact that she's kept the vibrant blue that is her signature style gives me a semblance of hope. Maybe she's the same girl she always was. Maybe we can be best friends again. She pins me with a pleading look. "I need to help."

"I don't think that's even possible." I go on to explain that the only way I know to get into Faerie is through The Gateway in Ireland, except the fae prince Casimir must have another way with his magic because he's taken me through the realms using his shadows. He can travel in ways that the rest of us can't, and he can take people with him. People he chooses. It's through Casimir that I intend to get Felix and Seth back.

She takes my hand and squeezes, and it feels like the first time in ages that I can relax again, even if it's short lived as she demands I still teach her how to get to Faerie through The Gateway. So I explain how the magical wards work, giving as many details as I can remember. She dutifully types it into her phone, and it makes me nervous because what if she somehow finds The Gateway and ends up trapped in Faerie with her brother? If both the Moreno children go missing because of me, I don't know how I could live with myself.

"Your parents can't lose you both," I plead. "Please, don't attempt to go there. It's not like here in the mortal world. It's so much more dangerous."

"I'm not scared of the fae," she snaps, sounding like she really means it.

I study her, admittedly a little bit confused. Last time I saw her, she was hiding in her bedroom and wouldn't even go outside because she was terrified of vampires. And now she's done research on supernatural beings and she's not scared?

"I've been going to lots of therapy," she says, placating my skepticism. A warm smile brightens her cheeks. "And also, I met someone."

She says that last part with an air of wistfulness that I've never heard from her before, not even when she fancied herself in love every other week back in middle school. My heart warms for my friend because she deserves to feel what I feel with Adrian. She always dated around but never had anyone serious. No relationship lasted longer than a month, that's if you could even call them relationships. They were more like passing flirtations. She would get bored quickly and move on to a new crush the same way other people scroll social media. Always something better to look at.

"Tell me about him."

She grins and opens up the photos on her phone. "His name is Dominic, but he goes by Dom." She pulls up a pic of a tall guy with closely cropped brown hair, soft green eyes, and a sexy smirk. He doesn't look too much older than us, but he's much, much bigger. His muscular tattooed arms are wrapped around her waist in the photo. She's smiling up at him like he's her own personal sun, and he's smirking at the camera.

"Where did you meet Dom?"

She closes her phone. "We met at college, actually. I know, I was only there for a month, but he was one of the people I met before I came home."

"Oh, wow, so is he still there?" She went to school up north but dropped out pretty quickly, deciding it wasn't for her, so I'm surprised she met a guy. She certainly never told me about him. I thought she was pretty much hiding out in her dorm room the whole time.

She shakes her head. "He just graduated, actually. He moved back home and only lives a few miles from here. He went to our rival high school if you can believe it. He was the star of the football team and everything," she snorts at that. "But he graduated three years ahead of us so it's not like we would've known him anyway."

This is a lot to take in. An older guy, already graduated college, big and tattooed and smirky. "Is he good to you?"

"He's amazing," she gushes, "he makes me so happy."

That makes me smile. She deserves happiness. We all do. But what will she say when I tell her about Adrian? Will she understand or will she judge me for it? I want to keep the information to myself, but I'm also really trying not to keep secrets from her since that's what broke us up in the first place.

"I'm dating someone too," I blurt out.

She side-eyes me knowingly. "Let me guess, you're dating Adrianos Teresi?" She bats her eyelashes. "*The vampire prince.*"

"How did you know?"

"Oh, I saw the way he looked at you that night in the alleyway. He wanted to do more than just drink your blood." She wiggles her eyebrows suggestively, and I snort.

Okay, so maybe she's not going to hold it against me.

"Do you love him?" she asks, becoming serious.

I nod. "I do. And he loves me back."

"Of course he loves you, what's not to love?" Her lips pucker. "But did you break my brother's heart?"

My own heart drops. "I don't think so, but I did hurt him. I'm really sorry."

"I was right, you know," she tuts. "You two never should've dated."

I nod because she was right, but what I don't say is she was also wrong in trying to force her opinions on us. We had to figure things out for ourselves, even if it meant doing it the hard way. But that's all water under the bridge now, and I don't want to go back there.

"Be careful with Adrian," she says coolly, and I can tell she doesn't like me dating him anymore than she liked me dating her brother. At least she's not lecturing me about it. She doesn't understand. I don't know if anyone really will. But it's not for them to understand because me and Adrian do.

And I am being careful, but not for the reasons she's thinking. She's still worried about my well-being, but I'm past that. It's my heart that's in the most danger. I've given it to the man––it's completely in his cold, dead hands––and if he decides to break it, I won't be able to stop him.

As lame as it sounds, that's scarier to me than anything else I'm dealing with right now. And I know that's selfish, that there are so many more important things than my love life, but it's the truth.

"I'm going to get your brother back," I promise her.

She hugs me again, and it feels like I'm the one with her heart in my hands now. Felix's life depends on what I do next, and I can't let her down. Not again. Nor can I let Felix and Seth down. Not like I did with Kenton.

The people I love keep getting hurt because of me, and it's time for that to stop. I just hope Casimir doesn't rip my head off when I betray him. But first, I've got to get Chloe into my dreams. Finally feeling brave enough to use her phone number, I text her before heading back to the casino.

Meet me at midnight.

––Eva

She'll know what that means.

Twenty-Five

I'm standing dead-center in the hunter's bank vault training facility. I'd recognize this place anywhere with its shiny glass dividers, concrete walls, and sense of righteous purpose permeating the air with the scent of sweaty coeds.

Spinning around, I find myself in the middle of the sparring mat where I first learned how to fight. I spent so much time here, it meant so much to me, but now I hate this place. I know what it truly is, who's behind it, and why. At least today the large room is empty and I don't have to face anyone I'd rather never see again.

"Hello?" My voice seems to be swallowed up by the walls. I turn in a wide circle, searching for her.

"I'm here," Chloe says, her voice ringing out.

She's suddenly standing right in front of me with her arms folded across her chest and a murderous expression on her heart-shaped face. She's wearing a black silk nightgown that hugs her curvy body in a way that makes me envious. My simple cotton shorts and tank top could never hold a candle to her outfit. "Well, you got me here, now what do you want?" she demands.

Oh...

The realization that this is a dream sets me off my axis and I nearly lose my balance. She rolls her eyes but grabs onto my arm, steadying me. When I was visited by Casimir in my old school playground I knew I was dreaming from the first second. This time, I didn't know until she pointed it out. I feel so out of sorts here.

And I feel guilty.

"Aren't you going to say something? My grandma is dead because of you," she sneers.

That accusation snaps me out of it. "She's dead because of her. And my father is dead because of her. Do you really believe everything you were taught by that monster?" I shift back from her, glaring. "I thought you were different, that you wouldn't really support genocide."

Her face goes red. "There's more to the story than you know."

I shrug. "I've got all night for you to explain it to me."

But really, I'm stalling for time because Casimir said if I got her into my dream, he would know and he would come for her.

So where is that prince?

My promise to Ayla depends on him showing up.

"Dreams don't really work like that," Chloe explains, annoyed. "You don't get unlimited time in here. Sometimes it will feel like we're here for minutes but it will be hours out there, and sometimes it can feel like hours in here but be seconds out there. I never know which one I'm getting until it's over."

"That actually makes a lot of sense. It explains why sometimes I can wake up from a full eight hours of sleep and feel exhausted. Or the other way around, sometimes I'll sleep and it will only feel like a couple minutes but really––"

"––I know you're stalling. Cut it out. If there's something you need to tell me, you'd better do it now before one of us wakes up because I'm not meeting you here again. I'd rather never see your face again."

I don't know what to say. I don't know how to keep her here. Or how to make Casimir show up. But I don't have to wait long because one of his strange silver doves with the ruby eyes pierces its way into our dreamscape, landing on her shoulder. She squeaks and swats it away.

"Dreams are so weird, aren't they?" I laugh. Black shadows descend on us, and I breathe out a sigh of relief.

Relief that is short lived the second Prince Casimir steps from the shadows. The man is a terrifying sight to behold, and when Chloe takes him in, her mouth thins to a line.

"Eva, what did you do?" she whispers.

"I'm sorry. I had to."

Casimir laughs. "She's not sorry. Neither am I."

He lunges for Chloe, and at the same moment, I lunge for him, grabbing onto his arm and holding tight. And all at once, the three of us are swept into his shadows, tumbling through the darkness. It feels like falling and being catapulted at the same time, my insides practically rearranging themselves.

We reappear moments later, the three of us sprawled out on a plush bed.

It's not Adrian's bed in New Orleans where I fell asleep.

No, it's a huge bed with tall posts and drapes of black and purple silk. And it has an elf lying between me and Chloe, laughing his head off.

Not what I expected.

At least we're no longer in a dream.

"You're a sneaky little devil," Casimir says, his eyes sparkling as he looks at me. "I think I like you after all."

I groan. I'm not here to be liked by him. I'm here to get my friends back.

"Did you come to join in the fun?" he questions. "I've shared my bed with multiple women before, so I assure you I know what I'm doing."

I scrunch up my nose. "You wish," I snap, but he just laughs again. And then he rolls over, pinning Chloe's body under his own. He looks down at her with a savage grin, like he's about to bite her.

"Get off me," she growls.

He doesn't move, though, he just stares at her for a long moment, his black hair hanging around the two of them as he studies her. Slowly, that grin falls into a frown of pure disgust, as if he hates her.

She spits at him, actually spits, and he curls his lip and rolls away, wiping his face clean. "You're a nasty creature," he growls. "I should whip you for that."

"It takes one to know one," she retorts, sitting up and folding her arms over her chest.

They kind of remind me of how we were when Adrian and I first met, and I hold back a smirk. There's a fine line between attraction and hate, and these two are obviously harboring attraction even though they want to kill each other. Despite everything, Adrian and I found a way to turn our hate into love. That was our miracle. These two? These two won't get a miracle. She's a nephilim, trained her whole life to hunt down his kind and kill them all. And he's an immortal fae prince, ruthless and cunning and just as prejudiced as she is.

"Remember our deal?" I say to Casimir. "You can't sacrifice me now, and you promised not to hurt Chloe either."

He levels me with an annoyed grimace while Chloe scrutinizes me like she wants to rip my head off. I can't say I blame her.

"I remember our deal," he says coolly, "and lucky for you that was never the plan for either of you, though, I'm sure my father won't hesitate to execute you should you prove yourselves to be villains."

I raise my hands. "Hey, I don't claim my nephilim family or their ways."

He nods once, turning his vitriol on Chloe. "But she does. She's all in on the nephilim ways."

"What do you want from me, fae?" she snaps.

"You'll see." He grabs her arm and tugs her out of the bedroom, and I scramble after them. He stops and turns on me. "You tricked your way into coming here, you can figure out how to get yourself back home."

"Don't you think I came for a reason? You people still have my human friends. I'm taking them home with me."

His face is glacial and unreadable. "They're not my property. I cannot return them to you."

"Who said anything about property?" I growl. "They're nobody's property, they're humans."

"Tell that to my father."

Then he turns back on his heels, still clutching onto Chloe, and drags her away. I have no choice but to follow. I got myself into this mess, and it seems the king is the only one who can get me out of it. The first time I met him, he terrified me and he knew it. This time, I'm sure he's still going to terrify me, but I'm not going to let him know it. There are too many people depending on me to be strong.

"Whatever you do, don't drink or eat anything here," I advise Chloe as I catch up to the pair.

"Obviously." Her natural sweet nature has all but turned sour toward me, but given the circumstances, I can't say I really blame her. "I never thought I'd have to actually worry about all those lessons about Faerie, so thanks a lot for this."

"If it's any consolation, you probably know a lot more than I do."

"It's not," she snaps.

"That's enough," Casimir orders, and when Chloe tries to argue, his creepy shadows sweep up to wrap around her mouth, silencing her.

"You're going to suffocate her!" That proves to be a stupid thing to say because he extends that shadow gag to me as well. It muffles the air around my mouth and silences my vocal cords. Panicked, I attempt to say something, but I can't. I swipe at him, but he easily out-maneuvers me.

"Just breathe. I didn't cut off your lungs or your nose."

Oh...

I relax as my lungs swell with oxygen. I shoot Chloe a conspiratorial look, but she just turns away from me. Okay, I deserved that.

We hurry through the castle corridors, ignoring the onlookers as we pass by. Glimpses of recognition hit me at many of the fae in all shapes and sizes. They come in all colors too, and most of them are beautiful, but some look like they crawled out of the depths of hell. None of them look all that human except for the elves with their pointed ears. I remember some of these people from my time here, but I was so drunk on wine and food half the time that I blush seeing them now. They witnessed me at my worst, but in my defense, it wasn't like I could starve myself for two weeks.

We enter the throne room, and King Orlyc gazes down at us from his creepy bone throne with equal parts amused pleasure and cunning strategy. He was expecting us.

"You both look so much like your namesakes," Orlyc says. "That's not a compliment, by the way. Your family should be ashamed of themselves. Anything you'd like to say?"

Our voices become freed from the shadows, and Chloe uses the opportunity to put her foot in her mouth. "I'm proud of my family name," she declares, standing tall. I want to kick her.

"Well, I don't claim them. My last name is Blackwood," I add because it's true, and also because I don't have a death wish.

"Ah, would you like me to change your DNA?" Orlyc cackles at me. "That could be arranged, though it's not something I would do lightly, and I would have to magick you to secrecy. . ."

I gape at him. "I have no idea what you're even talking about."

He grins. "Do you like being a nephilim?"

I frown. "I don't know. . ."

Chloe glares. "Touch my DNA and die."

Does my meek little cousin have no sense of self preservation? Her angelic gift can't save her from the fae, and it's not as if her family can follow her here. They obviously still haven't figured out how to cross The Gateway because if they had, the fae would either be sick and dying right now or already dead.

Casimir is quick to return those ghastly shadows to our mouths, silencing both of us for her stupid comments.

It's a damn good thing I love Felix and Seth.

The king turns to his son. "Why are there two of them? I thought we got rid of Eva." He nods at me, and my insides become like ice.

"I did as I was told and placed her in the vampire council," Casimir responds, shooting me a pointed look. "But I needed her to get to Chloe, and Eva was sneaky, grabbing onto me when I brought her cousin back."

A crease forms between Orlyc's eyebrows. "And why would she do that?"

"We still have her two human friends. She wants them back."

The king appears thoughtful before turning on me. "I'd forgotten all about those humans. Where are they now?" He motions to one of his attendants hovering near his throne, an elfin man with a dog-like swamp creature at his side. From what I remember of my studies, I think it's a kelpie. The little guy would be cute if its teeth weren't as long and sharp as knives.

"They've been entertaining the courtesans," the man replies simply. I have no idea what that means for Felix and Seth, but I just hope they're unharmed.

The king returns to me. "Ah, very well, I have no real use for your friends now that the novelty of humans has worn off on me. You can have them back, but I'd rather like some entertainment for myself first. I think you'll do just fine."

What does he want? Because I swear, if this is some kind of sexual advance, it's not happening.

As if reading my mind, his dark blue features contort in disgust. "I would never sink as low as to have sex with a nephilim. None of us would."

Good--because I'm not having sex with a fae.

But if not that, then what does he want from me? He's already surfaced my angelic gift and taught me how to feed, then threw me into the vampiric council's sacred circle in the eleventh hour. He's already taken weeks off my life that I'll never get back. What kind of entertainment can I possibly offer?

"How's her gift coming along?" he asks Casimir. "Still sharp?"

Flashes of his hands gripping my head, forcing my gift to burn from within my body out onto the surface, return to my mind. My stomach goes hard. Chloe shoots me a questioning look, but I ignore her.

"It's coming along well." Casimir's reply lacks emotion, and I wonder if this is how the prince always interacts with his father. "The light is under control, and her feeding is still happening naturally. Don't forget, she's still carrying vampire venom. Can't you smell it on her?"

Standing from his throne, Orlyc strides to me. I keep my posture straight, imagining a rod through my spine. I refuse to flinch when the imposing man leans down and sniffs me.

"Indeed," he says, stepping back. "I don't think I've smelled this much vampire venom on a nephilim in at least a century."

I don't think I'll ever get used to the immortals' sense of time, of how many lifetimes they can live, on and on and on until someone eventually kills them or they decide they've had enough.

Orlyc grins, and those creepy silvery-white eyes peer into mine as if he's looking down into my very soul. "Don't worry, I don't want you dead. I need your soul to stay bound to that council."

My soul?

"Your soul is stronger than I expected. That's good. You're very promising."

Uhh--what the heck? First he was talking about my DNA and now he's talking about my soul. They're two different things, neither of which I understand much about. Maybe I should start asking questions. Or maybe I'd better not. . .

"How about we play a little game? Complete a task for me, and you and your humans can go home. Fail, and you will still go home, but they will belong to me indefinitely."

He means every word he's saying. He doesn't care about humans. This is the Unseelie Court, and humans are of little consequence here. But how can he threaten such a thing? Do my friends truly mean nothing?

Casimir releases my vocal cords from his shadows, and I snap at the king. "My friends aren't your slaves. You need me in that vampiric council, it's all part of your secret plan. So I'm bargaining with you to get my friends back. Let them come home with me and I won't do anything to mess up my standing with the vampires."

I expect him to be angry, to demand I heed to his will. But he just laughs, and then he snaps his fingers. Seconds later, Felix and Seth are dragged into the throne room by a pair of warrior fae. My friends look very mortal standing between the elves in golden armor.

Without thinking, I run to them. "Are you okay?"

But they look at me with wide weary eyes. Confused. Lost.

It's like they're not even *seeing* me.

"What have you done to them?" I whip around on the king.

"You already know what our food and drink does to outsiders. They've been in Faerie for weeks now. I'm not sure how much longer their minds will be able to survive this realm."

He laughs again, more maniacal this time, and his people follow suit. They don't care. None of them do. This is all a game.

"How are you planning to keep them indefinitely if you're killing them?" I raise an eyebrow.

"Believe me, there are ways . . . now, are you prepared to win your friends back or do you want to keep arguing with me?"

"Fine. What do you want me to do?"

Twenty-Six

ADRIAN

She's gone, but at least this time I haven't forgotten her. She's burned onto my soul, a part of me, and I can't imagine forgetting her again. But it happened before, there's no denying that. It could happen again. I would continue on living with a gaping wound inside of me, never able to heal it, and driving myself mad trying to figure out why I was hurting in the first place. The fae need to be checked. What else are they capable of?

I've been scouring the hotel and casino security footage for over an hour, searching for signs of Eva but coming up with nothing. I left her in my bedroom earlier tonight, double checking that the locks and security cameras were working when I went. Hell, I even tested the motion detectors in the hallway outside the penthouse myself. All were intact. So where is she?

"Who would want her?" Mangus asks.

I give him a rageful glare, and he shrugs like this is the obvious place to start. Doesn't he realize I know that? "Everyone wants her. The nephilim, the fae, the council, Brisa . . . take your pick."

Mangus folds his arms over his chest. "Calm down, brother. This isn't like you."

"I need to get her back." I know I'm frantic, that I'm acting much younger than my age, that my normal demeanor is completely gone, but I can't help it. I'll do anything to get her back. I promised her my protection. I always keep my promises.

"You're in love." He tilts his head, assessing me with amusement. "I didn't realize it had come to that already."

Maybe I should be embarrassed, but I'm not in the slightest. "Yes, it has come to that. Now can you help me find her or not?"

"We need a tracker. I would say you should call Hugo but . . ."

I grumble and drop my face into my hands. A tracker isn't a bad idea, but I'd need more than just someone who can sniff out her blood scent and follow the trail. She straight up disappeared from our penthouse. Whatever happened to her had to have involved magic. Unless there's someone who has better tech than I do and has managed to override my cameras without my knowledge.

Both are possible.

Both are infuriating.

I need to follow all the leads until I find her, and the closest one I have to me right now is Kenton. Trying to break his blood bond to Brisa has been relentless. Everyday, while Eva sleeps, I go to him, and we try. And everyday the bond is too strong. But he's young and determined--we're so close. I just don't know how much more torture he can take.

"Go see if you can find out why Sebastian and Antara were talking to the fae coven in the French Quarter and report back to me," I command Mangus.

He rolls his eyes. "You know, I don't answer to you, Adrian. We're supposed to be equals." I open my mouth to argue, but he stops me. "I will take pity on you because I like you and Eva together. I never thought I'd see you fall in love. I'll admit it's a cruel form of torture for a man who recently lost his wife, but all the same, I want this for you."

With that, he leaves the security room. I follow shortly after, heading down to meet Kenton. It's time to find Brisa. I know for a fact she's been trying to get to Eva, so Brisa is the best place to start. And if she doesn't have her, then I guess I'm flying to Ireland because the fae are the next best lead.

Kenton is waiting for me. He's always waiting for me.

He wants this to be over, to be free of her. He also wants to be free of this afterlife, but I'm not sure I agree. He doesn't know what's possible for his future. If we can tame his bloodlust, he can live a good life without killing anymore. It doesn't have to be over for him, and I'm willing to take on the VEC on his behalf if he'll let me.

"Is today the day?" he practically begs.

"It has to be. Eva is missing. Brisa might have her."

Kenton's normally resigned eyes turn dark and determined. "Don't stop. Kill me if that's what it takes to get the information you need."

He doesn't deserve that. Getting to know him the last few weeks, I believe him to be a good guy. A lot of good people turn bad when they get a taste of the kind of power vampires have. Kenton partook in that power, but even still, he's still good deep down. I don't blame him for what he's done, not in the way he blames himself. I blame Brisa. And after she's dead, I plan to offer him a place in my coven. If he lets me, I'll help him, give him a new family and a job, something to live for.

But I don't think he will accept it.

He's still so stuck on the life he lost. Now that the initial bloodlust of being a newly turned vampire has worn off, he's ready to be done. I can't even blame him.

Sliding my hands into my leather gloves, I retrieve the silver knife and get to work.

It's different this time, maybe it's the sense of urgency, maybe it's that we both care about Eva, or maybe it's that we're both tired of Brisa getting away with things, but something starts to crack at a much faster pace than ever before. He sobs through the pain while simultaneously begging me to keep going. And I do. Even when I want to stop, I don't relent.

Finally, the cracks break wide open, revealing the truth. "Brisa's in the nearby countryside," he mumbles. Blood drips from his mouth. His eyes.

"Where exactly?"

Through the pain, he manages to explain the area. There's a certain look and layout of the house, there's a nearby forest and swamp. He remembers the numbers on the house and the name of the closest road. I'm sure with a little online searching I'll have an address within the hour.

"She's gathering an army," he warns me. "She kidnaps the strays, finds people that nobody will miss. She brings them in, has her new vampires feed on them until they're close to death, and then she turns the victims herself."

"And what's her plan with this army?" Now that he's able to speak, the confessions pour out of him. I still keep the knife lodged in his abdomen just in case, ignoring the scent of burning flesh.

"She wants to attack the council, but it's all a distraction to get to Eva."

"What does she want with Eva?"

"I don't know," he replies honestly. "I thought she still wanted to turn her, but sometimes she talked as if she wanted to kill her. Other times she would talk about her light. I can't say what her plan is, I honestly don't know, now please," he begs. "Let it be over. Please just kill me."

I release him just as he passes out. He's not dead, and he won't be getting a true death anytime soon, but he's going to be in a world of pain for the next hour as his body heals from the massacre of my knife. I'll come back for him later, will thank him, and will convince him to let me help him. He doesn't deserve to die, but if he truly decides that's what he needs, I won't stand in his way. I can't force this life on anyone, and I wouldn't begin to try.

But right now, I've got a vampire to kill.

Twenty-Seven

⟨⟨⟩⟩

I *seriously hate Faerie.*

That's all I can think as I stare at the nasty humanoid troll standing with me in the middle of the small dirt-floored arena. He's at least seven feet tall, with large yellowing teeth, pointy gray scales covering his bare back, long coiled hair on his bare chest, and hands the size of boulders. He's also hungry, and apparently he has a thirst for flesh––my flesh, if he gets his way.

"Don't worry," King Orlyc calls out from the overhead gallery, watching down on me while everyone laughs. "We won't let you die. Maybe just lose an arm or two, but we can heal those before we send you back to the mortal world. This is just for pure entertainment."

"And when I'm done *entertaining* you, you'll let me and my friends go home?" I call back up.

"That's our agreement." But the way he says it makes me think he probably has much more than this rolled up his sleeve.

Several of the spectators snicker at his response, and I grit my teeth. I need to stay focused. How in the hell am I supposed to kill this thing? Because that's the favor the king has asked for. Kill the troll. If I don't kill the troll, he'll still let me and my friends go home, but that's after I've healed. Because the troll is absolutely going to beat the shit out of me. And try to eat me, apparently.

This troll is an inmate on their fae-equivalent to a death row. It's here because it literally *ate* a fae child. Yup, it's disgusting, so either way, this creature is going to die. But why me? Why do I have to be the one to do it?

Again, it's all about games and entertainment. Just another day in the Unseelie Court.

"Sorry, buddy," I say to the troll. "You're dead either way, but I think you already knew that."

He grunts, and I jump into action, summoning my light and blinding the creature. It's a temporary advantage, but at least it's a start.

It's also a big mistake.

Because the troll snarls with intense rage and dives for my hands. Maybe I really will lose my arms in this fight. I crouch down and roll out of his way, and he slams into the stone wall that surrounds us, cracking it. But the wall instantly repairs itself with earthen elemental magic, and the people sitting on the benches above applaud gleefully. It's enough of a distraction that the troll gains ground, knocking me to the floor. I can't let him get me down—— if I do, it's all over.

I scramble up, using my levitation to fly above him. Several of the fae cheer at that while others shout disapproval. I catch sight of Chloe in the crowd sitting with Casimir. They both look downright miserable to be here. I catch Chloe's gaze, and she just looks away. Casimir does the same. *Well, I'm sorry, but are you two the ones fighting a troll right now? I don't think so.*

Refocusing, I come down on the troll's head, kicking it as hard as I can. I've got loads of vampire venom, so it should do something. Nope. Nada. He's like a steel mountain.

My legs buckle.

I cry out as I fall to the ground, pain rocketing through my lower half, and the back of my head hits the dirt floor with a thud. Stars shoot through my vision, and pain zaps at all my nerve endings. I scream, wanting nothing more than to end this, to call a truce and be done, but this isn't some sparring match.

And I can't stay down.

The troll is too quick, climbing on top of me and nearly crushing me with his weight. His smile is grotesque as his putrid breath surrounds me, reeking of coppery blood and rotting garbage. I gag, trying to squirm away. It's useless. I can't move, and we both know it. The crowd goes downright feral——they know it too.

He leans in, smelling my neck.

Sure, King Orlyc said he wasn't going to let me die, but at this moment I have zero faith in him. They say before you die that your life flashes before your eyes, but that's not what happens to me. It's not slow or surreal. It's frantic and terrifying, the emotions slamming me like a head-on collision with a semi truck, my life's memories coming at me all at once.

I don't want to die.

Using every ounce of strength and willpower I can muster, I free my hands from underneath him and thrust my palms into his face. I shine the light again, harder than ever before, brighter than I knew was possible. Blinding and hot. So hot that it burns.

The troll wails and rears back as heat blisters erupt across his body. I don't stop, letting it pummel him as I stand. My ribs are aching and my heart is pounding and the screams of the spectators are deafening, but I'm only focused on the troll.

I have to kill him before he kills me.

Guess I'm a killer afterall. Maybe none of us are all good or all bad. Maybe we're just doing the best we can with the shitty circumstances we have, and sometimes that means fighting a troll to the death. But I would rather be the predator than the prey. I'm done being anyone's prey. And I'm done holding back.

"You're going to die now," I announce. "I will make it as quick and pain-less as I can, not that you deserve that."

I don't have a weapon. I only have this angelic gift and the heightened senses and strength from the venom, but deep down, I know it will be enough to finish him. And King Orlyc must know it too. Maybe this is all part of his plan to show me what my gift is really capable of. It's more than just angelic light that streams from my hands, *it's angelic fire.*

The crowd is loving this: they're laughing, cheering, making bets, and most of all, they're feeding off the sickening energy of this fight. It's disgusting, but I can't worry about it right now. I just have to get it done.

But it's not working.

I'm burning him, he's in pain, he's down, but he's not dying. Maybe his skin is too thick? Am I not strong enough? Cruel enough?

Well, I know I'm not cruel enough to just stand here and let this continue.

Without pausing to overthink, I jump up and fly at the gallery, grabbing hold of the closest soldier. The elf cries out when I grab onto him, but I've surprised him enough to topple us both over the railing. We land on our backs on the arena's dusty and blood-soaked floor.

To do this, I've had to abandon the light, and the troll is back on his feet and furious. He's half burned, and he comes for me, but I push the soldier in his way. Just as I expected, the elf is quick, retrieving his long sword and pointing it at the troll. The troll slows to a stop and grunts with fury.

"End him," I instruct the soldier.

The man growls but quickly retrieves another weapon and hands me the sword. "I'll kill you for this," he sneers.

"Only if your king allows it." Which won't happen because the king wants me alive.

I wield my powerful new weapon, aiming it at the troll. The monster is circling us now, his beady eyes focused only on me. I'm the one he wants.

"So I take it you're not going to kill him for me?" I ask the elf.

"No, but I should let him eat you," he growls.

And that sets my resolve because I will not feel sorry for this damn troll.

He charges forward, and I jump and spin, the long silver sword cutting through the air in a circular arc and slamming into his neck. Using every ounce of strength I have left, I press down and slice through sinew and bone and muscle. Hot blood flies as his body crumples to the dirt, head rolling several feet away. Grimacing, I pick up the decapitated head by the oily hair and hoist it in the air like a trophy.

Half the crowd cheers wildly and the other half boos, but I don't care. I'm just glad it's done and I can go home.

"Are you happy now?" I call out to the king.

"Very." He nods, and the firelight of the many overhead torches reflects off his crown. "That was fun."

I suppose they get bored living as long as they do, but I'd rather not be the entertainment anymore. "Great, now send me and my friends back home."

When the king stands, the room grows silent. I drop the troll's head and step away, beyond grossed out that its blood is all over the combat clothing and boots the fae provided for this very event. I turn and hand the sword back to the soldier, who shoots me a glare before returning it to his sheath.

"Casimir will take you home after you dine with us," Orlyc says.

I snort. "I'm not eating your fae food. Good try, though."

"Then join us while we eat," he insists. He still sounds jovial, but his eyes are like ice. I don't trust him for a second. "I won't take no for an answer."

I agree, feigning resignation, but I'm actually more on guard than before. A troll was one thing. Dinner with the dark king? That's something else entirely.

Twenty-Eight

ADRIAN

There aren't a lot of basements in New Orleans because of the high water table. We built a several-levels deep basement into the hotel, but it took a substantial amount of money to engineer and complete. Most of the developers who bid for us discouraged the basement levels altogether, but I insisted on having an underground sanctuary for my coven. And a lavish one at that.

For as long as I've known her, Brisa never settled for anything less than total extravagance. I figured that she wouldn't hole up and plan my demise just anywhere. She would want to be in a luxury hotel or apartment somewhere close by, and probably somewhere that also had access to comfortable underground accommodations in case of an emergency. She'd definitely stay within the city limits, probably in the French Quarter. That way she could strike at a moment's notice.

But I was wrong––because she's not in the city at all.

She's in the swamp.

And so, I am in the swamp now too, hunting her down. It's filled with life, even in January, the croaking toads being the loudest of all. It's not even their mating season and they're obnoxious. There's no peace and quiet out here.

I wonder what Brisa thinks of that––she's not actually *in* the swamp, but she's taken over a property that backs up to it. The large antebellum house is old and gothic, but decently maintained. I wonder who owned it, and I also wonder if she killed them or turned them. I'm going to assume they're her children now after everything Kenton confessed.

Hovering over the dark swamp bordering the home, I catch a glimpse of the old graveyard on the other side of the property. That graveyard alone explains why she chose this estate for her plans. Graveyards can be hard to find in family estates like this. They're illegal in most places, but this one would've been grandfathered into the property. There shouldn't be any new souls resting here, but from the looks of several freshly dug graves, it's obvious she's been siring new vampires.

Kenton's still back at the casino, locked away, but he was right. She's building an army. I won't release him from his cell until after she's dead. And once she's gone, I'll have more new vampires without a master to deal with. That will create unintended consequences––I may be hunting new vampires for weeks. They won't be under the council bond like all others, so it will be best to kill them. It's going to be hard enough to get the council to agree to let Kenton live.

I've trusted five vampires to come with me tonight. After we left the car at the closest highway exit, I levitated and the rest came on foot. Mangus is leading William and three of Will's oldest and fiercest children. I hope the six of us will be enough because seeing the large house now makes me a little nervous. She's in there with God knows how many new children. They might even be waiting for us.

The others catch up, and I levitate down to meet them. "We'll go in and lure the new children out. Don't hesitate to kill them, they'll be instructed to do the same to you."

"You're sure we can go in?" William asks.

"Whoever owns this place is long dead by now. There's a family grave-yard on the other side of the estate. I'm certain that's why she chose this location."

"She could've turned a thousand vampires by now."

Mangus shakes his head. "We would've known. There would've been reports of people going missing. You can pick off loners here and there, but you can't pick off a thousand humans in a matter of weeks without notice."

"And it's a small graveyard," I add, "So no, not a thousand, but possibly a hundred. They're young, dangerous, and operating outside of the council's blood bonds. They all need to be eliminated."

A line forms between the eyebrows of one of William's men. He doesn't like the sound of that; he probably thinks I'm being cruel and ruthless. Well, I am. I have to be. There is no room for mercy in tonight's mission. I level him with a hard glare. "Do not hesitate," I repeat. "They won't hesitate to kill you, and it's either us or it's them." He nods, and I continue.

"We get in, we kill, and we find Eva if she's there. But leave Brisa to me. Got it?" They nod, their killer instincts come out to play. "Alright, let's go."

The six of us take off in a group, Mangus at the forefront and me just steps behind. We gather on the porch and he throws open the front door, the first to go in.

"It's clear," he whispers low, and we follow him inside.

I don't normally get nervous, but I'm a wreck right now. I can admit that. Because Eva could be in here. She could be hurt. Or worse. And the sickest thing about it is that I hope she's here, because if she's not, I won't be able to save her tonight. And I'm not going to stop searching until I do. I don't care if I have to comb through every corner on this planet, starting with the fae realm.

But right now, she needs me alive, and I need to stay focused. So I force her from my mind and think of Brisa instead. She's the one I want to question, that I need to kill.

But the house is eerily silent.

Did Kenton lead me to the wrong place, or did Brisa already move on to a new location? Or maybe they're off doing something else right now. For a second, I imagine her army has moved into the casino in my absence, that I've just walked into the perfect trap. That Kenton planned this all along.

We round the corner into the large kitchen, and Mangus points to the refrigerator. "Can you smell that?"

I inhale the scent of cold blood. It's being stored for later, and it smells fresh, like it was taken within the last twenty-four hours. She can't be too far.

"Split up," I instruct. "When you find her, call for the others." We're fast––it'll only take seconds for us to catch up to whoever finds her first.

We peel apart in different directions, and I head toward the back of the house, hovering inches above the floor to keep completely silent. I really hope I'm the first to find her. But the back of my neck prickles in an old familiar way, and that's when I know the truth.

She's found me first.

Twenty-Nine

~♦~

A pair of pixies bathe and dress me for the evening. They're barely a foot tall with large gossamer moth-like wings. They weave pink flowers into my hair and make me dress in a matching pastel pink tulle dress. "I hate this color," I mutter to myself, but the pixies take that as an insult and hiss, one of them pinching my cheeks.

"Ouch!" I try to brush her away, but she flashes sharp teeth at me, and I stop.

"This feels like some kind of cosmic joke." Chloe glowers down at her own pastel green dress. The dress looks way better on her than it does on me. "Thanks to you," she adds, shooting me an arched eyebrow.

"What would you do for Greyson and Bella? Or for your twin brothers? What about all the friends you made when you trained?" I smooth out the dress and release a breath. "Because I'm pretty sure you'd have done the same thing I did."

"You're asking a manipulative question, and I won't fall for it."

I sigh, overcome with exhaustion, and rub my eyes. A pixie hisses and swats my hand away, whining over the messed up makeup she just applied. "Geez, you're stronger than you look," I say to the pixie.

She giggles, snapping her sharp teeth again. "I'm a lot of things you'll never know, nephilim. Now let me do my job, or I really will bite."

Okay, note to self, they definitely bite and they understand English, so don't say anything that can't be repeated outside of this room.

But I really am beyond exhausted right now––I couldn't care less.

When Casimir brought us to Faerie, I was in another time zone sleeping.

I didn't get much sleep at all before being pulled here, and now the sun is rising here in Faerie. I assume we're somewhere near Ireland still, which makes me think it's setting or has already set back home. I really wouldn't know anymore, the time zones make no sense to me, especially adding in the fact that I'm no longer in the mortal world. All I do know is that I'm dying to get some decent sleep.

"I'm not trying to manipulate you." I return to my conversation with Chloe, stifling a yawn that earns me another hissing pixie. "I just want you to understand why I did what I did. They're not going to kill you, I made sure that was promised, and fae can't tell lies, but my friends would've been stuck here forever. They didn't deserve that."

She hums to herself, not yet convinced, but I can tell I'm cracking her shell. I still believe she's a good person deep down.

"And besides, they were kind to you. Don't you remember them? Seth and Felix lived at the Casa with us for a while." She stiffens, and I think I've almost cracked her. "And Felix is such a great guy. I've known him since I was a kid and believe me, he doesn't deserve to be stuck in this place. And Seth? Well, Seth is kind of a crotchety old man even though he's the young and broody type, but he's got a soft heart. "

"Fine," her voice drops an octave. "Whatever. I get it. You did what you had to do. Now can you stop talking? I'm still mad at you even though I understand."

Success−−I've got her!

"I'll take it." I offer her a wink, and she rolls her eyes.

The pixies finish with us, fashioning us into what looks to me like a pair of sugar-plum fairies from *The Nutcracker*. Casimir appears from the shadows of the dressing room, stepping out of them as if striding through a doorway. His creepy dove sits on his shoulder.

"What is that thing?" I ask him, not caring that he hates when I ask him questions about his magic.

He ignores my question completely, inspecting us, and taking way more interest in Chloe's appearance than my own. "This will do. Let's go."

We have no choice but to follow him outside.

The dinner has been set up in the castle's courtyard, and even though it's a cold winter's night, the air has been magicked to feel like a warm summer's evening. Little fairy lights flitter above the crowd, lighting the entire space. I squint up at the lights when I realize that they're actual fairies dancing around up there. They look to be enjoying a party all their own.

Long rectangular dining tables are set off to one side and covered in decadent food and drink. The dance floor is on the other side, already filled with dancers. Huge white roses overflow from centerpieces and archways. They're five times the size of any rose I've seen before, and the thorns tucked in their stems look sharp as knives. I take note to stay away from them.

The fae are dressed in some of the most beautiful gowns and suits I've ever seen. And also some of the strangest. They wear silks of every color, many covered in beaded embroidery or gems. And several with slits in the backs for wings. The wings are just as varied as the gowns are.

"Welcome to the Unseelie Court," Casimir says, sounding bored, probably because he's been to these parties a thousand times before. "You do know what Unseelie means, don't you?" He directs this question to Chloe.

"Evil and malevolent," she quips.

"That's one way to put it," he replies evenly. "There are light fae and there are dark fae. We are the dark fae. This is our side of Faerie."

The fae are comprised of many mythical creatures besides the elves, and I'm pretty sure all of them are immortals. They can still be killed, but they don't age once they reach maturity. For most that means they look to be in their twenties, and for others it's their thirties. But nobody here appears to be a day over forty. There's no way to tell who has the power, who has the secrets, and who belongs where. Aging and generations are such a human thing, but they just make sense to me. This? This is unsettling, to say the least.

I wonder what that makes of fae lives––do they still live it to the fullest? Or do they grow bored, coming up with malevolent games to occupy their time? I think I already know the answer to that question . . .

As far as I know, the elves are at the top of the fae food chain, ruling the Seelie and the Unseelie Courts. They're also the most like humans, but that's all I really know of them. There might be others in Faerie that challenge them, mages and such. It's not my place to know, nor do I really care so long as I can get out of here tonight.

"And does your father have a queen?" Chloe asks, gazing at the crowd. I think she's looking for King Orlyc, but he's nowhere to be found. "I'd like to talk to a woman about all this."

"There is no Unseelie Queen," is all Casimir replies, then he takes both of our arms and drags us to the head table. "Sit and enjoy yourselves." He sounds sarcastic, pushing us into chairs, but I wonder if he's actually being sarcastic or if he's filling a role. This could all be another game.

And then he's strolling away to go dance with an elf who has the prettiest hair I've ever seen. It streams down her back in a glossy red wave, sparkling like rubies in the dim light.

The king is the last to arrive, and when he does, everyone else takes their seats and begins to devour the food. It looks and smells delicious, but Chloe and I don't move a muscle. In fact, I sit on my hands, just in case. I'm not tempted this time because I know where it will get me. It also helps that I'm barely hungry.

We stay like that all through the dinner, and although we're sitting next to the king, he never speaks to us or even acknowledges our presence. It's as if he wants us here to be seen, but not to participate.

Fine by me.

After the dinner and dessert are finished, and after the people have started to grow tired of the dancing, King Orlyc motions to one of his servants. It's the very same elf that always has that kelpie dog at his side. Together, they scamper into the castle.

"I have your friends," Orlyc says, and my heart jumps. Then he turns to Chloe, "and I have someone I think you'd be very interested to meet."

The crowd parts, and Seth and Felix come strolling in. They look healthy, like their minds have been returned to them. At least compared to when I saw them a few hours ago, it's a night and day difference. I jump up and run to them, wrapping them both in a double bear-hug. Chloe follows close behind, though she refrains from hugging anyone.

"Eva, we've been so worried about you." Felix is the first to speak. "They sent you away and wouldn't tell us anything."

"I've been worried about you," I counter. "What have you been doing here?"

They exchange guarded looks. "Not now," Seth supplies. "But just know, we're okay. We're not traumatized. At least, I don't think we are."

Seeing their eyes so clear right now makes me wonder what the fae have done to make them return to their normal selves. There must be a safe way to survive this place if my human friends can go from being drunk on food and wine to being completely alert and sober like this. And it's only been a few hours. But it doesn't matter right now because we're leaving Faerie and never coming back.

"Let's go home." I turn back to the king to ask for just that when the crowd falls to complete silence, parting for a newcomer.

Thirty

T he tall elfin man saunters into the courtyard followed by several of his attendants, all of them dressed in gold and white silks. There's no question they belong together. The leader is stunning and impossibly tall, with golden ringlets that fall all around his face like a heavenly halo. A prickle of familiarity runs through me. I feel like I've met this man before, but that's impossible.

Is it impossible?

"Why have you requested an audience tonight, King Orlyc?" the man booms, seeming completely unaware of my little group huddled off to his right.

"Is it so strange for us to want to host our friends?" Orlyc teases.

The man responds with a deep scowl as massive white feathered wings explode from his back. The tips of the feathers seem to be ignited with an unearthly fire.

And that's when I realize how I know him.

"Oh, don't be like that." Orlyc laughs at this obvious display of power. He turns in a wide circle, arms outstretched in introduction. "Welcome King Alberich Mikael, High King of the Seelie Court." The party guests clap, but I don't. I can barely even move. I'm too stunned. "It's so kind of you to take time from your busy schedule to join us." He steps to the side, motioning Chloe forward. But she can't seem to move either. "How I've longed for you two to meet."

Chloe's knees begin to slump, and I grab her, helping her stay upright. Seth and Felix step forward as well. Chloe doesn't seem to notice any of us, though, her eyes are glued to the light fae king. And I get it, because as shocked as I'm feeling right now, she must be feeling complete betrayal. Her mouth hangs open. Eyes glossy. Unmoving.

"It can't be." Her voice cracks in equal parts horror and pain.

"Oh, but I assure you, it can," Casimir says, appearing at her other side. He frowns at her with pity, and that's almost worse than when he looked at her with disdain.

"That's right, your avenging angel is actually a light fae," King Orlyc confirms.

So it's true then. That is how I "know" Alberich. I saw him in Chloe's records.

"And to think, all along you thought our Al here was God's avenging angel, come down to command his precious nephilim seed to rid the world of supernaturals," Orlyc continues. "How wrong you are, Chloe. And how very wrong your ancestors were."

The fire on the light king's wings has only grown at this, as if it's tied to his fury. "This is why you brought me here, Orlyc?" His wings lift, as if he's preparing to take flight. "For these women? I don't have to entertain nephilim."

Orlyc rounds on Alberich. "The nephilim must be stopped. The truth is the only thing that will set us all free."

Alberich shakes his head. "I did what needed to be done in order to protect our realm from theirs. They were a virus, infecting our kind and diluting our bloodlines."

"And so you lied?" Chloe asks, growing bolder.

"It worked didn't it?" He stalks in close, and I hold on tighter to her shoulder, not willing to let her go. We're in this together. "I did what I had to do, and your kind easily believed it. They wanted something to do with themselves. They needed a purpose."

"You pretended you were an angel of God," Chloe hisses. "You spoke in tongues."

"I used elfin magic." His blue eyes bore down on her, and his wings flap once more, sending a gust of wind in our direction. "I did what had to be done to protect my kind. And I would do it again."

Prince Casimir's been watching this exchange with his mouth set in a grim line, not saying much, but at this he growls at the light king. "What you did cost thousands of innocent lives."

"But I saved generations of fae in the process. Do not act as if you understand the ways of kings, Prince."

Shadows dance around Casimir's knuckles, and I'm certain he's fighting the urge to set them loose on Alberich.

King Orlyc simply laughs––more entertainment to fill his evening. "The nephilim have a record keeper born to every generation, someone who can access the memories of what you did and continue to spread your message. The mission you tasked them with has never ceased. They've used it to justify countless deaths, claiming their God decreed it. But the truth is, the nephilim are mortals with watered-down angelic blood and nothing more."

He points to Chloe, and Casimir's shadows shove her forward, wrapping up her arms and legs in a cocoon of darkness.

"This is the current record keeper. Do you know what you've created? What kind of weapon this youth has become for her people?"

"Her *people* don't belong in our world, and we don't belong in theirs. I ensured they would drive the fae back into our world, which they did. The portals wouldn't have been sealed if it wasn't for my ingenuity." His wings are flapping again, that terrible fire growing taller and taller. "Yes, there were sacrifices. Yes, people died. But our kind has stopped mixing with the wrong bloodlines, and as a result, we're stronger than ever. We've returned to the old customs. Our courts have flourished. Our children grow up healthy. Our way of life is that of kings and queens. What does their mortal realm matter to us now that Faerie is thriving?"

Chloe's eyes release a well of unshed tears as she speaks the truth. "It matters because the war continues on in the mortal realm."

"Not my problem," he sneers.

She continues, "and because my people will find a way into Faerie, and when they do, they will unleash a weapon. A weapon the likes of which you've never seen. A weapon that will destroy this realm and everyone born of it."

Thirty-One

＊

C hoices are made quickly after Chloe's confession, mainly because King Alberich pulls his head out of his ass, and also because Chloe agrees to help the fae. She understands now that she's been as blinded by the records as the rest of her family, and she wants to set things right. Can we go back and save the thousands who've died in this centuries-long war? No. But can we stop it from continuing? We don't know, but we hope so––we believe it's possible.

The meeting winds down, and the exhaustion pulls me under. All I want right now is sleep. *Dreamless* sleep, if I can help it. I'm sure Adrian is losing his mind looking for me, but once I get home and tell him what happened, I'm going to bed.

Chloe doesn't know it yet, but I have a feeling she's going to struggle getting the truth out. She loves her family and believes the best of them, but I'm not so sure they'll accept her word on this. These prejudices are lifelong, are they really going to be able to give them up? What if they don't believe her or they find a way to twist her words into something ugly?

"Are you ready then?" Casimir says to the group of us ready to go back to the mortal world. He sounds bored by all of this, like there are more inter-esting things he could be doing with his time right now. His eyes flick to Chloe, and his nose wrinkles. "You're crying again. Please stop that."

She wipes at the tears. "Leave me alone, Casimir."

He stiffens at the mention of his name, like hearing it on her lips is an insult.

I'm quick to defend her. "She's just realized that her friends and family have been killing people for generations for no good reason and everything she was raised to believe is based on a lie. I would cry too."

"You would?" Her lip trembles. She sounds skeptical. That's what I get for having resting-bitch-face.

"I mean, probably. But if I didn't, it's only because I'm a bitter old hag."

"How old are you?" Casimir frowns in confusion. "You don't look old for a mortal."

"It's just an expression." I bug my eyes out at him. "Now can you take us home please?"

One of the party fairies has come down to buzz around Chloe, trying to collect her tears into a crystal vial. Chloe brushes her away, and the fairy throws sparkly dust in her face. Chloe sneezes. "I think I'm allergic to that stuff."

"It's pixie dust," Casimir says. "It's a gift."

"Does it make you fly?"

He frowns. "No. Wherever did you get that idea?"

"Never . . . mind," she mumbles but he seems genuinely curious.

"Let's get going." I shoot Casimir a pleading look, not really wanting to get into the tale of Peter Pan and Neverland. "Please take me to Adrian."

"I just want to go home." Chloe wipes up the last of her tears.

"Which home?" I snort. "Don't you people have houses all over?" Her eyes water again, and I backpedal. "Damn, I'm sorry. I didn't mean to make you upset."

Casimir bristles, giving me a death-glare. "What did I say about crying?"

Geeze, it's not my fault she's so sensitive.

"Take me to my brothers, Enzo and Nicco," Chloe interrupts. "Can you do that?"

I almost think he's going to say no, but he simply nods.

"Just take us to my house," Felix says.

I don't know how Casimir's magic works, that he can know where to take everyone, but he must because he stretches out his arms like what we're about to do is no big deal. He needed me to get to Chloe, so he must have some limitations, but I'm not about to slow us down by asking him questions he won't want to answer anyway. We all grab on at once and he pulls our group into his shadows.

We tumble through the darkness with no end.

Flashes of the twin's faces appear, and then Chloe is gone. We hover nearby for just a second, watching her reunite with her brothers in the living room of a home I don't recognize. It reminds me of when I was a kid and my mom would drop one of my friends off at their house. She'd always wait to make sure they got inside safely before driving away. Casimir is doing the same thing to Chloe right now. I try to speak, to ask him if he's developed a soft spot for her, but the shadows are cutting off my voice.

Chloe looks up, catching sight of us with her large caramel eyes, and then we're gone, falling back into the ether again. The inertia slams through my body at a sickening pace. We're moving much faster this time. It's like being on a horrible roller coaster, and all I can think is that Chloe got lucky to be dropped off first.

And then we're in the Moreno's kitchen where Felix and Seth are stumbling out of the shadows. But we don't stick around to make sure they're home safe, we're gone again.

Now it's just me and Casimir, and he turns his grip on me. It's so impossibly tight that I would cry out if I could speak, but the shadows keep me in silence. All I can do is hold on for the ride, everything spinning faster and faster, my mind nearly floating away.

I'm dropped in an unfamiliar place.

Catching my breath, I sit up and look around. I'm in a random backyard and it's night out.

Great job, Cas...

The grass is mossy and wet, the trees are tall and probably old, and up ahead looms a creepy antebellum mansion. There are no lights on, and it looks very much like it could be the set for a horror film. Except, this isn't a movie, this is my real life. I shiver and look around for Casimir, wanting to tell him that he dropped me in the wrong place, but he's gone. He didn't bother to stick around to make sure I made it home safe either.

Cursing the fae, I stand and brush myself off. At least the sunrise looks like it's coming soon. The sky is that shade of blue it turns when the sun is about to crest the eastern horizon. The one relief in all this is I won't have to try to find my way back to the casino in the dark. I take in the many gnarled trees and the huge weeping willows, the nearby croaking of toads and cicadas, and determine that a swamp is nearby. At least I'm probably in Louisiana, but how far to New Orleans?

I might be able to levitate back to the city, but I need to know where I am before I can know which direction to go, so reluctantly, I trudge up to the house. Let's just pray that whoever lives here isn't a "shoot first and ask questions later" type of southerner, but more of a "hospitality is our birthright" type. I almost channel light into my hands as a makeshift flashlight but decide better of it. That's a surefire way to scare someone. I'm already dressed in an ugly tulle pastel pink gown with loads of flowers braided into my hair. I look like a homecoming queen reject.

Just as I step onto the front porch, a guttural moan catches my attention. I pause to listen, a sense of foreboding creeping over me. The moaning continues, and I realize it's not actually moaning that I'm hearing. It's the sound of muffled speech.

This is the part in the horror film where I would be screaming at the television, telling the dumb girl to run the other direction. And I'd definitely be throwing popcorn at the screen when she goes to investigate the muffled voice. Rule number one of surviving a horror movie: don't put yourself in the wrong place at the wrong time on purpose. I guess today I'm that girl, because I back off the porch and head toward the noise.

All at once, three things happen: the sound grows urgent, the sun begins to peek over the trees, and my eyesight adjusts completely to the dim light.

And there he is.

Adrian.

Moments from death.

Thirty-Two

~∞~

He's tied to a tree with thick silver chains and a gag is shoved into his mouth.

I don't think, I just act.

Racing across the lawn, I reach him and begin frantically removing the chains. He groans hard as his exposed flesh sizzles against the metal. His eyes search mine, then dart back to the house, as if trying to tell me something.

It takes a second, but I pull the gag from his mouth. "How did you get here?"

His voice is ragged and more angry than ever. "Brisa's in there with her new vampires. Don't go inside. Untie me and get away from here."

"And what are you going to do?" I question as I work on the chains. My heart is going a million miles a minute because I know that rising sun is going to kill him soon.

"I'm going to go back in there to kill her," he snarls.

"Good. I'm going with you."

He levels me with a look that says he knows better than to argue with me but he's really not happy about it. "Fine." He breaks free of the chains. His body is weakened from the silver, and he needs time to heal. He also needs to get away from the sun. That house is not safe for either of us, but he's got thirty seconds at most.

He breaks a branch from the tree and fashions it into two makeshift stakes, handing me the sharper one. "Bring some of that chain," he instructs.

I pick the smallest length of it up and wrap it around my left hand, keeping the stake in my right. Then we race back to the house, crossing the threshold seconds before the sunlight hits the earth.

I have to hold my breath to keep from audibly panting. That was so close, and now we're walking into an equally dangerous situation because Brisa wants Adrian dead. Because she was surely watching everything we just did.

Because she knows exactly where we are.

Vampires come at me from all sides, and I don't have time to orient myself. I fight back immediately. I'm still tired and disoriented from the longest day of my life, and my movements are slower than normal. And there are just so many vampires. I can't count them all, but I'd guess at least thirty. Thirty of them, and there's only two of us. I manage to stake one, but seconds later another has me pinned against the floor. Meanwhile, Adrian is covered in them. He's so much faster and stronger, but he's vastly outnumbered. They're going to rip him to shreds.

Slamming my silver-wrapped fist into my current vampire attacker's face, the man rears back with a guttural roar. I jump to my feet, dropping both the stake and the silver, and channel my gift instead. I'm going to aim it at all of them. They're already dead as far as I'm concerned, and luckily Adrian is safe from my light since the council bond magic makes it impossible for me to kill him. The angelic firelight erupts from my hands, and I point at the attackers, spinning in a circle to make sure I hit them all. They scream and hit the floor, but I don't stop. And I won't stop. Not until they burn alive. And they do, one by one, crumbling into ash.

I never saw Brisa among them. She must still be in here, still hiding somewhere in this house. And I'm going to hunt her down and kill her for this.

I let my hands drop, the light disappearing for now. I cough, covered in the ash. I have to wipe it from my eyes.

I expect Adrian to be on the floor where I last saw him.

But he's gone.

My stomach roils with revulsion and adrenaline. I know I couldn't have killed him, so he must have been dragged away.

God, I hope I didn't accidentally kill him.

Ignoring my growing panic, I release a frustrated scream and race upstairs to search. I don't know why I think he's upstairs, but I just do. He could be anywhere in this huge house, but there's something about the grand staircase that calls to me.

It's *very* Brisa.

I go from room to room. The windows are all boarded up, but little streams of light are beginning to come through the cracks. It's enough sun to injure a vampire if they were directly in it, but I don't think it's enough to kill one. As far as I know, only full sunlight exposure can do that.

Jazz music begins to faintly play from a scratchy record player. I freeze. It's coming from a room farther down the hallway. A door cracks open, and what looks like candlelight flickers from within. It's a production, a show for my benefit, and it's creepy as hell.

Also, very Brisa.

Rushing forward, I slam open the door.

Adrian is lying on the bed, and Brisa is curled up at his side like a lover. But she's no lover because pressed to his heart, ready to kill, is a long wooden stake. And around his neck, coils a black and brown cottonmouth snake. It's one of the most poisonous snakes in the area, and seeing it sends a streak of panic through me.

Because she's controlling that snake . . .

I almost forgot that she can communicate with animals, commanding them to do things for her. And just beyond these walls is a swamp full of all kinds of dangerous creatures at her disposal. I imagine what she could do with all those snakes and gators, and my fear triples.

"Your girlfriend is here," Brisa whispers to Adrian in a breathy tone. "How very fortunate. I wanted her to see you die."

Thirty-Three

"Just tell me what you want from me. I'll do it, and you can stop this."

She tilts her head in my direction, her eyes narrowing into hateful slits. "I want my crown back. I lost it because of you. Once he dies, you're next. I don't care what you are or what you can do. I've made up my mind. I want you gone."

"Eva, don't," Adrian hisses, and she shifts her weight so she's straddling him, the tip of the stake never leaving its mark. She's not going to miss his heart. All it will take is one simple wrist movement, and he'll be gone forever. I'm not sure my gift would be fast enough to stop her in time. And still, the cottonmouth tightens around his neck, then turns to hiss at me, baring its fangs.

"Don't kill Adrian, and I'll help you," I plead.

She smiles her most calculated smile, the one that doesn't reach her eyes. "Here's what you're going to do," she instructs. "You're going to call a council meeting in three nights' time to meet in City Park at two a.m. sharp. You will ensure that every council member attends, insisting that the full moon requires another forging. Once you are all together, you will join bloodied hands, and I will arrive. That is when you will transfer the blood bond back to me."

"The hell she will," Adrian snarls, and she tuts, pressing the tip of her stake hard enough to pierce through his shirt and into his chest. He swallows a groan, shaking his head at me. He'd rather die than let her win. But I can't let him die. I just can't.

"And if word of my impending arrival leaks to anyone," she adds. "Not only will I kill Adrian, but I will hunt down anyone you've ever associated with, anyone at all, and I will kill them too. Friends, family, old teachers, co-workers--*anyone*."

I can see it in her eyes and hear it in her voice--she means every word. This is more than a threat, it's an oath.

"Okay," I agree, "I'll do my part, I will get them all there and help you do whatever you want. *But* if transferring the bond fails, you cannot blame me. You're forgetting that the fae are part of this equation too, it's their magic you want to change, and they already forged the bond. They said it couldn't be changed."

She smiles again, and this time it does reach her eyes. And it's terrifying. "I already have everything I need from the fae. You just make sure everyone arrives on time and that they don't suspect my arrival."

"And what about Adrian? You're going to have to let him go so he can show up with the rest of the council."

She mocks me with her tone. "Do you really think I'm foolish enough to do that? No, Adrian will come when I do. You'll have to cover for his absence."

Adrian stares at me with wide eyes, shaking his head over and over again. The snake grows agitated and bites him. He groans and stops moving, and the snake relaxes again. The snake's venom can't hurt him, but my heart still breaks to see him this way. To see him hurt and bound. Once again under Brisa's control.

He doesn't want me to do this. And I get it, because I wouldn't either if I were in his position right now. But I'm not, and if there's a chance to save him, I have to take it. I'll worry about the blood bonds when we actually get to that point.

"Please, just let Adrian go," I try one last time.

"Adrianos is mine. He will always be mine. It is my right to keep him alive or end him."

I shake my head. She's so wrong. "You have no right to anybody but yourself."

"Don't speak," she screams, then she speaks more calmly. "I will let him walk free once I have my royal bond returned to me."

I nod. There's nothing else I can do.

"Now leave."

"But--"

"Leave!"

The cottonmouth slips from Adrian's neck. It slithers off the bed quickly, snapping its fangs at me and hissing. I back away, but it doesn't stop coming at me. I turn and run, and the damn thing chases me from the house entirely. It's only when I'm fully outside that it finally doubles back to its master.

And even from way out here, I can hear the warning sound of Brisa's maniacal laughter.

Spinning around to take in my surroundings, I'm overwhelmed with panic. I don't know where I am. I don't have a phone. And I'm dressed in a pink gown, covered in blood and ash. What the hell am I supposed to do?

I could levitate, and I definitely will if needed, but I'm exhausted and worry I won't be able to hold it for long. Plus, it's daylight out. What if someone sees me? How will I explain myself?

Either way, I really hate snakes. There ain't no way I'm getting bitten by that cottonmouth, so I take off at a dead sprint away from the house and toward the long gravel driveway. It disappears into the trees up ahead, and I'm hoping whatever road it leads to will be an easy enough one for me to follow to civilization.

I run faster than I ever have before, but just as I'm about to hit the treeline, I notice a small cemetery off to my right. I've had enough cemeteries to last me a lifetime, and from the looks of this one, recent graves have been dug here.

Graves for all those new vampires I just killed.

It's probably stupid, but I don't want Brisa having any new children with her when she comes to the council meeting in three days' time. It takes three nights to make a new vampire, so she won't have time to make new ones to replace the ones I killed back in the house. But what if she has more buried here? Stifling a groan, I force myself to be brave and veer off toward the cemetery. I'll dig up any fresh graves and kill the vampires before they're fully turned. It's now or never.

Fighting back a nervous shiver, I swing open the wrought iron gate and edge my way inside. In this part of the world, bodies aren't able to be buried underground because of the water table, so the cemetery is a labyrinth of above-ground tombs and vaults. But vampires still have to be buried underground in order to turn, so I go straight to the areas of disturbed soil. There are several large holes, and I peer down into them to see open coffins at the bottoms.

Open and empty.

I exhale and find that I'm shaking so badly I need to sit down. But I can't. I have to search the place thoroughly, and then I have to go. And quickly, before Brisa realizes what I'm doing and sends her cottonmouth out here.

I shiver at the thought of having to dig up any graves should I find one.

At least all I'll have to do is open the coffins. If an actual vamp is in one, the sun can do the work in killing them for me. And if I find a half-dead human, I can help them to safety, lock them up somewhere until the three days are up.

I round a corner of a particularly overgrown area surrounding a tomb, and reluctantly find what I was looking for.

A row of four more disturbed graves.

There are four in all, each haphazardly piled with dark, wet soil. Falling to my knees, I set to work digging up the graves. I'm so much faster than I would've been when I was still human, and there's not that much soil to begin with, so it doesn't take long. And I'm already disgusting with blood and ash, what's some dirt going to do?

By the time I hit the first coffin, I want to puke from the nerves coiled in my belly. It's the last thing I want to do, but I throw open the coffin lid anyway.

A vampire hisses.

Thirty-Four

❧

I scramble back, holding in my scream. I expected to find a human, someone slowly being turned. Maybe they'd already be undead, maybe not. But the man in the coffin is a fully formed vampire in black tactical gear.

He reacts in a flash, pulling me into the coffin with him and slamming the lid shut overtop us. He's screaming, the sun already starting to sizzle his flesh, but I'm also screaming now. Because I'm trapped in a coffin!

"Let me out," I cry, pushing against the lid. Despite his fresh wounds, the creature holds me so tightly that I'm locked in a vice. I will the light to come to my hands when the man growls into my ear.

I know that voice.

"Calm down," Mangus says. "You're going to get me killed. And whisper, please. Brisa's hearing is excellent. She doesn't know where we are."

My heart rate is still beating a million miles an hour, but I shift my weight slightly to lie next to Mangus instead of on top of him. My eyes adjust to the complete darkness of this godforsaken coffin, and I take in the man pressed next to me. His hair is a tangled mess, his eyes are closed in pain, and he smells like burnt flesh.

"What are you doing out here?" I demand.

"There were five of us that came with Adrian to kill Brisa and look for you," he explains slowly, gritting his teeth as his body starts to heal itself. "Unfortunately, Brisa already killed William. And I hate to be the one to tell you this, but I think she killed Adrian, too. She had him tied up to a tree so he'd burn with the sunrise."

"No, I saved him," I quickly add, and he visibly relaxes. "*But* he's now her prisoner."

We both want the other to explain what they know, but I make him go first.

"After she killed William and tied Adrian up outside, she also tied us up and told us we were going to die after her children had a chance to play with us." He grimaces, but doesn't expand on that part. "Fortunately, her and her children all went to the other side of the house to watch Adrian burn. That's when we were able to get away. But we only had minutes to find somewhere safe to spend the daylight hours. It was by sheer luck that we found these coffins open. We quickly buried ourselves just as the sun was rising."

His story checks out. I was on the other side of the property with Adrian when they came over here, so I wouldn't have seen or heard them. I'm a little peeved that they didn't first go try to help Adrian, but there wasn't a lot of time.

"Now you explain how you got here," he says.

"I will when I have more oxygen." I'm trying to stay calm, but this coffin is really starting to feel like it's going to suffocate me. "I can't stay in here too much longer," I whisper. "I need air."

"Right, okay, I'll let you out in a minute, but at least explain what happened in there to make Adrian her prisoner."

I slow my breathing and nod.

This is still Mangus. I like him, but I don't necessarily trust him. I barely even trust Adrian, and I'm madly in love with the guy. But I do go into detail about Brisa's plan to get the council together and transfer the bond. I know she said I wasn't supposed to tell anyone, but I was never going to stick to that side of our agreement anyway.

"Adrian won't let you do it. We can't give her the royal bond. She'll have control over us again. He'd rather die, and so would I." Mangus is adamant about this, and I can't say I blame him.

"Obviously I don't actually intend to give her the bond, but we have to get her into our territory so we can kill her and save him."

He thinks on it for a long minute. "Or we just storm in there the second the sun sets and get it over with now." He wants revenge, and although I know he cares for Adrian, I think it has very little to do with Adrian, and a lot to do with his dead wife.

"Except when I questioned her on her plan, she told me that she already had what she needed from the fae. Don't you want to know what she meant by that? What if she has something big planned? And more importantly, shouldn't we find out who has been working with her so we can stop them too? As much as I want to storm in there and get Adrian back, we need to be more strategic about this." He doesn't have an answer to those questions, probably because he knows I'm right. "Besides, half the vampire council still wants to access my light. What if they're willing to work with Brisa to get to me? What if they'd even go so far as to give up their blood bond for it? If we just go in there and kill Brisa, we will lose our chance to find out the truth."

Mangus is still quiet. Too quiet. And I'm worried he's going to disagree with me again. I don't know what I'll do if he turns on me. "You're smarter than I gave you credit for," he finally says, much to my relief. "Now let me ask you this, who's the mole for the nephilim? Because we know that someone has been working with them and giving them information that only those deep within our organization could know. So, Eva, if you're so smart, tell me who it is?"

From the tone of his voice, I can tell he's desperate for me to know. All at once, the answer hits me, everything clicking into place at once.

The favor he owed Isadora.

How he seems to be everywhere in all of this, always in everyone's business.

And why he wants me to figure it out––to name the traitor.

Maybe this is a mistake, maybe he's going to kill me for this, but I whisper the truth anyway. "You are, Mangus. You're the mole."

He doesn't react. He doesn't even move. Which is the exact opposite of what I thought he was going to do.

I take a breath of the musty air and continue, "But I don't think you're a bad guy. I don't think you would've done this for just any reason. And I know you hate the nephilim."

"There's only so much I can say here . . ." he replies, practically admitting it.

"And that proves my point. You can't tell me anything because you've been spelled not to, which makes me think back to our interaction with the fae witch. She broke your bond to Brisa, but not without a favor. We were led to believe the favor hadn't been required of you yet, but actually, it was an ongoing one. It was something you had already started."

He's silent as only the undead can be, and that's all the affirmation I need.

"The fae wanted you to spy on the nephilim, but you couldn't do that unless you pretended to be on the nephilim's side. Turning on your own kind was the only way."

"The fae are tricky," he says bitterly. "They can make you do things you never thought you'd do, and even when you try to stop, if you've made an agreement with them that's been magicked, you will be forced to hold up your end."

"So you're basically a triple agent. You are trying to help the vampires, but you also have to help the nephilim so you can be the spy the fae demanded you to be."

"Well that sounds pathetic." His voice is lost and forlorn. He's still grieving, and he always will be so long as he's immortal.

"And meanwhile, the whole reason you even agreed to do this in the first place is gone," I say softly. "Brisa blamed your wife, used her as a scapegoat for something she was actually doing herself, and Katerina paid the ultimate price."

"And that's why we should go back in there and kill Brisa tonight."

"But we won't, because Adrian's life depends on this plan working. We're going to beat Brisa at her own game, and you're going to help me do it."

"And then we kill her," he growls.

"And then we kill her," I agree.

Thirty-Five

～

Three nights later, the moon is hanging like a silver dollar in the black sky, shining down on the vacant city park. Even though it's a beautiful winter's night, the chill that breezes through the trees is bitter. We're in the center of the large park, gathering our group in the middle of a clearing. The nearby trees hide us from the view of anyone who could be wandering through, but nobody's out here at this time of night anyway. Not even the homeless will hang around New Orleans for long these days. Too many things go bump in the night around here.

I stare up at the moon, equally mesmerized by its beauty and intimidated by its mysticism. There's something about full moons and new moons that the fae, especially the witchy kind, love, so it's only fitting that we're back out here during another full moon. That knowledge alone makes me feel like there is so much more to this world than I ever thought possible. Magic is proof enough of that.

It's been six months since I met Adrian, and so much about my life has changed since then. I know things I never wanted to know, but I can't go back, even if I wanted to. And I don't want to. I've accepted where I am now, accepted that this is the life I'm meant to be living. This is the way in which I'm going to help the world. Not by running around staking vampires, but by making it so that vampires don't need to be staked in the first place. It's no small feat, but I believe there's a way I can make things better for all people. Being on the council is just the beginning.

Working with the fae is also part of that.

And tricking Brisa . . .

There's a lot of loose strings to be pulled tonight. If I'm lucky, I'll be able to do it. And if I'm not, I'm going to create a big tangled web and a lot more dead bodies.

And even more ash . . .

"They're all here," Mangus says, sliding in next to me. He nods toward the shadowy trees where the other council members have appeared. I quickly count to make sure they're all here and release a slow relieved breath.

Antara and Sebastian are already exchanging conspiratory glances, setting off my inner alarm bells. I'm not sure if they are working with Brisa, but I think they are or else they wouldn't be so gleeful. Because I was right—they want power, but they want to be able to walk in the sun more.

They want my angelic gift.

And somehow, Brisa has promised to give it to them.

Which is funny, considering she told me she wanted to kill me. Maybe she thinks she can have both. Steal my gift for herself and then kill what's left of me.

My mind reels at that thought, and my insides go hollow.

We form a circle. Santino is the first to speak, his accent thicker than usual tonight. "Why did you call this meeting, Mangus? I had to travel all the way from Brazil for this. It had better be good."

"You're here because I wanted you here," Brisa's voice rains down like glass as she levitates from the darkened sky. She's dressed in a billowing bloodred gown. And she's alone. I glance to the thick trees, wondering who's eyes are watching us right now. And wondering where Adrian is.

"Where is he?" I demand, unable to wait a second longer.

She settles to the earth softly and presses her index finger to her lips. "Shh, you've done your part. Now be quiet and let the grown-ups talk."

Sebastian nods toward the forest, and several women dressed in long white fur coats amble out. Adrian comes stumbling out with them. Once again, he's wrapped in silver chains. His body heals fast, but the silver slows that process down, and he looks like he's been beaten within an inch of his life recently. Bruises purple up and down his arms and face. His lips are split open. But his eyes—his eyes are completely bloodshot, indicating that he's fed recently.

Good. He'll be stronger if he's fed. But I still want to cry seeing him like this. And I want to claw Brisa's face off.

"What's going on here?" Nadia demands. She's the councilwoman from Russia, a very take-no-prisoners type of personality. She turns on Sebastian. "Have you allied with Brisa? Are you working against us?"

Sebastian replies coolly. "I'm working for the betterment of our entire race, and that includes you."

Antara smiles softly, taking Nadia's hand like they're the best of friends. "Don't you see? Eva was given to us as a gift. We must use her now or else risk losing her forever. Don't forget, she's a mortal girl."

"Excuse me," I growl. "I'm standing right here, and I belong to nobody but myself."

Brisa addresses the group. "Evangeline belongs to the vampires, whether she agrees or not. Why else would she be bonded to the council?"

"What do you want, Brisa?" Mangus asks. "Stop playing pretty with your words and just tell us why you're here so we can get on with it."

She shoots him a nasty look but answers his question. "These fae witches have so graciously agreed to bring me into the council bond."

That's a bold-faced lie. She doesn't want to be brought into the bond, she wants to have the bond returned to her. She wants to be queen again.

Mangus snorts. "You'll never settle for a share of the power when you are used to having it all to yourself. You're selfish, you always have been."

Her eyes flare. "Quiet! You are not to speak to me that way."

"You've just proved my point. You're always going to think you're better than the rest of us."

"None of you would exist if it weren't for me!"

"Some of us didn't ask to exist," Adrian speaks up, his voice ragged and pained. His hair hangs down in his eyes, and he glowers at Brisa as if she were evil incarnate. My heart shatters for him, taking in his words more deeply than I ever have before. I know he didn't ask for this life, and I wouldn't wish it on anyone, but I'm also so glad that he's here, that I met him, that I love him.

"You were always so ungrateful," Brisa tuts at Adrian, "but I'm willing to overlook it." She points to the moon. "I'm here now. You have ten council members with Eva and need a tiebreaker to join your ranks, and that's what I am going to do. You don't have to like it or even agree, but it's happening." Then she crooks a finger toward the fae women. "Witches, come do it now while the moon is high enough to bless our sacred circle."

The women step forward, removing the furred hoods of their beautiful cloaks. They don't look like fae witches to me, they look like normal human women. What can they possibly do here? I still don't want to believe this is possible. This is Isadora's spell. They can't change it. It's already been forged. It's already done. But then the last woman removes her hood, settling it back against long tresses of white hair, revealing lovely green skin and pointed ears. My knees go weak.

Isadora . . .

Thirty-Six

Mangus and Adrian appear stunned, and I'm sure I do too, but I'm not giving up hope. Not yet. Her presence isn't the worst thing that could happen tonight. I expected that something like this might surprise us, which is exactly why we called the people we did, and why Mangus and I made our plan in that dank coffin.

"She doesn't want to join our council," I challenge. "She wants to take the bond for herself. That's why she called us here. This meeting wasn't Mangus's idea, it was hers." I nod toward Adrian. "Why do you think he's in chains? He's her leverage."

"And I can still kill him," she hisses. "If you don't shut your mouth, I will."

"Is this true?" Nadia demands.

"It's true I used them to get you here, that much is obvious. It's not true that I am trying to take the bond back. As much as I'd love to, it's not possible. All I can do now is be added to your circle." Her eyes sparkle, and she gives me a sly grin. "And help you take Eva's light as our own."

I'm horrified as we're pushed into a circle, Brisa included. *Myself included.* Adrian is at her side and still covered in chains. He looks two seconds away from murdering everyone aligning with Brisa. And about one second away from murdering Brisa herself. My hands are itching to unleash the angelic fire, but I hold back.

"Let's get started," Isadora instructs. "But first, we must remove the silver." She sets out to unwind Adrian's binds, and when he's free, I expect him to come to me, but he doesn't move from his spot next to Brisa. And when the blade is passed from person to person, I cut my own palms, forcing myself not to think about it. Adrian shows no emotion as he slices open his palms. Brisa does the same, and then Adrian takes her hand in his own.

My already shattered heart breaks even more, and tears spring to my eyes.

Should I just do it? Just kill her now? Would she have time to retaliate? To fight me? To hurt him? Because this is the last thing Adrian deserves. She won't have the same power as before, but if she joins the council, she'll always have something over him. She's the reason for most of his trauma. She deserves true death, not to be allowed into our sacred circle, and not to be in a position where nobody within this circle can ever attempt to kill her once the spell is done. And that's all assuming she doesn't get the bonds entirely to herself. I still don't trust any of this. She's not one to compromise so easily.

"I cannot remove the blood bonds," Isadora eases our fears. "The spell has already been forged and nothing can undo it, but I can add your maker to the council."

"We have to put it to a vote," Nadia insists.

"I vote no," Adrian snaps.

The vote will tie, at least that's what he expects, but when it gets to me and Mangus, we both vote to add Brisa to the council. Adrian stares at me like I've lost my mind and then at Mangus like he's just staked him in the damn back.

"Just stop fighting her," I tell him, and it nearly kills me to say those words that I don't mean. But it's all part of the plan, and it's going to work. It has to. "I don't believe they'll be able to get to my light anyway. It's not something that can just be passed around."

Brisa exchanges a knowing glance with Sebastian.

Mangus mutters, "It's better to have her as our ally than our enemy." And I'm pretty sure it just about killed him to say that.

"So it's settled." Brisa grins like we're old friends, but her eyes are still cruel, and I know she still plans to use me like she does everybody else. She turns back to Isadora, waving at her like she used to wave at her servants. "Now hurry, witch. We don't have much moonlight left."

The moon isn't going anywhere, though, and Isadora begins her chanting. It's eerily similar to the chants she used when she first cast the spell weeks ago, but at least this time I'm not being held down by vines. Not that this is much better. I'm currently clasping the hands of the vampires next to me––Mangus and Santino––our bloodied palms pressing together.

There are eleven of us in the circle now as the moon shines down, lighting all our faces in its silvery light. This light is so different to the angelic gift in my hands that seems to mimic the sun. I'm still not sure what the golden glow mimics, considering it doesn't hurt Adrian. For just a moment, I close my eyes and soak up the moonlight. It seems to compliment my gift, creating a calming balance deep down within me. For just a second, I imagine I'm alone out here, that I'm in meditation and not worried.

Crack.

My eyes fly open. Shadows have descended. Several of the vampires step back, widening the circle to its fullest as they try to drop each other's hands. They cannot.

And then none of us can move at all because we're being magicked. . .

Magicked by King Orlyc himself. The imposing man stands centered in our sacred circle, tall and magnificent and entirely fae. And he's not alone. He's brought seven other fae into the circle with him.

We're still unable to speak, which normally would piss me off, but I don't want to hear what the vampires have to say about this right now. When it's all over? Oh, absolutely, I can't wait to hear them bitch about it. But right now, everyone needs to let Isadora work her magic.

But then I catch sight of Adrian, his eyes narrowed on me in confusion, and I wish I could relay a telepathic message to him. *Hang tight. It's going to be okay.* But I'm not even sure I believe it because this is just the beginning of our plan, and there are still so many things that could go wrong.

Starting with trusting the Unseelie Court.

The fae have us right where they want us, and they could kill us if that was their endgame. It would be so easy. But I'm pretty sure they won't because that wouldn't solve the problem of the nephilim, nor does it create a lasting solution for anyone. And while most of the fae are prejudiced against other supernaturals, that doesn't make them murderers.

And besides, we have a plan.

The magic builds as Isadora continues her ancient chanting. It's obvious what's happening here––the Unseelie King is bringing himself and his most trusted allies into the council bond. The vampires must know it too, even though they can't move or speak. Because their eyes are huge––some angry, some awed, and all but Mangus's are shocked.

The shadows descend, thick and almost dark enough to block out the moon. Then one of Casimir's silver doves flies around the circle. I'm beginning to think his birds are like his own version of the Secret Service, always checking on things before Casimir himself arrives, always guarding him, ever present.

As expected, Casimir appears with the nephilim representation hanging off of him. Chloe, of course, and she's brought along Nicco, Greyson, Tate, her mother Lainey, two nephilim I don't recognize, and Remi.

Remi shoots me a thank you nod, and I'm happy to see they got her out of the casino prison. Casimir had said he wouldn't have a problem, and he was right. I'll admit, I'm happy that Remi is joining the council. She was always a kind person, and I know she'll be willing to fight for what's right. By now, the nephilim have seen Chloe's true memories. They had to agree to change in order to get an invite to come.

But the one person I wasn't expecting is the very same person I'd hoped I wouldn't see here tonight. Leslie Tate.

Everyone's packed tightly into the circle now. There are nine fae including Casimir, nine nephilim including myself, and ten vampires.

But I don't expect Brisa to last for much longer . . .

Without her, we'll have twenty-seven council members in all. Twenty-seven people prepared to govern the supernatural community.

But as I look at Brisa now, her chestnut hair billowing around her face with the rest of us, her eyes molten with rage, her hands clasped tightly onto Adrian and Antara, I'm suddenly worried she's about to be connected to us forever.

I should've just killed her. . .

Isadora's chanting grows louder. Stronger.

The magic continues to build into a crescendo, seeming to rocket from one bloodied palm to the next. I feel it when it splits, shooting into the people inside the inner circle and back out to us. Over and over again.

It's too much.

Chloe nearly falls over, but Casimir steadies her. King Orlyc continues to use his fae magic to hold the outer circle of vampires frozen while the people inside the circle form two inner circles facing outwards toward us. Even though there are three circles, we are all one.

The electric magic stabilizes.

"Now!" King Orlyc yells, and Chloe's eyes roll into the back of her head, going white. And then everything goes dark.

For all of us.

She immediately pulls us into her vision, right to those records stored within her mind. She shows us the past, when the wars first started, then she shows us what happened for her to recently learn the truth––and everything King Alberich of the light fae confessed that night in Faerie.

After seeing these records, I can only hope the rest of the council agrees that this is the right thing to do. The deadly consequences of the supernatural wars need to end. It's time for change, for new growth, and a better world for everyone.

My voice becomes free and I yell out, "Are we all in agreement?"

"Yes!" they all reply back, but I don't trust it.

Words are one thing.

Actions are another.

And intention is everything.

Which is why Isadora says what she says next, "Your hearts have been tested. Not all have proven worthy of this sacred bond."

And with that, two members are thrown from the circle. Physically tossed out. Removed. Hearts failed to be worthy of our common goal.

Brisa and Tate.

All at once, the moonlight brightens on those still in the circle, a blessing of magic. And then it stops, and King Orlyc releases our bodies. We can move again.

Brisa releases a rage-filled scream, charging right for me. One second I'm standing with the others, and the next I'm flat on my back. My vision blurs from my head slamming against the cold hard earth. Her knees pin down my hands, and she rears back, her fangs extending.

Her plan failed. Ours succeeded. And now I'm dead.

Thirty-Seven

J ust as her fangs sink into my neck, sharp and punishing and final, she's gone.

Nothing but ash.

I cough and sit up, gaping at everyone. Adrian's standing above me, a bloodied stake in his hand.

"Where did you get that?" Sebastian deadpans.

Mangus raises his hand and winks. "I may have brought one along, just in case."

Everyone stands there, stunned. In the quick seconds that Brisa was preparing to kill me, Mangus was tossing a stake to Adrian.

And Adrian finally got his revenge.

Isadora steps forward. "What was a vampiric council is now a supernatural council. Decisions made here will be for the betterment of all." She smiles, a blissful calm relaxing her sharp fae features. "The magic is three times stronger with the addition of nephilim blood and fae royalty. It would be impossible to break your council bond apart, but you may adjust members as necessary with my help."

"And what about me?" Tate steps forward from where he was tossed from our sacred space. I've never seen him look so much like an old man.

"You didn't make the cut," Chloe explains regretfully. "Your heart was tested by the magic. You're still hardened to better treatment for other supernaturals."

His jaw tenses, and he glares at us before motioning to Greyson. "Come along, son, we're leaving."

716

Greyson slowly shakes his head. "No, I'm not going anywhere with you." It's surprising, I never thought I'd see the sour-faced boy have a backbone for anything other than torturing people. "I'm tired of fighting demons for you."

I don't know what he means by that, but Tate goes still, then nods as if finally accepting the truth. He begins to walk away, but King Orlyc holds out his hand and Tate is physically moved back to us through Orlyc's power. He stops Tate right at his feet, glaring at the man.

"You have a weapon that can infect my world and kill my people. Where is it? It must be destroyed." Orlyc demands.

"It can't just be destroyed," Tate snaps.

"Do not lie to me. You do not want to know what I am capable of, what I will do to you if you keep this secret."

Tate's eyes are furious. "The weapon is a nephilim child. You cannot destroy it because it is a person. And didn't you just swear to protect all supernaturals?"

Orlyc's lip turns up. "That is up for debate."

"No, it's not, because this person has done nothing wrong."

I assumed the weapon was some kind of iron they were going to put in the water supply, but this? A person with the power to destroy an entire race? I glance down at my hands, understanding how that feels. The pressure of such an angelic gift is hard to fathom, but it's something I hold within my palms, that I could turn on vampires at any second and burn them alive. People will always want me dead for it. Or they'll always be trying to find a way to get it for themselves.

I look to the other nephilim, expecting one of them to confess more on this person who is the weapon, but all of their mouths stay shut.

"We cannot say any more than that," Chloe finally tells the king. "We've been oathed by one of our comrade's gifts not to confess. But I assure you, there's nothing to worry about. The person with the weapon is kind and gentle. They won't harm you. They never wanted to in the first place."

The king scowls, but there's nothing he can do. They're at a stalemate. "Consider this mutually assured destruction. You do one thing to hurt my realm, and I will rain hellfire down on all nephilim."

Everyone begins to bicker like school children.

"Okay, that's enough!" I yell. The group quiets, many of them looking at me with new eyes. "Are you forgetting that we're in a council bond together? We can't just go making these threats anymore."

"I'm not in the council," Tate grinds out defensively, but then he releases a long breath. "But I'm tired. I'm too old for this war. I just want to retire, go lie on a beach with Bianca, drink wine everyday, and enjoy the rest of my life."

"You're serious?" I question with a snort.

He shrugs, his bushy salt and pepper eyebrows coming together. "I'm being completely serious. Camilla was the driving factor in this family, and at this point, I'm just happy to pass the mantle down to the next generation. I've been fighting for so long, and what for? It was all a lie. So now I want to take my wife and retire on the coast, maybe I'll try writing or painting. I don't even have a hobby."

Okay, he actually does sound serious.

But it still doesn't make up for everything he did, for all the humans he manipulated and controlled. I still don't trust him as far as I can throw him, but I also have to find compromises here too. As much as I hate him, he's my uncle, and there are several people here who love him.

"Fine, but make one move against supernaturals and you will be executed," Orlyc states.

"Noted." He grimaces, and he really does look tired. But also, a little bit relieved. "If you need me, I'll be in Italy."

And with that, he walks away.

"Why do all this?" Adrian turns on the Unseelie King. "What's your endgame?"

The circles split apart, but King Orlyc stays rooted in the middle. "I wanted the nephilim to know the truth, that they are no better than other supernaturals, especially not better than immortal elemental fae." His words drip with royal snobbery. "I've long wanted to return to this realm, and after the vampires successfully returned to human society, I knew it would be possible for us to as well. The issue, however, were nephilim hellbent on killing us." His eyes land on me. "And then we found Eva."

My cheeks burn. "Mutual assured destruction is the only way we're all ever going to get along." Several of them nod, but others don't seem too happy about all this, especially Antara and Sebastian.

Orlyc continues. "Many of the original pieces of the council spell cannot be altered. Royalty who enter into this council cannot be removed. Everyone else here was voted in by their people, and new elections will still occur every decade."

"We already voted," Chloe explains. "I went to my people and showed them the truth. It's going to take some getting used to."

Everyone goes quiet for a moment, and then Adrian speaks up. "Since everyone traveled so far to be here, I propose our first council meeting to happen in this very spot tomorrow at midnight. Right now, however, the sunrise is fast approaching and the vampires need to get home."

We split up in our different directions, but I don't go with the nephilim. I'm with Adrian.

The trip back to the casino is uneventful. We have cars with drivers waiting for us, so at least we don't have to exert our energy on the way back.

I lie my head on Adrian's shoulder and recount everything that happened to get us to this point. I leave out the part about Mangus being the mole. It's not his fault, and I plan to keep that information to myself for as long as I possibly can. Maybe that's foolish, but I'd rather be a fool than be responsible for whatever will happen to Mangus if the vampires find out he's been magicked into being a traitor.

"You're a genius." Adrian chuckles, kissing me on the forehead.

"I don't know, the fae are pretty cunning. I couldn't have pulled this off without them."

"The fae don't hold a candle to you, Angel."

"You're grossing me out," Mangus complains from the seat next to us. "Can you two please wait until we get back?"

"You're just jealous," Adrian teases.

Mangus sighs. "I am. I miss my wife."

That sobers us up real quick, and I pat his knee. Nobody says another word.

We pull into the casino's parking garage a few minutes before sunrise. For the first time in ages, a sense of peace washes over me. We did it. Brisa is gone. Camilla's gone. Tate is no longer a threat. It turns out the half-fae witches that Brisa brought along with her actually went to Isadora a few weeks ago and brokered a deal for themselves. They'll have partial access to Faerie now that they've helped the fae.

And before leaving the park, I stopped Isadora for a quick chat. She assured me of a few things. First, that Brisa's plan to steal my gift and kill me required fae magic, but the fae double crossed her because they're loyal to me. And second, that my anti-vampire bargain in the original spell has now been voided. It was my one request of Orlyc back when we devised our plans to put this council together. I no longer need to worry about being forgotten or lost by the man I love. All in all, it seems like everything worked out.

I should know better than to let my guard down . . .

We're climbing from the armored cars to head inside when gunshots rain down. There's no confrontation, no time to plan, no time to react.

It just happens.

A bullet slams through my abdomen, and I go down.

Thirty-Eight

~∾~

My vision blurs, tunneling in on Adrian's face. He's lying beside me, wounded with what must've been silver bullets. Our blood puddles between us, and I have the stark realization that this is the end. He must think so too, because he reaches out, grabs my hand, and squeezes it three times. Each squeeze is weaker than the previous.

I squeeze back four times. *I. Love. You. Too.*

A man is walking up to us, heavy boots echoing on the pavement. He's got his wooden stake ready, pointed right at Adrian. "You really thought you could kill my boss and get away with it, didn't you?" he taunts. "This is for Armondo."

He swings the stake right for Adrian's heart.

But just before he hits the mark, someone is yelling, someone is pushing, someone is grabbing the attacker and getting staked instead.

Mangus.

The weapon slices into Mangus's chest at the exact same moment that Mangus rips open the attacker's neck. Both go down, crumpling on top of each other. But Mangus's body quickly turns to ash. And the man bleeds out.

A horrified sob wracks my stomach, and more blood gushes from the bullet wound. My whole body is cold. The sound of clattering against concrete draws my attention, and I find Adrian on all fours, the bullets naturally being ejected from his body. They fall like long silver raindrops. The same won't happen for me.

I'm going to die.

He could change me, could turn me into a vampire. But that's only assuming he could find a cemetery quickly, and I doubt I'd live long enough to make it through a three-night transition. But in this moment, I would take the very existence I feared most if it meant I would get to continue a life with him. Because I don't want to die.

Adrian scoops me into his arms. He's saying things, things about my life, things about holding on, but the words don't register. Nothing sticks. It's all fading too fast. He carries me out of the parking garage, outside into the fading darkness, and I give up the fight.

LIGHT. Everywhere. Beautiful, wonderful, golden, warm, eternal light.

I'm floating in the sunrise, made new by its rays.

And Adrian is here, kneeling over me. So this must be the afterlife, because vampires can't survive in the sun. But here we are together, the angel and the vampire. The pain in my abdomen is gone. My mind is returning.

"Are we dead?" I whisper, and his eyes go wild with relief.

"No, we're not dead." He laughs the kind of laugh I don't think I've ever heard from him before. It's so incredibly free. It's not the laugh of a vampire. "Well, you're not. I've been dead for a long time now."

Is he trying to make a joke? I blink and look around, but the light cocooning us is just so warm and bright, it's hard to see anything.

"Where are we?" My vision finally focuses, and I can see that we're not in a graveyard, nor are we in some kind of heaven. We're a few blocks from the casino, lying in a grassy area of the downtown riverwalk.

Lying in the hot pink sunrise.

"Adrian, no! You can't be out here."

He smiles, kissing my forehead. "How are you feeling?"

Is he serious right now? He's about to be burned alive, and he wants to know how I'm feeling? His mouth finds mine, and I'm momentarily lost in the sensation of being alive, of still being able to kiss him. But there's no time.

Is this a goodbye kiss?

I pull away, so utterly confused. "You didn't turn me?"

"I'll never turn you, not unless you beg me to. I'll never ever take that choice from you like it was taken from me."

More and more, my senses are coming back to me. I sit up and glance around, realization pounding against my ribcage. We're outside, the sun has risen, and Adrian isn't ash.

He's not ash, because he's *glowing*.

"You're golden," I breathe out, and he nods.

He's so beautiful. His hair sparkles like spun gold, and his skin looks warmed and healthy. This is a man that was always meant to be in the sun but was forced to live in the darkness. And seeing him like this? It's a treasure.

"How?" I mutter. Because somehow, maybe even by the grace of God, he's managed to make it out alive. My gift has saved him––I'm glowing too. And my bullet wound has been healed, which I'm assuming Adrian handled with his venom.

"Why are we out here? Why didn't you just take me back up to the casino?"

"You lost so much blood. I thought you would need the sun to heal."

The sun to heal? I blink at him.

He nods. "Haven't you noticed? When you spend time in the sun, you come back with more energy and your gift is stronger. You can feed your gift with human auras, and I think you've been doing it naturally every time we've been near humans, but I also think you've learned to feed your gift by going outside." He shakes his head. "I'm sorry I kept you cooped up in the casino. I'll never do that again."

Now that he says all that, I suddenly realize how right he is. It makes the most sense. Of course my gift would love the sun. "But what about you?" I counter. "You were just going to die to bring me out here?"

"For your life, I would gladly die. So I came to the place where I knew I could get you the most sun the fastest. We're only a few blocks from The Alabaster Heart."

"You healed me with your venom?"

He shakes his head. "No, you healed yourself with the golden light."

Realization hits me. *Of course.* My light is two sides of the same coin.

"And I stopped you from dying."

He nods, and I just stare at him. I still can't believe it. He was going to die to make sure I would live. And I was willing to become a vampire just so I didn't have to lose him. Laughing, I jump on his lap and wrap him into a hug.

I've never viewed my light as a gift, never wanted it, never asked for it, but it's a part of me. And maybe for the first time in my life, I accept every-thing that I am. The light and the darkness, the good and the bad. There are unspeakable things I would do for the ones I love. The killing white light is a part of me, but so is the golden healing light. And both have saved lives. I'm sure the good fight isn't over, but at least for today, we can put down our weapons.

I press my lips to Adrian's, and together we glow.

Thirty-Nine

TWO MONTHS LATER

The sprawling city of Rio De Janeiro, Brazil is a vista of asphalt and greenery stretched between the mountains and the sea. We came early so we could acclimate, and I've spent the last few days playing tourist, especially enjoying the landmarks and the white-sand beaches. I even swam in the South Atlantic Ocean, checking off a bucket-list item.

Rio is one big bucket-list item, actually.

From the cars honking down the streets, to the tropical flowers, the incredible food, and especially the grand mansions built right up next to rainbows of graffiti––there's just something so *alive* about this city.

I'll admit I've imagined myself living here with Adrian, daydreaming scenarios of what it would be like to be able to do everything together, to be able to go out in the sun every single day with him. Because this city needs to be enjoyed with some sweat on your neck and a little bit of a sunburn on your cheeks.

But we can't do that––not yet. We haven't told the vampires about what my gift can do for them. We've been putting everything together first, waiting for the perfect moment to present our case to the council.

That perfect moment is almost here.

Santino's coven has welcomed the entire supernatural council to their headquarters, an opulent building high in the mountains overlooking the city. We've all been given luxury accommodations for ourselves and our entourages. Just as with the New Orleans meetings, council members have flown from all over the globe for this event. The security is tight, but I'm not worried about getting attacked. The dust has settled, and the supernatural council has only grown stronger in popularity with all of our communities. Besides that, Adrian and his coven, the fae, and nephilim have my back. And I think everyone is going to like what I'm going to offer tonight.

We're meeting under the full moon to welcome our newest members onto the council. To even things out after Mangus's death and Tate's forced retirement, we needed one more vampire and one more nephilim in our ranks.

The vampires have elected a coven leader from Canada, and the nephilim have elected Dario. Adding a shapeshifter to the council has me nervous, but I guess what they say about keeping your enemies close is going to be proven true or false with this guy. Especially considering this is the shapeshifter who helped lead an attack on Adrian's coven, who tried to kill him. But we have to move on from all that, things are different now. At least, I really hope they are.

After sunset, the council pours out onto the sprawling lawn. It overlooks the city, which sparkles in the darkness like a million fireflies. Adrian takes my hand and squeezes. "Are you ready for this?"

I nod. "I've been ready for this since that first time I saw my mom giving blood in exchange for poker chips."

His eyes dim, and he threads his fingers through mine.

We all mingle for a bit, waiting for the moon to reach its peak position for our new members to be forged into our bond. Butterflies swirl in my stomach as I wait. And when it's finally time to join hands and bring the two newest members into our ranks, rounding us out at nine council members for each of the vampires, nephilim, and the fae, I still wait.

"I want to join you!" a male voice calls out from the darkness, interrupting our ceremony minutes before it's scheduled to start. A young man strides up to us, determination etched into his handsome face. Something about him is familiar, though I can't place it right away.

"And who are you?" Adrian demands. "This is a private meeting."

Not to mention, how the hell did he get past the security?

"I'm a werewolf," the young man says boldly.

"They are extinct. Do not lie to this council," Orlyc booms.

The supposed werewolf shakes his head, eyes narrowing toward the huddle of nearby nephilim. "They thought they wiped us out, but they didn't."

"If you're a werewolf, then where's your pack? And why are you able to stand here in this human form tonight?" Adrian points to the moon.

The wereboy laughs. "You don't know much about us, do you?"

Adrian stares at him for a long moment. "I'll admit werewolves have eluded most of the supernatural community for centuries. There weren't many to begin with."

"I don't have to disclose our secrets, but I will prove to you that I am what I say I am. It's why I am here, to demand my rightful place on this council." He says all this while simultaneously removing his clothing. He has zero sense of shyness about his nudity as he stands before us. And then his body changes, shifting into a massive dusty brown wolf.

The circle drops hands and stumbles back as he howls into the moon. Blood pools between our fingertips. Does he smell that blood? Does it call to him? I don't know a thing about werewolves or if I'm in danger right now.

But just as quickly as he did the first time, he shifts back into his human form and begins putting on his clothing.

"The nephilim have no objections to you joining our council," Chloe says softly. "Shall we put it to a vote?"

It's unanimous––nobody else has any objections either. He's only one more person on the council, not nine. How much damage could he possibly do?

"What's your name?" King Orlyc questions.

"I'm Dominic," he answers boldly. "That's all you need to know about me."

My insides go cold, and I rethink my vote––I know why he looks so familiar.

This is the boy that Ayla is dating.

I've only seen him in a few pictures, and seeing him out of context like this didn't jog my memory fast enough. As if sensing my distress, he turns and offers a smug wink, and then he cuts his palms with his damn teeth and forces himself into the circle.

I don't know what to do, I have too much else riding on tonight to worry about werewolf drama, but I wonder if Ayla knows this about her boyfriend. She must. Didn't she say she knew all about the supernaturals and the fae? This must be how she knows. *He told her.*

Taking a deep breath, I join the sacred circle and continue on with my waiting. It's harder to stay calm with these new questions swirling around in my head, but somehow, I manage.

And I wait, and I wait, all the way until the three new members are forged into our council bond.

Until Isadora has muttered her final word.

Until the electric magic flowing between us crawls to a stop.

And then I make my move.

"I have a proposal I'd like us to vote on tonight." My voice carries on the midnight breeze, and everyone turns on me.

"This can't wait until tomorrow?" Dario deadpans. "Some of us aren't nocturnal and would like to get decent sleep."

Touché. But in my defense, I am dating a vampire.

That said, I've mostly returned to a normal sleeping schedule. I've even started working at Pops again and am applying for college. I've decided I want to go to medical school and work in the Emergency Intensive Care Unit. It's going to take a lot of work and many years to get there, but I have enough time and self-confidence to know I'm going to do it. I also know I'll never have a normal life, but I'd still like to have one that I feel is my own. Not one that revolves around my boyfriend, even if I do love the guy.

"No, this can't wait," I say louder.

They gather around to hear me out, and Adrian offers an encouraging smile.

"It's no secret that the vampires have set up businesses that help them exchange human addictions for human blood. This has been a brilliant way for them to keep their kind well fed without having to bite anybody." I feel my cheeks burning as most of the vamps send me death-glares. "But I would like to propose a change to that system." I don't let myself stop to take questions. "I have access to light that will make it so vampires can walk in the sun. I know it works because I've successfully used it with Adrian."

Whispers erupt.

"Is this true?" Nadia demands, turning on Adrian.

"It's true," he confirms. "Now let her talk."

I clear my throat as they fall back to silence. "Thank you. I have two kinds of light. White angelic fire that comes from my palms and can kill . . . and warm golden light that can heal. Something about the healing light allows Adrian to survive in the sunlight."

"And how do you know this for sure?" Santino asks.

"The morning Mangus died, I naturally and unknowingly gave my light to Adrian. I believe I had been giving it to him for weeks . . . because I love him." Saying those three words in front of everyone is very uncomfortable for me, but it's an important part of my story. "I have talked with the fae witches, and they have assured me there's a way I can share it with more vampires. And I'm willing to do that, under a few conditions."

"Anything," Antara cries, her eyes going round. She suddenly looks less like an evil vampire and more like a young woman desperate to get her girl-hood back.

My heart squeezes––this was the right decision.

"If you agree to *pay* for human blood from now on, then I can magick my golden light to live within any vampires who are tested to have worthy hearts."

"What the hell does that mean?" Sebastian sneers. "Worthy hearts?"

"It means that you can't ever use the gift of walking in the sunlight to harm humans." I pin him with a knowing look. "No more big plans for world domination."

"You're asking too much."

"I'm not asking enough," I snap. "But I'll do it, and in return, you're getting what you've missed for so long."

He steps forward, his features going rigid. "You're asking us to give up our businesses. How are we supposed to pay for blood without those?"

I shake my head. "You can still operate your bars and casinos and whatever else, but no more exchanging vices for blood. No more of your shitty manipulation and compulsion to get these humans roped into horrible addictions just so they'll give you blood that you could just as easily pay for." My voice turns to ice. "If you want blood, then you use your profits to pay for it."

They're thinking about it . . . I can tell they're close to agreeing.

"You're young now," Sebastian carries on. "But what happens when you're gone in a few decades? We need more than a *mortal girl*, we need to extract your gift like Brisa had planned."

There. He said it. What I knew he wanted all along.

But I had a feeling this might happen. I knew he would still be looking for a way to take my gift away from me forever, probably at the cost of my life. That's why I did what I did. It's exactly why I chose to be brave. Why I recently traveled back to Faerie and made even more agreements with the King Orlyc––the very same king who has the ability to manipulate the magic within people, to change their DNA and turn them into something new.

I shake my head and then I turn to the group of fae. I first assumed they were wicked, but they're not. They're not all good either, they're like the rest of us––a menagerie of dark and light.

King Orlyc's eyes sparkle with mischief. Of course he demanded to be the one to announce the final reveal. This is the epitome of entertainment, and he's nothing if not a grand entertainer.

"She's not mortal anymore," he says boldly. His eyes sparkle with triumph as everyone turns on me. Pulling back the hair covering my pointy ears, I show the council what I've become: a fae.

"She's one of us now."

Epilogue

FOUR MONTHS LATER

"I'm going to melt if we sit out here much longer," I tease Adrian, though it feels true.

We're lounging on our hotel balcony, soaking up the late afternoon Spanish sun. After the July council meeting in England, the two of us set out on a month-long adventure through Europe. Well, the two of us and my ever-present vampire bodyguards. Now that I hold so much power to help both the vampires and the humans, I'm always protected. As we speak, three of them are standing outside the hotel door and several more are down below casing the lively city streets.

Spain is our last destination before heading back to New Orleans. We'll be home just in time for me to start college next week. I'll admit I wasn't sad to leave New Orleans behind for the hot summer months, but our week in Spain has turned out to be just as hot and humid. That's okay––the country is stunning, and the company isn't so bad either.

"Just five more minutes," Adrian mumbles, his eyes closed and his face raised to the sun. We've done this every day since coming out to the council. That's okay, Adrian needs this sunbathing just as much as I do.

Once we figured out what I could do that morning on the riverbank, I knew I had to use my golden light to help the humans. I also knew that I would never really be a human. And that's when I contacted King Orlyc to see if there was a way that we could use my gift to leverage the vampires. Orlyc was the one who helped me learn to feed. He was the one who helped me create the supernatural council. And with everything that happened to me in Faerie, I suspected he would be able to help me with this too.

Well, he was, but the price was my mortality.

As Unseelie King, Orlyc's throne allows him to not only manipulate magical gifts, but he can manipulate actual DNA. He can change people. And so we agreed to transform me into a fae so that I could become immortal. I don't even remember the ancient ritual--they made sure of that--but I was made fae a week before our trip to Rio.

At least my soul is mine. That will never change.

Even now, months later, I'm still adjusting. But I don't plan to go live in Faerie, and I'm not a natural born fae. Besides the fact that most will never accept me as one of their own, the natural fae have way more abilities than I do. They're also allergic to iron. I'm not. Lying hasn't been easy, though. Technically, I can still lie, but it takes a lot more effort and it's hardly worth it.

Basically, I'm an immortal nephilim with pointed elf ears and an aversion to lying, who is filled with vampire venom. I'll always be a nephilim by birth, and Orlyc says my angelic gift is mine forever because it's tied to my soul, but I'm now so much more than just part angel. Adrian teases me, calling me a triple threat. I guess he's right.

"I have a fantastic idea," I say. "How about we build a pool on the roof of the Alabaster? That way, we can both enjoy the sun and the heat without melting."

He grins, eyes popping open to gaze at me. "I like that idea. I'll get it done by next summer."

If Adrian says it's going to happen, then it's going to happen. His word is as strong as steel. Just like how he said he would keep me protected and hired the bodyguards, or how he brought me into his coven even though I'm not a vampire. Crazy enough, most of those people are starting to feel like family.

My actual blood relations are doing much better. I sort of have a relationship with my dad's side of the family, even though I doubt we'll ever be close. And my mom is doing amazing since getting released from rehab. She got a fancy new office job and hasn't stepped foot in a casino since returning from California.

And the Moreno family--my other family--are all doing great, too. We're not as close as we used to be, but my relationship with Ayla is at least doing better. She's still dating the werewolf, but she insists she can't talk about it. Felix is home and back in school full-time, and he's still hanging out with most of his same friends. Although last I heard, Seth isn't around as much now that he's come out and gotten himself an exciting social life with the LGBTQ community.

I'm just grateful they're not out hunting anymore.

"I've been thinking," Adrian interrupts my thoughts. "What if we found our own place and moved out of The Alabaster Heart?"

I freeze, and he sits up, taking my hands in his. "I mean it. I hate what The Alabaster did to you. I don't want you to have to keep living there just to be with me."

I imagine us playing house for a second, how nice it would be to have a life to ourselves, and then I shake my head.

"I'm okay with living there. Besides, I avoid the casino and stick to the hotel anyway. And I like our penthouse." He tries to argue, and I cut him off. "You're the coven leader. I don't want you to give that up for me. Maybe there will be a time when someone else can take over and you and I can have a break, but for now I don't want to change anything."

My mind flashes to Kenton. My friend has fit in with the other vampires far better than he ever imagined he could. Adrian got him into regular therapy with someone who specializes in this kind of thing, and he's been doing really well now that he's forgiven himself for what happened when he was a new vampire. He's moving forward with his new life.

"I think we should stay where we are," I reaffirm.

"Are you sure?"

I lean over and kiss him softly. "Yes. I like our home."

There was a time when I thought meeting Adrian was the worst thing that had ever happened to me. I was so wrong because he's the best thing. He sees all the sides of me. He loves me because of who I am, not despite it. And most of all, he's taught me how to do the same. Me, in love with a vampire? A year ago I wouldn't have taken that bet for all the money in the world.

I guess it's a good thing I don't gamble.

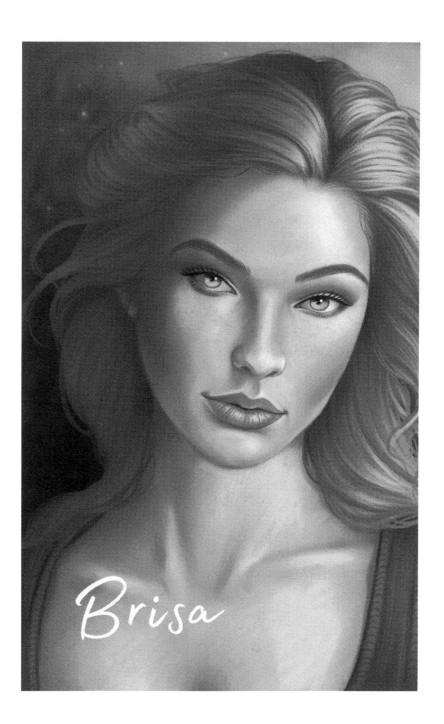

A Letter From The Author

Would you like to read the first kiss scene from Adrian's point of view? You can get that bonus chapter and other fun goodies by joining my Facebook reader group called "Nina's Reading Party". Thank you for taking a chance on *Vampires & Vices*. I've been working on this series for years, so to finally have it finished is a dream. If you liked it, please leave a quick written review, and please tell your reader friends.

Much Love, Nina

Also by Nina Walker

Young Adult Dystopian Fantasy Romance

The Color Alchemist (4 Book Series)

Dark Ocean Princess (Standalone)

New Adult Paranormal Romance/Urban Fantasy

Vampires & Vices (4 Book Series)

New World Shifters (4 Book Series)

New Adult High Fantasy/Paranormal Romance

Bleeding Realms: Dragon Blessed (3 Book Series)

Romance Standalones by Grace Costello

Twinfluence

Ivy League Liars

Beautiful Shattering

Acknowledgments

Thank you to everyone who championed this series.

Thank you first and foremost to all the readers, I couldn't do this without you. Thanks to the amazing fans and moderators in my Nina Reading Party FB group, to everyone on social media who shared this series, to my proofers Kate, Sarah, and Cassie, to my incredible editor Ailene Kubricky, to my character illustrator Kalynne Art, and my talented cover designer Clarissa at Joy Design. And of course thanks goes out to my supportive family, and especially my husband and best friend.

About the Author

Nina Walker writes paranormal romance, urban fantasy, dystopian fantasy and more. She lives in Southern Utah with her sweetheart, 2 kids, and 4 pets. She loves to spend as much time outdoors exploring the real world as she does exploring her own imagination.

Made in the USA
Columbia, SC
29 August 2024

40735103R00445